BARBARA CARTLAND

Five Complete Novels of

Love and Luxury

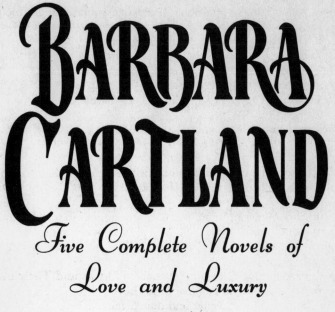

BARBARA CARTLAND

Five Complete Novels of
Love and Luxury

WINGS BOOKS
New York • Avenel, New Jersey

This omnibus was originally published in separate volumes under the titles:

Love Climbs In, copyright © 1979 Barbara Cartland.
From Hell to Heaven, copyright © 1980 Barbara Cartland.
Caught by Love, copyright © 1982 Barbara Cartland.
Riding to the Moon, copyright © 1982 Barbara Cartland.
Diona and a Dalmatian, copyright © 1983 Barbara Cartland.

This 1996 edition is published by Wings Books,
a division of Random House Value Publishing, Inc.,
40 Engelhard Avenue, Avenel, New Jersey 07001,
by arrangement with the author.

Wings Books and colophon are trademarks of
Random House Value Publishing, Inc.

Random House
New York • Toronto • London • Sydney • Auckland
http://www.randomhouse.com

Printed and bound in the United States of America

Library of Congress Cataloging-in-Publication Data

Cartland, Barbara, 1902–
    Five complete novels of love and luxury / Barbara Cartland.
       p.   cm.
    Contents: Love climbs in—From hell to heaven—Caught by love—Riding to the moon—Diona and a dalmatian.
    ISBN 0-517-18239-4
    1. Love stories, English.   I. Title.
  PR6005.A765A6   1996d
823'.912–dc20
                                 96-8054
                                     CIP

8   7   6   5   4   3   2   1

Contents

Love Climbs In

AUTHORS NOTE

─── ⚮ ───

THE DESCRIPTIONS IN THIS NOVEL of the tortures of the Climbing Boys is all historically factual—there was an actual case of a tiny boy of four years old who crashed down the chimney of a house in Yorkshire belonging to a family called Strickland. They found he was obviously well bred and he recognised a silver fork, saying: "Papa had forks like this."

The Stricklands learnt the boy had been stolen by a gypsy who tempted him from the garden where he was playing, to see a horse. He told them his mother was dead and his father was travelling abroad, but he was staying with his Uncle George. He had been bought from the gypsy by a Master Sweep for eight guineas.

Advertisements brought no reply, but the boy was eventually adopted by a lady who brought him up and educated him.

The Bill for the Abolition of Climbing Boys was accepted by the House of Commons in 1819, but thrown out of the House of Lords. It was not until 1875 that the country saw the last of the Climbing Boys. A Chimney Sweeper's trade card can be seen in the British Museum.

The horrors of St. Giles' persisted until 1847 when a new road was cut through it to be called New Oxford Street. The hovels, tenements and stinking alleys were rased to the ground and the rats dispersed to a thousand different holes.

CHAPTER ONE

— ❧ —

1817

"CAPTAIN WEYBORNE, M'LORD!"

The servant's voice rang out across the large Library with its richly bound books stretching from floor to ceiling.

It was a very elegant room designed by Adam, with furniture which would make any connoisseur's eyes glint.

At the far end of it the owner was lying back in a chair with one leg over the arm, a glass of champagne in his hand.

"Here you are, Freddie!" he exclaimed as the newcomer entered, "and about time!"

"I came as soon as I got your message," Freddie Weyborne replied, as he advanced over the Persian carpets towards his host. "What is the hurry?"

"Only that I wanted to talk to you before the rest of my guests get here."

Captain Weyborne accepted a glass of champagne offered to him on a silver salver by a flunkey resplendent in the Troon livery and wearing a powdered wig.

It was typical of the Marquis that he lived in the style which befitted his ancient title, even though his personal behaviour caused a number of his fellow Peers to raise their eye-brows.

5

"I cannot imagine what you want to talk to me about," Freddie Weyborne said, as the servants withdrew, "that you could not have said the day before yesterday, when I dined with you in London."

"Since then I have made a monumental decision," the Marquis replied.

He was extremely handsome, in fact his looks had made him the most admired man in London since Lord Byron had left the country.

But there was a hardness and a certain cynicism about his expression which belied the claims of those who said he was the equal of a Greek god.

He was also perilously near to being described as a Rake, and there was certainly a raffish, buccaneer expression in his eyes which women found irresistible, although his elders regarded it with suspicion.

His friend, Captain Weyborne, on the other hand was a typical type of English soldier, athletic and fresh looking, with a ready smile and a good humour which ensured that he had more friends than he could count.

The two men had been inseparable ever since they had been at Eton together and continued their education at Oxford. In that seat of learning they spent most of their time hunting, drinking and playing outrageous pranks on the other undergraduates.

They had both served with distinction in Wellington's Army but, while Captain Weyborne had remained in the Life Guards, the Marquis on his father's death had "bought himself out".

It had certainly given him more time to pursue not only the fashionable beauties of London Society, but also the "Fashionable Impures".

There was seldom a week when his escapades were not delighting the members of his Clubs but causing a frown between the eyes of mothers with eligible daughters who thought the position of Marchioness of Troon would become their offspring.

"Well, what plot are you hatching now in that over-fertile brain of yours?" Freddie Weyborne asked with a smile.

"That is just what I was about to tell you," the Marquis replied, "but first things first—I have decided to get married!"

"Married?"

If he had intended to surprise his friend he had certainly succeeded, and for a moment Freddie Weyborne's mouth dropped open from sheer astonishment.

When he could get his breath he asked:

"Why, in God's name? Why?"

"Lionel has become an ardent Radical and has announced that as soon as he inherits he intends to burn down this house and make the estate into common land for anyone who wishes to use it."

"That cannot be true!" Freddie Weyborne gasped.

"I have heard it from three different sources," the Marquis replied, "and frankly, it does not surprise me."

Freddie Weyborne was well aware that the Marquis's younger brother Lionel, Lord Stevington, had been a bone of contention for many years.

Every family in England who possessed a second son knew how they resented the privileges that were accorded to the eldest, but few of them were as aggressive as Lionel.

Freddie had often thought it was impossible to imagine two brothers who were more dissimilar, both in character and outlook.

Lionel had a fanatical hatred of his brother and everything he stood for. He refused to use his own title and was an extreme Radical in his politics.

But it was one thing to fight against the pricks of being merely the heir presumptive to his brother and another to threaten to destroy what was one of the most outstandingly magnificent houses in Great Britain and which contained treasures that were irreplaceable.

The Troon pictures were not only the envy of every Art Gallery and Museum, but also of the Prince Regent, who had exclaimed pettishly, on several occasions to the Marquis:

"However hard I try to emulate your collection, Troon, I doubt if I shall ever equal it, even if I live to be a thousand!"

"Lionel must be only bragging," Freddie said now. "He could not seriously mean to destroy anything so unique as this house."

"I would not put it past him to set fire to it and hope that I am burnt in the conflagration," the Marquis remarked laconically.

There was nothing bitter or even angry in his voice, he was simply stating a fact.

"So you intend to beget yourself an heir," Freddie remarked dryly. "Let us hope that Lionel does not kidnap him or do away with your wife before he is actually in existence."

"I intend to keep an eye on Lionel's activities," the Marquis said. "At the same time I suppose it is time I settled down. It is what my mother has been begging me to do ever since I came of age."

"I think the Dowager is right and it is time that you took life more seriously," Freddie said with a twinkle in his eye. "After all, no-one could have sown a finer crop of wild oats than you have!"

The Marquis laughed.

"If I die by Lionel's hand it is perhaps the only epitaph that will be laid on my tomb."

"We can always add it to the medals you won for gallantry in France."

Freddie was joking, but for the moment the Marquis did not reply in the same vein.

"You know, Freddie," he said after a moment, "what I miss is the danger and excitement of war."

"It was often hellishly uncomfortable while it was taking place," Freddie replied. "I cannot forget how hungry we were that time when the food wagons did not arrive and we marched for two days and nights on empty stomachs."

"All the same," the Marquis said, "we were doing something worthwhile. We were fighting the enemy and trying to out-wit them. We were using both our bodies and our brains to the very best of our ability."

A sudden thought came to Freddie's mind.

He was not as quick-witted as his friend, but although he was slower, he eventually reached the right conclusion.

"Is it because you miss the war and all its dangers," he asked, "that you have set yourself out to behave so outrageously since it ended?"

"I suppose so," the Marquis replied. "All I know is that I find peace is damned dull, and unless I can galvanize people into doing something amusing, I find myself yawning my head off."

"I have never heard such nonsense!" Freddie exclaimed. "Here you are, rolling in money, with horses any man would envy, and looks which make every 'Incomparable' fall into your arms like an over-ripe peach, and you find life dull? You are disgustingly ungrateful—that's what you are!"

"I am quite prepared to agree with you," the Marquis replied, "but the fact remains that I am bored."

"Do you think marriage will relieve your boredom?"

"I think it might even make it worse," the Marquis answered, "but it is the only thing I have not tried so far."

"And who is to be your partner in this desperate experiment?" Freddie asked sarcastically.

"Dilys—who else?"

Again for a moment Freddie seemed to be struck dumb.

"Dilys?" he managed to ejaculate after some seconds had passed.

"Why not?" the Marquis asked aggressively. "She is up to snuff and every bit of mischief I suggest to her. Besides which, she makes me laugh."

There was silence and after a moment the Marquis enquired:

"Well? Have you nothing to say?"

"Not that you would want to hear," his friend answered.

"Now look, Freddie, we have always been frank with each other, you and I, and we have been in some damned tough corners, one way or another. If you have any objections to Dilys as my wife, you had better say so now."

Again Freddie did not reply and after a moment the Marquis went on:

"If there is one thing that really makes me angry it is when you have that reserved, shut-in look on your face as if you could not trust yourself to speak. All right, let me know the worst. You have never approved of Dilys. You have made that pretty obvious."

"That is not true," his friend said. "I do not disapprove of her as your mistress, but a wife is a very different kettle of fish."

"In what way?"

"Oh, come on, Serle, you know as well as I do what I am trying to say. Dilys has made herself the talk of St. James's, but that is her business and not mine. But can you really see her taking your mother's place here at Troon? Or standing at the top of the stairs at Stevington House?"

Now it was the Marquis's turn not to answer, for Freddie had conjured up a picture in his mind which had often haunted him when they had been bivouacking on some barren mountainside in Portugal, or riding in the pouring rain over some wind-swept plain.

He must have been only six or seven when his Nannie had let him peep through the bannisters on the second floor of Stevington House to see his father and mother receiving a long line of guests on the floor below.

Standing at the top of the huge double staircase the Marchioness, blazing with diamonds which were almost like a crown on her fair head, had looked to her small son like a Princess who had stepped straight out of a fairy-tale.

His father resplendent in the evening clothes of a Privy Councillor with the Blue Ribbon of the Order of the Garter across his chest and his coat covered in decorations, had been almost as impressive.

His parents had stood for him at that moment for everything that was grand and at the same time stable in his life.

It was many years later, when he had watched the same picture enacted over and over again, that he had thought to himself that one day he would stand in the same place and receive everyone in the land who was important or distinguished enough to enjoy his hospitality.

Yet when his father had died it had not seemed practical for him to give huge Receptions at Stevington House, and he had gradually been drawn into the raffish, carefree set of young Bucks and almost without meaning to, had become their ringleader.

After following his train of thought for some minutes he said aloud:

"That sort of life is not for me."

"Why not? Is it not inevitable that you should, some time, take up the same position in the county and in the House of Lords, that your father filled so admirably?"

"Good God, what do I know about politics?" the Marquis enquired.

"You cannot go on being the *enfant terrible* for ever."

It was the Marquis's turn to look astonished.

"Really, Freddie, this is a case of *'et tu, Brute'!* I never expected you to preach propriety! What has come over you?"

"Old age!" Freddie replied, "and that is the truth, Serle, even if you do not wish to believe it. I am getting too old to drink myself stupid every night and go on parade feeling as if I had been hit on the head by a cannon-ball."

"I know the feeling," the Marquis remarked with a twist of his lips. "Perhaps that is why I intend to be married."

"An admirable resolve," Freddie said, "but not where Dilys is concerned."

"Ah! Now we are coming to the point!" the Marquis exclaimed. "Just tell me in words of not more than two syllables why Dilys will not make me the sort of wife I shall be able to tolerate."

"I have just driven here from London," Freddie replied, "and quite frankly, Serle, I do not feel like coming to fisticuffs with you. Besides, you always beat me."

"I am not going to hit you, you fool," the Marquis replied. "I would just like to hear the truth."

"All right then, if you want the truth," Freddie said, "I cannot imagine a worse fate than being married to a woman who is always looking over one's shoulder to see if someone more to her liking has just entered the room."

He looked defiantly at his friend as he spoke and saw the faint smile on the Marquis's lips.

"All right, I know exactly what you are thinking; that there would not be anyone more attractive than yourself. That may be true at the moment, but what as you grow older? What if you are ill? Do you think Dilys would sit sewing, or whatever damned thing women do, by your bedside?"

Freddie spoke with a sincerity that was unmistakable, and now the Marquis walked a little restlessly up and down the carpet.

"If it is not to be Dilys," he asked, "who is there?"

"A thousand women, all far more suitable for the position than she is!"

The Marquis went on walking and both men were thinking of the woman about whom they were speaking.

Lady Dilys Powick had startled London from the moment she became a débutante.

The daughter of the Duke of Bredon, she had the *entrée* to every important house and an invitation to every Ball and Reception that took place in the *Beau Monde*.

Six months after leaving the School-room she ran away with a penniless young man in a Foot Regiment and married him secretly.

She followed him to Portugal when his Regiment was sent there and behaved so outrageously amongst the camp-followers that she was sent home.

A few months later her husband was killed in action, but she hardly

bothered to give him a thought and certainly made no pretence at mourning.

She was, in fact, far too busy setting London by the ears.

Her behaviour caused her to be ostracised by all the leading hostesses,
but because she was beautiful, outrageous and undoubtedly amusing, her
house was invariably almost under siege from her numerous admirers.

She picked and chose her lovers in a manner which made those she
refused all the more determined to enjoy her favours.

But the Marquis of Troon had been *persona grata* from the moment he
appeared on Dilys's horizon, and for the last six months they had been
inseparable.

She had not only taken part in all his pranks but had in many cases,
instigated them and what she had said and done had lost nothing in the
telling, either in the Clubs or in the *Boudoirs* of those who hated her.

To the Marquis she had been a kindred spirit, which he told himself was
everything he required.

There was nothing too daring for Dilys to undertake, there was no
challenge she refused, and her love-making was as satisfying and fiery as
any man could desire.

As the Marquis continued pacing the carpet Freddie rose to help himself
to another glass of champagne from the bottle that had been left in a large
silver wine-cooler on a side-table.

"There is another thing you have forgotten, Serle," he said. "You may
think I am old-fashioned, but I think it is essential to marriage."

"What is that?"

"You are obviously not in love with Dilys."

"Not in love? Then what the hell do you think I feel for her?"

"Quite a number of things which I need not enumerate," Freddie replied, walking back to the fireplace, the full glass in his hand. "But none of
them are love."

"How do you know?"

"I have seen you through too many love-affairs for me to number, all of
which amused, fascinated, even captivated you for a time, but they were
none of them love, as I think of it."

"Then what is love 'as you think of it'?" the Marquis repeated in a
sarcastic voice.

"It is what my father and mother felt for each other, and what I would like to feel myself before I 'settle down'!"

"You will have to be a little more explicit than that," the Marquis said. "I knew your father and mother, and they were always very kind to me, but I never thought there was anything particular about their relationship with each other."

"It is not the sort of thing they talked about in public," Freddie said, in a slightly embarrassed voice. "But when my father died, my mother said: 'Freddie, dear, I have nothing to live for now, and all I want to do is to join your father.' She followed him four days later."

"I had no idea of that," the Marquis said after a pause. "You do not mean she killed herself?"

"No, of course not," Freddie answered. "But he was her whole life, and when he was no longer there she just gave up breathing."

"You never told me this before."

"I would not have told you now," his friend replied, "only I thought it might make you understand what I am talking about."

"I am not certain I do understand," the Marquis said, "but it is making me think."

"That is what I want you to do."

The Marquis sighed.

"Neither you nor I, Freddie, are likely to feel like that about any woman."

He paused before he went on:

"Yes, I do understand what you are trying to say to me. Of course I do! But I am not the romantic sort."

He saw the expression on his friend's face and laughed.

"All right! All right! There have been a lot of women in my life and would not pretend otherwise, some of whom have been damned attractive. Do you remember that little doe-eyed girl in Lisbon?"

The Marquis ceased speaking for a moment and then said:

"No, let us not get off the track. You are telling me that I have to feel some strange emotion I have never felt before—then I shall know that I am in love."

"That is part of it," Freddie said, "but I have a feeling there is something more."

13

"What do you mean by that?"

"I think that in every marriage there has to be a common ideal in the relationship, something you are aiming for together."

"What I am aiming for," the Marquis said, "is to have a son!"

"You are being deliberately obtuse. When we used to debate with each other and our friends at Oxford, you know we talked about a great many things we have not mentioned since."

"Of course we did," the Marquis agreed, "but it was a lot of high-flown balderdash, analysing our souls and worrying over what happened in the next world. I have often thought we wasted a hell of a lot of time talking when we might have been chasing the pretty girls."

"You did that too," Freddie said in a tired voice. "Try to concentrate on what I am saying, Serle, because it is important."

"To me, or to you?" the Marquis asked quickly.

"To both of us, I suppose," Freddie replied. "I will tell you one thing: our friendship will never be the same if you marry Dilys."

"Why not?"

Freddie did not reply and the Marquis said slowly as if the idea had suddenly percolated his mind:

"You are not telling me—you are not saying that you—and Dilys—?"

"That is not the sort of question you should be asking me," Freddie interrupted.

"Then you have!" the Marquis exclaimed. "Good God, I had no idea!"

"I think you will find yourself in the same uncomfortable position with a large number of your friends," Freddie said, after a moment, as if he was goaded into a reply.

The Marquis walked across to the window and looked out on the green velvet lawns stretching down to the lake lying below the house which was spanned by a stone bridge of perfect architectural proportions.

His eyes were on the swans moving slowly across the silver water, but Freddie was sure he was looking with a new perception into the future, seeing a very different picture from that he had conjured up before.

There was a long silence before the Marquis said irritably:

"I cannot think, Freddie, why you should come here and upset me and try to alter the plans I have made for myself."

"If I have upset them I can only say I am sincerely glad!" Freddie remarked.

"Damn you!" the Marquis said. "There are times when I actively dislike you, and this is one of them!"

He had not turned round as he spoke and Freddie looking at the squareness of his shoulders silhouetted against the light smiled a little ruefully.

He knew that his friendship with the Marquis was far too deep and too important to both of them to be destroyed by anything.

At the same time he thought it would be more pleasant if the problem of Dilys had not been raised the moment after his arrival.

Again there was silence until as if the Marquis suddenly made up his mind, he said in a different tone:

"Anyway, the question of my marriage can be shelved for the moment, at least until after tonight."

Freddie stiffened.

"What is happening tonight?" he asked.

"Well, it was intended as a grand gesture of good-bye to my freedom, and all that sort of thing."

Freddie looked apprehensive.

"You have not already proposed to Dilys, have you?"

"No, not in actual words," the Marquis said, "but I think she is already wondering whether or not she should wear a white veil at our wedding."

Freddie let out a sound of protest.

"God Almighty, Serle!" he began, "she would be the laughing-stock . . ."

He stopped.

"You are roasting me! I might have guessed! Well, let me hear the worst. What have you planned for tonight?"

"A Midnight Steeple-Chase," the Marquis replied.

"Is that all?" Freddie questioned. "I thought it would be something new and original. I hate your steeple-chases. You always win!"

"This one is going to be different," the Marquis said, "and what is more the prizes are well worth while."

"What do you call 'worth while'?"

"A thousand guineas!"

15

"That will cost you nothing. You always come in first."

"Five hundred guineas to the second and a hundred for third place."

"That gives somebody a sporting chance," Freddie admitted. "But what is so original about a Midnight Steeple-Chase? You have had them before. Your last one left my best horse lame for a month."

"You should be a better rider," the Marquis retorted, "and tonight you will have to be."

"Why?"

"I intend introducing certain handicaps."

Freddie groaned.

"I knew there was going to be something dangerous about it, in which case I am not going to take part."

"Can you really be so chicken-livered?" the Marquis jeered.

"Certainly!" his friend replied. "I consider my life too valuable to throw it away on some school-boy's taunt of: 'I ride better than you!' You should grow up, Serle."

"I will call you out if you talk to me like that," the Marquis said. "This will be a race for grown-ups, I assure you."

"If you think I am going to ride in my night-shirt with my eyes bandaged or sitting backwards in the saddle you can count me out!" Freddie retorted. "My father always said the Steeple-Chases were for fools who want to risk their necks, and the more foolish of them end up in the Church-yard. That is where I have no wish to be at the moment."

"Stop being a spoil-sport, Freddie!" the Marquis ordered. "Whether you take part or not there will be at least twenty competitors because they have already accepted."

"So you have been planning this nonsense for a long time."

"For the last three days since I decided to get married," the Marquis replied. "I told myself if I survived the Steeple-Chase, then I could survive marriage. It seemed there was nothing much to choose between them except that the Steeple-Chase would undoubtedly be more enjoyable."

"The truth is you are seeking danger," Freddie said. "Now tell me what the conditions are which make this particular Chase unique."

"I thought it would be amusing," the Marquis said slowly, as if he was choosing his words, "if every contestant rode as if he only had one arm and one eye. It is damned difficult, as it happens, to see with one eye when you are used to using two."

"And that means," Freddie said, "you will find it hard to take your fences and undoubtedly break your neck! It is too big a gamble. I will be the referee and use two eyes."

"Forsett has already agreed to do that," the Marquis replied. "He disapproves, but at the same time, he is completely just and everyone will accept his decision should there be any controversy."

Freddie knew this was true where Lord Forsett was concerned.

He was older than the Marquis and himself, and he had been too badly wounded in battle to be able to race his horses or to walk without a stick.

They all respected him as a brave man and it was true that whatever decision he made, they would accept.

"Forsett or no Forsett," Freddie said, "I only hope you have ordered plenty of stretcher-bearers to pick up the casualties and Surgeons to set broken arms and legs, besides grave-diggers to bury those who fall on their heads!"

"Stop being so gloomy," the Marquis commanded, "we are going to have the best dinner we have ever had. The wines will be superlative–the finest I have in the cellar. After that the majority of those present will be only too glad to compete for the prizes I am offering."

"That I can well believe," Freddie remarked, "but the more sensible of your friends will undoubtedly have an excuse which will prevent them from accepting your invitation. Who is coming?"

The Marquis gave him a rapid list of names, most of whom he knew well. Then as he added: "Sir Charles Lingfield," Freddie repeated:

"Lingfield? But he is too old!"

"Not really. I do not suppose he has reached his fortieth birthday."

"Then he *is* too old," Freddie protested. "You know as well as I do, Serle, that if the course is the same as we have ridden over on previous occasions the jumps are very steep for men of our age, let alone an older man."

"I like Lingfield, and his house is on my estate. I can hardly leave him out."

"If he had any sense he would refuse."

"Well, he has accepted," the Marquis said, "so what do you expect me to do? Say: 'Freddie thinks you are too old, so run home, my dear man, and come another day when things are easier'?"

"I suppose it is all right," Freddie said reluctantly. "I have seen Lingfield out hunting, he is a good rider."

"Then stop clucking over my guests like a mother-hen," the Marquis ordered. "Nobody is going to get hurt. If the course is too rough for them they can always pull off their eye-shade and unstrap their arm. It is as easy as that."

"I hope you are right," Freddie said disparagingly. "Personally, I think it all sounds like an unnecessary risk of life and limb to make a Roman holiday."

"Is that what you consider I am doing?"

"Of course you are! You are bringing in the sacrificial animals and a few Christians to amuse yourself, and personally I think it is all quite unnecessary."

The Marquis poured himself out another glass of champagne.

"What I would really like at the moment," he said, "is to have a call from Wellington to say he needs us both. I would like to shake the creases out of my uniform and ride off with you to the nearest Barracks, knowing there was an adventure ahead and that we would both be far too excited to suffer one moment of boredom."

"I know what you mean," Freddie said after a moment. "At the same time, I think we have to face the fact that we have to come to terms with a world without war. Personally, I am quite content as I am. I can find many amusements in London. I am looking forward both to the shooting and hunting in the autumn."

"One small fox," the Marquis said disparagingly.

"Did you really enjoy killing Frenchmen?" Freddie enquired.

There was a moment's pause before the Marquis replied:

"No, it was the chase that I liked. It was exhilarating, but I never wanted to think of the result of the objective."

"That is what I felt too," Freddie said. "I could not help remembering a great deal of the time that the French were men like us; ordinary men with a life to live, and perhaps, and this I could not bear to think about—a wife and children waiting for them somewhere far away in France."

"Are you insinuating that there is something wrong with me," the Marquis asked, "because I want to go on fighting?"

"No, I do not think it is that you want to go on fighting," Freddie replied. "It is the excitement and the danger you enjoy, and that is a very different thing."

The Marquis smiled triumphantly.

"That is exactly what I am giving you tonight."

"Oh, to hell with you!" Freddie explained irritably. "You always beat me in an argument. All right—you win! I will ride in your blasted Steeple-Chase, and I only hope that tomorrow my head is still on my body and you are not weeping beside my coffin."

"I think it is very unlikely that I shall be doing that," the Marquis said, "and although it has been a hard battle to get you to participate in my race, all I can say is that I should have been very disappointed if you had really been adamant about not taking part."

The Butler had glanced twice at the clock on the mantel-piece before the door opened and Freddie came slowly and a trifle unsteadily into the Breakfast-Room.

As he reached the table a footman hurried to pull out a chair for him and another placed a white linen napkin on his knees while a third went to the sideboard where a large array of crested silver dishes reposed on tripods beneath which burned oil soaked wicks with which to keep them warm.

However, before the dishes could be carried to Freddie's side for his inspection, he merely grunted in a hoarse voice which seemed somehow to be constricted in his throat:

"Brandy! What I need is brandy!"

"Of course, Sir."

The Butler made a gesture with his hand and the silver dishes were put back over the burning wicks as a footman hurried forward with a cut-glass decanter from which he poured brandy into a glass at Freddie's side.

Before he could raise the glass to his lips the door opened and the Marquis walked in.

"Good-morning, Freddie!" he said, and as his friend did not answer he said: "You look somewhat the worse for wear."

Freddie merely groaned as the Marquis went to the side-board where the footman raised the lids of the silver dishes so that he could inspect what was inside.

"I will have a lamb chop," he said finally and sat down at the table.

There was a smile on his lips as he looked at Freddie's pale face and the manner in which by now his elbow was on the table and his forehead was resting on his hand.

He waited until a lamb chop had been placed in front of him and the Butler had poured him a cup of coffee before he said:

"The trouble with you, Freddie, is that you mix your drinks. I noticed last night that you drank a considerable amount of port, while I followed the champagne with a very little brandy. It is always wisest to keep off red wines when one is riding."

Whatever he had drunk it certainly did not seem to have affected the Marquis's good looks, and the exercise of the night did not seem to have in any way diminished his usual vitality.

"It is not only what I drank," Freddie said after a moment. "It is that I am damned stiff, and my arm feels almost paralysed through having been strapped down for so long."

"You must have let them tie it too tightly," the Marquis remarked without much feeling. "As a matter of fact, Freddie, I thought you rode exceedingly well. It was just bad luck that Lingfield pipped you for second place. But at least you have come away with a hundred guineas to your credit."

"I would gladly pay more not to feel as I do now," Freddie replied.

The Marquis laughed.

"You will soon be better. Have something to eat. There is nothing worse than alcohol on an empty stomach."

"Leave me alone," Freddie said. "I know what is best for me."

"Very well," the Marquis answered. "Be it on your own head, but quite frankly I thought last night was a tremendous success. The dinner was excellent, you must admit that."

Freddie murmured something which was inaudible and the Marquis continued:

"You cannot deny that it was a triumph that only three riders failed to complete the course and not because they hurt themselves either. Bingham's horse went lame and so did Henderson's. Ironside fell at the water-jump which was not surprising. I have never thought much of his horses, although he boasts about them."

Freddie took another sip of brandy, then he said:

"You are right, Serle, it is my own fault. I feel as if my head is going to crack open. I should not have drunk the port and certainly not the claret we drank when we got back here."

"You will live and learn," the Marquis said. "I suppose it has never struck you that the reason why I win my own Steeple-Chases is that I am a damned sight more abstemious than the rest of the riders."

There was a somewhat wry smile on Freddie's face as he said:

"So to make sure of your success you tempt your guests like a Siren with all the delicacies which you feel they will not be able to refuse."

"That is, in fact, the first fence," the Marquis replied.

Freddie laughed as if he could not help himself.

"Really, Serle, you are incorrigible! I suppose I should accuse you of cheating."

"It is not cheating," the Marquis replied. "It is just using my brains and taking advantage of another fellow's stupidity. You know I never drink a lot when I am going hunting nor did I before a battle."

"That is true, now I come to think of it," Freddie admitted. "You were always in the prime of condition while a great number of fellows poured that filthy wine which was the best we could get, down their throats. I think really they were giving themselves 'Dutch courage'."

"Exactly!" the Marquis agreed.

He finished his coffee and the Butler hurried to his side with the silver coffee-pot.

As he did so the door opened and a man came into the room.

"Good-morning, Chamberlain!" the Marquis said. "Freddie you have not seen Graham Chamberlain since you arrived."

"No," Freddie agreed. "How are you, Chamberlain? Nice to see you again."

"Delightful to see you, Captain," Mr. Chamberlain replied.

He was a man of thirty-seven and he had served in the same Regiment as the Marquis and Freddie.

On his accession the Marquis had retired his father's Comptroller who was far too old to carry on and remembered a very intelligent and active officer in charge of Ordnance.

When it was suggested to him that there was a job which might be to his liking if he was thinking of leaving the Regiment, Lieutenant Graham Chamberlain, who had little chance of preferment, was only too delighted to accept it.

The Marquis prided himself, and he rarely made a mistake, on choosing the right man for the right job, and where Mr. Chamberlain was concerned that was certainly true.

He had taken over his new position with an enthusiasm which was only echoed by his commonsense and the knowledge that his Army training stood him in good stead.

Within six months he had swept away a lot of unnecessary extravagances, tightened up the administration of all the Marquis's houses, and in a gratifying manner, gained the respect of those with whom he worked.

"The race was a great success, Chamberlain," the Marquis said now.

"So I have heard, My Lord, but I am afraid I have bad news."

"Bad news?" the Marquis asked.

"Yes, Sir Charles Lingfield is dead."

"Dead?" the Marquis ejaculated. "But that is impossible! When he left here he was perfectly well and delighted at having won second prize. I saw him to the door myself."

"He had a heart-attack on the way home, My Lord, and was found early this morning at the far end of the Park, before he could reach his own house."

"I am extremely sorry about that."

"So am I," Freddie interposed. "I liked Lingfield. He was a decent chap, and I should imagine he was a good soldier."

"I am sure he was," the Marquis said. "Will you convey, Chamberlain, my condolences and sympathies to his widow?"

"Lady Lingfield died several years ago, My Lord. But he has a daughter. I know she will be very distressed by her father's death."

"Then convey my condolences to her," the Marquis said, "and of course, send a wreath. I suppose he will be buried in the village Churchyard?"

"I imagine so, My Lord, but there is something else."

The Marquis glanced up from the table at his Comptroller.

"No more casualties, I hope?"

"No, My Lord, but you will remember last night that you, I think jokingly, told anyone who was apprehensive about the ride ahead, to make a will."

"It was a joke," the Marquis said, "and some of the wills I read were certainly amusing."

He smiled thinking of how one man had left him a pack of fox-hounds with the proviso that every year they should be given a barrel of beer when the anniversary of their past owner's death came round.

"Do your fox-hounds drink beer, Guy?" he had enquired.

"That's what I want you to find out, ol' boy," the writer of the will replied.

The Marquis had learnt by the slur in his voice and the manner in which he spoke that he was in fact, "foxed."

Another will left him a collection of stuffed birds with the instruction that they should decorate the most appropriate room in his house.

Several suggestions were offered to which this room might be, and others of the diners had striven to produce even more outrageous bequests with the terms of which they averred their host would be obliged to comply.

"Are you telling me," the Marquis asked now, "that Lingfield made a will last night?"

"Yes, he did, My Lord, and what is more, he had it witnessed."

There was something in the way his Comptroller spoke which made the Marquis glance at him sharply.

"You are making me curious," he said. "What does this will contain?"

"Sir Charles, My Lord, appointed you the Guardian of his daughter."

"The Guardian of his daughter?" the Marquis repeated incredulously.

"Yes, My Lord, and I must inform Your Lordship that I consider the document in question to be completely legal!"

23

CHAPTER TWO

───── ❦ ─────

$\mathcal{V}$ALETA LOOKED HELPLESSLY AROUND the small but attractive Drawing-Room which she always felt had never been the same since her mother died.

It was a room that was very "lived in", and therefore contained an accumulation of treasures which had been collected over many years.

There were not only pieces of china that had come from her mother's old home, but there were also small objects that Valeta had either made or bought for her parents as gifts for birthdays and Christmas.

There was also a number of skilfully executed water colours, some framed, some unframed, and a number of silhouettes which Valeta had cut out and had quite a professional touch about them.

Besides these there were books not only in the elegant Chippendale bookcase, but because it was over-full, piled on tables and even chairs that were not often used.

Valeta looked around and knew that, if the Drawing-Room was full of a hundred things she could not bear to part with, her father's Study was worse.

Because he like her mother, enjoyed reading, in that room too there were books everywhere, piled high on the floor, on the chairs, on tables, and however hard she tried to keep the room tidy it was a sheer impossibility.

"How could I leave here?" Valeta asked herself, "and if I did, where would I go?"

She knew that every room in the house was a part of herself and while common sense told her that now her father was dead she could not afford to go on living at the Manor, there was no answer to the question—where else could she go?

She had already discussed it with her old Nanny who had been with her ever since she was born and who had said in no uncertain terms that she was too old at her age, to move about.

"But, Nanny, we cannot stay here."

"Why not?"

"Because we have to pay the rent and you know as well as I do, that without Papa's pension, we will not have enough to live on."

"If His Lordship has any decency about him, which I rather doubt," Nanny retorted, "then he'll charge you nothing to live here, considering it's his fault with his wild ideas that your father's not alive today."

Nanny had said this over and over again and because Valeta felt she could not bear it any more, she had gone from the kitchen to hide the tears in her eyes.

"Oh, Papa," she whispered when she took refuge in his Study, "how can I live without you? What shall I do now there is no-one to laugh with or talk to?"

Because she knew her father had always hated women to cry, she fought back the tears that came to her eyes and walked to the window to look out through the diamond-paned casement onto the garden.

It was ablaze with flowers because both her father and mother had enjoyed working in it, while old Jake had quite enough to do in growing vegetables and potatoes for the house without wasting his time on what he called "them there flowers."

It had been hard enough to keep her father happy, Valeta thought, after her mother had died, but because she had loved him they had somehow managed to hide from each other the ache that was always in their hearts and the inescapable feeling that something very vital was missing from both their lives.

"Now I am alone," Valeta told herself, and she knew she had to face it with the courage that had been so characteristic of her father.

He had not only been outstandingly brave when he was in the Army, but he had the courage which made him face every vicissitude of life with his head high and a determination that he would never be personally defeated by adversity.

"He died because he was brave," Valeta whispered and once again had to fight back the tears that flooded into her eyes.

25

She had only just managed to control them when she heard the door open and Nanny say in what Valeta knew was her disapproving voice:

"The Marquis of Troon has called to see you!"

"The Marquis?" Valeta repeated.

"And not before it's time!" Nanny said tartly. "If you asks me he should have paid you a visit before now to express his condolences."

Valeta was not listening.

She was smoothing down the skirts of her gown and patting her hair into place.

Then with an expression on her face which Nanny did not recognise she walked from the Study and across the small hall to the Drawing-Room.

When she reached the door she drew a deep breath as if she felt it gave her something she needed, then turned the handle.

The Marquis was standing at one of the bow-windows looking out, as Valeta had done a few minutes earlier, onto the garden.

He was, in fact, thinking how attractive it was with the sun-dial in the centre and beds of roses radiating out from it like the dial of a clock.

There was honeysuckle climbing over the roof of a small arbour and the flowers around it were planted so as to form great clumps of vivid colour that would have been the delight of any artist's eye.

As he heard someone come into the room the Marquis turned round and at first glance at Valeta, was astonished at her appearance.

Because Sir Charles had been a good-looking man he somehow had expected that his daughter would be attractive, but he had certainly not imagined she would be a beauty.

The girl he saw standing just inside the room had a small heart-shaped face which seemed to be filled with two large grey eyes fringed with dark lashes.

Her skin had the translucence of the finest porcelain and her hair, which was very fair, had golden lights in it which seemed to reflect the sunshine outside.

He thought she might have been dressed in black, but instead she was wearing a white muslin gown of what his expert eye recognised was a cheap material but which clung to her figure making her look like a Greek goddess come to life.

26

The only concession to her bereavement were two narrow ribbons of black velvet which had obviously been added recently to the gown and which outlined her small breasts.

For a moment neither the Marquis nor Valeta spoke. Then in a low voice she said:

"You wished to see me, My Lord?"

She made a small curtsey as she spoke and moved slowly towards the fireplace and the Marquis followed her.

She stood waiting but did not invite him to sit down.

Instead there was a look on her face he did not at first understand.

"I have called, Miss Lingfield," he said, "to express my very deep sympathy on your father's unfortunate death. I hope you read the card I attached to the wreath I sent to his funeral last week."

Valeta did not speak, she merely made a slight inclination of her head.

There was a pause and it was obvious the Marquis waited for some comment. As none came he continued:

"I have not called earlier because I felt it only right to give you time to get over the first shock of your loss, but now I feel there are certain things we should discuss."

"I presume, My Lord, you are referring to the rent."

The Marquis raised his eye-brows.

"Actually that had not entered my mind. I came to ask you first why you returned the five hundred guineas your father won at the Steeple-Chase."

Again there was silence, then as if she knew she must answer this question, Valeta said:

"You surely do not expect me to accept money which was the cause of my father losing his life!"

"I was afraid that might be your attitude," the Marquis replied, "although I was hoping you would not attribute your father's death to the race in which he rode magnificently."

He hesitated a moment before he said:

"I am informed by Dr. Moorland that your father had, in fact, suffered from heart trouble for some time."

"That is true," Valeta answered. "Dr. Moorland must also have informed Your Lordship that my father had been told not to exert himself unduly or place any unnatural strain upon his heart."

"In which case surely it was unwise to ride in a Steeple-Chase?" the Marquis ventured.

"Very unwise," Valeta agreed.

There was a note in her voice which made the Marquis say:

"I can understand that your father's sporting instincts overcame his sense of caution, but you can hardly hold me responsible."

"Who else?" Valeta enquired.

Then before the Marquis could speak she said:

"I suppose it has never struck you when thinking up some nonsensical amusement to pass the time that men like my father might risk their lives because they needed the prize-money?"

Valeta's tone was now scathing and the Marquis realised the expression on her face which he had not at first understood was one both of anger and contempt.

He was not used to having women, especially beautiful ones, looking at him in such a manner and for the moment he was nonplussed.

Then he said:

"I think that is an unfair accusation."

"It is the truth, My Lord," Valeta replied. "My father would be alive today if you had not offered such large money prizes for what I consider a degrading spectacle of grown men making fools of themselves."

"So that is what you think of my Steeple-Chase!" the Marquis remarked.

"It is!" Valeta replied, "it also applies to the others you have organised and which have been the talk of the neighbourhood and, if you want the truth, set a bad example to those who work on the Troon estate."

This was plain speaking and the Marquis thought that never in his life had a woman spoken to him in such a manner.

It was all the more wounding to his pride because Valeta was not only so lovely but so young, and for a moment he found himself almost speechless. Then he said with an effort at dignity:

"I am not in the habit of defending my actions to anyone, and I think we have other things we should discuss, Miss Lingfield, which are more important to you personally."

"I cannot imagine anything more important than the fact that my father has been killed through sheer stupidity," Valeta said. "And now perhaps you understand why I would not take the 'blood money' that was brought to me and which I considered in the circumstances to be an insult!"

"That is a very foolish attitude!" the Marquis said firmly. "You told me that your father rode in the race because he needed the money. He won the second prize riding, as I have already said, magnificently, and knowing Sir Charles in the past I am quite certain he enjoyed every minute of it."

He glanced around the room before he added:

"You need the money and it would therefore be absurd not to accept the five hundred guineas. However, as it happens that is not important."

"Nothing you can say will alter my decision, My Lord," Valeta answered, "but what is important is that, while I wish to stay on here in my home, since my father's pension died with him I cannot afford it unless Your Lordship will reduce the rent."

"The rent for the houses on my estate is not something I attend to personally," the Marquis replied.

"Then you should do!" Valeta answered. "I presume you realise that your tenant-farmers for instance, are finding it very hard to pay their rents, and I understand . . ."

She stopped.

The Marquis guessed she had intended once again to be rude, then thought better of it.

"If my farmers find their rents excessive," he said in an icy voice which would have made most of his acquaintances feel uncomfortable, "they are always at liberty to speak to my Agent."

"Your Agent, My Lord, can hardly be generous with your money unless you give him the authority to do so."

The Marquis gave a sigh of exasperation.

"Really, Miss Lingfield, I cannot see that this conversation is leading us anywhere. My rents are not a matter that should concern you."

"They should certainly concern you, My Lord!" Valeta replied. "Living in the depths of the country we still hear of your extravagances in London, the parties at which money is thrown away as it was thrown away on the grotesque spectacle of grown men behaving like clowns. I can only suppose that you are not aware that the agricultural community after the harvest failed last year, are reduced to praying that by some miracle they can survive this."

She made a little sound that was almost a sob as she said:

"Have you any idea what it is like, when you have nothing to live on but hope, to watch someone like Your Lordship throwing money away in such a profligate manner?"

She spoke aggressively, but because her voice was soft and musical and the lips that uttered the words were sweetly curved the Marquis surprisingly did not fly into a rage.

Instead deliberately he sat down in an arm-chair and crossed his legs.

"When I came here, Miss Lingfield," he said, "it was to talk about you. We seem to have diverged very far from the subject in question."

"There is no need for you to interest yourself in me, My Lord," Valeta replied, "except where it concerns the rent of this house."

"That is not true," the Marquis said. "I am, in fact, vitally concerned with your well-being."

"If that is because you feel responsible for Papa's death it is quite unnecessary."

"I consider it very necessary," the Marquis argued. "After all you are very young, and I am interested to know what you intend to do now you are alone in the world. Have you any relations with whom you could live?"

"That is my business, My Lord, but I would like to remain here."

"Alone?"

The Marquis's question seemed to ring out.

Valeta lifted her chin a little higher as if she longed to tell him to mind his own business.

Then as he was obviously waiting for her answer she replied slowly:

"I have my old Nurse with me who has looked after me since I was a baby. We will manage, one way or another."

"What does that mean?" the Marquis asked bluntly.

"We can grow a great deal of what we need to eat," Valeta replied, "and perhaps I can earn a little money."

"How?"

There was silence and he had the feeling she was not going to answer him.

"I want to know," he said after a second or two.

"Why?"

"Because, as it happens, I have a right to know!"

"A right?"

"That is another reason why I came to see you," the Marquis said. "Before your father left my house on the night of the race he made a Will."

"A Will?"

There was no doubt that Valeta was astonished.

"Some of my guests," the Marquis explained, "made Wills as a joke, but your father made his in all seriousness, and what is more, it was witnessed by the men sitting on either side of him at dinner!"

Valeta was looking at him suspiciously as if she did not really believe what he was telling her. Then she asked:

"What . . . did this Will . . . contain?"

"It appointed me your Guardian until you married or reached the age of twenty-five."

Although the Marquis had seated himself Valeta had remained standing.

Now, as if she felt her legs would not support her, she sat down on a chair opposite him and her eyes fixed on him seemed almost to double in size.

"My . . . Guardian?" she murmured beneath her breath.

"You can therefore understand," the Marquis said, "why I think I have a right to be concerned in your future."

"You cannot take this . . . seriously?" Valeta said. "My father, I think, made a Will which was deposited with his Solicitors and which left me everything he possessed."

"Which I gather," the Marquis remarked dryly, "is not very much."

"It is all I need," Valeta said defiantly.

"That is not true because if it was sufficient for your needs you would not need a reduction in your rent."

His logic was inescapable and Valeta said:

"What I want, My Lord, is to continue to live here and be left alone."

"I should have thought it was a somewhat unnatural life and a very uninspired ambition for a young woman."

"It is what I want to do."

The Marquis leaned back a little further in his chair.

"The question is," he said, "whether I will allow you to do it."

If he had meant to be provocative he succeeded and he saw the flash of anger in Valeta's eyes.

He thought with a feeling of amusement that at least he was getting his own back for her rudeness, and after a moment in a very much smaller voice she said:

"Could you . . . really prevent me from . . . doing anything I . . . want?"

"I am assured that your father's Will is legal," the Marquis said, "in which case, as your Guardian, I am responsible for you, and if you went to the Courts I think you would find that you had to obey me."

Valeta thought for a moment, then she said:

"The best thing that can possibly happen, My Lord, is to forget this absurd Will which my father made obviously after he had enjoyed a very good dinner."

The Marquis did not miss the inference Valeta was making that her father had been under the influence of alcohol and he asked bluntly:

"Did your father often drink to excess?"

"No, of course not!" Valeta replied hotly. "He was very abstemious, and always so before he rode in a race."

The Marquis smiled.

"In which case your father obviously intended his Will to be taken seriously because he thought he was doing the best thing for you. What is more, he could have had a premonition of what might happen to him."

He thought as he spoke that he had made a point, and felt almost as if he had been arguing with Freddie and, as they would have said to each other:—"That is Round One to you!"

Valeta was silent for a moment, then she said:

"You cannot really wish to . . . concern yourself with . . . me?"

"Naturally I am finding it rather a nuisance," the Marquis answered loftily, "but it is obviously my duty to carry out your father's last wishes."

"I should like to see this Will before I am convinced that it is in fact, valid."

"Mr. Chamberlain, my Comptroller, will show it to you any time if you would like to call at the house," the Marquis replied, "but as several people saw your father writing it and two eminently respectable gentlemen witnessed his signature, I think you would find it very difficult to prove it was a forgery or invalid."

Again Valeta was silent and now she looked down at her linked hands as if she was striving to find something with which to confront the Marquis.

As he looked at her bent head he was aware how long and dark were her lashes against the pale skin.

The sunshine coming through the window seemed to dance on her hair, which though it was not fashionably dressed, was the Marquis thought, a more attractive colour than he had seen for a very long time.

On an impulse he bent forward in his chair.

"Suppose, Miss Lingfield," he said in a tone which most women found irresistible, "we stop duelling with each other and get down to hard facts."

She glanced at him and he knew by the expression in her eyes that she was still hating him, but he went on:

"You have no wish to be my Ward and, I assure you, I did not seek the post as your Guardian. But I will certainly try to make it as easy as possible for us both if we can co-operate over the matter."

"In . . . what way?"

"Shall we start with the problem of your future?"

"I have told you that I want to stay here, with my Nurse."

"I think that might be possible for the time being until we can find you a suitable Chaperon."

Valeta stiffened.

"A Chaperon?" she repeated. "Why should I need a Chaperon?"

"I should have thought that was obvious," the Marquis replied. "It is not usual for an attractive young woman of your age to live alone with only a servant to keep her company."

"Nanny is more than that!"

"She was an employee of your father and mother's."

Valeta pressed her lips together.

"I do not want a Chaperon!"

"I cannot believe you would want to be the subject of ill-natured gossip."

She made a little gesture with her hands, then smiled.

"There are not many people who are likely to talk about me. My neighbours who were fond of my father and mother will, I am sure, quite understand my predicament at having lost them both and will not be inclined to be critical."

"That might have been true in other circumstances."

He saw that Valeta did not understand and explained, choosing his words with care:

"You are my tenant, but I am also your Guardian!"

For a moment the implication of what he had said did not penetrate Valeta's mind. Then for the first time since he had entered the room, she realised he was a young and handsome man and the colour swept into her pale cheeks.

After a moment she said in a hesitating voice:

"I . . . I suppose you could not . . . tear up Papa's . . . Will and just . . . forget about it?"

"That might have been possible if I was the only person who knew he had written it."

Valeta looked down again at her hands.

"What do you . . . want me to . . . do?" she asked.

"I want you to stay here for the moment," the Marquis said, "and think if you have any relative or friend who could come and live with you. If not, I suppose I must find someone."

He knew as he spoke, that this was a very unlikely contingency.

In the smart, pleasure-seeking, rather raffish Society in which he moved in London there was certainly no woman who would wish to bury herself in the country in a small unimportant Manor house.

As if his thoughts communicated themselves to Valeta, after a moment she said:

"I will try and think of someone . . . I promise you . . . because I want so much to . . . stay here."

"Most girls of your age," the Marquis said, "would want to be in London, meeting eligible gentlemen to whom they might be married."

"That is . . . impossible where I am concerned."

"Why?" the Marquis enquired.

"Because I cannot . . . afford to live in London," Valeta replied as if speaking to a rather stupid child.

"No, I can understand that," the Marquis agreed, "but perhaps something could be arranged."

Her eyes widened and she asked:

"What do you . . . mean by that?"

"I was just thinking," the Marquis replied, "that as your Guardian I ought perhaps to find someone who would introduce you to the fashionable world."

"That will be quite unnecessary," Valeta answered. "I have already told you that I want to stay here. I would like to make this quite clear: even if you are my Guardian I will not accept anything from you, nor will I ever forgive you for being responsible for my father's death."

The anger was back in her voice and because the Marquis could never resist a fight he retorted:

"That, if I may say so, is a very stupid attitude. You know as well as I do that your father was warned not to exert himself unnecessarily, and he must have known the consequences of riding in a very gruelling Steeple-Chase in which most of the riders were years younger than he was!"

"I can quite see," Valeta replied, "that you are trying to exonerate yourself from all blame, but when people are tempted beyond endurance we blame the Devil, not the temptation!"

"So that is how you think of me," the Marquis said.

"You can hardly expect me to think anything else," Valeta retorted, "and this is not the first time you have tempted men into injuring themselves simply, I suppose, so that you can wile away an idle hour."

"To whom are you referring this time?" the Marquis enquired.

"A young man who was not a particularly good rider broke his leg in the last Steeple-Chase you arranged," Valeta replied, "and he is still partially crippled."

"Who was that?"

"Nigel Stone."

"The General's son?"

"Yes."

"I knew he had broken his leg, but I had no idea that he was not restored to health."

"I expect those who participate in your 'fun' are easily forgotten, once the Circus is over."

The Marquis looked at her, then said slowly:

"You have a very unusual way of saying what you think, Miss Lingfield. Perhaps you are wise to bury yourself in the country. Such frankness might cause a furore anywhere else."

He thought that once again he had scored a point, but Valeta replied in what he knew was a deliberately demure voice:

"Papa always said that when a contestant resorts to personal abuse it means he has lost the argument."

Unexpectedly the Marquis found himself laughing, and saw as he did so, that Valeta was looking at him in surprise.

"I came here," he said after a moment, "expecting after I had offered you my sympathy and condolences to have to wipe away your tears and that you would be grateful for any generosity I could show you in the future. I find I am mistaken."

"Very mistaken, My Lord! As I have already said I have no intention of accepting anything that you might give me."

"I should not be too sure of that," the Marquis said. "As I have already pointed out, as your Guardian you legally have to obey me."

As he spoke he saw Valeta put up her chin and make a little movement as if she would have tossed her head.

He told himself that the interview had certainly been unexpected, and in a way more amusing than he had thought possible.

Now he was no longer angry he found it incredible that this small, lovely creature should defy him and look at him with a violent hatred in her expression that he had never before known—at least from a woman.

He rose to his feet.

"I will bid you good-day, Miss Lingfield. I think we both should have time to consider where our conversation has led us. I shall take the opportunity of calling on you tomorrow or perhaps the next day when we can discuss your future more thoroughly."

"I assure you, that is quite unnecessary," Valeta answered. "If I think of anything I wish to say I will send you a note by hand."

"I find it easier to talk than to write," the Marquis replied, "so I shall call in person."

Knowing that his insistence annoyed her, he walked towards the door with a faint twinkle in his eyes.

When he reached it he looked back to see that she had not followed him.

"Good-bye, Miss Lingfield or, as that sounds rather formal, perhaps owing to our new relationship I should call you Valeta."

There was no mistaking the anger in Valeta's eyes and the manner in which her lips parted as if to refuse him the privilege.

But the Marquis had already gone, shutting the door behind him and there was only the sound of his footsteps crossing the hall.

As he swung himself up into his Phaeton which was waiting outside the Manor House and drove his horses with a remarkable expertise down the small drive and out onto the road which would lead him back to Troon, the Marquis was smiling.

As she heard the wheels of the Marquis's Phaeton drive away Valeta, her hands clenched, stood where he had left her, aware that she was trembling with fury.

"How dare he treat me in such a cavalier fashion?" she said. "How could Papa have made him my Guardian?"

She knew that the only thing she wanted at the moment was to be sure that never again would she set eyes on the Marquis, never again listen to his drawling voice which seemed somehow indifferent to any insult she might hurl at him.

She had felt when he rose to say good-bye an insane impulse to strike him, perhaps to scratch his face, to behave in a manner which she knew would have horrified both her father and mother and indeed herself.

But never in her life, she told herself, had she met a man she hated more.

Everything she had heard about the Marquis had made her despise him, except of course, for his record in the war.

When her father had spoken of his gallantry and his courage she had felt a respect for the young man whose father had shown her family quite a considerable amount of kindness.

The old Marquis had been an autocrat who thought that few people deserved his interest and who could count his personal friends on the fingers of one hand.

Yet because he had liked Sir Charles Lingfield, he had often asked him to shoot and once or twice a year he and his wife had dined at the great house.

When the old Marquis had died Sir Charles had in fact, been genuinely sad at losing him, but when the new Marquis had left his Regiment the whole atmosphere at Troon had altered over night.

The parties he gave in London and in the country lost nothing in the telling.

The servants in both houses in the majority came from the estate and their relatives were regaled with stories which Valeta knew made the older folk feel as if their hair was standing on end.

Her father tried to find excuses for the new Marquis.

"It is the reaction from war," he said. "After all, he has been abroad fighting for a number of years and that takes its toll of every man."

"You do not behave in such an outrageous way, Papa," Valeta said.

Her father had smiled.

"I am too old and I cannot afford it."

"I do not believe, even if you could, you would ever do such things," Valeta said, "and the Marquis's money could be better spent in many other ways."

"Give him a chance," her father had pleaded good-humouredly. "He has generations of ancestors behind him who served their country in time of war and in time of peace."

It did not appear, Valeta thought, as if the young Marquis had any idea of serving anyone, except himself.

She heard of the presents he gave to the young women who graced the boards at Covent Garden and Drury Lane, and of the wild, daring exploits undertaken because he had been challenged to prove himself a better rider or finer pistol-shot than another man.

The whole estate learned of a Phaeton race from London to Newmarket which involved a collision between two of the competitors and resulted in three horses having to be shot.

"I have never heard before of a man of that age behaving in such a ridiculous fashion!" Valeta stormed.

Her father had sighed.

"He has certainly proved a disappointment so far," he agreed, "but I expect he will settle down sooner or later."

"The sooner the better!" Valeta had exclaimed. "It is time he took an interest in the estate. Andrews is too old to be the Agent and he does not like listening to stories of trouble or hardship."

"That is true," her father answered, "and it would be an excellent thing if the Marquis could only see for himself how much needs to be done here."

"Perhaps you could suggest it to him, Papa."

"You do not suppose I ever see the Marquis alone?" her father replied. "He is kind enough to ask me to his parties, but that is a very different thing."

"Very different!" Valeta agreed.

When her father was brought back dead the morning after the Marquis's Steeple-Chase she thought that she would have rejoiced if she had learnt that he had broken his neck at the same time.

"I hate him! I hate him!" she said to herself now, "and somehow, some day, perhaps I will be able to get even with him."

Then she told herself it was the wishful thinking of a child.

The Marquis was impervious to anything she could do to him, and what was more, he was her Guardian.

Valeta walked slowly across the Drawing-Room and down the passage which led to the kitchen.

She found Nanny as she expected, sitting at the kitchen-table sewing.

Valeta had asked her over and over again to come and sit with her in the more comfortable rooms in the house, but Nanny was used to the kitchen and it was where she said she felt more comfortable.

She looked up now as Valeta entered and there was no mistaking the curiosity in her tired old eyes.

"Well?" she questioned.

Valeta sat down at the table before she answered. Then she said:

"I think, without exception, the Marquis is the wickedest man in the whole world!"

"How has he been upsetting you?" Nanny asked sharply. "Surely he only came to make his apologies which he should have made before now?"

"There is more to it than that."

"What do you mean?" Nanny asked.

"I cannot believe it is true," Valeta replied with a desperate note in her voice, "but Papa made him my Guardian!"

Nanny put down her sewing.

"Is that true?" she asked.

Valeta nodded.

There was silence while the old woman began to fold up the nightgown she had been mending.

"Well," she said at length, "you might do worse. You certainly need a Guardian in the position you're in now, and the Marquis is a very rich man."

Valeta gasped.

"What are you saying, Nanny? Can you not see that it is the most terrible thing that could have happened?"

"I'm not so sure," Nanny answered. "It was worrying me what you would do with yourself with no money and nothing to look forward to. Well, if the Marquis does his duty, we should see a lot of changes in the future."

Valeta started to her feet.

"You are as bad as he is! My future is here with you, and not all the Marquises in the world are going to make me do anything different!"

"I shouldn't be too sure of that," Nanny replied. "After all, a Guardian's in the same position as a parent and His Lordship will have the right to say what you can and can't do."

"Nanny, what has come over you?" Valeta cried. "You sound as if you are pleased! How can you want this monster, this man who is responsible for Papa's death, to order me about and tell me what I am to do?"

"We'll wait and see, dearie," Nanny answered, "but it strikes me there might be some advantage in this for you, one way or another. Yes, we'll wait and see!"

CHAPTER THREE

———— ✦ ————

"I CONSIDER," THE MARQUIS SAID in an authoritative voice, "that you should have told me before now of the situation on the Estate."

"It has not been easy to have a private conversation with Your Lordship," the Agent replied, and added: "I wish, M'Lord, to resign my position. I've now served your esteemed father and Your Lordship for thirty-two years and it is time for me to retire."

The Marquis was silent for a moment. Then he said:

"If that is what you wish to do, Andrews, of course I understand, and I can only thank you most sincerely for all you have done for the Estate during those years."

The Agent bowed his head in acknowledgement of the compliment. Then he said hesitatingly:

"It's just a question, M'Lord—"

"You may choose a house that suits you," the Marquis interposed, before he could say any more, "or alternatively, accept a lump sum in lieu of accommodation, should you wish to live elsewhere."

"I was thinking, M'Lord, of returning to my own County which is Somerset, where I have an unmarried sister."

"In which case I am sure you will find that the pension to which you will be entitled and the capital sum which I have just offered will enable you to live in comfort to the end of your days."

"I thank Your Lordship."

The Marquis rose and the two men shook hands. Then the Agent walked from the room, closing the Library door quietly behind him.

The Marquis threw himself back in his chair and was staring into space when Freddie entered.

"I saw your visitor leave," he said. "What about that ride we planned?"

41

"He was not a visitor," the Marquis answered, "but my Agent, or rather, my ex-Agent, as he has just handed me his resignation."

"Does that worry you?" Freddie asked. "He looked to me a bit old for the job."

"He is," the Marquis answered, "and as I have just discovered, somewhat out-of-date in his methods. But that does not make it any easier for me to find a successor."

"You have no-one in mind?" Freddie asked.

"No-one, unless you think Lionel would be suitable for the job!" the Marquis replied.

"I have a suggestion to make," Freddie said ignoring the sarcasm in the Marquis's tone, "but I do not like to interfere."

"You are not interfering," the Marquis answered. "It is all that damned girl's fault! Since she needled me into looking into things, I find I am beset by problems, the chief of which is to find myself a new Agent."

"That is where I can help you," Freddie said, "and incidentally, 'that damned girl', as you call her, has done you a good turn."

"What do you mean by that?"

"I mean that it is about time you started to take an interest in your possessions, and I do not mean the pictures on the walls, or the wine that your guests imbibe so freely."

"I know what you mean," the Marquis said in a disagreeable voice, "but there is a hell of a lot to do and it is going to take up a great deal of my time."

Freddie started to make the obvious retort, then bit back the words.

"You were about to make a suggestion as to a new Agent," the Marquis observed. "You know of one?"

"A very efficient one, as it happens."

"For God's sake tell me about him."

"That is exactly what I am trying to do. He is the son of my father's Agent, and has been working with him for the last five years since he stopped a bullet in his leg and was invalided out of the Army."

"This is no place for cripples."

"He is not that, only it took him over a year to recover and so he stayed at home, learning under his father. He is an excellent man in every way."

"And you think he would come to me?"

"I am sure of it. My father was only saying last time I was home that he thought it was time John Stevens had a job of his own."

"I would certainly like to see him."

"I will send a letter off to my father immediately," Freddie said, "asking him to tell Stevens to come here with all speed. That at least will solve one of your problems."

"If I engage him," the Marquis conceded.

"Of course! The decision rests with Your Supreme Highness!" Freddie laughed mockingly.

"Shut up, Freddie!" the Marquis retorted. "You know it is important that I should like the man if I am to work with him."

"I am delighted to hear that you intend to supervise your land personally," Freddie said. "If you ask me, you will find it very interesting. I know my father says that he never has a dull moment and very few free ones."

The Marquis laughed.

"That is just what I am afraid of. What will the dressing-rooms of Drury Lane do without me? And I have a feeling that quite a number of 'Incomparables' will go into mourning."

"The trouble with you," Freddie said, "is that you are too puffed up with your own conceit. I suppose you have never asked yourself how many women would be left clinging round your neck despite your looks, if you had no title and no money."

"Fortunately that is a situation which is unlikely to arise," the Marquis replied, "so there is no point in speculating about it."

"I know it is a question I would ask myself, especially if I was getting married," Freddie said.

The Marquis shot him a quick glance.

"Still harping on about Dilys?"

"I had a letter from her this morning."

"You had a letter from Dilys?" the Marquis asked incredulously. "What about?"

"She wanted me to tell her confidentially what you were up to and why you had not gone back to London, as she understood you had intended to do."

"She asked you to spy on me?"

"I suppose you could put it that way."

"I know Dilys's methods only too well," the Marquis said. "You can tell her I am extremely occupied with the first love of my life, which happens to be Troon."

"She will be extremely suspicious of that piece of information," Freddie said, "and, although I know it is the truth, I doubt if she will believe me."

"It really does not matter whether she believes you or not!"

Freddie raised his eye-brows and the Marquis added:

"I have decided not to get married, at least for the moment. And what is more, I am too busy! Come on, let us go riding."

The Marquis walked ahead and he therefore did not see that Freddie's eyes were twinkling as he followed him.

They rode for nearly two hours, and when they turned for home their horses were moving more slowly and it was therefore possible to talk.

To Freddie's surprise the Marquis was obviously thinking deeply about his land and the way it was being farmed.

"I was just wondering," he said aloud, "whether we are using the most up-to-date methods possible. Who do you think would be in a position to show me what is being done in other parts of the country?"

"I believe Coke in Leicester knows more about agriculture than any other man in England. At least I have heard my father say so," Freddie replied.

"Then I shall make a point of visiting him," the Marquis said. "I feel sure we could improve our crops, although this year certainly looks promising."

Freddie was surprised, but he knew that when the Marquis really concentrated on a subject he considered it in all its aspects.

He thought to himself that 'that damned girl' had certainly started a new train of thought which might lead anywhere.

As they reached the great house which looked magnificent with the afternoon sunshine glinting on its hundreds of windows Freddie said:

"Do you mind if I go to the stables? I want to have a word with your Head Groom. One of the horses which I drove here seemed a bit off colour."

"Then Archer will soon tell you what is wrong," the Marquis replied. "But do not be too long. I thought we might have a game of tennis before dinner."

"A good idea!" Freddie answered.

Part of the out-buildings comprised a Royal tennis court where the ball game that had been popular since the reign of Henry VII was played and at which the Marquis excelled.

As it happened, he and Freddie were about equal performers and they found it an excellent way of taking exercise of which neither of them ever seemed to have enough.

A groom was waiting at the front door and the Marquis swung himself from the saddle, patted his horse's neck and walked up the steps into the Great Hall.

To his astonishment there appeared to be no footmen on duty, and he could hear raised voices coming from the Salon.

Putting his hat down on a chair, he walked across the marble floor, a frown between his eyes, as he wondered what could be causing such a noise and why the front door was left unattended.

He entered the open door of the Salon to see with astonishment that his Butler and footmen were all halfway down the room with their backs to him, having apparently an altercation with a large, extremely dirty red-faced man who was shouting abuse at both of them and at a slim figure standing in front of the mantelpiece.

It was impossible amid the turmoil to distinguish exactly what was being said, but the Marquis knew by a defiant attitude which he recognised that the latter was obviously the cause of contention.

For a moment he was stunned into silence by both the noise and the fact that such an altercation was taking place under his own roof.

Then as the voices seemed to grow louder he asked in a tone that cut like a whip through the confusion:

"What the devil is going on here?"

The Butler and the footmen turned hastily towards him looking guilty, but the big dirty man facing Valeta did not seem to hear.

"Oi tell ye ter hand 'im over!" he shouted, "or Oi'll get th' law t' tell ye 'e's mine."

"I will not let you ill-treat him any further!"

Even though Valeta spoke without raising her voice the Marquis could hear the anger beneath the surface as he walked towards her.

The footmen moved back hastily as the Marquis passed them and now the large dirty man realised something untowards was happening and turned his head.

"Who are you?" the Marquis asked, "and what are you doing in this room?"

Realising to whom he was speaking, the man was immediately obsequious.

"Oi be Cibber, the Sweep, M'Lord," he said, "an' engaged ter clean Yer Lordship's chimleys."

The Marquis looked towards Valeta.

"What is the trouble here?" he asked, "and why should it concern you?"

"It should concern anyone with any decency in them," Valeta replied. "Look at this child and see the way he has been treated!"

She stepped to one side as she spoke and the Marquis saw cowering behind her a small boy, black with soot except where his tears had washed rivulets down his thin face.

" 'E belong ter me," the Sweep averred before the Marquis could speak, "an' bein' foolish and none too good at 'is job, 'e's come down th' wrong chimley. Oi'll take 'im away, M'Lord, this moment an' teach 'im not to do it again."

"You will do nothing of the sort!" Valeta retorted. "The boy is ill, besides being abominably scared."

She turned her face to the Marquis saying:

"Look at the child's elbows. They are raw and bleeding, and so are his knees. I heard this man with my own ears threaten to thrash him to within an inch of his life for coming down the wrong chimney."

" 'Twere just a matter o' speech, M'Lord," the Sweep said quickly. " 'E's a stupid boy, an' if Oi sometimes give 'im th' rough edge o' me tongue it don't do 'im no 'arm."

"He—burned my—feet!" the child whimpered.

"I am sure he did," Valeta said, "and that is something he shall never do again."

" 'E lies!" the Sweep said. " 'E lies an' lies! Ye can't believe a word 'e says."

"I believe him, seeing the condition he is in," Valeta said. "I would not allow an animal to be treated as this little boy has been."

" 'E's mine, an' ye've no roight ter interfere!" the Sweep shouted.

It was obvious that his anger, which had been dampened down by the Marquis's appearance, was now rising again.

"That will be quite enough!" the Marquis said sharply. "You will be quiet and not speak in that manner to a lady in my presence. Is that clear?"

"Yus, M'Lord. O' course, M'Lord. Oi'll do wot ye say, M'Lord," the Sweep said. "But th' boy be mine an' nobody ain't got no roight to int'fere in 'is apprenticeship, 'as Y'Lordship well knows."

"You will wait outside," the Marquis said firmly, "while I discuss this matter. Andrews!"

The footmen had all disappeared from the Salon where they had no right to be in the first place, but the Butler had remained standing by the door.

"Yes, M'Lord?"

"Take this man outside and put him somewhere where he can wait while I discuss the matter of this climbing boy with Miss Lingfield."

"Very good, M'Lord."

The Butler with a disdainful expression on his face, beckoned to the Sweep.

"Come this way, my man," he said, "and be careful how you do so."

The Sweep looked at the Marquis as if he was about to challenge the order, but the expression on His Lordship's face made him know that he would be wise to keep his mouth shut.

He gave however, one furious glance at Valeta before he followed the Butler from the Salon and the door shut behind them.

"Now," the Marquis said, "perhaps you will explain what you are doing here, and what you expect me to do about that extremely dirty boy who is not improving the rug on which he is sitting."

"The rug can be cleaned," Valeta replied, looking down at the soot which had fallen from the boy's clothes.

As if she felt the Marquis had some right to demand an explanation she went on more quietly:

"I came here to see my father's Will, as you suggested I could do. I was waiting for them to find your Comptroller when this wretched child came

47

tumbling down the chimney. He was crying and as you can see for your-self his elbows and knees are bleeding."

She paused for a moment before she went on:

"Before I could ask him any questions the door burst open and that monstrous man came in threatening to thrash him within an inch of his life, as obviously he has done on many occasions before, for making a mistake. The child is terrified of him, and not surprisingly."

"He burned my feet!" the boy whimpered again. "He lights a fire un-derneath me so that I have to go up and up."

The memory of what he had suffered brought fresh tears and Valeta sat down beside him and taking her handkerchief gave it into his grimy hand.

"Do not cry," she said. "I promise you shall not go back to him."

The Marquis saw that her white gown was getting marks of soot on it from her contact with the small boy but it did not seem to trouble her.

There was a softness in her voice which was something he had never heard before.

"Come over here," the Marquis said. "I want to speak to you."

He walked as he spoke away from the hearth-rug towards the window and after a moment's pause Valeta rose to follow him. He saw her touch the boy's head with a consoling gesture before she left him.

When she reached the Marquis's side she looked down with an expres-sion of consternation at the soot on her hands.

With a faint smile he took a clean linen handkerchief from the pocket of his riding-coat and handed it to her.

"You cannot touch pitch," he said, "without being defiled."

He saw her eyes flash because she thought he was laughing at her, but she took the handkerchief and wiped her hands.

"He cannot go back to that man," she said as though nothing was of consequence except the child.

"You must be aware that an apprentice belongs to his Master," the Marquis said.

"Have you any idea how these children suffer?" Valeta asked.

She spoke in a low voice so that the boy could not overhear and the Marquis saw by the expression in her eyes how moved she was by his plight.

"Chimneys have to be swept," he replied.

"Have you read the findings of the Select Committee who were appointed to look into the plight of climbing boys?"

There was a moment's silence before the Marquis replied:

"As a matter of fact I have not, but I have heard there have been protests made against their employment."

"Then perhaps you are unaware," Valeta said, "that the official minimum age of these boys is supposed to be eight, but children of four to six are often forced up the chimneys."

The Marquis did not reply and she went on:

"They have to climb up half-blind and choked by soot, and either an older boy is sent up behind them to jab a pin into their bare foot to keep them going or they are driven up by the Master Sweep lighting hay or straw beneath them, as this fiend was doing."

"I will speak to the man about his methods," the Marquis said, "but, as I have already said, an apprentice belongs to his master."

"Not if he is a brute and practically a murderer!" Valeta flashed.

She stared at the Marquis disdainfully as she went on:

"The Society which has demanded the abolition of climbing boys has pointed out that there are alternative methods of cleaning and sweeping chimneys, but I suppose Your Lordship is not interested."

Now there was no disguising the contempt in her voice and the hatred in her eyes, and after a moment the Marquis said:

"Perhaps I had better send for Chamberlain and see what he can do in this matter."

"I should have thought it was a problem you could cope with yourself, if you wished to do so," Valeta retorted.

"What do you suggest I do?" the Marquis asked.

For a moment he thought she had no answer. Then she replied:

"Surely it would be possible to buy the child's freedom?"

The Marquis did not reply and she said:

"Perhaps it might cost the same as a brooch or a bracelet you would give to your lady-friends in London, or even as much as one of your much publicised parties, but at least you would have the satisfaction of knowing that you had saved a small child from a living hell."

The Marquis knew by the way she spoke that she doubted if he would

49

do such a thing, and he had an impulse to tell her that she was quite right in her opinion of him and that he would not stir a finger to help the boy.

Then he heard the child whimper and knew that much as he was reluctant to interfere Valeta was right and he could not give him back to his Master.

"You had better leave this to me," he said abruptly, and turning walked from the room.

Valeta gave a deep sigh as if some of the tension with which she had fought the Marquis went out of her.

Then she went back to the hearth-rug and knelt down beside the little boy.

When the Marquis came back into the room he found that Valeta had somehow managed to clean the boy's face of soot and he was no longer crying.

He realised that the blackened rag she held in her hand was what was left of his superfine linen handkerchief.

There was a cynical smile on his face as he looked down into Valeta's questioning eyes.

"You were quite right," he said. "The cost was the equivalent of a diamond bracelet."

"You . . . bought him?"

He could hardly hear the words.

"I bought his apprenticeship," he replied. "He is the first present that your Guardian has been able to give you. I only hope he does not prove to be too troublesome."

"You have bought him!" Valeta exclaimed. "Oh, thank you! Thank you!"

She rose to her feet and her eyes seemed to hold the sunshine in them.

"That was kind, very kind. You are quite certain that cruel man will not be able to demand him back?"

"If he tries let me know," the Marquis answered, "for I now have it in writing that Nicholas—that apparently is the boy's name—is no longer his apprentice."

"I am grateful, deeply grateful!" Valeta said. "Now I had better take him home."

"You have some mode of conveyance?" the Marquis enquired.

"A pony-cart."

"I will order it round from the stables, but first I think it would be wise to ask one of the servants to clean your new protegé up a little. He has obviously ruined part of my house, there is no reason why he should do the same to yours."

Valeta's lips twitched as she looked down at the mess on the rug.

"He is very dirty," she said, "and when I give him a bath it is going to make his wounds smart painfully."

"I only hope he appreciated the trouble you are taking over him," the Marquis said dryly.

Valeta was not listening, as she looked at the boy speculatively. Then she said:

"Perhaps if your Housekeeper can give me an old sheet we could bundle him up in it so that he would not make too much mess until I get him home."

"I am sure that can be arranged," the Marquis said. "You are quite certain you would not like my housemaids to clean him up a little?"

"Nanny and I will manage," Valeta replied. "Thank you very much for being so kind."

It was doubtful if the Marquis heard the end of her sentence for he had gone to the door and was telling Andrews to fetch a sheet as Valeta had suggested.

As the small boy sat on the hearth-rug looking at them apprehensively with wide eyes, the Marquis drew Valeta aside again to say:

"We will have to find foster-parents for this boy."

"I think the first thing is to feed him," Valeta answered. "You can see he is little more than skin and bone, and I have the feeling, although I may be wrong, that he is well-bred."

She paused before she said:

"He may even be one of the children who have been stolen from a decent home as was described in the report of the Select Committee."

She knew as she spoke that the Marquis was thinking she was making a fairy-tale out of it, but he merely said:

"I hope you are right, and I hope too, he will not prove so obstreperous that he wrecks your house before we can find more suitable accommodation for him."

51

The Housekeeper appeared with a large linen sheet and a surprised expression on her face.

When she saw the mess the boy had made on the hearth-rug she held up her hands in horror.

"It'll take me a long time to get that rug clean, M'Lord," she said, "and I've thought for some time we should get a better Sweep than that man Cibber. If you ask me, he doesn't know his job."

"This is your opportunity," Valeta said to the Marquis in a low voice, "to employ a Sweep who does not use wretched children to clean the chimneys."

"I had heard there are various alternative methods," the Marquis said, "before you mentioned it, but I have always been told they are not very effective."

He saw by the expression on Valeta's face that he had aroused her anger again, but before she could answer him he said:

"I promise you, however, that I will look into it."

"Thank you, My Lord," she said. "Unless you are a sadist I cannot help believing you will at least give a trial to another method."

"I am told," the Marquis said merely to tease her, "that in Ireland geese are sometimes drawn up chimneys."

"That too is disgustingly cruel!" Valeta exclaimed. "But perhaps Your Lordship and I can discuss it another time."

"I will call on you tomorrow," the Marquis answered, but Valeta did not seem to have heard him.

She had turned to the small boy and was drawing him very gently to his feet from the position into which he had collapsed when he had first come down the chimney.

She could hear the Housekeeper behind her making tut-tutting noises of disapproval as she looked at the amount of soot there was in the fireplace and on the rug.

Valeta said nothing, but merely went on wrapping the boy in the clean sheet before she said to him:

"Now, Nicholas, we are going for a drive behind my pony. You will enjoy that."

"You'll not give me back to Mr. Cibber?" the child whimpered.

It was obvious from the alarm in his voice that he was terrified of the man.

"No, no, you belong to me now," Valeta said. "That horrid man shall never hurt you again–I promise you!"

"You are sure?–quite sure?"

It struck the Marquis listening that the boy spoke in an unusually re-fined manner for a child from the back streets.

Perhaps Valeta was right and he was better bred than he appeared to be, covered as he was in soot and with his eyes swollen from crying.

She had wrapped the small child up like a cocoon in the big sheet but now Valeta wondered a little helplessly how she would get him out of the house.

It would be best, she decided, if she carried him and bent forward to pick him up when the Marquis said:

"Wait. I will send for your pony-cart and get one of the footmen to carry the boy."

"That's right, M'Lord," the Housekeeper approved. "He'll drop more soot on the rest of the carpet if he moves from there. I've never seen such a mess!"

"I am sure you will be able to clean it away," Valeta said, "and I think too you are right. That horrible man, Cibber, is a very inexperienced Sweep. There must be someone better you can employ."

"It's the rag-tag and bobtail in the sweep business nowadays, Miss," the Housekeeper replied. "Before the war the chimney sweeps were all skilled men, but now I'm told farm labourers have gone into the business hoping to earn more money."

"I am sure that is true," Valeta replied, "and boys are sold to them by their parents for three or four guineas."

"Is that a fact, Miss?" the Housekeeper asked. "Then it's a scandal! That's what it is!"

"I agree with you," Valeta said. "And in the report I read it said that a lot of the boys had even been kidnapped!"

"The Government should do something about it," the Housekeeper declared.

"Of course they should," Valeta agreed looking at the Marquis mean-ingfully as she spoke.

She thought she saw a cynical smile on his lips and hated him more than she did already.

"Little boys like this," she said to the Housekeeper, "are often given no food except what they can steal. They have to sleep on the floor and never get the chance of being washed, and their masters treat them with appalling cruelty!"

She was trying to speak calmly because she wished to make the Housekeeper agree that the climbing boys should no longer be used at Troon, but she could not help her voice breaking and the tears coming into her eyes.

Almost as if he was embarrassed the Marquis said:

"I think your pony-cart will be round by now, and here is James to carry your new acquisition."

A tall, stalwart young footman resplendent in his livery walked towards them as the Marquis spoke.

"Be very careful!" Valeta warned as he reached the child wrapped in the sheet. "He has been badly hurt."

The footman picked the boy up gingerly and although Valeta saw Nicholas wince he did not cry out.

They walked in a strange procession, the footman going first followed by Valeta, the Housekeeper, and lastly the Marquis.

The pony-cart drawn by one old pony which Valeta used to ride before she grew too big for it was waiting at the bottom of the steps.

Nicholas was placed carefully on the seat and Valeta picked up the reins.

"Thank you very much, My Lord," she said to the Marquis.

He inclined his head but did not speak as she drove off.

Only as she was going down the drive did he realise that Mrs. Fielding his Housekeeper was still standing beside him watching her go.

"That is a very determined young woman, Mrs. Fielding!" he said aloud.

"And a very kind-hearted one, M'Lord."

"Kind hearted?" the Marquis queried, thinking that was the last description he, personally, would have applied to Valeta.

"Yes, indeed, M'Lord. It's wonderful the way she's taken over her mother's good works in looking after the people in the village."

"Looking after them?" the Marquis enquired. "Why should they need looking after?"

Mrs. Fielding looked at him in surprise.

"Surely Your Lordship is aware that the Vicar has no wife? I'm told he often says he wouldn't know what he'd do without Miss Valeta helping him in visiting the sick, getting the children to Sunday-School, and a dozen other things for which a Clergyman depends upon his wife."

"Miss Lingfield seems very young for that sort of work."

"It's not a question of age, M'Lord, it's a question of heart, and when one has a big heart there's always others as benefits."

The Marquis said nothing, he merely walked back into the house.

The following afternoon Valeta was not surprised as she looked out of the window to see the Marquis's Phaeton coming down their small drive.

Her eyes lingered with appreciation on the magnificent horses which drew it, and although she hated him, she could not help realising that the Marquis was an intrinsic part of his ultra-smart turn out.

With his high-crowned hat at an angle on his dark head, his grey whip-cord coat fitting him like a glove, and his champagne-coloured pantaloons above his shining Hessians he was a picture of Fashion.

Yet at the same time he was so essentially masculine that his clothes were a part of him in a way which had been recommended by Beau Brummel.

Because she wished to be formal Valeta hurried into the Drawing-Room, seated herself by the empty fireplace, waiting until Nanny announced the Marquis:

"The Marquis of Troon, Miss Valeta!"

Without hurrying, Valeta rose to her feet slowly and gracefully telling herself it was absurd to feel her heart beating a little more quickly and that she was surprisingly nervous.

Ever since the Marquis's first visit she had sworn that she would not be intimidated by him, and she would never, in any circumstances be afraid of him.

And yet she knew because he was in himself, such an essentially positive person, she had the feeling that he overwhelmed her and she must fight desperately to preserve her own individuality.

He reached her and she curtseyed.

"Good-afternoon, My Lord!"

"Good-afternoon, Valeta."

She felt his use of her Christian name was an impertinence, but it was unimportant beside so much else that concerned her at the moment and she was not prepared to make an issue of it.

"May I sit down?" the Marquis asked.

"Of course," Valeta replied. "May I offer Your Lordship some refreshment?"

"No, thank you," he answered. "I wish of course, to know how your protegé is."

Her eyes lit up.

"I was right! I was absolutely right! He *is* well-bred and I am certain he was stolen from his parents."

"How can you be sure of that?"

Valeta seated herself opposite the Marquis and bent forward eagerly.

"First because he obviously found it quite natural to have a bath."

She gave a little smile as she added:

"Your Lordship will not know, but I can assure you that, if ever it has been necessary to bathe one of the village children, they have shrieked in horror at such an imposition. But Nicholas not only enjoyed his bath, but at the end of it he said: 'I feel clean'!"

"And have you done that?"

"We removed a great deal of the soot, but it is ingrained into the skin, and will obviously take time. I gather that his only bed has been sacks of soot in a damp cellar where that fiend kept his boys."

"Are there many of them?"

"Three others, but they are much older than Nicholas."

"What else did you discover about him?" the Marquis asked.

He found himself surprisingly interested.

He had thought when he was driving to the Manor that doubtless by this time Valeta would be disillusioned by her new toy, finding him as rough and foul-mouthed as were most of the boys who came from the slums of London.

He would not have been surprised if Valeta had pleaded with him to take the boy away immediately, saying that neither she nor her old Nurse could cope with him.

"He was cruelly beaten," Valeta was saying in a low voice. "There are weals from a whip on his back and on his legs, and because he has cried the soot has got into his eyes and they are still red and swollen."

She drew in her breath before she continued:

"But his features are refined and already he is beginning to forget the rough words he has learned from the other boys and to talk in the same way that I do, which I am quite certain is natural to him."

"How old do you think he is?" the Marquis asked.

"Six at the most. I have not questioned him yet about where he comes from, but when we gave him food to eat, he handled his knife and fork as any gentleman's son might do."

Her voice was excited as she added:

"This is important, he looked at a silver spoon and said: 'My Dadda had one like this'."

Valeta waited for the Marquis's reaction to her story.

"I am very interested in what you are telling me," he said. "Personally, I have always disbelieved stories of children being kidnapped, but I expect you are going to ask me to make enquiries from the Police, and I will do so, if that is what you wish."

"That is certainly one of the things I was going to ask you to do," Valeta replied. "I suppose the Police will help, although I believe they are shockingly under-manned."

"How do you know that?" the Marquis asked in surprise. But he was aware that she was speaking the truth.

Those who lived in London had been concerned about the lack of organisation of the Police and their hopelessly inadequate pay.

This inevitably resulted in too many of them being dishonest.

It was one thing, the Marquis thought, for him to know such matters, but how could Valeta, living in the country, be aware of what was happening in London?

She had, however, an answer to his question which he did not expect.

"I read a newspaper every day, My Lord," she replied, "and also my father and I studied reports of the last two enquiries that were published by the Select Committee of the House of Commons."

The Marquis was astonished.

Only a few men with whom he associated in the Social World took the trouble to read the findings of the Select Committees, and no woman of his acquaintance had even heard of such a thing.

As if she felt she ought to explain a little further Valeta said:

"My mother's father was the Bishop of London, and my mother was always deeply interested in the work that he and his clergy did to try to relieve some of the terrible suffering amongst the poor in the City."

"I had no idea," the Marquis murmured.

"Papa became interested too, and so I grew up realising that those who were fortunate to be born into a happy home, as I was, must try to help others in very different circumstances."

The way she spoke told the Marquis that she was utterly and completely sincere.

Yet as he listened to her he thought how lovely she would look if her hair was dressed in a fashionable style and there was a necklace of jewels round her throat and her gown had been made by a skilful dressmaker.

Such beauty is wasted, he told himself, on worrying over climbing boys, dishonest policemen and doubtless innumerable other vices and horrors that are the inevitable result of poverty.

"I think, Valeta," he said after a moment, "that while we are deeply concerned with the problem of Nicholas and his life, we have also to consider the problem of you!"

CHAPTER FOUR

———— ⚮ ————

"*D*O NOT WORRY ABOUT ME NOW," Valeta said quickly, "I want to talk to you about Nicholas."

The Marquis raised his eye-brows.

It was unusual for any woman of his acquaintance not to be interested in herself, but he was listening as Valeta continued:

"I have been thinking about the best way to get in touch with Nicholas's parents, and while I am sure they would have notified their local Police, if they had any, and the Magistrates, their loss may not have percolated to London."

"I follow your line of thought," the Marquis said, "but what else can we do?"

There was a little pause and Valeta looked embarrassed.

"It might be . . . expensive," she said after a moment, hesitatingly, "but might not the best thing be to . . . advertise?"

The Marquis considered the idea for a moment, then he said:

"I am sure you are right. The difficulty of course is that we must cover a very wide field."

"That is why I was . . . afraid it might cost a lot of . . . money, but I would like to pay some of it myself."

The Marquis smiled.

"That is something I should certainly not allow you to do. Even if we have to advertise in every newspaper in England, I do not think it will bankrupt me!"

He saw the gratitude in Valeta's eyes without her having to say the words, and he went on:

"I can see that the problem of Nicholas means a great deal to you, and I only hope you will not be too disappointed if your efforts to find his parents fail."

Valeta clasped her hands together as she said in a low voice:

"You will think it very foolish of me, but I have the unmistakable feeling that we shall find that somehow it was meant that he should come down the chimney at the precise moment when I had come to your house to see your Comptroller."

"I am afraid Mrs. Fielding will not agree that it was a destined occasion," the Marquis said dryly. "She informed me this morning that she believes the hearth-rug is irretrievably ruined."

"I am sure she is wrong," Valeta said quickly. "Let me try to clean it. I am very good at that sort of thing."

"That 'sort of thing,' as you call it," the Marquis said, "is not an occupation that befits my Ward."

He thought that Valeta might be abashed at his rebuke. Instead she burst out laughing.

"Are you really thinking of me in that capacity?" she asked. "What do you consider I should do? Sit on a silken cushion all day giving orders to a lot of non-existent servants?"

The Marquis did not smile.

"I have been thinking about your future," he said, "and I am more than ever convinced that you cannot stay here alone, with or without Nicholas as a protector."

"You would not wish me to . . . give him . . . up?" Valeta asked, afraid of the sarcasm in his voice.

"Supposing his parents do not turn up? You cannot expect to keep him for ever."

To the Marquis's surprise Valeta did not answer him, but rose to her feet to walk a little way from him towards the window.

"What are you thinking about?" he asked.

"I am thinking about Nicholas, and all the children like him who are suffering from intolerable cruelty which no-one does anything to prevent."

The little throb in Valeta's voice was inescapable and after a moment the Marquis said:

"You obviously do not know that the Chairman of the Select Committee who was appointed this year, Henry Grey Bennett, is trying to get a Bill passed through Parliament which will prohibit the use of small boys being used in the cleaning of chimneys."

"And you will support him?" Valeta asked eagerly.

The Marquis knew this was an important question to her, but he was not prepared to pledge himself to a course of action which he might not be able to keep.

"I am considering it," he said cautiously.

"Please . . . please," Valeta pleaded, "give it your full support. I cannot bear to think of sensitive little boys like Nicholas being forced into such an . . . appalling trade."

Her voice broke before she added:

"I suppose you have heard that they usually become the victims of what is known as 'The Chimney-Sweepers' cancer'?"

The Marquis rose to his feet.

"Now listen to me, Valeta," he said, "I think you are letting Nicholas's plight prey on your mind. At your age you should be wishing to enjoy yourself, to go to Balls and meet people of your own position in life."

He saw by the expression on Valeta's face that she was not impressed by what he was saying, and he added more forcefully:

"You have saved Nicholas. Now let that be enough. You cannot prevent people from wanting to have their chimneys swept, or using what is the easiest method of doing so."

He saw that Valeta was going to argue once again about the alternatives to using climbing boys and went on, before she could speak:

"As I have become involved in looking after you I promise I will do the same for Nicholas. We will arrange some schooling for him and later, I am sure, there will be employment for him at Troon. But I am not taking on a whole army of climbing boys and that is final!"

He thought for a moment that Valeta was going to protest. Then she said:

"I am grateful . . . very grateful that you will help Nicholas, and I do not want to be a . . . nuisance to you or bother you with my . . . prejudices. It is just that I loathe cruelty and it seems intolerable in a rich country such as ours that there is so much suffering from extreme poverty about which no-one seems to care."

The Marquis ignored the plea in her voice and said:

"Now let us get back to you, because it is a subject which has to be discussed sooner or later."

"I am . . . sorry to be a . . . trouble."

She spoke humbly. Then as if some pride within herself resented it, she added in a different tone:

"I have already asked Your Lordship to forget about me. Everything is perfect as it is, as long as I can stay on here."

"I am not going back over that argument," the Marquis said firmly. "What I have decided to do is to take you tomorrow to call on my mother."

61

He saw the surprise in Valeta's eyes and knew it was also a surprise to him because the idea had not come to him until that very moment.

"Your mother?" Valeta repeated.

"She does not live in the Dower House, as might be expected, but about fifteen miles away in a house which my father bought for her because she found it so attractive. Some people find her a rather frightening person and she is very much a law unto herself, but I would like you to meet her and I am sure she will have ideas of what you can do in the future."

There was silence for a moment. Then Valeta asked:

"Do you really . . . insist on my . . . meeting your . . . mother? I would much rather try to think of . . . someone who could come and live here with me if you . . . insist on a Chaperon."

"You have someone in mind?" the Marquis asked.

Valeta hesitated.

"I had a Governess of whom I was very fond. I am afraid she is old and not in particularly good health, but I am sure she could be persuaded to come to me, at least for a long visit."

Valeta did not add that her Governess and her Nurse had never got on well together.

She would not for a moment have suggested that Miss Colgrave should come to her except that she was afraid of the Marquis's plans for her future, and she wished to be involved with him as little as possible.

The Marquis thought the idea of any young girl as lovely as Valeta being shut up with two old women, one in ill health, was a quite ridiculous proposition, but aloud he said:

"I think it would be wise to try my way first, and for you to meet my mother. If you do not like her suggestions, then of course we will consider the idea of inviting your Governess to be your guest."

"At what time would you like me to be ready?" Valeta asked.

"I will send a groom to my mother to say that we will have luncheon with her," the Marquis replied, "so I will call for you at about eleven o'clock."

"I will be ready," Valeta said, "and perhaps I ought to thank Your Lordship."

"There is no need," the Marquis replied. "I am getting used to your reluctance to acquiesce in my plans and your efforts to twist me round to your way of thinking. But perhaps one day you will be obliged to acknowledge I am right."

"I am very . . . grateful to Your Lordship about Nicholas."

"We were not talking about Nicholas," the Marquis replied. "Nevertheless I will tell Chamberlain to send out advertisements immediately to all the County newspapers, and we will also advertise in *'The Morning Post'* and *'The Times'*."

"Thank you . . . thank you!" Valeta cried.

This time there was no doubting her sincerity.

The Marquis took his watch from his waist-coat pocket and was just about to say he must leave when Valeta asked:

"Would you like to see Nicholas?"

The Marquis had the feeling as Valeta spoke that she expected him to refuse, and because she expected it, he answered:

"Most certainly! I was going to ask you to bring him to me. I have a feeling I shall find it hard to recognise him."

"I will fetch him at once!" Valeta said eagerly and hurried from the room.

The Marquis found himself smiling a little ruefully.

He had found himself in a great many unusual situations in his life, but never before, he thought, had he spent any time with a young woman who looked at him with an expression of hatred and whose only thought was for a climbing boy.

It was obvious, although it seemed incredible, that there had been no *Beaux* in Valeta's life and she had not the least idea of how to be flirtatious, or how to coax a man into doing what she wanted.

She had instead, the Marquis thought, gone at him bald-headed, and he had the uncomfortable feeling that if he saw much of her, he would find himself forced into the position of attending long and dreary debates in the House of Lords on Social Inequality, and even voting with the Radicals.

The idea made him frown because it brought him thoughts of Lionel.

Only that morning he had received a letter from one of his friends in London saying that Lionel had been seen making impassioned speeches in Trafalgar Square against the iniquities of wealthy landlords and employers who ground down those who worked for them.

The writer had finished:

"The name of Stevington had always been respected, and it is most unfortunate that your brother should behave in this manner. I can only suggest that you remonstrate with him at the first opportunity."

The Marquis had thrown the letter down on the breakfast-table with a gesture of irritation.

He knew only too well that remonstrating with Lionel was a waste of time and always resulted in their both losing their tempers.

He was intelligent enough to understand that his brother's hatred of wealthy landlords was directed against himself and stemmed from jealousy and envy: he was not genuinely moved by the plight of the less fortunate members of society.

"What can I do about it?" the Marquis asked himself.

It made him think that Lionel with his sanctimonious and fundamentally insincere proselytising over the poor was bad enough, without having a Ward who had been thrust upon him by fate harping on more or less the same subject.

He was deciding that Valeta had definitely to be discouraged from becoming sentimental over such matters when the door opened and she came in leading Nicholas by the hand.

It would certainly have been impossible to recognise the soot-covered miserable child he had last seen sobbing on the hearth-rug in the good-looking, attractive little boy she led towards him.

Now that Nicholas's hair was washed it was fair, and his skin was pale.

As he looked at him, the Marquis realised that Valeta had been right in saying that his features were refined.

He was neatly dressed in clothes that were cheap and must have been purchased quickly from the village shop, but there was no doubt he carried himself in a manner which might easily be attributed to good breeding.

His hands, the Marquis noticed, had nothing coarse about them.

"Here is Nicholas!" Valeta said proudly to the Marquis, than added to the small boy: "This is the gentleman who saved you from that horrible Mr. Cibber. You must bow and thank him."

The Marquis was perceptive enough to notice that when Nicholas saw there was a man in the room, there had been a flicker of fear in his eyes.

Still holding tightly to Valeta's hand he bowed his head and said in a voice that shook a little:

"Thank you . . . for saving . . . me, Sir."

"I think it was really Miss Lingfield who did that," the Marquis said, "but you are safe now and so we must just forget everything that happened since you left your home."

Nicholas looked puzzled and the Marquis, to his own surprise, knelt down on one knee, so that he was face to face with the boy.

"Tell me about your home," he asked beguilingly. "Did your father have horses?"

For a moment it seemed as if the small boy did not understand the question. Then he said:

"I can ride. I have a pony."

"What is his name?" the Marquis asked quietly.

There was a pause, and it was obvious that Nicholas was thinking hard.

"Rufus!" he said at last. "My pony's name is Rufus!"

The Marquis straightened himself and looked at Valeta with a light of triumph in his eyes.

"That was clever of you," she said in a low voice. "I never thought of it, but of course at his age he would have ridden."

"It certainly gives us a clue as to his identity," the Marquis said. "Perhaps later he will describe to you the place he lived. It might save us from guessing whether it was the North, South, East or West of England!"

There was a sceptical note in his voice which Valeta thought she should resent.

Yet she was so grateful to him for being so pleasant to Nicholas that for a moment the hatred which flared every time she spoke to the Marquis seemed to have been dampened down.

"Now I must leave," the Marquis said. "I will call for you as we arranged at eleven o'clock tomorrow."

He was aware as soon as he spoke that Valeta was longing to dissuade him from doing anything of the sort, but without speaking she followed him, still holding Nicholas by the hand, across the small hall to the front door.

Outside the Marquis's Phaeton drawn by only two horses which he used when he was driving around the estate was waiting, the groom in his smart livery standing at the horses' heads.

Nicholas gave a little whoop of delight.

"A Phaeton!" he cried. "Like Dadda's!"

He disengaged his hand from Valeta's and ran down the steps looking at the Phaeton, then at the horses with obvious delight.

"You see!" Valeta said breathlessly. "I was right!"

"We must certainly try to find his parents," the Marquis replied.

"He is a dear little boy," Valeta said, her eyes on Nicholas. "I have a feeling when we do find them, I shall be sorry to see him go."

"I think it would be more sensible for you to be thinking of getting married and having a family of your own," the Marquis remarked dryly.

Valeta did not reply but merely stiffened, and the Marquis stepped into his Phaeton and picked up the reins.

The groom stood back from the horses' heads and as they started to move off, he ran to swing himself agilely onto the seat behind.

Nicholas stood in the driveway watching, then clapped his hands together.

"A Phaeton!" he said almost to himself. "A Phaeton, like Dadda's!"

The Marquis had plenty to think about as he drove back through the Park towards Troon.

As he neared the great house he saw there was a carriage waiting outside the front door and before he saw the servants' livery or recognised the crest on the doors he knew to whom it belonged.

He had the uncomfortable feeling that he was in for a scene.

Without really meaning to, he drew in his horses so that they trotted a little slower as he descended the drive towards the bridge and crossing the lake moved towards the long flight of stone steps which led up to the front door.

He hoped that Freddie, who had gone trout-fishing, was back now, but when he entered the Hall the Butler said:

"Lady Dilys Powick has called, M'Lord, and is in the Blue Salon!"

"Is Captain Weyborne here?"

"No, M'Lord. Captain Weyborne has not yet returned."

The Marquis gave a little sigh and walked across the Hall to what was known as the Blue Salon.

It was a room that was habitually used for callers and the one into which Nicholas had descended from the chimney.

Lady Dilys was seated on a high-backed arm-chair which she was aware showed to advantage her auburn hair and sensationally white skin.

She had slightly slanting eyes which were accentuated by a touch of mascara at the corners and which gave her what her admirers described as a bewitching look.

As the Marquis entered the room now she smiled at him in a manner which was calculated to drive most men to madness, and certainly to make the blood run quicker in their veins.

The Marquis however, seemed quite unmoved as he walked towards her to say:

"I was not expecting you, Dilys. Why did you not send word that you were coming?"

"There is surely no need for that where we are concerned?" Lady Dilys replied in a low, seductive voice. "I was tired of waiting for you and wondering what you were doing here in the country."

"There are a great many things to occupy me," the Marquis answered, "the most immediate being that I have engaged a new Agent and have to instruct him in his duties."

Lady Dilys threw back her head and gave a silvery laugh.

"My dear Serle, how pompous that sounds! Since when have you concerned yourself with Agents and doubtless also with cattle and pigs? Be careful, or you may become bovine!"

"There is always that possibility," the Marquis said. "Have you really journeyed all this way from London to see me, or are you staying in the neighbourhood?"

"I am staying with you," Lady Dilys said sweetly. "A second carriage containing my luggage and my lady's-maid is following."

The Marquis frowned.

"I am not entertaining at the moment, with the exception of Freddie, and therefore you cannot stay here!"

"Am I really hearing you aright?" Lady Dilys asked. "Why should I not stay with you as we have often done in the past?"

"Not alone at Troon," the Marquis replied.

"But in a great number of other places."

"That is different!"

"Why?"

"Because Troon is my home, and I must keep up certain standards."

Again Lady Dilys laughed and it was not such a pretty sound.

"What has happened?" she asked. "What has come over you, Serle? I cannot believe that you are refusing to give me a roof over my head, if only for tonight."

"It may surprise you, Dilys, but I have no intention of allowing you to stay here when there is no other woman in the house."

Lady Dilys stared at him in astonishment before she cried:

"I think you are going mad! We have been together now for a long time, and never, never in the whole of our acquaintance have you ever fussed about the proprieties or talked about our having 'another woman' with us. As though that would make any difference to the manner in which we behaved!"

"What we do in private is one thing," the Marquis said, "in public another!"

Lady Dilys narrowed her eyes.

"You almost sound as if you were ashamed of me!"

"Not in the slightest," the Marquis replied, "but here at Troon I do not wish to cause a scandal or invite local gossip."

"And I suppose you think they did not gossip about the party you gave a month ago of which I was a member, or your Easter party which certainly would not have satisfied ecclesiastical standards?" Lady Dilys asked mockingly.

"I am prepared to admit that the two parties you mention were in themselves somewhat regrettable," the Marquis said, "but that is all the more reason not to add fuel to the fire by flouting the accepted conventions."

"If that is what you feel," Lady Dilys said softly, "then let us, by all means, behave in a manner of which everyone would approve by getting married!"

The Marquis told himself he might have expected that was what she would say and what she had intended when she came here, but somehow it was a blow to hear the actual words and to know that this was a trap that he must avoid with some dexterity.

It suddenly struck him that he had no desire whatsoever although he had once thought differently, to marry Lady Dilys.

He did not know why, but he felt as if he was suddenly free of her and she no longer had the power to move him either to admiration or desire.

Always in the past, her beauty which was undeniable, had made him feel it was a sheer delight to see her face and be lost in admiration at the perfection of her features: to be beguiled by her slanting eyes and curving red lips.

There had also been something about her which invariably quickened his pulses and made him want to touch her.

But now, inexplicably and so suddenly that he felt himself jolted by the truth of it, the allurement or whatever it had been, had gone.

She was beautiful, there was no denying that, but she might have been a picture or a cold marble statue for all the effect she now had on him physically.

And she was waiting, waiting for him to reply to what had been a proposal of marriage.

With an effort at a laugh that was unmistakably contrived the Marquis answered:

"That is certainly a rather strange suggestion, Dilys, for you know that neither you nor I are the marrying sort. If we were tied to each other for life, I am quite certain we would be bored with each other within a few weeks."

"That is not true, Serle. We are eminently suited to each other," Lady Dilys replied. "We think the same, we enjoy the same pleasures, however outrageous, and we enjoy—each other."

Her voice deepened on the last two words and there was a deliberate under-current in her tone which the Marquis did not miss.

Also she looked up at him as she spoke and he knew she was inviting him in a manner that she believed was irresistible and which had always in the past, made him reach out to draw her into his arms.

But the Marquis did not move.

"I can only repeat, Dilys," he said, "that marriage with anyone would be my idea of unmitigated boredom!"

"If that is true," Lady Dilys said, "how delighted your brother Lionel will be!"

"Lionel?" the Marquis asked quickly, "what do you know about Lionel?"

"Ponsonby was telling me about the speeches he has been making against you. I am told there is a cartoon of him denouncing wealthy landlords like yourself, and inciting the rag-tag and bobtail with whom he associates, to burn down Carlton House."

There was a frown between the Marquis's eyes.

He knew how scurrilous cartoonists could be, but he had never thought any member of his family would figure in one.

"So you see, dearest Serle," Lady Dilys said, "the sooner you marry and produce an heir, the better!"

"There is still plenty of time for that," the Marquis said, "and not even to circumvent Lionel will I be forced up the aisle."

There was silence for a moment, and he knew that Lady Dilys was calculating her next move.

"If marriage does not concern us," the Marquis said briskly, "somewhere for you to stay the night does. I will send a note to Lady Forsett, asking her if she will put you up for the night. You will be quite comfortable and you will doubtless want to return to London tomorrow morning."

Lady Dilys rose gracefully from the chair in which she had been sitting.

As she did so, the ostrich feathers on her high-brimmed bonnet fluttered and the Marquis was conscious of the exotic fragrance which emanated from her.

It was a scent that was peculiarly her own and which all her lovers recognised as a haunting perfume which, the moment they smelt it, brought back irresistible memories of fire and passion.

The Marquis was forewarned of her intentions but he would not run away. Indeed, before he could do so, her arms were round him and she was pressing herself against him.

"Are you punishing me for some sin I do not know I have committed?" she asked, her lips raised to his. "I have come to see you, Serle, because I could not bear to be without you any longer. I want you, and I know you want me."

Her arms were round his neck, pulling his head down to hers.

He was not resisting her and was feeling the spell she always exercised

70

over him beginning to work. A second later her lips would have been on his, when the door opened and Freddie came in.

"Hello, Dilys!" he said. "I recognised your carriage outside."

The Marquis disengaged himself from Lady Dilys's clinging arms and she stepped back giving Freddie an undoubtedly baleful glance.

"Did you catch anything?" the Marquis asked.

"Two trout, but they were so small I threw them back," Freddie answered.

He walked to the hearth-rug to look at Dilys with an amused twinkle in his eyes as he said:

"Now why are you here, or need I ask? Were you afraid of Serle getting off the hook?"

"Go away, Freddie, and leave us alone," Lady Dilys said petulantly. "I came to talk to Serle, not to you."

"That of course, I expected, but he is very busy at the moment, and I doubt if he has time for one of your special 'talks'."

"He always has time for me," Lady Dilys replied. "Have you not, dearest?"

She put out her hand with its long thin fingers towards the Marquis, but he appeared not to notice.

"I have just been telling Dilys," he said, "that as she cannot stay here tonight, I have suggested that she goes over to the Forsetts."

Lady Dilys laughed, but her eyes were wary.

"I cannot think what you have been doing to Serle," she said to Freddie. "He has gone all respectable, which is something I never expected of him, not if he lived to be a thousand!"

Freddie glanced at the Marquis.

"Serle is right," he said, "although I dare say if you insist on staying we could rustle up a party. What about asking that pretty girl who has just lost her father?"

If he had intended to annoy Lady Dilys he succeeded.

"What girl?" she asked. "There were no girls at Troon the last time I came here."

"Things change," Freddie answered, "and I am sure if it is a question of emergencies, we could persuade the Dowager to come here for the night.

She does not live very far away, and then you and pretty Valeta Lingfield would be properly chaperoned."

Lady Dilys let out a little scream of rage.

"I do not know what you are talking about," she exclaimed, "and who is this Valeta Lingfield anyway?"

"Has Serle not told you that he has acquired a Ward?" Freddie asked. "Sir Charles Lingfield left him his daughter in his will, and of course, it is a legal obligation he cannot avoid."

Lady Dilys pressed her lips together and looked at the Marquis as if for an explanation, but his eyes were on Freddie's face knowing that his friend was deliberately baiting her and well aware in some subtle way he was getting his own back.

"Freddie is right," the Marquis said decisively. "If you want to stay, Dilys, we must get a party together. I am sure some of my more stodgy neighbours would love to meet you at dinner."

"You are behaving outrageously, as well you know!" Lady Dilys snapped. "I came here to see you because I could not bear to be without you any longer, and this is the reception I receive!"

"I am sorry," the Marquis replied, "but you should know me well enough by now to be aware that London is one thing and Troon is another."

"I know nothing of the sort!" Lady Dilys replied. "Something has happened to you, something I do not understand. If I go back to London, when will you join me?"

"I am not certain," the Marquis said evasively, "perhaps in a week, it depends when I can complete my arrangements here."

"What arrangements?"

"You would not understand if I told you, but they are, as it happens, important."

"What I suggest," Freddie interposed, "is that you sit down and have some refreshment. I am sure a glass of champagne would be very welcome after your journey. Then when the horses are rested, you can go back to London. You will be there in time for a late dinner."

Dilys looked beseechingly at the Marquis, as if she expected him not to agree to such an outrageous suggestion, but he had his hand on the bell-pull and when a servant appeared at the door, he ordered champagne.

Freddie sat down in a chair next to Dilys and asked conversationally:

"What is the latest gossip from St. James's? If anything is happening, I am quite certain you know about it."

"Go away, Freddie. Leave us alone," Lady Dilys said. "I want to talk to Serle."

"And I want to talk to you," Freddie said. "In a bachelor establishment such as we have here at the moment, a lovely woman is like a rainbow in the sky!"

He looked round at the Marquis to smile and say:

"That is damned poetical, is it not? Really, I shall have to find myself an 'Incomparable' who will appreciate such a Byronic style."

"You are a bore, Freddie!" Lady Dilys said vehemently. "I have told you to leave me alone with Serle."

"I shall do nothing of the sort!" Freddie replied. "You are only going to try and twist him round into letting you stay here against his better inclinations. Then you will have us at sixes and sevens with each other, which is something I most dislike."

Lady Dilys opened her lips to say something rude, but at that moment a servant entered with the champagne.

They all accepted a glass and as Lady Dilys sipped hers, Freddie said:

"Now tell us if you have done anything outrageous since we last saw you."

Lady Dilys made a little exclamation and said to the Marquis:

"That makes me think of something I came to tell you and which Freddie put out of my head. I have the most amusing idea for a practical joke."

"If it is like your other ideas in the past," Freddie said before Lady Dilys could go on, "Serle is not to hear it. Has he not told you he has turned over a new leaf and is now taking an interest in his broad acres and his tenants."

"They have managed quite well without him in the past," Lady Dilys retorted.

"That is just where you are wrong," Freddie answered. "They have not. Things have gone sadly awry, and Serle is going to put them to rights, and very efficiently."

"I think the Agent you have found for me will be a great asset," the

Marquis said as if he was following his own train of thought. "I was very impressed with his new ideas of harvesting about which he was telling me this morning."

Lady Dilys looked from one man to the other in perplexity.

"Is this true?" she asked after a moment, "are you really becoming interested in farming? You always told me the country bored you except when you were hunting or shooting."

"I think perhaps I missed something in the past," the Marquis replied.

"London is so dull without you, especially now the Regent has gone to Brighton."

"I am surprised you are not there," Freddie remarked.

For a moment Lady Dilys looked embarrassed, then she said quickly: "I loathe Brighton! The sea winds make my hair so untidy."

Freddie smiled.

He knew now why Lady Dilys was so anxious for the Marquis to return to London.

Most of the *Beau Monde* who surrounded the Prince Regent would be at Brighton, but Lady Dilys had gone too far at the last party at Carlton House when she had offended a number of the Regent's guests and was therefore in his bad books.

While the Regent's private life was outrageous in itself, he always displayed good manners in public and he had grown to dislike practical jokes.

Freddie had not heard the sequel to Lady Dilys's outrageous behaviour which had taken place the night before they had left London for Troon, but now perceptively he was quite certain that she had been told more or less bluntly to stay away from Brighton until she was back in the Regent's favour.

"Personally," he said aloud, "I think that London at this time of year, is hot and boring, and I intend to stay at Troon as long as Serle will have me."

"That is what I would like too," Lady Dilys said, "and I can hardly believe it possible that he should refuse to have me when I have driven all this way just to see him."

She bent forward in her chair, her face raised towards the Marquis who was standing with his back to the fireplace, a glass of champagne in his hand.

"Let me stay with you, Serle," she said pleadingly. "We will have such fun, and you know that I love you!"

It would have been difficult for any man to resist the appeal in her voice and the beauty of her face, and it seemed as if for a moment, both the Marquis and Freddie were hypnotised into stillness. Then the Marquis replied:

"If you insist on staying, Dilys, I will send a groom to my mother to ask her to join us, or if she cannot do so, I am sure she could spare her companion, a most respectable elderly widow."

Lady Dilys put her empty glass down with a slight slap on the table.

"I have no intention of staying where I am not wanted! Ponsonby is in London, so is Sinclair, and George Weston. They will look after me, and I am sure we shall find some amusements which do not smell of pigs or freshly manured ground!"

Her voice had a bitter fury which was unmistakable.

She rose to her feet with a rustle of silk and sweeping past the Marquis and Freddie walked down the room.

It was a dramatic exit, but both men were well aware knowing Lady Dilys as they did, that she expected them to stop her long before she reached the door.

The Marquis's eyes met those of his friend and Freddie knew without a word being spoken that he was being told to let her go.

They caught up with her only when Lady Dilys had reached the Hall and still without speaking a word she descended the steps to where her carriage was waiting.

A servant opened the door and handed her in and the Marquis and Freddie stood side by side on the top of the steps.

As the coachman drove the horses away they had a last glimpse of Lady Dilys's profile silhouetted in all its beauty against the dark background of the carriage. Then she was moving away from them down the drive.

Freddie put up his hand to his forehead as if he expected it to be wet with sweat and as they walked silently across the Hall and into the Library he said:

"God knows, Serle, I never thought you had it in you to turn down Dilys in such a manner. What happened before I came into the room?"

"She asked me to marry her."

"And you refused?"

"Of course. I do not intend ever to marry."

"That is nonsense, but at least it is not Dilys."

"No, and it was you who persuaded me it would not be practical."

"It would not be a great many other things," Freddie muttered. "I feel that I have pulled you back from a bottomless abyss."

"I suppose that is true," the Marquis said reflectively. "Do you know, Freddie, it is a damned queer thing, but I suddenly realised—and I cannot explain it even to myself—she no longer attracts me."

"I felt like that a long time ago," Freddie replied, "and I can only thank God, and I mean that in all sincerity, that you found out in time."

"Yes, I found out in time," the Marquis said. "What puzzles me is why it should have happened so suddenly in the way it has?"

"Perhaps you will never know the answer," Freddie said cheerfully, "but whatever it is, let us drink to our freedom! By God, I need a drink at this moment!"

CHAPTER FIVE

*B*Y THE TIME HER CARRIAGE HAD REACHED THE END of the drive Lady Dilys was shaking with anger.

She could not believe it possible that the Marquis had not prevented her from leaving.

On other occasions she had threatened a dramatic exit to gain her own way and had always been prevented from leaving at the last moment.

Once, she remembered, the gentleman in question had run after her coach and sprang into it when it was actually moving quite quickly to seat himself beside the fair charmer who had captured his heart.

On that occasion she had allowed the carriage to travel for nearly a mile before she had with a well-simulated reluctance given orders for her horses to be turned round.

Incredibly the Marquis had not followed her and she had the uncomfortable feeling that she might never see him again.

She had, in fact, been slightly perturbed, but not overwhelmingly so, when the Marquis had not returned to London and to her side as quickly as she had expected.

When he had left London she was quite certain it would be a question of his being away only a day or two, then irresistibly she would have drawn him back by the strong, fiery passion that linked them to each other.

That the Marquis could suddenly become immune to her blandishments, that he could assume an indifference to her pleading that she might stay with him, seemed so unlikely that Lady Dilys could not credit it had really occurred.

But as her horses plodded on, passing through the dusty lanes to reach the Highway, she told herself almost despairingly that she had lost the one man who mattered at this moment more in her life than any others.

She had made up her mind to marry the Marquis, not only because he was the richest and most important of any of her lovers, but also because he genuinely attracted her.

She liked his recklessness, which echoed her own, his daring and his spirit of fun, which made him so different in temperament from her other suitors.

She had decided some time ago, that she would marry him. There had however seemed no need for haste until after the scene at Carlton House, where she had learnt with some dismay that if she went to Brighton, the Regent would not acknowledge her presence there.

Lady Dilys admitted to herself frankly that she had gone too far and had not only antagonised the Regent himself, but far more dangerous, aroused the animosity of Lady Conyngham.

While Lady Dilys believed she could do anything with any man who was not blind, she knew that where women were concerned it was a very different story.

Women mistrusted and disapproved of her and, as Lady Conyngham had supplanted Lady Hertford in the Regent's affections and he was becoming more and more infatuated with her, there was no doubt that her approval was very important to those who wished to be invited either to Carlton House or to the Royal Pavilion at Brighton.

To be in Brighton and not take part in the huge dinner parties and musical soirees that took place almost nightly in the Royal Pavilion, was to be little better than a pariah.

However daring Lady Dilys might be, at the moment she had not the courage to brave Social ostracism in Brighton.

She therefore told herself that the obvious course was to marry the Marquis immediately.

She had known perceptively, because she was well experienced where men were concerned, that he was thinking of asking her to be his wife.

The words had, she was sure, trembled on his lips on one or two occasions without his actually uttering them, but Lady Dilys had thought triumphantly that it was only a question of time.

But now time was something she could not afford and she therefore decided that as the Marquis had not returned to London she would go to Troon.

She was quite sure that before she left Troon they would be betrothed and after that no-one in the length and breadth of the land would bar their doors to her.

What was more, because the Regent was genuinely fond of the Marquis his wife would be forgiven any misdeeds she might have committed in the past, and as the Marchioness of Troon she would be able to rule the *Beau Monde* from an unassailable social position with unlimited wealth to support it.

The more she thought about it the more attractive the idea seemed and the more she was determined the nuptial day should be fixed.

There were quite a number of protests from her adoring swains before she left London.

Despite the fact that they all knew she was the Marquis's acknowledged mistress, they had either enjoyed Lady Dilys's favours in the past or hoped to do so in the future.

She had quite a gratifying send off when she left the house in Curzon Street to drive to Troon.

Now she had the suspicion that they would speculate privately amongst themselves, if they dared not speak about it openly, as to why she had returned without the Marquis and with no promise, unless she invented one, of when he would be back in London.

"How could I have lost him?" Lady Dilys asked.

How could it have happened? How could any man, who had been as infatuated with her as the Marquis had been, suddenly become cold and aloof and indifferent when she had pressed her body against his and put her arms round his neck.

Something had changed him, she thought—but what?—Or who?

Carefully Lady Dilys went over every word that had been spoken since she had arrived at Troon.

She had known that Freddie was baiting her and she had been aware for some time, that he disliked her association with the Marquis.

Not because he was jealous—that she could have understood—but because his affection for his friend made him consider her a bad influence.

She had suspected in the past, she thought, that Freddie was really an enemy, but now he had shown her his true colours and she thought that if only she was a man, it would give her real pleasure to shoot him down and see him dying at her feet.

"I will get even with him one day," she promised herself, but knew her problem at the moment was not Freddie, but the Marquis.

If he would not marry her—and she had the uncomfortable feeling that was now very likely—to whom could she turn?

Lord Ponsonby, who had pursued her for years, whilst being an attractive man, had no money.

In fact, the only wealthy member of her circle at the moment was Sir George Weston, who might be extremely rich but was an unmitigated bore, both in bed and out.

Lady Dilys clenched her fingers until the knuckles showed white.

"How can I have lost Serle?" she muttered to herself. "He loves me, I know he loves me!"

But she could see again the expression in his eyes when she had pleaded with him and knew that in some extraordinary manner, he had withdrawn from her into a distant land where she could not reach him.

Then suddenly like a flash of lightning she remembered Freddie's talk of the pretty girl who had become the Marquis's Ward.

Vaguely she remembered that on previous visits to Troon she had met a good-looking, older man called Sir Charles Lingfield, who she had learned was a near neighbour.

She had not wasted any time with him, but the men she met were always stored in Lady Dilys's mind, just in case in the future they ever came in useful.

She thought over what she had heard; Sir Charles Lingfield had for some reason that was not explained, made his daughter the Marquis's Ward.

Could she be the reason for the change in the man that Lady Dilys had felt she knew so intimately, but who had in a few days, become almost a stranger?

Still it did not seem possible because the Marquis had always disliked girls and found them gauche and uninteresting, although actually despite the manoeuvring of ambitious mothers he had met very few of them.

"Valeta Lingfield!" Lady Dilys repeated almost under her breath.

There was a venomous expression in her eyes which would certainly have alarmed Valeta had she seen it.

The carriage proceeded at a good pace towards London until they began to encounter increased traffic on the outskirts.

As the Marquis had chosen and paid for the horses that filled Lady Dilys's stable, the journey was not as arduous as it would have been with inferior animals.

In fact, deep in her thoughts Lady Dilys was surprised when she realised they were not only inside the Metropolis but proceeding down Park Lane.

It was then she bent forward almost automatically to look at Stevington House.

She had been so sure when she passed it this morning on her way to Troon, that she would soon be its mistress and give parties as the Marquis's mother had done, in the great Ballroom, but for what Lady Dilys called "much more amusing people".

Now she told herself with a renewal of her anger that the picture of herself standing at the top of the stairs with the Marquis beside her was likely to exist only in her imagination and never become a reality.

Stevington House silhouetted against the last glow of the setting sun looked magnificent and had a grandeur that made it seem to eclipse all the other grand houses in the aristocratic road which overlooked Hyde Park.

It was then that Lady Dilys saw a familiar figure standing outside the house.

It was not hard to recognise Lionel Stevington, for he had an undeniable resemblance to his brother even though the expression on his face, bitter and cynical, made him unattractive and caused a number of his acquaintances to pretend not to have seen him or pass him with an indifferent nod.

He was standing now talking to a large, rough-looking man and Lady Dilys thought with a curl of her lip that he was doubtless abusing his brother while in reality he would give anything in the world to be the owner of Stevington House and Troon.

Lady Dilys was too experienced with men not to realise that Lionel's pretence of "helping the under-dog" sprang merely from envy, hatred and malice.

She had often warned the Marquis laughingly that one night Lionel would stab him in the back in some dark alley, and the following morning step into his shoes with alacrity.

The carriage had almost passed Stevington House when Lady Dilys peremptorily ordered it to stop.

The coachman drew the horses to a standstill and when the footman jumped down from the box to enquire her wishes she said:

"Ask the gentleman who is standing over there, to come and speak to me."

The footman hurried to obey her and she sat back in the carriage waiting, her eyes narrowing a little, her full lips set in a hard line.

"And what can Your Ladyship want of a poor unimportant fellow like myself?" a mocking voice asked at the window.

"Get in!" Lady Dilys said curtly.

Lionel Stevington raised his eye-brows, but the footman opened the door and he obeyed her, seating himself beside her on the back seat and throwing his high hat on the one opposite him.

It was typical that despite his alleged *penchant* for the working classes, he continued to dress as a gentleman of fashion, knowing that it made his revolutionary and radical prejudices sound more forceful when he did not look the part.

He leaned back very much at his ease and contemplated Lady Dilys in a manner which she knew was deliberately insulting, but which for the moment she was not prepared to challenge.

"Were you calling at Stevington House to see your brother?" she enquired.

"Of course."

"May I ask why?"

"It is no secret," he replied. "I am merely asking for some of the crumbs that fall from the table, or should I say the bed, of lovely creatures like yourself."

Lady Dilys ignored the rudeness.

"You are misinformed," she said. "Your brother is not spending his money on me at the moment, but on someone else!"

She saw that Lionel Stevington was surprised, but also interested.

"I thought you had His Lordship thoroughly tied up."

"So did I," Lady Dilys replied, "but I was mistaken."

"You amaze me," Lionel remarked.

"It has amazed me too," Lady Dilys agreed. "But I thought you should be the first to know, since it concerns you so closely, that your brother is in danger of being lured into matrimony with a young girl."

"Matrimony?"

Lionel Stevington stiffened.

Lady Dilys knew that he had never imagined there was any likelihood of such a union between herself and the Marquis.

"Yes, matrimony," she said, "for it is unlikely that he could offer any other position to Sir Charles Lingfield's daughter."

There was a frown between Lionel Stevington's eyes as he said:

"I remember Lingfield, but I had no idea he had a daughter."

"She is now your brother's Ward, and I am told, very pretty."

Lady Dilys thought to herself that her voice seemed to hiss the words as she spoke them, but she had the feeling that in some way, she was not quite certain how, she was striking back at the Marquis.

"Tell me about this girl," Lionel Stevington said after a moment.

Lady Dilys shrugged her shoulders.

"I was naturally not allowed to see her," she said. "I was only told of her existence and how preoccupied your brother is with her. In fact, in consequence, I was sent away from Troon, as if I was a servant no longer required, something I have not experienced until now."

He heard the chagrin in her voice and laughed.

"So Serle has turned you off, has he?" he asked. "Well, I expect you have had some good pickings off him, and I dare say there will be plenty of other fellows to take his place."

He leant forward to retrieve his hat from the seat opposite him as he added:

"I am obliged to you for the information."

"I thought it would please you to know that you could quite soon become an uncle," Lady Dilys said, "and after all, you have never had any real chance of inheriting the title. Your brother is young and very attractive."

Lionel Stevington knew that she was being spiteful because for a moment, he had got under her skin.

Again he laughed, and opening the carriage door, stepped out.

"I wish Your Ladyship good-day and good hunting!"

The innuendo in his words made Lady Dilys want to spit at him. Instead she watched him walk jauntily away back to where the large rough-looking man was still waiting.

As she drove on towards her own house, she wondered if she had gained anything by her conversation with Lionel Stevington.

She had the infuriating feeling that he in fact, had been more insolent to her than she had to him, and yet she might have struck a blow at the Marquis—she was not sure.

If Serle was unpredictable, so was his brother, and at the moment she loathed them both.

The Marquis received a note early the following morning from his mother to say how she longed to see him and would be delighted to meet Valeta Lingfield again, whom she had known as a small child.

But she unfortunately could not invite them to luncheon until the following day.

"I have promised for a long time," she wrote in her beautiful upright hand-writing, *"to take luncheon with your Aunt Dorothea. As She is over eighty, I would not like to inconvenience Her by changing My plans at the last moment. I know, dearest Boy, that you will understand and I look forward to seeing You on Thursday with little Valeta, and will expect You both here at a half after twelve o'clock."*

The Marquis gave the information contained in his mother's note to Freddie as they breakfasted together.

"I will have to drive over and tell Valeta that I will take her tomorrow instead of today," he said. "It will not take me long. Are you coming with me?"

"No, I want to read the newspapers," Freddie answered. "When you come back I want you to come and look at that horse of mine. Archer says he is definitely off-colour but can find no reason for it."

"If Archer does not know what is wrong," the Marquis replied, "the trouble either exists in your imagination, or it is really serious."

"I hope it is not that," Freddie said. "I paid a large sum for my team and I certainly cannot afford to lose any of them."

"I should not worry too much," the Marquis said, "I expect it is only a temporary indisposition. Some horses hate the heat."

"That may be the explanation," his friend said, "but I would still like you to look at him."

"Of course I will do that," the Marquis answered. "I must just tell Valeta not to put on her best bib and tucker until tomorrow."

He finished his breakfast and set off immediately driving a light Phaeton with a pair of perfectly matched horses that moved together in a manner which always gave the Marquis pleasure every time he handled them.

It took him only about ten minutes to reach the Manor House and he thought as he drove down the overgrown drive that Valeta would very likely be delighted that she did not have to endure his company on the long drive to his mother's, but could postpone the irksome experience until the following day.

The Marquis knew without conceit that most women would give

almost anything for the pleasure and excitement of driving alone with him anywhere he wished to go.

He wondered what his mother would make of Valeta, seeing that she was in every way different from anyone he had taken to meet her on previous occasions.

But those he had taken to luncheon or tea with the Dowager Marchioness had not included Lady Dilys.

He knew that to his mother she would not have been a welcome guest, and one reason why he had not proposed marriage to Dilys was the knowledge that his mother would disapprove of her as his wife and would have been much upset by the thought of Dilys taking what had been her place at Troon.

'Mama will be glad that I am going to see her for a very different reason,' the Marquis thought.

A turn in the drive revealed the Manor House ahead.

As the Marquis drew his horses up at the front door Valeta's old Nurse came running out through the doorway in a manner that told him before she spoke that she was upset.

"Oh, M'Lord, M'Lord!" she cried. "Thank God you are here! I was just about to send for Your Lordship—and now you've come!"

Her voice sounded so strange and her words were so incoherent that the Marquis quickly threw down the reins and as his groom went to the heads of his horses, stepped out of the Phaeton.

"What is the matter?" he enquired. "What has Nicholas been doing?"

"It's not Nicholas, M'Lord," Nannie gasped. "It's Miss Valeta! Oh, M'Lord, they've taken her away!"

"Taken her away?" the Marquis asked.

He had moved automatically through the front door into the small hall, and now he looked at the old Nurse in perplexity as the words came tumbling from her.

"Two men, M'Lord. They snatched her up and little Harry as she was a-talking to, covered them with cloths, threw them into a carriage and drove off."

Nanny was gasping for breath before she finished speaking and her hands were shaking in a manner which made the Marquis feel she might collapse.

Firmly he took her by the arm and sat her down on the seat at the bottom of the stairs.

"Now start from the beginning," he said quietly, "and tell me exactly what happened."

"Oh, M'Lord, 'twas terrible!" Nanny murmured.

"From the beginning!" the Marquis said firmly. "Where were you when this happened?"

"I was in the Drawing-Room, M'Lord," Nanny began, and the Marquis realised it was a great effort for her to speak more slowly.

"What were you doing?" he asked.

"I was brushing the carpet, M'Lord, and Miss Valeta was arranging the flowers."

She gave a gasp of breath before she continued:

"There was a knock on the door and Miss Valeta says to me: 'I will go, Nanny,' and she walks across the hall. I hears her speak to Nicholas as she passed him."

"He was in the hall?" the Marquis questioned.

"Yes, M'Lord, playing with some old toys Miss Valeta had found for him in the attic."

"Then what happened?"

"I heard Miss Valeta say: 'Good-morning, Harry! I see you have brought us some butter.' "

"Who is Harry?"

"He's the little boy from the Home Farm, M'Lord. We always buys the butter from Mr. Hopson and he sends it to us fresh from the churn twice a week."

"What happened then?" the Marquis asked.

"Miss Valeta calls to me, M'Lord: 'Harry is here, Nanny. Is there anything we want? Have we enough eggs?' and I says:

" 'We'd better have a dozen tomorrow.' You see, M'Lord, since we've had Nicholas with us, we've been trying to make him eat . . .' "

"Never mind about that now," the Marquis said. "Go on with what occurred."

"I was continuing with my brushing, M'Lord, when I hears Nicholas give a sudden shriek.

" 'They've come for me!' he cried. 'They've come! Save me! Save me!'

"I hears him running upstairs as quick as his legs could carry him."

"What did you do?" the Marquis asked.

"Thinking it was strange I put down my pan and brush and went into the hall to see what had upset him, and as I did so I heard Miss Valeta give a cry. It were a cry of fear, M'Lord."

"What was happening? Could you see?"

"Yes, M'Lord. There was a cloth over her head and a man were carrying her in his arms into a carriage that was standing outside the door."

"What sort of carriage?"

"I couldn't rightly say, M'Lord. 'Twas closed and was a bit old and dark, somehow."

"And they put Miss Valeta into it?" the Marquis asked.

"I sees the man push her into it, M'Lord, and another man was carrying young Harry, also with a cloth or sack over his head. He just throws him in and as I runs forward, having been so astonished I was unable to move, so to speak, they drives off!"

"There was another man on the box?"

"Yes, M'Lord. A coachman, but not in livery, or anything like that. Leastways, I don't think so."

"How many horses?" the Marquis asked.

Nanny thought for a moment.

"Two I think, but I'm not certain. I was looking at the carriage door thinking I might see Miss Valeta, but it was dark, and I couldn't see her, and I couldn't believe it had all happened."

"No, of course not," the Marquis agreed.

Tears were running down the old Nurse's face and now she put her hands to her eyes as if she was completely overwhelmed.

"Where is Nicholas?" the Marquis asked after a moment.

Nanny's voice was only a croak broken with tears as she answered:

"I expects he's under Miss Valeta's bed, M'Lord. It's where he always hides when he's frightened."

The Marquis went up the stairs two at a time.

He had to guess which of three doors opened off the landing into Valeta's bedroom, and opening the first door found he had made a mistake for the blinds were drawn and the bed was covered in dust-sheets.

87

He went to the next room and found the sun pouring in through the window.

There was a bed with a white muslin flounce matching the muslin skirt which enveloped the dressing-table.

It was, he thought, very much a young girl's room and smelt of lavender and roses, and was very different in every way from the bedrooms in which the Marquis had sported himself with women like Lady Dilys.

There was no sound except the song of the birds outside and the buzzing of a bee which had settled on some roses which stood in a vase on the dressing-table.

Then he heard a little whimper which he had heard before and knew who had made it.

"It is all right, Nicholas," he said quietly, "there is nothing to frighten you. I want you to come out and talk to me."

There was no response and the Marquis bent down and lifting the flounce looked under the bed.

There was a faint scream of terror and he saw Nicholas curled up like a small ball pressed against the wall.

"Listen, Nicholas," the Marquis said, "I need your help, and I need it very quickly."

"They will . . . take me . . . away!" Nicholas cried, and the Marquis could hear the terror in his voice. "They will take me . . . away and . . . burn my feet!"

"Who will take you away?" the Marquis asked.

There was no answer and he knew the child was terrified almost beyond words.

The Marquis knelt down on one knee as he had done before.

"Please help me, Nicholas," he said. "Those wicked people have taken Miss Lingfield away and unless you want them to harm her I have to find her very quickly. So you must please help me."

The small boy had hidden his head in his arms. Now the Marquis saw his eyes peeping at him and he went on:

"You do not want them to hurt Miss Lingfield, and I must know where they have gone. Come and tell me what you saw. Please, Nicholas."

For a moment the Marquis thought he had failed. Then Nicholas began to crawl towards him.

He came out from the flounce under the bed and then swiftly like a small animal that seeks sanctuary, he threw himself against the Marquis, putting his arms round his neck and holding onto him so tightly that the Marquis found it hard to breathe.

Slowly, so that the child did not become more frightened than he was already, he got to his feet, lifting him in his arms.

"No-one is going to hurt you," he said soothingly. "Look out of the window and you will see that the men have gone away. There is no-one there."

He carried the child to the window so that he could look down on the empty drive beneath them.

"You see—they have gone!" the Marquis said. "But they have taken Miss Lingfield with them and I have to catch up with them. So tell me, Nicholas, who they were."

Against his ear so softly that the Marquis could hardly hear, Nicholas whispered:

"I saw—Bill!"

"Who is Bill?"

"He—beat me and he—stuck pins into my—feet!"

The arms round the Marquis's neck clutched convulsively, but he managed to say:

"That is something he shall never do again, I promise you that."

He knew now what he had already guessed, that the men who had carried Valeta off had something to do with Cibber, but it seemed peculiar that they should have taken a strange boy with them, unless . . .

The Marquis carried Nicholas downstairs to find Nanny still sitting on the chair in the hall.

"What does the boy Harry look like, Nanny?" he asked as she rose a little uncertainly to her feet.

"He's got fair hair, M'Lord, and is nicely spoken."

"How old is he?"

"I don't rightly know, M'Lord, perhaps seven or eight years of age."

"And he looks something like Nicholas?"

"I wouldn't say that, M'Lord, except that they're both fair."

The Marquis was certain in his mind that Harry had been taken by mistake for Nicholas.

Aloud he said:

"I want you and Nicholas to come with me to Troon while I go and find Miss Lingfield."

"Oh, M'Lord, that's what I hoped you'd say. You'll bring her back, won't you? It's a-feared I am for her in the hands of those men."

"I will bring her back, Nanny," the Marquis said quietly. "You may be sure of that. But there is no time to be lost."

He saw Nanny look round as if she intended to fetch things and he said firmly:

"Come just as you are. We can send for anything you need later. I think Nicholas should feel he is safe, which he will not do while he is here."

Without waiting for Nanny to acquiesce the Marquis walked out of the front door with Nicholas in his arms and set him down in the Phaeton.

The child seemed for a moment reluctant to take his arms from around his neck, then the excitement at being high off the ground and driving behind two horses took his attention for the moment from his own personal fear.

Nanny climbed up beside him and they drove off with Nicholas sandwiched in between her and the Marquis.

The Marquis proceeded at a much quicker rate than he had on his journey from Troon.

He was trying to calculate what had happened and for what reason Valeta had been spirited away, presumably by Cibber. He had thought the man was quite satisfied with the money he had handed over in exchange for Nicholas.

It had, in fact, been far in excess of what an ordinary apprentice might pay to be released from his bond, but the Marquis was aware that Cibber had resented being beaten by a woman and he supposed this was in some extraordinary way his revenge.

They reached the main drive. Troon lay ahead of them magnificent with its windows glistening and the lake golden with sunshine at its feet.

The Marquis felt a sudden tremor pass through Nicholas and felt the small boy draw even closer to him than he was already.

"It is all right," he said looking down at him with a smile. "You will be quite safe here."

"Chimneys," Nicholas murmured, "lots and lots of—chimneys."

"Do not worry about them," the Marquis said, "and there will never be another climbing boy in them again."

The way he spoke surprised even himself, and he thought with a twist of his lips that Valeta had won a victory and would be delighted that he had capitulated to her demands.

Then he told himself that before she could learn of his decision he would have to find her, and it now struck him more forcibly that it might prove extremely difficult to do so.

He drew the horses up outside the front door and said to the groom:

"Go to the stables and tell them I require immediately my racing Phaeton and the new chestnut team to draw it."

"Very good, M'Lord."

The Marquis lifted Nicholas down to the ground and walking up the steps said to Andrews:

"Fetch Mr. Chamberlain and Mrs. Fielding. Where is Captain Weyborne?"

"In the Library, M'Lord."

"Tell all three I want them."

Footmen went hurrying in every direction and the Marquis stood waiting in the centre of the Hall, still holding Nicholas by the hand.

Mr. Chamberlain appeared from below the stairs as Mrs. Fielding appeared at the top of them and there was a surprised expression on both their faces as they hurried towards the Marquis.

"Nurse and the small boy are to stay here, and the latter is to be assured that he is in no danger and no-one will hurt him."

"Hurt him?" Mr. Chamberlain questioned.

"Miss Lingfield has been abducted, and a boy from the Home Farm who was talking to her and whom I am convinced they mistook for Nicholas, has been taken with her."

While Mr. Chamberlain's mouth opened in astonishment Freddie had come into the Hall and unnoticed by the Marquis had reached his side.

"What are you saying, Serle?" he enquired. "Valeta has been abducted. It cannot be possible!"

"It is very possible," the Marquis answered, "and Nicholas recognised one of the men who took her away as a man called Bill, who is in Cibber's employment."

"The Sweep?"

"Exactly!"

The Marquis turned again to Mr. Chamberlain.

"You have Cibber's address?"

"Yes, of course, My Lord. He sweeps the chimneys at Stevington House. That is why he came to Troon."

"From London?" the Marquis asked in surprise.

"No local Sweep could take on anything so large as this house," Mr. Chamberlain explained, "and as the chimneys had to be swept, I arranged for Cibber to come here."

"I see . . ." the Marquis said. "I never thought he might be a London man."

As he spoke he realised that this made it all the more urgent for him to find Valeta quickly.

"Give me Cibber's address," he said sharply, "and Freddie, we will take a couple of pistols with us."

"I cannot imagine what is going on," Freddie replied.

"This is no time for words," the Marquis said firmly. Then to the Housekeeper he said: "Take Nurse upstairs. See that she and the little boy are comfortable. You can send someone later in the day to collect their things from the Manor House."

"They are to stay here, M'Lord?"

"Until I return," the Marquis replied.

"And you'll bring Miss Valeta with you?" Nanny asked in a voice that broke. "Pray God, M'Lord, you'll be able to do that."

"I feel sure I will be able to," the Marquis replied firmly. "Look after Nicholas. He has been very frightened."

Nanny put out her hand to Nicholas but the small boy suddenly flung his arms round the Marquis's leg.

"I want to come with you," he said. "I'll be safe with you."

"You will be safe here until I come back," the Marquis answered, "and I think if you are very good, Mr. Chamberlain might be able to find a pony for you to ride."

"Like Rufus?"

"You must tell me if he is like Rufus," the Marquis answered.

He did not realise that hearing the gentle and understanding manner in which he was speaking to Nicholas, both his Comptroller and his friend were looking at him in astonishment.

The small boy loosened his grip of the Marquis's leg.

"You will be back very soon, won't you?" he asked wistfully.

"Just as soon as I can find Miss Lingfield for you."

"I'll be praying, M'Lord, I'll be praying every moment you are gone," Nanny cried. "Oh, how can this have happened? My poor baby! My poor baby!"

The Marquis glanced at the Housekeeper who put her arms round Nanny and began to draw her up the stairs.

Mr. Chamberlain took Nicholas by the hand.

"Suppose we go and look for that pony now," he said, and saw an expression of delight replace the one of fear in the small boy's eyes.

The Marquis turned to Freddie.

"You are ready?" he asked.

"These are the pistols you require," the Butler said stepping forward, "and here is that man Cibber's address. He left a card in the Pantry, M'Lord, when he was here last."

"It is the last thing he will ever leave in this house," the Marquis said grimly.

He took the card from the Butler.

It was a trade card such as many tradesmen had printed, to present to their patrons even though the Sweeps and their like could not read.

The Marquis read:

CIBBER
Chimney Sweeper & Nightman
9 Duck Lane
St. Giles
Begs leave most respectfully to inform his Friends and the Public in general, that he continues to sweep Chimnies of all Descriptions, cleans Smoke Jacks, Smokey Coppers, and extinguishes Chimnies when on Fire, with the greatest Care and Safety.

———

SMOKEY CHIMNIES CURED
Drains and Sesspools cleaned on the Shortest Notice.
CHIMNIES SWEPT BY THE YEAR.

Andrews now held out to Freddie the duelling pistols in their polished box.

Freddie put one in his own pocket and handed the other to the Marquis who was still looking at the card he held in his hand.

"St. Giles!" he murmured, and he was thinking as he spoke that he could not imagine a more terrible place for Valeta to be taken.

Anyone who lived in London was aware of the horrors that took place in the district of St. Giles' where there were a number of "Flash Houses" that even the Police avoided and would not enter unless in a band.

The Marquis had heard that over four hundred delinquents slept in one of the houses where the inmates were trained in crime from their very earliest 'teens.

The boys gradually becoming expert went out thieving, pilfering, picking pockets, injuring and even murdering those who resisted them, while the girls, who might be only twelve or thirteen years old, became prostitutes.

The Marquis had, in fact, read a report by one of the Select Committees of what happened in the "Flash Houses" and he could only hope this was not one that had come to Valeta's notice.

He knew that the horror and traffic of the "Flash Houses" would appal any woman who was gently bred.

He thrust the card into his pocket, took the second duelling-pistol, and walked towards the door.

As he did so the Phaeton he had ordered, drawn by a superb team of chestnuts which he had bought only a few months before at Tattersall's, came hurrying round from the stables.

The horses were fresh and it was difficult for the grooms to hold them while the Marquis climbed into the high driving-seat and Freddie joined him.

They moved off, driving from the very outset with a speed that made Freddie aware of the Marquis's sense of urgency to save Valeta from what they were both aware might well be a fate very much worse than death!

CHAPTER SIX

*V*ALETA WAS, AT FIRST, SO HELPLESS with the cloth over her head and shaken by the roughness with which she had been flung down onto the seat of the carriage, that it was difficult to breathe, let alone think.

Then as she heard and felt the wheels turning beneath her and heard Harry begin to cry from fright, she put up her hands to pull the cloth from her head.

"Leave it be!" a rough voice said, "or Oi'll toi yer up!"

She realised then there was a man sitting opposite her on the seat of the carriage with his back to the horses, and for a moment the harshness of his voice and the threat he had uttered made her speechless.

She tried to recall what had happened.

She had been talking to Harry when she had heard the sound of an approaching vehicle and seen two horses come round the curve of the drive.

She had thought it must be the Marquis and she felt, as always when he approached, a sudden constriction within her which she could not prevent.

Then as she looked at the horses she realised they were certainly not the type of animal the Marquis would drive and she wondered which tradesman they belonged to and why he should be calling on them when, as far as she knew, Nanny had ordered nothing.

Then the carriage which the horses were drawing came into view and she saw the driver of it was a rough-looking man with a cap pulled low over his forehead and a red handkerchief tied round his neck.

She watched the vehicle approach with curiosity and was just about to tell Harry that she wanted nothing more and he could go home when the carriage was brought to a standstill, the door of it opened and out jumped two men.

They rushed up to her, and before she could realise what was happening she was in darkness with a cloth over her head and was being carried forcibly in strong arms to be flung violently onto the seat of the carriage.

A second or so later she heard Harry cry as he was thrown down beside her.

Valeta struggling to think clearly tried to imagine what had happened and for what reason she was being carried off in such a manner.

She knew by now the carriage must have reached the end of the drive and had turned onto the road that led through the village.

She wondered if she screamed loudly enough or perhaps managed to reach the window whether any of the villagers would come to her assistance.

Then she had the uncomfortable feeling that long before she could attract attention the man who had spoken so roughly and was sitting opposite her, would force her into silence.

She did not like to think of the methods he might use to obtain it.

So she merely sat back in the seat knowing the carriage was a poor one, badly upholstered, and the wheels turning beneath her jolted and bumped in a manner which told her that any springing was non-existent.

'What will happen to me?' she asked herself and was afraid of the answer.

They must have driven for a mile and Valeta was now aware that they were out of the village and not far from the Highway. In a quiet and what she hoped was a conciliatory tone she said:

"Would it be possible for me to remove this cloth from my face as it is making me so hot and it is hard to breathe."

There was silence for a moment, then the man said grudgingly:

"Oi s'pose it'll be orl right, but if yer shouts or tries to attrac' attention Oi'll clobber yer!"

That, Valeta thought, was what she had expected him to do and she raised the cloth tentatively just to be certain he would not change his mind, then pulled it from her head.

Sitting opposite her was an exceedingly unpleasant-looking character.

He was a young man, she thought, of about twenty years or more. His features were coarse, his skin was pock-marked and he was extremely dirty.

He wore a cloth cap pulled low on his forehead and there was a torn handkerchief round his neck.

He was looking at her in a speculative manner which made her feel afraid, and she instinctively put her hands to her hair to tidy it, then looked down at Harry.

He was crying beneath the piece of sacking that covered him and which Valeta saw was ingrained with soot.

"May I take this off the boy?" she asked.

"Oi s'pose so," the man said grudgingly.

She pulled away the dirty sacking and threw it down on the floor. Then as Harry's frightened, tear-stained face looked up at her she heard the man opposite ejaculate:

" 'E ain't Nichilas!"

"No, of course not," Valeta said. "This is Harry, a local farmer's son, and I promise you there will be a great hue and cry when his father realises he is missing!"

"Oi wants to go back to me Pa!" Harry cried, his sobs breaking out afresh.

"Do not cry," Valeta said. "There has been a mistake and you should not be here at all."

She looked down at the soot-covered canvas on the floor, then at the man who was staring at Harry as if he could not believe his eyes, and said accusingly:

"It was Nicholas you were trying to kidnap, was it not?"

" 'E be like Nichilas," the man answered, as if excusing himself.

"Then as you have made a mistake," Valeta said, "I suggest you stop the carriage and put us down on the roadway. We will find our own way home."

" 'E be like Nichilas," the man said again.

"But he is not Nicholas," Valeta said firmly as if speaking to a child. "Therefore you have made a mistake in bringing him here. If in fact, you intended to kidnap Nicholas, it was exceedingly dishonest, considering His Lordship bought his apprenticeship."

It was obvious to Valeta that Cibber the Sweep had regretted his bargain and had not only accepted the money which the Marquis had paid him for Nicholas, but was now trying to steal the child back.

Although she knew Harry was frightened and she was sorry for the little boy, she could not help feeling an irrepressible gladness that it was not in fact Nicholas who was being subjected to a further ordeal at the hands of the man who had already treated him so badly.

It was only last night that she had said to Nanny after putting Nicholas to bed:

"Another child might have gone mad, being treated in such an inhuman manner."

"It's something that'll never happen again," Nanny answered, "and time will heal the agony of it in his mind."

"I hope so," Valeta said.

Twice the night before she had got up to go to Nicholas when he had cried out in his sleep.

Although Nanny wanted to have him with her, Valeta felt that he was her own special charge, and she therefore put him into the small dressing-room which led off the bedroom in which she slept.

By leaving the communicating door open she could actually see him lying in bed, and when she heard him turning and tossing and murmuring in his sleep, she had held him close in her arms and soothed him until he was no longer frightened.

To think of these monsters trying to take the child back again seemed a wickedness beyond anything she could imagine.

But with an effort she forced a smile to her lips as she said to the man opposite:

"Now you see it has all been a great mistake, so will you attract the attention of your friends, and tell them there has been a mix-up?"

As she spoke she was calculating in her mind that the moment she got back she must send for the Marquis and they must take Nicholas away to safety.

If Cibber wanted him so much he might try to kidnap him again, and she could not help feeling that the only place where Nicholas would be safe would be at Troon.

She thought the man opposite was going to respond to her plea, when he said with a grin that somehow was exceedingly unpleasant:

"Us might 'ave made a mistike about 'im, but not about ye!"

"Me?" Valeta questioned. "But why should you wish to kidnap me?"

"That's tellin'!"

Valeta looked at him wide-eyed.

"Is it possible that somebody has sent you not only to take Nicholas back to his cruel master, but also to abduct me? It cannot be true!"

"It be rite 'nough. Ye're wanted—that's wot yer are!"

Valeta remembered how she had defied the Sweep and the angry glance he had given her before the Marquis sent him from the room.

So this was his revenge!

Yet it did not seem possible somehow that any man engaged in a trade, however lowly, would dare to risk transportation, which was the punishment for abduction.

Then it struck her that perhaps he intended to use her to extort money from the Marquis as a ransom and she felt how uncomfortable such a situation would be, and how humiliating.

"I may be very stupid," she said aloud, "but I cannot understand why Mr. Cibber should want to saddle himself with a woman like me. Besides, you know as well as I do that the Marquis of Troon who is my Guardian will send the Police to find me, and that might prove very dangerous for all of you."

"Th' Markiss o' Troon," the man repeated, pronouncing the words wrong. " 'E be the bruvver, of Mr. Stev . . . !"

He stopped as if he realised he was being indiscreet, but Valeta was well aware of what he had been about to say.

Was Lionel Stevington involved in this? she asked herself.

She had heard her father relate often enough the disgraceful way he was behaving in London.

Their friends who genuinely worked to try to relieve some of the widespread suffering of the poor, always spoke of Lionel Stevington with contempt. They knew he did nothing really to help the people he professed to champion, but merely incited them to violence for his own ends.

"I think the old Marquis would turn in his grave," Sir Charles had said more than once, "if he knew how his younger son was behaving."

On one occasion Valeta knew he had discussed Lionel Stevington with the Bishop of London who had taken the place of her grandfather after he died.

"The Bishop says that Lionel Stevington is appealing to the young ne'er-do-wells, and sooner or later," Sir Charles had said, "he will cause a riot which will have to be crushed by the Military."

"Oh, I hope not!" Valeta had exclaimed.

She had been upset more than once by hearing of the riots that had taken place in London and various other parts of the country and which had been put down in an almost brutal manner.

This year, when the Regent had opened Parliament in January, he had driven through a very hostile crowd. Gravel and stones were thrown at the Royal carriage and some windows were broken.

The result of this had been that the Habeas Corpus Act was suspended, which meant that anybody under suspicion of causing trouble could be thrown into gaol and kept there.

Both Sir Charles and Valeta thought that in such circumstances quite a number of innocent people might be arrested when they had been doing nothing more sinister than walking peacefully about the streets.

Once in prison they had little chance of getting out unless somebody with influence interceded on their behalf.

Magistrates everywhere in the country had the power to send to gaol any person they thought likely to commit an act prejudicial to public order before they had even done so.

Sir Charles heard of cases where obstreperous boys pulling a face, or making a rude noise, had been shut away behind bars.

The terrifying thing was that there was nothing the ordinary citizen could do against this injustice.

It was no use trying to march to Westminster to present a petition against this abuse of power, because there was an Act prohibiting meetings of more than fifty persons within a mile of Westminster Hall.

Severe punishments for the slightest offence continued to be given simply because the real truth was the Government was frightened of revolutionaries.

So in the circumstances it seemed extraordinary to Valeta that an uneducated Sweep like Cibber, foul though he might be in his speech and cruel to his apprentices, would think of committing the outrageous crime of abducting a lady.

"Unless of course," she told herself, "he has been instigated by somebody of a very different class, and that person might easily be Lionel Stevington!"

But why? Why should Lionel Stevington be concerned with her when as far as she knew, he had never even seen her, much less spoken to her?

She herself had sometimes seen him riding through the Park when he was younger and living at home, and on several occasions recently when he had called to see his brother and left without staying the night.

From the Manor House it was possible to see the carriages passing down the drive, and as Valeta regularly used to walk in the Park for exercise she often had a good view of visitors on their way to or from the great house.

Lionel Stevington was, she thought, something like the Marquis in looks, but while she felt contemptuous of the Marquis for his rakish behaviour, he did not disgust or frighten her as a man.

Lionel Stevington did both, and she knew instinctively as he passed her with his grim, unsmiling face, that he was bad.

She thought she would make sure of her suspicions and after a moment she asked:

"Where am I meeting Mr. Stevington?"

" 'E said . . ." the man opposite began, then broke off to shout angrily:

"Will ye stop askin' questions. Oi b'ain't tellin' yer nothin'. D'yer und'stand?"

"I understand," Valeta said quietly, but she had learned what she wanted to know.

She busied herself talking to Harry and pulling him a little nearer for comfort, and put her arm around him.

He was a sturdy little boy and she thought once again how thankful she was that he was not Nicholas, sensitive and highly strung, who would have been in an abject state of terror if he were with her now.

They drove on and although Valeta made various efforts to converse with the man opposite, he made no response.

In fact she realised she was frightening him by her questions when he said:

"If yer go on talkin' Oi'll make yer cover yersel' up again. D'yer 'ear?"

"Yes, I hear," Valeta said.

101

Fearing he might put his threat into execution, she did not address him again, but talked only to Harry.

"Me Pa will be angry when I don't go home," the boy said.

"I am sure he will be, and he will come to look for you," Valeta replied. "Then Nicholas will tell him who has taken you away."

She saw by the look in the man's eyes listening that this possibility had not occurred to him.

"I suppose," she told herself, "that man Cibber thought he could just snatch Nicholas and me away, and nobody would know where we had gone. But now Nicholas will perhaps have recognised one of these men."

On the other hand there was always the chance that Nicholas intent on playing with his toys, had not paid any attention to what was going on outside.

But Nanny, Valeta thought, would find some way of letting the Marquis know what had occurred.

Then she remembered with a sudden leap of her heart that he was calling for her at eleven o'clock to take her to luncheon with his mother.

She had actually forgotten about it until this moment because being carried off in such a frightening fashion had put everything else out of her mind.

Now she remembered the Marquis would call and Nanny would tell him what had happened.

She felt the warm glow of relief flood over her and the fear that had been like a sharp dagger in her breast, although she tried to control it, receded a little.

What was the time now? she wondered. Not more than perhaps nine-thirty, but in an hour-and-a-half the Marquis would call at the Manor and learn that she had been abducted in this extraordinary manner.

It was such a comfort to know that he would soon learn of her terrible plight that she said to Harry:

"You need not be frightened. These wicked men will get their just desserts and perhaps sooner than they expect!"

"An' yer'll get wot's comin' to yer!" the man opposite her retorted.

"At least I shall not be transported across the sea," Valeta answered. "I understand the ships in which the convicts are chained are very uncomfortable and many of the prisoners die of starvation."

"Shut yer mouf, or Oi'll shut it for yer!" the man shouted angrily.

"I am sorry," Valeta said, "I am very sorry for you."

He looked over his shoulder as if somehow he wished to communicate with his friends on the box outside, but he made no effort to attract their attention and Valeta thought there would be nothing he could do until they reached their destination.

It seemed to take hours for the carriage to reach the outskirts of the city, and then begin to make its way through narrow and crowded streets which were rougher and more poverty-stricken than any Valeta had ever seen before.

Her father had described to her so often the horrors of the London slums and the misery of the inhabitants who were forced to live there.

It suddenly struck her that Cibber with his filthy sacks of soot and the miserable half-starved children he employed in his trade, might live in St. Giles'.

She had read and heard of the horrors that existed in a part of London which should have been swept away, Sir Charles always said, a hundred years ago.

It was there, Valeta knew, that the maimed and the blind beggars, the women with sick barefooted children (hired for the day), and soldiers and sailors with bogus wounds congregated.

"It is a camp," Sir Charles had said once, "for the lowest type of vagrant, the petty thief, and those who have sunk too low to be fit for even the roughest company elsewhere."

"My father has told me," Lady Lingfield said in her soft voice, "that they fill the old houses from garret to cellar, six or seven to a room, and the streets into which no light, let alone the sun, can percolate reek with the piles of decaying litter and all manner of offal."

"Something must be done about it," Sir Charles said firmly.

He went on saying the same thing after Valeta's mother was dead and he still tried to get organisations to help the pregnant women and save some of the children from becoming criminals from the very moment they could walk.

Valeta remembered learning some of the houses in St. Giles' had "schools" for the criminal training of the young.

Both girls and boys were taught the "kinchin-lay" "cly-faking", "wipesnitching," and how to "nim a ticker", and were sent out to work amongst the crowds.

"My father has often told me that when he was young and worked in those terrible streets," Lady Lingfield related, "above the nightly racket could always be heard screams of those who had come home empty-handed and were being beaten for it."

Valeta did not know why, but she was quite certain that was where she and Harry were being taken.

St. Giles'!

The area which made even the strongest young men in the priesthood draw in their breath, and which was a by-word for everything that was criminal and lawless.

She found herself praying that somehow the Marquis would save her, and yet how would he guess for one moment that his brother was involved in anything so reprehensible as a kidnapping?

If it was a question of a ransom, she supposed that sooner or later Lionel Stevington would get in touch with his brother.

She had known he was always hard up for money because that was an open secret amongst the employees on the Troon estate.

"Master Lionel be here again," she had heard one man say when he did not know she was listening. "I expects he's come to 'nick' anything he can't persuade His Lordship to give him, 'a sharpster', they tell is what he be called in London!"

It was not the way that anyone should speak of the Stevington family, Valeta had thought severely.

At the same time, how could those who had served the great house all their lives be expected to have any respect for Lionel when they learned of his revolutionary speeches and the manner in which he abused his brother and his own class in public?

The streets in which they were driving grew narrower and narrower and now Valeta knew with all certainty that they were in St. Giles'.

She could see the flaring lights of the gin shops at every corner, and she could see too the filthy drains running through the centre of the streets in which half-naked children with bare feet were playing.

She began to grow more and more apprehensive.

The people she could see through the windows of the carriage all seemed to have grotesque faces, many of them distorted by disease or debauched by drink.

At last the horses turned into a small yard and now Valeta knew they had reached their destination, for the yard was piled with sacks of soot.

The horses came to a standstill and the man who had been with them inside the carriage opened the door and jumped out.

She heard him telling the two men descending from the box that they had brought the wrong boy.

"It be th' wrong lad we 'ave 'ere. Nichilas be left a'ind. The woman says," pointing his finger at Valeta as she still sat inside the carriage, "that 'e'll tell as where 'em two 'as been took."

Valeta could not see clearly the faces of the two men who had been on the box, but she had a feeling they were shocked by the information.

Then the one who had been driving and was obviously an older man said:

"Put 'em two inside an' let's see wat Cibber 'as t' say abaht it."

The man who had been with them in the carriage came to the door.

"Aht yer git," he said, "an' sharp 'bout it!"

Valeta stepped out first, holding up her skirts as she followed the man who was walking ahead of them into the house.

The yard was filthy and there was the smell of soot and other things to which she had no wish to put a name.

The room they entered opened onto the street on the opposite side and was furnished with a rusty stove, a deal table and several hard-chairs, most of which had some part of them broken.

The walls were dark with dirt and smoke and what windows there were had their broken panes stuffed with rags so that it was almost impossible to see.

When Valeta would have stopped the man ahead beckoned to her and she was led round a corner into another room which was even more unprepossessing than the first.

Here, as in the yard, there was nothing but sacks of soot, many of them spilling out their contents.

There were no chairs, nothing on which to sit but the sacks which Valeta realised would make her black even to touch them.

She was about to ask a question of the man who led them there, but he was already moving out through the door and pulling it behind him.

"Wait a moment!" Valeta called. But he was gone and she heard him thrust home a bolt.

"Why have—those men brought us—here?" Harry asked in a frightened voice.

"I do not know," Valeta replied.

Then she put her fingers to her lips and moved a little nearer the door as she realised that she could overhear what the men were saying in the next room.

The door, while it kept them prisoner, was ill-fitting and several wooden panels were cracked so that the voices were very clear.

She heard the men quarrelling amongst themselves because they had brought the wrong boy.

" 'Ow was Oi ter know it weren't young Nichilas?" one man asked in an aggrieved tone. " 'E's got fair 'air, ain't 'e? 'E was wi' th' snazzy doll."

Valeta realised this was a reference to herself.

"Cibber won't loik it," one man said. "Nor 'is Nibs. 'E said over and over again that once they were 'ere nobody'd know where they'd gorn."

"Us'll 'ave to tell 'im."

"Ye can do that, seein' as 'ow yer picked oop th' boy."

" 'Ow was Oi ter know? 'Is 'air's th' same as Nichilas an' 'e's abaht th' same size."

"No, 'e ain't."

Valeta recognised the voice of the man who had been in the carriage with them.

" 'E won't get oop 'em smaller chimleys—Oi can tell yer that!"

Valeta drew in her breath.

As she had suspected, they intended to use Nicholas again as a climbing boy, and although she was glad he was safe from the horror of it, she could not bear to think of Harry's suffering when they subjected him to the torture of being forced up a chimney.

Where was the Marquis?

Surely, she thought, by now he must have learned what had occurred and be on his way to London?

Then, insidiously, the question came as to whether he would be interested. He had not wanted her for his Ward. Why should he put himself out now?

Perhaps he would send a servant, or Mr. Chamberlain, and she had a feeling that the latter might easily be hoodwinked by these ruffians while the Marquis would know them for what they were.

He had been so brave and so gallant in the war. He would not be afraid whatever the numbers against him.

"He will find us," Valeta said reassuringly to herself, "I know he will!"

Harry was holding tightly to her hand and she was just going to say something comforting to him when she heard the men in the next room say apprehensively:

" 'Ere 'e comes!"

There was the sound of heavy footsteps, then a loud aggressive voice that Valeta recognised as belonging to Cibber the Sweep.

" 'Ere yer be!" he said, shouting rather than speaking. "Oi meant ter be 'ere to meet yer, but Oi gets 'eld up. Th' blasted boy got stuck in a chimley an' half-suffocated, 'e were. But 'e'll recover."

Cibber must have walked into the centre of the room and when the three men did not speak, he said:

"Well? Wot've yer got ter tell me? 'Ave yer got 'em 'ere?"

"Yes, they're 'ere, in the next room."

"Well, that's satisfactory, that is! Th' Guv-nor'll be 'ere in a second or two, an' yer'll get yer money."

"Jus' one fing went wrong."

"Wrong?" Cibber asked. "Wot d'yer mean—wrong?"

"We ain't got Nichilas."

"Yer ain't got Nichilas? Why not?"

"Us picks up anuvver boy by mistike."

"Mistake?"

Cibber roared the word and it seemed to echo and re-echo. Because it was so loud Harry gave a little murmur of fear and moved closer to Valeta.

It was then that Valeta heard another voice, educated and yet somehow in its very manner sounding unpleasant.

"Here you all are! I gather from the fact that the carriage outside is empty, that our plunder is in the next room?"

"Yus, Guv'nor, in th' next room. Jus' like yer wanted 'em."

"The woman and the boy?"

"Yus, Guv—excep' . . ."

"Except what?"

The question was sharp.

"Us were jus' tellin' Mr. Cibber 'ere there's been a bit o' a mistike. Us brought th' wrong boy."

"You mean you left the boy Nicholas behind?"

"Yus, Guv, 'twas by haccident, so ter speak."

"That was an incredibly stupid thing to do."

Lionel Stevington's voice was sharp and biting as a whip.

" 'Twas a mistake, Guv, but us brung th' woman, jus' as yer said."

"I will deal with her, but I suppose you are aware that Nicholas will give us away if he recognised any of you?"

"Us never seed 'im, Guv'nor. Don't fink 'e were there."

"You are sure? Quite sure you didn't see him?"

"Nah, Guv. Not sight nor sound o' 'im."

Valeta realised that Lionel Stevington was thinking hard and wondering if he should believe them.

Then one of the men said:

"If us can 'ave our Jimmy o' gobbins, Guv, us'll be gettin' along."

"Very well. I suppose you did your best. It is extraordinary how there are always mistakes unless I do everything myself!"

There was no answer to this but there was the clink of coins, a low mutter which might have been gratitude, then the sound of the men's feet moving away.

"Damned fools!" Lionel Stevington exclaimed. "Why the devil could they not have brought the right child?"

" 'Tis ool right if Nichilas didn't see Bill."

"Can we believe them when they said there was no sign of the boy?"

"Oi 'opes so," Cibber said, "but t' make sure, Oi'll push this new boy off onto one o' me mates. Oi don' wanna be found wiv 'im on me 'ands, so to' speak."

"Yes, that would be the wise thing to do," Lionel Stevington agreed. "Then if you are short-handed it might be possible to get hold of the other boy again."

"Too dangerous!" Cibber said. "Oi don't like takin' risks, an' that makes Oi hask: 'Wot abaht th' woman?' "

"You need not worry about her," Lionel Stevington said. "Old Mother Baggott will be along very shortly and after that we shall hear no more of her."

"Be that safe?" Cibber asked. " 'Er'll talk."

"Not when Baggott's given her the juice of the poppy."

Cibber laughed an ugly rough sound.

"Oi'd always 'eard that as 'ow she works."

"It keeps them pliable for the first weeks until they are hooked on it. Then they have no wish to escape."

Valeta drew in her breath.

Any other girl of her age brought up in different circumstances might not have understood, but her father and mother had talked openly of the horrors that went on in London.

She was well aware that the procurers of young girls kept them either in a state of intoxication, or doped with opium until they were too bemused to know what they were doing.

She felt that what was being said could only be happening in a bad dream, and yet in a terrifying manner the words made sense and she could be in no doubt as to what lay in front of her.

She resisted an impulse to scream and beat her hands against the bolted door, but she knew that to do so would only attract attention and she would perhaps be made unconscious even sooner than was planned.

It seemed incredible that Lionel Stevington who had been born a gentleman should behave in such a manner, and yet now every tale, every innuendo in someone's voice, every disapproving look, came back to tell her that he was even worse than she had suspected.

How, she wondered, could she have hated the Marquis or found fault with his behaviour when his brother Lionel to all intents and purposes, was as wicked as the devil himself?

She was trembling and because he knew she was afraid Harry began to tremble too.

"What are we agoing to do, Miss?" he whispered, and Valeta could not find words or a voice in which to answer him.

She could only shut her eyes and pray weakly that if the Marquis did not arrive to save her she might die before the woman who was to take her into a bawdy house arrived.

Then she heard Cibber say:

"Oi thinks, Guv, oi'd best be gettin' along wi' th' boy. No point in hangin' abaht."

"No, off you go, Cibber. I will wait here for Mother Baggott. She will not let me down, and it will certainly be to her advantage not to do so."

There was an evil undertone in Lionel's voice, as though he was positively enjoying the idea of Valeta being handed over to such a woman.

Cibber must have turned towards the bolted door, for Valeta heard his footsteps coming towards them.

Instinctively she recoiled, pulling Harry by the hand.

There was very little room to move because of the sacks on the floor, and just as Cibber must have raised his hand to the bolt, there was the sound of a voice saying in a tone of authority:

"Is there a man called Cibber here?"

Valeta gave a little cry, but it could hardly pass her lips.

Then she felt her heart leap and begin to beat frantically, for she knew that the Marquis had arrived and was outside in the court-yard.

Cibber walked back to the other room as the Marquis was saying:

"What a surprise, Lionel, to find you here, but I might have expected it!"

"What do you want?" Lionel Stevington asked angrily. "Is not Troon enough for you that you have to come bursting into my part of the world?"

"If you consider this stinking place a possession of yours, then you are welcome to it," the Marquis replied, "but I understand that you and your hired felons have stolen something which belongs to me."

"And what can that be?" Lionel asked.

"There is no need to keep up any pretence," the Marquis replied, "although I am still somewhat at sea to understand why my Ward should be of interest to you."

"I have no idea what you are talking about," Lionel Stevington protested.

"Then let me put it into words of one syllable," the Marquis said.

110

"Cibber, who shall be taken before the Magistrates for this, has kidnapped the son of one of my farmers and he well knows the penalty."

"Oi didn't do nuffin' o' th' sort!" Cibber shouted in his usual manner. "Mr. Stevin'ton 'ere tells Oi 'e wants the boy brought t' London. Oi wasn't takin' 'im back in th' trade—not a'ter yer'd bought 'im from me, M'Lord. Nuffin' crooked abaht me!"

"You can say that at your trial," the Marquis said bluntly. "But what is your excuse, Lionel, for abducting a young girl who happens to be my Ward?"

"I have told you I do not know what you are talking about," Lionel Stevington repeated, "and you will find it very hard to prove your accusation."

Although she was certain that the Marquis would not be deceived by such blatant lies, Valeta could take no chances.

She beat on the door, calling out:

"We are here! We are here! Save us!"

The Marquis smiled.

"That sounds like pretty conclusive proof to me, Lionel. Now suppose you get out of my way and let me release my Ward and my farmer's son before I teach you a lesson which you will not forget in a hurry!"

As the Marquis spoke he told himself that while Lionel and Cibber might put up a fight, he and Freddie had them pretty well matched.

Granted Cibber was a huge, strong, beefy man, but the Marquis was quite certain he had only an elementary knowledge of boxing while he and Freddie were both pupils of "Gentleman Jackson's Salon" in Bond Street.

There were few of their friends who could beat them when it came to a fight.

At this moment it had not entered the Marquis's mind for one moment that he carried a loaded pistol and that Freddie who was standing just inside the doorway of the dirty room and who had not joined in the conversation, had another.

He was quite prepared to fight it out man to man and in fact, the idea was a pleasure.

This was the opportunity for which he had waited a long time, to give Lionel the thrashing he thoroughly deserved with no unfair advantage to either of them except that the premises in which they had to fight were somewhat restricting.

Then as he looked at his brother with a faint smile on his lips, knowing that Lionel was loathing him with the fanatical, unnatural hatred which he had shown ever since they had been children together, Lionel pulled a pistol from his pocket.

"Not so fast!" he said furiously. "If you are not out of here within three seconds, Serle, I will shoot you and Freddie down where you stand!"

"Do not be a fool, Lionel!" the Marquis said. "However much you dislike me, I am not worth swinging for."

"I will not do that," Lionel replied. "I shall be tried by my Peers and if there is an enquiry Cibber here will swear on oath that you attacked me first."

"I think you must be crazy!" the Marquis said. "Come on, Lionel, I have prevented you from committing a quite unnecessary crime, so be a sport and allow me to release Miss Lingfield and the small boy who is not climbing anybody's chimneys, and take them back to Troon."

The Marquis spoke in a conciliatory tone, but at the same time, his eyes were wary.

He saw an expression on Lionel's face that he had seen once or twice before and which he had told himself then, as he did now, was undoubtedly a look of madness.

He had, in fact, thought for several years, that his brother was becoming steadily insane and when he had mentioned his suspicions to the family Physician, the old man who had known the Stevington boys all their lives, had said:

"I've had a feeling for some time that your brother Lionel has something dangerously wrong with him. It may be an affliction of the brain, for the tantrums he indulged in as a child have obviously increased and he should be having medical treatment."

"I doubt if I could persuade him to do that," the Marquis replied, "even though I am prepared to pay for it."

The old Doctor shook his head and said nothing, but every time the Marquis saw his brother after that he was certain that the diagnosis had been correct.

Therefore he chose his words and spoke in a conciliatory manner which made Freddie look at him in surprise.

"Come on, Lionel," he said. "Stop pointing that unpleasant weapon at me, and let us have a laugh about this childish prank. I know as well as you do that you did not intend it to be serious."

"It is damned serious to me," Lionel said fiercely through clenched teeth. "How do you think I felt when that woman on whom you have been lavishing the family fortune told me you were going to marry a girl?"

His voice seemed to rise higher as he cried:

"Marry, and do me out of my inheritance? You will not have a son, if I can help it!"

He fired his pistol as he spoke, but the Marquis, who had seen his finger tighten on the trigger, flung himself on the floor a split second before the bullet crashed into the wall behind him, dislodging a large lump of dirty plaster.

The explosion from Lionel's pistol was followed almost instantaneously by another.

For a moment it seemed as if Lionel had not been hit. Then he fell slowly and almost ludicrously onto the dirty floor.

Cibber gave a shout of terror and stumbling over the fallen body ran from the house and across the yard to disappear into the crowds on the streets outside.

The Marquis picked himself up slowly.

"Is he dead?" he asked.

Freddie stepped forward to look down at Lionel who was now lying on his back, the blood seeping slowly over his shirt-front from a bullet hole just above his heart.

"I thought he had killed you!"

"I realised just in time that was what he intended to do," the Marquis replied.

He pulled the lapels of his riding-coat into place, walked across the room and pulled back the bolt on the door.

As it opened Valeta, frantic with fear, deafened by the sound of the pistol shots and unable to hear what had followed them, stood looking at him, her face as white as her gown.

Then she gave a little cry and moved swiftly towards him.

Neither was certain how it happened, but the Marquis's arms were round her and she was trembling against him, her face hidden against his shoulder.

"It is all right," he said. "You are safe!"

CHAPTER SEVEN

*V*ALETA DID NOT MOVE, but it seemed to the Marquis as if she was clinging to him as tightly as Nicholas had done.

Instinctively he held her closer as he said:

"It is really all right, and you need no longer be afraid."

"You . . . are not . . . hurt?"

He could hardly hear her voice, it was so low, and she was still trembling, although not so violently.

"I am unhurt," he said. "So let us get out of this ghastly place!"

He turned round to face the door, but kept his arm round her shoulder.

Somehow they managed to walk through it together and Harry followed them. Then just before they turned the corner into the next room the Marquis stopped.

"I want you to shut your eyes," he said. "I am going to carry you out into the yard."

Valeta did not speak, but he knew instinctively that she was asking why.

"There is something I do not want you to see," he explained.

As if she understood what it was, she said faintly:

"Harry?"

"Yes, of course," the Marquis replied, as if he remembered the child for the first time.

"Listen Harry," he said to the child behind them, "I want you to wait here until I come back for you. You are not to move, you are not to go any further. Do you understand?"

"Yes, M'Lord," Harry said obediently.

His face was streaked with tears, but he appeared to be no longer afraid and the Marquis liked the firm manner in which he spoke.

"That is a good boy," he approved. "Now wait until I come back."

He picked Valeta up in his arms as he spoke.

"Shut your eyes," he ordered, "and do not open them until I tell you you can."

She did as he told her and turned her face against his shoulder. He had the idea that she was feeling too limp to do anything but what she was told to do.

Freddie must have heard what the Marquis said, for he walked ahead of them into the yard and opened the carriage door which was standing where the men had left it, the horses unattended but too spiritless to move.

The Marquis set Valeta down on the back seat. As he did so she opened her eyes.

His face was very near to hers and for a moment they looked at each other without moving. Then almost abruptly the Marquis said:

"I will fetch Harry. Stay where you are and do not look out of the window."

He walked away and Valeta with a little gasp, leant back in the corner of the carriage.

She could hardly believe that what had taken place was not part of her imagination. Yet the Marquis had come and rescued her as she had prayed he might do, and now, as he had said, there was no need to be afraid.

But the horror she had felt when she listened to Lionel Stevington was still there like an evil shadow, and she felt as if her whole body was shrinking from a fate that was so terrifying that even now she trembled at the thought of it.

"He has . . . saved me!" she whispered to herself and heard the Marquis coming back with Harry in his arms.

"Now you can open your eyes, my boy," he said, "and do not be a nuisance to Miss Lingfield."

He turned back and Harry asked in a bewildered tone:

"What's agoing to—happen to us now—Miss?"

Because she knew the child was bemused by everything that had occurred, Valeta forced herself to say quietly:

"It is quite all right. The Marquis will take us home and you will be with your father and mother again."

Harry seemed to find this idea satisfactory, and Valeta closed her eyes fighting against a sudden faintness that seemed to seep over her like a mist rising over the water.

'I must be sensible,' she thought, 'it is all over, and I cannot be so weak and foolish as to swoon . . .'

But she felt herself drifting away into unconsciousness . . .

The next thing Valeta heard was the Marquis's voice saying:

"Have you a flask with you, Freddie?"

"There is not much in it," Freddie remarked. "I needed a drink myself after what happened just now."

"It will be enough," the Marquis said.

Valeta felt his arm behind her head, then something hard against her lips.

"Drink this!" the Marquis said firmly and because she had no will to oppose him, she did as he said.

She felt something fiery searing her throat and put up her hand in protest.

"Just another sip," the Marquis said, and because she could not argue with him, she did as she was told.

"I am . . . sorry," she tried to say as he took the silver cup from her lips.

Then unaccountably she had an almost uncontrollable desire to hide her face against him and burst into tears.

But with an almost superhuman effort she made herself say a little unsteadily:

"I . . . am . . . all right."

"I tell you what we will do, Freddie," the Marquis said, "we will drive this ramshackle old box to where we left the Phaeton. I am not allowing Valeta to walk through these filthy streets."

"A good idea!" Freddie agreed. "Shall I drive, or will you?"

"You drive," the Marquis replied, "if you think you are capable of making these tortoises move!"

"Can I—help, Sir?" Harry asked brightening up at the thought of going home.

"Come on then," Freddie said good-humouredly, "although whether we can turn the horses round in this hole I have not the slightest idea!"

He shut the carriage door and climbed up on the box with Harry following him.

The Marquis and Valeta were left alone.

He had not taken his arm from around her and his face was very near to hers.

As if she felt she must say something, if only to alleviate her shyness, she said:

"Thank . . . you for . . . saving us. I was . . . praying that . . . you would."

"It was fortunate that Nicholas recognised Bill, whoever that might be," the Marquis said.

"I . . . hoped he might . . . recognise somebody . . . but if . . . you had not . . . come . . ."

She shivered as she remembered the fate that Lionel had planned for her.

"Forget it," the Marquis said. "My brother, as I expect you realise, is dead."

"Did you . . . shoot him?"

"No, Freddie did when he tried to kill me."

"Supposing . . . just supposing he had . . . succeeded?"

"Would that have worried you?" the Marquis asked.

"He was . . . sending me to . . . a bawdy . . . house."

He could hardly hear the words. Then because even to think of it was so appalling, Valeta instinctively hid her face against the Marquis's shoulder.

She knew that for a moment he was tense with anger, then he said:

"My brother was mad. It is the only explanation I can give for this behaviour."

The carriage began to rock as with some difficulty and by moving the horses backwards and forwards Freddie turned round in the sack-filled yard.

The Marquis held Valeta closer and more firmly. Soon they were out in the narrow street, hearing the shouts of the children and the jeers of harridans propping up the doorways of their dirty houses, holding out the goods from their old clothes shops or handling food which was already in a state of stinking decay.

Freddie drove expertly with small boys running beside the carriage and ragged members of the populace shrieking abuse as the wheels threw up the filthy drain water from the gutter.

Then in a very short time they had moved into a wider and quieter street where the Phaeton was waiting for them.

Freddie drew the horses to a standstill and jumping down from the box, opened the door.

"What am I to do with this old Ark?" he asked, as the Marquis got out and turned to help Valeta.

"Send a boy to take it back to where it belongs," the Marquis replied. "I have no desire to be accused of being a horse-stealer on top of everything else!"

"A good idea!" Freddie agreed.

One of the bigger boys who had followed the carriage was gaping at them as they talked. Freddie beckoned him.

"You look an honest lad," he said. "If I pay you, will you lead these horses, and I mean lead—not drive them—back to Cibber's yard?"

The boy's eyes brightened.

"Yer'll pay Oi, Guv'nor?"

"I will certainly pay you," Freddie said, "but you have to promise me that you will deliver them safely and while you are about it, give the animals something to eat and drink."

"Orl roight, Guv'nor."

"Very well, I trust you," Freddie said, "and if you do not do as I tell you, I think you will find that Mr. Cibber will have something to say to you!"

He knew by the expression on the youth's face that this was quite a powerful threat.

Freddie handed him several silver coins which made him gasp with delight before he stowed them swiftly away in some obscure part of his ragged clothing from which there was no likelihood of their being pinched.

Then he walked away, leading the horses as he had been told.

The Marquis had already helped Valeta into the Phaeton.

"I will tell you what we will do first," he said. "We will go to Stevington House and have something to eat. Then I think, Freddie, you had better call on the Home Secretary and tell him that Lionel is dead."

"That is just what I was thinking myself," Freddie said. "As it happens, he is a friend of my father's so there is every liklihood he will believe me when I tell him the truth."

"It seems unkind," the Marquis said, "but I have a feeling that nobody will mourn Lionel and that those in high places who have resented his behaviour will actually rejoice!"

"Are you going to leave him where he is?" Freddie asked.

The two men had both been speaking in low voices so that Valeta should not hear what they said.

"No, of course not," the Marquis answered. "When I get to Stevington House I will make arrangements for his body to be collected and taken to Troon where he will be buried with due ceremony in the family vault."

"It is certainly more than he deserves," Freddie said. "It might have been you who were taken there in his place."

"I will express my gratitude on a more suitable occasion," the Marquis said, "but as it happens we are now even."

Freddie smiled for the first time since the conversation had begun.

"I have not forgotten that you saved my life at Waterloo."

"Nor have I," the Marquis replied. "I was wondering when you would repay the debt."

Freddie laughed and the Marquis swung himself up into the seat on the Phaeton.

"You can squeeze in beside Valeta," he said. "The boy on the floor. It will be a little cramped, but I will get you made into a more Savoy neighbourhood as quickly as I can."

The groom sprang away from the horses' heads and jumped up behind and they drove off, Valeta squeezed between the Marquis and Freddie, thinking that their close proximity made her feel safe in a manner that was curiously comforting.

Only when they reached the more fashionable streets did she suddenly become self-conscious, aware that she was wearing no bonnet and her hair after being covered by the cloth, was doubtless untidy.

She put up her hands to her head and the Marquis, as if he was aware of what she was thinking, said:

"Do not worry. You look very lovely."

The compliment was so unexpected that for a moment she stared at him wide-eyed.

"You are very brave," the Marquis said. "Most women having been through what you have, would be having hysterics."

"Of course they would," Freddie agreed, "and with reason. A more filthy, horrible place than that Sweep's house I could not imagine in a thousand years. Something ought to be done about it, and the whole of St. Giles'."

"I agree," the Marquis said, "and what is more, I am determined that something shall be done!"

Valeta who had turned her head towards Freddie when he spoke now looked back at the Marquis.

"Do you really . . . mean that?" she asked.

"I mean it," the Marquis confirmed. "The whole place should be demolished and burned to the ground, and the people who live there given the chance of a better sort of life."

Valeta clasped her hands together.

"If only Papa and Mama could hear you," she said. "It was what they always prayed would happen. Other parts of London are bad, but St. Giles' is the worst of the lot!"

"Something will have to be done!" the Marquis said determinedly.

And again inexplicably Valeta felt she was going to cry.

She was sure however, that both the Marquis and Freddie would despise her if she did so. So she bit her lip and blinked her eye-lashes forcing the tears away, but for some moments she was unable to speak.

By now they had moved swiftly into the wider streets of Mayfair and were only a short distance from Park Lane.

They drew up at the front door of Stevington House and when the servants in the magnificent livery hurriedly appeared to lay down red carpet, once again Valeta became conscious of her appearance.

The Marquis however, was already inside the Hall before Freddie could help Valeta from the Phaeton.

"I want luncheon to be served as quickly as possible," he said, "and ask the Housekeeper to attend to Miss Lingfield."

Then as Harry appeared he said to the Butler:

"Look after the small boy. He comes from Troon. Feed him, and I shall be taking him back with me this afternoon."

"Very good, M'Lord."

The Butler appeared to be quite used to receiving strange orders and in a few minutes a footman led Valeta upstairs to where the Housekeeper was waiting for her on the landing.

"If you will come this way, Miss," she said respectfully.

Rustling in her black silk dress she walked ahead to lead Valeta into a large and attractive bedroom.

"You must think it very strange," Valeta said, "that I have no bonnet, but . . ."

She was right in thinking that the Housekeeper was curious and she explained a little lamely that she had come to London at a moment's notice without time even to put on a travelling gown and pick up her bonnet and gloves.

She was quite certain that sooner or later the gossip about what had actually occurred would percolate from Troon, to Stevington House, but she had no desire at the moment to relate to anybody the terrible experience through which she had passed.

"Don't you worry, Miss," the Housekeeper said. "If you are returning to Troon with His Lordship this afternoon I'm sure I can find you something to wear, although it might not be in the very latest fashion."

"I shall be glad of anything," Valeta said. "I am afraid I would feel very untidy if I travelled in His Lordship's Phaeton without a bonnet."

"Leave everything to me, Miss," the Housekeeper said.

With her hair tidy, her face and hands washed, and several marks of soot sponged from her gown, Valeta went down the stairs a little while later feeling somewhat self-conscious.

In the magnificent house the Marquis was back in her mind as the authoritative, unapproachable Guardian she had thought him to be when she was at home.

It was embarrassing to remember how she had thrown herself into his arms when he had opened the door in the Sweep's house and how she had hidden her face against him in the carriage.

'Perhaps he will be shocked that I was so forward,' she told herself and blushed at what she imagined might be his condemnation of her behaviour.

Then she knew however much she surprised or even shocked him she could never be grateful enough for that moment when with the shots ringing in her ears and in terror at what might be occurring, she had seen him standing in the doorway.

At that moment he had been all the heroes of her childhood rolled into one: Sir Galahad, St. George and Perseus and certainly no longer the man she hated.

'Now he will save not only me but thousands of other people, if he keeps to what he said,' she told herself.

Because she was so excited at the thought she felt as if her feet had wings as they carried her down the stairs.

She had a sudden urgency to see the Marquis so that he could confirm what he had said and she could really believe there was hope for all the people whom her mother had worried over and whose plight had often made her father swear beneath his breath.

In the Salon, a glass of champagne in his hand, the Marquis was saying to Freddie:

"I have already sent to collect Lionel's body, and I have told them to notify the Magistrates and the Bow Street Police on the way, so that they can see the position of the body and that Lionel has a pistol in his hand that has been fired."

"I will explain it all when I get to the Home Office," Freddie promised.

"I am hoping you can arrange for neither of our names to be brought into it," the Marquis said. "I have a feeling they will not like the fact that the incident took place in St. Giles'."

"What makes you say that?"

"Because if they are not ashamed of the damned place they ought to be!" the Marquis said sharply.

The way he spoke made his friend turn and look at him with raised eyebrows.

"I seem to recognise that tone of voice! It is the one you used to use when you had seen the atrocities the French committed and you decided to have your revenge on them."

"That is exactly how I am feeling now," the Marquis said.

"If you are thinking of fighting such conditions," Freddie said half-jokingly, "it will take you a long time before you achieve a victory."

"It will certainly keep me busy," the Marquis said.

Freddie looked at him speculatively for a moment, then put down his champagne glass.

"I always rather fancied you as a Crusader, Serle," he said, "and with Dilys out of the way and no longer offering you all the temptations of Eve, you might even find it an interesting occupation."

"That is just what I was thinking myself," the Marquis said quietly.

"Perhaps after all, though it is infuriating to think so, Dily has done you a good turn," Freddie said.

"It will certainly be the first and the last," the Marquis said firmly.

As he spoke the door opened and Valeta came in.

Valeta awoke with a feeling that something strange had happened, but she was not quite certain what it was.

Then she opened her eyes and remembered.

She was at Troon, sleeping in a room that was ten times the size of her bedroom at the Manor and she could see the sunshine percolating through the sides of the curtains, picking out the gold cupids that climbed the posts of the great bed in which she was lying.

It had been late in the afternoon yesterday when they had arrived back at Troon to find Nanny frantic with anxiety and Nicholas overjoyed to see her.

As the Marquis drew up his horses outside the front door Nicholas who, Valeta learned later, had insisted on staying at one of the windows on the first floor all the afternoon waiting for her and watching the drive, had come tearing down the stairs to fling himself into her arms.

"You are back! You are back!" he cried. "Nanny said His Lordship would rescue you, but I was afraid, terribly afraid you were lost."

"I am not lost, dearest," Valeta said, holding him very tight.

A moment later Nanny's arms were round her and the old woman was shedding tears of thankfulness.

"It is not like you, Nanny, to cry," Valeta said.

"I'm getting old, that's what's the matter with me," Nanny said stoutly, "and I can't stand these shocks."

"It is all over," Valeta said comfortingly, "and His Lordship saved us both."

She saw as she spoke Nicholas run to the Marquis with a cry of joy, and to her surprise he bent down to pick the child up in his arms.

"You brought her back!" Nicholas exclaimed. "I knew you would, I knew it! Nanny cried and thought you might be too late, but she would not tell me what that meant."

"I was in time," the Marquis said.

Nicholas was looking over his shoulder at Harry who was standing a little forlornly just inside the door.

"Stop the Phaeton from driving away!" the Marquis said quickly.

A footman hurried to obey his command and the Marquis said to Harry:

"I think, Harry, you would like to go home in style, would you not? You can drive in the Phaeton and tell your father to come up and see me in an hour or so, and I will explain to him what happened."

Harry's face lit up with excitement and Nicholas cried:

"May I go too? I want to ride in the Phaeton."

"Very well," the Marquis said good-humouredly. "Jason will look after you, and both of you are to do exactly as he says."

"We will be good—very good!" Nicholas cried and he and Harry ran down the steps together.

Watching, Valeta thought how well the Marquis seemed to understand the two small boys and it suddenly struck her that he should have children of his own.

She did not know why, but suddenly that seemed not to be the happy thought it should have been.

Of course it was obvious that he should be married and have a wife to help him entertain in all his fine houses.

"I think, Nanny, we should go home," she said in a voice that suddenly sounded dull and a little bleak.

"Yes, of course, dearie," Nanny agreed.

"I feel that would be a mistake," the Marquis interrupted. "If you will come into the Salon, Valeta, I will explain why."

He did not wait for her reply but walked towards the Salon saying to the Butler as he went:

"Is tea ready in the Orangery?"

"In a few minutes, M'Lord!"

Knowing she must do what he asked, Valeta followed the Marquis only stopping for a second to take off the pretty but inexpensive straw bonnet which the Housekeeper at Stevington House had loaned her.

She gave it to Nanny saying:

"That has to be returned, but I will tell you about it later."

Then smoothing her hair with her hands she walked into the Salon and a footman shut the door behind them.

The Marquis had already reached his favourite place in front of the mantelpiece and he watched her advancing towards him thinking that unlike any other woman he had ever known before she was completely unselfconscious of her beauty.

Valeta reached his side and her eyes were wide and worried as if she expected what he was about to say was something with which she would not agree.

"I think, Valeta," the Marquis said quietly, "it would be wise for you, Nanny and Nicholas to stay here for a few days until we are quite certain there can be no recurrence of what happened this morning."

"But surely now that . . . Lord Lionel is dead . . ?" Valeta began hesitatingly.

"Cibber is alive," the Marquis said, "and until he has been arrested and put in prison for a great number of years, or transported I would rather have you safely beside me."

"I had not . . . thought of . . . that," Valeta admitted.

The Marquis did not speak and she went on:

"I kept on feeling grateful . . . although perhaps it was unkind to Harry . . . that Nicholas had not been frightened again by those horrible men."

She shuddered before she continued:

"They had meant to force him into being a climbing boy again, and

125

when they found that Harry was there by mistake, they were going to
. . . use him instead."

She gave an involuntary little cry as she said:

"It would have . . . killed Nicholas to have to go through all that
horror for a second time . . . I know it!"

"You once asked my support for a Bill to abolish the use of boys in the
cleaning of chimneys," the Marquis said, "and I will not only support the
Bill, but I will actively campaign to prevent boys being used in any of the
houses of my acquaintances."

Valeta gave a little cry of delight and said:

"How can I tell you . . . what it . . . means to me? How can I . . .
thank you?"

The Marquis looked at her, then he pulled her into his arms.

"Like this," he answered, and his lips were on hers.

For a moment Valeta was too astonished to think.

Then the Marquis's lips aroused a feeling that she had never known
before. It was so strange, and yet so wonderful that she could not struggle
or move, but only feel that she had stepped into a dream-world that was
more beautiful than anything she had imagined.

The Marquis's lips were gentle, as if she was infinitely precious, tender
and yet insistent and she felt as if, though he held her captive, she had no
wish to be free.

She felt as if the moment when she had thought he was Sir Galahad
come to her rescue, he had been enveloped with the glory that had surrounded the Knight.

He had also the determination of Jason and courage of Perseus, so that
all she had ever longed to find in her heroes was there in one man.

The Marquis released her lips and now he was kissing her eyes, her
cheeks, her small chin, then again her lips.

It was difficult to breathe as something warm and wonderful moved
from her breasts into her throat so that she could no longer speak.

The whole room seemed to be filled with an unbelievable glory and she
only knew that if this was love, it was perfect, ecstatic, as she had always
known it must be.

Then the Marquis raised his head to look down at her and he said in a
voice that she found hard to recognise:

"I love you! I suppose I might have expected this to happen when you came here hating me. But I love you, and there is nothing I can do about it except tell you so."

Valeta's eyes seemed to fill her whole face and the Marquis said with a smile:

"I think I know what you are feeling, as I am feeling the same. It has happened so quickly, so unexpectedly, and yet it is there!"

"You . . . love me?" Valeta asked in a tone of wonder.

"I love you," he replied, "as I have never loved anyone before. In fact, I did not know that love was like this."

"Nor did . . . I," Valeta whispered, "but it is love . . . real love?"

"Very real," the Marquis agreed. "My sweet, I know now that you are everything I want in my wife, everything I thought never to find. How soon will you marry me?"

Valeta's eyes seemed to grow wider than ever. Then she whispered:

"I do not know . . . what to say. You are so . . . grand . . . so magnificent. How could you marry anyone . . . like me . . ? I think I would be . . . afraid."

The Marquis smiled and it was very tender.

"You need never be afraid of anyone or anything when you belong to me," he said. "That I promise you."

Valeta gave a little laugh that was curiously unsteady.

"I was really . . . meaning I would be afraid . . . of you."

"Not if we love each other," the Marquis said. "I love you, and I want you to tell me that you love me."

Her eyes dropped because she was shy, and he said:

"Oh, my darling, I know it already. I was aware of it when you came into my arms when I opened the door, and when you trembled against me I knew I had to look after you and protect you for the rest of your life."

"It was . . . so wonderful to see . . . you there . . . when I had been . . . so afraid," Valeta whispered as if she must give him an explanation.

He put his arms round her and drew her close again.

"We have so much to say, so much to learn about each other," the Marquis said.

Then as he pressed his lips against the softness of her skin, he added:

127

"And you have so much to teach me."

He knew that Valeta was surprised and he explained:

"I have a new crusade: to save the climbing boys, clean up St. Giles' and rid London of much of its crime. Do you think I am capable of that?"

"I think you can . . . do anything you . . . want to do," Valeta answered, "as long as you let me . . . help you."

"Do you think I could do it otherwise?" the Marquis asked. "You have got me into this and now you have to work as hard as I shall have to do. Otherwise I might fall by the way-side."

He was teasing her and she laughed a little tremulously.

"I am so excited . . . so thrilled . . . I do not know what to say."

"Just tell me you love me," the Marquis said. "That is all I really want to hear."

"I do love you," Valeta said, "but I never thought it . . . possible I could do . . . anything but . . . hate you!"

"That is something you will never do again," the Marquis answered.

As he spoke, he kissed her, a slow demanding kiss that seemed to her to draw her very soul from her body and make it his.

Then after a long time when it was impossible to think but only to feel, the Marquis said:

"I had forgotten about your tea. It will be getting cold by now. Let us go and find it in the Orangery."

"I am so happy I feel as if I am disembodied," Valeta said, "and I will never want to eat or drink again."

"I feel the same," the Marquis answered, "but I suppose I have been inconsiderate. I should have given you your tea first, then told you I love you. But when I looked at you I wanted to kiss you so desperately that it was impossible to think of anything else."

He kissed her again before he said:

"Come along. I have to think about you, and you have had a very exhausting day."

"Now it is a very wonderful . . . marvelous day," Valeta whispered.

"If you say things like that and look at me with that particular expression in your eyes," the Marquis said, "you will not only have no tea, but no dinner and no breakfast tomorrow morning!"

Valeta laughed.

"I think the truth is that you want your tea," she said, "so let us go and find the Orangery. I have no idea where it is."

"I will show you," the Marquis said. "There are so many things I want to show you in this house, my darling, a house where we are going to spend a great deal of our time together, for I have a feeling you would prefer living here to London."

"We will have to go to London for you to attend the House of Lords," Valeta said.

"You are already driving me to work?" the Marquis asked laughingly.

"No, only hoping to . . . share it with . . . you," Valeta murmured.

He put his arm round her and drew her towards the door and kissed her again before they went out into the Hall.

The Marquis led her through passages filled with treasures which at any other time Valeta would have wanted to look at, but now she could only think of the man beside her.

The Orangery, with trees that had been brought from Spain nearly a century ago, was bright with sunshine and it glittered on the tea-table set amongst the flowers and beside a fountain in the basin of which swam goldfish.

Valeta looked at the profusion of silver, the silver teapot, kettle, milk-jug, and cream-jug, the sugar basin, all set on a magnificent silver tray embellished with the Marquis's coat-of-arms.

"You must pour out," the Marquis said. "It is something you will have to get used to."

"You are frightening me again," Valeta complained.

But her eyes were soft with love and as the Marquis looked at her for a moment they forgot everything but the enchantment of their feelings for each other.

Then with an effort Valeta poured out the tea and she thought that with the Marquis sitting next to her looking at her as if he had never seen her before, nothing could be more magical, more wonderful than to be alone with him in this beautiful place.

Then there was the sound of footsteps and the Marquis turned his head impatiently as if he resented the interruption.

It was Mr. Chamberlain who came towards them.

"Good-afternoon, Chamberlain!" the Marquis said. "What do you want?"

"I am sorry to interrupt Your Lordship," Mr. Chamberlain replied, "but I thought you would wish to know that a lady and gentleman have called in answer to the advertisement."

"What advertisement . . ?" the Marquis began.

But Valeta gave a little cry.

"The advertisement about Nicholas! Someone has actually called?"

"A Colonel and Mrs. Standish," Mr. Chamberlain replied. "They live the other side of London and have been travelling all day since the advertisement appeared in a Hertfordshire newspaper."

"Do you think they are really Nicholas's father and mother?"

"They told me their little boy disappeared when he was playing in their garden. There were some gypsies in the vicinity, and they could only think when the child vanished, that the gypsies had stolen him."

"It said in the report by the Select Committee," Valeta said, breathlessly, "that the gypsies were often accused of stealing children so that they could sell them to the Sweeps as climbing boys."

There was so much excitement in her voice that the Marquis put out his hand protectively to take hers.

"This is only the first answer to our advertisement," he said, "and these people may not be Nicholas's parents. I do not want you to be disappointed if we have to wait for some time to find his real ones."

"What else did these people tell you?" Valeta asked Mr. Chamberlain.

"They said their son was called Nicholas and had a pony called Rufus."

"Then it must be them! It must!" Valeta cried. "Oh, please, darling, let us go and see them."

The endearment had slipped out involuntarily and the Marquis seeing the astonishment on Mr. Chamberlain's face said:

"Perhaps I should tell you, Chamberlain, that Miss Lingfield has done me the honour of promising to become my wife."

Valeta blushed and said in a low voice:

"I . . . should not have . . . said that . . . perhaps you . . . wished to keep it a . . . secret."

"It is no secret as far as I am concerned," the Marquis said, "and I am the happiest man in the world. Congratulate me, Chamberlain."

"You know I do, My Lord, from the very depths of my heart," Mr. Chamberlain said. "And may I, Miss Lingfield, wish you every happiness, which I have a feeling you have both found already."

"We have!" Valeta said. "I did not know it was possible to be so happy."

She looked at the Marquis as she spoke and he smiled at her as if he had forgotten his Comptroller's very existence.

Just for a moment they were both very still, then Valeta said:

"Let us go and see these people, and they must see Nicholas. Where is he?"

"Anticipating that would be your wish," Mr. Chamberlain replied, "I have sent for the little boy and he should by now have reached the Hall."

"Then let us go and find him," Valeta said to the Marquis, "and how wonderful it will be if they really are his father and mother!"

The Marquis took her by the arm and followed by Mr. Chamberlain they walked towards the great Hall.

Nicholas was there playing with one of the valuable bronze ornaments that stood on a table.

"Look," he was saying to a footman beside him, "that is a big lion, and the man is killing it with his spear. Would you like to kill a lion?"

The footman had no time to answer before the small boy saw Valeta and the Marquis and ran towards them.

"I have found a lion on your table," he said to the latter. "Did you ever kill a lion?"

"As a matter of fact I have," the Marquis said, "and when we have time I will show you his skin, but now there is someone I want you to see."

He took Nicholas by the hand and walked towards the Salon.

As Valeta followed she sent up a little prayer in her heart that Nicholas had found his parents.

He was such a dear little boy and she knew that he ought to have a home of his own and people who loved him because he belonged to them.

The Marquis opened the door.

The two people were at the far end of the room, the lady seated in an arm-chair, the gentleman standing beside her.

For a moment no-one moved nor spoke, then Nicholas gave a cry which seemed to echo up to the ceiling and releasing the Marquis's hand he rushed towards them.

"Mama! Papa!"

It was impossible for Valeta to see what happened simply because tears flooded into her eyes.

It was too poignant, too moving and she was conscious only that the Marquis's arm was round her and he was holding her close as if he knew what she was feeling and felt very much the same himself.

Then without saying anything he drew her out of the room back into the Hall and shut the door.

"Let us leave them with their happiness," he said, "as we want to be alone with ours."

He turned to the Butler.

"We will be in the Library if the visitors wish to speak to us."

Walking into the Library he waited until the door shut behind them, then he was kissing the tears from Valeta's eyes.

"Do not cry, my darling," he said.

"They are tears of . . . happiness," Valeta sobbed. "If I had not . . . fought for Nicholas when I came . . . here to see . . . you, and if you had not . . . bought him from that . . . horrible . . . brutal man he . . . would have died . . . I know it."

"I forbid you to think of anything so unhappy at the moment," the Marquis said. "We are happy, Nicholas has found his father and mother, and all we have to do now is to hurry up and have a Nicholas of our own and perhaps some brothers and sisters for him to play with."

Valeta gave a little choked laugh.

"You are going too . . . quickly," she protested.

"There will be plenty of time for us to consider such things," the Marquis replied, "but there is one thing I am not going to wait for, and that is our Wedding Day!"

He kissed her again before he went on:

"Nicholas's father and mother will doubtless stay here tonight and tomorrow I will find another Chaperon for you. But I want you to myself alone, and it would be a bore to have other people with us."

"I, too, want . . . to be alone . . . with you," Valeta whispered.

"As you are in mourning, and I suppose I am too as far as the world is concerned, shall we just be married very quietly and secretly?"

"Could we . . . do that?"

"If you agree, and if you are prepared to be married without our friends gaping at us and receiving a profusion of wedding-presents which neither of us wants."

"How do you . . . know I do not . . . want them?" Valeta asked.

She wanted to tease him merely because she was so happy, but her heart was singing and she felt as if her head was enveloped in clouds of glory.

It was difficult to think of anything but the closeness of the Marquis and the feelings his lips aroused in her every time he kissed her.

"I will give you everything in the whole world you want," the Marquis said, "and throw in the moon and the stars, if you want those too."

There was a deep note in his voice which made Valeta say with her lips close to his:

"I think you have . . . given me those . . . already."

"Oh, my darling, I love you so much that I cannot think straight," the Marquis said, "and the only thing I want to say is that I love you, over and over again."

He drew a deep breath, then he asked:

"How can this have happened to me so unexpectedly? I never believed in this sort of love before! Yet it is true, it really can happen, that one can find the perfect person to whom one belongs and suddenly the whole world is changed."

"Has that . . . really happened to you?" Valeta asked. "Do you . . . really feel like that about . . . me?"

"It will take me a long time to tell you what I feel about you," the Marquis said, "but it will certainly be easier if we are married first."

He smiled, then his lips were on hers and he felt her respond and knew he had been right when he said this was different.

Never in the whole of his life and his many love-affairs had he known such ecstasy, such wonder and at the same time, a reverence.

He could not explain it.

He only knew deep down in his soul he had always been aware that

133

somewhere in the world there was a woman whom he had not yet met, but who was the right and perfect person for him.

That was why he had never married, that was why despite all his amatory adventures and his raffish behaviour there had been a sacred and untouched shrine within his heart which now in the flash of a passing second had been filled by Valeta.

He knew that in her purity, her innocence, her wise little mind and her compassion for others, she was exactly what he needed in his life—a life that was going to be very different from what he had lived before, and very much more worthwhile.

His lips became very demanding, more possessive and he felt the flames of desire flickering in his body.

Yet at the same time, he knelt at Valeta's feet because she was so different from all the other women he had known.

He took his lips from hers and with a little catch in her voice Valeta said:

"I . . . prayed for you . . . God sent you to save me . . . and He also gave me love. Oh, wonderful, wonderful Serle, our love is so perfect that it is divine . . . it is a part of God."

And that, the Marquis knew, was exactly what he believed himself.

From Hell
to Heaven

AUTHORS NOTE

———— ⌘ ————

A DEAD-HEAT AT THE DERBY STAKES begins this tale of love and hate, misery and happiness. There have actually been two dead-heats at the "Blue Riband of the Turf," the greatest horse-race in the world.

In 1828 the Duke of Rutland's *Cadland* dead-heated with *The Colonel,* owned by the Hon. Edward Petre. Under the then rules of racing, this dead-heat was run off later in the afternoon and *Cadland* won.

One of the most historic Derbies ever run took place in 1884. At the spring meeting at Newmarket, the Prince of Batthyány was in a high state of excitement as *Galliard,* a son of his much-loved *Galopin,* was expected to win the two thousand guineas. However, the strain was too much for the Prince, and he had a fatal heart-attack as he entered the Jockey Club luncheon-rooms.

His death undoubtedly altered the course of Turf History, as the classic nomination of his colt *St. Simon* was thereby rendered void according to the rule that then existed. *St. Simon* proved to be the greatest race-horse ever and certainly the greatest Sire ever known to the English Turf. There is no doubt that he would have won the 1884 Derby.

In his absence, the race resulted in a dead-heat between Sir John Willoughby's *Harvester* and Mr. John Hammond's *St. Gatien.* The Stewards gave the owners the option of having a run-off or dividing the race, and they unanimously decided to divide.

CHAPTER ONE

———— ❧ ————

1831

*T*HERE HAD BEEN A LONG WAIT, as was usual with a big field, then a number of false starts.

The Marquis of Alchester, with his glasses trained on the horses in the far distance, gave an impatient sigh.

"Feeling anxious, Linden?" Peregrine Wallingham asked.

"No, merely confident," the Marquis replied, and his friend laughed.

"That is exactly what Branscombe says."

The Marquis's expression darkened.

He was well aware that the Earl of Branscombe's *Gunpowder* was a definite danger to his own *Highflyer,* but, as he had just said, he was confident that his horse would be the winner.

The huge crowd sprawling over the hill was, as usual on Derby Day, different from the crowd at any other race-meeting.

The Derby Stakes, which was the Blue Riband of the Turf, was a day to which all sportsmen looked forward, and although it was not an official holiday there was hardly an employer in the country who did not expect his employees to absent themselves if they were anywhere within reach of Epsom.

"They're off!"

The cry went up with a big shout as the flag was down and the horses began the long run which led them round Tattenham Corner and up the straight in front of the stands.

This was a golden opportunity for pick-pockets, for necks were craned and the attention of everybody was on the horses.

In less than three minutes it would all be over, and confirmation of the race result would be signalled by a flight of pigeons circling up over the stands and carrying the name of the winner to the newspapers and book-ies in different parts of the country.

There were roars from the crowd all along the course.

In the stand of the Jockey Club, where the more important owners watched their own horses and those they had backed with a concentration that had no need for audible expression, there was silence.

Peregrine Wallingham was aware that on this occasion there was an extra tension owing to the rivalry between the Earl of Branscombe and the Marquis of Alchester.

They were old enemies, and because he was the Marquis's oldest and closest friend he disliked the Earl almost as much as the Marquis did.

One reason was that the Earl of Branscombe considered himself not only the finest sportsman in the country but of such importance that he conceded that only the King took precedence over him.

Dukes, Marquises, and other Earls he dismissed with a wave of his hand, and asserted with some truth that his blood and his ancient title made him superior to them and that it was only due to some quirk of fate that he was not in fact a candidate for the Throne itself!

What was so infuriating, especially for the Marquis, was the fact that there was justification for the Earl's assertions and he was indeed outstand-ing and exceptionally fortunate in the Sporting World.

Certainly his horses had in the last two years won many of the classic races, but then so had those belonging to the Marquis.

Both gentlemen were exceptional shots and outstanding amateur pugilists, and both could speak in the House of Lords so eloquently that their fellow Peers flocked into the Chamber to hear them, especially when they were opposing each other.

But while the Marquis was popular with his contemporaries, the Earl was not. Although both habitually gave themselves airs, the Earl was, everybody decided behind his back, almost intolerable.

Now the horses had rounded Tattenham Corner and were coming at a good pace up the last stretch of the course.

When there was a large field it was difficult to see exactly which was ahead until they drew nearer.

Then as the crowd began to chant the names it was easy to hear the cry of *"Gunpowder! Gunpowder!"* being drowned by the roaring of *"Highflyer! Highflyer!"*

They drew nearer, and Peregrine Wallingham murmured beneath his breath:

"My God, it is going to be a close finish!"

He knew that the Marquis at his side was aware of it too, not from anything he said, but because of a sudden rigidity about his long, athletic body.

Then on the other side of him Peregrine Wallingham heard the Earl mutter impatiently:

"Come on, blast you!"

Now the cries of the crowd grew louder, and as the horses drew nearer, Peregrine Wallingham realized that the two in the lead were riding literally neck and neck.

It was impossible to guess which one would pass the Winning-Post first.

The jockeys had their whips raised, but there was really no need to use them. Both horses were aware that they had to best the other and were striving with every muscle in their bodies to get ahead.

Then as they flashed past the Post there was a sudden sound which those familiar with racing knew was one of astonishment.

For the second time in fifty years, the Derby Stakes seemed to have finished in a dead-heat.

"Mine by a nose, I think!" the Earl said aggressively, taking his glasses from his eyes.

The Marquis did not deign to answer. He merely turned and walked from the Box, followed by his friend Peregrine Wallingham, and they hurried through the crowds to the gate through which the horses, when they had been pulled in, would leave the course.

"I have never seen anything so extraordinary!" Peregrine exclaimed as he walked beside the Marquis.

"I do not believe there was an inch between them," the Marquis replied, "whatever Branscombe may pretend!"

"You are right," Peregrine agreed. "At the same time, it is a pity you could not have won. Branscombe has been boasting for the last month that his horse was a sure winner, and I am certain in consequence he has shortened the odds."

The Marquis gave his friend a sharp glance.

"You surely did not back *Gunpowder?*"

"Of course not," Peregrine replied. "I put my shirt on *Highflyer,* but unfortunately I had not much of it left."

The Marquis laughed.

"You should stick to horses," he said. "In the long run they are cheaper than Cyprians."

"I found that out a long time ago," Peregrine agreed. "But that little dancer from the Covent Garden has a magnet which makes the guineas fly out of my pocket quicker than I can put them in!"

He spoke ruefully, but the Marquis was not listening.

He was watching his horse trotting back down the course and was aware that his jockey was having a violent altercation with the rider of the Earl's *Gunpowder.*

Only when the noise of the crowd cheering them from behind the rails made it impossible for them to hear each other could they concentrate on riding triumphantly through the lane cleared for them towards the Weighing-In Room.

As the horses entered the enclosure the Marquis was waiting and when his jockey dismounted he said to him:

"What happened, Bennett?"

"Bumped an' obstructed me 'e did, when we was coming into the straight after rounding Tattenham Corner, M'Lord. I'd have beat him easy, but for that!"

The Marquis was scowling.

"Is this true?" he asked. "You are sure of what you are saying?"

" 'E were behavin' as bad as be possible for a rider t' act, M'Lord, an' that's th' truth."

"I believe you," the Marquis said, "but I doubt if there is anything we can do about it. Get weighed in."

Carrying his saddle, the jockey went towards the Weighing-In machine, which the Stewards were supervising, and as he reached it the Earl's jockey passed him with a grin on his face.

As he did so he said in a voice only he could hear:

"Squeaking, are ye? Won't do ye no good!"

Bennett had been warned by the Marquis in the past not to brawl or to enter into arguments in front of the Stewards.

Right or wrong, it always reflected on both of those concerned, and although Bennett pressed his lips together in what was almost a grimace, he said nothing.

Only when he rejoined the Marquis did he say:

"I'll get that Jake Smith if it's th' last thing I does! 'E rides dirty an' that's why no-one w'd employ 'im till His Lordship took 'im on."

The Marquis's eyes narrowed.

"Is that a fact?" he enquired.

" 'Tis well known, M'Lord. Jake Smith were beggin' for a ride till three months ago."

The Marquis did not speak for a moment. Then he congratulated his jockey, promised the usual reward which was a very generous one for riding the winner, and rejoined Peregrine Wallingham.

He told him what he had heard, and Peregrine said:

"I heard that Smith was a questionable jockey before he was taken on by Branscombe, but he has never ridden a horse that I would wish to back. I will find out what I can about him, Linden."

"Do that," the Marquis agreed, "but now, I think, unless you particularly want to stay for the next race, we should be getting back to London. The crowds are going to make it an exhausting journey and the quicker we get away from the course the better."

"I am ready to go," Peregrine Wallingham replied.

"What is more," the Marquis went on, "I have no wish to return to the Box and hear Branscombe averring, which he is sure to do, that he is in reality the winner."

"It has been officially declared a dead-heat," Peregrine said, "so you share the prize money—twenty-eight hundred pounds."

"That will not prevent him from saying I am not entitled to it," the Marquis said grimly. "God, how I dislike that man!"

143

Peregrine laughed.

"That is obvious, and I admit his conceit and bumptiousness gets under everybody's skin, except of course the Monarch's."

The Marquis said nothing.

He was only too well aware that the new King, William IV, had been beguiled by the Earl's inflated estimation of his own abilities into thinking him an exceptionally good advisor.

The Earl had jumped at the chance, and as a Courtier had said somewhat bitterly:

"I have always found one Monarch enough, but when one has two of them, I find my position almost insupportable!"

Trusting, good-natured, and rather stupid, the King was anxious to make a good impression on his subjects, and with the help of his dowdy and dull little German wife to have a very different Court from that of his brother, George IV.

He had swept away the immorality and raffishness of the Court which had scandalised the country, but unfortunately the laughter had gone too, as those who attended the King at Windsor, Buckingham Palace, and Windsor Castle were sometimes dismayed to find.

The Princess de Lieven, wife of the Russian Ambassador, had complained to the Marquis that the Court was now intolerably dreary and dull.

"There is no possibility of even having a reasonable conversation," she had said bitterly. "In the evening we all sit at a round table. The King snoozes, and the Queen does needlework, and talks with great animation but with never a word of politics."

The Marquis had laughed.

He knew that the Princess, who was vivacious, witty, and usually very indiscreet, was undoubtedly suffering, and he only hoped that the Earl of Branscombe was finding his self-appointed position a bore.

Actually, when the Marquis was alone with the King he found him, although inclined to be repetitive, quite interesting on subjects on which he was an authority.

But he had in many ways to agree with the Duke of Wellington, who had said in his blunt manner:

"Really, my master is too stupid! When at table he wishes to make a speech, I always turn to him my deaf ear so as not to be tempted to contradict him."

The Marquis began to move swiftly throught the crowd of touts, gypsies, confidence men, and beggars.

There were dwarfs, clowns, acrobats, minstrels, and tipsters, all of whom added to the hubbub of the occasion.

As quickly as was possible the Marquis found his Phaeton, and as soon as he was driving his horses in the direction of London, Peregrine said:

"I presume the King, who knows little about racing, will be pleased that Branscombe's horse came in first, even if he is forced to share the honour and glory with you."

"Doubtless the King will believe that Branscombe would have won if *Highflyer* had not passed the Winning-Post at the same moment by a sheer fluke!"

The Marquis spoke bitterly and Peregrine was aware that the result rankled.

Actually, he thought it had been very exciting and certainly a surprise which few race-goers would have expected.

Because he was genuinely fond of the Marquis, he said consolingly:

"Well, you and I, Linden, know that he only won by a foul, but it will not do any good to say so."

"No, of course not," the Marquis agreed, "but I will do my best to see that damned jockey gets his desserts. I bet you any money you like that Branscombe knew what he was doing when he engaged the man."

"Of course he did!" Peregrine agreed. "He was determined to beat you by fair means or foul."

"That does not surprise me," the Marquis said. "Branscombe has always been the same ever since he was at Eton. He has to be top, and, if you remember, even there we were always running neck and neck for some position or other."

Peregrine laughed.

The rivalry between the two boys had been the talk of the School and the other scholars had divided themselves equally behind one or the other. It had been very much the same when they had both gone to Oxford.

He himself had always disliked the Earl because he knew that despite his success in the field of sport, he was fundamentally unsporting.

145

He was not averse to taking an underhanded advantage in any contest, and he intended always to be the winner.

Some boys and young men sense with an almost clairvoyant perception the flaws in each other, and Peregrine had always been quite sure that somewhere in the Earl there was a canker of which few people were aware.

The Marquis was different.

Although he had his faults, he was in his friend's mind a gentleman who would never do anything that was not completely straight and honourable.

"What are you thinking about?" the Marquis enquired as they cleared the worst of the crowds and the horses were able to move more quickly.

"You, as it happens."

"I am flattered!" the Marquis said sarcastically. "But why?"

"I was comparing you to Branscombe, to his disadvantage."

"So I should think, and I am not looking forward to the dinner this evening."

The Derby Dinner given by the Stewards of the Jockey Club was always an important occasion, and every winner of the Derby enjoyed the congratulations and the honour that was accorded to him on that particular evening.

It would be particularly irksome, as Peregrine knew, for the Marquis to have to pretend that he enjoyed the Earl's company and to repress the knowledge that their horses had been equal owing only to foul riding by his jockey.

"Let us hope we need not stay long," Peregrine said in an effort to cheer up his friend. "There are some very attractive little 'bits of muslin' arrived from France at the Palace of Pleasure, whom you may find interesting, as soon as we can get away."

The Marquis did not reply. Peregrine remembered that his friend usually found such Houses a waste of time, and he said quickly:

"But I expect you have arranged to meet Lady Isobel."

There was just a note of doubt in the question, as if he realised that recently the Marquis had not been seen with Lady Isobel Sidley as often as might have been expected.

This was surprising, for she was not only an acknowledged beauty in London Society but was also quite obviously wildly, passionately in love with the Marquis to the point where the whole Social World was aware of it.

Lady Isobel had, Peregrine often thought, been born too late. Her impetuous indiscretions were such as had been admired fifteen years ago by the Regent.

He had loved pretty women and he had certainly not wished them to be moral or prudent.

Unfortunately, Lady Isobel had never learnt to control her feelings, and her infatuation for the Marquis, which she had made no attempt to disguise, had already shocked the Queen.

There was a distinct pause. Then with his eyes on his horses the Marquis said:

"No. I shall not be seeing Isobel. To tell you the truth, Peregrine, I am no longer interested."

His friend turned to stare at him incredulously.

He had thought that perhaps the Marquis might remonstrate with Isobel or curtail some of the time they were seen together in public, but that he should have finished with her completely was incredible.

"Do you really mean that?" he enquired.

The Marquis nodded.

"I am bored."

There was no obvious reply to that, and again there was silence as they drove on.

Peregrine was thinking that it was typical of the Marquis to be so ruthless in making a decision which most men in his position would find hard to implement.

But the Marquis was very blunt, and, if he was bored, whoever was boring him would be shown the door immediately, and there would be no appeal against his decision to finish either a love-affair or a friendship.

"Does Isobel know this?" Peregrine asked at length.

"I have not yet told her in so many words," the Marquis replied, "though I intend to do so when the opportunity arises. But I think she must have some inkling, as we have not seen each other for over a week."

Peregrine remembered seeing a groom in Sidley livery delivering a letter at the Marquis's house when he had been with him that morning.

He was certain that Lady Isobel would be very voluble on paper if she could not get the chance of saying what she thought in person.

Suddenly he saw storm-clouds ahead, and he only hoped that he would not be involved in them.

Then as if he knew that this was the moment when he must tell the Marquis what was on his mind and what had been worrying him considerably all day, he said:

"Are you ready to hear something which will annoy you?"

The way he spoke, rather than what he said, made the Marquis look at him sharply.

"Does it concern Isobel?"

"No, it has nothing to do with her," Peregrine said quickly. "It is something I feel I have to tell you, and I have been waiting for a propitious moment."

"Which you think is now?"

"I suppose it is as good a time as any," Peregrine said a little ruefully. "As a matter of fact, I was remembering that in the old days Kings cut off the heads of messengers who brought them bad news."

The Marquis laughed.

"Is that what you are afraid will happen to you?"

"At least for the moment your hands are engaged with the reins!" Peregrine replied.

The Marquis laughed again.

"I will not hit you, you fool, whatever you tell me, and now that you have aroused my curiosity I am naturally speculating as to what it can be."

"It concerns Branscombe."

The Marquis groaned.

"I am trying to forget him before I have to see his smug face at the dinner tonight."

"According to him, Her Majesty admires him enormously and thinks he looks just as a gentleman should."

"God help us!" the Marquis ejaculated. "And incidentally, Branscombe does not consider himself a gentleman but a nobelman, which entitles him to be more self-satisfied, more blown up with his own importance, and more bumptious than he is already!"

"It is a pity we cannot tell him so," Peregrine said, laughing.

"What are you going to tell me about him that I do not know already?"

"I will be surprised if you do!" Peregrine remarked. "You are aware that the Queen is anxious that those who are in attendance at Court should be 'properly and respectably' married?"

"The Princess de Lieven told me," the Earl replied, "that the Queen said: 'We want all those dear people who are closest to the King to be as happy and compatible as we are.' "

The way the Marquis mimicked the Queen's voice made it sound sickly sentimental, and Peregrine said quickly:

"Be careful, Linden, or Her Majesty will have you up the aisle before you are aware of it!"

"I assure you she will do nothing of the sort!" the Marquis retorted. "I have no hesitation in declaring that I have no intention of marrying any woman before I wish to do so, even if for disobeying the Royal Command I am sent to the Tower!"

"That I can well believe," Peregrine smiled, "but Branscombe has agreed with the Queen that it is an excellent idea and has already mentioned privately to one or two people the name of the woman he intends to marry."

The way Peregrine spoke told the Marquis that what he was saying was significant, and because he knew it was expected of him, he asked:

"I presume you intend to tell me who the unfortunate female is?"

"The Princess de Lieven told me in confidence, because she said she was too frightened to tell you herself," Peregrine replied, "that Branscombe intends to marry your Ward as soon as she arrives in England."

The expression on the Marquis's face was one of sheer astonishment.

"My Ward!" he exclaimed. "Who the devil . . . ?"

He stopped.

"You cannot mean Mirabelle?"

"Exactly! Mirabelle Chester!"

"But the girl is still at School. She has seen nothing of the world, and anyway she is not arriving in England for another month."

"That is true," Peregrine agreed, "but naturally people have been talking about her."

"By which you mean," the Marquis said sharply, "that they have been talking about her fortune!"

"As usual, you have hit the nail on the head!"

The Marquis gave an exclamation that was almost an oath.

"You are not telling me that Branscombe needs money?"

"The Princess told me, again in confidence," Peregrine replied, "that he has secretly been looking for an heiress for some time. Apparently he said to someone who reported it to the Princess that, much as he disliked you, he could not deny that the Chester blood was nearly compatible with his own!"

The Marquis exploded.

"Nearly, indeed!"

"When he heard of the extent of your Ward's fortune," Peregrine went on, "he decided that she is exactly what he needs."

The Marquis's lips tightened before he asked:

"But for Heaven's sake, why?"

"I gathered, from the Princess's rather garbled explanation, that he found on his father's death that the old Earl had not left him all he expected."

"He will marry her over my dead body!" the Marquis exclaimed. "As Mirabelle's Guardian, I would never give my permission for her to marry Branscombe."

There was silence. Then Peregrine said:

"You will have to give substantial grounds for your refusal."

The Marquis did not answer for a moment, but his friend knew by the expression on his face that he was realising it would be very difficult for any Guardian to refuse the Earl of Branscombe as a suitor.

Whatever might be felt about him privately, publicly he was the holder of a great and honoured title, the possessor of an Estate that, like his ancestors, was part of the history of England, and he certainly enjoyed the favour of both the King and Queen.

The Marquis had already considered his responsibilities towards the daughter of his first cousin.

Edward Chester, who had died two years ago, had been one of those brilliant but restless people who was happy only when he was exploring strange parts of the world or risking his life quite unnecessarily in adventures that would have appalled more-cautious men.

Although his travels had often been extremely uncomfortable and dangerous, in the course of them he had become enormously wealthy.

Someone who had befriended him had left him shares in a gold-mine which had suddenly borne fruit, and in another part of the world, land he had written off as a dead loss had become valuable overnight when oil was found in it.

Perhaps because he was not particularly interested in stocks and shares, those he had bought in a haphazard fasion always seemed to bloom the minute he acquired them.

When he was killed, as everybody expected he would be, attempting to cross a range of mountains which were considered impassable, his daughter Mirabelle found herself to be the possessor of a huge fortune and a Guardian to administer it for her whom she had never even seen.

Mirabelle's mother had been half-Italian, and when Edward Chester had left on his last expedition, from which he had never returned, he had deposited his wife and daughter in Italy.

It was unlikely that the letter which had been despatched to him telling him of his wife's death had ever reached him, and the Marquis had learnt first of Mrs. Chester's death, then of his cousin Edward's, within a month of each other.

All this had happened last summer, and while he was wondering what he should do he had received a letter from Mirabelle's aunt with whom she was staying in Italy.

The Contessa told him that as her niece was attending an excellent School in Rome, she thought it would be a mistake for her to come to England until she was out of mourning.

The Marquis had agreed.

"Next year, when she is eighteen," he had told Peregrine, "she can be presented to the Queen, and I have plenty of relatives who will be only too pleased to chaperone her."

"Are you also going to sit on the dais with all the Dowagers?" Peregrine had teased.

"I am not going to do anything except fight off the fortune-hunters," the Marquis had replied. "By God, Peregrine, do you know how much this girl owns?"

When he heard the answer to this question, Peregrine had agreed with the Marquis that it was far too much for one young woman and would undoubtedly result in all the wasters swarming round her like hornets.

"I am going to marry her off to the first decent man who comes along, then I shall be free of responsibility," the Marquis had said. "Because I was fond of Edward, eccentric though he was, I will not let his daughter be imposed on by one of those titled ne'er-do-wells who think all a rich woman wants from them is a coronet."

Those sentiments were extremely laudable, Peregrine was thinking now. At the same time, nobody could say that the Earl of Branscombe was a ne'er-do-well and had nothing to offer except a title.

Peregrine was aware that the Marquis was determined not to inflict a man he loathed and despised on the daughter of his cousin for whom he had had an affection.

But it was going to be extremely difficult to think of a plausible refusal which would not result in the Earl causing a scandal by immediately calling him out.

William IV had expressly forbidden duelling, but where there was a will there was a way, and in certain circumstances gentlemen could, if they wished, settle their differences by the time-honoured method of firing at each other, without there being any scandal.

It was difficult to know who, if such a duel did take place, would be the winner, but it was something Peregrine knew must be prevented at all costs.

Aloud he said:

"I know exactly what you are feeling, Linden, but if Branscombe has set his heart on marrying your Ward, it is going to be damned difficult to prevent him from doing so."

The Marquis's lips tightened before he said:

"It is just like him to say he is going to marry a woman without having the courtesy to ask her first!"

"He knows only too well that no girl would refuse him," Peregrine replied. "The Earl of Branscombe, the highest in the land, the King's favourite! It would be a fairy-tale come true!"

"Except that you and I know under all that tinsel he is not Prince Charming or ever likely to be."

Peregrine nodded.

"Do you remember Rosie?"

The Marquis did not reply, but they were both thinking of the little dancer whom the Earl had deliberately seduced away from the Marquis when he was out of London attending a race-meeting in the North.

On his return he found that the Earl had installed her in a far larger house than the one he had provided for her, with now four horses instead of two for her carriage, and her jewellery was dazzling.

Knowing that it was a deliberate way of scoring off him, the Marquis had been annoyed, but because he had been too clever to show his annoyance the Earl did not have the satisfaction out of the episode that he had expected.

In fact, the Marquis had said openly in the Club, knowing it would be repeated, that he was extremely grateful to the Earl for relieving him of a young woman who he had already found had a very small repertoire and none of it worth repeating.

What he had not expected was that his and the Earl's animosity towards each other had ended the girl's career.

Because he was annoyed by the Marquis's reaction, the Earl had deliberately taken his revenge on her.

He had not only deprived her of everything he had given her, which was against all the rules of such liaisons, but he had gone out of his way to see that she was dismissed from the Theatre and was unable to find any engagements elsewhere.

She had come to see the Marquis in desperation because she was actually almost starving.

She had been afraid that he would punish her for the way she had treated him, and she had appealed to him only as a last resort.

The Marquis had not only been extremely generous but had got her an engagement in a touring-company playing the larger towns in the Provinces in a show which had eventually come to London.

He was no longer interested in her as a woman, and he would not have stooped to pick up the Earl's leavings, but she had thanked him for his kindness with tears in her eyes.

The Marquis had merely added another notch on the tally he was marking up against his enemy.

Now he said with an urgent note in his voice:

"What am I to do, Peregrine? You have to help me with this."

"I want to," Peregrine replied, "but how can we set about it?"

"We could, of course, write to the Contessa and ask her to keep Mirabelle in Italy and not let her come to London this Season."

"Surely that will only be postponing the evil hour? And if Branscombe has made up his mind to marry her, he might even go out to Rome."

The Marquis drove on and they must have travelled for nearly half-an-hour before he said:

"There must be something we can do!"

"Only find him another heiress!" Peregrine replied. "And there are not many girls about as rich as Mirabelle Chester."

"I know," the Marquis agreed, "and although I have not seen her since she was a baby, I am told she is pretty and has a sweet nature."

"I do not suppose Branscombe is particularly interested in her nature," Peregrine said cynically.

"I have to stop this marriage," the Marquis snapped. "If Edward were alive he would whisk her off to the top of the Himalayas or across the Gobi Desert. But personally I should be unable to look after myself in such outlandish places, let alone a young girl!"

"There must be something we can do," Peregrine repeated. "There must be other heiresses in London waiting to make their curtseys to the Queen."

"If there was anybody outstanding we would have heard about her," the Marquis said, "and certainly the Princess de Lieven would know. There is not a piece of gossip in circulation small enough to escape her sharp ears!"

"Shall we ask her?" Peregrine suggested.

"For God's sake, no!" the Marquis ejaculated. "I swear Branscombe shall not marry my Ward, but you know as well as I do that the Princess would not be able to resist telling him I had said so, which would make him more determined than ever."

"I do not suppose anything will stop him," Peregrine said, "not if he really wants money. And if it comes to that, who does not really want money except you?"

"We are talking about Mirabelle," the Marquis said, as if he felt he must keep to the point. "I suppose I could persuade her to say she would not accept him."

"That is all very well," Peregrine said, "but you know perfectly well that all your relatives would think it a splendid match. Among the available eligible bachelors, compared to Branscombe there is no-one as suitable except yourself, and you can hardly marry your own Ward."

"You are right about that," the Marquis said. "Besides, I have no intention of marrying anyone, especially not an unfledged School-girl."

"Then we are back to where we started," Peregrine said, "with Branscombe the villain or the hero of the piece, whichever way you like to look at him, and the heroine, young, unsophisticated, sweet, and innocent, with no idea what she is in for as she walks into the arena!"

He spoke dramatically, expecting the Marquis to laugh.

Instead he said sharply:

"Say that again!"

"Say what?"

"What you said just now. It gave me an idea!"

"I said: 'with Brans—' "

"No, not him. What you said about the girl."

"I said: 'and the heroine, young, unsophisticated, sweet, and innocent,' " Peregrine repeated slowly.

"That is it!" the Marquis exclaimed. "That is it! And Branscombe has never seen her!"

"What are you talking about?"

"It is obvious. All we have to do is find a young, unsophisticated, sweet, and innocent girl to take the place of my Ward. Branscombe will propose to her because she is rich. But it does not have to be Mirabelle! He will only think it is she."

"Are you suggesting that you produce a fake Mirabelle," Peregrine asked, "and palm her off on Branscombe as your Ward?"

"Exactly!" the Marquis said. "That is what I intend to do! If he can cheat me and my horses out of winning the Derby Stakes, I can cheat him when it comes to his winning his future wife!"

"You may have an idea there," Peregrine conceded, "but whom do you have in mind?"

"I have no-one at the moment," the Marquis replied, "but we are going to find this 'young, unsophisticated, sweet, and innocent girl' and we are going to groom her secretly in our own stables, so to speak, until we think she is ready for the matrimonial stakes which Branscombe thinks is going to be a walkover!"

"But who will she be?" Peregrine asked.

"That is the crux of the joke," the Marquis said. "I will tell you exactly who she will be."

He paused before with a hard, metallic note in his voice he said:

"Branscombe is a snob, so she will come from the gutter; Branscombe wants money, so she will be penniless; Branscombe wants a blue-blooded wife of whom he can be proud, so she will be a nobody! That will teach him a lesson he will never forget—and nor shall I!"

CHAPTER TWO

———— ❧ ————

"*I* CONGRATULATE YOU!" PEREGRINE SAID as they drove away.

The Marquis, intent on tooling his Phaeton, smiled, which told his friend that everything had gone as he had expected.

Last night when they had arrived at the Marquis's country house in Hertfordshire, they had sat up late, arguing as to whether they would be able to find the type of girl they had in mind with whom to deceive the Earl.

Peregrine had been insistent from the beginning that she would have to be an actress, but the Marquis had said firmly:

"If she was acting it would soon become obvious, and that is something we must avoid at all costs. He has to actually marry our fake before we expose her and make him look a fool."

"I can see your point," Peregrine said reluctantly.

"What is more," the Marquis went on, "I have no intention of laying myself open to an accusation of trickery."

"What do you mean?"

"I mean," the Marquis said firmly, "that whatever girl I produce, she will in fact be my Ward."

Peregrine looked at him in astonishment.

"How do you intend to contrive that?"

The Marquis's lips twisted in a wry smile.

"If I were in the East I could doubtless buy in a slave-market, but as we are in England we have to acquire her by more subtle means."

"You are not suggesting employing one of those old harridans who entice young girls up from the country into bawdy-houses and sell them to the type of man who likes them young and innocent?"

"I would certainly not sink to that sort of trick," the Marquis said sharply. "But there must be girls who would be only too pleased to have a rich Guardian."

"Orphans, for instance," Peregrine agreed.

The Marquis gave an exclamation.

"That is the answer!" he said. "Of course, orphans, and I maintain two Orphanages."

"Then we must certainly visit them," Peregrine said, "and with no relatives to turn up unexpectedly and make a scene or try to blackmail you, everything should be plane-sailing."

"We first have to choose the orphan," the Marquis remarked.

At the same time he was smiling, and Peregrine had to admit that his idea was a clever one.

All the way driving down to Alchester Abbey they talked of nothing else.

The Marquis's ancestral home, built before the Dissolution of the Monasteries, had been a Cistercian Abbey and architecturally was one of the most beautiful buildings in the whole of Great Britain.

It had been converted into an extremely comfortable house. At the same time, the exquisite Cloisters, the great Refectory, and the medieval Chapel were still there.

Peregrine always thought that Alchester Abbey had an atmosphere that was different from that of any other house in which he had stayed.

He felt it was not something he could say to the Marquis, although he often wondered why the holiness of it did not soften his whole attitude towards the world outside.

There was no doubt that now the Marquis was determined, where the Earl was concerned, to live up to his reputation of being ruthless and at times extremely hard.

Yet the Earl deserved everything that was coming to him.

This was confirmed when, before they left London the morning after the Derby Dinner, the Marquis was told that his jockey would like to speak to him.

"Do you want me to leave you?" Peregrine asked, as they walked from the Breakfast-Room into the Library.

The Marquis shook his head.

"No, I want you to hear what Bennett has to say. It will be useful for me to have a witness, if it is what I suspect."

Peregrine held up his hands in horror.

"I refuse, absolutely refuse, to be involved in your row with Branscombe! He is an unpleasant enemy and I am not up to his weight."

"I am not asking you to fight him," the Marquis said, "I will do that. I merely want your moral support, which I have always had in the past."

"Morally, it is all yours!" Peregrine said with a smile. "Physically, I am inclined to run for cover!"

The Marquis laughed.

"I never thought you were a coward!"

"I simply know when discretion is the better part of valour!"

They were both laughing as the Butler announced:

"Bennett, M'Lord!"

The jockey came into the room looking anxious.

Peregrine thought that without the colours and cap which gave jockeys a certain glamour, in their ordinary clothes they always appeared small and insignificant.

"Good-morning, Bennett!" the Marquis said. "I hope, as you are here, that my secretary has given you the reward you were promised."

"Yes, M'Lord, and I'm very grateful, M'Lord, considering I were only entitled to half o'what you've given I."

"I thought you rode an excellent race, Bennett, and did the best you could in the circumstances."

"Which is what I wanted to speak about to Your Lordship."

"I am listening," the Marquis said.

"After th' meeting was over, Smith were a-drinking with 'is pals, and having been watching 'is weight before th'race, 'e has a few over the odds, so to speak."

"So he was drunk," the Marquis said.

"Yes, M'Lord, and 'e were a-talkin' free-like."

"What did he say?"

"That 'e were resentful, M'Lord, as 'e'd been told that as 'e hadn't won as 'e'd been instructed to do, 'e'd receive no extra fee."

The Marquis stiffened.

"Are you seriously telling me, Bennett, that the Earl of Branscombe is not giving Smith anything extra for carrying his horse past the Winning-Post, even though it was a dead-heat?"

"That's what 'e says, M'Lord," Bennett confirmed. " 'E were a-grumblin' that 'twere a mean action on th' part o' 'is Lordship, considerin' 'e'd done 'is best to carry out 'is instructions."

"Did he say what they were?"

" 'E made that clear enough, M'Lord," Bennett answered. "As 'e were a-leavin' 'e comes across to me an' says:

" ' 'Tis yer fault, Bennett, that I'm skint. Next time I'll take me whip, as 'is Lordship tells I, ter ye and yer damned 'orse.' "

"What was your reply?" the Marquis enquired.

"I didn't get a chance to say anythin', M'Lord. Two of the Branscombe grooms was there with 'im. They realised 'e were sayin' things in 'is cups 'e wouldn't say out loud if 'e were sober, an' they 'ustled 'im away."

The Marquis was silent for a moment, then he said:

"Thank you, Bennett, you have told me exactly what I expected, and I am glad to have it confirmed. I shall offer you the choice of the three horses I am entering for the races at Ascot. I feel sure that if things go well, you will make certain of the Gold Cup for me."

Bennett's grin stretched from ear to ear.

"Thank ye, M'Lord. Thank ye very much! It's a chance I've always wanted. And I'd rather ride fer Your Lordship than any other owner; ye've always been fair and square and no rider can ask more than that."

The jockey was smiling when he left the Library, and the Marquis turned to Peregrine.

"You heard what he said. Branscombe deliberately told his jockey to prevent my horse from winning the race."

"There is nothing you can do about it now," Peregrine said. "If Bennett repeated what he just said in front of the Stewards, his word would not be taken against that of Branscombe, who would obviously deny it."

"I am aware of that," the Marquis said. "That is why I have no compunction about playing a trick on him which will definitely not be as unsporting as what he tried to do to me."

"There I agree with you," Peregrine replied, "but it is not going to be easy."

However, they set out from the Abbey to visit the Marquis's Orphanages with the hope that there they would find exactly the right type of young girl who, with careful grooming, would be able to deceive the Earl.

On most important Estates the owner in some century or another had built Orphanages and Alms Houses.

The Marquis explained that the newest one, which they were to visit first, had been built by his grandmother.

"My grandfather was an extremely raffish character with a large number of love-children. I always felt that my grandmother meant it as some reparation for his sins."

"If you are expecting to find one of your relations from the wrong side of the blanket there, I think you will be unlucky," Peregrine remarked. "They would be too long in the tooth to pass off on Branscombe as suitable young women."

"I know that," the Marquis replied. "I was just explaining to you why this particular Orphanage was built, and it is, I have always understood, a model of its kind."

It was apparent that the Marquis had not spoken idly.

The Orphanage was attractive to look at, and the orphans, about twenty of them, seemed healthy and happy.

The Matron, a motherly woman, was delighted and a little overcome by the Marquis's visit.

She showed them with justifiable pride that everything was clean and tidy, and the orphans themselves showed good manners in their bows and curtseys.

There was, however, one snag which both the Marquis and Peregrine realised immediately.

All the orphans were very young, and when he commented on it, the Matron explained:

"As soon as the orphans reach the age of twelve, M'Lord, they leave; the boys are apprenticed to a trade, the girls are sent into Domestic Service."

"At twelve years of age!" the Marquis exclaimed.

"Yes, M'Lord. I sent my two eldest girls up to the Abbey a month ago, and I understand they are doing well in the scullery."

The Marquis glanced at Peregrine and they both knew their visit had been fruitless.

Having pleased the Matron by his expressions of approval, the Marquis climbed back into his Phaeton, and as the groom released the horses' heads and jumped up behind, they drove off.

"It was a good idea," Peregrine said, "but how were we to know the orphans are disposed of as soon as they are old enough to work?"

"Do you suppose that is true of all Orphanages?" the Marquis asked.

"I expect so," Peregrine answered.

"We do not know that for certain," the Marquis said, as if he resented being thwarted in his original plan. "We will therefore visit my other Orphanage, which is on the south side of the Estate."

It took them a long time to drive to where the land seemed more thinly populated and the villages through which they passed were smaller.

"I cannot remember ever having been here before," Peregrine remarked.

"We have hunted here," the Marquis replied, "but the woods do not give as much sport as those nearer the Abbey. I do not think we have ever shot here."

"You own too much, Linden," Peregrine said with a sigh. "I am sure it is impossible for you to keep track of everything that goes on on this Estate and on your others."

The Marquis laughed.

"I have Agents and Managers to look after things for me, and so far there are no complaints."

Peregrine thought that if there were any, the Marquis would not be likely to hear of them.

He spent a great deal of his time in London, and when he came to the Abbey it was usually with a large party of amusing people to keep him from being bored.

It was difficult, Peregrine thought a little enviously, to imagine how anyone in the Marquis's position should ever be bored when he was rich enough to have everything he wanted.

There was not a beautiful woman in London who would not be only too willing to take Isobel Sidley's place, now that he had finished with her.

"The trouble with you, Linden," he said aloud, "is that you are too good-looking, too rich, and too successful!"

The Marquis laughed.

"Whatever I have done to provoke that outburst, I certainly do not intend to dispute it."

"You are growing more conceited than Branscombe!" Peregrine exclaimed.

"If you say that again," the Marquis replied, "I shall set you down here in the middle of nowhere and make you walk home."

"I thought that would annoy you!" Peregrine chuckled.

The Marquis was just about to make some retort when the Orphanage came in sight.

It was a long, low building, set back from the road on the outskirts of a hamlet consisting of a few cottages, a village green, and a black and white Inn.

The Marquis drew up his horses with a flourish, and as the groom ran to the horses' heads, he fastened the reins to the back-board before he and Peregrine stepped down.

It struck the latter as they walked up to the door that it needed painting, and when he lifted the knocker he noticed that was dirty.

"We will not stay long," the Marquis said, "and if we are not successful here we shall have to think of some other way of finding the girl we require."

"You are not going to be lucky here," Peregrine warned him. "It looks as if no-one is home."

He raised the knocker again, making a rat-tat that certainly sounded noisy outside the house.

"I am sure if the place is empty I should have been informed," the Marquis said vaguely.

Then they heard footsteps on the other side of the door and a moment later it opened.

The girl who stood there was an unprepossessing sight.

She was wearing an apron of sacking that had holes in it, a dress that, although clean, was threadbare, and her hair, scraped back from her forehead, fell in lank wisps over her ears.

She looked ill and emaciated and the bones of her cheeks seemed unnaturally sharp as she stared first at the Marquis, then at Peregrine, with an expression of surprise on her face.

Then with an obvious start, as if she remembered her manners, she dropped a curtsey.

"I am the Marquis of Alchester," the Marquis said. "I wish to see over the Orphanage. Is Matron here?"

"Y-yes . . . My Lord."

The question obviously agitated the thin girl.

She spoke with a cultured voice and opened the door a little wider for them to pass through into the Hall. It was bare of furniture and at the end of it was a staircase on which, Peregrine noticed, a number of the bannisters were broken or missing.

The girl moved towards a door.

"P-perhaps . . . Your Lordships . . . should . . . come in here," she said in a voice that seemed to tremble.

As she spoke there was a scream from upstairs. It was the scream of a child in pain, and it was followed by another, and yet another—screams which seemed to echo and re-echo round the empty Hall.

"What is happening?" the Marquis asked sharply. "Has there been an accident?"

"N-no . . . it is . . . Matron."

"Matron?" the Marquis enquired. "What is she doing? Why are those children screaming like that?"

It was difficult to make himself heard above the noise.

Now the girl, who had been gazing upwards, said:

"I must . . . stop her! She will . . . kill little Daisy if she goes on like . . . this!"

She did not wait to say any more, but started to run up the uncarpeted stairs as quickly as she could, and after a moment's hesitation the Marquis and Peregrine followed her.

They reached the landing and saw the girl ahead of them hurry down a short passage which obviously led to a room at the back of the house.

The screams were coming from there, and as they followed the girl through the open door they saw her run towards a woman at the far end of the room who was hitting the children round her with a heavy stick.

She was holding one, a small child of about five or six, and as the others, trapped between her and a number of beds, were trying to escape she was striking at them too.

They were all screaming and one was lying on the floor with blood pouring from a weal on her back where a blow from the stick had broken the skin.

"Stop, Mrs. Moore! Stop!" the girl cried.

She rushed down the room just as the Marquis and Peregrine entered it, and, seizing the woman's arm, she tried to force it upwards to prevent her from striking again the child she was holding with her other hand.

"Don't you interfere with me!" Mrs. Moore shouted furiously. "These little varmints has woken me again after I told them to be quiet. I'll teach them to obey me orders. I'll beat them until they're unconscious!"

"No, Mrs. Moore! You cannot do that! And you cannot . . . hit Daisy again. She is too . . . ill."

The woman was just about to scream abuse at the girl when she caught sight of the Marquis and Peregrine standing in the doorway.

Her jaw dropped open and she lapsed into silence so that the girl was able to pull the stick from her hand.

Mrs. Moore found her voice.

"Who's this?" she asked.

"H-His . . . Lordship . . . the Marquis!" the girl answered.

Dropping the stick down by one of the beds, the girl put her arm round the small child on whom Mrs. Moore had now relinquished her hold and who was sobbing convulsively.

"It is all right, dearest," she said. "It is all right. She will not hurt you any more."

The other children had already stopped screaming at the sight of the Marquis, and, with the tears running down their thin cheeks, they merely stared at him as if he were an apparition from another world.

The room was a dormitory containing a number of iron bedsteads, most of which were broken and tied up with rope or wire.

The blankets on them were torn and stained, and the pillows appeared to be nothing but bundles of rags.

The Marquis, however, looked at Mrs. Moore as she walked towards him, and he realised from the unsteadiness of her gait and the heightened colour in her florid face that she had been drinking.

She was a largely built, voluptuous creature, dressed in a manner which was a complete contrast to the orphans who were in her charge.

They were in rags, as was the girl who had opened the door, but Mrs. Moore was elegantly attired in a gown that would have been more suitable for a Lady than a working Matron.

There were rings in her ears and on the fingers of her fat hands.

"Your Lordship—this's a shurprishe!" she said, slurring the last word.

She attempted to curtsey and almost fell over in the effort.

"Are you the Matron?" the Marquis asked sharply.

"Yes, indeed, Your Lordship," the woman replied ingratiatingly, "and if you'll come to my Sitting-Room I'll tell you about the difficulties I have here."

The Marquis was looking round the dormitory and at the now-silent, tattered children.

The girl who had let him in was kneeling beside the child lying on the floor, attempting to wipe away the blood from her back.

"Why is this place in such a state?" he asked harshly.

"It's the children. Horrible little varmints they be! Like animals, destroying everything they touch."

Mrs. Moore was obviously now on the defensive, and her dilated eyes and slobbering lips made the Marquis feel physically sick.

He walked away from her towards the girl who was kneeling on the floor.

"It is true that the children are out of control?" he asked.

The girl looked up at him and to his surprise he saw that there was an undoubted look of hostility in her face.

"If they make a noise," she answered, "and commit the crime of waking Matron, it is because they are hungry."

There was an unmistakable note of condemnation in her voice, and for a moment the Marquis felt she blamed him for what they were suffering.

Then as he looked at the children he realised that what she had said was the truth.

Of course they were hungry. He could see it in the hollowness of their eyes, the way their cheekbones protruded, and the pallor of their skin.

He saw too that the wrist-bones of the girl as she staunched the blood on the child's back were unnaturally sharp.

"Why are they not given enough food?" he asked, and his voice was angry.

He saw that the girl was about to tell him the truth, but even as her lips moved she looked towards the Matron and was afraid to speak.

It was then Mrs. Moore gave a cry that was almost as poignant as that of the children.

"Don't you listen to her, M'Lord! Don't you listen to a word she says!" she screamed. "She's a liar, and she encourages the children in their wickedness!"

"That's enough!" the Marquis said sharply.

At his voice of command, the words Mrs. Moore had been about to speak died in her throat.

"As I can see you are incompetent to run this Orphanage, which bears my name," the Marquis said, "you will leave immediately—within ten minutes. I have no wish to hear anything you have to say, and I will take care that you do not ever have such a post as this again."

Mrs. Moore gave a scream, but the Marquis merely pointed towards the door.

"Go!" he said.

It would have been a brave person who could have argued with him.

166

However, the Marquis turned away from the Matron and back to the girl on the floor to ask:

"Is there no food in the house?"

She shook her head.

"She spends the money on drink and her own clothes."

The Marquis was about to ask her other questions but instead he said:

"Where can we get some food immediately?"

"You mean you will . . . send out for . . . some?"

"My man will procure anything that is obtainable here and I will send more from the Abbey when I return home."

The girl rose to her feet and carried the child she was holding in her arms to one of the beds. She laid her down and covered her with a torn blanket. Then as the child whimpered and tried to cling to her, she said to one of the older girls:

"Look after Daisy while I tell His Lordship where to buy us some food."

The word "food" seemed to galvanise the silent children into speech.

"Oi'm hungry!" one of the boys shouted.

Then they were all clamouring at once:

"We're hungry! We're hungry!"

For a moment there was an uproar, then the Marquis said firmly:

"Listen to me!" As their voices died away he went on: "I'm going to get you some food immediately, and after this you will be properly fed, but meanwhile you will have to wait and be patient until I can find out what is obtainable. Do you understand?"

It seemed as if they did, and they looked at him with unnaturally large eyes which made him think of small animals which had been ill-treated and did not understand why.

The girl was standing beside him.

"Now, how do I start?" he asked.

"There is a shop that sells . . . bread," she said breathlessly, "and there will be . . . milk at the . . . farm."

"You had better tell me exactly where it is."

"You mean . . . you will . . . fetch it?"

"There does not appear to be anybody else available," the Marquis replied.

167

"No, there is no-one."

"Explain to me where these places are."

As he spoke, he thought a bread-shop would not be hard to find in such a small village.

"Perhaps . . . the farmer's wife will have a . . . ham at the farm," the girl suggested as if she had suddenly thought of it, "unless . . . it would be too expensive."

The Marquis frowned.

"You must be aware that I am not considering the expense. I wish you to tell me who is responsible for the condition of this place."

He saw by the expression in her eyes that she was well aware who it was.

"Tell me!" he said sharply.

"Please . . . let us eat . . . first," she begged. "The children have had nothing . . . today and very little . . . yesterday."

"Very well," the Marquis agreed. "Come downstairs and explain where I should go."

He started to walk towards the stairs as he spoke, followed by Peregrine and the girl. As they reached the Hall he said:

"I suggest, Peregrine, you stay here and see that that ghastly woman leaves without making any further contact with the children. I will not be longer than I can help."

"I have a better idea," Peregrine replied. "I will go and buy what is necessary and you find out the reason for this sorry state of affairs. After all, it is your Orphanage."

There was a faint twinkle of amusement in the Marquis's eyes, as if he realised that Peregrine had no wish to be left in an uncomfortable position with the drunken Matron.

"Very well," he agreed.

He opened the front door, and as Peregrine got into the Phaeton and picked up the reins, the Marquis said to his groom:

"Help Mr. Wallingham, Jason. You are to buy everything that is obtainable in the village for a large number of hungry children. It does not matter what you get as long as it is food. Do you understand?"

"Yes, M'Lord."

"P-please . . ." a small voice said beside the Marquis, "get the smaller children plenty of milk . . . if they eat too much after being hungry for so long, they will be sick. The farm is just past the Green Man Inn. You cannot miss it."

"I'll find it, Miss," Jason said.

"You had better pay your way, Jason."

The Marquis drew a net purse from his pocket and held it out to the groom.

"I expect they'd give you credit, M'Lord," Jason said with a smile.

It was an impertinence, but the Marquis let it pass.

"Hurry!" he said firmly. "The children will be counting the minutes until you return and so shall I."

Jason took the purse, touched his forehead, and scrambled up onto the Phaeton as Peregrine moved off.

The Marquis turned back to the house.

"I want to talk to you," he said to the girl. "There are a number of questions I have to ask."

The girl seemed to hesitate. Then she opened the door of a room which was very different from those the Marquis had seen so far.

The Marquis realised it was the Matron's Sitting-Room. It was small and comfortable, with a sofa and arm-chairs set in front of a blazing fire.

But much more significant was a table on which there were a number of bottles and a glass from which somebody had recently been drinking.

"She will be in her bedroom, packing, My Lord," the girl said.

The Marquis stood with his back to the fire.

As if she suddenly realised how ragged and dilapidated she looked in contrast to his elegance, the girl undid the sacking-apron and, folding it, set it down on a chair.

The dress she was wearing looked hardly better than the apron. It was worn until the material itself had given way, and so although darned the darns did not hold.

Unnaturally thin though she was, the dress was still too tight and was strained across her thin chest. Because it was too short, the Marquis was aware that she had grown out of it.

"Let me start by asking your name," he said.

"It is . . . Kistna, My Lord."

"Kistna?" he questioned.

"I was born in India."

"How long have you been here?"

"For three years."

The way she spoke told him it had been a long time.

"And your age?"

"I am . . . eighteen, My Lord."

He was just about to ask her why, being so old, she was still in the Orphanage, and as if she knew what he was thinking she explained:

"When my father and mother died of cholera, I was sent here by the Missionary Society with my sister who was only eight."

"She is still here?" the Marquis enquired.

"She . . . died a year ago . . . from the cold in the winter . . . and . . . lack of food."

Now there was no doubt that the note of condemnation was back in Kistna's voice.

"How long has Mrs. Moore been here?" the Marquis asked.

"Nearly two years. There was a kindly Matron here before, but Your Lordship's Agent, Mr. Harboard, retired her as being too old."

"And was she?"

"Not really . . . but I think he wanted to put . . . Mrs. Moore in the position because . . . she was prepared to help him in the . . . way he . . . wished her to . . . do."

The Marquis noted that as she spoke the last sentence Kistna's voice dropped to barely a whisper, and having finished speaking she glanced towards the door almost as if she was afraid that Mrs. Moore would come in to contradict what she had said.

"Do not be afraid," he assured her. "There will be no repercussions, I promise you. I intend to see that what has happened here never occurs again."

Kistna clasped her hands together.

"I hoped Your Lordship would say that. I have often thought I should get in touch with you, for I could not believe you would have countenanced—nor would any decent man—the conditions in this terrible place."

"Tell me about it," the Marquis said. "And I suggest, because you look as if you could do with a good meal, that you sit down while we talk."

Kistna gave a little sigh.

"Thank you, My Lord."

She sat down on the edge of the sofa, but the Marquis remained standing and after a moment he said:

"I can hardly believe what I see when I have just come from the other Orphanage I maintain."

"Things were all right when I first came here," Kistna said, "and Mrs. Owen, who looked after us, was kind and very conscientious."

She paused before she went on:

"My sister was not well and was very unhappy without my mother, so Mrs. Owen allowed me to stay and look after her instead of trying to get employment as I intended to do."

She paused and the Marquis prompted:

"And after your sister's death?"

"The new Matron, Mrs. Moore, found me . . . useful. She and Mr. Harboard sacked the women who came in to clean and cook, and I . . . took their . . . place."

"Why did they do that?"

Kistna's eyes flickered. Then, as if she felt he compelled her to tell him the truth, she said:

"They . . . thought they could . . . save on the wages, as they did not have to . . . pay me."

"What you are saying," the Marquis said slowly, "is that the money they should have been spending on the Orphanage was going into their own pockets."

"I do not think Mrs. Moore got a lot of money," Kistna said. "Mr. Harboard gave her drink, which she craved, and paid for most of the gowns she wore. He also gave her . . . other presents."

"Why?" the Marquis enquired.

He saw a flush on Kistna's face and as it turned crimson he knew she was too embarrassed to find the right words, and he said quickly:

"I understand. Go on!"

"I used to hear them talking, and I think this was not the only place from which Mr. Harboard was obtaining money."

Again as she spoke she saw the Marquis's expression change, and she said quickly:

171

"Please . . . forgive me . . . I should not have said that. It is none of my . . . business, and Mr. Harboard is your . . . servant."

"Not for much longer," the Marquis said ominously. "And I have asked you to be frank with me and tell me the truth, Kistna. There is no-one else to explain to me what has been going on here. I promise you it will never occur again."

"Thank you," Kistna said. "It has been terrible . . . like a nightmare . . . to see the children . . . suffering. Three of them . . . died last year from the cold, although Mrs. Moore tried to explain it was of a . . . fever."

She gave a little sob as she said:

"They used to lie awake at night, because they were so hungry, and though I pleaded and pleaded . . . with Mrs. Moore . . . she would not . . . listen."

"As I have already said, this sort of thing must never happen again! Do you think the last Matron—what was her name?—Mrs. Owen?—would come back?"

"I am sure she would if Your Lordship asked her," Kistna said. "She lives in the village and used to come and call, until Matron told her to keep away and forbade me to open the door to her."

"I will persuade her," the Marquis said, "and I suppose she will know where to buy clothes for the children, blankets for the beds, and so on."

"It was . . . terrible last . . . winter," Kistna said almost beneath her breath.

Then as she spoke she gave a little gasp, for the door opened and Mrs. Moore came in.

She was dressed in a bonnet and cape.

She looked first at the Marquis, then at Kistna, with an expression on her face that was an ugly one.

"I can see Your Lordship's listening to a lot of lies about me," she hissed. "Well, I'm leaving, but them bottles is mine and I'm taking them with me."

She went to the table as she spoke, and, picking up the bottles one by one, she put them into a basket she was carrying over her arm.

When the table was bare she turned to Kistna, who was regarding her with frightened eyes, and said:

"I hope, you little sneak, you die as your sister died, and good riddance to you and the rest of 'em! I've had enough of children to last me a lifetime!"

She flounced round at the last word and went out of the room, slamming the door behind her.

The Marquis saw that Kistna was trembling.

"Forget her," he said. "She cannot harm you! You can be thankful I came here today, or this situation might have gone on for years."

"If it had, we would . . . all have been . . . dead," Kistna replied.

Even as she spoke they heard Mrs. Moore's voice rise as she spoke to somebody and a man replied. Kistna jumped to her feet.

"I think your groom must be back, My Lord, and with the food!"

She did not wait for the Marquis's confirmation but ran across the room and pulled open the door.

She was right.

Jason had come into the Hall carrying a huge basket filled with loaves of bread, and Mrs. Moore was just disappearing down the path which led to the road.

"You are back!" Kistna exclaimed unnecessarily. "And you have brought some food!"

"Mountains of it!" Jason replied with a grin. "Wait till you sees what Oi've got in th' Phaeton."

He spoke to Kistna in a familiar tone. Then as he saw the Marquis in the doorway, he added in a more respectful voice:

"Oi buys everything as was available, M'Lord, as Your Lordship tells me."

"Quite right," the Marquis approved.

As if the word "food" had somehow penetrated through the closed door leading to the dormitory—or rather, as Kistna guessed, the children had crept along the passage and were listening to what was happening below—there was a sudden cry and they all came rushing down the stairs.

Because it was impossible for Kistna or Jason to stop them, they seized the loaves of bread in their hands, pulling them apart and stuffing large pieces into their mouths in an effort to assuage the hunger in their empty stomachs.

The Marquis would have stepped forward to try to restore some order,

173

but as she realised what he was about to do, Kistna shook her head and, picking up two loaves, put them in his arms.

"Let them eat what they can," she said. "Hold these while I go and heat the milk for the small ones."

Before the Marquis could speak or reply that he was not in the habit of holding loaves of bread, she had run out through the front door, and he saw to his amusement that Peregrine was not only controlling the horses but at the same time keeping them from upsetting a large milk-churn.

Kistna was trying to move the milk-churn by the time the Marquis, still carrying the loaves, was beside the Phaeton.

"I suggest, Peregrine," he said in an amused voice, "that you help Kistna with the milk while I control the horses."

"What you are implying is that it is my turn," Peregrine replied.

He handed over the reins, looking with some surprise at the loaves the Marquis held in his arms.

Then he found himself carrying the milk-churn up the path and into the kitchen of the Orphanage.

On reflection it struck both the Marquis and Peregrine how efficiently Kistna managed to get the older children to put out plates and cups on the kitchen-table and help her cut the loaves into small pieces and soak them in milk for the youngest of the orphans.

There were six of them, including the little girl with the injured back, and Daisy, who still seemed half-conscious from the beating she had received at the hands of Mrs. Moore.

They were all fed while Peregrine and the Marquis cut up the hams which Jason had produced from the back of the Phaeton, and there was also a cooked chicken, which the farmer's wife had sold them.

Fortunately, a man appeared from the village to take care of the horses, and Jason was invaluable in keeping the older boys from snatching the food from the younger ones.

By the time everything was distributed evenly and the greediest of them were unable to eat any more, the Marquis had gone in search of Mrs. Owen and brought her back in triumph.

She was just the type of woman who he thought should be in charge of children, and she even wept a little as she told the Marquis how upset she had been at the way they had been treated.

She also related that everybody in the village had been scandalised at Mrs. Moore's behaviour but had realised that as she was a very close personal friend of Mr. Harboard, there was nothing they could do.

"You could have written to me," the Marquis suggested.

"I thought of it, M'Lord," Mrs. Owen said simply, "but we knew Mr. Harboard was in charge of the Estate, and with you away so much in London, we thought perhaps you would never get the letter."

The Marquis told himself angrily that never again would he neglect his responsibilities on his Estate or delegate them to people who were not worthy of his trust.

He seemed to remember far back in his childhood his Nurse saying: "If you want something done properly, do it yourself!" and that, he told himself bitterly, was the truth.

"What I am asking, Mrs. Owen," he said, "is for you to put things right for me and see that the children have everything they need. I assure you that at the moment no expense need be spared in having things exactly as you think they should be."

He felt that in the circumstances no woman could resist such an opportunity, and he was right.

Mrs. Owen drove back with him in his Phaeton, saying she would send for her personal belongings later, and the children, now that they were fed, and looking quite different from what they had before, greeted her with undeniable pleasure.

"Have there been no new children here since I left?" Mrs. Owen enquired of Kistna.

She shook her head.

"I think Mrs. Moore was offered some more," she replied, "but she always said we were full up, which was not true. There are two empty bedrooms."

She gave a little glance at the Marquis as she spoke, which told him, without her elaborating the point, that Mr. Harboard had undoubtedly collected money for children who were not there and for the same reason had not reported that any of them had died.

By the time he and Peregrine were ready to leave he was in a towering rage at the behaviour of his Agent and was determined to sack him as soon as he got back to the Abbey.

He shook hands with Mrs. Owen, promised her that he would send more food as soon as he got home, and was just about to depart when Peregrine drew him to one side.

"Have you not forgotten something, Linden?" he enquired.

"I hope not," the Marquis replied.

He and Mrs. Owen had discussed the children's clothes, the furnishings, and the women who were to come back to clean and cook as they had always done.

He had agreed to the re-employment of the gardeners who, like the other servants, had been sacked by Mr. Harboard so that he could take their wages for himself.

"The reason we came here," Peregrine prompted.

The Marquis looked at him uncomprehendingly and he went on:

"Surely the girl, Kistna, is just what we are looking for?"

For the moment the Marquis was astonished. Then he looked back down the passage and through the open door of the kitchen where he could see Kistna still at the table, trying to coax Daisy to swallow a few mouthfuls of bread and milk.

She had the child on her lap, and as the Marquis watched her, Daisy, too exhausted to eat, hid her face against her shoulder.

Kistna smiled and kissed her hair.

Then, holding the under-nourished child close in her arms as if she were a baby, she came walking down the corridor.

"I am putting Daisy to bed," she explained to the Marquis as she reached him, "and if she is no better in the morning . . . do you think we might send for . . . the Doctor?"

She spoke a little anxiously, as if it was an unheard-of extravagance.

The Marquis knew without being told that however ill any of the children had been, Mrs. Moore had never allowed a Doctor to be called in.

Their sufferings had meant nothing to her, and if they died it was just more money in her lover's pocket.

"Of course send for the Doctor, and tonight, if it is necessary," he answered.

He saw a sudden light come into Kistna's eyes and realised that because she was so thin, they had sunk into her face.

Then as she gave him a smile and started to walk up the stairs, he realised that Peregrine was waiting for his answer.

"You are right," he said. "She is quick-witted, and if we feed her she may look more prepossessing. We will collect her tomorrow morning."

CHAPTER THREE

———— ◈ ————

"*I* DO NOT UNDERSTAND," KISTNA SAID.

The Marquis paused as if he was choosing his words before he replied:

"It is quite simple. Because I feel responsible that you have suffered so much these last three years, I intend that you shall become my Ward."

"Your . . . Ward?"

He saw that she did not understand exactly what that entailed, and he said slowly:

"It means that I, as your Guardian, will look after you, provide you with clothes, and when you are restored to health and feel you can face it, I will introduce you to Society."

For a moment Kistna stared at him incredulously. Then she said in a voice that trembled:

"D-do you . . . really mean . . . that?"

"I assure you that when I make a promise I always carry it through," the Marquis replied.

"Then it is the most . . . wonderful thing I can possibly . . . imagine could . . . happen to me," Kistna said, "and I only wish Papa and Mama could thank you. It is . . . difficult for me to find the . . . right words."

"I do not want to hear them," the Marquis said.

Peregrine, who was listening, felt that he was a little embarrassed.

They had discussed last night what they should say to Kistna and they had agreed that she must be convinced that she was really the Marquis's Ward.

177

"The less acting and pretence there is about the whole plan, the better," he said. "We must not forget that Branscombe in his own way is intelligent."

Peregrine had agreed that the Marquis's idea of making Kistna in actual fact his Ward was a good one.

They had sat up late discussing the whole idea, and Peregrine had wondered what Kistna's reaction would be. He thought now her gratitude was touching.

There had been many things to do after they had left the Orphanage yesterday. First, the Marquis on his arrival back at the Abbey had sent for his Agent and told the man to leave his employment immediately, adding:

"You know as well as I do what are the penalties for theft, and the lightest sentence you would receive would be one of transportation. However, because I do not wish your appalling behaviour to be known to the outside world, I am letting you go free."

He thought there was an expression of hope in the man's eyes, and he added:

"But you will leave with nothing, not even your personal belongings, which have doubtless been purchased with the money you have stolen from me. You will go only with what you stand up in."

"I have to live, M'Lord," the Agent said in a surly tone.

"If you are hungry it will give you some idea of what those wretched children felt when you refused to feed them," the Marquis said sharply. "Now get out! If I ever see you again I will have you arrested!"

When the Agent, white-faced and shaking, had left the Abbey, the Marquis sent for his Housekeeper.

Mrs. Dawes had been at the Abbey for over twenty years. She had a kindly nature but her department of the house was run with a rod of iron.

She came into the Study in her rustling black silk dress, her long silver chatelaine hanging from her waist.

She dropped the Marquis a respectful curtsey and he said:

"Good-evening, Mrs. Dawes. I need your help."

He guessed that by now Jason's story of what had happened at the Orphanage would have reached the upper servants in the Abbey, and he knew by the expression on Mrs. Dawes's face that she was wondering in what way he would expect her to help the orphans.

"You may have learnt," he began, "that the Orphanage in Westbury Village is a disgrace and the conditions I found there must never be repeated."

"It's something that wouldn't have happened, M'Lord, if certain people who shall be nameless had been trustworthy."

"Things are being put right by the previous Matron," the Marquis explained. "But while I was there I found that through a most regrettable error, my Ward, who had come from India, had been sent to the Orphanage rather than to me here at the Abbey."

This was something Mrs. Dawes obviously had not anticipated, and the Marquis was aware that he had aroused her interest.

He had already decided that Kistna should always be known by her Christian name. It would not make the change, when it came to deceiving Branscombe, too difficult.

" 'Tis a terrible thing to have happened, M'Lord."

"It is indeed, and that is why we must make reparation in every way we can, Mrs. Dawes, for the years she has suffered quite unnecessarily."

"What does Your Lordship wish me to do?"

"First thing in the morning I shall send a carriage to London," the Marquis replied, "to bring back a dressmaker who I know will be able to provide the right type of clothing, but she will naturally require Miss Kistna's measurements."

Mrs. Dawes nodded but did not speak, and the Marquis went on:

"One difficulty, Mrs. Dawes, is that Miss Kistna is actually in rags, and I have no wish for the story of her neglect to be known outside these four walls."

"Of course not, M'Lord!" Mrs. Dawes agreed in a shocked voice.

"You must therefore find her something to wear in which she can receive the dressmaker, and I also require, Mrs. Dawes, a cloak and a bonnet in which to convey her from the Orphanage to the Abbey."

"I understand, M'Lord," Mrs. Dawes said, "and it should not be too difficult. Your Lordship's guests have often left behind gowns for which they had no further use, and which I have kept in case they should come in useful. Mrs. Barnes, the sewing-woman, is at the moment in the Abbey and can alter anything as soon as the young lady arrives."

"Thank you, Mrs. Dawes," the Marquis said.

When the following morning he and Peregrine set off for the Orphan-age, he saw that one of the servants had placed a small trunk and a hat-box at the back of the Phaeton.

He was therefore prepared that Kistna should look a little different when they drove back to the Abbey, after there had been a touching farewell to the rest of the children.

They too, the Marquis thought, already looked different. They were cleaner and seemed to be better clothed, and he gathered that they had been provided with garments by the villagers until Mrs. Owen could buy exactly what was required from the nearest town.

One child told him with pride that they had had eggs and bacon for breakfast and another added that there had been honey and hot milk.

They spoke as if, as Peregrine said jokingly, it had been "manna from Heaven."

The Marquis noticed as he drove away with Kistna towards the Abbey that she was very silent, and he guessed it was because she felt that every-thing that was happening was like being in a dream and she was half-afraid that if she spoke she would wake up.

Now, looking at her in the gown provided by Mrs. Dawes, into which she had changed before she came down to luncheon, he thought that because she was so thin she was ugly, almost to the extent of being gro-tesque. But that was no reason to assume that with good food and freedom from worry she might not become passable in appearance.

He appreciated that the gown she was wearing was too old for her, and although the seamstress had obviously taken large tucks in at the waist it was still far too big.

But at least she was decently covered, although the bones protruding at her wrists, the hollow shadows around her eyes, and the sharp lines to her chin and cheek-bones were all too obvious.

She was like a very young bird without its feathers, the Marquis thought, and if she looked as she did now when the Earl saw her, he would refuse to marry her, however rich he might think her to be.

Then he consoled himself with the thought that good clothes could make a difference to any woman, and he had always been told that starva-tion was extremely disfiguring.

Now as he saw the tears of gratitude come into Kistna's eyes he felt uncomfortably that he was being a hypocrite in evoking such a response for something he was doing entirely for his own ends.

Then he pacified his conscience by reflecting that there was hardly a woman in the length and breadth of the country who would not be only too eager to marry the Earl and occupy a position in the Social World that was second to none.

"It is a very great . . . honour that I should be your . . . Ward," Kistna was saying, "but . . . suppose I disappoint you and you become . . . sorry that you did not leave me to earn my own living . . . as I intended to do when I first came to England?"

"At fifteen?" the Marquis enquired.

"I thought . . . perhaps I could be . . . apprenticed to a . . . dress-making-shop."

The Marquis remembered that he had heard that apprentices had a very hard time. In fact, many of them received such meagre wages that they were as hungry as Kistna had been in the Orphanage.

Aloud he said:

"I think you will find that being my Ward is far more comfortable and definitely more enjoyable."

"But of course," Kistna agreed. "It is only that . . . I am a little afraid."

She looked round the room as if she was realising for the first time how large and luxurious it was.

Then she said in a small voice:

"Papa and Mama were very . . . poor because they were . . . Missionaries, and I am afraid I shall make many . . . mistakes because . . . the way you live is . . . very grand."

The Marquis, however, had already noticed that at luncheon Kistna had watched which cutlery he and Peregrine used and did not pick up a knife or a fork until they had set her an example.

He thought it was intelligent of her and he saw too that she ate delicately, and from the educated way she spoke it was obvious that her parents had been gentlefolk.

"What I am suggesting," he said, "is that until you feel well and have put on a little weight, and have all the clothes with which I intend to provide you, we stay here quietly at the Abbey so that no-one sees you."

"I cannot imagine any . . ., place that could be more . . . beautiful!" Kistna exclaimed.

"That is what I hoped you would think," the Marquis replied, "and Mr. Wallingham and I will instruct you about the etiquette you will have to know when I take you to London."

He knew as he spoke that Peregrine looked at him a little questioningly.

They had not really discussed any details of how they should produce the Marquis's Ward, and Peregrine had in fact thought it would be wiser for the Earl to hear that she was at the Abbey and invite himself to stay.

Then he suspected that the Marquis was deliberately making Kistna realise how hard she must work if she was to be a success in the Social World with its Balls and Receptions and endless other forms of entertainment.

Watching Kistna while the Marquis talked to her, he thought she was exceptionally sensitive, and her emotions seemed to mirror themselves in her eyes.

Like the Marquis, he wondered what she would look like when she was not so pitiably thin and emaciated.

Then the Marquis said:

"I expect Mrs. Dawes has told you that later this afternoon the dressmaker will be arriving from London with a number of gowns that you can wear immediately, and she will make you many more. Do you think it would be wise to rest until she arrives?"

"Yes . . . I will do that," Kistna said obediently, "but please . . . My Lord . . . would it be . . . possible for me to have some books to . . . read? There are many in the Library."

"You like reading?" the Marquis enquired.

"It has been agonising these past three years when there was nothing I could read in the Orphanage except for my Bible."

She gave a shy little smile as she said:

"It is now the only possession I own, because all the other things that came with me from India have either fallen to bits or I have given them to the children."

As she spoke, the Marquis knew that she would have given the children who were suffering from hunger and cold all the warm clothing she owned.

Because he thought it was a mistake for her to go on thinking about the past, he said:

"There is a large selection of books in the Abbey, and you must get my Curator to show you the shelves on which you will find the latest novels, including those of Sir Walter Scott."

"There is so much I want to read," Kistna said in a rapt voice.

Then there were tears both in her eyes and in her voice as she said to the Marquis:

"Is this true? Really . . . true that I am here and will be your Ward? To live in this . . . wonderful . . . magnificent house?"

"It is true."

"How can I thank you . . . except by asking . . . God to do that for me."

"You have thanked me," the Marquis said firmly. "Too many protestations of gratitude will make me embarrassed, so I would prefer it, Kistna, if you give me your thanks in actions, and not in words."

"How can I . . . do that?"

"By doing exactly what I tell you, and by putting some flesh on your bones as quickly as possible."

Kistna gave a little laugh.

"That is exactly what Mrs. Dawes said to me, and she has already made me drink two huge glasses of milk since I arrived!"

"You will find that Mrs. Dawes invariably knows best," the Marquis said, "and as I also like having my own way, you must do exactly what we tell you."

"You know I want to . . . please you," Kistna said simply.

When she left them the Marquis turned to Peregrine with a smile on his face.

"What do you think of our *protégée* so far?" he enquired.

"She is definitely intelligent," Peregrine said. "I am just wondering how long it will be before she puts, as you said, some flesh on her bones."

"Clothes will make a difference and will give her confidence."

"I know you are an expert on what clothes mean to a woman," Peregrine teased, "but I think where Kistna is concerned it will not be only her looks that count but her character."

The Marquis held up his hand in protest.

"Oh, for Heaven's sake!" he ejaculated. "The last thing we want is a girl with character! What we require is a nice, complacent creature who will do exactly what we tell her and accept the idea of marrying Branscombe as being a gift from Heaven itself!"

Peregrine was silent for a moment. Then he said:

"I think Kistna is different from the average girl. She has lived in India with her father and mother, and she has certainly suffered in England. I doubt if she will ever be the fat, complacent cow that you are imagining in the part you wish her to play."

"Very well then," the Marquis said, as if he must defend himself. "She is intelligent, and therefore when we get to the point of telling her exactly what she has to do, that she has to pretend to be Mirabelle, she will see at once that it is very much to her advantage. Even being Branscombe's wife is preferable to starving to death in an Orphanage."

"I am sure if she gives her mind to it she will be admirable in the part," Peregrine replied. "I am only wondering if she will have an opinion in the matter."

"If she has an opinion it will be to thank her lucky stars that she will live in extreme comfort for the rest of her life and that, if Branscombe is angry at being deceived, there will be nothing he can do about it."

The Marquis spoke sharply. Peregrine decided that there was no point in continuing the conversation and suggested that they go riding.

When they returned several hours later, it was to find that the dressmaker had arrived and was waiting to see the Marquis.

She was a sharp-faced, clever woman who had made her business one of the most successful in Bond Street.

The Marquis had in the past accompanied a number of his mistresses and his social *chère amies* to Madame Yvonne's dress-shop.

She was known to be discreet and she never made the mistake of letting the woman the Marquis was providing with an expensive gown be aware that she had served him on other occasions.

Now she dropped him a curtsey and waited politely for him to give her his orders.

"I want you, Madame, to dress my Ward in the very latest creations," he said, "and provide her with a wardrobe which will excel that of every other debutante in Society."

Madame Yvonne could not conceal the glint of excitement in her eyes, but she replied in a quiet tone:

"I will, as usual, do my very best to please Your Lordship."

"There is one condition attached to this order."

"Yes, My Lord?"

"It is that for the moment I do not wish anyone in London to know that my Ward is here with me at the Abbey."

He saw the surprise in Madame Yvonne's expression, and went on:

"You will understand when I explain that Miss Kistna has been ill, and nothing could be more of a handicap for a young girl than to be thought to have ill-health or to suffer from temporary or permanent ailments, whatever they may be."

Madame Yvonne nodded her agreement and the Marquis continued:

"That is why, Madame, I have no intention of allowing anyone to know that my Ward is here, until she is well enough to grace your gowns and the Ball-Rooms where she will appear in them."

"Of course, I understand, My Lord," Madame Yvonne said, "and I promise that not a word about the young lady will pass my lips."

"Thank you," the Marquis said. "And now make sure that everything which you provide is of the finest and best quality."

He paused before he added:

"My Ward is a great heiress and there is no need to cheesepare in any manner."

As he spoke he knew this meant he would doubtless be overcharged on a great number of items on the bill.

At the same time, he had planted the idea in Madame Yvonne's mind that Kistna was an heiress, and he suspected that later she would not be able to prevent herself from dropping a hint to those in the Social World that his Ward was very rich.

It all fitted in like a puzzle to the general plan, the Marquis thought, and congratulated himself on his eye for detail.

He decided to tell Mrs. Dawes that quite a number of gowns would be left for Kistna today, and others would be arriving almost daily as soon as they were ready.

"What does Miss Kistna feel about her new clothes?" the Marquis asked.

"I've never seen a young lady so excited or so thrilled with the gowns which Madame Yvonne brought her," Mrs. Dawes replied. "In fact, now that the excitement's over I've put her to bed, and I'll be exceedingly surprised if she's not fast asleep, M'Lord, and sleeping like a child, from sheer exhaustion!"

"I knew I could leave her in your capable hands, Mrs. Dawes," the Marquis said, and the Housekeeper was delighted with the compliment.

He did not see Kistna again until she came down to dinner that evening, when she certainly looked very different from the ragged orphan he had first met.

As she was so pale and obviously anaemic from lack of food, Madame Yvonne had not dressed her immediately in the traditional white of a débutante.

Her gown was of soft periwinkle blue, and its full skirt and large balloon-like sleeves concealed the skeleton-like slimness of her figure.

There was little that could be done about her face except to add a little rouge to her cheeks.

But either Mrs. Dawes or one of the housemaids had concealed Kistna's lank hair with skilfully arranged bows of satin ribbon which matched her gown.

There was a narrow band of velvet of the same colour to encircle her long neck.

She came into the Salon a little shyly, where the Marquis and Peregrine were waiting, and as she walked towards them they both saw that the Marquis had been right in thinking that clothes could change a woman.

He felt that because she was so thin and therefore very light, Kistna walked with a special grace that reminded him in a strangely poetical manner of a flower moving in the breeze.

When she smiled at him he saw that Madame Yvonne had advised her to wear a little lip-salve, which certainly prevented her lips from looking so pale and bloodless.

"Fine feathers make fine birds!" Peregrine said, before the Marquis could speak.

"That is what I . . . hoped you would . . . say," Kistna replied with a little laugh, "and I do indeed feel like a peacock spreading my tail in this beautiful gown."

186

She glanced at the Marquis and said in a low voice almost as if she spoke to him alone:

"I want . . . to . . . thank you . . ."

"I have told you, I dislike being thanked."

As he spoke, he thought he had never in his whole life seen such an expression of overwhelming gratitude in a woman's eyes.

He remembered how offhand Lady Isobel had been about a diamond necklace she had wanted for Christmas, and when he had given it to her she had complained that he had omitted to purchase the bracelet that went with it.

He remembered too other jewels he had given to attractive Cyprians whom he had installed in one of his houses in Chelsea in the manner that was expected by their profession.

They had extorted everything they could from him, and, as Peregrine had said: "had a magnet which drew the gold coins out of his pockets." But their gratitude had always sounded contrived.

It struck the Marquis as rather touching that this girl had such a joyous delight in being well dressed, and as he met her eyes he found himself thinking it was a pity, in a way, that there had to be an ulterior motive for giving her the clothes.

Then he told himself that this was not the moment for becoming senti-mental. Besides, they had a long way to go before he was ready to cheat the Earl as he had been cheated.

Merely to think of it made the Marquis scowl, although he had no idea that he was doing so, until Kistna said in a frightened little voice:

"You are . . . angry? Is it . . . something I have . . . said or . . . done?"

"No, of course not!" the Marquis replied. "And I hope never to be angry with you or to make you afraid that I might be."

"I should be very . . . very afraid if you were . . . angry with me."

"You would have reason to be," Peregrine interposed, "for I assure you the Marquis can be very overpowering when he is in a rage, and what makes it worse is that he never raises his voice."

Kistna gave a nervous little laugh.

"I agree . . . that is much worse than someone . . . who shouts."

She paused before she went on:

187

"Papa was never angry if someone did anything wrong. He was only hurt and upset and that made one penitent immediately."

"How do you behave when you are angry?" Peregrine asked.

"Sometimes I lose my temper," Kistna admitted, "but it is over quickly, and then I am sorry . . . very, very sorry . . . and want to apologise."

"That is the right and generous way to behave," Peregrine approved.

"I am sure I could never be angry in such beautiful surroundings as these," Kistna said. "There are two things that make people angry—ugliness and injustice."

"Particularly injustice," the Marquis said in a hard voice.

Once again he was thinking of the Earl, and, as if Peregrine thought it was a mistake for his mind to dwell on his enemy, he quickly changed the subject and when they walked into dinner all three were laughing.

To Kistna it was a fascination that she had never known before, not only to dine in such luxurious surroundings but to eat food that she thought must taste like the ambrosia of the gods.

It was also an enchantment she found hard to express to be alone with two such distinguished, elegant, delightful men.

Thinking back into the past, she knew her father had always seemed rather serious, although he laughed when they were together as a family and there was a warmth and love in everything they said to each other.

But it was not the same as listening to two Gentlemen of Fashion who exchanged witticisms almost as if they duelled with each other not with swords but with words, and every cut and thrust of their tongues had a subtle meaning.

Because Kistna felt that over the last three years she had been starved not only of food for her body but of food for her brain, she found every moment that she listened to the Marquis and his friend as stimulating as any lesson she might have been given by the most experienced teacher.

Because she was no longer hungry, she could appreciate the subtlety of a word, of a turn of phrase, and could concentrate on the Marquis and his friend without her mind slipping away as it would have done a few days ago.

Sometimes they talked to her, but more often they appeared to forget that she was with them.

They discussed sport or their acquaintances with the freedom of two

men who are so close to each other that much of what they said had no
need for elaboration.

Peregrine talked to the Marquis of his chances of winning the Gold Cup
at Ascot. Then he said, as if he suddenly remembered Kistna's presence:

"Are you fond of horses?"

"I love them!" Kistna replied. "But I have never had a chance of riding
the sort of horses you are talking about. All we could afford in India were
the small-boned little animals, which were very spirited and often bolted in
a manner which was almost impossible to control."

The Marquis smiled.

"Do I understand that you are longing to ride one of my horses?"

Kistna gave a little cry.

"Please . . . please . . . could I have a habit? Then perhaps you
would . . . allow me to ride with you and Mr. Wallingham."

"I have ordered you two habits, as it happens," the Marquis replied,
"and they are what you will need for the summer. You will require something warmer when winter comes."

Instead of thanking him, he saw that Kistna was staring at him with a
look of bewilderment.

"What is it?" he asked.

"I cannot understand how you can know . . . exactly what a woman
needs. Madame Yvonne was saying today that you have such excellent
taste, and I wonder how, as you are unmarried, you have learnt about
gowns, bonnets, and even habits?"

There was a pause as the Marquis wondered how he should reply to
such an artless question.

He was well aware that Peregrine's eyes were twinkling and that he had
been as surprised by it as he was himself.

Kistna was waiting for his answer and after a moment he said:

"I may be a bachelor, but I have a large number of female relatives."

"Oh . . . of course! I never thought of that!" she exclaimed. "Mrs.
Dawes told me that your mother was very, very beautiful, and I expect she
taught you about how much clothes mean to a woman, especially someone like me . . . who has never had any."

The Marquis glanced across the table at Peregrine and, without speaking, dared him ever to tease him about this conversation.

189

Then, as if she sensed what they were thinking, Kistna looked from one to the other and asked:

"H-have I said . . . something wrong? Was it . . . incorrect of me to . . . question His Lordship's knowledge of what . . . pleases a lady?"

"No, of course not!" Peregrine said reassuringly. "When you know the Marquis better, you will find he is extremely knowledgeable on every subject, whether it appertains to women or to horses."

"There is so much I want to learn about horses," Kistna cried, and the awkward moment passed.

After dinner the Marquis and Peregrine played piquet, gambling fiercely against each other and betting large sums on each game.

Kistna watched them for a little while, then she moved down the Salon, looking at the objets d'art, which were extremely valuable, and the paintings, each of which held her attention for a long time.

The game finished and the Marquis walked across the room to stand beside her.

He found she was looking at a very beautiful Poussin where nymphs gambolled in the foreground against a forest glade and misty mountains.

"Do you like that painting?" he enquired.

"It is . . . difficult to put into words . . . what I feel about it," Kistna said in a rapt little voice.

The Marquis was interested.

"I would like you to tell me, however difficult it may be, what you feel."

She did not answer for a moment, then she said:

"When we were in India there were many strange carvings on the Temples which shocked the English, and they complained to Papa."

"What did your father do about them?"

"I asked him what he was going to do," Kistna said, "and he told me that he tried to understand why the Indians had carved such erotic figures on what to them was a place of sanctity."

She looked up at the Marquis to see if he was listening, and went on:

"Papa said that each Indian craftsman used the life-force within himself to create through his fingers something that to him expressed his faith and his belief."

She paused and again looked at the Marquis, this time a little appealingly.

"I am not explaining it well," she said, "but I think Papa was trying to say that each man who creates anything to which he gives his heart is like God and is, in his own way, a creator."

"I have never heard that theory before," the Marquis said.

"You asked me what I felt about this painting," Kistna went on, "and I feel that Nicholas Poussin poured his own life-force into it, and it is therefore a creation not so much of his mind as of his soul and his heart."

The Marquis stared at her in sheer astonishment.

It seemed to him incredible that this girl, whom he still thought of as an inmate of the Orphanage, could not only think so profoundly but could express herself so ably in a way that he might himself have found very difficult.

"Do all paintings make you feel like that?" he enquired.

"I have never seen one like this before," she said, "nor like any of the others here in this room. But India is full of paintings and India itself is sheer beauty."

"You speak as if you miss it."

"I miss the happiness I knew there," Kistna said, "and because it is the only beautiful thing I have had to think of these last few years, it is very vivid in my mind and very real."

The Marquis could understand that the only way in which she could escape from the horror of her surroundings was through her imagination and her memories of the past.

Because she made him feel sentimental, he said sharply:

"Now that you have beautiful things in the present, you must think of them and, because you are young, of the future. That is what matters— what lies ahead."

"Yes . . . of course," Kistna agreed. "But it is only today being here with you that I have felt for the first time that I have a future. Before, it was only a matter of time before I died as my sister died of the cold and hunger."

She spoke quietly in a voice that was not dramatic in any way, which somehow made it more poignant and more moving.

The Marquis had a strange impulse to put his arm about her shoulders, hold her against him, and tell her she need never be frightened again.

He knew it was what he would have done to a child, but he remembered that Kistna was not a child but a grown-up young woman who would doubtless misunderstand such an action on his part.

"Now you have a great, positive future, and I think a very exciting one!" he said.

The way he spoke seemed to break the spell that had existed for some moments between him and the girl standing beside him.

Later that night when Kistna was alone in the darkness of her bed, she found herself thinking of the Marquis's words and the way he had said: "A very exciting future," almost as if he knew what would happen to her.

"What could be more exciting than being here and becoming the Marquis's Ward?" she asked herself.

And yet, perceptively, she knew there was something more; something she felt was in the Marquis's mind ever since she had met him.

She remembered that her mother had often said to her father:

"There is something about India, darling, that makes one intuitive, or is it perceptive?"

"The two are almost synonymous," the Reverend John Lovell had said with a smile.

"Not to me," his wife had replied. "It is difficult to express what I mean, but at times I feel I am closer to the Other World, the world in which both you and I belong, darling, than I am to this world."

"I think perhaps that happens to everybody who comes to India," Kistna's father answered. "It is as if the faith of the people is intensified by the heat and the dryness until one can feel it vibrating everywhere."

"I am sure that is it," Mrs. Lovell said. "The vibrations of your faith, and you, my dearest, make you very real."

They smiled at each other across the table, and Kistna had thought that she could feel the vibrations of their love as clearly as her mother felt the vibrations of faith.

Looking back, she was sure that their house, small though it was, had been filled with the love and happiness that is rich beyond the dreams of avarice.

"We were so happy," she would cry despairingly when she lay in the darkness on the hard bed in the dormitory. "Oh, Mama, Papa, how could you . . . die and leave me . . . all alone?"

She tried to tell herself that they were near her and to find them she had only to reach out from the confines of the material world.

But somehow, because she was so cold and hungry, it was difficult to link with the unseen or with the love she had lost.

Now she felt as if her mother and father were beside her again, talking to her, guiding her, and she knew that her love for them and theirs for her was as strong as it had ever been.

"I am lucky, so very, very lucky," Kistna told herself.

Perhaps it had been her mother who had guided the Marquis to the Orphanage to save her and the children from a hell which had seemed to stretch endlessly into an empty future.

Now there was tomorrow, the next day, and the day after that, and she would be with the Marquis, who, almost like a Medieval Knight, had destroyed the dragon in the shape of Mrs. Moore.

"He is wonderful, Mama!" Kistna said in her heart. "So wonderful and so handsome! He is very kind to me and has given me all these wonderful clothes. At the same time, there is . . . something I do not . . . understand."

She thought and tried to put it into words.

"It is something he is thinking about me; something that is not just kindness but something else."

She tried to express it, but the words would not come.

She knew only that behind the Marquis's eyes there was a mystery she could not solve and that vibrating from him there was something different from what she had expected.

It made her a little afraid.

It made her feel that even in the dream-world into which he had taken her, where she lived in the most fantastically beautiful house she had ever imagined, where she was waited on and dressed as if she were a Princess, there was still something that she found herself questioning, like a note of music that was not quite true.

Then she thought she was being absurd.

"I am lucky . . . so very . . . very lucky," she said aloud. "Thank You, God, for sending him, and thank You for making him my Guardian."

CHAPTER FOUR

─── ❦ ───

"*I* WONDER IF WE ARE BEING MISSED in London?" Peregrine asked.

"I imagine there is plenty of speculation about our absence," the Marquis replied drily, "especially in certain quarters."

Peregrine knew he was referring to Lady Isobel, and he thought she would not only be bewildered but curious to know why, when there were so many attractive gaieties in London, the Marquis had chosen to retire to the country.

Almost as if their conversation had evoked a response, the Marquis's secretary, Mr. Barnes, came to the door to say:

"There is a letter from London for Your Lordship and a groom has been told he is to wait for an answer."

He held out a note as he spoke, and the Marquis, without taking it from him, saw the flamboyant crest on the back of the envelope and said:

"Send the groom back with a message to say that you are unable to get in touch with me and it would be useless for him to wait for me to return to the Abbey."

Mr. Barnes's expression did not alter. He merely replied: "Very good, My Lord," and left the room.

"Isobel?" Peregrine questioned.

The Marquis nodded.

"She is extremely persistent, but I have no intention of being embroiled with her again. I realise now it was a mistake from the very beginning."

"I could have told you that," Peregrine said, "but I doubt if you would have listened."

The Marquis did not answer, and he went on:

"Even though she is a beauty, I have always thought that at heart Isobel

194

is a bad woman, and that is not something I say about many 'Fair Charmers.' "

Again the Marquis did not respond, and as Peregrine knew he disliked talking about his love-affairs, even to his most intimate friends, he was not surprised.

At the same time, because he was extremely fond of the Marquis he was glad that he had realised in time that Isobel was not only no good but also dangerous.

Because the new situation was uppermost in both their thoughts, Peregrine, having dismissed Isobel, was thinking once again of Kistna.

"Have you noticed how different she looks after only four, or is it five, days of decent food and pretty clothes?" he asked the Marquis.

"She has certainly put on a little weight."

"I have the feeling," Peregrine said, "that by the time we have finished her rehabilitation she will turn out to be a beauty."

"Do you really think so?" the Marquis remarked.

He did not sound particularly interested, and Peregrine replied almost aggressively:

"Where are your eyes, Linden? Personally, I find it fascinating to notice the change which I can see taking place every day, or I could almost say every hour. She is certainly no longer the little scarecrow she was when we first saw her at the Orphanage."

He gave a little laugh.

"Now that I look back, I can think of nothing more fantastic than that moment when we arrived and Kistna, in rags, looking as if she might die at any moment, opened the door."

He saw that the Marquis was listening and continued:

"Then there was all that screaming upstairs and we found that devilish woman beating those wretched children. It was just like something out of a book."

"I will certainly never allow such a thing to happen again on any property of mine," the Marquis said harshly.

"How is Rodwell shaping up?" Peregrine enquired.

"I like him," the Marquis answered, "and as he has always lived on the Estate and knows everything and everybody, he is a far better Agent than the last swine I employed."

"You were wise to take him on," Peregrine agreed. "It is always a mistake, I think, to bring in a stranger."

"I agree, and, as you say, I have been wise in this particular."

"And a great many others as well," Peregrine said with a smile. "Now, to get back to what is the really important question—when are we going to produce Kistna like a rabbit out of a hat and start tricking Branscombe into proposing marriage?"

"She is not yet ready!"

"Personally, I do not think we have far to go."

"What you are really saying is that you are bored with being here and want to get back to London."

"I have said nothing of the sort!" Peregine objected sharply. "I always enjoy being with you, Linden. And as long as I have superb horses to ride and your wine-cellar at my disposal, I have no complaints."

"What about Molly, or whatever her name was?" the Marquis enquired.

Peregrine grinned.

"I never could really afford her, and being with you here I am not only saving on her board and lodging but on all the things I should undoubtedly have been persuaded into giving her, even though I could not pay for them!"

"I am glad to be of service!" the Marquis remarked.

Peregrine laughed.

"I am enjoying myself and there is no pretence about it! I have the feeling, although I may be wrong, that I can say the same thing about you."

The Marquis did not answer him immediately, and Peregrine was certain that even if he would not admit it, he was not half as bored as he had been before the Derby.

There had been no doubt then that nothing interested him particularly, and, with his liaison with Isobel coming to an end, there was little to look forward to except the familiar round of entertainments and the same crowd of friends and "hangers-on."

There was no doubt, Peregrine thought shrewdly, that Kistna had brought something into his life that had been lacking.

The Marquis in fact was concentrating very seriously on seeing that she acquired all the graces and attributes that were required of a debutante.

"More than that," he said to Peregrine, "Mirabelle is different from most young girls her age."

"In what way?" Peregrine enquired.

"Because she has always been so rich," the Marquis answered, "she has had the best teachers, not only for her education but also for all the other talents a young girl is expected to produce for the 'Marriage Market.' "

Peregrine raised his eyebrows.

"The 'Marriage Market'?" he questioned.

"What else is it?" the Marquis enquired. "Their parents groom them like show-horses and bring them to London to parade them before bachelors like you and me, hoping to captivate our fancy."

He spoke so cynically that Peregrine looked at him in surprise. Then he laughed.

"What else do you expect them to do?" he enquired. "A woman's sole aim in life is to get married."

"And a man's is to avoid it!"

Peregrine thought this over. Then he answered:

"That is not quite true. After all, unless my elder brother has a regrettable accident, it does not matter if I remain a bachelor for the rest of my life, but you have to continue the family and sooner or later produce a son, or rather two or three to be on the safe side!"

"It was drummed into my head almost from the moment I was born that that was my duty towards the family," the Marquis remarked with a note in his voice that told his friend he had always disliked the idea.

"It is strange," Peregrine ruminated, "that you have never fallen in love."

"I have taken damned good care not to get involved in the 'Marriage Market,' " the Marquis said. "In fact, I cannot remember when I last met a girl of Kistna's age, which makes it rather difficult."

"In what way?"

"I am not certain how much she should know, or how ignorant she will appear among other débutantes."

"If you ask me," Peregrine said, "she is so quick-witted that she will make most of them seem like suet-puddings."

"She is still too thin," the Marquis said sharply.

"The curves are there, and that is the important thing," Peregrine said. "I remember my father saying: 'A woman should be curved and a man straight.' He was looking at the Prince Regent's stomach as he spoke."

"Poor old 'Prinny'! He was very ashamed of it," the Marquis smiled, "especially the last years when he used to drive out only in a closed carriage, and when I visited him at Windsor he always kept the blinds half-drawn."

"He ate and drank too much and had done so all his life," Peregrine said. "I do not mind betting, Linden, that you will keep your figure until you reach the grave."

"I certainly hope so," the Marquis replied. "Which reminds me, the horses are waiting and I told Kistna she could come with us."

"I thought that would be the reason why we were not leaving earlier."

"She had to have her French lesson," the Marquis said. "Incidentally, we were fortunate to find that woman to teach her. Her accent is perfect, but then she is Parisian."

"I have a feeling that by the time you have finished with Kistna she will be stuffed like a Christmas goose. Men hate a clever woman, and if she entered the 'Marriage Market' of which you are so scathing, she will frighten her suitors away rather than attract them."

"With her fortune?" the Marquis asked cynically.

"You have not told her yet that she has to pretend to be Mirabelle?" Peregrine enquired.

"No, of course not!" the Marquis replied. "You know we agreed that we would train her together, and I would not dream of taking such an important step in her development without discussing it with you first."

"I am glad you are being cautious," Peregrine said. "I may be wrong, but I have the feeling she will not like pretending to be another woman."

"I am not concerned with her feelings," the Marquis said in a lofty tone. "She will do as she is told, and personally I anticipate no difficulties of any sort."

"Why not?"

"Because Kistna is so grateful for what I have done for her that I am quite certain she would obey any order I give her, whatever it may be."

Peregrine was about to argue, then changed his mind.

He could not help thinking that the Marquis was over-confident and that women, however young they might be, were invariably unpredictable.

But there was no point in saying so, and he kept silent.

Kistna, having said good-bye politely to her French mistress, had run on winged feet to her bedroom to change into her riding-habit.

It had been difficult for the last quarter-of-an-hour of the lesson to concentrate on *Mademoiselle's* voice and not to watch the clock, knowing that by the time the hands reached eleven she would be free and could be riding with the Marquis and Mr. Wallingham.

She had never thought her life could change overnight from misery and despair to a happiness which seemed to make everything golden and sparkling like the sun.

When she looked back to the moment when she had opened the door to the two most handsome and elegant gentlemen she had ever seen in her life, how could she have imagined that they were taking her from an old world to a new one, where everything had an unmistakably dream-like quality?

'It cannot be true,' she said to herself as she put on one of the habits which had arrived from London.

'It cannot be true!' she thought as she ran down the carved gilt staircase to find the Marquis and Peregrine in the Hall, with three magnificent horses waiting for them outside.

The Marquis was himself teaching her to ride, and he was extremely insistent that she hold the reins in the right way and sit in her saddle like a born equestrian.

She learnt to take her fences in a manner which brought her the enthusiastic approval of Peregrine, if not of the Marquis.

She had learnt, however, to know when he was pleased by the expression in his eyes. But it was not only in riding that he was her tutor.

He taught her when she came into a room to walk at a measured pace, to stop at exactly the right place, to drop a curtsey, and to carry her head at precisely the correct angle as she did so.

He made her rehearse it over and over again until he had obtained the perfection he desired. Then there were similar instructions for greeting people, for saying good-night, and for proceeding to the Dining-Room for meals.

"If you ask me, you expect too much," Peregrine had protested once or twice.

"If she is pretending to be my Ward, I expect her to be faultless in her behaviour in any and every circumstance," the Marquis answered.

He thought Peregrine looked sceptical, and he added:

"Make no mistake—Branscombe, who is a stickler for etiquette and protocol, will notice the slightest fault, and we have no desire to make him suspicious until the knot is tied."

Peregrine had to agree that this was common sense and certainly Kistna made no complaints.

She appeared to be as anxious as the Marquis was that everything she did should be perfect.

Riding now through the Park and into the fields beyond, Kistna was on a horse that was spirited but well trained and responded to almost everything she required of him.

As they drew in their mounts after a long gallop, she said with a little sigh:

"I never imagined it would be possible to move so fast. Since your horses must be swifter than anyone else's, I am not surprised you win so many races."

"I am certainly hoping to win the Gold Cup at Ascot," the Marquis replied.

"Will I be able to see it?"

The Marquis turned to look at her and she knew this was something he had not considered.

"Please . . . let me!" she pleaded. "It would be . . . so exciting to see your horse first past the Winning-Post."

"Actually," the Marquis said, "I had not thought of your being there."

He looked at Peregrine and they both realised it would be a mistake for Kistna to be seen at such a fashionable gathering. There might well be someone present who had met Mirabelle in Italy.

She looked from one man to the other and was aware that there was something passing through their minds that she did not understand.

"Am I . . . doing something . . . wrong?" she enquired.

"No, of course not," the Marquis said. "It is just that I had not considered taking you with us to Ascot and it is something I must think about
before I agree."

The way he spoke told Kistna that it would not be an easy decision for
him to make, although why there should be any difficulty about it she did
not understand.

More than either the Marquis or Peregrine she was aware of the difference in her appearance.

In fact, every day that she was at the Abbey she was becoming more
like the girl who had come confidently from India to England, thinking
that while it might be different she would soon find a way of looking after
herself and eventually her younger sister as well.

Because she had been so happy in her home life, Kistna had never
known fear—either of people or of living.

It was only when Mrs. Moore had come to the Orphanage that she
found herself trapped in an appalling terror from which she could find no
way of escape.

To begin with, she could not leave her sister to try to earn her own
living in the world outside.

Then when little Indira died, Kistna had not the will-power or stamina
to break away, besides which she had a feeling that Mrs. Moore would not
have allowed her to go.

She had thought that all that lay ahead of her was death—a slow, humiliating, agonising death from hunger, cold, and misery because she must
watch the children suffering and dying round her.

Then like a miracle everything had changed and it seemed to her as if
the Marquis were the Archangel Michael lifting her from the darkness into
the light.

It was the light which she had left behind when she had been taken
from the warm sunlight of India into the fog, the mist, and the cold that
she found in the Orphanage.

At night when she had lain with only a thread-bare blanket to keep out
the cold, she had tried to imagine the sun beating down on the roof of her
father's bungalow.

She had seen the flowers which her mother loved brilliant in the small
garden, and had felt the warmth percolating through her starved body, so

that she felt as if she were part of the sunshine which turned to gold the river whose name she bore.

Because she had been brought up in a world which was beautiful wherever she looked and wherever she went, it was the ugliness of the Orphanage apart from everything else which seemed to eat into her very soul.

The ugliness of the chilly rooms, the broken beds, the dirty floors, her terror of Mrs. Moore with her face flushed with drink and her voice screaming abuse, and the children with their protruding bones and tattered ragged clothes.

Finally there was the ugliness and pain of hunger; the tears of helplessness and despair.

Kistna would remember how much her father had loved beauty and especially the beauty he had found in India.

It was in fact a desire to discover a new land, one to which his mind and heart had been drawn long before he saw India, which had made the Reverend John Lovell volunteer for Missionary work in a country where the evangelical fervour of reformation had not yet been known.

The gentlemen of the East India Company had not originally intended to govern India but merely to make money there.

This they had done very effectively in the Eighteenth Century, gradually assuming more and more responsibility, until in 1813 the Company's trade monopoly with India was abolished and for the first time public opinion in England began to have some direct effect upon British administration.

The East India Company had hitherto forbidden Christian Missionaries to come to India, but with the Crown appointing a Governor-General and the board from Westminster having ultimate authority, the ban was lifted.

The Reverend John Lovell had learnt the previous year that this would happen, and it was one of his relatives in the East India Company who had suggested to him that here was a country where he would find Missionary work preferable to being an underpaid Curate in England.

"You may not convert many of the heathens," his relative had said, "since the Indians are religious enough in their own way not to want any alien faith. But you will have a good time and it will certainly widen your horizons."

John Lovell had jumped at the chance of going abroad, especially to the East, and while he was considering it there was another reason, a very personal one, which forced him to make up his mind quickly and to leave England towards the end of 1812.

He was therefore first in the field, and when the next year the Company ban on Christian Missionaries was lifted, they swarmed in in their hundreds to look with horror at the wickedness they found in this enormous and strange country.

The savagery, the hideous customs of widow-burning, infanticide, and religious extortion, convinced them that they had to fight a crusade against the devil himself.

But they found what John Lovell had already discovered: the religious faith of the Indians was so deep-seated, an intrinsic part of their very breathing, that Christianity had no appeal, no attractions to offer a people who believed that every sin or virtue in this life was punished or rewarded in the next.

The Reverend John in fact made very little effort to convert those who believed fervently in one set of gods into embracing another faith.

Because he was an extremely intelligent man, he found that the history of India and its different castes fascinated him.

Instead of being a teacher he became a pupil.

It was doubtful if he ever made a convert, but because he was sincere and because the Indians knew they could trust him, he made friends in every sect and caste from the untouchables to the Brahmans, from the lowest sweepers to the Maharajahs.

Therefore, as Kistna grew up she met an amazing variety of Indians and learnt through her father to recognise the differences in their beliefs and creeds, their characters and outlooks.

To the other English whom they met first at Calcutta, and later when they travelled up-country, anyone with coloured skin was a "native." But to the Lovells they were people and each was more fascinating than the last.

In fact, though they did not realise it, John Lovell and his wife were like the first pioneers of the East India Company who had developed a trading policy and had little wish for anything else.

They had no wish in those first years to convert the Sub-continent, which would have seemed a preposterous ambition.

They had treated the native Princes with respect and often affection and had tolerated the religions of the country. Often they were men of aesthetic sensibilities who responded sensuously and appreciatively to the beauty of India.

Kistna could remember her father standing looking at a sunset or across the silver river to the desert beyond, and saying with reverence in his voice:

"Could anything be more beautiful, more a part of God?"

She felt that he found the God in whom he believed in the exquisitely carved Temples, in the chanting of the pilgrims as they bathed in the holy water of the Ganges, in the flight of the birds, and even, perhaps, in the chattering of the monkeys in the blossom-covered frangipani trees.

Everywhere there was beauty. Then, from that and the love that had been so vital and inescapable in her home, she had come to England and misery.

Now at the Abbey she had found again what her father had always sought—beauty.

She would stand in front of the Marquis's painting, entranced by the loveliness of a sunset by Turner; while the rich colours of a Rubens made her think of the silks, satins, and jewels worn by the Maharajahs.

Her mind would thrill to the mystic mythology of a Poussin and the spiritual perfection of the Italian masters who had portrayed the Madonna in countless different paintings.

Kistna could remember that she had seen that same expression of sanctity on the faces of the Indian women when in their colourful *saris* they would kneel in the dust before a wayside Shrine or scatter flowerpetals in the incense-filled Temples.

There was beauty too, she thought, not only in every room inside the Abbey but in the green Park with its huge ancient oak trees and in the lake, where the swans who moved over it looked like ships in full sail. Above all, there was beauty in the Marquis himself.

Never had she imagined from that first moment when she had seen him standing outside the door that any man could look more handsome, more commanding, more magnificent.

He made her think of the Governor-Generals she had seen bowling through Calcutta in a high-wheeled gilded barouche, with foot-grooms running beside it and with an escort of Cavalry behind.

She had thought then that nothing could be more dashing or more important.

But the Marquis exuded the same atmosphere of power and authority just by being himself. At the same time, omnipotent though he appeared, his kindness made her want to cry.

"How could any man be so wonderful?" she asked herself, as she touched with gentle fingers the fine lingerie trimmed with lace which Madame Yvonne had sent from London.

Never had she imagined that she would know such softness against her skin or feel as if she were wrapped in a silken web woven by fairies.

"He is wonderful! Wonderful!"

She found herself repeating the same sentence not once but a dozen times every day.

Because she wanted to please him, she strove to do everything he asked of her and to do it well, if not to exceed his requirements.

"How could I be so fortunate or so blessed as to become the Ward of such a man," she asked herself, "who lives like a King and is certainly a King among men?"

She liked Peregrine Wallingham, and she knew that if the Marquis had not been there, she would have been impressed by him.

He teased her and laughed with her and she thought him charming and good-humoured, but the Marquis was wonderful and god-like.

Looking at him riding a horse, she knew instinctively that he was a better rider and a better horseman than any other man could be.

So she tried desperately hard to ride as he would wish her to do, so that she would be a worthy companion and he would be proud of her.

There were so many things to remember and so many small points of etiquette which apparently were of importance that sometimes Kistna felt despairingly that she would fail not only the Marquis but herself.

When she made mistakes she would lie awake at night wondering how she could have been so stupid and feeling ashamed that she should have failed his demand for perfection.

Sometimes she thought of her future, but for the moment nothing seemed important except the present.

Because it had a dream-like quality, it was impossible to think ahead, except to hurry in dressing, changing, and getting through the darkness of the night so that she could see the Marquis again.

"Your hair certainly has new life in it, Miss Kistna," Mrs. Dawes said one morning.

"Are you sure?" Kistna asked.

"It's a fact, Miss," Mrs. Dawes replied.

She was brushing out Kistna's long hair, and, seeing it spring out from the brush, each hair seemed charged with a separate life of its own.

"Yes, it is better," Kistna agreed, "it really is!"

"And so are you, Miss," Mrs. Dawes answered. "I said to Ethel only yesterday: 'Miss Kistna's growing real pretty now that she has some flesh on her bones. You mark my words, she'll be a beauty before she's finished!' "

Kistna bent forward to look at herself in the mirror.

'Is that possible?' she wondered to herself; and if she was pretty, perhaps even beautiful, would the Marquis notice it?

She had been too miserable and hungry at the Orphanage to worry about how she looked. Now in the beauty of the Abbey, with the Marquis's grey eyes on her, she longed desperately to look like her mother.

There was no doubt that her mother had been beautiful and not only in the eyes of her husband, who had adored her.

As Kistna had grown older she had been aware that every Englishman who had come to their house would look at her mother, then look again, with an expression that she grew to recognise first as one of incredulity, then of admiration.

It was almost as if they said aloud:

"How, here in India, married to an obscure Missionary, could one expect to find such a beautiful woman? And one who apparently is content with what must be a very restricted life?"

Sometimes they would further a casual acquaintance by calling again and again at the small poor bungalow, arriving in luxurious carriages which belonged to the Governor with servants wearing the flamboyant red-and-white uniforms affected by the servants of the Raj.

They would start by being a little condescending, a little patronising, only to find incredibly that the beautiful Mrs. Lovell, while polite and listening attentively to what they had to say, was not the least interested in them as men.

It was then that they became more insistent and, Kistna would think, very much more sincere.

If her father came home while they were there, she often thought it should be impossible for them not to understand why her mother did not press them to stay or to come again.

When her father's footsteps sounded on the verandah, her mother would jump to her feet, and her face, beautiful though it had been before, seemed to have a new beauty which made it impossible not to watch her.

"John!"

She would breathe the word and her eyes would be shining.

Then she would run across the poorly furnished room to her husband, and even though they had been with each other only an hour or so before, his arms would go round her and he would hold her against him.

It was as if they had been reunited after a long passage of time, and Kistna, when she was old enough, began to understand that every minute they were not together did in fact seem to them a century of emptiness and frustration.

"That is love," she had said to herself, "and it is very beautiful."

It was love she missed at the Orphanage, and because there was no love, there was no beauty.

Now, at the Abbey, it was hers again, perhaps not the beauty of the love her father and mother had known, but at least the kindness and under-standing of two men who apparently found her interesting and to whom in gratitude she poured out the emotions of which she had been deprived and starved for three long years.

"How do I look, Mrs. Dawes?" Kistna asked that evening.

She had put on a gown that had arrived at midday from London.

It was white, embroidered with silver thread, and Madame Yvonne had hidden her thin arms under voluminous sleeves of diaphanous gauze speckled with silver and had draped the neck with the same gauze that shimmered in the light of the candles when she moved.

There was a velvet ribbon at the neck, on which was attached a little spray, of silver and white flowers, and there were the same flowers for her hair, from which ribbons fell down her back and were a further clever disguise for the sharpness of her bones.

"You look real pretty, Miss Kistna!" Mrs. Dawes exclaimed. "There's never been a young lady staying in this house as could hold a candle to you."

"Do you mean that?" Kistna asked. "Oh, Mrs. Dawes, I do hope you are telling me the truth."

"I can assure you, Miss Kistna, I never lie, and I'm not saying a word that could not be spoken over the Bible itself!"

"I hope His Lordship agrees with you," Kistna said almost as if she spoke to herself.

Mrs. Dawes gave her a sharp look. Then she said in a different tone:

"I'm sure His Lordship will be pleased, and soon he'll be inviting young people of your own age here to meet you, and that's as sure as sure!"

She saw Kistna look at her enquiringly, and she went on:

"I expect as soon as you are well enough His Lordship will be finding you dance-partners amongst the young gentlemen of the neighbourhood, and you'll find plenty of them in London."

"I do not want . . . dance-partners when I might dance with . . . His Lordship and Mr. Wallingham," Kistna said.

Mrs. Dawes gave a laugh that somehow sounded affected.

"Oh, it's young gentlemen I'm thinking of, like young Lord Barrowfield, who lives on the next Estate. Twenty-two he'll be next birthday, and a nicer young man it'd be hard to meet. Perhaps His Lordship will have him in mind as a husband for you."

The words startled Kistna and she turned to look at Mrs. Dawes as if she thought she could not have heard her aright.

"A . . . h-husband?"

"Yes, of course, Miss," Mrs. Dawes replied. "You're eighteen, and most young ladies want to be fixed up before their nineteenth birthday. If you're thinking there's lots of time—time soon passes."

She tidied some things on the dressing-table as she went on:

"Don't you worry your head, Miss Kistna. I'm sure His Lordship has your future in mind, and a lovely bride you'll make, really lovely! It would be nice for you to be married here at the Abbey. It's a long time since there's been a Wedding Reception in the Ball-Room."

Kistna did not answer. She merely rose to her feet and said in a voice that somehow seemed incoherent:

"I must . . . go downstairs . . . His . . . Lordship will be . . . waiting for me!"

She did not look at or speak to Mrs. Dawes again as she left the bed-room, and the Housekeeper stood watching her go, an expression on her face that was one of anxiety.

"Poor child!" she said beneath her breath. "It's what I expected would happen, and how could it be otherwise, with His Lordship so handsome and women flocking round him like flies round a honey-pot?"

Because the idea annoyed her, Mrs. Dawes set the silver-backed hair-brushes sharply down on the dressing-table.

Downstairs, Kistna paused before she entered the Salon.

She felt as if she must pull herself together, although why she should do so or what had made her feel so strange she did not wish to explain even to herself.

She only knew that she was afraid, and there were no words in which to express it.

A footman had opened the door and was looking at her wondering why she did not go into the Salon.

Then as she did so, she saw the Marquis standing at the far end in front of the mantelpiece.

Dressed in his evening-clothes, he was very impressive and, Kistna thought, very magnificent.

Then, because she would not help herself, because fear was making her heart beat in a strange way, because he was looking towards her with a smile on his lips, she felt that he stood for security and what she wanted more than anything else—beauty.

Forgetting her lessons, forgetting all he had taught her, she started to run towards him.

CHAPTER FIVE

———— ⌒⦵⌒ ————

KISTNA WAS LAUGHING at something Peregrine had said as the three of them rode back through the Park towards the Abbey.

It was nearly luncheon-time and Kistna had begun to feel hungry even though she disliked knowing that their ride had come to an end.

It was a joy that was inexpressible to know that every morning she could ride the Marquis's magnificent horses, and with him.

Today they had gone farther than usual and had raced each other on a flat stretch of land that was over a mile long.

It was inevitable that the Marquis should win, but Kistna managed to beat Peregrine by a short head and he congratulated her.

"Who would have thought that that miserable girl who looked like a lamp-post," he said teasingly, "and had ridden nothing better than an Indian donkey should dare to prove herself an Amazon and beat me!"

Kistna laughed.

"I am delighted I have been able to do so, and as it happens I never rode a donkey in India!"

"Then it was either an elephant or a camel," Peregrine retorted, "but certainly nothing as swift as what Linden produces from his stable."

"There I agree with you," Kistna said. "They are the most marvellous horses one could imagine, and if I were an Amazon I would steal one and gallop away."

"Where would you go?" Peregrine asked.

Kistna had been speaking lightly, trying as she always did to out-do Peregrine in repartee.

Now, suddenly serious, she glanced at the Marquis and beneath her breath she murmured:

"Nowhere!"

Peregrine followed the direction of her eyes, and, like Mrs. Dawes, he realised at once what had happened and wondered what he should do about it.

He thought that Kistna had already suffered enough to last her a lifetime, and it would be cruel to have her break her heart as so many other women had done over the Marquis.

Peregrine better than anybody else was aware that no woman, however attractive, had ever held his attention for long.

He had the feeling, which he had never expressed before even to himself, that the Marquis was searching for some ideal, some mythical woman he would never find.

As they rode on, with Kistna edging her horse a little nearer to the Marquis's, Peregrine was wondering if he should warn her.

Then he thought it would be useless.

Love, he told himself with uncharacteristic seriousness, was something that one could not prevent or control. It happened, and when it did, there was little one could do about it.

'She is young, she will soon get over it,' he tried to think.

But he found it difficult to imagine Kistna with Branscombe.

He had not been with her every day and nearly every hour for the past ten days without realising that not only was she, as he thought at first, quick-witted, but there were also depths to her character which he had certainly not found in any other young woman of the same age.

'It is because she has lived abroad,' he thought, but he knew it was more than that, and sometimes when they were talking together he felt that Kistna was as old as, if not older than, he and the Marquis.

'It is a question of thinking and feeling,' he decided with an unusual perception.

Then at something Kistna said to him they were all laughing again and he kept them amused until the Abbey was in sight.

"What are we doing this afternoon?" Peregrine asked as they rode over the bridge that spanned the lake.

"I have planned something rather interesting," the Marquis replied, "which will be a surprise."

"I will say one thing about you, Linden," Peregrine replied, "you are a superb host. I was thinking last night, I have never had a quieter time at the Abbey or a more interesting one."

211

"I would not wish you to be bored," the Marquis said mockingly.

"There is no likelihood of that," Peregrine said in all sincerity.

As he spoke, he thought that it was something his host should be saying; for it was the Marquis who had been bored in London, bored at the races, bored at the last Mill they had attended, and bored with Isobel.

As they rode on towards the house they saw that there was a carriage standing outside the front door.

Peregrine looked at it casually, then as he saw its up-to-date, expensive lines and the four horses drawing it, he looked sharply at the Marquis and realised he was as aware as he was who was calling.

They reached the front door, and as the grooms came hurrying to the horses' heads, the Marquis dismounted and went to Kistna to assist her to alight.

As he did so, he said in a low voice:

"Go upstairs and stay in your room until I send for you."

Kistna's eyes widened in surprise, but he did not bother to explain and merely walked ahead up the steps and into the Hall, knowing that she would obey him.

As he handed his hat, riding-gloves, and whip to one of the footmen, the Butler said:

"Lady Isobel Sidley has called, M'Lord, and is waiting for Your Lordship in the Silver Salon."

The Marquis did not reply, and there was a scowl between his eyes as he walked in the direction of the Silver Salon, thinking that a scene was inevitable and it was impossible for him to avoid it.

Isobel was looking extremely beautiful as she rose from the chair on which she had been sitting and held out both her hands to him.

"Linden!" she said in a voice that meant she was deliberately being alluring, "I decided that as Mohammed would not come to the mountain, the mountain must come to Mohammed."

"I am surprised to see you, Isobel!" the Marquis said.

He raised one of her hands perfunctorily to his lips, then somehow extricated himself from her fingers though she was obviously trying to cling to him.

"How can you be so heartless, so cruel, as to leave London without telling me where you were going or when you would return!"

"I was not certain of that myself," the Marquis replied. "Have you really come all this way to ask me questions, or are you staying in the neighbourhood?"

"I am staying with you, or at least I hope so," Isobel replied.

She glanced at him from under her eye-lashes in a way which made most men feel the blood rush to their heads. But the Marquis appeared to be unmoved.

"I am afraid that is impossible," he said in an uncompromising voice which she knew only too well.

"Why?"

"Because Peregrine and I are here alone and I have no wish for a party."

"You are lying!"

The accusation was almost spat at the Marquis and he stiffened.

"I know you are lying," she went on. "I was told that you were out riding with Peregrine Wallingham and your Ward! I did not realise that Mirabelle Chester had arrived in England."

If the Marquis was disconcerted at Kistna's presence being revealed, he did not show it. Instead he said:

"Mirabelle is still a School-girl and cannot even be considered a débutante until she has made her curtsey to the Queen at Buckingham Palace."

"People have been talking of her arrival in this country and of her great fortune."

"People will talk about anything," the Marquis remarked in a lofty tone. "But I must persuade you to return to London this afternoon, even though it may seem inhospitable."

"I want to be with you," Isobel insisted, and now she was pouting.

"Then I am delighted to invite you to stay to luncheon, but as I have just returned from riding, I must go and change."

Lady Isobel moved a little nearer to him.

"Let me stay the night, Linden," she begged in a low voice. "I want to talk to you, and be with you."

The invitation in her dark eyes was very obvious but the Marquis was already walking towards the door.

"I am sure Peregrine will be delighted to entertain you with a glass of

213

champagne," he said, "and you must tell him all the gossip that has accumulated since we have been away from London."

He walked out of the Salon and saw Peregrine halfway up the stairs.

He waited, and as the Marquis caught up with him he said:

"What does she want? Or is that an unnecessary question?"

"I have told her she can stay to luncheon but must leave this afternoon," the Marquis replied. "She has been told that Mirabelle is here, and I am going to tell Kistna to have luncheon upstairs. I have told Isobel she is only a school-girl and not yet entitled to be treated as a débutante."

Peregrine raised his eye-brows but said nothing, and the Marquis went on:

"I am going now to tell her to keep out of sight, and then I must change my clothes. But there is no need for you to change yours, so go and ply Isobel with champagne! If she asks you about Mirabelle, say indifferently that she is nothing but a School-girl who will need a lot of grooming before she appears in Society."

The Marquis did not wait for an answer but hurried up the stairs two at a time.

Peregrine, with a twinkle in his eyes, turned and went down again.

'I might have anticipated,' he thought, 'that this sort of situation would arise.'

It amused him to see how the Marquis was striving to keep control of events, though he might soon find that beyond his power.

The Marquis went to Kistna's bedroom and knocked on the door.

She said: "Come in!" but when he entered she did not turn her head.

She was standing looking out the window, and although she had taken off her hat, she obviously had not rung for her maid or begun to change her riding-habit for a gown.

She was in fact wondering who Lady Isobel was, being certain in her own mind that she was someone who loved the Marquis and whom perhaps he loved in return.

"Kistna!"

As the Marquis spoke her name Kistna started and turned round.

She had been expecting a maid, and when she saw him standing just inside the door there was a sudden light in her eyes and a radiance in her face which made it seem as if the sunshine had come inside the room.

For a moment the Marquis looked at her. Then, as if he remembered why he was there, he said:

"Somebody has called to see me whom I am anxious you should not meet. I therefore wish you to have luncheon up here in your *Boudoir*. As soon as she has gone I will send a message to let you know and you can come downstairs."

Having given his instructions, he would have turned away, but Kistna asked:

"Why should I not . . . meet this . . . lady? Are you . . . ashamed of me?"

"No, of course not!" the Marquis answered quickly. "It is nothing like that."

"Then . . . why am I to stay . . . out of sight?"

"One reason," he explained, "is that you are staying in the Abbey unchaperoned. You must be aware that it would be correct for an elderly or married woman to be present."

Because she had expected a different answer, the radiance which had faded from Kistna's face when the Marquis had first told her what she was to do was back again.

"Is that all?" she asked in such a tone of relief that he looked at her curiously.

"What else did you expect?"

What Kistna had really thought was that the Marquis wanted to be alone with the lady who had called. It was an inexpressible relief to know that his reason was merely a conventional one, and she said:

"Of course I will have my luncheon up here as you want me to, but please, My Lord, do not let your visitor . . . spoil the afternoon. I am so looking forward to the . . . surprise you have planned."

She was suddenly very child-like in the way she pleaded with him, and the Marquis smiled as he answered:

"I promise you I will do my best."

Yet, as he left her he had the feeling that he was being unkind, and when he went downstairs again he was very conscious of the fact that there was a lonely young woman eating alone while Isobel was waiting for him.

Luncheon was in fact an uncomfortable meal, because Lady Isobel was determined to hold the attention of the Marquis and undoubtedly resented Peregrine being there.

She made spiteful replies to some of the things he said, and when he lapsed into silence and the Marquis made no effort to talk, Isobel attempted to keep the conversation concentrated on herself but was not very successful at it.

Instead of the lavish meal usually served at the Abbey, Peregrine suspected that the Marquis had cancelled at least two courses, because luncheon was finished far quicker than was usual.

"I will order your carriage, Isobel," he said as he rose from the table.

"I wish to speak to you alone, Linden."

She walked with an air of defiance towards the Silver Salon.

As she entered it the Marquis hung back for a moment to say to Peregrine:

"Order her carriage. I only hope this will not take long."

"I am sorry for you," Peregrine replied.

The Marquis closed the Salon door behind him and moved towards his guest in a casual manner.

At the same time, he was uncomfortably aware that Isobel was determined to have a scene.

However, she tried a different tactic from what he had expected by throwing herself precipitately into his arms the moment he reached her side.

"Oh, Linden, I love you!" she said, lifting her lips to his. "Kiss me, and I will tell you how much."

The Marquis looked down at her beautiful face and as he did so he realised that she no longer had the slightest attraction for him.

In fact, it was difficult to remember why he had ever found her irresistibly fascinating or how in the past she had easily managed to evoke a fiery response from him by an overture such as this.

With an ease which came from long experience of evading clinging women, the Marquis managed to extricate himself from Lady Isobel's arms.

"I think, Isobel," he said, as he stood with his back to the fireplace, "we are both old enough and experienced enough to know when an *affaire de coeur* such as we have both enjoyed comes to an end."

"There is no question of it coming to an end as far as I am concerned."

Lady Isobel's voice rose a little as she spoke, and the Marquis was aware that she was angry because he had avoided her wiles.

"What I suggest," he said, "is that when I return to London I will give you a present that will commemorate the very happy times we have spent together in the past. And I hope there will be no recriminations or regrets and that we shall always be friends."

As he spoke, he thought that what he had said sounded priggish and slightly pompous, but he knew from past experience that there was really nothing else he could say to a woman who still wanted him while he had no further interest in her.

But while many of his discarded loves had wept, sulked, or merely accepted the inevitable, Isobel was made of sterner stuff.

Having been spoilt all her life and having a very inflated idea of her own charms, she was not only furious at losing the Marquis but was also insulted that he no longer desired her as a woman.

Incensed almost beyond control, she spat out her venom at him, berating him in a manner that he thought would not have come amiss in a Billingsgate fish-wife, and with every second that passed he found her more unpleasant.

By the time she finished he had come to the conclusion that he positively disliked her and had decided that there was no-one to blame but himself for having had the bad taste to find her desirable in the first place.

When finally Isobel could find nothing more to say and had already repeated herself a dozen times, she picked up her gloves and her reticule and said in a bitter and acid voice:

"I will leave you, Linden, as you are so anxious for me to do so, but let me make this absolutely clear—I loathe and detest you for what you have done to me! I gave you my heart and you trampled it under your feet. One day you will be paid back in your own coin."

Her eyes narrowed as she went on:

"One day you will suffer and some woman will hurt you as I have been hurt, and I shall rejoice that she has the power to do so!"

The Marquis did not reply. He merely inclined his head.

Then with a violent sound of exasperation Lady Isobel swept down the

Salon towards the door. The Marquis followed her slowly, thinking only how glad he would be to see the last of her.

They reached the Hall where one of the footmen was waiting with the silk pelisse that matched the gown Lady Isobel was wearing.

As she allowed the flunkey to help her into it, she looked up at the ceiling in the Hall, then down to where the flags hung over the mantelpiece and to the Marquis standing waiting for her to leave.

She was, in her heart, cursing the Abbey and the owner of it, but to Kistna peeping at her through the bannisters she looked so exquisitely beautiful that it was an indescribable agony to see her.

Never had Kistna thought that any woman could look so lovely or be so exquisitely gowned.

Her bonnet trimmed with ostrich-feathers and her gown with huge sleeves and a full skirt gave Lady Isobel a glamour and an elegance which had made her the undisputed toast of St. James's.

'She is the most beautiful person I have ever seen, and the exact . . . counterpart to the . . . Marquis,' Kistna thought.

Then as if she could not bear to go on looking at the woman below, she ran back along the passage to her own Sitting-Room, wishing that her curiosity had not made her leave it.

It had, however, been impossible for her to resist her desire to see the reason why she must have luncheon alone.

Now she could understand why the Marquis would not want a complete stranger to be present when he talked intimately to somebody belonging to his world, as she would never be able to do.

"I am just an . . . outsider," Kistna whispered to herself.

She felt she could see nothing but Lady Isobel's beautiful face, and the picture she made with her eyes looking upwards at the ceiling, then descending slowly to rest on the Marquis, was, Kistna thought, engraved on her heart.

She felt a pain that seemed to strike into her like a dagger.

Then as she felt as if even the beauty of the Abbey could no longer help her, nor the sunshine outside, nor the pretty gown she was wearing, the ugliness was back in her life, and this time it lay within herself.

It was the ugliness of pain, and she recognised it for what it was: the pain of jealousy.

"How can I be jealous of a woman I have seen only for a fleeting second?" she asked herself.

But she knew the answer.

She was jealous because she loved the Marquis and he filled her whole life!

She supposed she should have known the truth a long time ago and acknowledged it. Now she felt almost as if it struck her like a blow.

And yet it was so inevitable, already so much a part of her living and breathing, that it was almost absurd to think she had not been aware of it.

Of course she loved him! She had loved him from the very first moment when she had seen him standing outside the front door of the Orphanage.

She had loved him even while she had been blaming him for the agony they had suffered from Mrs. Moore.

She had loved him when he had put things right, and when he had fetched her that first morning to take her to the Abbey.

She had lain awake the first night fearing that the promise he had made was something he would never substantiate.

"He did not mean it," her rational mind had tried to tell her.

But her heart believed him, because already she loved him. He was St. Michael coming to save her, attended by his angels, and she was ready to go down on her knees and worhsip him.

She knew now that her love had grown more and more every day and every minute that she had been with the Marquis.

She had awakened each day with a feeling of wild excitement because as soon as she was dressed and downstairs she would see him.

She had gone to sleep thinking of him, to dream of him, and when she awoke she thought of him again.

"I love him! I love him!" she said now, a hundred times, as she walked restlessly round the attractive flower-filled *Boudoir* which opened out of her bedroom.

When she had first seen it she had thought it was the loveliest room one could ever imagine. Now it seemed like a cage, a prison which kept her from being with the Marquis when he was somewhere else.

She had a sudden fear that if the beautiful lady was going back to London, the Marquis would go with her. Then even as the thought seemed to shoot through her, leaving a streak of pain behind, there was a knock on the door.

With difficulty Kistna managed to answer.

"His Lordship's compliments, Miss," one of the footmen said, "and he wishes you to join him ready to go driving."

Kistna felt her heart leap.

She ran into the bedroom to put on a pretty bonnet that went with the gown she was wearing and to pick up a silk shawl and her gloves which the maid had left ready on one of the chairs.

Only as she ran towards the door did a sudden thought take her instead to the dressing-table to look at herself in the mirror.

For a moment she did not see her own reflection but the beautiful face she had seen below in the Hall, and with difficulty she prevented herself from giving a cry of despair.

How could she be so silly? How could she expect for one moment that the Marquis would so much as notice her when there were lovely women who looked like angels competing for his favours?

"It is hopeless!" Kistna told herself despairingly.

At the same time, she was feminine enough to realise that now that her eyes were no longer sunken in her head they looked very large, almost too large for her face, and as her cheeks had filled out her mouth seemed smaller and properly curved.

Her chin was still a sharp line but her neck was round, and her skin was smooth and no longer sallow but white.

She stared at herself for a few seconds, then turned away because she had only one thought in her mind—to be with the Marquis!

She seemed to fly rather than walk down the stairs to where he would be waiting for her.

"You realise," Peregrine said later that evening when Kistna had gone to bed, "that Isobel will undoubtedly tell all London that Mirabelle has arrived. That means that Branscombe will be on our tracks."

"I have thought of that," the Marquis replied. "The best thing we can do is to sit tight and let Branscombe make the first move."

"You are quite certain he will do so?"

"I do not believe he would change his intention so quickly, unless he has come into a fortune in the meantime."

"I cannot understand how he can possibly need money," Peregrine said, "but if he does, then Mirabelle Chester is obviously the answer to his dreams."

As he spoke, Peregrine noticed that there was almost a cruel smile on the Marquis's lips, and he knew without being told that his friend was thinking of the satisfaction he would feel if their plot succeeded and they made the Earl look a fool.

"We have little more than a week before Ascot," he remarked, "and if Branscombe has not come up to scratch by then, what do you intend to do about Kistna?"

"I am quite certain he will not let the grass grow under his feet," the Marquis replied. "In fact, with Isobel abusing me from the roof-tops you may be quite certain that we shall have some response from him within the next twenty-four hours."

"You are very optimistic."

"I do not make many mistakes when dealing with men of Branscombe's calibre," the Marquis said. "And I consider myself to be a good judge of character."

He spoke with a tone of satisfaction, then as he met Peregrine's eyes he laughed a little ruefully.

"That only applies to one sex," he said. "I admit where Isobel is concerned I made a grave error of judgement."

"No-one, unless he is a magician, can ever be sure what a woman will be like," Peregrine said consolingly, "and if they all ran according to form, they would certainly be boring! It is their unpredictability that makes the chase a gamble from start to finish!"

"I agree with you," the Marquis said with a smile. "At the same time, I can promise you I shall be very much more careful in the future!"

"I doubt it," Peregrine said. "But thank goodness you are at least human when it comes to women!"

"What do you mean by that?"

"I mean," Peregrine replied, "that you are too damned successful in every other way, and it is a sheer relief to ordinary mortals like myself to find that one of his gods has feet of clay!"

"Hardly a very apt metaphor," the Marquis remarked. "At the same time, it expresses the truth and I must accept it. I only hope I am not so easily taken in another time."

There was silence, then Peregrine said:

"What really concerns me at the moment is what you are going to do about Kistna."

"Kistna?" the Marquis queried. "You know exactly what I am going to do about her. Marry her off to Branscombe, and watch him discover what it is like to be tricked and cheated!"

There was silence. Then Peregrine said:

"I presume you realise that if he is angry he will take it out on her?"

"I have thought of that already," the Marquis replied, "and I shall make sure he provides for her."

"In what way?"

"I am going to make him settle money on her before I give my permission for the marriage."

"Will he not think that rather strange, when the alleged Mirabelle is a thousand times richer than he is?"

"I will make my request sound convincing," the Marquis said, and his voice was hard.

Again there was a pause before Peregrine said:

"I suppose if Kistna gets some money and an undoubtedly distinguished title she will think the bargain worthwhile."

"Good God, Peregrine, why should she be anything but delighted?" the Marquis asked. "You saw the condition she was in when we found her and how much she enjoys having pretty gowns. Well, I will see that she can afford them for the rest of her life, and there is certainly no reason for her to go hungry in the future."

Peregrine felt he could say no more.

The question in his mind was whether Kistna would find that enough.

He was quite certain that she was already in love with the Marquis. The signs were all too obviously there, but once again he told himself that as she was very young, she would forget.

Besides, the Earl was a very presentable, good-looking man.

Glancing at the Marquis sitting opposite him on the other side of the hearth-rug, he wondered if he was really as obtuse as he appeared, and if it had never struck him that the girl was in love with him.

Then he told himself that the Marquis was too busy concentrating on having his revenge on the Earl to be concerned with anything else.

At the same time, Peregrine did not like to think of Kistna being unhappy.

He had learnt these last days how sensitive she was to everything the Marquis said or even thought, and he knew that after what she had been through in the Orphanage she would find it hard, if not impossible, to live in a house however grand where she was hated and despised.

'What will she feel when she knows she has been part of a plot and that Linden's generosity was merely a means to an end?' Peregrine wondered to himself.

Yet somehow it was impossible to say so to the Marquis, or to let him think that he was beginning to disapprove of his whole plan of revenge.

"We had better go to bed," the Marquis said unexpectedly. "We have to be ready for tomorrow, when anything might happen. I intend first thing to warn the household that they are not to mention Kistna as they did today when Isobel arrived, and that if anyone asks for Miss Mirabelle Chester, they are referring to her."

"When are you going to tell Kistna of the part she has to play?" Peregrine enquired.

"I was going to tell her tonight," the Marquis answered, "but it seemed to me she was a little under the weather. She appeared rather quieter than usual and not as happy as she had been all day."

Peregrine had also noticed that, but he was surprised the Marquis had.

"What do you think has upset her?" he asked.

"Why should she be upset?" the Marquis parried.

"I thought perhaps she might have resented having been sent upstairs when Isobel arrived."

"I explained that it was because she was here unchaperoned, and she seemed to think it was quite a reasonable excuse."

"It is a good thing Isobel did not see her," Peregrine said. "She would have been quite convinced that you had taken on a new love before being free of the old."

The Marquis laughed.

"A ridiculous idea, but one which would undoubtedly occur to Isobel. She would never believe I was interested in any woman unless I found her desirable."

Peregrine was silent for a moment, then he said:

"I am rather sorry in a way that we are not taking our *protégée* to London and letting her have a run for her money before she gets tied up with Branscombe."

"Why should you want to do that?" the Marquis asked.

"Because it would be interesting to see if she was as successful as I am sure she would be."

He saw that the Marquis did not understand, and he exclaimed:

"Good God, Linden, you must realise by now how attractive she is! Her eyes are fantastic, and now that her face has filled out, the rest of her features have fallen into place. Personally, I find her straight little nose entrancing! It certainly looks as blue-blooded as anything the Chesters can produce."

He spoke lightly, but there was no doubt that the Marquis was scowling at him.

"Now listen, Peregrine," he said. "If I find you messing about with Kistna I will murder you! We have taken all this trouble over her for one reason and one reason only!"

"I was only intimating that there are quite a number of men who would not only find her attractive but would be willing to marry her. So if Branscombe fails to come up to scratch, we can always let her find a man she can love."

The Marquis rose to his feet.

"I do not know what has got into you, Peregrine," he said. "You have been helpful and understanding up to now. I cannot think why you are putting obstacles in my way at the last minute."

"I am doing nothing of the sort!" Peregrine protested. "I am only saying that knowing what we do about Branscombe, we also know that anyone as sweet-natured and sensitive as Kistna is too good for him, and I wish it were possible to marry her to somebody we both like and admire."

"Get it into your head," the Marquis said sharply, "that Branscombe may cheat on race-courses and behave like an outsider in many ways, but he is still of great distinction and a favourite of the King. Can you imagine any woman not being delighted and extremely grateful at finding herself married to such a man?"

"I hope you are right," Peregrine replied. "I just feel that Kistna is different."

"It is useless to discuss this any further," the Marquis retorted, "and I forbid you, I absolutely forbid you to upset Kistna in any way. Do you understand?"

The Marquis did not wait for Peregrine's answer but walked out of the Library.

Peregrine gave a sigh.

He had never known the Marquis to be so unpredictable or indeed so bad-tempered when they were talking intimately.

He rose from his chair and stretched himself.

'I expect Linden is right,' he thought, 'and he is providing for the girl in an extremely generous manner.'

Nevertheless, as he went up to bed and there was no sign of the Marquis to say good-night to him, he had the feeling that a volcano might erupt at any moment.

In her own room, Kistna was awake, lying in the darkness, finding it impossible to sleep.

Normally she was so happy with her thoughts of the Marquis and the things they had done during the day that she would fall asleep immediately.

But tonight she could think only of her love for him and of the beautiful lady who had visited him for luncheon and whom she had not been allowed to meet.

She told herself she had been stupid to think even for a moment that the wonder and delight of being alone with the Marquis could continue.

She did not question at first how strange it was that he should stay in the country with only Peregrine and herself, rather than be with his friends and the King at this particular time of year when London was gayer than at any other time.

Because she had been curious, she had talked to Peregrine about the things they did when they were in London, and he had told her about the

Marquis's house filled with treasures, of his importance in the Social World, and of his skill and success at every sport.

She had of course been intensely interested in his successes on the Turf, but although Peregrine had told her his horse had dead-heated for first place in the Derby Stakes, he had not added that it was due to the crooked riding of the Earl's jockey.

He had been aware as he talked that Kistna listened to him with wide, excited eyes because he was speaking of the Marquis.

"Why has His Lordship never . . . married?" she asked.

Peregrine shrugged his shoulders.

"It is not for want of trying on the part of almost every unattached woman he meets, but he does not fall in love with them, not to the extent of wanting to be tied."

There was a silence, then Kistna said:

"Would he be very . . . bored?"

Peregrine laughed.

"He would! And the truth is that the Marquis, like myself, enjoys being a bachelor. We have a great deal of fun together, and quite frankly it is more amusing to entertain a pretty woman one night and change her for an even prettier one the next, than to be tied to somebody who, pretty or ugly, is a wife for life."

Peregrine was talking in the amusing manner which always made those who listened to him laugh.

Then he realised that Kistna was taking him very seriously.

"I suppose I understand that," she said, "but if one were in love . . . really in love . . . one would want to be with the same person all the time . . . and not keep changing."

She was thinking of her father and mother as she spoke, and without thinking Peregrine answered:

"The Marquis likes a change—and who shall blame him? If you could fill a huge stable with the finest horses, why should you ride the same one every day and neglect the others?"

Again he was speaking lightly and frivolously. Then as he saw the expression on Kistna's face and remembered she was a Parson's daughter, he added:

"Perhaps one day the Marquis will find the right woman and so shall I.

Then we shall settle down and be extremely dull and doubtless very pompous."

"There is no reason why you should be that."

Again Peregrine did not realise that Kistna was thinking of her father and mother and how when they were together they always found everything delightful and enjoyable because they could share it.

Peregrine thought he had somehow been indiscreet, and, trying to smooth things over, he said:

"There is no reason to worry your head about me or the Marquis. All you have to do is to concentrate on yourself, and when we find you a nice husband, you will undoubtedly find marriage a very enjoyable institution."

"But you have just said that most men do not wish to be married," Kistna replied, "and perhaps no-one will . . . want to marry me."

"I can assure you they will," Peregrine answered, "and if you had any money and I could afford it, I would bet you that by this time next year you would be a respectable married lady with a gold ring on your finger!"

Kistna laughed and shook her head.

"Who would want to marry me?" she asked.

Then as if she suddenly remembered something, she added:

"Except, of course . . . if I am the Ward of . . . somebody very important . . . I suppose that would count as a very . . . considerable advantage."

"It certainly will," Peregrine agreed.

Because he felt he was getting involved in a conversation he should never have started in the first place, he had been relieved when the Marquis appeared.

Kistna had gone over the conversation in her mind that night, and the nights that followed.

Now she thought that as the Marquis did not wish to get married, she would perhaps be able to stay with him for a long time and they could be happy as they were now.

Because it was something she wanted more than she had ever wanted anything, she found herself praying:

"Please, God, let me stay here with him. Please make him content to be in the country and not want to follow that beautiful lady to London."

Then as she thought of her father and mother and how deeply they had loved each other and how the very air round them had seemed somehow redolent with love when they were together, she knew that was how she loved the Marquis.

"I love him with my mind . . . my heart, and my . . . soul," she whispered into the darkness.

Then, although it seemed wicked and presumptive, she added:

"Please, God . . . let him care for me a little . . . just a very . . . little . . . and even if his love only lasts a week . . . a month . . . a year, then I could . . . die having known . . . real happiness."

CHAPTER SIX

————— ❦ —————

WHEN THEY CAME BACK FROM RIDING, the Marquis said to Kistna:

"When you have changed I want to speak to you. I will be in the Library."

Because there was a note in his voice that did not sound normal, she looked at him in surprise.

Then when he did not wait for her reply but walked away in the direction of the Library, she ran upstairs.

While she was changing into what she thought was one of the prettiest gowns Madame Yvonne had sent her, Kistna wondered what the Marquis had to say to her.

She could not imagine she had done anything wrong, but she thought now that this morning when they were riding he had been a little aloof and more silent than he had been on other rides.

Peregrine had made her laugh but the Marquis had not joined, and now she was afraid that something was wrong.

"What could I have done? What could I have said?" she asked herself.

She could find no obvious answer, and as she went downstairs there was a look of anxiety in her eyes.

As Peregrine had said to the Marquis, her eyes were now not only very expressive but also beautiful, and they seemed to dominate her whole face so that it was difficult to notice her other features, good though they were.

She opened the door of the Library and went in to find the Marquis, as she had expected, sitting at the huge flat-topped desk in the centre of the room.

There was a gold ink-pot on it, made in the time of Charles II by one of the greatest goldsmiths in the land, and Kistna admired it every time she saw it.

Now she could see only the Marquis, and as always she felt her heart give a sudden leap at the sight of him, then seem to beat more quickly within her breast.

She walked towards him, but he did not look up until she stood directly in front of him.

Then he said:

"Sit down, Kistna. I have something to say to you."

Because she was nervous, she sat on the very edge of the chair and clasped her hands together.

It seemed to her that the Marquis looked at her searchingly for a long moment before he said:

"I have decided your future, which would be a very brilliant one for any young woman, but I need your help in assuring it."

He paused, and because Kistna felt he was waiting for her to reply, she said in a voice he could barely hear:

"W-what do you . . . want me to . . . do?"

"I expect like all women you have been wondering, now that you are eighteen, whom you will marry. Of course, in the circumstances in which I found you, it was unlikely you would ever meet a man, let alone one suitable to be your husband."

"I . . . I have no . . . wish to be . . . m-married," Kistna said quickly.

She saw the frown between the Marquis's eyes before he said sharply:

"That is an absurd statement for anyone of your intelligence. Of course

229

you wish to be married, and as your Guardian I have in fact chosen a suitable husband for you."

Kistna gave an audible gasp. Then she went very pale and clenched her fingers together.

As if he knew it was impossible for her to speak, the Marquis continued:

"Because you are my Ward, and because I feel I must recompense you for your sufferings in the Orphanage, I have chosen as your husband a man who will give you what is undoubtedly the most brilliant social position in England today."

Again he paused, and he realised as he looked across the desk that Kistna was staring at him with huge frightened eyes that seemed to fill her whole face.

It struck him that there was a stricken expression in them. Then he told himself that he was being absurd and her expression was merely one of astonishment.

"The man I am talking about," the Marquis continued, "is the Earl of Branscombe. He is the possessor of an ancient and noble title, he is a sportsman of high repute on the Turf, and he enjoys the trust and friendship of the King and Queen."

The Marquis waited, and this time it was obvious that he expected Kistna to make some response.

After some seconds had passed she asked incoherently:

"W-why should he . . . wish to . . . marry me?"

"Because he thinks you are my Ward," the Marquis replied, and his voice was hard, "and while I do not consider the Ward he had in mind suitable for him, I feel that you, as another Ward of mine, will make him an admirable wife."

"But . . . but he might not . . . like me . . . and I might not like . . . him," Kistna stammered.

"You must be aware," the Marquis said loftily, "that in the aristocratic families in England, as in the East where you have lived, marriages are always arranged."

"But in India," Kistna said, "and . . . I suspect in England, the marriages are arranged because both the bridegroom and the bride obtain some . . . financial advantage from the . . . union."

For a moment the Marquis was taken aback.

Then he thought he might have guessed that Kistna was too intelligent not to be aware that an arranged marriage was a business transaction from which both sides benefitted.

It took him a second or two to find the answer, but finally he said:

"The Earl of Branscombe considers that because you are my Ward, that is the advantage he requires."

"How can he want to marry somebody he has never seen . . . and whom he does not . . . love?"

"I have already explained to you that this is an arranged marriage," the Marquis said with a note of irritation in his voice, "and as the Earl is a very prepossessing man, and you are a very attractive young woman, love will come with marriage, if that is what you want."

He spoke as if it was something completely unimportant, but Kistna, thinking of her father and mother, said in a frightened voice:

"Please . . . I do not . . . wish to . . . marry in such . . . circumstances."

The Marquis leant back in his chair.

"That remark is foolish and over-emotional," he said. "You must be aware that I am offering you a marriage which would be the height of the ambitions of any girl in England, and to most of them it would be an alliance beyond their wildest dreams."

He looked at Kistna almost angrily as he continued:

"Surely you have not forgotten already the condition you were in when I found you at the Orphanage? You said at the time it might only have been a question of a year or even a few months before you died from starvation and cold. In contrast, what could be more advantageous from every point of view than for you to become the Countess of Branscombe?"

Because Kistna could not bear to see the anger in his eyes she looked away from him and stared down at her hands. She felt as if the irritation in his voice vibrated through her body, making her feel almost as if he hurt her physically.

"Apart from anything else," the Marquis went on, "I think you should be grateful to me for giving you the opportunity of such a golden future."

"I am . . . very grateful . . . for everything you have . . . done for me," Kistna said, and now there was a sob in her voice.

"Then if you are grateful," the Marquis answered, "you will do what I tell you to do, without making difficulties. I cannot think that is too much to ask."

There was a pause. Then Kistna said:

"I am . . . grateful, My Lord . . . and I will do what you . . . tell me to do."

"Good!" the Marquis approved. "Now listen carefully."

He bent forward with his arms on the desk as if to intensify the importance of what he was about to say.

"The Earl of Branscombe has already announced in London that he intends to marry my Ward. When he arrives here I shall introduce you to him as my Ward, which indeed you are. But he has no idea that you even exist and he has asked in fact for my other Ward, who is in Italy at the moment. Her name is Mirabelle Chester, and that is who you will let him think you are."

Kistna raised her head.

"Do you mean . . . I am to . . . deceive him?" she enquired.

"What does it matter?" the Marquis asked lightly. "One Ward is as good as another."

"I do not . . . understand! Why should we not tell him my . . . real name?"

"Because," the Marquis said slowly, "I wish him to believe that you are Mirabelle Chester, and I am asking you to help me and yourself by doing what I require."

There was silence. Then Kistna said:

"But . . . will you not explain to me . . . why this . . . deception is necessary?"

"No," the Marquis said firmly. "It is my business and mine alone. As I have already pointed out, Kistna, I am ensuring that your future will be one which ranks high in the Social World and you will be the envy of every other young woman. What more can you want?"

To the Marquis's surprise, Kistna rose from her chair and walked away towards the window.

He found himself, without meaning to, admiring the grace of the way she moved and the lines of her figure. She wore a gown of pale pink gauze trimmed with ribbons of the same colour.

'She is like a flower,' he thought, then told himself sharply that she was being difficult.

With her back to him, Kistna stood looking out at the sunshine on the Park. Then she said:

"Will you be very . . . angry if I . . . refuse to do what you . . . want?"

The Marquis started, then brought his hand down sharply on the desk in front of him.

"I will not only be angry," he replied, "but I should think you half-witted, which is something I have never thought before."

Kistna did not speak or look round and he went on:

"If you will not marry Branscombe as I wish you to do, have you thought of the alternative? You can hardly stay here with me indefinitely, unchaperoned and with nothing to look forward to except an attempt to find another husband. It would certainly be impossible for me to produce one who could equal the Earl in any way."

"I could perhaps . . . earn my own . . . living."

"How?" the Marquis enquired. "What talents have you for earning money in a very competitive world?"

She did not reply and he went on:

"Perhaps you are thinking of working in an Orphanage, but I should have thought you would have had enough of that sort of existence, even in one better equipped than the place where I found you."

Again Kistna felt almost as if he had hit her, and because she knew she could not bear him to be angry with her, she turned back to say:

"I am . . . grateful for your kindness and for . . . thinking of me . . . and I will try to . . . do what you . . . want."

Her voice broke a little on the last word, but she controlled herself and as she stood in front of him at the desk, the Marquis said:

"I thought you would see sense. Now, remember, Kistna, that your name is Mirabelle Chester. You are the daughter of my cousin Lionel, who was a wanderer over the face of the earth—I think he called himself an explorer—but he is dead and his wife is dead also."

"So Mirabelle is an . . . orphan . . . like me!"

"Exactly!" the Marquis said. "In fact, as you are the same age you will see that you have several things in common."

He looked at Kistna as he spoke and thought she looked very pale, almost as if she might faint.

He rose to his feet.

"Come and sit down in a comfortable chair," he suggested, "and I will tell you more about Mirabelle so that you do not make any mistakes."

He walked from behind the desk towards the fireplace and Kistna followed him slowly to sit down on one of the big comfortable armchairs.

Because it had been so warm for the last two days, the fire was not lit. Instead, the fireplace was filled with a magnificent arrangement of flowers and plants from the Marquis's own greenhouses.

Kistna could smell their fragrance and she thought it was very much part of the beauty of the Abbey and very different from the smell of the dust, dirt, and misery she had known at the Orphanage.

Living in India had taught her to use her senses and she thought that it was not only what one could see and hear which made a picture in the mind that remained in the memory, but also the smell of places and even people.

To her the Abbey had a scent that was a mixture of the fragrances of flowers, bees'-wax, cigar-smoke, and the cleanness of the fresh air outside.

It was all associated in her mind with the Marquis, and as he sat down opposite her, he looked so handsome and so irresistibly attractive that she felt her whole body vibrate with love.

"Mirabelle, since her father died, has been living in Rome," he was saying, "and finishing her studies at a very good School. But I expect you will find that you know quite as much as she does and perhaps, because you have experienced a very different life, in many ways you know even more."

"I do not . . . speak Italian."

"No, but your French is coming along," the Marquis replied, "and I think it is very unlikely that the Earl speaks any foreign language except French."

"Suppose he . . . asks me questions I cannot . . . answer?"

"I imagine you are quick-witted enough to avoid being caught out," the

Marquis said, "and it is always best in such circumstances to say as little as possible."

"When are you . . . planning I should . . . be married?" Kistna asked.

The Marquis was just about to reply: "As soon as possible!" when he thought that might frighten her.

Instead he answered deliberately vaguely:

"We shall have to discuss that, of course, with the Earl, and I suggest you leave the arrangements in my hands. Just think how very lucky you are, and that if your father and mother were alive they too would be grateful to me for taking care of your future in an exceptional manner of which they could not help approving."

The Marquis thought as he spoke that he was being somewhat ponderous but undoubtedly reassuring.

What he did not expect was that Kistna should look at him wildly, as though she was going to protest or say something that might cancel out everything she had agreed to before.

Then, as if with a tremendous effort, her expression changed, but the tears came into her eyes and made them look even bigger than they were already.

With an incoherent little word of apology, she rose from the chair and ran from the room, leaving the Marquis staring after her until he could no longer hear her footsteps running down the passage.

"A visitor!" Peregrine exclaimed as they drove down the drive.

He looked at the Marquis as he spoke and they simultaneously knew whose Phaeton was standing outside the door of the Abbey.

When they drew a little nearer there was no mistaking the yellow-and-black wheels and upholstery, while the same colours were echoed in the coachman's livery, which were also the Earl's racing colours.

"Who do you think it can be?" Kistna asked. "And do you want me to . . . hide until they . . . leave?"

There was a little tremor in her voice as she asked the question, because she thought that perhaps the beautiful lady who had called on the Marquis yesterday morning had returned.

They had driven over to one of the farms in the Marquis's Phaeton and

Kistna had been entranced by the newly born lambs and the calves that were just able to stand on their spindly legs.

Because she had been so happy to be with the Marquis, she had for the moment forgotten her unhappiness of the morning, and she had found everything at the farm so entrancing that her enthusiasm had communicated itself both to the Marquis and to Peregrine.

"Mama told me how beautiful spring was in England," she said. "But although I expected golden daffodils under the trees, and the shrubs and hedges coming into bud, I had forgotten there would be lambs like this and fluffy yellow chicks and waddling baby ducks!"

She picked up a little yellow chick as she spoke and held it in the palm of her hand for the Marquis to look at it.

"Could anything be more adorable?" she asked.

Watching her, Peregrine thought the same adjective might apply to her, and he wondered why the Marquis did not realise how attractive she looked with the chick in her hand and her eyes soft yet radiant with happiness.

Now the happiness was dimmed as Kistna looked ahead.

"What I want you to do," the Marquis said, and there was a definite note of satisfaction in his voice, "is to go upstairs and put on your prettiest and most expensive-looking gown. Get your maid to arrange your hair, and be ready when I send for you to meet your future husband, the Earl of Branscombe."

"He is . . . here?"

There was no doubt of the dismay in Kistna's voice.

"That is his Phaeton," the Marquis replied. "As you see, it is a very expensive vehicle, and I direct your attention to his horses, which are always outstanding!"

There was a little sting in the way he spoke, and Kistna looked at him. She did not speak, and after a moment he said:

"You promised to do what I ask you, Kistna! Be careful to remember that your name is Mirabelle, which is how I shall address you."

"I have . . . not forgotten," Kistna said in a low voice, "but I was wondering why . . . when you wish me to marry him . . . you do not . . . like the Earl."

"Who said I did not like him?"

"I heard it . . . in your voice."

"I think you are being over-imaginative," the Marquis said coldly.

They had reached the gravel sweep outside the front door and he drew his horses to a standstill behind the Phaeton belonging to the Earl.

They stepped out, and because she knew she must obey orders Kistna hurried up the staircase to her room.

The Marquis turned to Peregrine with a smile on his lips.

"You were right!" he said in a voice the servants could not hear. "The fish has risen to the fly and now all we have to do is to land him!"

"I will leave you to do that," Peregrine replied, "but just remember one thing, Linden."

"What is that?"

"You are playing a game with people, not chessmen."

The Marquis looked at him in perplexity but Peregrine had already turned away and was climbing the stairs towards his own room.

A footman opened the door of the Salon where the Earl was waiting.

As the Marquis entered he saw him at the far end and was instantly aware of a feeling of dislike and distrust.

But he appeared both genial and surprised as he moved forward to say:

"Good-afternoon, Branscombe! This is an unexpected visit!"

"I was on my way to stay with Verulam at Gorhambury," the Earl replied. "As I wished to see you on a personal matter, I hope you will forgive me for not notifying you of my arrival."

"Of course," the Marquis answered. "Do sit down. I see my servants have brought you some refreshment."

The Earl had a glass of champagne in his hand. Now he put it on a side-table and did not sit, as the Marquis had suggested, but stood in front of the mantelpiece, as if he found what he had to say easier if he was on his feet.

The Marquis poured himself a small glass of champagne and waited, knowing that the Earl was finding it somewhat embarrassing to know how to start.

"I have been aware for some time, Alchester," he began at last, "that I should get married. As you will know, it is the wish of Their Majesties that those in constant attendance on them, like myself, should have a wife."

He paused. Then as the Marquis did not speak, he went on:

"My wife would of course be singularly fortunate in that she, as hereditary 'Lady of the Bedchamber,' would be not only a companion for Her Majesty but also a friend."

As the Earl continued standing, the Marquis seated himself in one of the armchairs and, crossing his legs, leant back.

He thought he was enjoying more than he had enjoyed anything for a long time seeing the Earl in the unaccustomed position of being, in effect, a supplicant.

"As the Queen is so young," the Earl continued, "twenty-six next birthday, it would therefore be pleasant for Her Majesty to have a younger person round her than she has at the moment. I am sure you will agree with me."

"Of course," the Marquis murmured.

"That is one reason why I have decided, after a great deal of thought and consideration, that I need a wife who is young in years, but naturally one who by birth and breeding qualified for the position she will hold not only at Court but as my wife."

Again he waited for the Marquis to speak, but he merely nodded his agreement and took another sip of champagne.

"It is not always easy to find exactly what one wants in life," the Earl said, "but I think that there is one young woman who I could say in all sincerity fulfils my requirements in almost every particular, and that, Alchester, is your Ward—Mirabelle Chester."

The Marquis gave a well-simulated start.

"Mirabelle!" he exclaimed. "But she has not yet made her debut."

"However, she is, I believe, eighteen," the Earl remarked.

"That is true, but I had not thought of her being married so quickly after her arrival in England."

"I cannot see any point in waiting."

The Marquis put down his glass.

"You have certainly taken me by surprise, Branscombe. Of course, as Mirabelle's Guardian I can see the advantages she would gain by marrying you, just as I can also see the advantages to you."

There was no need to say more, and he saw the flicker of greed in the Earl's eyes as he asked almost too casually for it to be natural:

"I believe she has a large fortune?"

"Very large!" the Marquis agreed. "In fact, an astronomical one, and it is likely to increase."

"Then I presume I have your permission," the Earl said with an undoubted note of triumph in his voice, "to pay my addresses to your Ward and ask for her hand in marriage?"

"Of course I cannot refuse such a request," the Marquis replied formally, "but there is one condition."

"Condition?"

"It is that since whoever Mirabelle marries will have the handling of her entire fortune when he marries her, I want my Ward to receive a certain sum of money from her bridegroom which will be hers unconditionally, and for life."

As he spoke, the Marquis thought he had phrased what he had said so cleverly that he had not in fact lied but had manipulated the words "Mirabelle" and "Ward" so that he spoke the truth.

He was aware that the Earl was looking at him in astonishment.

"What would be the point of that?" he enquired.

"I wish my Ward to feel independent of her husband."

"I assure you I will always be extremely generous."

"At the same time," the Marquis continued, "we all know of cases where a rich woman has been unable to obtain a penny of her own fortune once it became by marriage legally her husband's property."

"As I have said, I am known to be generous," the Earl boasted.

"I still have to safe-guard my Ward's interests," the Marquis persisted.

There was a little pause, then the Earl asked:

"How much are you proposing I should settle on her?"

"I was thinking, considering that Mirabelle's fortune is so colossal," the Marquis said, "that my Ward should receive on her wedding-day a capital sum which would bring her in a thousand pounds a year!"

"That is impossible!" the Earl snapped.

"Impossible?" the Marquis queried.

"I did not expect you to make such a strange request," the Earl said aggressively, "but as you have done so, I have to admit to you, of course in confidence, that it would be very difficult if not impossible for me to do what you ask."

"I find that incredible," the Marquis replied.

The Earl walked to the table where there was a bottle of champagne in a silver ice-bucket, and without asking permission he helped himself to another glass.

"I will be frank with you, Alchester," he said after he had drunk some of the champagne, "and explain something which few people know about, but which has left me in a somewhat embarrassing position."

The Marquis waited, thinking this was something he had not expected.

"My grandfather was a rich man," the Earl began, "but a very extravagant one. He also had a large family, all of whom he provided for in what my father, as the eldest son, thought was an over-generous manner."

The Marquis smiled slightly, knowing that it was traditional in aristocratic families that while the eldest son had everything, the younger members were usually kept on very short commons.

"My grandfather," the Earl continued, "was also, as I am, extremely proud of our ancestry. You will therefore understand that when Prince Frederick of Melderstein suggested that he should marry his youngest daughter, my grandfather was delighted."

The Marquis raised his eye-brows.

"I know Prince Frederick, but I had no idea that his wife was your aunt."

"She is not," the Earl said, "and that is the whole point of what I am telling you."

The way he spoke told the Marquis he did not like being interrupted, and he went on:

"The marriage was arranged, and because it was made quite obvious to my grandfather that the Prince expected a very large dowry with his bride, he behaved in what I consider a very reprehensible manner."

"What did he do?" the Marquis asked, already knowing the answer.

"He settled a considerable sum of money on my aunt, and, for some reason I have never been able to ascertain, made it over to her on the day before the wedding actually took place."

The Marquis was listening intently but he did not interrupt, and the Earl said dramatically:

"Then she disappeared!"

"Disappeared?"

"On the night before the wedding! As she took no possessions with her, it was thought at the time, and I still think so, that it was a case of foul play. She was obviously murdered!"

"But you have never been able to prove it?"

"How could we when there was no sign of her body?" the Earl asked sharply.

"And what this means," the Marquis said slowly, "is that you cannot touch the money that was settled on her by your grandfather."

"That is so," the Earl agreed. "At least the Courts informed me I cannot do so until after a lapse of twenty-five years. Then, I believe, she will be assumed dead and the money will revert to me."

"How much longer have you to wait?"

"Another five years or so."

The Marquis's lips twisted in what Peregrine would have thought was his cruel smile.

"I understand your predicament, Branscombe," he said, "but you will understand that in the light of these unfortunate circumstances I could not give my permission for you to marry my Ward."

"You would *refuse* me?"

The Earl's voice shook with astonishment.

"I am afraid so," the Marquis replied, "unless of course you could scrape together enough money to make my Ward independent."

He gave a little laugh.

"It should not be difficult to borrow any sum you fancy on such expectations."

The Earl walked restlessly across the hearth-rug, and, having drunk the champagne he had in his glass, once again he helped himself.

The Marquis waited and finally the Earl said:

"If I settle enough to bring in your Ward five hundred pounds a year, would you be satisfied?"

"Supposing we make it seven hundred fifty pounds?" the Marquis suggested. "After all, with our horses winning the Derby side by side, we should be able to come to an amicable agreement on slightly lower stakes."

The Earl thought for a moment. Then he said:

"Very well, but I consider you have driven a hard bargain which I had not expected, Alchester."

"I am not thinking of you but of my Ward," the Marquis replied. "I presume now you would like to see her?"

"Of course," the Earl agreed. "And I would like to suggest that the marriage take place without much delay. I know that would please the Queen, and I have my own reasons for not wishing to wait unnecessarily long before my marriage."

The Marquis had the idea that his reasons were wholly financial, but he merely rang the bell and when a footman appeared he said:

"Ask my Ward to join me."

"Very good, M'Lord."

As the door was shut again, the Earl said:

"I was thinking that I would like to introduce Mirabelle to London as my wife, rather than have you taking her there first as a débutante and then announcing our engagement."

The Marquis thought that the Earl must be in more urgent need of funds than he had intimated.

That he was in such a hurry certainly coincided with his own plans. But he had no intention of appearing too eager.

"Do you think that would be a good idea?" he asked. "Surely your relatives will think it very strange if they do not meet your future wife before you are married? And I suppose my own family would wish to meet you."

"I see no reason for those extremely boring family gatherings," the Earl said sharply. "What I think would be far easier for both of us would be for the marriage to take place here in your private Chapel, and then we can astound the Social World when it is a *fait accompli.*"

"That is certainly something that commends itself to me," the Marquis said, "because if there is one thing I really dislike, it is a wedding. At the same time, it is something I would first wish to discuss with my Ward—and alone."

He thought as he spoke that if the Earl suggested a hasty marriage to Kistna without his preparing her for it, she might easily refuse to entertain such an idea. Worse still, she might give the whole game away.

The Earl had no time to acquiesce when the door opened and Kistna came in.

She was looking lovely, the Marquis decided at first glance. He also knew she was very frightened.

Her green gown was an elaborate and fashionable creation that was obviously extremely costly. Her hair was equally elaborate and she wore a tiny cluster of real snowdrops at her neck which made her look the embodiment of Spring.

She advanced towards them, the Marquis noted, at exactly the correct pace, stopping at the right place to curtsey. Then, with her eyes very wide, she looked only at him.

Because he knew how nervous she was, the Marquis took her hand in his and felt her fingers trembling like the wings of a captured bird.

He gave it a gentle pressure to give her confidence and said:

"I want to present, my dear, the Earl of Branscombe, who has asked if he may pay his addresses to you, and I can only commend him as a most suitable husband."

With difficulty the Marquis kept the sarcasm out of his voice.

The Earl bowed and there was no doubt that with his skilfully tied cravat, his close-fitting whipcord riding-coat, and his highly polished Hessian boots, he was a very handsome and fashionable man.

"Your Guardian, Miss Chester," he said to Kistna, "has given his permission to our union and I therefore have the honour to ask you to be my wife."

He put out his hand as he spoke, and the Marquis, feeling that Kistna was incapable of speech or movement, gave the hand he had been holding to the Earl.

He raised it to his lips.

"I feel sure," he said, "that we will deal extremely well together."

Still Kistna did not speak, and the Marquis said hastily:

"I think this calls for a glass of champagne, and I must of course drink your health."

He moved towards the table and poured champagne into two glasses, one for himself and one for Kistna.

He carried them back to where she was still standing, while the Earl had begun a monologue which made him sound more conceited with every word he spoke.

"As your Guardian will doubtless tell you," he said, "His Majesty relies on me greatly for advice and support, and the Queen asks my opinion on everything she does. It is a great responsibility and one which I hope my wife will share with me, just as I hope she will share the many demands made on me in Hampshire where the Branscombes have for many centuries played the leading part in County affairs."

The Marquis put a glass of champagne into Kistna's hand, then he raised his own to say:

"Let me drink to both of you! May you have many years of happiness!"

"Thank you," the Earl said.

He drained all the champagne that was left in his glass, while Kistna took only a tiny sip.

She was so pale that the Marquis thought suddenly that she was as white as the snowdrops at her neck, and he was afraid she might faint.

"Why do you not fetch Mr. Wallingham?" he suggested. "I am sure he would wish to hear the happy news."

"I . . . I will . . . do that," Kistna said in what seemed to be a strangled voice.

She put down her glass on the nearest table and hurried towards the door.

"She is young and shy," the Marquis explained, as if he felt he must make some excuse for her silence.

The Earl smiled.

"That is an attribute I find desirable in my future wife."

There was something in the way he spoke that made the Marquis want to hit him.

Then as he moved towards the bell to ask for more champagne, he was sure that Kistna would not return and he hoped that the Earl would not find such shyness suspicious.

As the Marquis had suspected, there was no sign of Kistna when Peregrine arrived to drink to the Earl's health and complimented him in such an insincere manner that he was forced to frown at him.

The Earl, however, was so supremely confident of his own importance that when he had finally driven away, the Marquis was quite sure he had never for one moment thought either that his suit would be rejected or that his future bride and her Guardian were not delighted at the idea of such an advantageous marriage.

"Blast him!" the Marquis said to Peregrine as they turned away from the front door. "I dislike him more every time I see him! All I can say is that if the King can put up with Branscombe, he certainly should not jibe at the Reform Bill."

This was a point of bitter controversy in the Houses of Parliament and over the whole country, with the King making every possible excuse not to approve any of the reforms which were long overdue.

Peregrine, however, was not listening.

"What did Kistna think of him?" he asked.

"I have no idea, as she did not speak."

The Marquis had thought that in fact it was rather a good thing that she appeared so shy. At the same time, he thought it was unlike her, as she had too much character to behave in such a hesitant fashion.

"Where is she now?" Peregrine asked.

"Upstairs, I suppose," the Marquis replied. "I will send a servant to find her."

"If she is upset, perhaps it would be best for me to go and look for her," Peregrine suggested.

Then he hesitated and added:

"No—I think you should go. It will be you she wants to see."

The Marquis did not argue. He merely said:

"She will be in her Sitting-Room, I suppose, but I need a drink first. I cannot tell you how intolerable the Earl was, harping continually on his position at Court and of course his own importance."

"What have you done about Kistna's future?" Peregrine asked. "When he knows the truth, I am quite certain he will treat her as he treated Dulcie and chuck her out without a penny."

"I have thought of that," the Marquis said, "and I have given my consent only on condition that he settles a capital sum on her to bring in seven hundred fifty pounds a year."

His lips twisted before he added:

"I tried for a thousand, but Branscombe informed me that he was extremely short of money, and I even had to suggest that he borrow the money to provide the seven hundred fifty pounds on which we finally agreed."

"Why should he be so hard up?" Peregrine asked. "I always thought he was warm in the pocket."

"So did I," the Marquis agreed, "but apparently his grandfather, who was as big a snob as he is, settled a large sum on his aunt because she was to marry Prince Frederick of Melderstein. But she disappeared before the wedding, and although Branscombe is convinced that she was murdered, they have never been able to find the body."

"Now that you mention it," Peregrine said, "I remember my father telling me about that scandal. Apparently there was a tremendous commotion at the time because as it was a Royal Wedding, Crowned Heads had arrived from all over Europe."

He laughed.

"So not only the bride was lost, but so was the money which was settled on her! Can you imagine how much it must irk Branscombe not to be able to get his hands on it?"

"Now I know why he was so mad-keen to win the Derby," the Marquis said. "Apart from the honour and glory, two thousand eight hundred pounds is not to be sneezed at!"

"No, of course not," Peregrine agreed, "and he will try even harder for the Gold Cup. You will have to watch him, especially if he employs Jake Smith again."

"He had better not try any tricks at Ascot," the Marquis said. "If he does, I swear I will have both his horse and his jockey disqualified. I only wish I could disqualify him as well!"

"You will have punished him quite enough when he realises that Kistna has not a penny to her name."

"That, as I have now found out, will hurt even more than I thought it would," the Marquis said with satisfaction.

Then, as if speaking of Kistna brought her to mind, he said angrily:

"What the hell is she waiting for? Branscombe has gone, and I want to talk to her!"

CHAPTER SEVEN

―――― ◦⳽◦ ――――

"*D*INNER IS SERVED, M'Lord!"

The Marquis looked round at the Butler from the hearth-rug where he was standing talking to Peregrine.

"Miss Kistna is not down yet," he said sharply.

"Mrs. Dawes asked me to tell Your Lordship that Miss Kistna will not be coming down for dinner."

The Marquis did not reply, but there was a definite scowl between his eyes as he put down his glass and walked with Peregrine towards the Dining-Room.

When he had gone upstairs to speak to Kistna after the Earl had left, he had knocked on her door and it had been opened by Mrs. Dawes.

To the Marquis's surprise, she had stepped out into the passage, closing the door of the *Boudoir* behind her.

"I want to see Miss Kistna," the Marquis said sharply.

"I think, M'Lord, it'd be wise, if Your Lordship'll excuse me saying so, to leave her be," Mrs. Dawes answered. "She's upset at the moment and I'm trying to persuade her to lie down."

The Marquis's lips tightened.

There were several things he wanted to say, but not to Mrs. Dawes.

"Then tell Miss Kistna I shall be looking forward to seeing her at dinner," he replied.

Now when she refused to appear, he found himself feeling annoyed, although there was another emotion involved to which he did not wish to put a name.

Dinner as usual was excellent, but the Marquis helped himself absent-mindedly to the dishes he was offered, and his conversation with Peregrine was spasmodic, there being moments when they both sat in silence.

Finally when both gentlemen refused port and the servants left the room, the Marquis said:

"I have been thinking that my revenge on Branscombe will be even more effective than I expected. If he has to borrow the money I require for Kistna, he will doubtless have to pay a high rate of interest."

Peregrine did not reply and after a moment the Marquis said:

"You do not seem very elated. I thought you disliked Branscombe."

"I do," Peregrine replied, "but I do not like what your hatred of him is doing to you."

"Doing to me?" the Marquis asked in surprise.

Peregrine felt for words.

"My mother used to say that hatred is a boomerang that will come back to hurt the person who hates more than it hurts their victim."

"I understand what you are trying to tell me in a somewhat garbled manner," the Marquis said in a lofty tone. "At the same time, you can hardly expect me to let Branscombe get off scot-free, considering the way he behaved at the Derby."

Peregrine did not answer and the Marquis went on:

"I consider my plan to avenge myself very subtle, and, what is more, it will not only humiliate him but hurt him where he will mind it most—in his pocket!"

"I am sick of talking about him," Peregrine exclaimed irritably. "The whole thing is turning you into a monster, and I would rather Branscombe cheated his way to victory in a dozen Derbies rather than watch you plotting and intriguing in what I consider an extremely undignified manner."

The Marquis was astounded.

In all the years he had known Peregrine, when he had often thought they were as close in their friendship as if they were brothers, he had never been spoken to in such a manner.

He was just about to reply aggressively when he realised that the servants would be waiting for them to leave the Dining-Room and might conceivably overhear what they were saying.

Instead he rose to his feet, and as he did so he rang the gold hand-bell which stood on the table in front of him.

The door to the Pantry opened immediately.

"You rang, M'Lord?" the Butler enquired.

"Bring the decanter of brandy into the Library."

The Marquis walked from the Dining-Room, considering, as he went, how he could refute Peregrine's accusations and show him that he was being exceedingly unfair and was, to all intents and purposes, championing the Earl.

They reached the Library, where the Marquis preferred to sit if he was alone or had only masculine company.

Although it was not yet dusk, the candles were lit and the colourful leather-bound volumes decorating the walls up to the exquisitely painted ceiling showed to their best advantage in the soft light.

The Marquis, however, was intent on his own thoughts, and as the Butler set down the cut-glass decanter on the table beside the armchair, having first proferred a glass to Peregrine, the Marquis asked:

"I presume you have sent Miss Kistna her dinner upstairs?"

"I sent up the first course, M'Lord," the Butler replied, "but it was returned untouched with a message that the young lady did not require any dinner."

He left the Library as he finished speaking and the Marquis said angrily:

"I have never heard such nonsense! Of course she wants dinner when she is still weak from years of starvation!"

"She is obviously upset."

"Upset?" the Marquis questioned. "What has she to be upset about? I thought when I looked at Branscombe, obnoxious though we know him to be, he is quite a fine figure of a man from a woman's point of view."

"Presumably Kistna does not think so."

"Why should you say that?" the Marquis asked.

"I should have thought the answer to that question was obvious."

"Because she is sulking upstairs? What is the matter with the girl? God in Heaven, she has the chance of making the most brilliant marriage any woman could desire! She certainly has a better future than the one she had in mind of earning her own living."

"Is that what she suggested she should do?"

"She said something about it," the Marquis said vaguely. "Of course I told her the only qualifications she had were for working in an Orphanage, and I should have thought she had had enough of that."

"Really, Linden, such a remark was needlessly brutal!" Peregrine said scathingly.

Once again the Marquis looked at him in astonishment.

"I was attempting to make Kistna understand how fortunate she is. After all, she knows nothing about Branscombe. Why should she not want to marry him?"

There was silence. Then as the Marquis was obviously waiting for an answer, Peregrine, as if he was goaded into a reply, said:

"Why should she want to, when she loves—someone else?"

The Marquis's lips parted as if to question such a statement. Then the expression on his face changed and for a moment he just stood staring at Peregrine as if he had never seen him before.

Then abruptly without another word he went from the Library, slamming the door behind him.

He walked along the corridor, through the Hall, and up the Grand Staircase.

He moved forcefully and determinedly until he reached Kistna's *Boudoir,* where he stood still, as if he was considering what he should say, or perhaps questioning his own feelings.

Then he knocked.

There was no answer and he thought she must have gone to bed as Mrs. Dawes had wished her to do.

He went to the next door and knocked again. He heard a movement, then the door was opened and it was Mrs. Dawes who stood there.

When she saw the Marquis there was an expression of surprise on her face.

"I came to enquire how Miss Kistna is," he said. "I was worried when I heard she had refused to have any dinner."

"I thought Miss Kistna was with you, M'Lord."

The Marquis shook his head.

"I cannot understand it!" Mrs. Dawes exclaimed. "I was told downstairs that she had refused her dinner, and I thought she must be poorly, so I came up as soon as I'd finished my own meal, only to find the room empty."

As if he would see with his own eyes, the Marquis moved past the Housekeeper into the bedroom.

One glance told him that although the bed had been used, it was empty.

"When I came in a few minutes ago," Mrs. Dawes was saying, "I felt certain Miss Kistna had changed her mind and gone downstairs to Your Lordship. The wardrobe door was open, as Your Lordship can see, and I thought she must have put on one of her pretty gowns and done it up herself."

"She is not in the Library," the Marquis said, "and I can hardly imagine she would be sitting alone in the Salon."

"No, of course not, M'Lord," Mrs. Dawes replied. "But now I thinks of it—that could have been Miss Kistna!"

"What could?"

"I never thought it at the time," Mrs. Dawes said, "but when I came into the bedroom a short time ago I realised the curtains had not been pulled, so I went to the window. As I did so, I thinks I sees someone in white crossing the lawn towards the lake."

"I cannot believe Miss Kistna would want to go there at this time of the night," the Marquis said.

"She might have thought she needed a little fresh air," Mrs. Dawes answered. "She was upset, very upset, M'Lord, and it's not good for her to be in such a state when she's still so weak from what she went through in that terrible place."

"No, of course not," the Marquis agreed.

"I've never known her so unhappy, M'Lord. It broke my heart to see her. It was almost as if she'd had bad news."

The Marquis was aware that Mrs. Dawes was consumed with curiosity. Then as he did not reply, she said:

"If I was you, M'Lord, I'd see if I could find her. It's not right for her to be walking about in the dark, and in the state she's in. Accidents can happen at night."

The Marquis looked sharply at the Housekeeper. Then without saying a word he went from the bedroom.

He did not return by the way he had come down the Grand Staircase, where footmen were on duty in the Hall, but instead went very quickly down the corridor to where there was a secondary staircase.

This led to the East Wing of the great house, where there was a door which opened directly onto the garden.

It was locked, but it took the Marquis only a few moments to turn the key and pull back the two bolts. Then he was out on the lawn which stretched from the house down to the lake.

He realised, from what Mrs. Dawes had said, that the person she thought might be Kistna had been moving towards the end of the lake which was obscured from the house by trees and shrubs.

It was strange, he thought, that she should be going in that particular direction. Then a sudden idea came to him which made him quicken his pace.

It came back to his mind how as they were crossing the bridge which spanned the lake, Kistna had looked down at the sunshine playing on the water and asked:

"Do you ever swim here? I am sure you must have done so when you were a boy."

"Very often," the Marquis had replied with a smile, "but only in this part. The other end is dangerous."

"Why?" Kistna had enquired.

"It has what the gardeners call 'shifting sands,'" the Marquis had replied. "There are certain undercurrents as well, and a man was drowned there many years ago. My father put it out-of-bounds to me and to everybody else."

"I am sure you obeyed him," Kistna had said laughingly.

"Of course," the Marquis had replied. "I was a model child!"

Now the light-hearted conversation came back to him in a sinister way, but he told himself that even to entertain such an idea was quite ridiculous.

At the same time, he began to move faster, and now as he reached first the banks of shrubs, then the almond and cherry trees which, covered in blossom, were very beautiful, he began to move even quicker.

He tried to tell himself that the white figure Mrs. Dawes thought she had seen was undoubtedly the white lilac, or perhaps, as it was growing dusk, it was merely the petals lying on the ground which had given the illusion of there being a figure.

Yet, because he was afraid, he began to run.

He had forgotten what a long way it was to the end of the lake and how thick the lilac and syringa had grown in the past years.

Then when he was feeling breathless and, despite being extremely fit, his heart seemed to be pounding in his breast, he emerged through a thick belt of trees to see the end of the lake—and Kistna.

He was relieved that she was there and at the same time was almost embarrassed by his own fears, and he came to a standstill in the shelter of the trees and stood looking at her.

He saw that she was standing where the bank was high above a pool at the spot which was considered dangerous and where the man had been drowned.

Kistna appeared to be bending over. The Marquis was unable to see what she was doing and thought she must be picking flowers, which seemed odd at this time of the evening.

Then he saw that on the bank beside her was something large and bulky.

He stared, wondering what it could be, and in the faint light coming from the last of the sunset he realised that it was a brown linen bag.

He recognised it as being one of the laundry bags in which the house-maids collected the sheets and towels which were to be taken downstairs to be washed.

The Marquis wondered why Kistna had brought the bag with her.

Then he saw that now she was bending down to tie something round her ankles.

He stared as she knotted it several times before he saw that there was a cord attached to the bag.

Kistna straightened herself and turned to look at the water beneath her. With a shock of sheer horror the Marquis realised what she intended to do.

He reached her in a few strides, and when he was beside her and his hands went out to take hold of her, she gave a little cry.

"No . . . no! Go . . . away! Leave me alone . . . you are not to . . . stop me!"

She tried to struggle with him as she spoke, and he knew that she was standing on the very edge of the pool and that with one unwary move-ment she would topple over and into the water.

He held her close against him and tried to lift her to safety but found that the heavy bag to which her ankles were attached made her immobile. He guessed then that it contained stones.

"How could you think of doing anything so wrong—so wicked?" he asked.

"I cannot . . . help it," she answered.

"Of course you can," he scolded.

His voice was raw because he had been so afraid.

"If you had only come a . . . few seconds later . . ." she whispered, "it would have been too . . . late . . . I would not be here . . . and no-one would ever have . . . found me."

The Marquis's arms tightened about her. Then he said:

"Why should you want to do anything so crazy and so utterly and completely mad?"

He was still holding her close against him and she made an impulsive little movement as if, despite his being there, she would still do as she had intended and drown herself.

The Marquis's arms held her still, and as if she knew that any further struggle would be futile, she suddenly went limp and her head rested against his shoulder.

"I do not understand," he said. "How could you even think of anything so terrible?"

"Papa would have . . . thought it . . . wicked of me," Kistna said in a voice he could barely hear, "but . . . Mama . . . would have . . . understood."

"What would she have understood?" the Marquis asked, as if he were speaking to a child.

"That I . . . I cannot . . . marry that man! He is . . . bad . . . I knew it when he . . . touched my . . . h-hand."

"Bad?" the Marquis questioned. "Why should you say that?"

"I am . . . sure of it. There is . . . something about . . . him . . . something that made me . . . afraid . . . and besides . . . I cannot . . . m-marry anyone!"

"Why not?"

He saw that she was about to reply. Then, as if she realised to whom she was speaking, she turned her face and hid it against him.

"I want you to answer that question," the Marquis said, and his voice was gentle.

"N-no . . . I . . . cannot . . . tell . . . you."

The Marquis put his fingers under her chin and turned her face up to his.

"Look at me, Kistna!" he said. "Look at me and tell me why you cannot marry anyone!"

As he looked down at her, he could see the unhappiness in her eyes and the tear-stains on her cheeks.

It seemed to him for a moment as if she looked as pathetic and miserable as she had when he had first seen her.

Yet, with her body close against his, he knew that during the time she had been at the Abbey she had changed and become very different from the miserable, starving creature who he had thought at first was so ugly.

Now she had a beauty that was different from anything he had seen in any other woman, and as he felt her trembling because of his questions, he knew that never before in his whole life had he felt as he was feeling now.

Because she was so young and because she had come to him from the Orphanage, it had never struck the Marquis that Kistna was a desirable woman, like Isobel or any of the other women with whom he had amused himself.

He had been so intent on educating her and preparing her to be the Earl's wife that he had not thought of her as a human being but merely as an instrument he could use to injure the man he hated.

Now as she looked up at him and he saw her answer in the depths of her expressive eyes, and as he was aware that she was quivering against him, not from fear but because he was touching her, he felt a strange rapture sweep over him.

"Tell me," he said, and now his voice was very soft and beguiling, "tell me why you say you will never be married and why you cannot marry the Earl."

He knew that the deep note in his voice and the nearness of him affected her. Then, as if he took her will away from her and it was impossible for her to withstand him, her eyes looked into his, and in a broken little voice that was very near to tears she whispered:

"I . . . I . . . love   you . . . I . . . c-cannot . . . help   it . . . I love . . . you . . . how could I . . . let . . . another . . . man . . . t-touch me?"

"No other man shall!"

His lips were on hers.

He felt her stiffen as if from sheer shock, then she surrendered herself to the insistence of his kiss.

He did not know a woman's mouth could be so soft, sweet, innocent, and yet at the same time so exciting in a way he had never known before.

As his arms tightened round her, the Marquis knew that he had found something he had always been seeking. While it had eluded him and he was not quite certain what it was, he had known that it was there, only out of reach.

Now it was his and he recognised it as love, the real love that had nothing in common with the fiery but easily quenched passion he had known with so many other women.

To Kistna it was as if the Heavens had opened, and the Marquis, who she had identified long ago as St. Michael, carried her up into the divine light which she had always been aware was part of love.

She heard music and there were the songs of angels combined with the scent of flowers.

This was the ultimate wonder, the beauty she had always looked for but which in all its perfection could only come to her through somebody she loved.

She knew that she loved the Marquis as her mother had loved her father, and his lips holding her captive gave her a beauty which was a part of God.

When the Marquis raised his head, she said in a voice that vibrated with the rapture he had aroused in her:

"I . . . I love you . . . and what I . . . wanted before I . . . died was for you to . . . kiss me. . . ."

"How can you wish to die when you belong to me?" he asked. "And I know now that I can never lose you—never let you go!"

It seemed for a moment as if the last rays of the sun lit her face, and she stammered:

"D-do you . . . mean I can . . . stay with you . . . and not have to . . . m-marry. . . ?"

"You will marry me!" the Marquis said firmly.

The start she gave told him that the idea had never crossed her mind, and he said:

"You must try to forgive me, my darling, for having been so absurdly blind, so stupid as not to realise until now that I love you and you are everything I want my wife to be."

"Do you . . . mean that . . . do you really mean it?"

"I love you!" the Marquis said simply.

He was kissing her again, kissing her with long, slow, demanding kisses which seemed to Kistna to draw her soul from between her lips so that she became his and she was no longer herself but part of him. . . .

A long time later, when the first stars were coming out overhead, the Marquis said in a voice which sounded strange and very unlike his own:

"I think, my precious one, we should move from this very precarious position. If you fell into the lake now, we might both be drowned!"

Kistna gave a little cry of horror.

"You must be careful . . . very careful."

The Marquis smiled.

"That is what I should be saying to you, to stand very still and hold on to me while I untie that rope from round your ankles."

As he spoke he bent down and released her, then he picked up the linen sack, which was in fact very heavy, and threw it into the water.

As it splashed and sank out of sight, the Marquis knew with a shudder that if he had been just a few seconds later it would have been impossible to save Kistna and she would have drowned as she had intended.

Nobody would ever have known what had happened to her, and it was doubtful if her body would ever have been recovered.

As if he was afraid even to think of anything so horrifying, he lifted her in his arms and carried her away from the water's edge towards the trees.

"I ought to be very, very angry with you!" he said.

"P-please forgive me," Kistna pleaded. "It was . . . only because I . . . loved you so . . . desperately . . . that I would rather . . . die than leave you."

"You will never leave me!" the Marquis said. "I know now, as I should have known long ago, that I cannot contemplate life without you."

"I thought," she said in a low voice, "that if you . . . would love me
. . . for a month . . . a week . . . even a d-day . . . I would be . . .
grateful and try to ask for . . . nothing more."

"I intend that you shall have a great deal more," the Marquis replied.
"Me, for instance, as long as we both shall live!"

Kistna gave a little cry.

"That is what I want, to be with you . . . to love you and be in . . .
Heaven."

The Marquis set her down on the ground in the shade of an almond
tree.

"If Heaven is here on earth," he said, "that is what I shall give you, but
you will have to make it a Heaven for me too."

"That is what it will be . . . if you are . . . there," Kistna answered,
and lifted her lips to his. . . .

Later they walked slowly back to the house, taking a long time over it.

Everything Kistna said seemed to the Marquis to invite her kisses, and
when they stepped out of the darkness into the light, he thought that love
had given her a beauty that was like the sun. She radiated a happiness
which was linked with the vibrations coming from himself.

Holding hands, they walked into the Library to find Peregrine asleep in
an armchair with the *Times* on his knees.

But before they could speak his name, as if in his dreams he sensed
their presence, his eyes opened and he jerked himself into wakefulness.

"Where have you been. . . . ?" he began.

Then as he saw the expressions on their faces, he gave a cry and rose to
his feet.

"What has happened?" he asked, knowing it was an unnecessary question.

It was Kistna who answered him—Kistna who looked so different from
the way she had ever looked before that it was hard to recognise her.

"We are . . . to be . . . married!" she said, and it was a paean of
happiness.

Peregrine gave a cry of delight and flung the *Times* high in the air.

"Hoorah!" he cried. "That is what I hoped! Congratulations, Linden! I
thought sooner or later you would see sense!"

"Sense?" the Marquis questioned. "Is that what you call it?"

He spoke lightly, then turned to smile at Kistna, and as Peregrine saw the expression in his eyes, he knew that all he wanted for his friend had come true.

After a great many false starts and a number of disappointments, the Marquis had won the race for love which had always eluded him.

Peregrine knew as they looked at each other that he was for the moment forgotten and that he intruded on something so beautiful that it was almost a shock when he said:

"We must drink to this! May I order a bottle of champagne?"

"I think it is more important that Kistna has something to eat," the Marquis said.

"I am too happy to be hungry," she replied.

"Nevertheless, because it is good for you I want you to eat something to please me."

"You know I would do . . . anything that . . . pleases you," she said in a low voice.

They were standing close to each other and once again they were looking into each other's eyes as if they spoke without words and could hardly believe the glory they found there.

"You rang, M'Lord?" the Butler asked from the door.

With an effort the Marquis came back to reality.

"Ask the Chef to prepare a light supper for Miss Kistna, and bring a bottle of champagne."

"Very good, M'Lord."

The Butler was just about to shut the door when there was a footman at his side and he took from the man a silver salver on which there reposed a letter and brought it to the Marquis.

"This arrived, M'Lord, a few minutes ago. It reached the Post Office, I understand, too late to be delivered at the usual time, but as it is marked 'Urgent' and comes from abroad, the Post Master sent his son up to the house with it."

The Marquis took the letter from the salver.

"Thank him," he said to the Butler, "and reward the boy."

"I'll see to it, M'Lord."

The Marquis, looking down at the letter, said with a smile:

"It is from Rome and it must therefore concern my Ward, Mirabelle."

He smiled at Kistna and added:

"There is no need now, my darling, for you to have to impersonate her or anybody else. All I want is that you should be you, and my wife!"

"H-how soon can we be . . . m-married?"

"I have no intention of waiting for one moment longer than is necessary," the Marquis replied. "Nor do I intend to have a large and fashionable wedding."

Kistna gave a little cry.

"Oh, no, please . . . we want nobody there but . . . ourselves."

"And Peregrine," the Marquis added. "He will have to give you away, and be Best Man and our witness!"

"Thank you," Peregrine said wryly. "I am only surprised you do not wish me to play the organ as well!"

"I would make you do that if I thought you were capable of it!" the Marquis teased.

"Of course we want him at our wedding," Kistna said.

Then she looked at the Marquis and said almost nervously:

"It is . . . true? It is really . . . true that you will . . . marry me?"

"Very true!" the Marquis said definitely.

Then as if he could not help himself he put his arm around her and drew her close to him.

She put her cheek in a caressing little gesture against his shoulder. Then as if she was embarrassed by her own emotions she said:

"Open the letter. After all, it is marked 'Urgent.' "

As she spoke she was afraid that it might contain something which would prevent the Marquis from being married as soon as he intended.

As if he too felt anxious, the Marquis walked to his desk and, picking up his gold and jewelled letter-opener, slit the envelope and drew out a thin sheet of paper.

He read it while Kistna watched him with eyes which Peregrine thought expressed her love very eloquently.

The Marquis finished the letter and looked up and smiled.

"They say that lightning never strikes twice," he said, "but obviously one marriage breeds another!"

"What has happened?" Peregrine enquired.

"Mirabelle's aunt writes to tell me that she has fallen in love with the young Prince di Borghese, and he with her. As he is an extremely rich young man, there is no question of his being interested only in her fortune, and she therefore hopes I will give my permission for them to become engaged and for the marriage to take place before the end of the summer."

The Marquis put out his hand towards Kistna.

"I think, my darling," he said, "you and I might include Rome in our honeymoon tour and attend my Ward's wedding, which will be very different in every way from ours."

"Our honeymoon!" Kistna murmured, feeling that word was more important to her than anything else the Marquis had said.

"Our honeymoon abroad," the Marquis said with a smile. "I want us to be alone, which would be difficult in England, where everybody will want to meet you."

Kistna gave a little cry.

"Then please . . . please . . . let us go abroad . . . I want to be . . . alone with you."

The way she spoke was very moving, and the Marquis threw the letter down on his desk and put his arms round her.

"We will be married the day after tomorrow," he said firmly. "I will send Anderson to London to get a Special Licence, and before anyone is aware of what has happened we will be on our way to Paris!"

"No, to . . . Heaven!" Kistna said softly. "Our Heaven . . . yours and mine."

The room in which they had dinner was small but very attractive. As Kistna had said when she first saw it, the small Manor the Marquis owned a little way off the Dover Road was just like a doll's house.

"What can you want with a house there, when you have the Abbey?" she had asked when the Marquis told her where they would spend the first night of their honeymoon.

"I keep a change of horses on the Dover Road, and I prefer them to be in my own stables rather than in those of a Posting Inn."

"You are very grand!" she teased.

"No—practical," he answered. "I must have known, through some inner sense, that one day the Manor would be a perfect place in which to start our honeymoon."

They had been married in the Chapel at the Abbey and it had seemed to Kistna redolent with the faith of ages.

She fancied that the monks who had first worshipped there were joining in the prayers said by the Marquis's Chaplain and that she could hear their deep voices behind the music of the organ.

It was on Peregrine's arm that she had walked into the Chapel to find the Marquis waiting for her.

"Mrs. Dawes says it is unlucky for a bridegroom to see his future wife on their wedding-day, before the service," Kistna had said, "and I want to be very, very lucky, so I will just stay in my room until I meet you in the Chapel."

"You have brought me luck already," the Marquis replied. "I have never felt so happy, so content, or so excited about the future."

"That is what I want you to feel. But supposing I . . . bore you, as I have been told you have been . . . bored by so many . . . beautiful women?"

"What I feel for you is very different," the Marquis said firmly, and knew that was the truth.

Now as he looked at Kistna across the small table which had been decorated with white flowers, he wondered, as he had a thousand times already, how he had not recognised her as his ideal from the moment they had first met.

In the candlelight, wearing a white gown with real orange-blossoms in her hair, she looked so lovely, and the very embodiment of youth, beauty, and happiness, that the Marquis thought only music could describe her adequately.

"I love you!" he said.

As if there were no other words that could express what they were both feeling, Kistna replied:

"I love . . . you . . . but I also . . . worship you because to me you have always seemed to be . . . St. Michael . . . who who came to rescue me from the darkness of Hell and lift me into the light of Heaven."

"My precious!" the Marquis said in his deep voice.

Then as if he could not bear there to be a table between them, he stretched out his hands to draw her to her feet.

They walked from the Dining-Room, where they had sat for a long time, up the twisting oak staircase to the old-fashioned bedroom with its oak four-poster bed.

The room was lit by only three candles on a small table beside the blue-curtained bed, and Kistna was aware that neither her maid nor the Marquis's valet was waiting up for them.

As the Marquis shut the door behind him, she felt an excitement seep over her which he thought once again gave her a beauty that was so exquisite and so spiritual that it could only be part of the Divine.

Then as his arms went round her and his lips sought her, he knew that their love was very human.

He kissed her passionately, demandingly, before he said:

"I adore you! But I will try to remember how young you are and that I must not frighten you, my precious little love."

"I shall never be frightened by you except when you are . . . angry with me," Kistna answered. "You love me and I know that everything you do is perfect and part of God."

"My darling, my wonderful little wife, I adore you."

Then the Marquis was kissing her until there was no need for words and the light of love enveloped them until they were dazzled by the glory of it.

A long time later, when the candles were guttering low, Kistna said:

"I have just remembered something!"

"What is it, my precious?" the Marquis answered.

Then as he looked at her lying against his shoulder he put out his hand to touch her hair.

"How can you be so beautiful?"

"You are . . . quite sure you still . . . think so?"

He smiled.

"Every moment I am with you, every time I touch you," he answered, "you seem more beautiful, more adorable, until I am afraid."

"Afraid?" she asked.

"That you might tire of me!"

She gave a little laugh of sheer happiness.

"That is the most marvellous compliment you could pay me, and when

I think of how I looked when you rescued me, words like that are a present of the stars, the moon, and the sun, and no woman could ask for more."

"There are so many things I want to give you," the Marquis said, "but I agree that they could not compare with the stars, the moon, and the sun!"

He pulled her closer, and with his lips against the softness of her skin he said:

"I love you: the things you say, your quick little mind, your soft voice, and your eyes! And as Peregrine said once, you have the most adorable little nose."

"Peregrine said that?" Kistna enquired.

"He said a great many things about you," the Marquis replied, "but if you allow him to flirt with you or you become too fond of him, I shall be jealous."

"There is . . . no need for you to feel jealous of anyone," she said, and now there was a passionate note in her voice. "I love you . . . and now that you have taught me how perfect and beautiful love can be, you can understand there is . . . no other man in the whole world . . . but you."

The Marquis would have kissed her, but she said:

"I was telling you what I have remembered, and it is something I must do on my wedding-day."

"What is it?"

"I promised Mama that when I was married I would open a letter she gave me."

"A letter?" the Marquis questioned.

Kistna's voice was low as she said:

"I think Mama had a presentiment that she and Papa might die from the cholera."

The Marquis pulled her closer to him as she went on:

"There were only a few cases at first, but the authorities were worried, and of course Papa insisted on doing everything he could to help."

Kistna paused, as if she was looking back into the past.

"One day Mama sat for a long time writing at her desk. Then she said to me: 'Bring me your Bible, the one Papa gave you.'"

"I fetched it from my bedroom and she very carefully opened the leather cover where it was attached inside."

"Why did she do that?" the Marquis asked.

"She slipped the letter she had written into it and sealed it," Kistna answered. "Then Mama said: 'I do not want you to read this or even think about it until you are married. Then, on your wedding-day, open it, unless I have told you in the meantime what the letter contains.' "

"You must have been curious," the Marquis remarked.

"I was, in a way," Kistna answered, "but it did not seem very important and Mama never spoke of it again."

"But the Bible has always been with you."

"I told you, it is the only possession I have."

"Very well," the Marquis said. "Open it now, before I prevent you from doing so."

He kissed her shoulder as he spoke, and she pushed the curtain aside and reached out to take her Bible, which was on the table beside the candles.

Then she sat up in bed and the Marquis lay back against the pillows, watching her.

He thought it would be impossible to find anyone so lovely and so attractive and at the same time so completely unselfconscious and so sensitive.

He knew it was not only her love but also an intuition which most young girls did not have which made her responsive to everything he asked of her.

He realised when he made love to her that he had found in one very young woman the completion of himself.

Because he loved her and was thinking more of her feelings than of his own, they had both been aroused spiritually as well as physically to an ecstasy which was to the Marquis an experience he had never known before and which seemed to him perfect in every way.

He knew now that his love for Kistna, which he had been so stupid not to recognise at first, had already deepened and developed until he was confident that he would make her as happy as she made him.

As he looked at her he thought that no other woman could arouse him as she did.

Nor had he ever known before a physical satisfaction combined with a spiritual rapture which ignited within him ideals and new ambitions which he was aware would, in the future, enrich his life.

Kistna had drawn the closely written sheets of paper from the cover of her Bible.

She opened the folded sheets and the Marquis knew there was an expression of sadness in her eyes as she thought of her mother.

He felt as if she moved away from him, and instinctively he put out his hand to touch her.

As if she understood, she turned her head and smiled at him.

"Shall I read you what Mama says?" she asked. "I want to share this with you as we share everything else."

"Of course, my precious."

Kistna held the letter so that the light from the candles shone on it, and in her soft, musical voice she read:

"My dearest, most beloved daughter:

Just in case anything should ever happen to me, I want to tell you a secret about which I have no wish to speak to you at the moment, and especially in front of Papa.

You know how happy we have been together, your father and I, and how I am the most fortunate woman in the world to love and be loved by a man who is so wonderful in every way that he could only have been sent to me by God. But, Kistna, to marry your father I had to do what most people would have said was a very reprehensible act, although it was a courageous one.

I have never talked to you about my family because it was too dangerous for Papa's sake for me to do so.

Had my father been able to find him, I know, because he was a very powerful and in many ways a vindictive man, he would have made us both suffer, and perhaps he would even have destroyed Papa."

As if she was astonished by what she had just read, Kistna looked quickly at the Marquis as if the very sight of him gave her comfort and a feeling of security.

"Go on, my precious one," he said gently, and she continued:

"My father was in fact the seventh Earl of Branscombe! I was his younger daughter, and I think without conceit he was fonder of me than of any of his other children. He was therefore very proud when Prince Frederick of Melderstein asked for my hand in marriage.

Needless to say, I was not consulted as to whether or not I wished to marry him. I was just told how fortunate I was and that I should be overwhelmed with gratitude at the thought of wearing a Royal Crown.

I too might have thought it would be an advantageous position in life, had I not already fallen in love so overwhelmingly, so completely, that for me there was no other man in the whole world."

Kistna gave a little cry.

"That is what I feel for you," she said to the Marquis.

"I will tell you what I feel for you, my lovely one," he replied, "but finish the letter."

Kistna continued:

"I had met your father when I was arranging the flowers in the Church. It was something I did every Saturday and it was one of the tasks that had been allotted to me for several years.

He introduced himself as being the new Curate, and we talked, and after that we met every week, although of course my father and mother had no idea of it.

And because, as you yourself see, he is so handsome and so very, very lovable, I fell wildly in love with him and I knew, although he said nothing, that he loved me too.

When I was told that my father had agreed I should marry Prince Frederick, we both broke down and confessed what we felt for each other, but we knew it was hopeless.

Your father said he could not bear to stay in Europe when I was married to the Prince, so he arranged through one of his relatives in the East India Company to go out to India as a Missionary.

It was known that the ban on Missionary work in India was to be lifted, and because your Papa was so eager to get away, his relative agreed to help him with the fare so that he could go before the other Missionaries had their passages arranged for them.

It was not of your father's choosing, but he learnt that the ship in which he was to sail would leave Tilbury the morning of my wedding-day.

By the time I was beside myself at the thought of losing your father and being forced to marry the Prince, I found it impossible to take any interest in my trousseau, the presents, or the expensive preparations that were being made for my wedding.

Then when the moment came to say goodbye, I knew it was impossible to live without your father, and if I could not be with him, I would rather die."

Kistna glanced at the Marquis and she knew what they were both thinking. Then she went on reading:

"We met in the Church, which was already decorated with the white flowers for my wedding-ceremony the next day. Your father was dressed in his travelling-clothes, and he was to catch the stage-coach which stopped at the cross-roads near the village, at five o'clock that evening.

When we met, I knew that I could not let him go. 'Take me with you!' I begged. 'Please take me with you! If you leave me behind, I will kill myself, because I cannot marry anyone but you!'

For a moment your father did not believe me. Then when he realised that I spoke the truth from the very depths of my heart, he put his arms round me and I knew that I need no longer be afraid and the future was ours!

I went with your father on the stage-coach just as I was. I did not go back to the house for anything in case they should stop me from leaving. We were married early in the morning by a very old Parson, who, fortunately, when I told him I was older than I was, was too blind to see clearly. We went aboard the ship together and nobody troubled about two unimportant missionaries.

We learnt a long time later that there had been a terrible commotion over my disappearance on the night before the wedding and that it was suspected that I had been murdered. I was only glad that everyone should think that and not search for me, for otherwise your father might have been accused of abducting a minor or, worst of all, my father might have tried to annul the marriage.

When you read this, dearest little Kistna, it will mean I am no longer with you. But remember that I have been the happiest woman in the world because I was married to the man I loved, who loved me and who gave me the crown of love which is more valuable than anything else.

Bless you, my darling, and I hope that as this is your marriage-night you will find the same happiness that I have had, the same marvellous love which will keep and protect you all through your life."

Kistna's voice broke on the last words. Then she put down the letter and the Marquis pulled her into his arms.

"Your mother and father loved as we love," he said, "and we will be as happy as they were."

Vaguely at the back of his mind he knew that the revenge he had wanted on the Earl of Branscombe was complete, and that because he could prove that the money the seventh Earl had settled on his daughter was now Kistna's, he would remain financially handicapped until he could find another heiress.

It was poetic justice, but it did not matter and the Marquis knew that his revenge was quite unimportant.

What mattered was that he had found Kistna, and love.

She had changed his life and he knew he was not the same man, nor would he ever revert to being hard, ruthless, and, as Peregrine had said, "a monster" again.

He was wildly, deliriously happy and he wanted other people to be happy too. Perhaps not the Earl—that was too much to expect!

But at least he no longer felt vindictive towards him, nor would he allow him to sour his feelings in the future as he had in the past.

As far as he was concerned, the only thing that mattered was Kistna's happiness, and he knew because she loved him it was in his power to give it to her.

There were tears in her eyes now because she was moved by what she had read, and the Marquis kissed them away.

Then he kissed her little nose and her lips.

He kissed her until her sadness vanished and he knew that the fire that was rising within himself had ignited a flame within her that had flickered when he had made love to her before.

Now it was more intense, and as his lips moved over the softness of her neck and she quivered against him, he knew that he evoked in her new sensations she had not experienced before.

269

"I love . . . you," she whispered breathlessly, "and you . . . excite me."

"As you excite me," the Marquis replied. "I want you—God, how I want you!"

"I am . . . yours . . . oh, love me . . . love me!"

Then as his hands touched her, and his lips held hers once again captive, and as his heart beat against hers, he knew she believed that he was St. Michael carrying her up towards the glory of Heaven.

He felt as if they touched the stars, the sun was burning within them, and a light enveloped them.

Then there was only love and they were one.

Caught by
Love

AUTHORS NOTE

———— ⌘ ————

THE CATO STREET CONSPIRACY was exactly as I have described it. Thistlewood, the renegade gentleman who had been in prison, planned to murder the entire Cabinet when they were dining at Lord Harrowby's home at 44 Grosvenor Square on February 23, 1820.

Lord Harrowby was warned on the morning of the dinner-party. The Duke of Wellington warned the Prime Minister not to alter the arrangements, but other Members were not so eager to meet the assassins.

So the dinner was cancelled, although none of the members of Lord Harrowby's staff, including his French Chef, were told.

One of Thistlewood's spies, hiding in the Square, saw guests arriving for a dinner-party two doors away, at the home of the Archbishop of York, and thought they were the Cabinet arriving at Lord Harrowby's.

He reported back to Cato Street that all was well, then just as the conspirators were ready to set out, a party of Bow Street Officers appeared at the foot of a loft-ladder.

Thistlewood killed their leader with a sword. Someone snuffed the candles, and a terrible fight took place, during which he escaped.

In the middle of it, Captain Fitzclarence arrived with a troop of Goldstream Guards. He was late, as he had lost his way, but the soldiers arrested nine of the criminals, including Archie Ings, the butcher, a bootmaker, and a cabinet-maker. Thistlewood was caught the next day.

Five of the conspirators, including Thistlewood and Ings, were ordered to be hanged, and the rest were transported to Australia.

A crowd of thousands watched the hanging outside Newgate Prison.

CHAPTER ONE

————— ✦ —————

1820

$\mathcal{T}$HE MARQUIS OF BROOME STIFLED A YAWN.

He was finding the hot, airless atmosphere of Carlton House more intolerable than usual and he wondered how soon he would be able to leave.

Although he admired the Prince Regent for quite a number of reasons, he was growing increasingly bored with the endless parties that succeeded one another and about which there was little variety.

The only thing that ever changed was the Regent's heart. At the moment, the Marquis thought that Lady Hertford was on her way out and that her place as Royal Favourite would doubtless be taken very shortly by the Marchioness of Conyingham.

Whichever large, fat, elderly woman it might be, he thought, her conversation would be very much the same, and she would betray her ignorance of the feeling in the country every time she opened her mouth.

One thing which the Marquis really enjoyed at Carlton House was the collection of paintings, to which the Regent added almost weekly, together with the furniture, the statues, and the objects d'art which made the Royal Residence look more and more like a Museum.

He yawned again, and this time one of his friends, Lord Hansketh, who was passing, stopped to say:

"Are you bored, Ivo, or merely tired from your excesses of last night?"

"Bored!" the Marquis replied briefly.

"I thought you chose the pick of the bunch," Henry Hansketh continued. "I found my 'charmer' talked too much, and if there is one thing I find tiresome it is a yapping woman as the dawn breaks."

The Marquis did not reply, and his friend remembered that it was one of his rules never to discuss the women in whom he was interested, whether they were Ladies of Quality or "bits o' muslin."

"I should think 'Prinny' will retire soon," he said, to change the subject. "It is one blessing that as he has grown older he does not wish to stay up so late."

"I agree with you," the Marquis replied. "I remember times in the past when it was inevitable that the sun should be in the sky before the Prince of Wales struck his feathers."

Lord Hansketh laughed and repeated:

" 'Struck his feathers!' I must remember that, Ivo. It is one of your better *bons mots!*"

"I will make you a present of it," the Marquis drawled. "You will doubtless use it anyway."

His friend grinned.

"Why not? You are always more witty than the rest of us, and it is therefore one thing we can steal from you with impunity."

However, the Marquis was not listening. He saw that the Prince Regent was offering his arm to Lady Hertford, which meant that he was getting ready to escort her from the Chinese Drawing-Room.

He calculated that with any luck he would be able to leave Carlton House in the next ten minutes.

As if his intention had transmitted itself, Lord Hansketh said:

"What is your next appointment, Ivo? I wonder if I can guess who will be waiting for you."

"You can save your more odious innuendoes for somebody else," the Marquis replied. "As it happens, as soon as I leave here I am driving to Broome."

"At this time of night?" Henry Hansketh exclaimed.

The Marquis nodded.

"I have a horse I am particularly eager to try out before the Steeple-Chase next Saturday."

"Which of course you intend to win!"

"That depends on how good this particular stallion is."

There was silence for a moment. Then Lord Hansketh exclaimed:

"Of course! I know what you are talking about. You bought quite a number of animals at poor D'Arcy's sale, and I suppose this is one of them."

"You suppose right," the Marquis said drily. "And as it happens I was very annoyed when D'Arcy purchased *Agamemnon* at Tattersall's one day when I was unable to be there."

"*Agamemnon!*" Lord Hansketh repeated. "I remember the animal! A magnificent beast! It caused a commotion when it took at least three men to bring him into the ring."

He saw a faint smile on the Marquis's lips before he said:

"I was told how wild he was, and although I offered to buy him from D'Arcy, he was intent on keeping him so that he could force up the price. But he never had a chance of controlling the animal himself."

"Which of course you will be able to do easily!" Henry Hansketh said mockingly.

"It is what I intend to do," the Marquis answered quietly.

He spoke with a self-assurance and confidence in his own ability, which was characteristic.

An extremely handsome man, he was taller than most other men in the room, and there was not an ounce of superfluous flesh on his slim, athletic body.

The Marquis of Broome was greatly admired for his successes in the sporting world. In fact, he had a public following and was cheered on every race-course.

At the same time, those who considered themselves his friends found him unpredictable and in many ways an enigma.

Although every beautiful woman was prepared to lay her heart at his feet, he was known to be so fastidious about those in whom he showed an interest that he had earned the reputation of being heartless and often completely callous.

"He is cruel—cruel," one Beauty had sobbed to anyone who would listen.

This was strange, because the Marquis was violently opposed to any form of cruelty where sport was concerned.

He had been instrumental in making bull-baiting taboo in the Fashionable World and had been known to thrash a man with his own whip if he saw him ill-treating a horse.

But the tears of a woman left the Marquis unmoved, however pathetic she might appear or however lovely she looked when she was weeping.

As was fashionable, the Marquis like all his contemporaries regularly had a "Fair Cyprian" under his protection.

This was invariably an "Incomparable" who was pursued by the Bucks and Beaux of St. James's Street, and whom he carried off under their noses, much to their chagrin and jealousy.

"If you ask me," Lord Hansketh had said at White's Club confidentially to a friend, "I do not believe Broome has the slightest interest in the women he installs in his house in Chelsea and covers with diamonds, except that it infuriates all of us who are unable to compete when the stakes are so high."

"If you are telling me that Broome did not really want Linette, I think I shall blow a piece of lead through him," replied the man to whom he was talking.

Henry Hansketh laughed.

"You have as much chance of doing that, Charlie, as flying over the moon. Have you forgotten how quick Ivo is with a pistol? Nobody has ever been known to win a duel against him yet."

"Damn him! Why does he always pass the winning-post first, whether it is with horses or women?"

Henry Hansketh laughed again.

"You are envious, that is what is wrong with you. But because I am very fond of Ivo, I realise he is not really a happy man."

"Not happy?" Charlie exclaimed incredulously. "Of course he is! How could he not be happy with all that wealth and so many possessions that I have ceased to count them?"

"I still think Ivo is missing something in life," Henry Hansketh persisted.

"And what is that?" Charlie asked aggressively.

Lord Hansketh did not reply.

As he had driven home from White's to his lodgings in Half-Moon Street he was thinking that in all the years he had been a close friend of the Marquis, he had never known him to fall in love.

They had been quite young men when they had first served in Wellington's Army, and there Ivo, who had not yet inherited his father's Marquisate, had been not only the best-looking Officer in the Life Guards but also the most dashing, the bravest, and undoubtedly the most admired.

When he and Henry were off duty they had enjoyed the company of attractive women, whether they were of the *Beau Monde* or were "Ladies of the Town."

But while their friends sighed over, pursued, and captured the women of their fancy, Ivo remained completely self-sufficient, and if he ever yearned after a woman, his closest friends were not aware of it.

But women certainly yearned after him, and Lord Hansketh, who was continually with the Marquis, was well aware of the numerous scented notes that arrived from first thing in the morning until last thing at night at his house in Berkeley Square.

Whether he opened and read them and whether he ever replied remained a mystery, but they were undoubtedly there.

Yet it was true to say that the gossips found it hard in their endless chatter to find anything about the Marquis's love-life which indicated marriage.

Henry Hansketh was at this moment wondering if the Marquis was going to Broome alone or whether he would suggest that he should go with him.

If there was one thing he really enjoyed, it was riding the Marquis's superlative horses. Moreover, they had been friends for so long that they always had a great deal to discuss, and the hours they spent together were not only intellectually enjoyable but inevitably amusing.

Then Henry Hansketh remembered that unfortunately he had promised the Regent he would be in attendance tomorrow morning when he visited Buckingham Palace to enquire after the health of the King.

His Majesty was deteriorating day by day, and now in his eighty-second year he was greatly emaciated.

Because the eternal waiting depressed the Regent, he usually asked somebody he trusted and of whom he was fond to accompany him on his calls of duty.

"When will you be back?" Lord Hansketh asked now.

The Marquis, who was watching the Regent making a number of somewhat prolonged farewells at the end of the Drawing-Room, replied:

"I am not sure. Wednesday, or perhaps Thursday."

"If you have not returned by then, I shall come and join you," Lord Hansketh said.

"That will certainly encourage me to stay in the country," the Marquis answered. "I cannot think why anybody wants to be in London when there is hunting to be enjoyed."

"I agree with you. We should keep all this bowing and knee-bending until after the hunting-season is over."

"The one blessing is that the King is supposed to be really dying this time. 'Prinny' is talking of cancelling his parties, and that should let us off the hook for a little while."

"You have cheered me up," Henry Hansketh replied. "At the same time, I cannot help suspecting that this filial affection will not last for long."

The Marquis did not reply, but there was an expression in his eyes which was more eloquent than words, and Henry Hansketh was quite certain that while he himself would find it impossible to escape any of the Carlton House parties, the Marquis would somehow manage it.

The Regent was now definitely moving towards the door, while all the ladies as he passed sank down into a deep curtsey and the gentlemen bowed their heads from the neck.

Fat, florid, and yet with an indefinable charm which no-one could deny, the Prince, with Lady Hertford clinging to his arm, finally disappeared from sight, and the Marquis exclaimed:

"Now I can go! Can I give you a lift, Henry?"

"No, thank you," his friend replied. "I have two or three people to talk to before I leave. Do not stay at Broome longer than you have to. All the same, I envy you the fresh air, and of course the battle you will enjoy with *Agamemnon*."

The faint twist on the Marquis's lips told his friend that that was what he was looking forward to.

"I think it would be best," the Marquis said after a slight pause, "if you definitely joined me on Thursday evening or Friday. Then, however much we are needed here, we need not return until Monday."

"All right, Ivo," Henry Hansketh agreed. "I had promised to dine with a certain very attractive lady on Friday night, but I will make my apologies and join you at Broome."

The Marquis did not wait to hear his friend's acceptance, taking it for granted, and was already walking quickly from the Chinese Drawing-Room, having avoided with some dexterity the Princess de Lieven, wife of the Russian Ambassador.

She was an acknowledged wit and had also pursued the Marquis for some time without gaining her objective.

He hurried down the graceful double staircase, which had amazed those who saw it when the house was first finished, and into the splendid Hall decorated with Ionic columns of brown Siena marble.

A flunkey placed a fur-lined cape over his shoulders, then he walked out through the front door under the high Corinthian portico, where Linkman immediately appeared and called out:

"The carriage of the Most Noble Marquis of Broome!"

The Marquis had already instructed his servants that he would be leaving as early as possible, and as it drew up a few seconds later where he was waiting, all eyes were on the six perfectly matched and superbly bred jet-black stallions.

The chariot they were drawing had only recently been delivered from the carriage-maker and was so light and so well sprung that it appeared as if its brightly painted yellow wheels hardly touched the ground.

The Marquis stepped into it, the footman put a sable rug over his black satin knee-breeches; then, having shut the door, which was emblazoned with the Broome coat-of-arms, the man sprang up onto the box as the horses were already moving.

One thing the Marquis particularly disliked was taking a long time on any journey.

While he expected his coachmen to drive with the expertise he had himself, he also demanded a speed which usually left any passengers who were with him sitting tense on the edge of their seats and wondering if they would ever reach their destination alive.

The Marquis had no such qualms, unlike many Corinthians who disliked being driven, being such expert hands with the reins themselves, for he had complete trust in his coachmen, who had all been with him for many years.

As soon as the horses moved out of the traffic in Pall Mall into St. James's Street, and then into Piccadilly, the Marquis leant back against the well-padded seat of the chariot, lifted his silk-stockinged legs, and put his feet on the opposite seat.

It was heavily padded, and it needed to be, because it was not only a seat but also a safe with a very special lock in which valuables were carried on long journeys.

Highwaymen, if they were intrepid enough to bring the carriage to a halt, were unaware of its existence.

The Marquis had in fact designed this particular safe himself, making sure that it was deep and wide enough to hold all the valuables he might wish to carry with him. At the same time, it was comfortable if used as a seat by his guests.

However, at the moment he was thinking not of his chariot but of the pleasure he would derive tomorrow when he rode *Agamemnon* for the first time.

He was looking forward to his struggle with a horse which he knew would demand all his expertise as an outstanding rider to bring it under control.

He was also, as Lord Hansketh had surmised, slightly fatigued.

It took a great deal to tire the Marquis, but he had been out extremely late the night before and for several previous nights in succession.

But however late he was, it never prevented him when he was in London from riding very early in the Park before the presence of other riders made it difficult to exercise either himself or the horse he was riding in the way he wished.

What was more, this morning after breakfast he had gone to Wimbledon to watch a mill between two pugilists, to one of whom he had given his patronage, and who not unexpectedly had won the contest.

After this he had had luncheon with the Prime Minister and a Member of the Cabinet, when they had discussed certain problems in which the Marquis was particularly interested.

He was concerned with the outbreaks of violence, revolutionary behaviour, and fierce threats against the social order which had been such a feature of the year 1815 and which seemed to be beginning again.

A number of the more optimistic Statesmen thought this an exaggeration of the position.

But Lord Sidmouth had supported the Marquis, saying he had little doubt that "the clouds in the North would soon burst," and as he had said to the Lord Chancellor, Lord Elton, he wished he could convince himself of the "sufficiency of the means, either by law or force, to curb the spirit of revolt."

Very few of the Marquis's social friends, except for Lord Hansketh, had any idea how at such private meetings his opinions were listened to with interest and his ideas noted.

"Something has to be done, and done quickly!" he told himself now. "Otherwise we shall undoubtedly have trouble, because reform is long overdue."

He started to enumerate to himself the measures he would bring in if he were Prime Minister.

By now his horses had carried him out from the suburbs into the open country and were travelling at a tremendous pace over roads that were dry after quite a long spell without rain and with only a mild frost at nights.

As the Marquis had known when he planned his journey, there was a full moon, and therefore the coachman did not have to rely on the inadequate lantern-light of the chariot.

He could see his way quite clearly beneath the Heavens ablaze with stars and the moonbeams that lit the land.

It would take, as the Marquis knew, less than two hours to reach Broome, which was situated in the Surrey hills.

He was almost asleep when he was alerted, not by any movement of the chariot but by the fact that for some reason he could not understand his feet were being pressed upwards.

At first he was just vaguely aware that they were rising. Then it crossed his mind that the lock of his safe could not have been closed properly.

This was something that annoyed him in that he expected perfection in everything round him.

Angrily he lifted his feet onto the floor, pushed aside the rug, and bent forward to feel if the lock was loose, indicating that it had not been fastened as it should have been.

Then to his astonishment the top of the seat rose even higher, and in the moonlight coming through the windows he realised that it was being lifted from the inside.

"What the Devil . . . ?" he began to say beneath his breath.

Then, going into action, he put his hand into the dark aperture beneath the raised cushion-top to clasp with fingers like steel what was beneath it.

There was a cry of pain, and the Marquis, feeling something warm and soft in his grasp, drew it out into the carriage.

To his astonishment, he found that what he held was a young boy who fell at his feet, exclaiming accusingly:

"You hurt . . . me!"

"Who are you and what are you doing here?" the Marquis demanded angrily.

"I was hiding."

The boy, sitting on the floor, was rubbing his neck with his hand as he spoke, and the Marquis could see that his head was covered with fair curls.

He was a very small boy, which accounted for the fact that he had been able to hide in the empty safe.

"I presume you were trying to steal something from me," the Marquis said harshly, "but we moved before you could escape."

The boy did not reply, but went on rubbing his neck, and after a moment the Marquis asked:

"What I want to know is how you knew there was a hiding-place beneath that seat, and how you opened it when it should have been locked."

Now the boy looked up at him and he saw that his face was small, with an oval forehead, a pointed chin, and eyes that appeared very large.

There was silence until the Marquis said:

"I am waiting for an answer, and I advise you to tell the truth before I hand you over to my servants to punish you as you undoubtedly deserve."

284

"I did not steal anything from you," the boy replied. "As I told you, I was hiding."

"From whom, and why in my carriage?"

"Because it is drawn by six horses."

The Marquis was suddenly aware that the boy's voice was cultured and unusually musical.

It was also surprising that he seemed not as frightened as he should have been, but was sitting quietly on the floor, his legs under him.

The Marquis saw now that he was wearing a short jacket, the type that he himself had worn when he was at Eton, but instead of the conventional white collar he wore a dark silk scarf tied in a bow.

"I suppose you have some explanation for your behaviour," he said, "and I am certainly entitled to hear it."

"I was not doing anything wrong," the boy replied, "except taking a lift without asking your permission. Once you have carried me out of London I will disappear and you will not be bothered with me any further."

He paused before he went on:

"With any luck you would not have known of my existence, except that I was so cramped and it was so airless that I could not stand being cooped up any longer. I was afraid I might die of suffocation."

"It would have served you right if you had," the Marquis said grimly, "but I still want to know how you got into my coach in the first place and how you know of that particular hiding-place."

He knew the boy smiled before he replied:

"As it happens, my uncle, as a prevention against Highwaymen, has had exactly the same type of safe fitted into the travelling-chariot he has just purchased."

The Marquis stiffened.

"I do not believe it! It was my own invention, and the coach-builders assured me on their honour that there would be no replicas of it sold in any circumstances."

The boy laughed, and the Marquis thought it was a mocking sound.

"You must have a very trusting nature! Some men would sell the secrets of the Tower of London if you paid them enough money."

"Dammit, I will never give that firm another order!" the Marquis exclaimed.

"As a matter of fact, it was not the firm but one of their employees, whom they dismissed for taking bribes."

The Marquis's lips tightened and he said:

"I find what you have told me as reprehensible as the fact that you are here. Who are you and what is your name?"

"I do not have to answer that question," the boy retorted with unexpected dignity. "All I ask is that you will put me down in any town that you pass through before you reach your destination, and then forget that you have ever seen me."

"It seems a very strange request," the Marquis replied, "and I would like to know a little more about you before I agree to what you have asked me."

"There is no reason why you should be interested in me," the boy answered. "As I have already said, you would not have known I was here if I had not felt it so difficult to breathe that I thought I would faint."

"You are not fainting now," the Marquis said, "and I suggest you sit down in the seat opposite me, so that I can look at you, and tell me the truth about yourself."

The boy laughed, and the Marquis thought it was a very young, spontaneous sound.

"I doubt if you would believe me," he said, "but let me assure Your Lordship that it would be much better for you to remain in complete ignorance about me and the reason why I am accepting your hospitality for a short distance."

The way the boy spoke made the Marquis's lips twist slightly in amusement before he said:

"I presume you are running away from School or your Teachers! Let me tell you that it is not only a very unwise thing to do, but one that is likely to prove dangerous."

"That is my business!"

As the boy spoke he moved from the position in which he had remained ever since the Marquis had drawn him out from his hiding-place.

Rubbing one of his legs, which obviously hurt him, he sat down as the Marquis had instructed on the seat which was now closed and continued to rub his leg.

"If you are in pain," the Marquis said coldly, "you have nobody to blame but yourself."

"I know," the boy answered, "but I am suffering from 'pins and needles' as the blood comes back into my leg, and it is extremely unpleasant."

As he spoke he pulled his leg up so that his foot was on the seat on which he was sitting, and raised his trouser-leg to rub his ankle.

"It hurts!" he said. "It was so numb that I could not feel it at first."

"You will receive no sympathy from me," the Marquis replied, "and the sooner you return home, the better."

"I have no intention of doing that," the boy said positively, "and nothing you or anyone else can say will make me!"

The Marquis could not see very clearly even in the moonlight, but the boy's voice was not broken, and as he was small and his hands and his bones seemed delicate, the Marquis was sure he was very young.

"Now listen to me," he said in a different tone. "All boys at some time in their lives feel like running away from their family and their lessons. But you have no idea of the difficulties you will encounter in the world outside the security of your home. Go back and do not be a young idiot!"

"No!" the boy said defiantly.

"How long do you think you will last on your own with no money?" the Marquis enquired.

"I have quite a lot of money on me."

"Which no doubt will be stolen from you by the first tramp you meet! You will be lucky if he does not knock you about as well."

"You are trying to frighten me," the boy said, "but there is nothing you can say that can frighten me half so much as the cause of my running away."

"Suppose you tell me what it is?" the Marquis suggested.

"You would not believe me."

"How can you be sure of that? I have heard a lot of strange stories one way or another in my life, and if they seemed truthful and genuine I have always tried to help."

"Are you offering to help me?"

"I am."

There was silence. Then the boy, putting down his leg, said slowly:

"In a way I would like to trust you . . . but I think it would be a . . . mistake."

"For you or for me?" the Marquis enquired with a smile.

"For both of us, but especially for you. I can assure you that if you encumbered yourself with me, it is something you would undoubtedly regret. That is why, as soon as your horses stop, I am going to get out and you will never see me again."

"You cannot imagine how infuriating I shall find it if you leave me wondering who you are and what has happened to you," the Marquis said. "So now, my young friend, you must pay your way by revealing to me the story, whether it is true or false."

The boy gave an unexpected chuckle.

"You make me sound like Sheherazade."

"Sheherazade was a woman!"

There was silence. Then the Marquis said slowly:

"I think, unless I am mistaken, that I have found the answer to the first puzzle!"

For a moment he thought that the small figure opposite him was going to deny it. Then she asked:

"Was it so obvious? I thought if I cut my hair short nobody would ever guess I was not a boy."

"If I had seen you in the daylight I should have guessed sooner," the Marquis answered. "A boy's voice, even at the age you appear to be, would be deeper and certainly rougher."

"Do you think anyone would guess except you?"

"I am sure they would."

"I do not believe you!"

"I think it would be a mistake to put it to the test," the Marquis said drily.

There was a pause before she said:

"Now you have ruined everything! I was so confident that I would get away and remain undetected until I reached France."

"France?" the Marquis exclaimed. "Is that where you are going?"

She nodded.

"I have a friend in Paris. She is French, and I think if I could reach her she would hide me, and nobody would find me however hard they looked."

"And you really think you can travel from here to France by yourself? It is not only impossible but an extremely foolhardy idea!" the Marquis said.

Now that he had realised that he was talking to a girl and not a boy, he could see that she was undoubtedly attractive.

He thought he should have known sooner that the softness of her voice and its musical tones could never have belonged to anybody who was not feminine.

"Now you definitely have to help me," she said. "Will you find me a Courier to escort me to Paris? I can pay for his services."

"How much money have you?" the Marquis enquired.

"Twenty pounds in notes and coins," she replied, "and these . . ."

She put her hand into the pocket of her trousers and brought out two pieces which glittered in the moonlight.

The Marquis could see that one of them was a large crescent-shaped brooch set with diamonds, and the other was a collet of the same stones, which was undoubtedly worth a great deal of money.

"I can sell these," the girl said, "and live in comfort, I imagine, for quite a long time."

"And to whom would you sell them," the Marquis enquired, "even if you managed to cross the Channel in safety?"

She did not reply, but he knew she was attentive and listening as he went on:

"Any jeweller, seeing you dressed like that, would cheat you, and even if your friend will take you in and hide you, I imagine your parents will be searching for you and will find you sooner or later. Also, you will find that what money you have will not go very far in France."

"You are just making difficulties to scare me," the girl said accusingly.

"It would make things easier if you were frank with me," the Marquis said. "Start at the beginning. What is your name?"

"Cara."

"Is that all?"

"No, I have another name, but I do not intend to tell you what it is."

"Why not?"

"That is a leading question which I cannot answer."

"You must realise it is impossible for me to help you if you keep everything so secret."

"The only way I want you to help me is to get me to France. Surely that is not very much to ask?"

"It is a great deal," the Marquis replied. "First, you hide away in my carriage, in a place that I thought was inviolable from thieves. Secondly, you pretend to be a boy when you are a girl, and thirdly, you will not give me your name. What do you expect me to do, except perhaps hand you over to the Magistrates to deal with as they think best?"

The girl gave a little cry of horror. Then she said:

"You are frightening me! You know quite well you would not do such a thing."

"Do not be so sure."

"I am sure, even though you have a reputation for being heartless and ruthless."

The Marquis was startled.

"What do you mean by that?"

"Everybody talks about the Most Noble Marquis of Broome."

"Well, if they do, it is only fair that I should be able to talk about you. Give me your name."

"I refuse, utterly and completely refuse!"

"Why?"

"Because if I did, I know you would not help me."

The Marquis stared at her in surprise.

"I cannot imagine for a moment why you should say that. Actually I have helped a great number of people in trouble."

"That is not your reputation."

There was a pause before the Marquis said:

"I am not going to give you the satisfaction of being curious about me. I am trying to talk about you."

"Yes, I know, and as I have no wish to do so, it is far easier for us to discuss you. Other men are very jealous of you, but I expect you know that."

The Marquis laughed.

"I do not believe you are real," he said. "I must be dreaming this whole ridiculous situation. And incidentally, why are you wearing an Eton jacket?"

"It belongs to my cousin, who has outgrown it," Cara replied. "I smuggled it down from the attic and hid it in the back of the wardrobe until I was ready to run away."

"So you have been planning this for some time?"

"For over a week. I tried to think of another way of escaping, but this was the only way that seemed possible."

"You cut off your hair, dressed as a boy, then hid yourself in my chariot. How did you know it was mine?"

"I saw your coat-of-arms on the door, but actually I did not choose it because it belonged to you."

"Then what was the reason?"

"Because it was drawn by six horses, I knew it was going out of London tonight, which was what I wanted to do."

The explanation was so simple and reasonable that the Marquis smiled.

"So you would have taken any coach or carriage that looked as if it might be travelling a long distance?"

"Yes, but I am glad it was yours."

"Why?"

"Because whatever else they may say about you, you are a sportsman. That is why I know you will not turn me over to the Magistrates, and while you frighten me with talk of tramps robbing me and knocking me about, you will not abandon me."

The Marquis had to admit to himself that it was intelligent thinking, and he said after a moment:

"This is all very well, but I have to do something about you."

"I have told you what you can do."

"Are you prepared to give me the name of your friend in France?"

"No!"

"Why not?"

"Because you might later be forced into telling those who will undoubtedly pursue me where I have gone."

"Do you think I might be questioned?"

"I doubt it, but one never knows. There will be a hue and cry, and it would be much better if you were not involved too deeply."

"I think I am that already," the Marquis said. "And if there is a hue and cry, as you say, am I to pretend that I have never seen you, that you never travelled with me from London to the country?"

"How could you think of giving the enemy unnecessary information and encouragement?"

"They are your enemies, not mine."

Cara gave a little laugh.

"That is what you think!"

"What do you mean by that?" the Marquis asked.

"Nothing, but few men have as many enemies as you have. They are of course envious of your possessions and jealous of your personal successes, especially when it concerns lovely ladies."

The Marquis sat upright.

"How dare you talk like that!" he exclaimed. "I was obviously mistaken when I thought you were well bred."

Cara laughed again, and she was obviously not in the least abashed.

"What you are really saying is that you do not like the truth. If I was dressed in a ball-gown, simpering behind my fan, I would flatter you in the way you expect. But because I am pretending to be a boy I can say what I think."

"If I treated you like a boy, I would give you a good spanking!" the Marquis said grimly.

"I always understood that brute force was the last resort of idiots!" Cara retorted.

For a moment the Marquis glared at her. Then he leant back in his seat and chuckled.

"You are incorrigible!" he said. "Nobody has ever talked to me like this before."

"Then it is doubtless a salutary experience," Cara answered. "Although you will never see me again, perhaps you will remember what I have said to you and will be aware that there are those who will stab you in the back when you least expect it."

The Marquis laughed as if he could not help himself.

"If that happens, I shall doubtless remember what you have said too late."

"That will be your fault, now that I have warned you," Cara remarked.

CHAPTER TWO

———— ∞ ————

BY THE TIME THE MARQUIS HAD RIDDEN *Agamemnon* to the far end of the Park, both he and the horse were breathless.

By this time *Agamemnon* was beginning to acknowledge that he had met his master, and although he had tried every trick he knew to unseat him, the Marquis was still firmly in the saddle.

Both man and beast had developed a respect for each other during what had been a fiery and tempestuous battle from the moment they had left the stableyard.

Now *Agamemnon* moved with a certain dignity, to show that he was still aware of his own consequence, but in the direction that the Marquis guided him.

He was thinking with satisfaction that he had a horse that was worthy of his own expertise, and that he would doubtless enjoy innumberable further battles with *Agamemnon,* but with the knowledge that they each had a wholesome respect for the other.

At the edge of the Park there was a flat piece of grassland on which the Marquis saw a number of his own horses galloping, ridden by stable-lads who were competing with one another.

He watched them for a few minutes, then rode towards his trainer, who held a watch in his hand.

The Marquis drew up beside him but did not speak until the man looked towards him and he was aware that he had finished his calculations.

"Well, Johnson?" the Marquis asked. "What is the verdict?"

Ted Johnson, who had been with the Marquis for six years and was acknowledged as one of the most experienced trainers in the country, smiled.

"*Fly-catcher,* M'Lord, will win the first big race in which Your Lordship enters him."

"You are sure of that?" the Marquis enquired.

"Very certain, M'Lord."

"And what about *Rollo?*"

"Given equal conditions, we shall certainly beat him," Ted Johnson replied with satisfaction.

The Marquis's eyes were on the horses trotting back to him now that they had finished their test-gallops.

They were all superbly bred. At the same time, there was one which any man with an eye for horses would know was outstanding, and that was *Fly-catcher.*

The Marquis had raced him in only one public race, then had withdrawn him into obscurity.

He knew without being told that he had what all owners dreamt of finding: a horse that was undefeatable in any race in which horses of the same age were running.

The previous year the Marquis had been confident of winning the Derby with a very fine horse which had been tipped to win quite early in the season.

Then, almost at the last moment, a rival had appeared on the scene in the shape of the Earl of Matlock's *Green Dragon.*

Naturally the Marquis, who if nothing else was a great sportsman, would have acceped his horse's defeat by *Green Dragon,* if he had not been suspicious of the way the Earl's horse had run.

His jockey had asserted that he had been "bumped and bored" in a manner that was definitely against the rules.

But the Marquis had been aware that it was no use complaining to the Earl, whom he disliked and with whom he had had a number of skirmishes already over different Classic Races in which they both competed with a rivalry which had something very personal about it.

To put it in simple terms, the Marquis despised the Earl and the Earl detested the Marquis.

Although it was difficult to prove, the Marquis was quite certain that the Earl's instructions to his jockeys were to prevent his horses from winning, whatever methods they chose to use.

The Marquis, realising the brilliance of *Fly-catcher's* promise, had therefore taken him from his stables at Epsom and brought him and a number of his other horses down to Broome.

Keeping them out of sight of the racing fraternity, he had decided to produce *Fly-catcher* only at the last moment, as the Earl had done the previous year with *Green Dragon*.

There was no doubt that *Red Rollo* was an exceptional horse, but that was the only one belonging to the Earl that really constituted a threat to the Marquis's stable.

Because the Marquis had lain low, as it were, until now, *Red Rollo* was already being heavily backed, and when the time came the odds on him would shorten considerably.

"You are satisfied, Johnson?" the Marquis asked now. "He certainly looks in fine condition."

As he spoke he was watching *Fly-catcher* trot past him.

He knew by the grin on his rider's face that the horse had certainly come up to his expectations.

The other horses were being ridden by the stable-lads, but Bateson, who was a distinguished and well-known jockey, rode *Fly-catcher* up beside the Marquis.

"Good-morning, M'Lord!"

"Good-morning, Bateson," the Marquis replied. "What is your verdict?"

"Need Your Lordship ask?" Bateson answered. *"Fly-catcher's* the most outstanding horse I've ever had the privilege of riding!"

"I know that is high praise from you, Bateson."

"Keep him out of sight, M'Lord, or the first time anyone sees him he'll be an odds-on favourite."

The Marquis smiled.

He did not bother to say that he never betted on his own horses.

What he enjoyed was the satisfaction of being the winner. He disliked the type of owner who was concerned only with how much a horse could win him personally in hard cash.

Because he had no more to say, Bateson rode away, following the other horses who were returning to the stables.

The Marquis turned *Agamemnon,* and as he rode beside him Ted Johnson said:

"It'll give me great satisfaction, M'Lord, to beat His Lordship after the way he crowed over us last year."

The Marquis did not reply and Ted Johnson went on:

"I didn't know at the time, M'Lord, that Harwood, who were a-riding our horse, got two weals across his back when the Earl's jockey struck him."

The Marquis stared at his trainer before he asked:

"Do you mean to say that he was deliberately struck with a whip?"

"Yes, M'Lord," Johnson replied. "But Harwood's a quiet man and he'd no wish to make accusations against the Earl, which he said he'd find hard to substantiate in front of the Stewards."

"I have never heard anything so disgraceful!" the Marquis exclaimed. "If you had told me at the time . . ."

He stopped and said:

"No, Johnson, I think Harwood was right. It is always difficult to prove exactly what happens during a race, but you and I know that Harwood is a truthful man and would not lie about a thing like that."

"Exactly, M'Lord! And that's why he made no mention of it at the time. But he told me confidentially a little while ago that he'd no wish, even if Your Lordship asked him, to ride in this year's Derby."

"Why not?" the Marquis asked sharply.

"Because, M'Lord, there've been some unpleasant stories lately of jockeys who beat the Earl of Matlock having accidents on a dark night, and in one case being picked up in a ditch more dead than alive."

The Marquis stared at his trainer incredulously.

"Are you telling me the truth, Johnson?"

"It's what Harwood told me, M'Lord, and we both know that he's a Chapel-goer, known for being abstemious, and certainly no loose-mouthed talker."

"That is true," the Marquis conceded, "but I can hardly believe that the Earl of Matlock would sink to doing anything so utterly despicable and against all the rules of the Turf."

There was silence before Ted Johnson said:

"I've heard, M'Lord—but of course it's only the gossip of the race-course—that the Earl's in deep water and finding it hard to pay his debts."

The Marquis nodded his head as if it was no more than what he had expected.

Then, knowing it was a mistake to gossip for too long with one of his employees, he touched *Agamemnon* with his spur, which made the horse as restless as he had been before.

After a few bucks it was obvious that any further conversation would be impossible, and the Marquis rode him away.

He did not return to the house, but took *Agamemnon* over the gallop at a speed which satisfied them both.

He then rode for an hour over the fields to the west of the Park before returning at a more leisurely pace towards the house.

All the time he was riding the Marquis was thinking of the Earl of Matlock, who he had known for some time was an avowed enemy.

He was wondering how he could prevent him from causing a scandal which would bode ill for the whole racing world, which was something that the members of the Jockey Club, like himself, tried to avoid by every means in their power.

It was only as he was riding over the bridge which spanned the lake that he remembered he had another problem on his hands, and that was Cara.

The hard lines in which his lips had set while he was thinking of the Earl relaxed a little as he remembered her unexpected appearance in his carriage.

He recalled with some amusement the manner in which she had refused to tell him of her identity and various other details on their journey home.

She had sat opposite him, refusing to answer his questions about herself and sparring with him in a manner which he found original if extremely impertinent, until she said:

"As I am very cold without an overcoat, I think, if you do not mind, I will share your fur rug, and it would be far more comfortable if I sat beside you."

She did not wait for him to agree, but getting up and sitting down on the back seat beside the Marquis, she pulled the sable rug which covered his knees over her until it reached her chin.

As she did so, she gave a little shiver and said:

"Although I have no wish to impose upon you, I am thinking that if you are to help me travel to France, I shall have to borrow a cloak of some sort or I may die of cold on the journey."

"If you do, it will be your own fault!" the Marquis said unsympathetically. "You must have realised that this was the wrong time of year in which to travel."

"Of course I realised it," Cara answered, "but I would have braved the snows of the Himalayas or the ice of Antarctica rather than endure the fate that was awaiting me in London."

The Marquis looked towards her expectantly, thinking that perhaps she was going to tell him a little more about herself.

But she was sitting beside him in the shadows where the moonlight coming through the window did not reach, and he could only vaguely see the top of her head.

Cara gave a little chuckle.

"I know what you are expecting to learn," she said, "but you can just forget it. The only problem is whether you will be generous enough to send me to France with a Courier. Or, as I have already suggested, put me down in the nearest town to fend for myself."

"There is a much better alternative," the Marquis said, "and that is that you should return to where you come from. However unpleasant the conditions waiting for you there, you will encounter, I assure you, far worse in France, or even in some quiet market-town where the yokels will undoubtedly consider you a figure of fun."

"Do let us talk about something more interesting," Cara pleaded, "or perhaps you prefer not to talk while you are travelling."

"That is certainly an idea," the Marquis replied.

"Papa always said chattering females were intolerable, and never more so than when the movement of carriage-wheels loosened their tongues and they became indiscreet."

The Marquis smiled a little cynically, thinking that when he was alone with a woman it was not only her tongue that became loose, but that was something he could not say to Cara.

There was a little silence before she said:

"Now that I am beginning to feel warm, I also feel sleepy."

"Then I should go to sleep."

"I will," she answered, "if you promise not to take the opportunity of depositing me in a ditch, or returning me on a Stage-Coach to London."

"Do you really imagine I would do either of those things?" the Marquis asked.

He was aware from the movement of her body that she shook her head.

"No, you would consider that unsporting," she replied. "So I trust you to wake me first, whether it is when we reach Broome, or . . . when I have to . . . leave you. . . ."

Her voice trailed away on the last word and the Marquis was aware that she had fallen asleep.

A little while later her head slipped lower against the cushions in the corner of the carriage, and he lifted her legs up on the seat beside him.

He was aware that she was completely unconscious, lying curled up like a child in her cot.

He put out his hand and pulled the rug a little farther over her, then sat back and closed his eyes, thinking that he too would sleep.

Finding it impossible to do so, instead he puzzled as to who Cara could be and what in fact he was to do about her.

It was obvious that she was well bred and well educated, and he also had the idea that when he saw her in the daylight she would be attractive.

He knew that he would have to come to some conclusion about her before he reached Broome, for that he had brought from London a young woman dressed as a boy would be a piece of gossip that would sweep through the *Beau Monde* as if it were carried on the wind.

"I want no scandal!" the Marquis decided.

It was obvious that in that case the best thing he could do would be to agree to Cara's request that he set her down in a small market-town which they would pass through about half-an-hour before they reached the drive-gates of Broome.

Then he knew that such an action was impossible.

If Cara was unaware of the dangers she would encounter either as a young boy dressed as a gentleman, or worse still, as a girl dressed as a boy, the Marquis was not.

Because there was unrest over the whole country, which was something he had brought to the notice of the Cabinet again and again without much response, he was aware that in the towns where there was a great deal of hardship, it had naturally resulted in violent protests and a considerable amount of crime.

Three-quarters of the Cabinet were Peers of the Realm, and despite everything they heard and the Marquis's warnings, they were determined to repress the fomenting seeds of social revolution.

Freedom of speech had largely been lost during the Napoleonic Wars, and this suppression was still maintained.

Of the fifteen hundred men in the North of England who marched in protest at the price of bread, twenty-four had been condemned to death. Men were imprisoned, transported, or even hanged for protesting against low wages and their intolerable conditions of life.

The Marquis was convinced that there was a great deal more trouble ahead in the easily foreseeable future.

It was therefore impossible for him to think of leaving alone a young girl who had no idea of the conditions that existed both in Urban and in Rural England.

Her money, which she thought ensured her independence, would be taken from her as soon as she was noticed by any hungry labourer, and if she struggled, there was every likelihood of her losing her life, or being treated in a manner which did not bear thinking about.

"The best thing I can do," the Marquis decided, "is to send her to France as she wishes. Then she will no longer be my responsibility."

But the idea of washing his hands of a young woman who was undoubtedly a lady made him feel uncomfortable.

He had not decided exactly what he would do when he realised that his horses were already turning in at the lodge-gates of Broome and proceeding down the long drive of ancient oaks which led to the house.

Putting out his hand, he shook Cara by the shoulder to bring her back to wakefulness.

"What . . . is it? . . . What is the . . . matter?" she asked, sitting up straight.

"Wake up," the Marquis said. "We have arrived at my house, and I suppose, reluctantly, I must offer you a bed for the night."

Cara yawned, and the Marquis realised that she had been in a deep sleep when he had disturbed her.

"A . . . bed for the . . . night," she repeated, as if she found the words reassuring, then asked: "Tomorrow will you send me to France?"

"I will consider doing so," he replied, "but for the moment I would rather my servants did not see you in that extremely disreputable disguise."

As he spoke he slipped his fur-lined cloak from his shoulders, saying:

"You had better put this on, and for God's sake try to hide your trousers before I hand you over to my Housekeeper."

Cara chuckled.

"Do they shock you?"

"I am both surprised and shocked that a young woman of your age should be so immodest!"

"Rubbish!" Cara retorted. "If you are not shocked at the parties you give with your friends, and which are whispered about as being outrageous, you are certainly not shocked by me!"

The Marquis was about to ask her what she had heard about his parties when he realised that the horses had almost reached the front of the house and the servants were standing at the open door, from which a golden light poured over the stone steps.

"Cover yourself!" he ordered sharply.

He made it a command such as he might have given one of his troopers, but Cara merely chuckled.

At the same time, the Marquis was aware that he was pulling his extremely expensive fur-lined cape over her shoulders.

As he had already determined, she was very small.

By the time they reached the lighted Hall with its great carved gilt and ebony staircase, he was aware that she was completely covered by his cape, which reached almost to the ground and looked fairly respectable.

"I have an unexpected guest with me, Newman," he said to the Butler. "Ask Mrs. Peel to come to me as soon as possible."

"Very good, M'Lord," the Butler answered.

His impassive face expressed no surprise that the Housekeeper, who was nearly sixty, should be expected to get up and dress to accept His Lordship's instructions at two o'clock in the morning.

Without saying any more, the Marquis strode ahead into the Library, where he knew there would be sandwiches which were always ready for him on his arrival home.

Some hot soup would already be on its way up from the kitchen, where the Chef had been waiting, doubtless impatiently, for his arrival.

Only after the footman had offered the soup to Cara, which she had accepted, and the Marquis had taken a sip from a two-handled silver cup, did he say:

"Is there anything else you would like?"

It was the first time he had addressed Cara since they had entered the house, and he had in fact not even looked at her face, partly because he was afraid of what he might see.

Now as she sat beside the log fire which was burning brightly in the open grate, wrapped closely in his fur cape, he saw that she was different in appearance from what he had expected.

Because he was aware that she had fair hair, he had thought it would be complemented by blue eyes, and perhaps the "rose" look that was expected of a typical English maiden.

Instead, Cara had a heart-shaped face, and her eyes instead of being blue were decidedly green, slanting a little at the corners, which gave her a mischievous, provocative expression which the Marquis thought was somewhat in keeping with the manner in which she talked to him.

There were dimples on either side of her lips, which also curved upwards, and her face was balanced by a very small, straight, aristocratic nose.

As the Marquis inspected her with a penetrating look which those who were in awe of him said made them feel apprehensive and nervous, Cara's eyes twinkled, and her two dimples showed as she smiled before she asked:

"Am I worse or better than you thought I would be?"

"I am trying to make up my mind," the Marquis answered. "From your point of view it is definitely worse, because it would be impossible for me to send you to France looking as you do, even with a Courier."

"What do you mean by that?" Cara enquired.

"You are too young, you are too attractive, and you undoubtedly come from a respectable family," the Marquis answered.

"How can you be so ridiculous?" she asked. "You know nothing about

302

me. I am just a tiresome stranger who has intruded on your privacy because I was in need of a lift. I have no wish to be treated as if I were a Lady of Fashion—which I am not!"

"That, I think, is for me to judge," the Marquis replied, "and even if you are not a Lady of Fashion, you are certainly young and at an age when, whether you like it or not, you require a Chaperone."

Cara drank a little more of her soup before she said:

"What a bore you are! I shall now have to run away from you, as well as running away from . . ."

She stopped as if she realised that what she had been about to say would be too revealing.

Then as if she was aware that the Marquis was listening intently, hoping to catch her out, she said:

"As you are kind enough to give me a bed for the night, I would like to go to it now. I am so tired that I may otherwise be indiscreet, and that would be something I should very much regret in the morning."

"I will allow you to go to bed on one condition," the Marquis answered.

"What is that?"

"That you give me your sacred word of honour, that you swear on the Bible or anything else you consider holy, that you will not run away until you have discussed with me what would be the best thing for you to do."

There was silence for a moment. Then Cara said:

"Supposing I refuse?"

"Then regrettably," the Marquis said, "I shall either have to see that you are locked in for the night, or, which would be more uncomfortable as far as you are concerned, my Housekeeper will arrange for a maid to sleep in your room to make sure you do not escape."

Cara sat bolt upright, and there was no doubt that her eyes flashed at him as she said:

"How dare you suggest such a thing and make yourself responsible for me in a way I consider an imposition!"

The Marquis laughed.

"Now you sound more like a small tiger-cat than a young lady," he said. "Nevertheless, even a tiger-cat has to be put in a cage at night."

"Perhaps I made a mistake in choosing your carriage to convey me out of London," Cara said. "I did consider travelling with a young Buck who had only four horses, but as he had certainly had too much of the Prince Regent's wine to drink, I could doubtless have left him without his being aware of it."

The Marquis thought that she was too innocent to know that she might have found herself in a very unpleasant situation with a drunken Buck, but there was no point in his saying so, and he merely replied:

"My Housekeeper will be arriving at any moment. Do you wish to have one of the housemaids sleeping with you, or are you prepared to give me your word of honour?"

"How do you know I will keep it?" Cara enquired.

"In the same way that you know that I am a sportsman," the Marquis replied.

As he spoke the door opened, and as if the sound forced her to make up her mind, Cara said quickly:

"I give you my word of honour."

There was a faint smile on the Marquis's lips as he turned to greet his Housekeeper, who, bustling in black silk, looked quite unperturbed at being ordered from her bed at so late an hour.

The Marquis handed *Agamemnon* over to two grooms, who took the stallion's reins somewhat apprehensively.

He then walked up the steps, thinking that Cara might be as difficult to tame as the horse to whom he had just given a lesson which he would not forget.

In the Hall he handed his tall hat, gloves, and riding-whip to a footman, and Newman, the Butler, went ahead of him to open the door of the Breakfast-Room.

As he did so he said:

"I think the young lady has already begun breakfast, M'Lord. I told her you would not wish her to wait for Your Lordship's return."

The Marquis did not reply. He was aware that *Agamemnon* had made him nearly two hours late, but he had no intention of apologising to an unwanted and uninvited guest.

He only walked into the room, wondering as he did so what Cara would look like.

She was sitting at the round table in the window, and putting down her knife and fork she rose when he entered and dropped him a small curtsey.

She was dressed in a pretty but simple gown, which at first glance seemed to fit, but the Marquis's experienced eye realised a second or so later that it was too large round the waist and was therefore confined with a sash.

"As you have been riding, I wish you had let me come with you," she said reproachfully.

"Good-morning, Cara!" the Marquis said loftily, as if he reminded her of her manners. "If I had thought of it, which I did not, I would hardly have expected you to have in your pocket the requisite clothes for riding."

Cara gave a little chuckle as she sat down again at the table.

"I suppose you would not have considered letting me ride astride?"

"Most certainly not!"

The Marquis helped himself from the silver dish presented by one of the footmen while another poured out the coffee which he invariably drank on returning from riding, unlike his contemporaries who preferred brandy.

The Butler placed a rack of toasted bread in front of him, moved a silver dish containing a pat of golden butter from his own Jersey cows a little nearer, and put a bell at the Marquis's left hand.

Cara watched these attentions with an undoubted twinkle in her eyes before she said:

"No wonder you do not get married! There is no need when you have so many servants to cosset and fuss over you. Mrs. Peel talks about you as if she were a mother hen and you a wayward chick!"

The Marquis repressed a desire to laugh.

"If you are trying to provoke me, Cara," he said, "it is too early in the morning. What is more, I am hungry."

"Only because you have been riding," Cara remarked. "I call it very inhospitable of you not to have let me come with you. I am quite certain somewhere in this house there is a riding-habit that I could wear."

"Why should you think that?" the Marquis enquired.

"Because, although I could hardly believe it, Mrs. Peel has a whole wardrobe of clothes that have belonged either to your relatives, alive or dead, or to guests who have stayed here and left some of their garments behind, and there are also suits that you yourself have grown out of."

"Those you will kindly leave alone," the Marquis said sharply.

"There are a great many of them," Cara replied, "and they are far more suitable for me than the Eton suit I was wearing. If I am going to France, I would travel more comfortably dressed as a young man."

"If I find you wearing my clothes," the Marquis said, "I promise you I will treat you as a man, and give you a good hiding! It is what you deserve anyhow!"

"Now we are back to where we were last night," Cara said. "What are you going to do about me?"

"I have not decided," the Marquis replied, "but before I do so, I want you to tell me a great deal more about yourself than you have up to now."

There was silence until after a moment Cara asked:

"What exactly do you want to know?"

"First, who you are," the Marquis replied, "and secondly, why you have run away."

Cara pushed her plate to one side and put her elbows on the table, resting her chin on her hands.

Looking at her, the Marquis thought that with the light from the window on her hair, she looked exceedingly pretty, very young and different from any woman he had ever seen before.

He was used to conventional beauties, who, after being married for several years and having presented their husbands with several children including the much-needed heir, were prepared to enjoy themselves by flirting with the most attractive man they knew, who was invariably himself.

It was an unwritten law in the Social World that when a flirtation became an *affaire de coeur,* it should be kept as secret as possible, and husbands, even if they might suspect what was happening, had no wish to have their suspicions confirmed.

The Marquis of Broome, in his imperious, fastidious manner, had enjoyed the favours of some of the most lovely women in England, and there was no doubt that the Regent collected round him at Carlton House beauties whose attractions were unsurpassed by those of any other women in the world.

The Marquis could not quite determine why Cara's face had something irresistible about it that made him think it would be difficult, having once seen her, to forget what she looked like.

It might, he thought, be the effect of her short hair, which she had cut a little untidily and which was not arranged on her head.

Instead, it rioted in a manner which he was quite certain would seem irresponsible to any of the Dowagers who considered themselves to be leaders of the Social Scene.

At the same time, it had an attraction of its own which he had noticed before only in Lady Caroline Lamb.

Whatever he felt about Cara, there was one thing that was obvious: she was a lady by birth, and as such he could not send her out alone, even with a Courier, on the long journey to France without behaving in what by his code was an irresponsible manner.

Without realising it, he had been staring at Cara, and now once again she interrupted his scrutiny to say:

"I hope you are taking in all my good points and not deliberately concentrating on my bad."

"I am not admiring you as a woman," the Marquis said sharply. "I am trying to decide what I should do about you as a person."

"Then as a person, or rather as an unwanted package which you have acquired by chance, send me to France!" Cara retorted. "I will go either as a boy or a girl, whichever you prefer, and having rid yourself of me, you need never think of me again."

The Marquis had a strange feeling that this might be difficult, and although it seemed incredible on such a short acquaintance, he had the uncomfortable feeling that he would worry about her.

"What I am going to suggest," he said, "is that you allow me to eat in peace. I will then decide, after you have told me your story, how and in what way I will help you. But I think I should warn you—I am very astute in knowing when somebody is lying to me."

Cara's laughter rang out, and it was a very spontaneous sound of delight.

"Really, you are so stupid," she said. "Do you suppose I do not know that? Of course no one could lie and you not be aware of it! You have an instinct, as I have, and my instinct tells me you will help me, however much you may prevaricate or try to wriggle out of the net in which I have caught you."

"Net?" the Marquis asked.

"Oh, do not be frightened," Cara said hastily. "If you think I am trying to trap you into matrimony, you are very much mistaken. I have decided I will never get married, and that is final! And I do not intend to argue about it with anybody!"

She spoke so vehemently that the Marquis looked at her in surprise before he said:

"I presume, and now I am being intuitive, that the reason why you are running away is that you were to have been married."

Cara smiled at him.

"That is quick of you," she said, "and quite frankly, I am surprised that you are so perceptive."

"I find that remark almost an insult," the Marquis retorted.

"Not really," Cara answered. "Few men have any intuition at all. They just make up their minds what women are like, and they put them into a sort of pattern that has been evolved over the years, probably by their Nurses, their Governesses, their Tutors, and naturally by their mothers and fathers."

She gave a little laugh before she added:

"That means of course that to them a woman is a puppet, a doll, who has no feelings and certainly no intuition of her own."

"Is your suitor like that?" the Marquis asked. "And is that why you have no wish to marry him?"

He expected this to be too obvious a question for Cara to answer, but she gave a little shiver and said:

"He is horrible! Odious! Revolting! I would rather die than be his wife!"

"That might easily happen if I do not look after you," the Marquis said lightly. "But I do not suppose the gentleman in question is the only man in the world."

"He is the only man I am allowed to marry."

"And there is somebody else you would prefer?" the Marquis questioned.

She looked up at him.

"Now you are trying to embellish the story, to make it seem more romantic. No! As I have already told you, I have no intention of marrying anybody, and that is why you are quite safe from me, if that is what is worrying you."

The Marquis threw back his head and laughed.

"You are certainly frank, my dear Cara, but not particularly complimentary!"

"Why should I be?" Cara enquired. "I have heard about your attractions and how women flutter round you like stupid moths round a flame, and I can assure you, if you went down on your knees and begged me to be your wife, I would say: 'No!' To be honest, I hate men—all men!"

Once again she was spitting out the words as she had last night when the Marquis had called her a "tiger-cat," and after a moment he asked quietly:

"What has a man done to you that you should speak like that?"

It was as though Cara drew in her breath, and there was an expression in her strange eyes he could not interpret. Then she said:

"I refuse to talk about the past. I am interested only in the future, and because you appear to have some sensibility, please try to understand that I must get away quickly, in case I am discovered here or anywhere else in England."

"And if you are?" the Marquis asked. "What will happen then?"

She looked at him, and he saw a fear in her eyes that he had never expected to see in any woman's before she said:

"You may think I am being theatrical or overdramatic, but I will kill myself rather than accept what has been planned for me, which I can assure you is worse than any hell that was ever thought up by the Bible-thumpers."

Because although her words were dramatic she spoke in a low, quiet voice, they rang in the Marquis's ears with a sincerity he could not ignore.

He did not laugh or argue with her.

He merely rang the bell, and when the Butler came hastily into the room he accepted another dish that was hot from the kitchen and waved away two others.

Without speaking, he had his cup replenished with coffee.

Only when the servants had once again left them alone was he aware that Cara was sitting back in her chair, looking at him appraisingly in the same manner in which he had looked at her.

He ate several mouthfuls of food before he asked:

"Well, what are your conclusions? Have you found my good points?"

Cara laughed.

"A few. I think you are authoritative, autocratic, and that you frighten most people, although you do not frighten me."

"Why not?" the Marquis asked.

"I will answer that question a little later, when I discover if I am right in what I am thinking about you now."

"I am disappointed," the Marquis said. "I thought after all you have said that you are so quick-witted that you make up your mind in a flash."

"I know I can trust you, if that is what you mean, and when you say you will help me, you will. But actually, I was considering you just now as a man."

"A species you tell me you dislike," the Marquis remarked.

"I loathe all men!" Cara replied. "But you have certain qualities that remind me of my father."

"As I hope that is a compliment, I would like to hear more," the Marquis said.

"Surprisingly, for it is certainly something I had not expected, I think you have a sense of humour."

"Thank you," the Marquis remarked somewhat mockingly.

"If you want to be flattered," Cara said, "there are plenty of women to do that, and from all I have heard, they include those not only of the *Beau Monde* but of an under-world which I am told no lady should know exists."

"Then why are you talking about it?" the Marquis asked.

"Because men like yourself find it attractive, and it interests me to learn why, when you have so much that is beautiful, fine, and perfect round you, you should also look at the gutters, or rather the Dance-Halls and the Houses of Pleasure, which no lady should mention."

"Then you should not be talking about them!" the Marquis said sharply.

"They interest me simply because it makes the world so much more complex and in a way more intriguing than the life that I am told I must enjoy as a débutante!"

She sighed before she went on:

"Which to my mind seems incredibly boring, and nothing more than a Marriage Market in which one sets out to catch a fish, and the bigger, the better!"

Again she was spitting out the words, and the Marquis laughed.

"Your metaphors are certainly very mixed," he said, "but I understand what you are saying. But surely no one can force you to marry someone you do not wish to marry?"

Cara stared at him before she said:

"Now that is the first really stupid remark you have made since we met!"

"Who is forcing you into marriage?" the Marquis asked. "Your father, or is it a Guardian?"

"You are being clever and trying to twist out of me what I do not intend to tell you," Cara answered. "If I tell you what you want to know, you will take me back a prisoner and hand me over to what I swear to you will be my certain death."

"I do not believe you!" the Marquis exclaimed. "What is more, I dislike hysterics at breakfast."

He spoke in a way which would have crushed most people he knew. Men or women, they would have either apologised or stammered into an embarrassed silence.

Cara merely laughed, and the sound seemed to ring round the Breakfast-Room and join with the wintry sunshine which was peeping through the grey clouds in the sky.

"You are very, very subtle," she said, "and I take back what I said about your being stupid. You are trying to make me lose my temper so that I will tell you what you want to know!"

She laughed again and went on:

"It is an old trick. In fact, it was thought out by the French Revolutionaries when they interrogated the aristocrats and forced many of them to incriminate themselves by their own words."

"How do you know that?" the Marquis asked with an amused smile.

"Curiously enough, unlike most girls of my age, I read!" Cara replied. "I will now whet your curiosity a little further: nothing I have read is half as bad, pernicious, or degrading as what I have encountered in real life."

311

She spoke in a way that made it difficult for the Marquis to say that he did not believe her or that she did not know what she was talking about.

She looked so young, yet, by again speaking in that quiet, controlled voice, she gave him the feeling that she was old and experienced.

He pushed his plate away and sat back in his chair.

"I wish you would trust me, Cara," he said. "If I am to help you as you want me to, you must be sensible enough to tell me the truth and let me judge whether it is as bad or as terrible as you believe it to be."

As he spoke he looked directly at Cara and met her eyes.

For a moment it seemed as if they were linked together by something magnetic, yet invisible, something which joined them in a way which made it difficult for her to look away from him.

Then as she told herself that she must not listen to him, and that once again he was trying to trap her and find out what she had no intention of saying, the door of the Breakfast-Room opened.

"The Earl of Matlock, M'Lord!" the Butler announced.

For a moment the Marquis felt he could not have heard correctly what the servant had said.

But into the room came the man he most disliked, followed by two others.

There was silence.

Then Cara gave a little scream like that of a small animal caught in a trap.

"Uncle . . . Lionel!" she exclaimed, and her voice vibrated with fear.

CHAPTER THREE

$$\text{───}~\infty~\text{───}$$

*F*OR A MOMENT THE MARQUIS COULD ONLY STARE at the Earl in astonishment.

He was a middle-aged man and had been considered good-looking when he was young, but his eyes were too close together.

He now not only looked debauched, but the enmity and hatred with which he regarded the Marquis had etched lines on his face that were unmistakable.

As he entered the room he was smiling unpleasantly and there was a light of triumph in his expression which the Marquis at first found hard to understand.

Deliberately he did not rise to his feet but asked:

"May I enquire why you are here, Matlock, so early in the morning?"

As he spoke he realised that the Earl was in riding-clothes, his boots were covered with dust, and he was holding in his hand a thin riding-whip.

It was obvious that he had ridden hard and fast, and a glance at the two men with whom he had come told the Marquis the same story.

One was a sharp-faced, long-nosed, sandy-haired individual, not unlike a ferret; the other, to his surprise, was wearing the white bands of a Cleric beneath his riding-coat.

He had grey hair and a thin, cadaverous face which gave the impression that he was half-starved.

Ignoring Cara, the Earl walked across the room to the breakfast-table to confront the Marquis.

"I am here, Broome," he said, "to inform you that at last I have you where I have always wanted you—at my mercy!"

The Marquis's expression did not alter, but there was a wary look in his eyes as he replied:

"I have not the slightest conception of what you are talking about, and I think, Matlock, you should explain not only yourself but also the presence in my house of two other people I have not invited."

"Let me introduce them," the Earl said with a grandiose gesture. "My Solicitor, Israel Jacobs of Lincoln's Inn, and the Reverend Adolphus Jenkins, whom you are unlikely to have met, as his clients are mostly from the Fleet Prison."

He spoke mockingly. At the same time, there was an undeniable note of spite in his voice, which echoed the elation he was feeling.

His two companions stood just inside the door, and the Marquis was aware that Cara had retreated from the table until she stood against the panelled wall as far from the Earl as it was possible to get.

The Marquis also had the idea that she was longing to bolt from the room, which was impossible owing to the fact that the Earl's companions were standing by the door, and the windows which opened onto the garden were tightly closed.

"I am still at a loss to understand why you are here," the Marquis said after a moment's ominous silence.

"Let me put it to you more plainly," the Earl replied. "I am accusing you, Broome, of abducting and doubtless of ravishing a minor."

The Marquis stiffened but did not move, and the expression on his face did not change, while Cara gave another shrill cry.

"That is a lie! He did not abduct me. I hid myself in his carriage."

The Earl did not turn his head as she spoke, and indeed he gave no indication that he had even heard what she said.

His eyes were on the Marquis as he said slowly and distinctly:

"I am prepared, Broome, to give you a choice between standing trial for a crime which entails transportation, or marrying my niece and giving me ten thousand pounds for the privilege."

As he finished speaking there was a silence that seemed to the Marquis to be more eloquent than any words.

He saw only too clearly that the Earl held a trump-card in his hand and would not hesitate to play it.

He was well aware that not only had the successes of his horses over the Earl's enraged and embittered him as a rival, but he had on numerous occasions found it necessary to report to the Jockey Club infringements of the laws of racing which involved the Earl's jockeys and the Earl's horses.

On one occasion a horse had actually been disqualified after the Earl had ostensibly won the race, and the prize had gone to the Marquis's, which had come in second.

He had known then that the Earl would never forgive him, and now it flashed through his mind that he had inadvertently put himself at the mercy of a man who was an avowed enemy and was overjoyed at the chance to take his revenge.

What was so galling was that the Marquis had for years escaped every bait offered to him and every trap set for him as the most eligible bachelor in the *Beau Monde*.

There was no aristocratic family in the length and breadth of England which would not welcome him as a son-in-law.

But he had long ago decided that he had no wish to be married and no intention of being caught by the ambitious parents who thronged the Mayfair Ball-Rooms.

This decision, once it was known, had evoked a great deal of gossip and had even been lampooned by the satirical pens of the cartoonists.

Vaguely he had thought that at some time he must beget an heir, and he knew exactly the type of wife who would fulfil his requirements as the Marchioness of Broome.

This certainly did not involve espousing himself to some unfledged, ignorant girl with whom he knew he would become bored stiff within a few weeks of the Wedding Ceremony.

There was plenty of time for him to pick and choose and, with his fastidious, critical taste, to take a wife who would fit into the pattern of his life and do exactly what he required of her.

That he should be confronted with an ultimatum such as the Earl had brought him now was something that had never occurred to him even in his wildest nightmares.

Quickly and intelligently he sought a way out.

In his usual calm, rather dry manner, he said:

"I can scarcely believe that what you are saying, Matlock, is not some poor joke in very bad taste."

"It is no joke, I assure you," the Earl replied sharply. "Mr. Jacobs is prepared, if you refuse, to take my petition, which I have already signed, to the Chief Constable of the County. You can then expect to be arrested within a few hours and taken to the Old Bailey to await trial."

He paused to see the effect of his words before he continued:

"On the other hand, the Reverend Mr. Jenkins has in his possession a Special Licence which I obtained before I left London, which will enable him to marry you to my niece in your private Chapel. The choice is yours!"

The Marquis drew in his breath.

He was just about to say that he would see the Earl and his underlings damned first, when Cara gave another scream and walked into the centre of the room.

"If you think I will marry the Marquis in such circumstances," she said furiously, "then you are very much mistaken! I ran away because you tried to marry me to that filthy, beastly man, and I have made up my mind that I will not marry anybody ever, and you cannot make me!"

The Earl turned to look at her for the first time since he had come into the room, and as the Marquis watched him there was no doubt of the hatred he could see in his eyes.

"Are you again defying me?" he demanded. "Well, I am prepared to concede that you have chosen for yourself a more impressive lover than Forstrath, but you will marry him and I will have no hysterics!"

"I am not hysterical!" Cara replied fiercely. "I am only telling you that I will not marry the Marquis or that beast Sir Mortimer Forstrath, and no Marriage Service is legal if the bride says: 'No'!"

Her eyes were blazing as she spoke, and her words seemed almost to tumble over one another.

Without replying, the Earl raised his hand and struck her so violently on the side of her face that she fell to the ground.

Then, so quickly that the Marquis could hardly believe it was happening, the Earl transferred the thin whip he had been holding in his left hand to his right, and brought it down with all his strength on Cara's body as she lay on the floor at his feet.

He hit her twice before the Marquis jumped to his feet, shouting:

"Stop! How dare you strike a woman in my house!"

He pushed the breakfast-table in front of him to one side and was advancing towards the Earl with his fists clenched menacingly when Israel Jacobs moved from the doorway to confront him.

To the Marquis's astonishment, he held a pistol in his hand.

"Stay where you are, M'Lord," Israel Jacobs ordered. "A Guardian has his rights and is within the law if he punishes his Ward as he sees fit."

As his Solicitor spoke, the Earl glanced over his shoulder before he struck Cara again.

"That is right," he said, "and by the time I have finished with this tiresome little renegade, she will marry the Devil himself, if I tell her to!"

He raised his whip again, and as it struck her back Cara gave a shriek of pain.

The Marquis calculated that by moving quickly he might be able to knock the Solicitor's pistol from his hand, and the chances of success without having a bullet blown through him were about fifty-fifty.

Then as he flexed his muscles he became aware that the Parson also was pointing a pistol at him, and while it was held in a shaky and certainly unprofessional hand, it was still an unmistakably lethal weapon.

With two muzzles pointed at his heart, the Marquis knew he had not even an odds-against chance of escaping injury, if not death.

As he stood irresolute, Cara screamed again, and feeling as if he signed his own Death Warrant the Marquis said:

"Very well, Matlock. You win this skirmish, which I concede is a well-thought-out piece of criminal blackmail."

The Earl lowered his arm.

"I am glad you appreciate it, Broome. And now perhaps we can get down to business."

The Marquis, with tremendous self-control, did not reply.

He only walked across the room to stand in front of the fireplace, wondering desperately as he did so if there was any possible escape and, if so, what it could be.

The Solicitor and the Parson lowered their weapons but did not replace them in their pockets, and as the Earl looked down at Cara, the Marquis had an undeniable impression that he just barely restrained himself from kicking her.

"It is a pity," the Earl said to her, "that your future husband has, by surrendering so quickly, prevented me from giving you the thrashing you so richly deserve! How dare you run away from my house!"

He waited as if he expected her to reply, then went on:

"But who knows? I may be able to turn your position in the Social World to a better advantage than I would have gained by your marriage to Mortimer Forstrath."

As he spoke in a sneering, unpleasant manner that seemed almost to poison the atmosphere, the Marquis was suddenly aware of whom he was speaking.

He was not acquainted with Sir Mortimer Forstrath, who was a man he would never have acknowledged as a friend, knowing that he was greatly disliked in the Clubs of which he was a member.

He could not recall at the moment the specific reason for this attitude, but he could well believe that Forstrath was not a suitable husband for Cara.

As the Earl finished speaking he walked towards the Marquis and stood a few feet from him, and the two men glared at each other like pugilists in a ring.

Then the Earl said in the same unpleasant, sneering tone of voice and with a smile on his thin lips:

"I shall require your cheque first, Broome. The ceremony can take place immediately afterwards."

As he was speaking, Cara dragged herself from the floor up onto her feet.

She was very pale, except for one cheek which was red from the impact of her uncle's hand when he had struck her down.

The weals across her back were agonising, but her only thought was that if she could leave the room she would somehow get to the stables and, taking a horse, gallop away before anyone could stop her.

It flashed through her mind that the money and jewellery she had brought with her were upstairs, but at the moment that was immaterial.

What was important was that she should escape before she was forced to marry the Marquis, for she knew that her uncle was not speaking lightly.

When she had run away last night from his house in Grosvenor Square, she had known that nothing she could say, no pleading or begging for mercy, would prevent him from marrying her to Sir Mortimer Forstrath.

He wanted the money, he wanted to be rid of her, and he had already threatened to beat her unconscious if she argued with him any further.

It had never entered her head that in imposing herself on the Marquis, her uncle would not only find her but would use the situation as a means of providing himself with the money he so desperately needed, and at the same time of having his revenge on his greatest enemy.

Slowly, step by step, hoping that nobody was noticing her, she crept towards the door.

But just as she reached it, Israel Jacobs moved several steps backwards to stand in her way.

There was no need for him to speak, he just stood there, and with a little sigh Cara realised that she was defeated.

From the other side of the room the Marquis said:

"Let us talk this over sensibly, Matlock. I will give you the money, but as you are well aware, I did not abduct your niece, and there is no reason for me to marry her. She was well chaperoned last night by my House-keeper, a very respectable woman."

"No Magistrate, Jury, or Judge would consider a paid servant a suffi-cient Chaperone for a young innocent girl who has spent a night with the noble Marquis of Broome!" the Earl sneered.

As if he wished to provoke the Marquis even further, he added:

"You have had your fun, Broome, and now you must be a sportsman and pay for it!"

Only by exerting the greatest control did the Marquis prevent himself from knocking the Earl down.

"I will make it fifteen thousand pounds," he said quietly.

The Earl laughed.

"You are a very rich man, Broome, and it will be a considerable advan-tage for me to be able to claim a close relationship with you. I shall hope to enjoy a great deal more than money in the years ahead."

What the Earl was saying was irrefutably true, and the Marquis knew that he would make the very most of a family connection between them. It was infuriating that he should also demand an astronomical sum in recom-pense.

As if he felt he had driven the Marquis too far, the Earl said briskly:

"Suppose we get on with the business on which I have come? As I imagine you do not keep your cheque-books in the Breakfast-Room, I propose we should repair to your Study, if that is where they are."

That the Earl was taking command and ordering him about in his own house was in itself an insult which was hard to stomach, but the Marquis merely walked across the room and opened the door.

Cara was standing by it, and he glanced at her perfunctorily, and waited, obviously expecting her to precede him.

Moving slowly, as if in pain, she walked ahead, the Marquis followed, and behind him, delighted by the success of his campaign, came the Earl and his two attendants.

Because she did not know the way, Cara waited until the Marquis was beside her; then, knowing that there was nothing she could do, she let him lead her to the Study door, which was opened hastily by a footman.

They entered the large, comfortable room where the walls were hung with paintings by Stubbs, the chairs were covered with leather, and there was a flat-topped desk furnished with a huge gold ink-pot and a blotter on which was the Broome coat-of-arms.

As the Marquis walked towards his carved, high-backed writing-chair, Cara wondered once again if there might be a chance of escaping.

But with her uncle and his two henchmen behind her she knew it was impossible, and because she felt her legs could no longer hold her, she sat down on the hearth-rug.

Turning her back to the room, she held out her hands towards the big log-fire.

As she did so she was unaware that the blood from the weals on her back caused by her uncle's whip had begun to seep through the thin gown she was wearing.

The Marquis looked up from his desk and saw them, and his lips tightened into a harder line than they were already as he opened the drawer in front of him.

As he started to write the cheque, the Earl saw that in the corner of the Study was a table containing a grog-tray on which were various decanters.

Without asking permission, he walked across to it and poured for himself and the two men with him a large amount of brandy.

320

They took the glasses from him eagerly. Then he raised his own in the direction of the Marquis to say:

"I am of course prepared to drink, My Lord, to your happiness."

The Marquis did not even look up, and the Earl continued mockingly:

"You will find Cara hard to handle and extremely headstrong. So I think it appropriate that my wedding-present to you should be the whip I use to make her obey me. You will certainly need it yourself in the future!"

As he spoke he walked towards the desk and flung down in front of the Marquis the whip he had still been carrying in his hand.

The Marquis ignored both the act and the Earl's remark. He merely signed the cheque, then rose to his feet, leaving it on the table.

The Earl reached out and appeared almost to snatch it in his desire to make it his.

Then he looked at it carefully as if to see that he had not been tricked, and said:

"That is satisfactory. Now perhaps, Broome, you will show us the way to your Chapel, which I presume you as a God-fearing man keep in use?"

Again he was sneering, but the Marquis merely looked towards Cara, who at her uncle's words had turned her face from the fire.

Realising that they were all waiting for her, she slowly rose to her feet.

She was even paler than she had been when they had left the Breakfast-Room, except for the imprint of the Earl's hand, which was like a red flag on her cheek.

She walked past her uncle with her chin held high, and only as the Marquis opened the door for her and she started to walk through it did an idea flash into her mind.

As she stepped outside into the passage, she turned suddenly, slammed the door to, and turned the key in the lock.

Then, lifting her skirts, she was running as swiftly as she could towards the Hall and out through the front door.

As she had anticipated, the three horses which had brought her uncle and the two men with him to Broome were outside, each held by a groom.

Cara sped down the steps and literally flung herself into the saddle of the first horse she came to.

She made no pretence of riding side-saddle but sat astride, and picking up the reins set off before the grooms could grasp what was happening.

As they stared after her she rode the horse away from the house and towards the bridge which spanned the lake.

She had not gone far before she realised that the horse she was riding was tired after what had been a long and doubtless exhausting journey from London.

She guessed that it had been quicker for her uncle to ride across country than to take the road.

Because he must have been afraid that she might leave Broome before he had arrived, he had travelled at a speed which had exhausted the horse under him.

Cara had no whip and no spurs, and although she dug her heels into the horse's sides, she found before she had reached the end of the drive that the animal would go no faster than a trot.

She glanced over her shoulder, and as she reached the lodge-gates she could see in the distance that there were two horses following her.

It was not difficult to guess that her uncle had forced the Marquis to ring the bell, or had done so himself, and a servant had answered the summons to unlock the sliding door.

Outside the lodge-gates was a road running both right and left, and because she remembered that the way to London was to the right, Cara turned to the left.

It was nothing more than a small lane which twisted along the side of the high brick wall which at this point bordered the Marquis's Estate.

She rode on, doing everything in her power to hurry her mount, but knowing that she was having little effect.

Then, because she was afraid of the two men following her, when she saw an open gate which led to a field in the centre of which was a small copse, she rode towards it.

She hoped that she might hide there, but even as she reached the first trees she looked back and saw a rider coming down the lane she had just left, and she knew with a constriction of her heart that it was her uncle.

She realised then that the two riders who pursued her must have divided at the lodge-gates and her uncle had turned to the left.

He was beating the horse on which he was riding so that it moved at a far greater speed than anything she had been able to produce from her horse.

As the hedges were low and leafless at this time of the year, Cara was aware even as she was about to enter the wood that her uncle had seen her.

Because she now realised that her effort to escape was hopeless, she thought it more dignified to turn and ride back towards him.

He was red in the face from his exertions, and as he met her in the middle of the field, he shouted furiously:

"Damn and blast you! What the hell do you think you are doing?"

"Trying to escape from you, Uncle Lionel!" Cara replied with a flash of spirit, which was echoed by a feeling of despair at her fruitless effort to get away.

"You will come back with me!" the Earl said. "If the Marquis has run away in the meantime, I will beat you until you wish you had never been born."

"I have wished that often enough since I have been with you!" Cara retorted.

Her uncle turned his horse back towards the gate through which they had entered the field, and because there was nothing else she could do, Cara followed him.

When they reached the road and were riding side by side, the Earl said:

"If you were not so pig-headed you would realise I am doing you a good turn in marrying you to Broome. Your social position will equal that of any other woman in the land who is not Royal."

"I shall also be married to a man who will loathe and despise me because I am your niece!"

Instead of being angry, the Earl chuckled.

"At last I have beaten him!" he said with a tone of satisfaction.

Cara did not speak, and he went on:

"He has sneered at me, condescended to me, and has been a thorn in my flesh for the last five years! Now I am the winner, and 'Mr. High and Mighty' has to eat the dust!"

"You have the money you wanted," Cara said. "Let me go, Uncle Lionel. Say you could not find me and have no idea where I have gone. I will disappear and you will never see me again."

"I am not going to argue with you," the Earl replied. "You will marry

Broome, and thank God, if there is one, on your knees! No Guardian could do more for a niece who has been nothing but a headache since he has known her."

"You are not doing it to please me," Cara said. "You always hated Papa because you were jealous of him, and that is why you hate me. The only reason I shall thank God is because I shall no longer have to live with you!"

The Earl chuckled and it was an unpleasant sound.

"So you have still got some spirit in you, have you?" he asked. "I hoped I had beaten it out of you. It is a pity you are not marrying Mortimer Forstrath, for he would have had no nonsense with you."

Cara did not answer.

She merely saw the house lying ahead of them and knew that her uncle was right in that whatever her life with the Marquis might be, it would be infinitely preferable to what she would have suffered as the wife of Sir Mortimer Forstrath.

She suddenly felt limp and faint, not only from losing the battle against her uncle but also because of the weals on her back, which were hurting intolerably.

She rode ahead so that she need not listen to the Earl's sneers and jeers, and because she was afraid that she might collapse, she tried to think only of keeping in the saddle until she reached the house.

Somehow, she managed it.

As a groom went to the horses' heads, she swung her leg over the saddle and slid to the ground.

Only as she reached it and knew that she must somehow walk up the steps did she feel a darkness coming up from the earth beneath her feet to swallow her up.

Cara came back to consciousness to find herself sitting in a carved wooden pew in the Marquis's private Chapel.

Somebody was holding a handkerchief dipped in *eau de Cologne* against her forehead, and another hand held a glass of brandy against her lips.

She tried to push it away, then she heard the Marquis say in his dry, impersonal voice:

"Drink it. You will feel better."

Because it was easier to obey than to argue, Cara took a sip and felt the fiery liquid seep down her throat and into her body.

It took away a little of the darkness that was still hovering round her, and she knew from the way the Marquis moved the glass against her lips that he wished her to drink again.

She did so, and now the last remnants of the darkness cleared and she realised where she was and what had happened.

"She will be all right now," a voice said.

The handkerchief was moved from her forehead, and as she looked up she saw that the Marquis was standing beside her.

It was difficult to read the expression in his eyes, but she knew by the tightness of his lips and the squareness of his chin that he was very angry, although she thought it was not with her.

"Would you like a little more?" he asked, and although his voice was impersonal, she had the feeling that he was in fact somewhat compassionate.

She shook her head.

"No-no . . . thank . . . you."

"In which case, let us get on with the ceremony!" her uncle said sharply.

Cara turned her head.

She saw that he was leaning against another pew and that the Parson he had brought with him was standing at the altar-steps, holding a Prayer-Book in his hand.

In his dusty riding-boots and with the only sign of his Holy office being the two white bands at his neck, he looked shockingly incongruous.

But Cara was quite certain that her uncle would have seen to it that he was properly ordained and that the Marriage Service said by him and the Special Licence would be entirely legal and binding.

She knew in that moment that she had failed and there was no escape, although any marriage in such circumstances was a farce and an outrage against a Sacrament of the Church. But there was nothing she could do about it.

The Marquis was not looking at her but had walked a few paces away to wait for her to come stand beside him.

Almost instinctively and without conscious thought she glanced towards the back of the Chapel and saw that in the doorway, either to prevent her from leaving or to prevent people from entering, Israel Jacobs was standing.

His eyes were on her and she felt as if he too mocked at her helplessness.

Her uncle crossed to her side.

He put out his hand, and because she could not bear to touch him, she held on to the pew in front of her and pulled herself to her feet.

As she did so, she knew that the scars on her back were stiffening, and it was with difficulty that she prevented herself from giving a murmur of pain.

Then, because she would not be treated with derision, and if nothing else she still had her pride, she put up her hand, even though it was painful, to pat her untidy curls into place.

Then, without even glancing at her uncle, she walked the short distance up the aisle to stand beside the Marquis.

He did not look at her as the Parson began the Service, reading slowly and at times inaudibly from the Prayer-Book he held in his hands.

"I, Ivo Alexander Maximilian, take thee, Cara Matilda, to my wedded wife."

Cara heard the Marquis repeating the words calmly and quite expressionlessly, and she felt she must be dreaming.

Then, as if it were a dream, she heard her own voice:

"I, Cara Matilda, take thee, Ivo . . ."

Even as she spoke, she knew that she had lost not only her freedom but also her dreams.

Although she had sworn never to marry, somewhere far away at the back of her mind she had believed that one day she would find a man who was different from all the others she had known.

But that had seemed impossible when she was hating first her uncle, then the monster he had produced as her future husband.

Then, with a terror that had seemed to sweep through her body like forked lightning, she had believed that all men were fiends, or rather wild animals who pursued her and from whom she had to escape.

Her uncle's cruelty, the hatred she felt for him, and the horror that she had known when she had met Sir Mortimer had combined to make her determined that never, never would she be owned by a man!

She would remain free, unless by some miracle, which seemed very unlikely, she found a man whom she could trust because she loved him.

Now, when she least expected it, when she thought she had run away to become independent, she had been captured and was to be chained to the Marquis for the rest of her life.

"Those whom God hath joined together let no man put asunder!"

As the Parson spoke the words it seemed to Cara that it was the voice of doom.

She knew that somehow, in some way she could not for the moment envisage, she had to escape from the Marquis.

CHAPTER FOUR

———— ◦⊗◦ ————

*T*HE MARQUIS STOOD at the door watching the Earl and his two companions ride away under the oak trees.

Only long years of exerting control over his feelings prevented him at the last moment from striking the Earl and wiping the smile of satisfaction and derision from his face.

When they left the Chapel, the Earl had said in the same sneering voice he had used before:

"I presume, Broome, you are not hospitable enough to offer us a glass of champagne to drink on this auspicious occasion?"

The Marquis had not replied. He had walked away from Cara's side the moment they were married and strode ahead along the passage which led from the Chapel back to the Hall.

When they reached it, he did not speak but merely stood looking at the Earl in a manner which told him in no uncertain terms that he was to leave his house.

He knew by the expression on the Earl's face that he was trying to decide whether to provoke him further, or whether it would be wiser to leave him in silence.

Finally he chose the latter, and walked through the front door and down the steps to mount his tired horse in a manner which was a flourish of defiance, if nothing else.

The Solicitor and the Parson followed him, and they rode away with the Marquis watching them with such hatred vibrating from him as would have intimidated any ordinary man.

Then with a last glance at the three riders vanishing into the distance, the Marquis called to one of the grooms who had been holding their horses and were now preparing to make their way back to the stables.

"Ben!"

"Yes, M'Lord?"

"Saddle *Thunderer* and bring him to me immediately!"

"Very good, M'Lord."

The Marquis, feeling that he could not face Cara, did not go back into the house.

Instead, he walked from the front door across the gravel sweep in front of it and down over the lawn towards the lake.

When he reached it, the thin cover of ice that had been there first thing in the morning had broken, and now the ducks and swans were swimming on the water in the centre of it.

A pale sun was seeping through the dark clouds to throw a golden light on them.

The Marquis did not see it. Instead, he saw and felt only the humiliation he had just endured at the hands of an enemy.

It was, he thought, the first time he had been defeated in a battle in which he had never had a chance of being the victor.

It had all happened so quickly that he could hardly believe that what had occurred was not just a figment of his imagination.

And yet it was an undeniable fact that he was now married, and to a woman he had seen for the first time only last night in strange and not particularly admirable circumstances.

"Married!"

The word seemed to echo round him, and for the moment his brain could not be stimulated into telling him how he could cope with a situation he had never envisaged, and which was completely incompatible with everything that he had planned for himself now and in the future.

He stood staring at the lake until he heard the sound of a horse's hoofs behind him and the clinking of harness, and turned to see one of his finest stallions approaching.

The horse was fresh, and the Marquis knew that only by taking violent exercise could he somehow assuage the tumult that seemed to be flooding over him like a tempest.

He flung himself into the saddle, and without a word to the groom he galloped away, taking a route through the Park to where he knew he would be able to ride *Thunderer* until they were both exhausted.

In the house, Cara, having seen her uncle depart, walked towards the staircase and climbed it slowly, feeling that every step was an effort as the pain in her back increased.

For the moment, because she was concerned with the physical agony she was enduring, she could not think clearly of her marriage to the Marquis or what it entailed.

All she wanted was to lie down and be alone.

Only when she reached her bedroom did she know that after the beating her uncle had given her and her collapse when she returned to the house after trying to escape, she was too exhausted to care.

Wearily she struggled towards the bed, and lying down on it slowly so as not to hurt her back, she closed her eyes and hoped that she might become unconscious. . . .

Hours later Cara awoke from a sleep that had been half a faint to begin with; then, because she had no wish to face reality, she had gone into what was a self-induced coma.

She tried to turn and found that the blood from the wounds on her back had dried onto the pillow on which she was lying, and she gave a little cry of pain, which brought somebody to her bedside.

It was Mrs. Peel, the Housekeeper, and Cara found it hard to remember who she was.

"Are you awake, M'Lady?"

"I . . . suppose . . . so."

"I wonder if Your Ladyship feels strong enough to move to another room? Everything's prepared for you, and I think, Your Ladyship, I should put some salve on your back, then you can get into bed properly and rest."

Because it was easier to agree than to argue, Cara let Mrs. Peel lead her from the room she occupied and down the corridor to the South Wing of the house.

She was too tired to be interested, and it was only later that she realised she had been put in a bedroom that had always been occupied by the mistresses of Broome and had last been used by the Marquis's mother.

But when she first entered it she was aware only of pain and exhaustion, and like some small animal that had been hurt she wanted to crawl into a hole out of reach of everything that was frightening.

It was very painful when her gown was being removed, but the salve was some comfort as Mrs. Peel applied it to the broken skin, then covered it with a soft lint.

She was given something warm to drink, which she thought was honey and milk, but she was not curious enough to enquire.

Then, half-lifted by Mrs. Peel, she found herself in the large bed with massive posts carved and gilded which supported a canopy of cupids rioting amongst leaves and flowers.

But this had no reality for Cara, who could think only of putting her head down on the pillow and shutting her eyes.

The curtains were drawn over the three long windows, and left alone she tried to close her brain against thought and concentrate only on trying to sleep.

The Marquis did not return to the house until late in the afternoon.

As he walked in through the front door, the Butler, taking the Marquis's tall hat, gloves, and riding-whip, thought he looked drawn and considerably older than he had that morning.

The servants were naturally agog at what had happened, being well aware that their master had been in the Chapel with a Parson and the strange young lady who had arrived unexpectedly the night before.

Although Mrs. Peel was the soul of discretion, the housemaids could not resist relating below-stairs that the young lady who had arrived had short hair and wore an Eton suit under His Lordship's fur-lined cloak.

Speculation as to who she could be and why she had come to Broome in such a strange manner had been the sole topic of conversation from the knife-boy to the eldest housemaid.

"There's a gentleman arrived from London to see Your Lordship," the Butler said respectfully to the Marquis. "I've shown him into the Study, M'Lord."

"From London?" the Marquis queried.

For a moment he thought it might be Henry Hansketh, then knew it was too soon to expect him.

His first impulse was to say that he wished to see nobody, but convention and good manners told him that was something he could not do when somebody had journeyed all the way from London.

Accordingly, knowing that what he wanted was a bath and something to eat, he walked towards the Study, hoping his unexpected caller would not keep him long.

A footman opened the door, and as he entered the room he saw to his surprise that the gentleman, who apparently had not given the Butler his name, was a member of the Royal Household.

"Good-afternoon, Bingham," the Marquis said. "I must apologise if I have kept you waiting. I was not expecting you to visit me."

"I thought it right to bring you the information myself," Mr. Bingham replied, "that His Majesty expired at thirty-two minutes past eight o'clock last night."

"The King is dead!" the Marquis exclaimed.

It came actually as a surprise, even though it was something that had been expected for so long.

Like the Regent, the Marquis and many other Courtiers had begun to think that the King would never die.

"He is dead," Mr. Bingham replied, "and as today is the anniversary of the execution of Charles I, the Proclamation of the new King's accession will not be made until Monday."

"And of course he expects me to be present," the Marquis said almost as if he spoke to himself.

"That is why I came here with all speed, My Lord. His Majesty is already asking for you."

"Thank you, Mr. Bingham," the Marquis said. "And now let me offer you a glass of wine, or would you prefer brandy?"

"Wine, if you please, My Lord."

"You will of course stay the night," the Marquis went on, "and we will leave for London first thing tomorrow morning."

"The earlier the better, My Lord! His Majesty received the news with a burst of grief, and there is nobody he prefers to have with him in such trying circumstances as yourself."

The Marquis received the compliment somewhat wryly. He knew how emotional the new King could be.

All through his life he had over-dramatised every situation from the time when at the age of twenty-two he had stabbed himself in a frenzy because he was determined to make Mrs. Fitzherbert marry him.

Since then he had on every possible occasion resorted to hysterical outbursts or floods of tears to express himself.

As the Marquis poured Mr. Bingham a glass of champagne from the bottle resting in a silver wine-cooler, he thought that the King's over-dramatisation of his father's death was the last thing he wanted at this particular moment, and that made him remember Cara.

If he had to go to London, what was he to do about her?

And what was more, how was he to announce his marriage to his friends?

Something the Marquis hated more than anything else was any scandal connected with himself. Yet, for the moment he could not imagine how he could present to the Social World the fact that he had a wife whom nobody had seen or heard of before.

He knew it would be as startling in its own way as was the death of the King.

However, as the thoughts raced through his mind he appeared quite calm, as having handed Mr. Bingham a glass of champagne he poured one out for himself.

As he picked up the glass he realised that his visitor was not drinking but was looking at him in a speculative way, as if he waited for him to make a move.

The Marquis understood what was expected of him.

He lifted his glass to say slowly and distinctly:

"The King! God bless him!"

"The King!" Mr. Bingham repeated, and drank the champagne as if he was sorely in need of sustenance.

A little later the Marquis, having instructed the Butler to show Mr. Bingham to his room, went upstairs and, turning towards the South Wing, walked quickly towards his bedroom, knowing that his valet would have a bath waiting for him.

While he bathed he wanted to think over this new problem which made it impossible now for him to stay in the country as he had intended to do.

He had almost reached his own room when from out of a doorway ahead of him appeared Mrs. Peel.

As he saw her the Marquis knew without being told that Cara had been moved into the room next to his.

This meant that the whole household was now aware of his marriage, she was being treated as his wife, and she would in future sleep, as was traditional at Broome, in the Marchioness's bedroom.

For a moment he felt a surge of anger that they should have anticipated his instructions and, what was more, put Cara in a bedroom that had not been occupied since his mother had died.

If he could have obeyed his impulse he would have thrown Cara out to sleep in the attics or anywhere, as long as it was not close to him.

Then as Mrs. Peel curtseyed to him respectfully, once again his self-control made him acknowledge her and listen expressionlessly as she said:

"Her Ladyship seems a little better, M'Lord, and although at first I did think of asking Your Lordship to send for a Physician to look at Her Ladyship's back, I do not now think it will be necessary."

The Marquis stiffened.

He was well aware that if the local Physician examined Cara it would be impossible for him to keep to himself the fact that the new Marchioness of Broome had been beaten until the blood flowed, and chattering tongues would carry the story from one end of the County to the other.

"I have no wish, Mrs. Peel," he said in his most commanding voice, "for anybody to be aware of Her Ladyship's injuries, and I trust you to see that it is not spoken of either inside the house or outside!"

"I'll do my best, M'Lord," Mrs. Peel replied.

She curtseyed again as the Marquis walked past her to open the door of his own room, and having passed inside to close it in a manner that was suspiciously like a slam.

Mrs. Peel gave a little sigh and walked away down the passage.

The Marquis would have been surprised if he had known how distressed and upset she was that he should have been married in such a strange, unaccountable manner, and to a young lady who not only had been ill-treated in a way she found appalling, but who was also not the type of lady she had expected to welcome as the Marquis's wife.

"Short hair and trousers!" Mrs. Peel murmured to herself as she moved towards the other part of the house. "What's the world coming to, I ask myself?"

The Marquis and Mr. Bingham dined together and discussed discreetly what would happen now that after waiting for so many years the Regent was at last on the throne.

"I can only hope, Mr. Bingham," the Marquis said, "that His Majesty will listen, as the Prime Minister and the Cabinet will not, to my continual demands for some sort of reform before it is too late."

Mr. Bingham, who was an intelligent man, shook his head.

"Things are getting worse in the North, My Lord," he replied, "but unfortunately everybody in power seems to think that if they ignore what is occurring, the menace of it will go away."

The Marquis's lips tightened.

He knew that the measures known as the "Six Acts," by which the Government was endeavouring to curb the activities of the Revolutionaries, had only made things worse.

He thought too that letters like the one from the Duke of Cambridge, who said that "nothing but firmness" could quell the "abominable revolutionary spirit now prevalent in England," were just a lot of "hot air."

He had in fact spoken to the Regent very firmly, telling him that something must be done, and His Royal Highness had been made personally aware of the necessity when hissed by an immense mob outside his own front door.

Lady Hertford, his latest fancy, had been all but pitched out of her chair into the street and had to be rescued by the Bow Street Runners.

"What is wanted," he said aloud "is cheaper food, higher wages, and somebody to make the working people feel that their problems are understood."

"I am sure His Majesty would become aware of what is required if Your Lordship would explain it to him," Mr. Bingham said.

The Marquis knew that the new Monarch, beset by problems of his own, the most notable being the behaviour of his wife, the Princess Caroline, would find it hard to listen.

The more he thought of the King's unhappy marriage, the more he was reminded of Cara lying upstairs at the moment.

Ever since the Princess's arrival from Brunswick in August 1814, Caroline had been providing Europe with scandal after scandal.

She had dressed her gentlemen in a startling new livery of gaudily embroidered coats and plumed hats.

At Genoa she had appeared at a Ball dressed *en Venses,* or rather not dressed above the waist.

At Baden she had pranced at the *Opera of the Widowed Margraviere* into the box shouting with laughter and wearing an outlandish peasant's head-dress ornamented with candles and flapping ribbons.

At Genoa she had driven through the streets in a glittering mother-of-pearl Phaeton, dressed in pink and white like a little girl, and showing a large expanse of middle-aged bosom and two stout legs in pink top-boots.

At Naples at a Ball she was alleged to have appeared *"in a most indecent manner, her breasts and arms being entirely naked."*

In Athens she had *"appeared almost naked and danced with her servants."*

One by one these incidents, which had lost nothing in the telling, flashed through the Marquis's mind.

With horror he saw himself suffering in the same way from his wife, and having people say, as Lady Bessborough had:

"Having seen the Princess at a Ball, I cannot tell you how sorry and ashamed I felt as an Englishwoman."

Although he did not talk about it, the Marquis was exceedingly proud of his heritage.

His ancestors were part of the history of England, and the Bromleys, which was the family name, had played their part not only in attendance at Court but on every notable battlefield whether on land or on sea.

He himself had been very careful never to do anything that would defame or dishonour the coat-of-arms which was carved over the front door of Broome and which decorated his carriages in London.

Then he told himself, as if he must soothe down the temper rising within him, that Cara, even though she had appeared dressed in an indecent manner, and with her hair cut in order to run away, was only a child compared to the plump, over-boisterous Princess Caroline.

It was ridiculous for him to think that he could not make a girl of eighteen behave properly in the future and obey him.

"After all, I have had command of a great number of troops," he consoled himself.

But he had the uncomfortable feeling that a woman, whatever her age, could be more difficult than a whole Battalion of men who were trained to take orders.

He went on talking to Mr. Bingham, and when at last the Courtier retired to bed, saying that he would like as much sleep as possible, knowing how many duties awaited him in London, the Marquis knew he must advise Cara of this sudden but unavoidable change in his plans.

He supposed she would not be well enough to travel tomorrow, but he had no wish to leave her for long on her own at Broome.

Although it might be awkward in London, he had the uneasy feeling that it would be best for her to be near him so that he would know what she was doing and planning.

"She is my wife," he told himself, "and the sooner I make it clear that I will have no nonsense, the better!"

Having said good-night to Mr. Bingham, he walked down the passage to his own room.

He had looked at the large clock in the Hall before he ascended the stairs, and seeing that it was not yet ten, he thought there was no reason to suppose it was too late to disturb Cara.

One thing was perhaps a blessing in disguise. If the King was not to be acclaimed until Monday, it would certainly be a mistake for him to announce his marriage until after the Proclamation was over, so he might even delay it for several days.

"I shall wait until I am in London and see exactly what is happening," the Marquis thought.

He reached the door which led into the room where Cara was sleeping, then hesitated.

He decided it would be more natural if he came to her through the communicating door between their rooms with only a *Boudoir* between them.

This was the room in which his mother had spent much of her time. It was very feminine, being furnished with all the things the late Marchioness had particularly treasured: pictures of her son and daughters when they were children, a portrait of her husband on the wall, and some delightful paintings by French artists which the Marquis thought showed that her taste had been as good as his own.

As he entered the *Boudoir* from his own bedroom, having given his valet instructions to start packing immediately, he resented the fact that anybody should be using it, especially a wife he did not want.

He told himself that what was most important at the moment was that he should establish his relationship with Cara in a way which would leave her in no doubt as to who was the master and that she must behave as would be expected of his wife.

As usual, in accordance with the Marquis's orders, everything at Broome House was ready for immediate use, and the *Boudoir,* although he had not entered it since he had come home, was filled with flowers and the candles were lit.

This was something that happened every night when he was in residence, and although he had never opened the communicating door from the *Boudoir* into his own room, he was aware that everything was ready on the assumption that he might do so.

He felt now, however, with a darkening of his eyes, that the room had been prepared for Cara.

He deliberately did not glance at the portrait of his father over the mantelpiece or a very lovely one of his mother by Sir Joshua Reynolds on the other wall.

Instead he walked quickly towards the door opposite his own, which led into the bedroom.

For a moment as he put out his hand to turn the handle he had a feeling of revulsion, and every instinct in his body cried out against the woman who had taken his much-valued freedom from him.

Then he told himself it had not been her fault, and it would be an unsportsmanlike gesture to blame her entirely for what had occurred.

He turned the handle, only to find that the door was locked, then turned it again to make quite certain he was not mistaken.

Because he could not believe that Cara would deliberately lock him out or anticipate that he might wish to see her, he thought that by some stupid lapse on the part of a housemaid, the door must have been left locked even after the bedroom was occupied.

He debated with himself whether he should go into the passage and try the other door, then instead he decided to knock.

He raised his hand and knocked on the wooden panel, not loudly, for he had no wish for his valet, who was in his bedroom, to know what was happening, but loud enough for anybody inside to hear.

There was silence and he knocked again.

"Cara!"

For a moment he thought that she had not heard him, but after a moment she replied:

"What is . . . it?"

"I want to talk to you. Open the door!"

There was a pause. Then she said distinctly:

"No!"

"It is important that I should speak to you," the Marquis insisted.

There was no reply, and he thought perhaps she was getting out of bed and coming to the door. When she spoke again, he was sure that was what had happened because her voice sounded nearer.

"What do you want to see me about?" she asked.

"My plans have changed, and I have to tell you about them."

"You can tell me through the door."

The Marquis felt his temper rising.

"Stop being ridiculous," he said sharply. "I can hardly talk to you through a closed and locked door."

"Why not?"

"Because it is foolish and unnecessary."

"I have gone to bed . . . I want to sleep."

"I can understand that," the Marquis said patiently. "But I still want to speak to you. I am your husband."

"I know, but I have no wish to talk to you at this hour of the night."

"It may be late," the Marquis agreed, "but I was told earlier that you were asleep, and I am leaving for London first thing tomorrow morning."

He thought she was considering what he had said.

"Open the door, Cara!" he ordered. "I will tell you what has happened."

"No!"

The monosyllable had a very final ring about it.

The Marquis resisted an impulse, which was very unlike him, to put his shoulder against the door and break the lock.

"I insist on your doing what I tell you to do," he said. "It is important that you should know why I am going to London."

"You can leave me a note," Cara said, "unless you wish me to accompany you. But I do not think I shall be well enough."

"No. I was not going to suggest that," the Marquis answered, "but it will be necessary for you to join me in a day or so."

"Very well," Cara replied. "When I am better I will try to carry out your instructions."

As she spoke, the Marquis heard her voice fading away and knew without being told that she had moved back to the bed.

He could hardly believe that she was deliberately disobeying him and ignoring his request.

But a moment later he heard her voice in the distance as she said: "Good-night, My Lord!" and knew that their conversation, if that was what it could be called, was at an end.

Mrs. Peel did not bring Cara's breakfast to her the following morning until some hours after the Marquis had left for London.

Propped against the silver-crested dish which covered a plate of Crown Derby china was a letter inscribed with a strong, upright handwriting. Cara thought she would have recognised it as belonging to the Marquis wherever she had seen it.

It was, she thought, characteristic of him: authoritative, determined, and, in a way, overwhelming.

Deliberately, because she thought it would annoy him if he knew, she ate her breakfast before she read it.

Because she felt very much better than she had the night before, she enjoyed the eggs and the fresh country butter from the Marquis's Jersey cows, which she spread with home-made quince jam, a specialty of the Broome Still-Room.

Only when she had eaten almost everything that was on the tray did she pick up the Marquis's note and open it.

It stated, without any preliminary:

"His Majesty King George III died on Saturday evening. The new King will be proclaimed today and requires my presence. I am therefore going to London and will be at Broome House in Park Lane.

If you are well enough, I suggest that you join me tomorrow or the next day, as apart from the fact that I think you should be with me when I announce our marriage, you will require clothes which can only be provided for you in London.

If you will inform Mr. Curtis, who is in charge of the household, on which day you are prepared to travel, he will make all the arrangements for your comfort, and also for a maid to travel with you."

I. B.

The Marquis had not signed his letter but merely added his initials entwined at the bottom of the page.

Cara read what he had written, then read it again.

She was interested to learn that the King was dead, and she thought that after waiting so long the new King would be thrilled and delighted at being at last on the throne and having the power to do as he wished.

'If I were King I would abolish matrimony,' Cara thought, with only herself in mind.

Then she remembered, as the Marquis had done, that the King was married to a woman who had humiliated him by her behaviour and had become a laughing-stock not only in England but in Europe.

Some of her uncle's friends had met Princess Caroline when they had been abroad, and they had talked about her behaviour interspersed with roars of laughter, which Cara had thought was insulting not only to her husband, the Regent, but also to the English people.

"I wish you could have seen her, Lionel," one of her uncle's friends had said, "when after her English attendants had left her she filled their places with a collection of French chamber-maids and cooks, Arab footboys, Austrian postillions, and Italian footmen!"

"Good God!" the Earl had ejaculated. "Is that true?"

"They are overbearing, and their insolence is beyond description," his friend replied, "and their entrance into any territory is as much regretted as an incursion of free-booters."

"I hope His Royal Highness knows this," the Earl sniggered.

"You may be quite certain that somebody will tell him," his friend replied. "I heard that he swore like a trooper when he heard how his wife had ridden into Jerusalem on an ass."

The way they were talking made Cara feel not only embarrassed but as if she too was humiliated as the Regent would be.

She had learnt that her uncle hated the Regent and gloried in hearing anything about Princess Caroline that was degrading and derogatory.

It struck her that the Marquis would doubtless expect the same kind of behaviour from her because she was her uncle's niece.

'I hate him because he is my husband,' she thought. 'At the same time, Papa and Mama would expect me to behave like a lady, whatever Uncle Lionel is like.'

Because her back was still very painful, she decided it would be foolish to go to London to join the Marquis until she felt very much stronger.

If she was horrified and angry at finding herself married to him, she knew that his feelings at being married to her would be equally violent.

She had not heard her uncle deriding him and disparaging him as the owner of successful race-horses without knowing that in character the Marquis was everything that the Earl was not.

At the same time, he was a man, and she had no wish to be married to any man. More than anything else, she was concerned with considering if she would break the marriage.

If not, she must try in some way, however difficult it might be, to escape to an independence where she would belong to no man and could be herself.

It was not going to be easy, she was well aware of that, and as the day progressed she learnt, and it infuriated her, that the Marquis was having her carefully guarded in case she should make an attempt to run away from him as she had done from her uncle.

She realised he was perceptive enough to know that she had no interest in the social position she had attained on becoming his wife, and she was still intent on either reaching France; where she could be with her friend, or on disappearing.

She did not ask herself how she knew that the Marquis was thinking this, but because she was intuitive she felt quite certain that this was the truth, and that without saying anything to her he had made it impossible for any form of escape from Broome to take place.

Explanations were offered, and very plausible ones, for her guards.

"I thought you might want something in the night, M'Lady," Mrs. Peel said, "so I have told Robinson to sleep in your dressing-room next door. You only have to call out and she will be at your side within moments."

"Thank you," Cara said, but she had known at once why Robinson, an elderly housemaid, was there.

On the third day she decided she would join the Marquis in London and when she went downstairs was not surprised to find that she was to journey not only with Robinson but also with Mr. Curtis.

He travelled with her in the coach, sitting beside her on the back seat, while Robinson, looking exactly as a lady's-maid should in a black bonnet and wrapped in a heavy black cape, sat opposite them.

Mrs. Peel had excelled herself in finding an elegant travelling-gown that Cara could wear for the journey to London.

It was extremely becoming and had a very pretty coat that went with it, heavily trimmed with sable, with a small muff to match.

"Who could have left these pretty things behind?" she asked Mrs. Peel.

"They belong to His Lordship's younger sister, M'Lady, who is now abroad in a hot climate and has no need of furs. I'm sure she won't mind Your Ladyship borrowing them. Later I'll put them back in moth-balls to keep them safe until her return."

There was no mention of what had happened to the Eton suit in which Cara had arrived at Broome, and she was too shy to ask Mrs. Peel what she had done with it.

She thought with a little twist of her lips that perhaps it would be kept in Mrs. Peel's wardrobe for some youth in the future who might be short of just such an outfit.

The bonnet with which Mrs. Peel provided her was definitely not as fashionable as those Cara had seen in London, but it was quite pretty.

The seamstress who worked in the house had added a few ostrich-feathers from another source to make it more suitable for the new Marchioness of Broome.

Because she could not prevent herself from being curious, Cara asked Mrs. Peel before she left:

"How did you know, or did he tell you, that I was married to His Lordship?"

For a moment Mrs. Peel seemed disconcerted, then she said:

"Your Ladyship must be aware that little goes on in the house without Mr. Newman or myself being aware of it."

"I suppose that is the same in any big house," Cara said with a smile.

Because of the way Mrs. Peel had mentioned the Butler, Cara was sure that every word her uncle had said in the Breakfast-Room had been listened to outside the door.

And the fact that they had gone straight to the Chapel only confirmed that the servants had overheard while eavesdropping.

She did not know until she arrived in London that the Marquis, intent on attending His Majesty, had been furious when he opened the morning newspapers to find that the Earl, determined to have the last say, had sent an announcement of their marriage to *The Gazette*.

However, he had no time to express his anger before he hurried to Carlton House to stand in the cold air beside the King, the Royal Dukes, and Prince Leopold, and listen to the aged Garter King of Arms read out the traditional formula of accession in a slow and quavering voice.

The next day the new King had inflammation of the lungs, and a bulletin was issued with the grave news that His Majesty was severely indisposed.

The Marquis visited Carlton House to find that the King could not sleep, had a racing pulse, pains in the chest, and great difficulty in breathing.

On Wednesday he was close to death, and everybody walked about speaking in whispers.

The Princess de Lieven, who always had something pertinent to say on such occasions, said to the Marquis:

"If he should die, Shakespeare's tragedies would pale before such a catastrophe. Father and son in the past have been buried together, but two Kings? I hope this one will recover."

"I hope so indeed!" the Marquis agreed in a heart-felt voice, wondering if he died whether the Queen would make an attempt to be accepted as Regent.

The idea was so horrifying that he was disliking Cara more than ever when on returning to Broome House he was told that she had arrived.

Because he had been thinking of her in the image of Queen Caroline, he was expecting her to be large-bosomed, red-faced, and truculent.

But when he entered the Drawing-Room, where he was told she was waiting for him, he found it difficult for the moment to recognise her.

As he approached, she rose from the chair in which she had been sitting, and he saw how very small she was, and her hair curling on top of her head seemed to hold the sunshine.

Her eyes seemed enormous as they turned up at the corners and were not in the least aggressive.

She curtseyed, and the Marquis bowed formally, then looked down at her. As he did so, he realised with a shock of genuine surprise that she was frightened of him.

CHAPTER FIVE

———— ❧ ————

WOMEN HAD LOOKED AT THE MARQUIS in many different ways—with love, desire, jealousy, anger, and reproach—but he could not remember any woman before looking at him with an expression of physical fear.

For the first time since his marriage he was thinking not of his own outraged feelings but of Cara's, and he realised that the punishment she had received from her uncle had been enough to terrify any young woman and make her afraid of all men.

Without a great deal of difficulty he forced himself to smile at her in a way that most women had found irresistible.

"Are you better?" he asked.

"Yes, thank you," Cara replied. "I waited until I felt well enough to travel."

"That was sensible," the Marquis said. "And now that you are here, we have a great deal to talk about. Suppose we both sit down?"

He noticed that Cara did so carefully, as if her back was still stiff, and that she sat upright on the edge of the chair, with her hands in her lap.

As he sat down opposite her he saw that the expression in her strange eyes was still wary and there was an undoubted touch of fear in their green-gold depths.

The Marquis had meant to start by telling her about the King and the anxiety his illness was causing both at Court and in the country.

Instead, because he was curious, he asked:

"Has your uncle often beaten you?"

Cara looked away from him and there was just a faint touch of colour in her cheeks as if she was embarrassed.

"Whenever I have annoyed him," she replied.

"It is intolerable that he should have treated you in such a manner!" the Marquis ejaculated.

"He hates me because he hated Papa!" Cara said simply.

"Why should he hate your father?"

There was a little pause before Cara answered:

"My father was the elder son, and Uncle Lionel was, I think, desperately jealous of his position as soon as he was old enough to understand it."

The Marquis did not speak, and after a moment she went on:

"Papa was in every way different from my uncle. He was a sportsman, brave, kind, and everybody loved him, just as they . . . loathe Uncle Lionel!"

There was a sudden violence in her voice, which told the Marquis very clearly what she too felt for the Earl.

"Perhaps it would be easier for us both," he said, "if you would explain

345

to me a little about your family and how your uncle became your Guardian. I presume that not only your father but also your mother is dead?"

Cara nodded.

"Mama died . . . last year."

"And your father?"

"He died five years ago. Two days before he would have inherited the title from my grandfather."

As she spoke there was a note in her voice that was so strange that the Marquis looked at her enquiringly, and when she did not elaborate, he remarked:

"I feel that there is some mystery about your father's death."

Cara looked at him swiftly, as if she was surprised that he should be so intuitive, but when she did not reply the Marquis said:

"I think, Cara, the most important thing in trying to make our strange marriage work smoothly is for us to be absolutely frank with each other, and that is something I am prepared to be with you."

"Very well," Cara replied, "if you want the truth, I believe, although I cannot prove it, that my uncle . . . murdered Papa!"

Her words were a shock, even though the Marquis thought he might have anticipated them.

Then he told himself that Cara, in making the accusation, was influenced by her personal hatred of her uncle.

In a quiet and calm voice, which those who consulted him politically would have recognised, the Marquis said:

"Suppose you tell me exactly what happened?"

As Cara began to speak, his eyes were on her face as if he was minutely weighing everything she said, to be quite certain whether it was true or false.

Cara gave a little sigh before she began:

"We all lived, Papa, Mama, and I, in the big house which the Matlocks have owned for two hundred years. Grandpapa liked us to be there with him because otherwise he would have been very lonely, and in fact he loved Papa very much."

She paused before she said in a voice that told the Marquis she was speaking more to herself than to him:

"We were very . . . very . . . happy."

"Then what happened?" the Marquis prompted.

"Grandpapa became ill, and although Uncle Lionel never came home except when he wanted money, Papa thought it only right that he should inform his brother that the Doctors thought that Grandpapa might die."

The way she spoke told the Marquis how worried and distressed they all had been.

"I had not seen Uncle Lionel for some years," Cara went on, "and I suppose that because now I was older, the moment he appeared I knew exactly what he was like. I knew too that he was planning how much he could obtain for himself if Grandpapa died, and how much he loathed Papa for being the heir."

"Did your father realise this?" the Marquis enquired.

"Papa had always tried to help Uncle Lionel and had even given him money, which we could ill afford, to help him meet his debts."

"I presume he was in debt on this occasion?"

"Very deeply, as we were to learn afterwards, when he sold everything in the house that was not entailed."

Cara thought the Marquis looked surprised, and she explained:

"That was after Papa was dead and he inherited."

"How did that happen?"

"Two days before Grandpapa died, when we all knew there was no hope of saving him, Papa and Uncle Lionel went out riding together . . . but he returned alone."

For a moment it was difficult for her to continue. Then she forced herself to say:

"According to Uncle Lionel, they had both taken a very high fence, but Papa's horse had fallen, throwing him to the ground so heavily that he broke his neck."

"But you did not believe it was an accident?"

"Papa was a brilliant rider and knew every fence and every jump on the Estate. He would never have let his horse attempt anything that was too high!"

"Why should you suspect that your uncle was responsible for his death?" the Marquis enquired.

"Papa was brought home on a gate carried by farm-workers," Cara answered, "and it was a long time later in the evening when I asked Uncle

Lionel about Papa's horse, which was the favourite he always rode and with which he had never had any difficulty."

"What had happened to it?"

"Uncle Lionel said that the fall had broken its leg and he had therefore shot it."

The way she spoke told the Marquis without any further words exactly what she suspected. He knew that if a man was wicked and unscrupulous enough to shoot a horse at the moment when it was taking a high jump, the result must be a precipitate fall which could quite easily kill its rider.

There was silence before the Marquis asked:

"Could you really accuse your uncle of such a dastardly crime?"

"Mama thought, as I did, that that was what he had done," Cara answered, "but she said that accusations would not bring Papa back to life, and it would only make things between us much more unpleasant than they were already."

Cara drew in her breath before she finished:

"Also, we were completely dependent financially upon Uncle Lionel. Papa had no money of his own, although Grandpapa had made him an allowance in the same way as he made one to his other son!"

She paused, as if she was thinking back, before she went on:

"Because agriculture had suffered during the war when so many men were away fighting with Wellington's Army or at sea, we had not had good harvests, and the tenants were behind with their rents so that we too had to make very strict economies."

"I think things are the same throughout the country," the Marquis said, "and I can understand that it meant your mother had no money in hand."

"We had practically nothing," Cara replied. "Uncle Lionel turned us out of the big house and gave us a small cottage on the Estate. He would barely furnish it, and he allowed us to have nothing that was of any value."

The Marquis could understand that this had been very humiliating.

"Fortunately," Cara continued, "Mama could prove that Grandpapa had given her two of the horses as presents, one at Christmas and one on her birthday, so at least we had something to ride."

She looked at the Marquis as if she thought he must know how important that was, then went on:

"Uncle Lionel closed the country house and went to London. He sacked the servants, refused to give them pensions, and behaved in a manner which made me ashamed of my own family."

The Marquis thought it was the type of behaviour he would expect of the Earl.

But there was no point in saying so, and he was concentrating on learning what had happened to Cara.

"This must have been in about 1815," he said aloud.

It was the year the war had ended, and he had still been on the Continent, following Wellington's victory at Waterloo.

"There was a great deal of hardship and often hunger when the men began to come home after they had been dismissed from the Forces," Cara said, "but Mama was more concerned with seeing that I was given a good education."

Her voice softened as she continued:

"Fortunately, she had a few pieces of jewellery which Papa had given her over the years. These she sold so that I could have the best Teachers available in the neighbourhood, but it meant we had to live very frugally and could not afford extravagances of any sort."

Now there was a new note of aggression in her voice, and the Marquis understood that she did not want pity, least of all from him.

She was telling her story exactly as it had happened, which was what he had asked her to do.

He did not speak, but his grey eyes were on her face, which was very expressive as she went on:

"Then last year Mama became ill. She had always been very unhappy without Papa, and although it was an agony for her to leave me, I knew she would be happy again once she was with him."

The Marquis felt that this statement was very revealing as to Cara's beliefs, and he thought how few of the women he knew were religious enough to have faith in an "after-life" where the man they loved was waiting for them.

"After Mama was buried," Cara continued in a different manner altogether, "Uncle Lionel arrived."

"You had not seen him for some time?"

"No, not since he had closed the house, and I had been only thirteen at the time."

Now there was something like horror in her voice as she said:

"As soon as he came into the cottage, I realised he was surprised by my appearance and that I looked different from what he had expected."

"You mean that he admired you?" the Marquis interposed.

"What I knew," Cara answered, "and I cannot tell you why I knew it, was that he thought my looks might be useful to him. I hated him as Papa's murderer, and now I was afraid for myself in a way I cannot explain."

"Did he say you were to live with him?"

"He ordered me to pack what clothes I had and come with him to London," Cara replied, "and I had no choice but to obey him."

"When did this happen?" the Marquis enquired.

"Just before Christmas, and as we drove away he said:

" 'You will not wear mourning for your mother, and I want no weeping and wailing in my house. The only asset you have is that you are of marriageable age, and I will find a suitable husband for you.' "

"What did you reply?"

"I told him I had no intention of marrying any man unless I loved him."

"I suppose your defiance annoyed him."

"He struck me!" Cara answered. "And when we reached his house in Grosvenor Square in London, and I repeated what I had already said, he . . . beat me with a whip!"

The expression on her face told the Marquis what a horrifying experience it had been, but she went on quickly:

"There was nothing I could do. He bought me some gowns, having said that everything I owned was fit only for the rag-bag. I tried to think of how I could possibly escape, but I had not a penny to call my own."

The Marquis looked puzzled, knowing that she had told him she had twenty pounds in the pocket of her coat, and also some jewellery.

"I knew that it was hopeless to run away without being able to pay my way," Cara went on, "and until Christmas came there was no chance of my possessing even a shilling."

"What happened at Christmas?"

"A friend of my uncle's came to stay at Grosvenor Square, and she was very rich."

"What was her name?"

"She called herself *La Marchesa* di Cesari," Cara said, "but I found out from the servants that she was nothing of the sort. She was a singer who was always under the protection of rich men, and she had the most fantastic jewellery, besides being very generous with her money."

The Marquis was beginning to see the whole story, which had puzzled him, falling into place like the pieces of a jig-saw puzzle.

He listened intently as Cara went on:

"The *Marchesa* was impressed by Uncle Lionel because he had a title, and he was enamoured, or pretended to be, of her."

"It was hardly the right sort of society for you to be in," the Marquis remarked. "I am quite sure your mother would not have approved."

"At first I was not allowed to attend the parties they gave," Cara replied. "Then one night the *Marchesa,* who was really quite a kindly woman, said to Uncle Lionel:

" 'Oh, let the child have a bit of fun. After all, Christmas festivities were meant for children.'

"I found it exciting to go downstairs in a pretty gown for the party," Cara continued, "although the guests were a strange collection and I think Mama would have been shocked not only by the women but also by the men."

She paused before she added:

"And . . . most especially by . . . Sir Mortimer Forstrath."

The Marquis remembered that he had intended to make enquiries about that particular gentleman, but the new King's illness had put it out of his head.

"That was the man your uncle wanted you to marry," he said.

"The moment I saw him he made me creep!" Cara replied. "I did not like the way he looked at me, and when he touched me it gave me 'goose-pimples.' I felt, as the servants say, 'as if a ghost was walking over my grave.' "

"What was wrong with him?"

"I did not know what it was that made him so repulsive right from the start," Cara answered. "Then Emily, the maid who looked after me and had grown fond of me, told me about him."

"What did she say?"

Cara's voice dropped almost to a whisper as she replied:

"She said . . . that he went frequently to a wicked house that . . . belonged to a Mrs. Barclay . . . where gentlemen like him paid large sums of money . . . to whip . . . young girls."

The Marquis stiffened and looked at Cara incredulously.

He knew whom she was talking about and was well aware that Mrs. Barclay's house of ill-repute was notorious.

It was the sort of place he would never visit himself, but the fact that the woman had made a fortune out of debauched and usually elderly men who liked such exotic pleasures was well known in the Clubs of St. James's.

"How can the maid-servant possibly have told you about such things?" he asked.

"Emily was worried about me," Cara replied, "and she had heard about Sir Mortimer from Uncle Lionel's valet. He also told her that Sir Mortimer was prepared to pay ten thousand pounds to Uncle Lionel if he would permit him to marry me."

The Marquis understood now why that particular sum had been extorted from him by the Earl.

It seemed utterly incredible that any man who called himself a gentleman could sink to such a level of obscenity, and he thought that his dislike of the Earl of Matlock, which had existed ever since he first knew him, was certainly justified.

"Now you can . . . understand," Cara said in a small voice, "why I ran . . . away."

"And to do so you took jewellery and money belonging to the *Marchesa!*"

"I helped her up to bed after her Birthday Party, which went on until the early hours of the morning," Cara said. "I was allowed to be present because Sir Mortimer wanted me there, but I had a miserable time trying to avoid him."

Her voice sharpened as she said:

"At one moment I thought of stabbing him with a knife. Then I knew I would doubtless fail to kill him and the result would simply be that I would receive another beating from Uncle Lionel, who had grown more and more violent every time I said I would never . . . never marry such a man!"

"So you stole the *Marchesa*'s jewellery while you were helping her to bed!"

"Her lady's-maid was downstairs, enjoying herself with the rest of the staff," Cara answered. "Most of Uncle Lionel's servants behaved in a manner that neither Papa nor Grandpapa would have allowed. Mama always said that 'a bad master breeds bad servants.' "

"That is true," the Marquis agreed. "So you put the *Marchesa* to bed and took her jewellery."

"Not the jewels she was wearing, that would have been very stupid! But when I put them away in her big jewel-box, I saw at the bottom of it two pieces she never wore, and as you know, I still have them."

"I had forgotten that," the Marquis said. "They must certainly be returned to their rightful owner. I can hardly allow you as my wife to be prosecuted for being a thief!"

Cara's eyes widened before she said:

"Uncle Lionel would be delighted if I was hanged for such a crime! Please let me give you the jewellery. I am sure you can think of some clever way of returning it to the *Marchesa* without her being aware that it is missing."

Then, before the Marquis could agree, she gave a little cry and said:

"Emily would do that for me if I could get in touch with her."

"We will consider it carefully," the Marquis said, "but first finish your story."

"I took the brooch and the collet to my room and hid them," Cara said, "and the next day the *Marchesa* was very ill, too ill to get up. She asked me to fetch her a handkerchief from one of the drawers, and while I was doing so I saw that she had a great amount of money thrown there untidily amongst her other things."

Cara looked a little embarrassed as she explained:

"I knew it was what she had won at the party and when she had been gambling with Uncle Lionel at one of the places they often visited in Mayfair."

There were a number of Gaming Houses, as the Marquis knew, that catered only for the aristocrats and which were therefore considered private houses and outside the jurisdiction of the Gaming Laws.

"I was quite certain she had not counted it and could have no idea of how much she had won," Cara went on. "She was very stupid about English money and always said she could not understand what any of our coinage meant."

"So you helped yourself!" the Marquis said drily.

"It was either that or stay and marry Sir Mortimer! Uncle Lionel had already told me he was arranging for our marriage to take place within two weeks, and I was to order for myself a wedding-gown."

"Now I understand why you decided to run away, and perhaps in the circumstances it was the best thing you could do."

For the first time during this conversation Cara's eyes twinkled.

"Are you really approving of something I have done, My Lord?" she enquired mockingly.

The Marquis laughed.

"You are leaving me no other alternative."

"I had found the Eton suit in the attic earlier when I had been exploring the house," Cara said. "There were several there, and I think they must have belonged to Papa or Uncle Lionel when they were boys. There were also costumes which were at least a century old."

"The attics of every house in London are full of treasures," the Marquis said. "I know my mother once found a gown at Broome that had real diamonds sewn on it, and it had been in the attic for a hundred years!"

"I shall certainly have a treasure-hunt if I return there!" Cara exclaimed.

The Marquis realised that she had said "if" instead of "when."

As she was aware that he had noticed the slip, she said quickly:

"I want to talk to you about that."

"Yes, of course," he said, "but may I say first, Cara, I am glad I have heard the whole story of your attempted escape from your uncle, and I can understand now why you felt it imperative to do so."

"I am afraid it was unfortunate for you that I chose your travelling-chariot because it had six horses," Cara said, "but I suspect that whoever it was who saw me climb into it and told Uncle Lionel, the result, as far as I am concerned, would have been the same."

It flashed through the Marquis's mind that she might not have chosen either such a rich man who could be blackmailed into marrying her, or, from the Earl's point of view, an enemy over whom he could score such a satisfying revenge.

But there was no point in saying so, and after a pause he said:

"What is done cannot be undone, and I hope, Cara, that we are both intelligent enough to make the best of what for us both is an unfortunate situation."

"Surely it is possible for you to break the marriage?" Cara asked. "After all, Uncle Lionel blackmailed you into it."

"Nevertheless, we were legally married by Special License and by a Parson," the Marquis replied.

Because he resented it so much, he had no idea how his voice altered when he spoke, and became cold, sharp, and contemptuous.

"I have a . . . suggestion to . . . make," Cara said in a very small voice.

"What is it?"

"If you had no wish to be married . . . neither had I, and if I . . . disappear when after a year or two you will be able to . . . assume that I am . . . dead, you will be free."

"If that idea was practical I suppose we might consider it," the Marquis said. "But you must be aware that if you disappeared, your uncle would undoubtedly accuse me of having murdered you and create such a scandal that the whole country would be searching for you."

Cara looked at him with startled eyes.

"Do you really think Uncle Lionel would do that?"

"I am sure of it," the Marquis said, "if for no other reason that he could then force me to pay him to keep silent!"

"I hate him! I hate him!" Cara said furiously. "How can he be allowed to flourish in his wickedness? I am sure he killed Papa, and perhaps a great number of other people, for all we know!"

"Such suppositions are quite useless without proof," the Marquis said coldly.

"What can I do?"

"The answer is quite simple," he replied. "You are my wife, and it should not be difficult for you to behave outwardly in the way the world will expect of anybody in such a position."

Cara laughed.

"I am quite certain you know the answer to that," she said. "Why should I stay with somebody who hates me because I am my uncle's niece?"

"I will try not to labour that point," the Marquis promised, "since you are well aware that it would be most unfair. You may be the niece of a man whom I despise and am ready to condemn, but you are also the daughter of your father and mother."

Cara rose from the chair in which she was sitting and walked across the room to stand looking out the window.

Outside was a small paved garden with, in the centre, a very beautiful statue standing above a carved stone goldfish-pool.

Because it was winter there was no water in the pool, and in the garden itself there was no colour except for a few dwarf-sized shrubs which were evergreen.

Cara's eyes were looking at them, but actually she was considering her life with the Marquis and thinking that although it was unlikely he would beat her or physically ill-treat her as her uncle had done, it would be an existence without love.

She felt she could not face an atmosphere of hate and loneliness such as she had experienced while she was living in Grosvenor Square.

'I shall have to run away,' she thought. 'Whatever he may say, it is the only thing I can do.'

"What are you thinking, Cara?" the Marquis asked.

"At least my thoughts are my own!" she snapped.

"Perhaps I can guess them," he said. "I have a feeling you are still intent on leaving me. Let me make it quite clear that I will not allow you to do so."

Cara turned round to look at him.

"Why should you be so foolish," she said, "as to want me to stay when you know as well as I do that you will find my presence here intolerable? Every time you look at me you will remember how you have been humiliated by Uncle Lionel, and however much you try to forget, it will be a constant irritant that will make our lives a hell!"

The way she spoke was more surprising than what she actually said, and the Marquis rose from his chair to walk across the room and stand beside her.

She did not speak but merely stood looking up at him, her strange, slanting eyes seeming to hold a question which was impossible for him to answer.

He did not speak for a moment, then he said:

"You puzzle me, Cara, because you are quite unlike any young woman I have ever met before. But you constitute a problem which I have every intention of solving, and it would be far easier if we tried to solve it together."

"Now you are being very subtle," Cara said. "You want to get me on your side so that I shall obey you without actually realising I am doing so."

The Marquis laughed.

"In fact, I was thinking how uncomfortable it will be if we continue bickering and fighting from morning to night! I had thought when the war ended I had finished fighting enemies."

"I am not your enemy!" Cara flashed.

"No, that is true," he conceded, "and while I am quite prepared to fight with enemies outside the house, it would be an impossible situation if one very important one was inside."

"Now you are being conciliatory, and that, I feel sure, is far more dangerous than when you bristle aggressively and threaten me with every weapon within reach!"

The Marquis laughed again, and it was a spontaneous, whole-hearted sound.

"You certainly have a very unusual turn of phrase," he said. "I have a feeling, Cara, that as long as we can laugh, if not together, at least at ourselves, things will not be as black as they appear at the moment."

Cara looked away from him again into the garden, and the Marquis said:

"Because I have so much to do for His Majesty, who keeps demanding my presence at his bedside, could we for the moment call a truce?"

"I suppose we might do that," Cara conceded.

"Very well," the Marquis said with just a touch of satisfaction in his voice. "This is where you start by buying yourself a trousseau."

As he spoke he felt it would be impossible for any woman to refuse such a generous suggestion. In fact, he knew that any Beauty, in whatever strata of society she existed, would in the past have been wildly elated at such a suggestion coming from him.

But Cara appeared to be hesitating, and he could not understand why.

"I want my friends to admire my wife," he said, "and I think it extremely important from the point of view of both of us that they should believe we were married because we were attracted to each other, and not because we were compelled into it by your uncle."

"You do not think he will . . . tell everybody what really . . . happened?"

"I doubt it," the Marquis answered. "He has won what to him is a tremendous victory, and I think that while he will undoubtedly attack again, he will wait for the moment to see the result of what he has achieved so far."

Cara gave a little shiver.

"He . . . frightens me."

"Let me promise you one thing," the Marquis said. "Now that you are my wife, if he ever touches you again, I will kill him!"

The way he spoke without raising his voice was very impressive, and Cara turned to look at him with startled eyes.

"Do you . . . mean that?"

"I mean it!" the Marquis said positively. "I loathe and detest cruelty in any form! I am always prepared to mete out punishment to any man who ill-treats one of my horses, and I can only tell you that I am not speaking lightly when I say I would murder a man who frightened you."

Cara was looking at him wide-eyed, and he saw the colour come into her cheeks almost as if his reassurance had brought her to life.

Then she said:

"What you have just said . . . makes me feel safe for the first time since . . . Mama died."

"I assure you that you are completely and absolutely safe so long as you remain with me."

"Thank you," Cara said. "Thank you very much."

"I have been thinking," the Marquis went on, "that perhaps your uncle will realise his plan has misfired if he finds I am quite content with the situation he has created, and if I can convince my friends, who will be curious as to why we were married in such a strange manner, that it was something we did willingly because it was what we wanted to do."

Cara clasped her hands together.

"That is clever . . . very clever," she approved.

"I thought you would appreciate the subtlety of it," the Marquis said. "But we have to play our hands carefully to see what turns up, and be prepared to fight your uncle fairly and squarely when the occasion arises."

Cara nodded to show that she understood, and the Marquis went on:

"The first step is for you to look beautiful, because my friends will expect me to have married a beautiful woman, and secondly, in public at any rate, we must both appear happy in each other's company."

"You mean that it can be an act put on for Uncle Lionel's benefit, which he will find disconcerting," Cara said, as if she reasoned it out to herself.

"Exactly!" the Marquis agreed. "That is why I suggest that while I am busy in attendance upon the King, you buy yourself a trousseau that will make all the other women's eyes pop out with envy."

Again there was that unexpected little pause and he asked:

"What is troubling you?"

Cara looked up at him and said:

"I . . . I think perhaps I am being . . . very foolish but I have been so poor with Mama . . . and the only clothes I have owned were the ones she and I made together . . . and I am therefore afraid I would not have the . . . good taste or the . . . knowledge to choose the sort of clothes I should wear as . . . your wife."

The Marquis smiled and there was no need to force it to his lips.

"I understand what you are saying, Cara," he said, "and it was foolish of me not to know that was what you might feel. There is, however, a quite easy solution."

"What . . . is that?" Cara asked doubtfully.

"The dressmakers can come here, and we will choose your clothes together."

As he spoke, he thought how many gowns he had chosen not only for the mistresses whom he had kept in his comfortable house in Chelsea, but also for the Beauties who, while they loved him wholeheartedly, still expected to be able to dip their fingers into his large and generous purse.

They were always begging him for a gown for some special occasion, furs because they were cold, or perhaps a muff into which he could put his hand to warm their cold fingers.

After that there had been an avalanche of accessories to make them look beautiful in his eyes—bonnets to frame their gold, red, or raven-black hair, sunshades to protect their delicate white skins from sunburn, and of course jewels to embellish their long necks, their tiny shell-like ears, and their slender wrists.

'This at least will be the first time I have bought a trousseau for my own wife,' the Marquis thought.

Quite unexpectedly, he found it amusing.

CHAPTER SIX

"*T*HEY'RE REELLY BEAUTIFUL, M'Lady, they are reelly!" Emily said in awe-struck tones as Cara showed her the clothes that had arrived daily from the dressmakers.

She thought the same herself, and she was honest enough to acknowledge that it was due to the Marquis that all the garments which had been made for her were so glamorous and alluring, for she would not have had either the experience or the good taste to know exactly what suited her.

She lifted down from the wardrobe a gown in pale green which matched her eyes, and when she held it up against her Emily exclaimed:

"It makes you look like a bit o' spring, M'Lady, and that's the truth!"

Because she was curious about what was going on at her uncle's house in Grosvenor Square since she had left it, Cara had been pleased when she was told that Emily had called to see her.

"It might seem a bit presumptuous, M'Lady," Emily had said humbly, "but I've wondered about you ever since you runs away, and the master was so furious he were like a madman 'til Tim said as how he'd seen you gettin' into a chariot outside Carlton House."

"So it was Tim who saw me!" Cara exclaimed.

Tim was the scullery-boy who she had always thought was rather a tiresome character and not quite normal.

He could be shrewd when it suited him, but the servants disliked him because he was spiteful and often told tales about them to the Earl.

"Yes, 'twas Tim right enough," Emily said. "He's always going to Carlton House to watch the Gentry going in and out, just as he watches the houses in the Square. I often wonders why it interests him."

In a way, Cara was glad to learn who had been watching her.

She had lain awake sometimes wondering how she could have been so unfortunate as to have attracted anybody's attention when she slipped into the Marquis's chariot, hoping that she had escaped from her uncle forever.

Although she still played with the idea of escaping again, and this time from the Marquis, she had found it an absorbing interest to be able to buy as many clothes as she wanted.

Also, it had been exciting to talk to the Marquis and to his friend Lord Hansketh.

She was actually never alone with her husband except after the dressmakers had fitted her with the gowns which he had ordered, when she went downstairs to show them to him when he was writing letters at his desk in the Study.

When he was not out of the house he always seemed to have a great deal of writing to do.

Cara gradually realised that he played an important part in the debates and business of the House of Lords, as well as being constantly in attendance upon the King.

His Majesty had recovered slowly from the inflammation of the lungs, and although he wished to attend his father's Funeral, his Physicians strongly urged him not to take the risk of doing so.

The King gave way to their entreaties and remained indoors, but he insisted on the Marquis being with him.

Now that he was no longer physically ill, he was exceedingly worried about his wife and in fact could speak of nothing else, and the Marquis was regaled with every incident of the Queen's behaviour in Europe.

He was also forced to read the long statements that the King was compiling in the hope that he might be able, sooner or later, to divorce her.

The whole story was so sordid that every time he came home the Marquis began to think that Cara at any rate was very different from what he had feared.

As he had realised when he first met her, she was quick-witted and had a gift of repartee that Henry Hansketh at any rate found very amusing.

"One thing about your wife, Ivo," he said to the Marquis in private, "is that she will never bore you as so many of your lady-loves have managed to do."

"Why should you say that?" the Marquis asked somewhat truculently.

"She has an original mind and a most unusual way of saying what she thinks," Lord Hansketh replied. "There are very few women like that, especially when they are young."

The Marquis had to admit this was true, but he was still resenting the manner in which he had been blackmailed into marriage by the Earl, and he still felt infuriated that Cara had shackled him.

At the same time, he had to admit that in the evenings when he, Henry, and his wife dined *a trois,* she contributed intelligently to the conversation and was also a good listener.

To Cara it was an experience she had never had before, which, although she did not admit it to herself, was sweeping away her fear of the male sex.

Because the Court was in mourning, no parties were being given, and the Marquis had said it would be a mistake for her to start to meet his friends until he could present her to them formally and make it, as he expressed it, a "grand occasion."

She knew this meant that she had to look right, and he wanted to show that there was nothing strange about their marriage, which had just been kept quiet until the King was well enough to be present.

"At the same time," she told herself, "I expect he is ashamed of me really, because I am not in the least the sort of wife he would have married if he had had the choice."

Just as Mrs. Peel had spoken about the Marquis almost as if he were a god, the Housekeeper and the rest of the servants at Broome House in Park Lane did the same.

Most of them had known him ever since he was a boy, and his successes first at Oxford, then in the Army, lost nothing in the telling.

They were ready to show Cara momentoes of every stage in his growing up, and because they believed her to be deeply in love with him, they assumed she would find every momento and anecdote about the man they admired something she would treasure and remember.

In the face of such adoration it was impossible to appear indifferent to what they wished to tell her, and she thought it would not only be ungracious to do so but also unkind.

She therefore found herself beginning to look at the Marquis in a very different light from the way she had before.

It was his secretary, Mr. Curtis, who told her of his importance in the political world and how the Prime Minister and Members of the Cabinet consulted him.

"Do they ever come here?" Cara asked, thinking she would like to see the Prime Minister and also the good-looking Lord Castlereagh, who was Secretary of State for Foreign Affairs.

"Sometimes they do," Mr. Curtis replied, "but usually they meet at Lord Harrowby's house in Grosvenor Square."

"I know that house!" Cara exclaimed. "It is next door to my uncle's. He lives at Number Forty-three; and Lord Harrowby lives at Number Forty-four."

"That is right," Mr. Curtis said. "When the Cabinet was dining at Lord Harrowby's house on June 21, 1815, the Duke of Wellington's *Aide-de-Camp*, Major the Honourable Henry Percy, burst into the Dining-Room with the story of the victory of Waterloo and brought the Duke's despatch to Lord Bathurst, who was then Secretary of State for War."

"How exciting!" Cara exclaimed. "I wish I had been there!"

"I am afraid those dinner-parties do not include ladies," Mr. Curtis said with a smile.

"I think it is unfair that men have all the fun," Cara complained, and Mr. Curtis laughed.

She wished that when she was living with her uncle she had known of the exciting parties that were taking place next door, and she said now to Emily:

"Has Lord Harrowby, who lives next door to my uncle, had many guests lately?"

"I don't rightly know, M'Lady," Emily answered, "but I can soon find out."

"How can you do that?" Cara asked, and Emily looked coy.

"Well, as it happens, M'Lady, one of His Lordship's footmen has been courting me, so to speak. He makes all sorts of excuses to come round and see me. He's something of a chatter-box, and I expect he'll tell me anything I want to know."

Cara thought perhaps she should not ask outright for such information, and changing the subject she said:

"Has my uncle had any parties since I left?"

"Not big ones, M'Lady," Emily answered, "but there's a very strange man as comes to the house who Tim tells us has been in prison for abusing Lord Sidmouth."

Cara had heard the Marquis and Lord Hansketh speaking of Lord Sidmouth and knew he was the Home Secretary.

"Why should my uncle want to have anything to do with a man who has been in prison?" she asked.

"His name's Thistlewood," Emily said, "and Tim says he's a nasty customer."

"What does he mean by that?" Cara questioned.

"I don't know, I don't listen to what Tim says. He's always saying things to make our flesh creep. But do you remember Albert? He was saying last night that this Mr. Thistlewood and the master are planning something, and he wouldn't be a bit surprised if it didn't include murder!"

Emily lowered her voice as she spoke to make what she was saying sound creepy.

"You cannot mean that," Cara said lightly.

Then she remembered that she had suspected her uncle of murdering her father, and if he could commit such a crime once, there was no reason why he should not do the same again.

She put the gown she was holding back in the wardrobe and said:

"I expect Albert is exaggerating, but tell me what he heard."

As she spoke, she knew that Albert must have been listening at the door of the room in which her uncle had been talking to this man Thistlewood.

"I thinks Albert talks a lot of nonsense!" Emily said. "I don't listen to half of what he says, but by the time I next comes to see you, M'Lady, I'll have got the whole story out of him."

After Emily had left, Cara thought over what she had said and decided it was unlikely that her uncle would involve himself in any activities which might be proved criminal.

At the same time, servants usually were surprisingly well informed about what was going on.

She was especially interested in Lord Harrowby's parties because she knew the Marquis attended them.

Because of the way he had talked to his friend Henry in front of her, she had begun to grow more and more interested in politics. She knew they were both deeply concerned that unless something was done there would be a social revolution with an attempt to overthrow the Government.

Often, she thought, they forgot that she was present and talked so seriously and so interestingly that she wished she could note down everything they said so that she would not forget it.

"I must find out about this man Thistlewood," she decided. "Perhaps he is the sort of person they fear may stir up trouble."

That evening the Marquis came back very late from the Palace, where the King had kept him while he railed furiously against the caricatures and satirical pamphlets that were appearing in the shops and were sold in the streets.

George Cruikshank, William Home, and a host of other satirists and artists championed the Queen and ridiculed the King.

In fact, there was only one print-seller who ventured to purvey Loyalist prints.

"Something must be done!" the King cried frantically, but the Marquis had no ready solution to the problem.

Every day produced dozens more aggressive and vulgar libels against the Monarch which were hawked in all the streets, and it was useless to make any attempt to check it.

"They must be aware that this will encourage the Queen to behave even worse than she is already!" the King said bitterly, and the Marquis could only feel desperately sorry for him.

It was quite a relief, after hours of talking about the Queen and going over her misdeeds for the thousandth time, to find Cara waiting for him in the Drawing-Room.

She was looking very young and, as the Marquis admitted to himself, exceedingly lovely in one of the new gowns he had bought her.

It matched her eyes, as a number of others did, simply because the Marquis had found that one particular shade of pale green made her skin seem dazzlingly white and brought out the lights in her hair and in her eyes.

It also, he thought, gave her a somewhat elfish appearance which was unlike anything he had ever noticed in any of the women with whom he had been involved and which, although he still did not admit it, he found attractive.

Cara jumped to her feet as he entered the room.

"You are very late!" she said. "I wondered if something had happened to you."

"His Majesty kept me, and it is such a usual experience that I am almost tired of apologising."

"There is no need for you to do so," Cara replied. "Just as I accept it, so does the Chef, and I am sure that dinner will not be spoilt."

"It will not take me long to change," the Marquis answered, and hurried upstairs to his bedroom.

By the time he came downstairs again, Henry, who had been told that dinner would be later than usual, had arrived and was talking to Cara.

They were sitting together on the sofa, and the Marquis thought they were talking somewhat intimately as he came into the Drawing-Room.

It flashed through his mind that Henry, who had said that he admired both Cara's looks and her intelligence, might be making love to his wife.

Then he knew that the idea was not only disloyal but an impossibility.

However, during dinner the thought occurred again and again and began to irritate him.

"I was asking Lord Hansketh before dinner," Cara said as dessert was put on the table, "if he had ever heard of a man called Thistlewood."

"Her Ladyship suspects him of being a bad character who has been in prison," Lord Hansketh said.

"I have heard of him, and I have no idea why Cara should be interested in such a person," the Marquis said coldly.

He noticed that both Cara and Henry looked at him curiously, and he went on:

"Thistlewood is a renegade gentleman who gambled away all his money, then made a nuisance of himself by importuning Members of Parliament."

"I understood he went to prison for twelve months for abusing Lord Sidmouth," Cara said.

"I suppose you read about it in the newspapers," the Marquis replied. "He has certainly behaved abominably, and Sidmouth was quite right in taking a strong hand with such a trouble-maker."

"He is out of prison now," Cara insisted.

"If he is, and if he continues to make a nuisance of himself, he will soon be back there," the Marquis said.

"He might make a lot of trouble in the meantime," Henry remarked.

"I think it unlikely," the Marquis said crushingly, then changed the subject.

When Cara went to bed, she thought over what had been said and was sure that the Marquis, if he became aware that Thistlewood was seeing her uncle, would suspect that they were plotting something unpleasant.

For all she had heard from the conversations between the Marquis and Lord Hansketh, it seemed certain that the revolution they both feared would not take place until those who wanted to rebel had the right sort of leader.

She was imaginative enough to realise that what the Marquis had called a "renegade gentleman" would be just the sort of person to organise a rebellion and give it direction and purpose.

'I must find out more from Emily,' she thought.

As Henry was leaving he had asked:

"Are you riding in the Park tomorrow morning, Ivo?"

"Of course," the Marquis replied with a smile.

"Then I will meet you there," Henry said. "I bought a new horse

367

yesterday, and before I send it down to my place in the country I want you to have a look at him."

"I would like that," the Marquis answered, "and as soon as I can get His Majesty's permission, I intend to take Cara to Broome, and I hope you will accompany us there."

"You know I never refuse one of your invitations," Henry said, "nor the opportunity to ride your horses."

"As it happens, I am looking forward to riding one of my own," the Marquis said. "You have not yet seen *Agamemnon.*"

"That is an animal I am very eager to meet," Henry said with a smile, "after all you have told me about him."

Cara listened with interest.

She was aware by now how much his horses meant to the Marquis, and she noticed that when he talked about them there was a very different note in his voice from when he talked about anything else.

"Perhaps he should have married a horse!" she told herself with a little smile, and wondered if he would ever love a woman as much as she was certain he loved *Agamemnon.*

She knew that it irked him to have to be in London for so long, and the only compensation was that he rode very early in the Park, when he had the place almost to himself.

'When my riding-habit is ready,' she thought, 'I will ask if I can accompany him.'

She had the uncomfortable feeling that he would think her superfluous to his enjoyment and would prefer her to continue as she was doing now, driving with a groom later in the day to get the air and not taking any really active exercise.

'When we go to Broome,' she thought, 'perhaps I will be able to demonstrate to him how well I can ride.'

Because they had been estranged from the very moment of their marriage, she found it difficult to ask for special favours which concerned her own enjoyment.

She still vaguely thought of the idea of leaving the Marquis, and she asked Emily to bring her another suit from the attic in Grosvenor Square.

"What've you done with the one you ran away in, M'Lady?" Emily asked.

368

"The Housekeeper at Broome looked at it with horror, then doubtless burnt it!" Cara replied.

Emily laughed.

"I always thought 'twas very brave of you, M'Lady, going off on your own like that, not that I blamed you, with His Lordship beating you like a dog and saying as how you had to marry that horrible gentleman."

"I shall always be very grateful to you for telling me about him," Cara said. "If you had not done so, I might have been married to him by now!"

She shivered as she thought of it, and told herself that although she might dislike being married to any man, at least the Marquis did not beat her.

Although automatically she had locked the communicating door between his room and hers and the door into the passage at night, ever since the first evening when he had said he wanted to talk to her, she knew he had never again made any effort to come to her.

When on that first night he had knocked on her door, she had been frightened.

It had seemed impossible, when he had been forced into marriage by her uncle in such a barbarous manner, that the Marquis should think of her as a woman.

And yet she could not be sure.

Because of what she felt about her uncle, Sir Mortimer, and in fact all men, she had been terrified that the Marquis might try to touch her.

Now that she knew him better, she was certain that he was not in the slightest degree interested in her as a woman and was in fact concerned only that she should not shame him while she bore his name.

She had gradually began to relax; her heart no longer jumped with fear when he came into the room, nor did she watch him apprehensively as if he were a wild animal who might pounce on her at any moment.

Just as the scars were beginning to fade from her back, and by now could barely be seen, so her mind was adjusting itself to living with the Marquis in comparative friendliness.

The next morning she heard him leave his bedroom at seven-thirty and knew he would be going riding in the Park.

For the first time she had a sudden urge to go with him and be with him, and she decided that when he returned she would definitely ask if she too could ride when the Park was empty.

Then it crossed her mind that perhaps, although she was unaware of it, he went to meet somebody he found attractive and who had ridden with him in the past before they were married.

The servants had not omitted to relate to her amongst their other memories what a success the Marquis was with the famous Beauties of the *Beau Monde*.

"I thought at one time His Lordship might marry the daughter of the Duke of Newcastle," the Housekeeper had said. "A lovelier young lady you never saw, and she would certainly have looked her best wearing the Broome diamonds at the Opening of Parliament and at the Balls given at Carlton House."

"Oh, I never believed she'd a chance!" Robinson had replied, who was still maiding Cara.

"Who did you fancy then, may I ask, Miss Robinson?" the Housekeeper had enquired.

"There were plenty to choose from," Robinson replied, "but I always thought the loveliest lady of them all was Lady Aileen Wynter, and there's no doubt she laid her heart at His Lordship's feet."

"Let me think—oh, I remembers her now, and very sad for her it was when her husband was killed in Spain."

"She forgot about him when she met His Lordship," Robinson said with a smirk.

Then, feeling that they were being too indiscreet in front of Cara, they had hurriedly gone back to tales about the Marquis when he was a small boy.

Because he was so handsome, Cara thought, there were bound to have been numerous women in his life, and yet he had not wished to marry any of them, but had wanted to remain single and independent as she had wanted to do.

"If I run away, he will never find me and he will be free," she told herself.

Then she realised that she was back at the same place where her fantasies always began and ended, seeking freedom but unable to know how she could get it.

* * *

"Here you are, M'Lady, and I think it'll fit you as well as the other one did," Emily said.

She had arrived late in the afternoon when Cara had come back from a drive in the Park.

As she spoke, Emily opened a rather untidy parcel and produced another suit consisting of trousers and a coat which Cara thought must have belonged to her father when he was a boy.

"It is rather bigger than the last one," she said, "and the trousers are too long."

"You can turn 'em up at the bottom," Emily said, "or I'll stitch 'em up for Your Ladyship."

"I will not bother now," Cara replied. "But I will hide it away so that it is here if I want it."

"I can't think that you should want it, M'Lady," Emily said. "You don't want to run away from His Lordship! He's a fine man! His Royal Highness thinks the world of him."

Cara had been told this before, and she asked:

"Have you anything more to tell me about Mr. Thistlewood?"

"I were just going to tell you about him, M'Lady," Emily answered. "Albert says there's ever such strange things going on, and he thinks Lord Harrowby himself is in danger."

"Why should he think that?" Cara enquired.

"Mr. Thistlewood told His Lordship that if they could dispose of Lord Harrowby and the Members of the Cabinet, then they'll be able to make the mob who're fed up with the whole Government march on all the important buildings, starting with the Barracks in Hyde Park."

Cara stared at Emily incredulously.

"What are you saying, Emily?" she asked. "Start at the beginning and tell me exactly what Albert overheard."

Because she had spoken sharply, she thought Emily might be frightened and refuse to talk. So she added quickly:

"We both know that Albert listens at the door, and I am not saying I disapprove, because I am sure my uncle and Mr. Thistlewood are up to no good, and it is important for us to know what they are concocting."

"Yes, of course, M'Lady, but you knows what Albert's like when he tells a story. Half of it may be true and the other half false."

"Yes, I know that," Cara agreed, "but tell me what he said anyway."

"This Mr. Thistlewood, from all I hears," Emily began, "has a whole band of people as follows him, and Albert thinks they're planning when Lord Harrowby next gives a dinner-party to break into Number Forty-four and murder them all!"

"I do not believe it!" Cara exclaimed incredulously.

"That's what he told the master. They've got it all planned out."

Cara was silent for a moment. Then she said:

"Where does Mr. Thistlewood live?"

"Albert doesn't know that," Emily said. "He meets those he leads in a stable-yard in Cato Street."

"Where is that?" Cara enquired.

"Somewhere off the Edgware Road, and Albert heard them say they've all sorts of weapons there, and their revolution when it does start'll be a big one!"

Cara shivered.

It was, she felt, just the sort of intrigue her uncle would enjoy.

However, it seemed impossible to believe that he would really plot with Revolutionaries to overthrow the Government or even to make trouble.

She had read in the newspapers what was happening in the North.

She knew that last year at St. Peter's Field, which had been almost like a battlefield, fifty thousand unarmed cotton operatives had been fired on by the Yeomanry.

There had been a great deal of anger about it, and yet, Members of the Government were still asking for stronger and more repressive measures against any form of rebellion or protest.

"I'll find out more from Albert," Emily was saying. She obviously enjoyed supplying Cara with the information she had asked for.

"Yes, do that," Cara said. "How often do these men meet Mr. Thistlewood?"

"I think every night, M'Lady. Albert said he heard the master say this morning in the Library:

" 'You tell them what I've said, Thistlewood, and report to me tomorrow morning.' "

Cara said nothing more and Emily hurried away. Not long afterwards, Robinson came to her room to help her change for dinner.

She put on one of the beautiful gowns that had been made for her in Bond Street, and thought as she looked at herself in the mirror that the Marquis would be pleased that this one in particular would be exactly as he wished it to be.

It was white, trimmed with small bunches of magnolias with their very dark green leaves, and it made the gown very striking and quite different from any gown Cara had ever seen before.

She thought it must be unusual for a man to know so much about dresses. Then she suddenly realised why he was such an expert in this field as in others.

It had never struck her until this moment that she was not the first woman for whom he had chosen clothes.

She did not know why, but she suddenly felt dissatisfied with her own appearance and petulantly turned away from the mirror.

Then she glanced at the clock and realised it was later than she had thought.

"I must hurry," she said to Robinson. "His Lordship will be annoyed if I'm late and spoil the dinner."

"I don't think His Lordship's back yet, M'Lady," Robinson replied.

"Not back? But it is nearly quarter-to-eight!"

Without saying any more, Cara opened her bedroom door and ran downstairs.

Bateson, the Butler, was in the Hall.

"Is His Lordship back?" she asked.

"I was just about to send upstairs to tell Your Ladyship that His Lordship has sent a message with the carriage," the Butler replied, "to inform Your Ladyship that he deeply regrets he cannot return home for dinner as His Majesty requires him."

For a moment Cara did not answer. Then in a voice that sounded a little flat she said:

"Please tell the Chef I am ready for dinner."

"Very good, M'Lady."

* * *

373

The Marquis, driving back to his house, was thinking not of his wife, who had had to dine alone without him, but of the King and his problems.

Of these, however, he was heartily sick, and he had already informed the Lord Chamberlain that he intended to leave for Broome the day after tomorrow.

"I must get away," he said, "and the sooner the better."

Then, as if he felt he must explain, he added:

"I have promised to dine with Harrowby and the Cabinet tomorrow, but that is the last engagement I intend to have in London for at least a week, or perhaps two."

"I cannot blame you," the Lord Chamberlain replied. "With the late King's death and His Majesty's illness, you have not yet had a honeymoon."

"That is true!" the Marquis exclaimed, but he did not elaborate on the matter.

Now as he neared Broome House he thought it might be a good idea for him to get to know Cara better when they were in the country.

He was already aware that she was a good rider, and he thought it would interest her to try out some of his horses, not those which were as wild as *Agamemnon* but which needed a strong hand.

'It is certainly an interest we have in common,' he thought.

He found himself thinking how attractive she had looked the previous evening in one of the gowns he had practically designed himself, and in which he realised, once social festivities recommenced, she would stand out.

The carriage drew up outside his house and the footman ran to open the door.

The Marquis stepped out, and as he walked into the Hall, Bateson said:

"Excuse me, M'Lord, but a young woman, a woman called Emily, insists on seeing Your Lordship. I told her it was too late, but she waited and asked me to tell you that it's a question of life and death!"

Bateson spoke with the supercilious manner of a servant who relays a message in which he does not believe.

For a moment the Marquis wondered where he had heard the name "Emily" before, then remembered how Cara had told him it was Emily who had helped her to escape from her uncle's house.

"I will see the young woman in the Study," he said.

He walked into the room in which he worked, and wondered what he was about to hear and why Emily had not first discussed with Cara what she had to say.

He glanced at the clock, and seeing that it was nearly midnight, he thought that Cara would be asleep and that was why, quite rightly, Bateson had not disturbed her.

The door opened and Bateson said in a very disapproving voice:

"The young woman to see you, M'Lord!"

His first glance at Emily told the Marquis that she was a respectable-looking girl, neatly dressed in black and wearing a black bonnet trimmed with ribbons that tied under her chin and with a heavy woollen shawl over her shoulders.

She curtseyed and stood just inside the door, waiting for him to speak to her.

"Good-evening!" the Marquis said. "I understand your name is Emily and you are a housemaid Her Ladyship knew when she lived in Grosvenor Square."

"That's right, M'Lord, and I had to see Your Lordship—I had to reelly!"

"Is something wrong?" the Marquis enquired.

"Very, very wrong, M'Lord, and it's my fault. But I swear I never imagined Her Ladyship would do anything so foolish when she asked me to get her another suit of clothes. I just thought she was planning some sort of escapade. But nothing like this, I swear it, M'Lord!"

The agitated way in which Emily spoke made the Marquis stare at her in surprise.

Then he sat down at his desk, indicating an upright chair at the other side of it.

"Suppose you sit down, Emily," he said, "and tell me what all this is about. At the moment, I cannot understand what you are saying."

Emily crossed the room to the chair almost as if her legs would barely carry her there. Then she sat down, clasping her hands together in an agitated manner.

"When Tim tells me he'd seen Her Ladyship, I didn't believe it!" she said.

"Who is Tim?" the Marquis interrupted.

"He's the scullery-boy, M'Lord. He's always snooping and prying about, and it's him as told the master that Her Ladyship climbed into your carriage when she ran away."

"I understand," the Marquis said. "And what has he seen now?"

"He sees Her Ladyship going into that place where all them murderers hang out. When I tells her about it, I'd no idea she'd do such a thing! If they finds her, they'll kill her, M'Lord!"

The Marquis looked bewildered.

"What murderers? And how do you know where Her Ladyship has gone?"

"Tim seen her, M'Lord! Seen her not two hours ago, and when he comes back and tells me, I could hardly believe my ears!"

"Where did he see her?" the Marquis asked.

His voice was calm.

He had known when he interrogated men during the war that it was the greatest mistake to shout or hurry them, because then they became completely inarticulate.

"It's the place in Cato Street, M'Lord," Emily replied, "where them Revolutionaries meet as is led by Mr. Thistlewood!"

The Marquis stiffened.

"Did you say Thistlewood?" he enquired.

"Yes, M'Lord. He's the man as has been coming to the house to talk to the master, and Albert—that's the footman—overheard what they said."

"What did they say?"

"They're planning, M'Lord, at the next dinner-party to be given at Number Forty-four, to murder Lord Harrowby and all his guests."

For a moment the Marquis was too surprised to speak. Then he said:

"And you told Her Ladyship about this?"

"Yes, M'Lord, but I never realised—I never thought she'd do anything about it or visit them murderers herself."

"And you tell me this is what she has done now?"

"Yes, M'Lord. Tim sees her. Sees her dressed in the suit I brought here from the attics, going into the stable just before Mr. Thistlewood and them as follows him arrives."

The Marquis's lips tightened and he said, still in his calm voice:

"Did Tim tell you how many men there were?"

"Two dozen or so, M'Lord, perhaps more."

"And you say this place is in Cato Street?"

"Yes, M'Lord, and Tim says if they find Her Ladyship, they'll kill her for sure!"

"Then let us hope they do not do so," the Marquis said. "Thank you, Emily, for being brave enough to come and tell me what is happening."

"I had to, M'Lord. I had to! Even if it loses me my job, I couldn't let Her Ladyship be killed or hurt by them thugs, could I?"

"No, of course not," the Marquis agreed.

He looked at Emily, then he said:

"What I am going to suggest, Emily, is that you do not go back to Grosvenor Square, where you might be in danger for bringing me this information. Instead I suggest you stay here. My Housekeeper will find you a bed, and tomorrow we will discuss what can be done about you in the future."

Tears ran down Emily's cheeks.

"Thank you, M'Lord, thank you!" she said. "I was sure they'd think it strange when I runs out of the house after what Tim told me. They knows I love Her Ladyship an' would never let anything happen to her."

"Nothing will, and you will be safe here," the Marquis said.

He rose to his feet and strode from the Study into the Hall. While he was giving his orders sharply to Bateson, he was wondering if and how he would be able to save Cara.

CHAPTER SEVEN

———— ∽✦∾ ————

$\mathcal{D}$RIVING TOWARDS CATO STREET in the closed Brougham that he sometimes used in London, the Marquis could hardly believe that what Emily had told him was true.

Now he remembered saying to Cara:

"I am dining in tonight, but not tomorrow, as I have to meet the Cabinet at Lord Harrowby's."

She had made no comment at the time, and he had not thought that to be significant.

But now he was sure that the reason she had gone to Cato Street was to find out if Emily's story was true and they really intended to murder the Cabinet at Lord Harrowby's house the next evening.

It seemed incredible, and yet, as the Marquis had said so often, the seeds of revolution had been growing steadily and nobody had done anything about it.

To make certain that Cara was actually out and not asleep in bed, when he had gone upstairs to change from his evening-clothes he had opened the door of her bedroom.

If it had been locked as it had been every night since she had married him, he would have known that his fears were unnecessary.

But when the door opened, even before he could see by the light in the passage that the bed was empty and unslept in, he knew that Cara had impulsively done the most crazy thing in her whole life.

The Marquis did not underestimate the danger she was in, and after he told his coachman to wait in a quiet square off the Edgware Road, he walked alone towards Cato Street, keeping in the shadows.

As by now it was after midnight, everything was very quiet and there was very little traffic.

There was not even the usual number of unsavoury characters looking in the gutter for scraps or anything they could beg or steal from some gentleman returning home after imbibing too freely.

Anyway, the Edgware Road was not a place for drunken Bucks, and when the Marquis did see somebody in the distance, he kept out of sight in case he should get involved in anything unpleasant.

He found Cato Street quite easily, having a good idea of where it was situated.

It was a small, insignificant street with a few dilapidated stables facing some squalid houses that were badly in need of repair.

Some of these were empty, but there was a Tavern, its windows throwing a golden light onto the cobbled road and illuminating a stable opposite, which the Marquis, more by instinct than anything else, felt must be the place Emily had described to him.

The door, which was broken at the hinges, was ajar; but he did not go near it. Instead he waited in the shadow of a doorway on the other side of the road.

After a minute or so he realised that the house against which he was standing was empty, the windows were broken, and the door itself was ajar.

He therefore let himself in, being careful to avoid a creaking and broken board, then stood watching the stable opposite.

He thought a flicker of light came from within the building, but he could not be sure.

Everything seemed very quiet and, as such, menacing.

It was then that he began to be desperately afraid for Cara.

"How could she possibly," he asked himself, "do anything so rash as to go alone dressed as a boy and listen to the plots and plans of men who will think nothing of murdering anybody who might betray them?"

He had to admit that she certainly had tremendous courage, and he could not imagine that any other woman of his acquaintance would take such risks.

Yet, ever since he had known Cara she had been unpredictable.

She was so small, delicately made, and lovely that he could not bear to think of her being handled roughly and perhaps tortured to tell what she knew before she was killed.

For the first time since he had left home, he thought that perhaps he should have brought help with him.

Yet, if Emily was right and there were twenty-four men plotting in the stable opposite, he would have required at least an equal number to face them, and where could he have got so many at this time of night?

Then as he began to think that waiting to see what would happen was intolerable and he would have to take some course of action, slowly and quietly the broken door of the stable was pulled open.

The Marquis held his breath, then saw a man peep out to look up and down the street.

Obviously reassured to see that there was nobody about, he opened the door a little wider and they came trooping out.

They were exactly the type of men that the Marquis had expected to be engaged in such a plot.

They were not humble labourers who had every reason to protest against hunger and unemployment, but malcontents of a higher class who were always prepared in any argument to use brute force rather than words.

There were large men and small, all with the stamp of rebels on them, the Marquis thought, and also the look of buccaneers who were prepared to risk life and limb if the plunder was worthwhile.

They emerged in absolute silence, which made it more sinister than if they were talking with one another.

Then they hurried away, separating in different directions as if they had been told not to keep in a group, until last of all came a man who the Marquis was sure was their leader—Thistlewood.

He was obviously a man of better birth and would pass as a gentleman.

At the same time, although it was hard to see his face clearly from across the road, the Marquis was sure he was a brutal and callous type who was thinking entirely of his own interests rather than of the men he was leading into trouble.

He pulled the stable door to behind him.

There was no lock, but the Marquis knew this was a positive recommendation, for any door bolted and barred in this sort of street would give an indication that there was something inside to steal, and the place would immediately be broken into.

When Thistlewood had shut the stable door as close as he could, he squared his shoulders, then hesitated and glanced at the Tavern as if he felt in need of a drink.

He took a few steps towards it, and in the light coming from the windows the Marquis could see him more clearly and knew that he was looking at a man who was born to be a criminal.

There was something cruel about the thin tightness of his lips, and the Marquis thought too that he looked elated, presumably at the result of the meeting, and there was an unmistakable stir of triumph about him.

Then he obviously changed his mind and walked away down Cato Street in the direction of the Edgware Road.

The Marquis waited until he was out of sight. Then, stepping out of the house in which he had been hiding, he hurried to the stable.

He opened the door very quietly, knowing from his experience of war that men had often lost their lives when they thought the enemy had left a certain post, only to find that one had been left behind as a guard.

Only after he had waited for a second or two, having opened the door, did he step inside the stable.

It was dark and smelt of musty hay, and just in front of him he could see the loft in which the conspirators had met.

There was no sign of a ladder anywhere, but he thought that before he left Thistlewood would undoubtedly have hidden it in case it should be stolen.

The Marquis walked farther into the darkness, then stood still, listening.

There was only silence. Then very softly, making his voice little more than a whisper, he called:

"Cara!"

For a moment he thought he was mistaken and she was not there.

Then he heard a murmur of surprise and a moment later her voice asked:

"Is that . . . really . . . you?"

"I am here," he replied. "Where are you?"

"I . . . cannot get . . . down."

Because it was impossible to see anything in the direction from which her voice came, the Marquis pulled the door open a little farther, then walked deep into the stable, where he stopped to ask again:

"Where are you?"

"I am . . . here," she replied, and her voice came from above his head.

He realised then that she had climbed over a broken manger and up into the hay-rack above it so that she was just below the floor of the loft above her.

He walked to stand immediately below her and put up his arms.

"I will not let you fall."

She put one leg over the side of the hay-rack and leant over, her arms going out towards him to hold on to his shoulders.

"You are quite safe," he said. "Let yourself go."

She did as he told her and fell into his arms.

He had braced himself for the impact, then he was holding her tightly against him, and as he did so he felt her arms go round his neck, and she said in a terrified whisper:

"They are . . . going to . . . kill you! Oh . . . Ivo, they are . . . going to . . . kill you . . . and everyone else . . . tomorrow night!"

He knew as she spoke how frightened she was, and he could feel her heart beating frantically against his.

His arms tightened and he looked down in the darkness to where he knew her face would be and said:

"How could you come here? How could you do anything so incredibly . . ."

He stopped.

Then as he knew he held her safe and there was no need for words, his lips found hers and he kissed her.

As he did so he knew that he was in love.

While he was waiting on the other side of the road he had been desperate with anxiety and fear, but now the relief of knowing that she was safe was sweeping over him with an irrepressible joy that could only be love.

He had never thought, never imagined for one moment, that he would fall in love with Cara, who was everything he disapproved of in a woman.

But now as his lips held hers captive he knew that, although he would have never admitted it even to himself, every day she had entwined herself closer and closer round his heart until he was in love as he had never thought it possible to be.

To Cara it was as if the Heavens opened and she found herself in a blaze of light instead of in a darkness in which there was only horror and fear.

Without even knowing she was doing so, she pressed herself closer to the Marquis and her lips responded to his.

How long they were held together by that kiss neither of them had any idea.

But at last the Marquis raised his head and felt as if he had come back to reality as he said:

"For God's sake, let us get out of this place! I was so afraid those devils would kill you."

"They . . . intend to . . . kill you," Cara murmured.

Yet, he knew by the way she spoke that for the moment the words meant nothing and she had been swept, as he had been, by the ecstasy of their kiss into the sky and it was difficult to come back to earth.

Still holding her in his arms, the Marquis walked towards the door.

Only when he reached it did he stop, as the first of the conspirators had done, to look up and down the street before he emerged.

There was nobody about and the place seemed quiet and deserted.

Then hurriedly, because he was still afraid for Cara, he carried her across the road and back the way he had come after leaving his carriage.

She did not speak, and he knew without being told that she was still caught in the rapture they had felt when their lips had touched, and it was hard to think of anything else.

Only when the carriage was in sight did she ask:

"Do you . . . want me to . . . walk?"

"Stay as you are," the Marquis said. "I am still desperately afraid of losing you."

His arms tightened as he spoke, and Cara felt that she had never known such safety or such happiness.

At the sight of them the footman jumped down from the box and opened the carriage door, and the Marquis laid Cara gently down on the back seat before he stepped in himself.

The footman put the fur-lined rug over their knees and asked:

"Home, M'Lord?"

"Yes, home," the Marquis replied.

Then, when the footman had shut the door and scrambled up on the box and the horses set off, the Marquis put his arm round Cara.

A question came to his mind that he was longing to ask her.

Then by the candle in the silver lantern fixed above the seat opposite them he saw her face tipped up to his, her eyes wide and excited as she looked at him enquiringly, and he knew that the only thing of importance was that he should kiss her.

As if he was still haunted by the dangers through which she had passed, he pulled her almost roughly against him, and once again his lips were on hers, kissing her fiercely and possessively because he was afraid he might have lost her.

As he did so, he knew that the feelings rising within him were different from anything he had ever felt in his life before.

He realised that they had been activated by fear, but he knew there was something else in this kiss that was different from any he had given or received before.

It was not only that he desired Cara as a woman and that her lips were soft, sweet, and very innocent beneath his.

There was also something intensely spiritual in his feelings, which told him, through an instinct which had never deceived him, that she was what he had been seeking all his life and never found.

He could not explain it, he knew only that it was there and that he loved her with an emotion which no other woman had ever aroused in him.

He wanted to protect her and at the same time to give her a happiness that came from something Divine within them both.

Only when they had driven quite a long way towards Berkeley Square did the Marquis raise his head, and Cara said in a rapt little tone he had never heard from her before:

"I . . . love you . . . oh, Ivo . . . I love you but I did not . . . know it until I . . . heard those wicked men . . . plotting to . . . k-kill you!"

At last the Marquis was able to say what he had wanted to say earlier.

"How could you do anything so crazy, so mad, as to go to that place alone? How could you have risked your life?"

"I had to be . . . certain that Albert was not making it up . . . that if . . . you went to . . . Lord Harrowby's dinner tomorrow . . . night you would . . . d-die."

Her voice broke on the last word, and the Marquis asked:

"Would that have worried you? I thought you wanted to be free of me."

"I love you, although I did not realise it," Cara replied. "But I . . . do, and . . . please . . . I want to . . . stay with . . . you."

For a moment the Marquis did not answer, and she said quickly:

"You are not . . . angry with . . . me?"

"I am not angry," the Marquis assured her, "you only frightened me as I have never been frightened before. Oh, my darling, do you swear to me that you will never do anything like this again?"

He felt Cara quiver at the endearment, then as if her feelings were too much for her she hid her face against his neck.

"If you . . . let me . . . stay with . . . you," she whispered, "I will be safe . . . but I must be . . . sure that you will be . . . safe too."

"I will be," the Marquis answered, "because, thanks to you, Harrowby's dinner-party will not take place tomorrow evening."

He felt Cara give a deep sigh of relief, but when he would have turned her face up to his to kiss her again, he was aware that they were back in Berkeley Square.

There was only a night-footman on duty in the Hall, because the Marquis before leaving had deliberately told Bateson to go to bed and not wait up for him.

He had known how Cara would be dressed and had no wish for more servants than necessary to see her in trousers.

"Go straight to your room, my precious," he said as the carriage came to a standstill. "I will bring you something to eat and drink. Then you can tell me what happened."

From the light streaming through the Hall he saw the smile she gave him, and he thought that, strangely dressed though she might be, nobody could look more beautiful.

As the footman opened the door of the carriage, she slipped past him and was running up the stairs almost before the man realised what had happened.

The Marquis took his time dismissing his coachman and came into the house to hand over his tall hat and cape to a flunkey.

Then, going to his Study to collect the bottle of champagne which he knew would be there and a plate of pâté sandwiches, he carried them up the stairs, thinking as he did so that he felt happier than he had ever felt in his whole life.

It was as if the curtain were rising on a Play he had never seen before, but which he knew would be more thrilling than anything he had ever dreamt of or encountered because Cara was waiting for him.

When his valet had helped him to undress and put on a long silk robe that reached the ground, holding the champagne and sandwiches in one hand, he opened the communicating door between his room and Cara's.

He knew that tonight it would not be locked.

As he went through it he saw her sitting up in bed, and he thought that in her transparent nightgown and with her gold curls glinting in the light from the candles, nobody could look more exquisitely feminine and excitingly desirable.

He put the champagne and the sandwiches down on a table.

Then, as if it was impossible for the moment to think about them, he sat down facing Cara on the side of the mattress to say in his deep voice:

"You are here! I have brought you back safely, and for the moment I can think of nothing else."

"I had to . . . go to . . . see if you . . . really were in . . . danger," Cara said, "and, oh, Ivo, now you must save all the . . . others because they . . . intend to kill them."

"You must tell me about it," the Marquis said vaguely.

But his eyes were on her face and the softness of her lips.

"I love you!" he said. "How could I not have known it before now? You must never in any circumstances ever risk your life again, because you belong to me."

"Do you . . . really love me?" Cara asked. "I cannot believe it."

"I will make you believe it," the Marquis said, "and, darling, I know now that what I am feeling for you is what I have always wanted, searched for, and longed for, although I was unaware of it."

Cara gave a little cry of happiness. Then she said:

"How can I have been so stupid as not to know the moment I saw you that you were the man I dreamt might be . . . somewhere in the . . . world, and whom I could . . . love as Mama loved Papa?"

"And as I love you."

As he spoke he bent forward to put his arms round her.

As her head fell back against the pillow, he looked down at her for a long moment, as if he must engrave her beauty on his heart forever before his lips found hers.

Then he was kissing her with a long, slow, passionate kiss which was more ecstatic, more marvellous than their kiss had been before, until Cara's arms went round his neck to draw him closer, and still closer. . . .

* * *

A long time later, Cara stirred against the Marquis's shoulder to ask:

"How could I have been so . . . foolish as to waste so much time in thinking I . . . must leave you, when I know now that if I had done so . . . all I would want to do would be to . . . die?"

"You are not going to die, my beloved," the Marquis answered. "You are going to live with me, belong to me, and, as I told you once before, I will kill anybody who attempts to take you from me."

"No one will be able to do that," Cara said. "But I did not . . . know that love was so . . . wonderful and so overwhelming."

"I did not frighten you?" the Marquis asked.

"How could I be frightened when I adore and worship you?"

"You were frightened of me the first night you came here," the Marquis said, "and it has worried me ever since."

"I will never be frightened *of* you again, only *for* you, in case that horrible man Thistlewood or Uncle Lionel should hurt you."

As if her words brought back the agonies they had both been through, the Marquis pulled her even closer to him, and his lips were on her forehead as he said:

"I suppose, my adorable one, you will have to tell me what happened tonight, but for the moment I can think of nothing but you and the happiness you have given me."

"It is . . . so . . . wonderful that you . . . love me," Cara said, "but you will have to save Lord Harrowby and the Cabinet."

"I will do that," the Marquis said, "but first, tell me again that you love me and that I am not dreaming this whole situation."

Cara gave a little chuckle of delight.

"It does seem incredible, does it not?" she agreed. "I made Emily bring me another suit because I was vaguely thinking I must run away from you. Then tonight, when she told me that Uncle Lionel was plotting with that man Thistlewood to kill everybody who goes to the dinner with Lord Harrowby tomorrow night . . . I knew I had to . . . save you."

"You could have warned me about it without taking such risks," the Marquis said.

"I did not think you would believe me," Cara answered, "and I felt as if Fate was driving me to go find out for myself. Only when I was listening to the evil things they were planning did I know how much I . . . loved you and that even if they . . . killed me I had to save you."

Her words made the Marquis hold her closer still. Then he kissed her cheeks and was seeking her mouth before he said:

"Tell me the whole story. Then we can think only about ourselves and forget the conspirators at least until tomorrow morning."

Cara put her hand across his chest as if she would protect him.

"I found my way to Cato Street because Emily had said the men met there in a stable, and I looked at all the stables before I found the right one."

"How did you know which one it was?" the Marquis enquired.

"The others either had horses in them, or the lofts had collapsed completely from neglect and it would be impossible for anyone to sit in them."

"Go on," the Marquis prompted. "Having found the stable, what did you do then?"

"I realised that if I was discovered I would be in terrible trouble," Cara said, "but as the door was open, I saw the broken manger and rack above it, and I knew that if I could climb into it, no one entering through the door was likely to see me. Also, as my head would be against the floor of the loft, I would be able to hear what was said."

"That was clever of you," the Marquis said, "but still dangerous."

"I only had to wait for about fifteen minutes," Cara went on, "before the first man appeared. He set up the ladder, which had been hidden, fortunately at the other end of the stable, and climbed into the loft. Then they all began arriving, one after another, and they sat talking amongst themselves until Mr. Thistlewood came."

"How did you know it was him?" the Marquis enquired.

"Because they spoke very respectfully to him when they said 'good-evening.' He told them he had seen Uncle Lionel, who had insisted that the first person they . . . murdered was to be . . . you!"

There was so much horror in Cara's voice that the Marquis held her even closer against him and felt her heart beating against his.

"It is all over now, my precious," he said softly, "but you have to tell me what else occurred."

"Mr. Thistlewood went through the whole plan and they decided that one of their number should call at Lord Harrowby's house while dinner was in progress, and he would pretend he was a messenger with a special despatch."

The Marquis listened intently as Cara continued:

"While he spoke to the footman, the rest of the conspirators, who would be hidden in small groups in the Square, would be watching."

Her fingers tightened on the Marquis's bare shoulder as she said:

"Oh, Ivo, they have planned to murder the entire Cabinet, including the servants if they resist, and a man called Ings, who is a Butcher, said he intended to cut off the heads of Lord Castlereagh and Lord Sidmouth!"

The Marquis drew in his breath incredulously, but he did not interrupt, and Cara went on:

"He had two bags for them, and he said he also wanted the right hand of Lord Castlereagh, which he felt would be a valuable souvenir!"

"They must all be mad!" the Marquis ejaculated.

"They sounded mad," Cara agreed, "and when they have killed everybody they plan to fire a rocket from the house as a signal to their friends."

"What will happen then?"

"An oil-shop, which they said was near Grosvenor Square, is to be set on fire to gather the crowds."

"Did they really say that?" the Marquis enquired. "What was the idea?"

"Mr. Thistlewood said the fire would collect a huge mob which would become wild with excitement at the sight of the mangled remains of the Cabinet. They would then be able to capture the Barracks in Hyde Park."

"I have never heard such a crazy scheme in the whole of my life!" the Marquis exclaimed.

"That is not all. Thistlewood said that if they take hundreds of rioters with them, they will sack the Bank of England, occupy the Tower of London, and throw open the gates of Newgate Prison."

"Such a plan seems absolutely incredible!" the Marquis said. "And you really think your uncle is aware of this?"

"Mr. Thistlewood spoke of him proudly," Cara answered, "and I am sure it was Uncle Lionel who told them that they will be able to establish a Provisional Government and proclaim it on the steps of the Mansion House."

The Marquis remembered the Earl boasting that he had him at his mercy. Now he knew that the tables were turned: the Earl was at his mercy and would be hanged as a traitor.

However, he did not say so to Cara, but merely asked:

"What else did they say?"

"They checked the number of guns, pikes, and hand grenades they had, and Mr. Thistlewood arranged for them to collect all these before they go to their hiding-places in the Square tomorrow night. He also said that Uncle Lionel had given him a large sum of money to buy more weapons, especially pistols."

The Marquis was sure the Earl imagined that the gratitude of the conspirators would ensure him a high place in the new Government and that he would be able to make a considerable amount of money out of the revolution.

"What happened then?" he asked Cara.

"They all swore their allegiance to Mr. Thistlewood and said they would follow him faithfully and place him in the seat of power as Governor of the country, once everybody in the present Government was dead."

The Marquis could hardly believe that what he was hearing was the truth.

Yet, if the conspirators did not manage to achieve all their ambitions, they could certainly do a great deal of harm, and twenty-four of them without any difficulty would be able to murder all those who were present at Lord Harrowby's for dinner tomorrow.

"It was very brave and wonderful of you, my darling," he said gently, "to find out what you have, and I know how grateful the Prime Minister and especially Lord Harrowby will be when tomorrow night the rebels are arrested and imprisoned. At the same time, I cannot have you involved."

Cara looked up at him, and he explained:

"As my wife and the Marchioness of Broome, it would cause a great deal of undesirable gossip if it were known that you had listened to the eavesdropping of a servant, and disguised as a boy had overheard the plans of cut-throats and Revolutionaries."

"I understand."

"I shall therefore tell only the Prime Minister how I obtained the knowledge that I will impart to him tomorrow morning."

"All that matters is that you should be safe," Cara said. "I do not want to talk about it or even think about it. I only know that I heard them saying you must be killed, and I felt as if a dagger had been thrust into my . . . heart."

"Now you know, my darling, how I felt when I waited outside, fearing that at any moment those evil men might discover and perhaps torture you."

Cara gave a little cry, and the Marquis said:

"But you are safe, completely and absolutely safe, and never again, never, never, will I let you take part in anything so dangerous."

"I have no wish to do so," Cara said. "Because I love you, all I want to do is to please you and do what you want me to do."

The Marquis looked down at her with a tenderness in his eyes which no one had ever seen before.

"I love you just as you are," he said. "Actually, that is a very strange thing for me to say, but it is true."

"And I love you," Cara said. "When I said I hated men and was afraid of them, how could I have thought that I should love you until I feel that my whole body is throbbing with love? I want you to kiss me, and love me until I can remember . . . nothing else but you and only . . . you."

The way she spoke, with a little touch of passion in her voice that had never been there before, made the fire come into the Marquis's eyes.

He was intelligent enough to realise that Cara's defiance and her hatred of men had come from the treatment she had received from her uncle and the fact that she had been alone and helpless in a world that was very frightening.

But because she had so much character and spirit, it had not crushed her as it might have done another woman.

Instead, she had fought back, determined to survive, determined to be herself. Yet, even while she gave hatred for hatred, she was craving for love.

Feeling that his own emotions rising within him were so overwhelming, so irresistible, the Marquis turned Cara's face up to his and, looking at her, said:

"What have you done to me, my beautiful one, to make me feel like this? And what have I ever done to deserve anybody so perfect and so adorable as you?"

"Do you really mean that?" Cara asked. "I wanted you to admire me, although I did not understand that what I really wanted was to be . . . loved. Now I am so happy that I feel as if you are carrying me . . . up to the sky and I can . . . touch the stars. There is only beauty and music round us, . . . and nothing . . . horrid or . . . cruel."

She gave a little shudder as she said the last word, and the Marquis knew she was remembering how her uncle had hit her and beat her.

"Forget him!" he said softly. "He is finished. After tomorrow night he will be in the Tower, and if he does not take his own life, he will be tried by his peers and condemned to death!"

As he spoke he was quite certain in his own mind that when the Earl learnt that the conspiracy had been discovered and the rebels arrested, he would shoot himself.

There was no chance of his not being implicated. Thistlewood would undoubtedly betray him, and amongst his own servants, apart from the rebels, there were witnesses to his guilt.

Normally the Marquis would have felt satisfaction at the defeat of his enemy, but now he was thinking primarily of Cara and that the horror the Earl had brought into her life would gradually fade from her mind.

Enveloped by his love and the love she had for him, she would forget, and there would only be the glory and joy of being together.

As if she knew what he was thinking, Cara said softly:

"I love you! How can I make you . . . realise how much I love you . . . and that . . . nothing else in the world . . . matters except . . . you?"

"That is what I want you to say," the Marquis answered, "and go on saying it not once but a thousand times."

He turned round in bed so that he could look down at her and thought that with her eyes brilliant with happiness filling her small face, he had never seen real beauty before.

Then the warmth and softness of her body and her fingers holding tightly on to him as if she was afraid she might lose him made the Marquis feel the flames rising from the fire she had lit within him.

He told himself that he must be very gentle because Cara was so precious, and while he would awaken her to the love which raged within him like an inferno, he would do so slowly and tenderly, so that she responded to it like a flower opening its petals a little more each day.

Because he was a very experienced lover, he had already evoked in her a response which he felt, as Cara had, lifted him into the sky.

But he knew this was only the beginning of the ecstasy they could arouse in each other, which would grow and grow.

He knew that never in his numerous love-affairs had he ever had to teach anybody so young or so exquisite, and it was in fact the most exciting thing he had ever experienced in his life.

When he looked at Cara he knew that all the women who had come and gone, who had tried to hold his attention and failed, had been but a shadow of the reality he felt now.

Like pale ghosts they had already disappeared into the past, and he would never think of them again.

His instinct, which Cara had recognised joined with hers, told him that he had found the real love which all men seek with the woman who is the other part of themselves.

He thought that with Cara's courage and resilience, and with her personality, which was very unusual in anybody so young, she was in fact the complement to his own character that he would have looked for if he had understood his need of her as fully as he did now.

He felt not only a desire for her rising steadily and insistently, but also a deep, mysterious gratitude to the fate that had brought him the El Dorado that all men seek.

As if she was a little puzzled by his silence and the way he was looking at her, Cara asked:

"Are you . . . thinking of . . . me?"

"Only of you, my lovely one. You fill my eyes, my mind, my heart, and my soul—if I have one."

"That is what I wanted you to say, because it is the same way that I . . . love you."

Then she said very softly:

"Will you tell me everything you want me to do so that I will not disappoint you? Because I love you, I want to be perfect, absolutely perfect, but it will be difficult if you do not help me."

The Marquis drew in his breath.

"You just have to be you, my darling. It is as easy as that."

She smiled so that he saw her dimples and an irresistible twinkle in her eyes as she answered:

"Have I really captured the elusive Marquis? I thought it was an impossibility!"

"I thought it was, too," the Marquis admitted, "but I have also caught you, and I promise you there is no escape. You will never run away and I will never, never lose you."

"Make me . . . sure of that," Cara whispered. "Love me, Ivo, and make me sure, please . . . please I want . . . you to love . . . me."

As she spoke she moved closer to him, and the Marquis felt as if he could feel the little flame that had awakened within her flickering against his body.

Then as his arms went round her and his heart beat against hers, he knew they were no longer two people but one. They were flying into the sky and leaving behind everything that was sordid, evil, and cruel, and nothing would ever hurt them again.

Riding to the Moon

AUTHORS NOTE

———— ❦ ————

STEEPLE-CHASES WERE INSPIRED by the hell-for-leather match races run all through the ages, across any naturally fenced country which was available. The winner proved that he could get his horse from one place to another faster than anyone else.

During the Regency it became fashionable to have private Steeple-Chases, and this involved erecting special fences and marking out a course with flags.

Steeple-Chasing was popular with sportsmen from its very beginning but was frowned on by the established authorities of flat racing.

The most famous Steeple-Chase in the world—the Grand National—started in 1839. It was four miles across country, with twenty-nine jumps, and the purse was twelve hundred pounds.

The poems quoted in this novel come from *Shih Ching*, the first anthology of Chinese poetry, about 561-579 B.C., and from the T'ang Dynasty, 618-907 A.D.

CHAPTER ONE

————— ✦ —————

*T*HE MORNING-ROOM AT WHITE'S CLUB was rapidly filling up with its aristocratic members, both famous and infamous.

The Bow window looking onto St. James's Street, which Beau Brummell had made famous, was already full, and there was not a brown leather chair available when Lord Frodham and his friend Sir James Overton walked into the room.

They stopped to talk to a friend with whom they had spent the previous evening, and as they did so they heard a voice say:

"You are becoming as boring as George Byron on the subject of love, which I can assure you is nothing but desire tied up with pretty ribbons."

There was laughter at this, and Charles Frodham said in a low voice to Jimmy Overton:

"Ardsley, at his most cynical! I have always believed he was crossed in love when he was young."

"Nonsense!" Jimmy Overton replied. "He has never been in love with anybody except himself and his horses!"

Charles Frodham laughed, and moved a little nearer to the Bow window to hear what else the Marquis of Ardsley had to say on the subject.

Somebody was obviously arguing with him, and he said scathingly:

"Women have two uses—to amuse and to produce the necessary heir. Otherwise, a man of any intelligence has other interests to fill his life."

"That is all very well, Ardsley," a notorious Rake exclaimed. "But you know as well as I do that life would be very dull and colourless without pretty women in our arms and in our bed."

"There speaks the expert!" somebody exclaimed, and there was a roar of laughter.

"Every man to his own taste," the Marquis replied, when he could make himself heard. "At the same time, I was reading this morning that poor Oliver Markham has made a damned fool of himself, and somebody ought to have warned him."

"You mean that he should not have married an heiress?" the Rake asked incredulously. "It is all very well for you to sneer at money, Ardsley, but those of us who have pockets to let know that it is the only way we can keep up our ancestral homes and put decent horses in our stables."

"There are heiresses and heiresses," the Marquis said coldly. "Do you not realise that Markham has married the daughter of a tradesman?"

The scathing condemnation in his voice was almost like the bite of a cold wind.

"Perhaps he had no other choice," somebody ventured.

"Nonsense!" the Marquis said. "Markham comes from a very old family, and, thank God, blue blood and a respected title still have their established value in the Social Marriage Market. He has been a fool, and I shall not hesitate to tell him so."

"It is too late, Ardsley," the Rake said. "He is married, and doubtless we shall all be delighted to be asked to the parties which Oliver will give! Personally, I have always been very fond of him."

"And fonder still, now that he can afford to entertain you," somebody said mockingly.

"I blame myself and you too," the Marquis said in a serious tone. "When we realised that Oliver was serious in pursuing this unspeakable creature, we should have prevented him from marrying her."

"I heard," another man said tentatively, who had not spoken before, "that she is very attractive, and that Markham is in love with her."

"Love! Love!" the Marquis exclaimed. "Now we are back to that nonsensical emotion all over again! Let me make it quite clear: where marriage is concerned, love is the least important consideration to any man who has any sense."

"Like yourself!" the Rake mocked.

"Of course," the Marquis answered. "When I marry, which will not be for many years, I shall choose somebody with a pedigree to equal my own, and who will not offend me or shame the position she will hold as my wife by her low-class manners and low-class ideas."

"You are quite certain you would recognise her for what she is?" somebody asked.

"If I did not know a Thoroughbred when I saw one, I would give up racing," the Marquis answered sharply, "and I can assure you it is easier to detect the finer points of a woman than of a horse."

There was silence for a moment. Then someone asked:

"Are you telling me, Ardsley, that just as you claim you are an expert on horse-breeding, you can tell how a woman, or a man for that matter, is bred when you meet them, without a form-book to guide you?"

"Of course I can," the Marquis said positively. "However pretty, however attractive, however good an actress a woman might be, I can assure you I am never deceived."

"I would like to have a bet with you on that," the Rake said, "but as I have the uncomfortable feeling I would lose my money, I shall not ask for the Betting-Book."

The Betting-Book at White's was one of its most famous possessions.

Since 1743 members had entered their bets in the book, which was kept in a safe place in the Club, and which thereby became a sacred commitment on which no member would welsh.

Some of the bets were serious, but many were frivolous.

Births and marriages were almost as popular subjects for bets as death: "Would Lord E. marry Lady B.'s daughter in duty-bound?" "Was Lady C. in the family way?"

Lord Eglington in 1757 made a bet that he would find a man who could kill twenty snipe in three-and-twenty shots, and Lord Alington on a wet day bet three thousand pounds on which of two raindrops would first get to the bottom of a pane of glass.

During the war with France, Wellington's campaigns provided material for innumerable wagers, and many of the members believed firmly in Napoleon's invincibility, only to lose their money.

As the Rake finished speaking, Charles Frodham looked at Jimmy

Overton; then, because they knew what each other was thinking, they walked away from the Bow window to the far end of the Morning-Room and sat down to order a drink before Charles Frodham said:

"Do you think anybody would lay us twenty-to-one on his being deceived sooner or later?"

"Not a chance!" Jimmy Overton replied. "I expect what he says is the truth, and no woman could take him in."

"I do not believe it," Charles remarked. "Women are born actresses, and if we could find one who was as clever off the stage as Madame Vestris is on, she could lead him up the garden-path and make a fool of him."

"I would love to see that," Jimmy replied. "He gets under my skin because he is so damned pleased with himself. But I am sure he is like a fox-hound on the scent and would know an imposter before she could even open her mouth."

"You are as bad as he is!" Charles said crossly. "And because I intend to prove to you how wrong you are, I will find a woman somewhere, and I will bet you one hundred guineas that Ardsley will be unaware she is not *crème de la crème* for at least three days after he has met her."

"Done!" Jimmy answered. "But you have to play fair."

"That is what I should be saying to you," Charles protested. "I do not trust you to avoid losing one hundred guineas. How do I know you will not tip off Ardsley so that you will win?"

"Now you are insulting me," Jimmy cried, "and if you are not careful I will call you out and drill a hole through you!"

"You have no more chance of doing that," Charles laughed, "than of making Ardsley apologise when we prove him wrong."

"That is something I would really enjoy!"

"I do not like Ardsley," Charles said. "He is always laying down the law about women, and if you ask me, it takes away some of the enjoyment we have in them, which is exactly what he intends."

"I too dislike Ardsley, and I always have," his friend replied. "At the same time, I have to admit that he is a 'top-notcher' when it comes to sport, and his horses are better than anybody else's."

"So are his women, whatever he thinks about them," Charles agreed.

"If you want the truth, I will never forgive him for taking Clarice away from me."

"I can understand that," Jimmy said sympathetically. "She was lovely! Quite the most alluring 'bit o' muslin' you ever pursued."

"Hopelessly, thanks to Ardsley!" Charles exclaimed bitterly. "That is why I would like to get even with him. If I could find another Clarice, and convince him that her blood was as blue as his, he would not only have to eat his words, but he would look damned foolish when we revealed that she was actually straight out of the gutter."

Jimmy put back his head and laughed.

"Really, Charles, you are crazy to have such ideas. You know as well as I do that any woman who is as lovely and as fascinating as Clarice is quite certainly not going to be accepted at Richmond House, nor by any other of the great hostesses. Ardsley may think he can detect a social imposter, but no-one is more astute than other women."

"That is true," Charles admitted. "My grandmother has every debutante's pedigree at her fingertips and scrutinises them through a magnifying-glass before she offers them to me as prospective brides."

"I am sorry for you! Your grandmother frightens me, and I do not know how you have managed to evade matrimony for so long."

"It has been difficult at times," Charles admitted, "and I expect I shall eventually be caught."

There was silence for a moment between the two friends. Then Jimmy said:

"Well, what about having luncheon and forgetting this rather gloomy discourse?"

"Certainly not!" Charles said sharply. "I am going to call for the Betting-Book and record our bet in it."

"Do not mention Ardsley by name."

"No, of course not," Charles replied. "I am not as birdwitted as that."

He raised his hand, and instantly a steward came to his side.

"The Betting-Book."

"Very good, M'Lord."

The leather-bound book was brought and set down at Charles Frodham's side, together with an ink-pot and a quill-pen.

Charles thought for a moment before he wrote carefully:

1st May 1818.
Lord Frodham bets Sir James Overton that he will deceive a certain nobleman for
three days without his being aware of it.

"Is that ambiguous enough?" Charles asked.

"It will make everybody who reads it damned curious," Jimmy replied.

"It will give them something to think about," Charles said with a grin. "Come on, let us go up to the Coffee-Room."

He put down the pen and the steward carried the Betting-Book away. Then the two friends started to wend their way through the Morning-Room, which had grown fuller still since they had been talking.

They had just reached the door when a voice behind them said:

"Frodham! Overton! I wanted to see you! I am running a Steeple-Chase and I would like you both to take part in it."

The eyes of both the young men lit up.

The Marquis's Steeple-Chases were famous, not only because they were well run and most enjoyable, but also because the house-parties he gave with them at Ardsley Hall were legendary. An invitation to one of them was more prized than one to Carlton House or the Royal Pavilion at Brighton.

"Thank you very much," Charles Frodham said before his friend could speak. "Jimmy and I will look forward to it."

"Send your horses on ahead of you," the Marquis said carelessly, "to give them a chance to rest before the big event, and I shall expect you both on Thursday night. The race will take place on Saturday, and I expect there will be a lot of competitors."

"I am sure there will be," Charles said. "I have a new horse which might even defeat Your Lordship's."

The Marquis laughed.

"You can try," he said, "but I shall be extremely annoyed if my new one, which I have not yet tried out, is not the victor."

He walked away as he spoke, supremely sure of himself and moving through the Club in a majestic manner that invariably aroused a respect that other men were not accorded.

Charles and Jimmy went upstairs to the Coffee-Room and sat down at a table in the window where they could be alone.

"Do you really think you have a chance of beating the Marquis?" Jimmy asked.

"I said that to annoy him," Charles admitted. "I expect he will win, he always does."

"That is what is so intensely irritating!" Jimmy agreed. "I know my horses have not a chance against his, but I shall enjoy the Steeple-Chase and also the party. I wonder who will be there."

"Beauties galore," Charles said casually.

"Somebody told me last night that the Marquis actually danced with Lady Beris at Richmond House," Jimmy said, "and the Duke had visions of having him as a son-in-law."

Charles laughed.

"Not a chance! He spends his time, I am told, with a new charmer— Lady Sinclair—although I doubt if she will hold him for long."

"The Countess of Martindale is one of the prettiest women I have ever seen," Jimmy said. "Ardsley dropped her in a month, so how are you going to find a 'gutter-snipe' to compete with her?"

"I will find someone," Charles said confidently. "But not a gutter-snipe. I think she will have to be an actress."

"That will cost you a pretty penny."

"I shall have your hundred guineas towards expenses."

"I have never before made a bet I have been so certain of winning," Jimmy answered provocatively.

"I think it only fair that just for once he should be in the wrong," Charles said as if he was speaking to himself.

He was frowning as he spoke, and Jimmy knew he was still feeling angry at the way in which the Marquis had swept Clarice away from him in a high-handed manner that would have annoyed anybody, especially Charles Frodham.

Very good-looking, wealthy because his father had died while he was still a minor, and the owner of a very charming if not particularly impressive Estate in Huntingdonshire, Charles was run after by the most attractive women in the *Beau Monde* and courted by ambitious mothers for their young daughters.

He had good grounds for being conceited and proud of himself, but it was no use pretending that he was not eclipsed by the Marquis of Ardsley.

Jimmy Overton was not ambitious and was quite content to be only comparatively well off. Yet, he had enough money to enjoy himself in London and to keep up the delightful Seventeenth-Century Manor he owned in Essex.

As his mother ran it very competently and was in no hurry to move to the Dower House, he was not pestered as his friend was to settle down and get married.

He had therefore every intention of enjoying himself and remaining free for a great number of years before he asked any woman, however attractive or suitable, to be his wife.

Because he and Charles had been close friends at Eton and at Oxford, they enjoyed life together, hunting as a couple, being welcomed not only by the great hostesses at every Ball, Reception, and Assembly, but also by the Madams in the "Houses of Pleasure" and the Dance-Halls, where the prettiest "Cyprians" ran towards them with open arms.

Jimmy knew that Charles's pride had certainly been bruised if not deflated by the way in which the Marquis had taken the lovely Clarice from him at the very moment when he was considering setting her up in a small house in Chelsea and taking her officially under his protection.

"What are you thinking about?" Jimmy asked now.

"The pleasure I shall enjoy at seeing Ardsley discomfited."

"You cannot say that until you have found this paragon who I am convinced does not exist," Jimmy said practically.

"I will prove him wrong if it is the last thing I do!" Charles said aggressively.

Jimmy laughed as he said:

"Actually, I would willingly pay five hundred guineas to see Ardsley 'bite the dust,' which is strange when you think about it, because he has never done me any harm."

"It is insufferable that any man should walk about as if he were God!"

"That is rather a good description," Jimmy said. "At the same time, the sort of god you really mean is the fellow we read about at Oxford—what was he called?—the one who drives his Chariot across the sky by day."

"Apollo."

"That is right."

"We saw a statue of him when we were in Rome, and Ardsley does look like him," Charles remarked.

"That is the answer, then," Jimmy said. "He is Apollo, a god, and we poor devils are just humans."

"Even gods, if my mythology is not at fault," Charles said, "were susceptible to pretty women, but I have the uncomfortable feeling that it was the male gods who disguised themselves, rather than the goddesses."

"Oh, well, you can rewrite the whole of Greek—or was it Roman?—mythology to suit yourself," Jimmy said with a smile, "but Apollo or no Apollo, I am hungry."

It was a week later when Lord Frodham and Sir James Overton set off from Charles's house in the country to drive to Ardsley Hall.

Their horses had left two days earlier, both gentlemen having given their grooms strict instructions to take them easily and to make sure that they were in perfect condition for the Steeple-Chase on Saturday.

Besides thinking of his horses, Charles had given a great deal of his time to searching for a young actress with whom he intended to deceive the Marquis into believing that she was as blue-blooded as he was.

"If you are going to give her a fictitious name," Jimmy said, "you will have to be careful to choose one of which the Marquis will not be suspicious. I am quite certain he knows the genealogical tree of every family in the country."

"That is the least of our worries," Charles said after the third day and night of searching the Theatres and Dance-Halls and even the "Houses of Pleasure" for a likely candidate.

Once or twice they had seen a face that was so attractive and so pretty that Charles had thought his search was at an end.

But the beauty in question had only to open her mouth to betray an accent that no possible amount of tuition could disguise from anybody as astute as the Marquis.

"Of course, we may have to teach her how to speak," Charles conceded, "but perhaps if she was a foreigner it would be easier."

"I have always been told that the Marquis of Ardsley is very good at languages," Jimmy said. "In fact, I remember hearing that he has helped Lord Hawkesley at the Foreign Office on various occasions."

Charles's lips tightened, but he made no comment, and they moved on to look elsewhere for a creature who Jimmy was already convinced was as rare as a dodo-bird.

Jimmy actually had found the chase most enjoyable, although he was sorry for his friend, and now as they drove through the countryside at a spanking pace behind Charles's team of bays he said:

"I ought to have insisted that we have a time-limit on our wager, otherwise I can see us spending the rest of our summer searching for the unobtainable, with you growing more and more grumpy in the process."

"I am not grumpy," Charles replied, "and I have not given up hope! But I have begun to think that we are looking in the wrong places."

"What do you mean by that?"

"The sort of woman we want is more likely to be found in the country than in London. You know as well as I do that if she was beautiful enough for our requirements, she would have been snapped up the moment she set foot in one of those overcrowded Dance-Halls. And if she was on the Stage, her dressing-room would be full of followers."

"You certainly have something there," Jimmy replied, "and I was just thinking that when I was young, the Vicar of the family Church to which I was taken every Sunday had an extremely pretty daughter."

Charles turned from his contemplation of the road ahead to look at his friend and ask:

"Where is she now?"

Jimmy laughed as he replied:

"Married, with a large family!"

"Then why the hell are you talking about her?"

"I was only agreeing with you that pretty girls are not the prerogative of London."

"If they are pretty enough, it is the one place they want to go."

"That is true," Jimmy agreed. "So what you have to do, Charles, is to trap 'em before they get there!"

"You are laughing at me," Charles said, "and so damned sure of taking my hundred guineas off me that you are getting as bad as Ardsley himself!"

Jimmy sighed as he said:

"I want to topple him off his perch! At the same time, I am quite prepared to eat his superlative food, stay in the most comfortable house in England, and applaud him as he wins the first prize at his own Steeple-Chase."

"If you say one more word," Charles threatened, "I will turn you out of the Phaeton and make you walk."

"In these Hessians?" Jimmy exclaimed. "For God's sake, Charles, it would be a Chinese Torture!"

They both laughed as they drove on.

The sunshine, which had been somewhat fitful earlier in the day, had now disappeared behind dark clouds.

Then, after luncheon in a comfortable Inn, where Charles changed his team of bays for four perfectly matched chestnuts, the sky was not only overcast but there were rumbles of thunder in the distance.

"Damn!" Charles said irritably. "We are going to get wet. I should have thought of travelling in my fastest Chariot so that we could put the hood up."

"It will be very unpleasant to arrive looking like a drowned rat," Jimmy said reflectively. "I am quite certain that the Marquis, if he were in our place, would manage to control the elements."

"I agree with you, but there seems to be nothing we can do about it, and we still have at least another hour's driving before we get there."

Ardsley Hall was in Hampshire, and now, too late, Charles thought that if they had started earlier in the morning, they might have reached their destination before the storm broke.

A sudden flash of forked lightning made the horses nervous, and as he was not certain that if the lightning grew worse, the comparatively young team would not panic, he said:

"There is an Inn about half-a-mile from here. I have never been there, and I expect it is rather scruffy, but it might be wise to take shelter. I do not believe the storm will last long."

"I think you are wise," Jimmy said. "I have heard of nasty accidents taking place in thunderstorms."

As he spoke, he was thinking that four horses were difficult to control at the best of times, and although Charles was an extremely good and experienced driver, he was not a Corinthian like the Marquis.

However, it was something he was far too tactful to say aloud, and as the lightning flashed again and the crash that followed it seemed nearer than it had been before, he was thankful when Charles drove into the courtyard of an attractive old black-and-white Inn with diamond-paned windows.

The groom clambered down from the back seat and began to give orders to the ostlers who came running from the stables.

Charles put down the reins and climbed from the Phaeton while Jimmy descended on the other side of it.

They walked into the very low-ceilinged Inn, and a large, fat man who was obviously the Landlord came hurrying towards them, wiping his hands on his apron.

"Good-evening, Sirs, you're very welcome!"

"I am Lord Frodham," Charles replied, "and I and my friend will be staying for the duration of the storm. We would like a private Parlour."

"I'm afraid it's small, M'Lord, but it's all we've got," the Landlord replied.

He led the way through an open Lounge in which a large log fire was burning to where at the far end it had obviously been divided by a somewhat makeshift wall of panelling that did not match the rest of the room.

The Parlour was small, as he had said, but there was a fireplace, two armchairs, and a table on which fastidious guests who did not wish to mix with the hoi-polloi could eat in private.

The Landlord bent down to light the fire, and Charles said:

"Bring me a bottle of your best claret. I presume you have no champagne?"

"Afraid not, M'Lord," the Landlord replied, "but th' claret's good, and the brandy, which be French, be very good indeed!"

The way he spoke made it quite clear that the brandy had come across the Channel and no Duty had been paid on it.

"Bring a bottle of both," Charles ordered.

Bowing, with a gratified expression on his face, the Landlord left the room.

There was a small window which looked onto an untidy piece of ground which could hardly be described as a garden, and Jimmy walked towards it.

As he did so there was a flash of lightning which illuminated both the outside and the inside of the Inn, followed by a resounding crash of thunder, and he started back almost as if he had been struck.

"Thank God we are out of this!" Charles exclaimed. "The horses would go mad!"

"We were only just in time," Jimmy agreed. "Another few minutes and we would have been drenched."

Almost as if it were an echo, as he spoke they heard a woman's voice say on the other side of the wall:

"My carriage and horses are drenched. May I stay here until the storm has abated?"

It was a soft, rather attractive voice, and Jimmy thought that in some strange way she sounded a little frightened.

"Yes, of course, Ma'am," he heard the Landlord reply. "Perhaps you'll sit by the fire? And can I offer you a cup o' tea? I feel sure you'd not take wine."

"No, no, of course not," the woman replied, "and a cup of tea would be very pleasant. Thank you."

"I'll see to it at once, Ma'am."

As the Landlord finished speaking he opened the door of the private Parlour and came in carrying a bottle of French brandy and one of claret.

He also had a tray in his hands with four glasses on it, and he set everything down on the table, saying as he did so:

"It's an ill wind that doesn't blow a Landlord some good. I weren't expectin' any visitors today."

He drew the cork from the brandy bottle and as he put it down on the tray Jimmy said:

"I heard you talking to a lady."

The Landlord looked at him, then said in such a low voice that it was almost a whisper.

"A Nun, Sir!"

"A Nun!" Jimmy exclaimed.

The Landlord nodded.

"I wondered why you were so certain she would not take wine," Charles said. "Now I understand."

"It's not often we sees Nuns in this part of the world, M'Lord, and driving in a smart carriage with two horses."

411

As he opened the bottle of claret the Inn-Keeper added:

"If there's anything else you gentlemen wants, let me know."

"We will," Charles replied.

He walked to the table, poured out half-a-glass of claret, sniffed it, then tasted it tentatively.

"Not bad!"

"I prefer brandy," Jimmy said, "but not too much. As you know, Ardsley's cellar is famous, and I am keeping myself for dinner."

"If we ever get there!" Charles reacted.

The thunder was still deafening overhead, and the rain seemed to increase until the ground outside looked like a pond.

It was such a depressing sight that Jimmy walked to the fire.

"It is overhead," he said, "and I have no wish to endure more than an hour of this."

"Nor have I," Charles agreed. "We are fortunate that when the storm started we were so near to a place of shelter, whatever it might have been like."

"Thank God for it."

As Jimmy spoke he sat down in a comfortable armchair, and his friend sat opposite him.

Because it was hard to make their voices heard above the noise of the rain, they both were silent, sipping their drinks and feeling sleepy from the warmth of the fire.

They had been sitting quietly for quite some time when suddenly there was the sound of a door opening noisily, footsteps, then a cry from the woman they had heard earlier.

It was a cry of fear, and they heard a man's voice saying:

"So here you are! What the hell do you mean by running away and being dressed up like that?"

"I . . . I am going . . . into a . . . Convent . . . and nothing you can . . . say will . . . stop me!"

"I've a great deal to say, and you'll listen to me!"

The man's voice was rough, and although it was educated, there was something about it which told Charles and Jimmy that he was not a gentleman.

"You've put me to a lot of inconvenience," the man said, "and as soon as this storm is over, I'm taking you to London, where you'll do as I tell you."

"If you think I have any intention of marrying Lord Bredon or obeying you in any other way, you are very much mistaken!"

"You'll do as you are told!" the man said sharply. "You ought to be grateful to me, instead of behaving in this mad-cap manner. Going into a Convent indeed! I've never heard of such a thing! Besides, they might not want you."

"I have every intention of becoming a Nun, and they will be only too pleased to accept me . . . and my . . . fortune!"

"So that's your idea, is it? Well, you'll not give your fortune over to any Convent while I'm in charge of you."

"In charge of me?" the woman replied scornfully. "You are not in charge of me. You were employed by my father as his Solicitor, and he would not engage you for a day more if he were still alive."

There was a little tremor in her voice as she said the last word, and Charles and Jimmy, who were listening with undisguised curiosity, thought her father's death must have taken place quite recently.

It was almost as if they were in the audience at one of the melodramatic plays which held spell-bound those who paid to see them.

"Now listen to me, Mr. Jacobson," the woman said, and it was obvious from her voice that she was young and, Charles was sure, frightened. "I will pay you anything you ask, even if it is a large sum, when I am twenty-one and have control of my fortune."

The man laughed, and it was not a pleasant sound.

"Do you really think I am going to wait for three years? Lord Bredon has promised me ten thousand pounds the day he marries you—and the sooner the better, from his point of view and yours."

"What do you mean . . . and mine? I will not marry . . . Lord Bredon. I hate him . . . as I hate all men . . . and I do not . . . intend to . . . marry anybody!"

For a moment it seemed that Mr. Jacobson was stunned before he said:

"You've got bats in your belfry, that's what you've got! All women want to get married, and Bredon's a gentleman all right, and you'll look pretty in a coronet."

"I daresay he has pawned that with everything else," the woman said

413

scornfully. "If you think I want to marry a bankrupt to save him from being taken to the Fleet Prison as a debtor, you are the one who is mad! Papa would be appalled by your behaviour."

"Your father's dead and there's nothing you can do about it," Mr. Jacobson said roughly. "And if it's not Lord Bredon, it will be another fortune-hunter of some sort, and you'll find there is not much to choose between any of them."

"I am not going to choose. As I have already told you, I am going into a Convent, and there is nothing you can do to stop me."

Mr. Jacobson laughed.

"That's what you think! You will come to London with me willingly, or I'll take you unconscious. That's the only choice you've got. What's more, we're going now, and if you get wet, you've only yourself to blame."

"I will not . . . come with you . . . I will not!"

Her defiant words ended in a scream, and Charles and Jimmy knew that she was fighting against Mr. Jacobson, who was dragging her towards the door.

They looked at each other and without saying anything rose to their feet.

They put down their glasses and, pulling open the Parlour door, walked out into the Lounge.

As they both expected, Mr. Jacobson, an unpleasant, foxy-looking man, was dragging the woman towards the outer door of the Inn.

She was resisting in every way possible, but she was small while he was large, and there was no doubt how the contest would end.

In the struggle the woman's veil had fallen off, and Charles, who had walked out first, had a glimpse of thick red tresses falling over her black-draped shoulders before he punched Mr. Jacobson hard with his clenched fist.

The Solicitor immediately released the woman's wrist and put up his own hands.

But he was too late.

Charles hit him again, this time on the chin, and he fell to the ground, out for the count.

Jimmy turned from the satisfaction he was receiving from watching his

friend in action, to see two very large eyes looking up at him and hear a
voice say fervently:

"Oh, thank you . . . thank you!"

He was just thinking that she was one of the prettiest girls he had ever
seen in his life, when Charles turned round.

"What shall I do about him now?" he asked.

The girl, for she was nothing more, was looking apprehensively at Mr.
Jacobson lying unconscious on the floor.

"I . . . I must get . . . away!" she said, "but the horse . . . that
. . . brought me here from Southampton is very tired . . . and I am
afraid that when he revives, Mr. Jacobson will . . . catch up with me
. . . again."

Charles looked at Jimmy and smiled.

"I think we can prevent that from happening."

"Of course!" Jimmy replied.

As he spoke he looked round and saw that there was a heavy curtain
that could be pulled over the outer door in the winter to keep out the cold.

It was caught back now with what appeared to be a tough rope of the
same material.

He unhitched it from the hooks, letting the curtain fall forward, and
handed it to his friend.

Bending down, Charles tied the Solicitor's legs together, turned him
over somewhat roughly, and, pulling a handkerchief out of his pocket, tied
his wrists behind his back.

As he did so he said with a note of laughter in his voice:

"We need yours to gag him."

"Yes, of course," Jimmy agreed obligingly.

He took his handkerchief from his pocket, then as if there was no need
for them to speak of what was required, he lifted Mr. Jacobson up by the
shoulders, Charles took his legs, and they carried him through the door
which led into the yard.

There was nobody about because it was still teeming with rain, but still
they carried the unconscious Solicitor a little way down the road from
which they had approached the Inn.

"This will do," Charles said.

He and Jimmy swung the still-unconscious man backwards, forwards,

415

and then back again, before they flung him into a deep ditch at the side of the road.

There was a splash as he fell, then without waiting to see whether or not his head was above the water, they ran quickly back into the Inn.

The girl was waiting for them, her hands clasped together almost as if she were praying, and as they came into the Lounge, shaking the rain off themselves like two dogs, she said in a voice that trembled:

"What have you . . . done with . . . him?"

"Thrown him where he will not be found for a long time. At least, not until we have all got away from here."

"Are you . . . sure?"

"Quite sure," Charles said reassuringly, "and as it has been a shock, I suggest you have a little brandy. It will make you feel better."

The girl did not refuse, and when Charles opened the door of the Parlour, she went ahead of them and sat down in a chair by the fire.

For the first time Charles looked at her, and with her red hair glinting in the firelight, her huge eyes in her very small, pointed face raised to his, he thought he must be dreaming.

Never could he have imagined that he would see anybody so attractive, so lovely, and playing a part in a drama which he had found exceedingly enjoyable.

It was almost, he thought, what he and Jimmy might have encountered when they were at Oxford, and they had both found life less exciting and much duller since they had left.

With an engaging smile which many women had found irresistible he said:

"Now suppose you tell us about yourself and why you are travelling alone, pursued by a swine like that?"

For a moment she did not answer but looked up at him a little nervously, until as if he would reassure her Charles said:

"Let me introduce myself. I am Lord Frodham, and this is my friend Sir James Overton."

"How do you do," the girl said. "I do not know how to begin to thank you or to tell you how . . . grateful I am that . . . you came to my . . . rescue."

"Perhaps you should start by telling us who you are," Charles suggested.

The way he spoke told Jimmy he was very curious.

"My name is Indira Rowlandson."

"That is a very beautiful name," Jimmy remarked.

"It is Indian, and I have just arrived from India, where I was with my father . . . until . . . on the voyage home he . . . died."

Indira gave a little sob before she went on:

"He contracted a fever of some sort, and almost before I realised how ill he was, he had died . . . and was . . . buried at . . . sea."

"I am sorry," Charles said. "But surely you have some relations you can go to?"

"That is what I meant to do," Indira said, "but Papa had written to his firm of Solicitors, saying that they were to meet us at Southampton, and . . . Mr. Jacobson was there . . . waiting."

She shivered.

"How could your father have chosen such a horrible man to handle his affairs?" Charles asked.

"It was, I believe, quite a reputable firm when the Senior Partner was in charge," Indira replied. "But he is now very old, and Mr. Jacobson told me he now runs everything."

"What happened?" Charles asked.

"Mr. Jacobson said he would look after me and there was no reason for me not to trust him. He said he was taking me to London, but when I talked about finding my relatives, he told me what he was planning."

She drew in her breath as she went on:

"He said that one of his clients, Lord Bredon, was deeply in debt and had to marry an heiress in order to save himself from going to prison."

"So you are an heiress," Jimmy interposed.

"Yes, Papa was very rich, and he left me everything he possessed. I have the handling of it if I marry, or rather my husband will, but until then I can use only the income until I am twenty-one, and then I can control the whole fortune if I have not found anyone I want to marry."

It was, Charles thought, a sensible Will that a clever man might make, to safeguard his daughter, but Mr. Rowlandson had obviously not expected that his Solicitor would prove to be crooked.

"Do you really want to go into a Convent?" Jimmy asked.

"There is nothing . . . else I can . . . do," Indira replied. "Anything would be better than to marry a man who only wants my money and was stupid and dissolute enough to lose his own."

She spoke scathingly, but there was also, as the two men listening were aware, a touch of terror in her voice.

"I will be safe in a . . . Convent," she said as if she spoke to herself, "then I will not be . . . frightened by men, whom I . . . hate!"

She spoke spontaneously, hardly aware that she was speaking to two of the species, then added quickly:

"Oh, please . . . do not think I am being . . . rude when you have both been so kind . . . and I am very . . . grateful to you, but ever since Papa died it has been very, very . . . difficult for me. There were . . . men on the . . . ship, and then . . . Lord Bredon."

As she was so attractive, there was no need to tell Charles and Jimmy what had happened, and after a moment's silence Charles said:

"You must have some idea where your relatives are."

"My father has an aunt, but she must be very old, and I am sure there are cousins, but I never troubled to make a list of them, nor to listen at all carefully when Papa was talking about them. There were so many other things that made him so exciting to be with, and when we were in India, England seemed very far . . . away."

There was something wistful in the way she spoke. Then there was a little pause, and Charles looked at Jimmy, and they each knew what the other was thinking.

Almost as if fate had taken a hand in their affairs, Charles said:

"I can understand you wanting to go into a Convent, but I think I have a better idea, and if we have helped you, perhaps you would be kind enough to help us."

"I will if I can."

"There is a question I have to ask you first," Charles said. "First, what exactly was your father's position in life, and why did he have so much money?"

Indira hesitated. Then, as if she was thinking exactly what she should answer, she replied:

"It is rather difficult to put into words, but I suppose you could say he was a trader in many different fields."

There was a smile on Charles's face, as if this was what he had expected.

Then he said:

"And now, Miss Rowlandson, will you please listen to me?"

CHAPTER TWO

———— ⌗ ————

"*I*T IS IMPOSSIBLE, I could not do anything like that!" Indira exclaimed.

"Why not?" Charles enquired. "You are far too pretty to go into a Convent. But if you are intent on it, there is nothing to stop you from doing it later."

Indira was obviously reflecting on what he had said, and looking so lovely as she did so that Jimmy was staring at her almost as if he felt she could not be real.

Finally she asked:

"This Marquis who says such unkind things about women . . . what is he like?"

"Tall, handsome, and irresistibly attractive to the female sex," Charles replied.

The way he spoke made Indira look at him speculatively for a moment before she said:

"He has obviously . . . hurt you . . . personally in some . . . way."

Jimmy laughed.

"That is very perceptive of you. Of course he has! He took away a very lovely—lady on whom Charles had set his heart, and that is such a familiar

story in London that there is hardly a man who does not bear him a
grudge in one way or another."

The way Indira looked at Jimmy as he was speaking made Charles
wonder if she had noticed the perceptive pause before Jimmy had said the
word "lady."

Then he told himself that the girl they were talking to was far too
young to know anything about "Cyprians" and "Ladybirds."

As if he thought it was a subject to be skated over quickly, he said:

"What my friend and I are begging you to do, Miss Rowlandson, is to
help us win a bet and at the same time to teach the Marquis of Ardsley a
lesson. I cannot believe that you would approve of any man who is so
stuck up and so very pleased with himself."

"No, of course not," Indira agreed. "In fact I hate all men, and that is a
very good reason why I would like to go to a Convent."

"You will hate that," Jimmy said. "Think of being shut up for the rest of
your life with a lot of women who will loathe you because you are much
prettier than they are."

Indira's eyes widened and she looked at him in a startled fashion.

"Do you think that is true?" she asked. "I thought Nuns were too
dedicated to God to feel jealous or envious of other women."

Charles laughed.

"If you ask me, however many prayers she may utter, a woman will still
be a woman, and quite frankly, Miss Rowlandson, you are far too beautiful to be a Nun."

"Then what . . . can I . . . do?" Indira asked helplessly.

"Do what we suggest!" Charles said. "We promise you we will protect
you, and we will certainly stop anybody like that ghastly Solicitor from
forcing you into a marriage with a fortune-hunter."

He paused before he said:

"When our little adventure is over, which is what it will be, and you
have confounded the Marquis, I promise you I will find you somewhere to
go."

He realised as he spoke that Jimmy was looking at him questioningly,
and he added:

"I have a mass of relations, and so have you, Jimmy, who would be
only too pleased to chaperone Miss Rowlandson or to travel with her."

The two young men looked at each other and they each knew the other was thinking that because she was very rich as well as beautiful, the world was at Indira Rowlandson's feet.

It was certainly true that both of them could find relations who would be more than willing to undertake the task of looking after such an attractive girl and to introduce her to Society, in which she would undoubtedly shine.

It was obviously impossible for her to enter the *Beau Monde* as the daughter of a tradesman, but there were a great number of people who were not so particular, especially in the country.

Both Charles and Jimmy were already mentally making a list of their poorer relations who they were quite certain would be interested in such a proposition.

Almost as if Indira knew what they were thinking, she looked from one to the other before she said:

"It is very . . . kind of you . . . but of course . . . when I have time I am sure I can find some of Papa's . . . relatives."

She made an exasperated little sound before she said:

"How could I have been so foolish as not to listen to Papa when he was telling me what we would do when we reached England? But I was thinking of the big house that he intended to rent in London, and the horses he wanted to race at Newmarket and Epsom, and I was not particularly interested in who would be with us, as I so much liked being alone with him."

As she said the last words there was a note in her voice as if she wanted to cry at losing him, and Charles said hastily:

"I am quite certain your father would not want you to do anything so foolish as to incarcerate yourself in a Convent just because you are alone and have been upset by the behaviour of that swine Jacobson."

"That reminds me," Jimmy said. "It would be wise to leave here as soon as we can. When he regains consciousness he might somehow manage to get back here and make a scene."

Indira gave a little cry and started to her feet.

"You are quite right! I must get away at once! Please, do not let us stay here a moment . . . longer than we . . . have to!"

421

While they had been talking, the storm had passed and the rain had ceased.

Charles looked out the window, then at Indira. With her red hair streaming over her shoulders she certainly looked very lovely.

At the same time, he thought he could hardly arrive to stay with the Marquis with a woman who was dressed as a Nun.

"Have you any other clothes with you?" he asked.

"Yes, of course," Indira replied. "There are three trunks and a bonnet-box in the carriage that I hired to bring me here. I think it was because they are heavy that Mr. Jacobson was able to catch up with me."

Jimmy walked towards the door.

"I will have them sent upstairs," he said, "and I suggest you change as quickly as possible. Charles will tell you what to wear."

Jimmy went from the small Parlour, and Charles said to Indira almost as if he were talking to a child:

"Now what we must do is to concoct some tale to explain why we are bringing you to Ardsley Hall. I think perhaps it would be easiest to say we had to rescue you from Highwaymen."

Indira laughed.

"That sounds very exciting!"

"Only in retrospect," Charles said. "When it happens, it is exceedingly unpleasant, as I know to my cost."

"You have been held up by Highwaymen?"

"Yes, but I will tell you about it another time," Charles answered. "Now listen to me carefully."

"I am listening."

She raised her eyes to his as she spoke, and Charles thought she had not only beautiful eyes but very strange ones.

They had a sort of mystery about them that he had never seen before, and he told himself with satisfaction that the Marquis was going to find her very intriguing.

Then, as he realised that Indira was waiting for him to speak, he began:

"You are a Lady of Quality who has just arrived in this country from India. It is always wise to keep as near to the truth as possible. You were chaperoned on the voyage by some extremely respectable people."

He paused and said quietly:

"Jimmy and I will think of names for them later. And when you arrived at Southampton, to your surprise there was nobody to meet you."

"Our Mr. Jacobson!" Indira murmured, but Charles continued as if she had not spoken:

"You therefore very bravely hired a carriage to take you to London, only to be held up by Highwaymen who fought with the Coachmen, leaving them too bruised and battered to take you any farther, and stole your horses."

Indira laughed.

"That is certainly dramatic, and just like a story in a book."

"I am rather pleased with it myself," Charles admitted. "That is how we found you, and as we did not like to disappoint our friend the Marquis by not turning up as he expected, we decided that rather than escort you to London, we would bring you to stay with him."

Indira clapped her hands together.

"That is a marvellous tale!"

"What is?" Jimmy asked, coming in through the door.

Charles quickly repeated what he had just said to Indira.

"Good gracious!" Jimmy exclaimed. "You will be writing a book if you are not careful."

"I might consider that," Charles said loftily. "In the meantime, that is what happened, and we must all tell the same story."

"Yes, of course," Jimmy agreed.

"I will go change," Indira said.

They both realised that she was nervous in case Mr. Jacobson reappeared.

"Yes, hurry!" Charles exclaimed. "Jimmy and I will try to think of a grand title for you, because do not forget that your pedigree must be impeccable. Moreover, it must not be one he might suspect to be a fraud, and therefore check it for authenticity."

As he spoke Charles looked worried.

He was astute enough to realise that this was the weak link in his and Jimmy's story.

As the Marquis was so knowledgeable about the genealogy of the people he knew, it would be dangerous to invent a title, and perhaps even more dangerous to pretend to a relationship which could not be substantiated.

While he was thinking, Indira was already moving towards the door through which Jimmy had just entered.

As he held it open for her he said:

"You will find your trunk being taken to the best bedroom, which is just at the top of the staircase."

"Thank you," she said with a smile.

"Wear the smartest travelling-clothes you possess," Charles said.

She turned her head to smile at him, then stopped.

"I have a suggestion."

"What is it?"

"If you are really going to make me out to be so important, I think it would be difficult for the Marquis to suspect I am not the daughter of the Earl of Farncombe."

"Who is he?" Charles asked.

"The Governor of Madras. Papa and I knew him in India."

"Farncombe!" Jimmy exclaimed. "If he is an Earl, then I am quite certain that the Marquis will have heard of him."

"But this Marquis has not been to India?" Indira asked.

"If he has, I am sure that we would know about it," Charles replied.

"Yes, I am sure we would," Jimmy agreed. "We would doubtless have had a lecture too on how the Indian women under the skin are just the same as the European variety."

The two men laughed, and Indira went on:

"The Earl of Farncombe in fact has a daughter just about my age. Her name is Lady Mary Combe. Even if some of the Marquis's friends have been to India, they would never have met her because she has been very ill for the last two years and has been living in the hills, where it is cooler, and only very close personal friends have been allowed to visit her."

Charles looked at Jimmy.

"It sounds a perfect alias," he said. "Thank you, Indira. That is very helpful."

"The Earl has also lived in India for many years without coming home," Indira said, "so it is very unlikely that your Marquis will have met him."

She did not wait for Charles and Jimmy to reply, but ran across the Lounge and up the oak staircase at the end of it.

Jimmy shut the door behind her.

"Fate has certainly taken a hand in our affairs," he said. "I never dreamt that we would be lucky enough to find anybody so attractive and exactly what we need."

"I listened very carefully," Charles said, "and she never mispronounced a word in a manner which might have given her away as being a tradesman's daughter."

"She has obviously been very well educated," Jimmy said. "But of course no real Lady would have travelled alone."

"How could she help it when her father died?"

"I do not know, but I expect the Captain would have found her a Chaperone or someone like that."

The two men were silent until Jimmy said:

"When we have confounded the Marquis with her, we will have to look after her and see that that swine Jacobson does not harass her again."

"I have met Bredon," Charles said reflectively.

"You have?" Jimmy exclaimed. "What is he like?"

"Ghastly! He got sacked from Eton, and when he came into the title after his father's death, he gambled away every penny he possessed in two years."

"No wonder he has been looking for an heiress," Jimmy remarked.

"The only thing he has left to sell is his title," Charles said, "and when I last saw him at some Dance-Hall about six months ago, he looked dissipated and down-at-heel. He was also very unpleasantly drunk."

"Well, we have saved the pretty redhead from him for the moment."

"Pretty?" Charles exclaimed. "She is lovely! And I am sure we can find her a decent husband who would be kind to her."

"I am even prepared to be kind to her myself," Jimmy said, "but I think my family would shoot me if I married a tradesman's daughter."

"So would mine," Charles agreed.

"Well, I am quite certain that at the suggestion of any other position in our lives, she would be off to the Convent again."

"I am sure she would," Jimmy said. "At the same time, it is the greatest bit of luck that she dislikes men. It means she will keep the Marquis at

425

arm's length, and that will surprise him. Apart from anything else, he is quite certain he is irresistible."

"He is," Charles said drily. "We established that a long time ago."

He spoke so bitterly that Jimmy decided to change the subject.

"One thing I will say is that our lady-friend is exceedingly sporting. Most women do not have the guts, as you and I well know, to run away on their own from a blackguard Solicitor, or to agree to the extraordinary proposition we have put to her."

"She is exceptional," Charles agreed. "I am only rather nervous in case the Marquis penetrates her impersonation the moment he sees her."

Jimmy gave a cry of horror.

"Now you are inviting disaster! If you are afraid he may be suspicious, then perhaps he will read your thoughts, or if you are obviously on edge he may suspect that something is up."

"You are right," Charles conceded. "I remember one of those old bores at the Club who was always droning on about how he rescued people during the French Revolution saying: 'The art of disguise is to think one-self into the part'!"

"Exactly! And we have to believe absolutely in the tale we tell the Marquis, and make sure Indira Rowlandson does the same."

"The same what?" a voice asked, and as the two gentlemen rose to their feet Indira came into the Parlour.

She was looking very different from when she had left them, and for a moment both Charles and Jimmy stared at her, speechless with admiration.

She was wearing an exceedingly smart travelling-coat of sapphire-blue satin edged with braid which made a pattern round the hem and round the sleeves.

Her bonnet, which was in the very latest fashion, had a high, pointed brim which was edged with a row of lace, and the high crown was decorated with tightly curled ostrich-feathers of the same blue as her coat.

Her shoes, gloves, and bag all matched, and it flashed through Charles's mind that they were in fact being deceived and to be so smartly dressed she must have come straight from London.

As if she understood his astonishment and could read his thoughts, Indira said:

"You look surprised, but Papa's organisation is so splendid that my clothes were made in Paris and sent out to India, or wherever we were, every six months."

"You look magnificent," Charles said, recovering his voice, "and exactly as we wish you to look."

"Thank you, My Lord, but now let us be on our way. I am so afraid that Mr. Jacobson will reappear and I will have to start running away all over again."

"You are not running anywhere except with us," Jimmy said firmly. "I will see to your trunks being put on the Phaeton, or perhaps we will be able to hire some sort of vehicle to follow us."

"Oh, please," Indira said quickly, "if possible let us take my trunks with us. Now that Papa is dead, I feel they are the only things I possess, and I am so afraid of losing them."

"Yes, of course," Charles said soothingly. "I understand exactly what you are feeling."

He paused before he said:

"I do not want to seem inquisitive, but will you be able to get hold of any of your money without having to contact that reptile who has behaved so badly towards you?"

"Oh, yes," Indira answered. "I can go to Papa's Bank in London and I am sure when I identify myself they will let me draw on his account. I know too that they hold some securities which are in my name."

Charles looked at her in admiration, thinking that few young women would be so knowledgeable or so sensible about their finances.

Then he thought that as a tradesman's daughter she would understand the handling of money, while a débutante in the Social World would never have to bother her pretty head with such mundane matters.

There was no time for any more conversation, for Jimmy came hurrying back to say that the trunks were being strapped on the back of the Phaeton, and although it meant their groom would have to hold Indira's hat-box on his knees, they could take everything.

"Let us go at once!" Charles said. "It is a good thing you are slim, Miss Rowlandson, because three is always a squeeze in a Phaeton which is made for two."

"I would put up with anything to get away from here and be quite certain that Mr. Jacobson will not be able to find me."

"I doubt if he will be in a position to find anybody for the next twenty-four hours," Jimmy said. "Of course, there is also a chance that he may have drowned in the ditch, in which case you will not have to worry about him ever again."

"I suppose it is wicked of me to say so, but that would give me a great deal of . . . pleasure."

"Wicked or not, I feel the same," Charles added.

She laughed.

They drove out of the courtyard of the Inn, with the Landlord bowing them good-bye, having been handsomely reimbursed for his hospitality.

Only when they had driven on for a short while did Jimmy say:

"Forgive me for asking you, but what did you do with the Nun's robe you were wearing? It would be a mistake for the maids who will unpack for you at Ardsley Hall to discover it."

"I thought of that," Indira replied, "and because I was aware it might be incriminating evidence if Mr. Jacobson was searching for me, I stuffed it up the chimney."

Charles and Jimmy both burst into laughter.

"You are magnificent!" Charles said when he could speak. "And I am quite certain I shall win my bet."

"I am feeling somewhat apprehensive that you may," Jimmy replied, "but you have a long way to go yet."

"Now, tell me more about the Marquis," Indira said. "Supposing after all the trouble you have taken in introducing me into the house, he takes no further interest in me and . . ."

"He will take an interest in you," Jimmy interrupted. "You are the most beautiful girl I have ever seen, and I think I know every beauty in London by this time. I know Charles will say the same."

"Beauty means different things to different people," Charles remarked, "but if the Marquis is not bowled over by Miss Rowlandson, then I am a blind man."

There was a little pause. Then Indira asked:

"What do you . . . mean, 'bowled over'? You are not . . . expecting that he will fall . . . in love with . . . me?"

The way she spoke made Charles and Jimmy aware that she thought it so horrifying that she might now, at the very last moment, refuse to go on with the act.

"No, no, of course not," Charles said soothingly. "Ardsley has never been in love with anybody. You can be quite certain about that. We just want to make sure that he finds you extremely attractive and believes you to be *crème de la crème,* which is what, with his infallible instinct, he expects in a woman to whom he offers his friendship."

Charles emphasised the word "friendship" to reassure Indira, but as Jimmy knew she was still anxious he said:

"Because he will believe you to be a Lady of Quality and unmarried, I assure you he would not try to kiss you, or anything like that."

Indira gave a little cry of horror.

"Are you sure . . . quite sure? If he did, I should have to . . . run away again, and . . . nothing you could say would . . . persuade me to . . . stay."

"I promise you will be quite safe," Jimmy said, "but it will certainly surprise him if you do not wish to flirt with him."

"Flirt with him!" Indira exclaimed. "I have no wish to flirt with anybody! The men on the ship . . . after Papa was . . . dead would . . . never leave me . . . alone."

Because she was sitting between Charles and Jimmy and they were so close together, they were both aware of the shudder that ran through her body as she remembered what had happened.

"Then," she went on, "when Mr. Jacobson told me I was to marry a man I had never seen, and would not listen when I told him I would rather die than do so, I was frightened, very, very . . . frightened that somehow he would . . . force me to . . . obey . . . him."

"That is what he might have done," Charles said, "and that is why you must be very careful not to encourage the Marquis or any other man in the house-party."

"What do you mean—encourage?"

"Be polite, somewhat aloof, and do not laugh too loudly or too frequently at what they are saying, and . . ."

He paused, then said:

"Oh, go on, Jimmy, you can explain better than I can."

"What Charles is trying to say," Jimmy began, "is that real Ladies of Quality, like this daughter of the Earl you are pretending to be, would be somewhat reserved and would not encourage a man to pay her compliments. If he did, she would seem shy and a little bashful."

"In which case," Indira said in a low voice, "he would not . . . force himself upon . . . me?"

"Not if he was a gentleman," Charles said sharply, "and certainly not if we are about. What you have to do, Miss Rowlandson, is to think of us as if we were your brothers."

Indira gave a little sigh.

"I always wished I had a brother, and Papa was very, very disappointed when I was not a boy."

"Well, you have two brothers now," Jimmy said. "Charles and I will look after you and see that no-one insults you in any way or does anything you do not like! You can be quite certain of one thing: we will keep away any brutes like Jacobson or fortune-hunters like Bredon."

"Of course," Charles agreed, "and there is something else you must remember: you are not rich, and you rely entirely on your father for any money you have. He is generous, but you own nothing personally."

"I understand," Indira said.

Charles thought that her father had trained her well and felt quite certain that a Society Girl would have asked innumerable questions on this particular score alone.

"I will tell you another thing we have to think of," Jimmy said. "Where was Lady Mary supposed to be going when she hired the carriage at Southampton?"

"I have thought of that already," Charles replied. "About ten miles away from here I have two very boring old cousins. They never do anything or go anywhere. I know they are both alive because my mother had a letter from them about ten days ago."

"So Lady Mary was going to stay with them!" Jimmy interposed.

"Exactly!" Charles agreed. "They were friends of her father's, and actually I believe my cousin Harold was in India about a century ago."

"You do not suppose the Marquis knows them?"

"I am quite certain if he has ever heard of them he would make every effort to avoid them," Charles said. "I have told you, they are bores, and no-one in their right mind would want to entertain them, although they are highly respectable."

"What is their name?" Indira asked.

"Colonel and Mrs. Toddington," Charles answered, "and I will tell the Marquis that I have sent a message to them to say that you will not be arriving until we can escort you there safely after the Steeple-Chase is over."

"Really, Charles, you are a genius at improvisation!" Jimmy exclaimed. "I had no idea you had such imagination! There is almost a magical quality about it!"

"I think he is very clever," Indira said. "And now that I know the whole story of my background, I think also that as I have been through such an unpleasant experience with the Highwaymen, I would not want to talk about it."

"That is sensible," Charles approved. "I have always been told that one lie leads to another, and the less you say, the less you will become involved."

"It is certainly an . . . adventure that I did not expect," Indira said in a small voice, "and since I am with you I find I am not really as frightened about meeting the Marquis as I was at the thought of . . . begging the Convent to take me in."

"How did you know about the Convent in the first place?" Charles asked, curious.

"There was a Nun on board ship who was very kind to me after Papa died. She nursed him when he had the fever."

"So she told you about it?"

"Yes, she said if ever I was in trouble I was to go there and mention her name, and they would look after me."

"The Convent is not the right place for you," Charles said firmly.

"I am beginning to think that myself," Indira agreed. "But when Mr. Jacobson met me when I came off the boat and took me to an Hotel, and told me what he had planned for me, I was absolutely frantic."

"So you got hold of a Nun's habit in which to escape from him."

"I thought he would not be looking for me dressed as a Nun," Indira said simply. "So I bribed the chambermaid to buy me a Nun's robe."

"How on earth did she know where to buy one?" Jimmy enquired.

"She was very clever about that," Indira answered. "She was sure there would not be one in the shops, so she offered one of the Little Sisters of the Poor, who work in the slums round the dockyard at Southampton, five pounds for her robe. I presume she had two, and the money was tempting."

"I can see you are a born adventuress," Charles said, "and not only brave but undefeatable."

"I hope so," Indira replied, "but I am very . . . afraid of the . . . future without Papa to . . . look after me."

As there was nothing they could say to this, they drove on in silence.

It was Indira who broke it by saying:

"You may think it . . . foolish of me, but I am so nervous that I may forget my own name or not answer when I am addressed as Mary."

Jimmy turned his head to look at her and Charles was listening as she went on:

"Would it be possible when you got to know me . . . better to call me Indira? We could say I was Christened 'Mary Indira.' "

Jimmy did not answer for a moment and she said hastily:

"Not if you think it would be a mistake. But it would make me feel I was still . . . close to . . . Papa."

"Of course you can be Indira to us," Charles said, "and I think it's a charming and original name."

"Thank you . . . thank you!" Indira cried, and gave him such a beguiling smile that Jimmy thought no-one could be lovelier.

They drove for another half-an-hour and the light was fading when Charles exclaimed:

"There it is—that is Ardsley Hall!"

There was a gap in the trees which bordered the road, and through it on a high rise Indira could see a magnificent building of grey stone.

It was certainly architecturally attractive, and at the same time it was large enough to house a Regiment.

The Marquis's standard was high above the roof-tops, and as they turned in at the imposing wrought-iron gates with lodges on either side constructed to look like small Castles, Jimmy thought that no girl who had just come from abroad could fail to be impressed.

Indira did not say anything, but he was aware that she was tense, and as

432

they reached the end of the drive and the house seemed to loom above them, vast and somehow menacing, he felt that Charles was tense too.

A large dome rose above the centre of the building and commodious wings extended on each side. A great flight of grey stone steps led up to the front door, and as Charles brought his horses to a standstill, grooms came running to their heads.

A red carpet was run down the stone steps up which they were to walk.

"Keep your chin high," Jimmy said in a whisper to Indira as they reached an enormous Hall where there were a great number of footmen wearing powdered wigs, white knee-breeches, and a resplendent livery in the Ardsley colours.

A white-haired Butler bowed to Charles.

"Lord Frodham, I believe. His Lordship is expecting you and your— party."

It was obvious from the way the Butler spoke that his eyes rested on Indira with a slight expression of surprise.

He went ahead of them with pompous dignity, and only when he reached a pair of mahogany doors did he pause to ask:

"May I have the names of your friends, M'Lord?"

"Lady Mary Combe and Sir James Overton."

The Butler opened the door and announced them in a voice that seemed to ring out round the large room and reach the four people at the other end of it.

The Marquis came towards them, and as he did so Charles thought however infuriating he might be, there was no doubt that their host was an extremely handsome man and had, when he chose to use it, an undeniable charm.

"How nice to see you, Frodham," he said, holding out his hand. "I was growing worried that you might have had an unpleasant journey owing to the thunderstorm."

"It certainly delayed us," Charles admitted, "but there is another reason why we are later than we intended."

The Marquis was already holding out his hand to Jimmy, saying:

"It is a pleasure to see you, Overton!"

And now he was looking at Indira questioningly.

"May I introduce the Marquis of Ardsley?" Charles asked her, then said to the Marquis, "This is Lady Mary Combe, whom Jimmy and I have just rescued from an appalling experience with some Highwaymen who not only stole her money but also her horses."

"Highwaymen!" the Marquis exclaimed. "What a terrible thing to happen!"

Indira gave him a little curtsey and put her hand in his. The Marquis, holding it firmly, was aware as he did so that her fingers trembled.

"You are suffering from shock," he said, "and it is not surprising. Come and sit down. Let me bring you a glass of champagne."

"Thank you," Indira murmured. "It was . . . very frightening."

Without relinquishing her hand, the Marquis drew her towards the fireplace, where he introduced her to his other guests—two men and a lady—all of whom exclaimed in horror and consternation at what she must have been through.

"The Highwaymen are becoming a perfect pest on the roads!" said one of the gentlemen, whose name she had not heard. "Something ought to be done about them, and I intend to raise the question in the House of Commons."

"I wish you would do that, Edmund," the Marquis said. "What we need is a local Police Force to keep a watch on the main highways. As it is, when they are sent for the Military always arrive too late."

"That is true," Jimmy said. "My father always complained that in our County it is impossible to catch a Highwayman, who has in every case several hours' start of his pursuers."

The Marquis had fetched a glass of champagne, which he handed to Indira before he offered any to Charles and Jimmy.

Then he sat down beside her on the sofa and said:

"I am sure you do not want to talk about your experience, and because I know how frightening it must have been, I suggest we talk of other things. Let me say first how delighted I am to be able to offer you my hospitality tonight. I hope that wherever you are going we can persuade you to stay and watch the Steeple-Chase."

"That is very . . . kind of . . . you," Indira said in a small voice.

Charles turned to Indira.

"I told you we were right to bring you here and that His Lordship would welcome you."

Indira smiled in a manner which he thought looked shy and reserved, and he explained to the Marquis:

"At first Jimmy and I thought we should take her on to where she was going. But it is at least fifteen miles in the opposite direction, and there was every likelihood of it starting to rain again, so we thought it best to come straight here."

"I think it very sensible of you," the Marquis approved, "but surely Lady Mary was not travelling alone?"

"I was unaccompanied after a long chapter of accidents," Indira said before Charles could reply. "I have just . . . arrived from . . . India."

"From India!" the Marquis exclaimed.

"Yes. My father . . . died . . . on the voyage."

There was a little pause before she went on:

"We were supposed to be met by a Courier and, I believed, several relatives, but when the ship docked there was nobody!"

"Blame the post!" Jimmy exclaimed. "It is getting ridiculous how bad the overseas mail is, despite the fact that the Government boasts about its efficiency."

"I agree with you," one of the Marquis's other guests affirmed. "My father is in Egypt at the moment, and I have not heard one single word from him since he left, although he always writes to me at least twice a week."

"It is a scandal," the Marquis agreed. "But tell us, Lady Mary, what happened."

"I thought the best thing I could do would be to hire a carriage and drive to the house of my father's friends, where I was to stay. I had quite a pleasant journey until . . . the Highwaymen . . . held me up."

Her voice faltered, and both Charles and Jimmy thought she was acting her part admirably.

"You must have been very frightened," the Marquis's lady guest replied. "I know I should have fallen into a swoon, or screamed for help."

"There was no point in my doing either of those things," Indira said, "because I was in an empty lane, and although the Coachman and the footman on the box tried to defend me, the Highwaymen knocked them to the ground, then stole the horses. That was what they were really interested in."

"But they took your money too."

"Fortunately, I did not carry a large amount in my bag, and because Lord Frodham and Sir James appeared, the Highwaymen did not have time to rifle my trunks."

"You poor, poor thing!" the lady exclaimed. "My heart bleeds for you. How lucky that these two charming gentlemen came to help you."

"I am very . . . very . . . grateful to them for . . . saving me, and driving the men away, who were very . . . frightening," Indira said.

"I am sure what you would like to do now," the lady suggested, "is to have a little rest before dinner. Shall I take her upstairs, Seldon?"

"Yes, of course, Rosie," he replied.

As he spoke her Christian name, Charles and Jimmy gave each other a knowing look.

As Charles had said in White's, Lady Sinclair, who was described as a "Rose of England," had captured the attention of the elusive, fastidious, and at the same time discriminating Marquis of Ardsley.

Now both young men were thinking to themselves somewhat dismally that because Lady Sinclair was at Ardsley Hall, it was unlikely that the Marquis would be "bowled over," as they had put it, by their protégée.

At the same time, there was no doubt that Indira was the more spectacular of the two.

Lady Sinclair, while very lovely in the conventional English pink, white, and gold manner, paled a little, in their estimation at any rate, in comparison with Indira's flaming red hair.

Her white skin, which they had not appreciated until now, was, in the light of the candles that had been lit in the Salon, like the petals of a magnolia.

"Thank you very much," Indira was saying to Lady Sinclair. "I would like to go upstairs and, as you suggest . . . lie down."

She rose to her feet before she said to the Marquis:

"It is very kind of you, My Lord, to have me here as an unexpected and uninvited guest. I hope I shall not prove a bother for tonight, and I think perhaps it would be . . . best if I would . . . leave tomorrow."

"I am quite certain," the Marquis replied, "that we can persuade you to stay and watch your two rescuers, Lord Frodham and Sir James, competing in my Steeple-Chase. They are very experienced riders, and I may tell you they are up against some stiff competition."

"Especially where it concerns our host," Charles added. "We were thinking, My Lord, that it would be a sporting gesture, since you have the best horses and know the course better than we do, if you were severely handicapped."

"It is an idea, but it is certainly one I would not agree to with any enthusiasm," the Marquis said.

"I was afraid of that," Charles replied, "in which case, Lady Mary, you will see your host receive the Steeple-Chase Cup which he himself has provided and which, however hard we compete for it and for how ever many years, is likely to remain at Ardsley Hall."

Everybody laughed, and the Marquis threw up his hands in dismay.

"What can I say but suggest that we abandon the whole idea of a Steeple-Chase and instead make it merely a Show with a prize for the most beautiful woman on horseback."

As the Marquis spoke, Charles noticed that Lady Sinclair gave a self-conscious little laugh, as if she was quite certain who would win the prize.

At the same time, he did not miss the fact that the Marquis was looking at Indira, and her eyes in the light of the candles seemed even more mysterious than they had in the Parlour when he had first noticed them.

Too, he had the feeling that as Lady Sinclair linked her arm with Indira's and drew her towards the door, she was glad to take her out of the Marquis's orbit.

'So far, so good!' he thought to himself, and knew that Jimmy was thinking the same.

As they walked up the stairs, Lady Sinclair said to Indira:

"You must be feeling very shaken and distressed. I am sure if you would rather retire to bed and have a light meal sent up to your room, our host would understand. Everything in this house is done to make the guest feel happy and at home, and perhaps after your traumatic experience it would be wiser to take things very easy."

"Thank you for your concern," Indira replied, "but perhaps after I have rested I shall be able to decide what is best for me to do."

"That is very sensible," Lady Sinclair agreed, "but you must not take any risks with yourself. Shock often has a delayed action, as I know to my own cost."

She went into a rather incoherent tale of what had happened after she had once had a shock from being involved in a fire.

When she had finished it they had reached the room where Indira was to be sleeping and where two maids were already unpacking her trunk.

"I will leave you now," Lady Sinclair said, "and do not hesitate to stay in bed, if you feel it is an effort to rise again."

"Thank you for being so kind," Indira replied.

However, she was astute enough to realise that Lady Sinclair's kindness was not entirely concern for her health.

As the maids unpacked her things, she thought with satisfaction that her gowns, which came from Paris, would certainly not look out-of-place at Ardsley Hall, magnificent though it was.

The maids helped her to undress and she got into bed, and when they had left her and she was alone, she lay thinking of how lucky it was that she had been able to escape, with the help of Lord Frodham and Sir James, from that horrible Mr. Jacobson.

"How could I have known that he was a crook?" she asked herself. "If Papa were alive he would be furious at his behaviour!"

She had been so close to her father and he had discussed so many things with her that she thought that the wise thing for her to do would be to go to Coutt's Bank and explain to the Manager what had happened.

She would ask him to find her a new firm of Solicitors who would take over her business affairs, and whom the Bank would vouch for as being both reliable and honest.

Even as she reasoned it out calmly, she found herself afraid of being without her father, who had meant everything in her life since her mother had died.

She had loved him and he had loved her, and because they were constantly travelling about, she had been truthful when she told Charles and Jimmy that she was not certain how she could find her relations in England or indeed who they were.

It was over ten years since she had last been in her own country, and as she had been only eight years old at the time, she could hardly remember anything about it.

Her father's interests were in the East, and while England was at war with France, he had thought it not only a waste of time but dangerous to attempt the long sea-voyage home.

But because her father was determined that she should be properly educated, her Governesses and Tutors travelled with them as they moved from one Eastern country to another.

Because he was so rich and of such importance in his own world, a large entourage of those he employed always accompanied them.

Since they were never intrusive when her father wished to be alone with her and she with him, it was quite easy to forget the company of paid employees whose special charge they were.

Now suddenly her father had died and she was completely alone.

Because the majority of those they had employed over the years were foreigners, they had set out to return to England with only a lady's-maid for herself and a secretary and a valet for her father.

The former had succumbed to the same fever as had killed him, and the valet, whom Indira had never particularly liked, had left at Cape Town.

Her lady's-maid was French, and when the ship stopped at Marseilles she had begged Indira that she might go to Paris and see her mother before she rejoined her in London.

Indira was perceptive enough to realise that once she had arrived home she would never see the woman again.

She did not think it would matter much, being sure that it would be a mistake after the long years of war for her to arrive in England with a French servant.

She had thought there would be the usual crowd of attendants waiting for her at Southampton, and she knew that her father had instructed his Solicitors to arrange everything for their convenience.

It was therefore a shock and a very unpleasant one when there was only Mr. Jacobson, who abruptly and rudely told her she was to be married to Lord Bredon, so that she could come into her father's money three years before she would possess it otherwise.

At first she could hardly believe she had to listen to such an outrageous idea, but when he became unpleasantly threatening, she told him she wished to retire to her bedroom, feeling exhausted after her father's death and the long voyage.

Mr. Jacobson had agreed, and when she was alone, Indira had made up her mind to escape.

She fortunately had a lot of money with her because her father never travelled without considerable sums of ready cash.

The difficulty was, what could she do?

It was then that she thought with horror of the trouble she had had on the voyage when she was alone without her father's protection, when men of all ages pursued her relentlessly, and whether it was because of her looks or her money was immaterial.

She then decided that the only possible way she could escape them and Mr. Jacobson was to go into a Convent.

With the same efficiency that had characterised her father's dealings, she had put her plan into operation.

She was relieved when she drove away from the Hotel at dawn the next morning before Mr. Jacobson could make enquiries as to what time she would be ready to leave with him for London.

It was only because the carriage provided for her was not of the quality that she was sure would have been obtained by her father that she did not get as far on her journey as she had hoped.

In another hour-and-a-half, she reckoned, she would have reached the Convent the Nun had told her about, but Mr. Jacobson had appeared, and she had been rescued only at what seemed to her to be the very last moment.

Now by some strange quirk of fate for which she was very grateful, she was lying in an extremely comfortable bed in a magnificent room with a painted ceiling in the type of house that her father had often described to her as being very much a part of England.

"If only Papa were here," Indira said to herself. "It would be so exciting to see it all with him, and hear him tell me about these people. He would not be as much impressed with them as they are with themselves!"

She knew as soon as she had met the Marquis that the way Lord Frodham and Sir James had described him was very true, if a little unkind.

He was very conscious of his own consequence, and she compared him with the men she had seen in India who governed it with pomp and circumstance besides a pride which made the Indians very conscious that they must bow to their conquerors.

"At least it will be interesting to stay here for a day or so," Indira told herself, "and it will give me time to think of what I can do and where I can go."

She was aware that Lord Frodham was prepared to make plans for her future, but she was not certain if she wanted a future which depended on the kindness or the patronage of any man.

"I want to be independent of them all," she said aloud.

She thought that however kind Charles and Jimmy might seem, they were still men, and she unfortunately was a woman.

CHAPTER THREE

AS THE LADIES LEFT THE DINING-ROOM, Indira was aware that Lady Sinclair was regarding her with undisguised hostility.

Before dinner the Marquis had introduced other members of the house-party who had arrived, then said:

"I think I must honour our unexpected guest tonight, to assure her not only how delighted we are to have her here at Ardsley Hall, but also to apologise for the unpleasant treatment she received on her arrival in England, instead of the welcome she might have expected."

The story of Indira's treatment at the hands of Highwaymen had lost nothing in the telling.

One after another the guests had come up to her before dinner to say how intolerable the situation had become in the country, and that theft, robbery, and violence were becoming so habitual that something would have to be done about it.

"Of course," one Peer said, "if these felons are caught they are hanged, but that is no deterrent to a man who finds it impossible to get employment of any sort and must either starve or steal."

The argument grew quite heated and naturally the Government was

441

blamed for being weak in providing proper protection for its citizens, and worst of all for pursuing a policy of low wages and the import of foreign goods.

Indira listened to everything that was said, and Charles and Jimmy thought approvingly that she was acting the part they required of her with an expertise that could not be equalled.

To begin with, not only did she look lovely, but her gown was obviously the envy of the lady guests, outshining theirs beyond dispute and making them, Charles thought with satisfaction, look quite dowdy in comparison.

He was knowledgeable enough about women to be aware that Indira had a grace that was unusual, which together with her red hair and white skin would have made her outstanding in any company, however many other beauties were present.

He thought she had certainly listened to him and Jimmy attentively when they had told her to seem quiet, reserved, modest, and a little shy.

Charles thought with a slight smile that, like himself, every man in the room was only too ready to protect her from Highwaymen or anything else that menaced her.

It was certainly a satisfaction to the two friends when the Marquis seated Indira on his right with Lady Sinclair on his left.

They were aware that the spoilt beauty was infuriated at taking second-place and equally aware that the Marquis, intent as usual on doing what he wished, was not in the least perturbed by her pouting red lips and the flounce with which she went into the Dining-Room on the arm of another man.

Indira was actually very hungry because she had been too frightened to linger at the Posting-Inn where her Coachman had changed horses.

She had therefore eaten only a little bread and cheese and drunk a glass of cider before she was ready to proceed on her journey and put as many miles as possible between herself and Mr. Jacobson.

She was quite certain that he would not let her get away easily, but she thought he would have no idea that her destination was a Convent.

It was only after she had driven for some hours that she had realised with dismay that she had been obliged to tell the Posting-Inn at Southampton where she was going and that when Mr. Jacobson made enquiries he would get the information he required.

She therefore sat tense in the back of the carriage, willing the horses to go faster and still faster, knowing that the animals were of inferior breeding and that the last two had been too old to travel more quickly than what she considered to be a "snail's pace."

But she had been saved, and now she thought she could never be sufficiently grateful to Charles and Jimmy.

Because they seemed to her to be young and lighthearted, she was trying to think of them as if they were in reality her brothers, and not the men she hated, who without the protection of her father made her desperately afraid both physically and mentally.

She was afraid physically because they obviously considered her beautiful, and on the ship she had been terrified that by some unscrupulous means of their own men would intrude on her in her cabin either in the daytime or at night.

After her father's death, she had ensured her safety at night by insisting that her lady's-maid sleep in her father's cabin, which communicated with her own.

Even then, she left the door open between them and instructed the woman at the slightest disturbance to run for the ship's officer who was on duty.

Fortunately, there had been no need for such dramatics. At the same time, Indira would lie awake shuddering at every footstep she heard, and feeling that even in the dark she could see men's eyes desiring her.

It was only when her father was no longer with her that she realised how protective he had been all her life and that his company of secretaries, couriers, and valets, wherever they had travelled, had all contributed to the wall of security she had always felt round her and yet had taken as a matter of course.

Now that it was no longer there, she told herself, she had to become self-sufficient.

Mentally she was too astute and too intuitive not to realise the difficulties, and it was only when Mr. Jacobson struck real terror into her that she knew that only her quick wits could save her from being married to a man she had never seen but already loathed and despised.

'I must never be in such a position again,' she thought.

She wondered if despite everything Charles and Jimmy had said it would not be better for her to enter a Convent.

She obviously could not go to the one which was now known to Mr. Jacobson, but it would not be the only Convent in England, and she was quite certain she would be accepted somewhere.

But for the moment she was safe, and as she looked down the long table at the Marquis's glittering guests, she thought it was the sort of company that her father would have wished her to be in, and it was almost as if he had had a hand in bringing her here.

"You are very quiet, Lady Mary!" the Marquis remarked beside her.

"I am sorry if I appear rude," she replied, "but I am in fact very hungry."

"Then I hope my Chef will not disappoint you."

"I am sure he will not do that. But as you say he is a Chef, can it be possible that he is French?"

"Of course he is French," the Marquis replied firmly. "No people in the world can cook as well as the French, or have such an appreciation of food."

"I have always found the Chinese cooking very good," Indira remarked.

"I have heard that," the Marquis replied, "but I cannot ever remember eating Chinese food."

"You should try it sometime. It is exciting and imaginative, and the Chinese have for generations known how to appeal to the palate because they have studied health as well as philosophy."

There was an expression of surprise in the Marquis's eyes as he said:

"Are you really interested in those subjects?"

"Of course," Indira replied, "and I hope in a great many others besides."

"Such as?"

As he spoke, the Marquis thought a little cynically that with such astounding good looks, the most obvious subject for Lady Mary would be love, and he wondered if she would be brave enough to confess it.

"I find the Eastern religions," she said in reply to his question, "fascinat-

444

ing and absorbing. Perhaps Buddhism is the most mystic, the most understandable of them all, and the one which draws me most."

"Why is that? Because of its belief in reincarnation?" the Marquis
asked. "And who do you fancy you were in your previous life: Cleopatra,
or perhaps the Queen of Sheba?"

He spoke mockingly, thinking that whenever the subject had arisen in
the past, which was not very often, any woman present had always been
convinced that she had been one of those exotic and enticing women.

However, Indira did not answer, and after a moment he said:

"I am waiting for your reply to my question."

"I thought we were talking seriously," she said quietly, "and as it is
obviously a subject which bores Your Lordship, shall we talk of your
horses, which Lord Frodham tells me are outstanding."

The way she spoke, the cold note in her voice, and the expression he
saw in her eyes made the Marquis feel as if she had suddenly confronted
him with a naked sword.

Never in his experience had any woman slapped him down in such a
surprising manner, and certainly not anybody who looked as young and
lovely and, he thought, amenable as Lady Mary.

"Forgive me," he said after he had drawn in his breath. "I was not
taking you seriously for the simple reason that it is very unusual in England to find any woman of any age who knows anything about the East."

Again to his surprise, Indira did not enthuse over his apology but
merely inclined her head as if she accepted it as her just due.

"Are all these gentlemen here," she asked, "taking part in your Steeple-
Chase?"

"Now you are deliberately being unkind to me," the Marquis protested.
"I have apologised, and quite frankly, I want to continue with our conversation about the East, and go back to when I asked you why you were
drawn to Buddhism more than to the other religions you have studied."

For a moment he thought that she would refuse to answer him. Then as
if she felt that politeness demanded an answer, Indira said:

"It is the only logical way of explaining the different circumstances in
which we are born, and there is a justice in the Wheel of Rebirth that I
cannot find in any other religion."

"You do not think the Christian attitude of promising a repentant sinner a front seat in Heaven after death if he has suffered in this world is a reasonable one?"

"No."

The Marquis waited, and when she obviously did not wish to elaborate on her reply, after a moment he said:

"I have some books in my Library which I feel sure you will find interesting. One of them, Shih Ching, was brought back to England from China many years ago by my great-great-grandfather. There is also an early edition of the *Vedas,* which I do not think can be found in any other Library in Europe."

Indira turned her head to look at him, and now there was a light in her eyes that had not been there before.

"Is that true?" she exclaimed. "How can you be so fortunate as to possess anything so unique? And please, will you allow me to see them before I leave?"

"I shall be delighted to show them to you."

"Some of the Chinese have the most magnificently illustrated manuscripts in their houses," Indira said, "but they are always very secretive about their possessions, and will only show their books, their porcelain, and their really precious drawings to somebody they think will understand the hidden meaning in them."

"They believed that you could do that?"

"I was lucky enough to be my father's daughter."

As she spoke she realised she was thinking of her real father and not the Earl of Farncombe, whom she had adopted for her pretence role.

To divert the Marquis's interest, she said quickly:

"I have always found it fascinating that every great Eastern religion always had an esoteric and secret side to it which was revealed only to the initiated. I expect you will remember reading that the ancient Egyptians, for instance, could conjure up fire by merely speaking a certain word from *The Book of the Dead,* which was read only by their specially chosen Priests."

"You are bringing back to me memories of things I have not thought about since I was at Oxford," the Marquis replied. "There, as it happens, I studied Oriental history, and I found it most intriguing."

"Then when you left Oxford you promptly forgot all about it," Indira said lightly.

"I did not forget," the Marquis contradicted, "but I placed it at the back of my mind. It was Napoleon who spoke of 'the cupboards of his mind,' and that is what I think we all do in one way or another. Although certain subjects may be shut away, you have only to open the door to rediscover them."

"I am sure that is true," Indira agreed, "but some people have very few cupboards, and some a 'Bluebeard's Chamber' where it is best to leave the door closed."

She was talking as if she were with her father, and they were exchanging points of view and arguing as if they were two Dons fencing with each other in words.

The Marquis was just about to reply when Lady Sinclair put her hand on his arm and said plaintively:

"You are neglecting me, Seldon! And it is something that has never happened to me before. I am feeling very hurt by such unkindness."

She spoke in a little-girl's voice that he had found rather intriguing when he had first met her.

Like all strong, positive men, he believed he liked women to be small, clinging, and feminine, and Lady Sinclair with her pink-and-white beauty appeared to be all that.

She was also astute enough, after a long succession of lovers, to know exactly what appealed to men.

She turned her large blue eyes up to the Marquis as if she felt the child-like appeal in them would never go unrequited, but to her surprise he merely said:

"I am sure, Rosie, that Lord Neville is only too ready to make up for my shortcomings."

As he spoke, he looked across her at her partner on her other side, a dashing Rake, the youngest son of a Duke, who was looking for a suitable heiress to keep him in the comfort in which he had been brought up and which only his eldest brother had any hope of enjoying in the future.

"If you think anybody could take your place, Seldon," he replied to the Marquis, "you are very much mistaken. We have all tried, and failed.

447

Instead, we hobble along behind you, grateful for the crumbs that fall from the rich man's table."

The Marquis laughed.

"You are very modest all of a sudden, and that, I may tell you, Neville, is not your reputation."

"I am merely envious," Lord Neville said. "I am also flattering you, Seldon, so that you will give me one of your best horses to ride in the Steeple-Chase. I have nothing in my own stable good enough to compete with yours, so if you want me to finish the course in style, you must provide me with the means to do it."

The Marquis had anticipated this, and he said:

"I have two horses for you to choose from, Neville, and I shall be interested to see which you prefer."

Lord Neville looked extremely satisfied at his host's reply. Then, as if he thought he must ingratiate himself further, he said to Lady Sinclair:

"Will you come tomorrow to help me choose the winner of this contest? I suppose you know that as well as the Challenge Cup there is a prize of two thousand guineas, which I could well do with at the moment."

"Are you seriously asking me to help you to defeat Seldon?" Lady Sinclair enquired. "It is useless, because he will win. He is too magnificent and too omnipotent to be defeated in any activity in which he competes seriously."

Her voice was very moving, but unfortunately the Marquis was no longer listening.

He had turned once again to Indira, only to find, to his annoyance, that she was talking to the gentleman on her other side.

He was a middle-aged but still raffish Peer who had a dull and conformable wife who never accompanied him to the Marquis's parties.

He was in consequence prepared to make the very most of his freedom.

"I do not believe," he was saying to Indira, "that anything so exquisite or so overwhelmingly beautiful as you could possibly have come from India or anywhere except Paris. You have French *chic* written all over you, and an allurement that has a special magic peculiar to French women and is quite inimitable."

As he uttered the fulsome compliments he moved his face nearer to Indira, and it made her recoil from him.

The Marquis was aware that she was repulsed in a way he found hard to understand.

Without replying, she turned to him and he saw an expression of fear in her eyes, which surprised him.

He was intrigued, and yet he was too wise to refer to it, but merely continued his conversation quietly on the subject of books.

It was only when the gentlemen joined the ladies in the Drawing-Room that the Marquis found himself, almost without meaning to, gravitating towards Indira, who was seated on a sofa near the fireplace.

Because it was still chilly in the evening and the storm during the day had left a damp atmosphere outside, the fire had been lit and Indira was glad of its warmth.

She was well aware that after a few desultory words when they reached the Drawing-Room, the majority of the ladies had left her alone while they gossiped amongst themselves.

Lady Sinclair in particular ignored her, while she made it very clear to the other women who was the most important person at the Marquis's party.

"Dear Seldon has arranged this Steeple-Chase especially for me," she was saying in her child-like way. "It is the first time that ladies have been allowed to ride with the men, and it will be a great triumph if I can win. But of course, as you know, Seldon likes to be first in everything."

"You mean we can ride too?" one of the ladies exclaimed. "Why did the Marquis not tell us when we were invited? I would have brought a horse with me who is a magnificent jumper!"

"I am sure it would be a mistake for you to compete except on your own horse," Lady Sinclair said quickly. "After all, the course will be very dangerous, and the jumps are very high."

"I am sure, dearest Rosie, if they are safe enough for you they will be safe enough for us," one of the ladies said in a spiteful voice, "unless you are doing a little bit of cheating by having special places in the fences made easy for you."

"I am sure dear Seldon would not do anything that was not completely honourable," Lady Sinclair replied, "and he considers me a very fine rider."

"Well, I think it is unfair that we were not told!" another lady insisted.

Indira, listening, thought with amusement that Lady Sinclair had definitely asserted herself in a way they seemed to resent.

She wondered if there was any chance of her riding one of Charles's or James's horses which they told her had been sent on ahead.

She had no idea how good Englishwomen were as equestriennes, but she herself had ridden every sort of horse, including some very fine Arabian mares in Arabia.

She knew she would love to compete, not because she wanted the prize but for the thrill of jumping English fences and riding on an outstanding English horse.

She thought she would ask Charles or Jimmy about it as soon as they came from the Dining-Room, but the Marquis reached her first, and as he sat down on the sofa beside her she realised that he was a man, and instinctively, without questioning whether or not he would notice it, she moved away from him.

He did notice, and it surprised him.

He had never yet met a woman who was not eager to be as close to him as possible, and who sooner or later invariably irritated him by the way in which she made every excuse to touch him with her hands or to press her shoulder against him.

That any woman, and especially one as young and lovely as his new guest, should deliberately widen the distance between them made him want to ask her the reason for it.

Then as he looked at her he saw what appeared to be a flicker of fear in her strange eyes, which made him extremely curious.

Then as if she forced herself to think of something other than his sex, Indira said:

"The ladies are all talking of your Steeple-Chase, and I gather it is the first time they have been allowed to compete in it."

"Only over the first half, which is easier than what comes later," the Marquis replied. "Are you telling me that you would like to join it?"

There was a little silence before Indira said:

"It is something I would enjoy doing, and I have looked forward to riding in England, but I may not be good . . . enough . . . I do not know."

"You will have a chance tomorrow to see the course, and that will give you the answer better than I can."

"Can I really do that?" Indira asked eagerly.

The Marquis smiled.

"I can see it is going to be a choice between my stables and my Library, and I wonder which will win."

"If I were really forced to choose," Indira replied, "I should say the Library."

"I will be generous and allow you to sample both."

"Thank you . . . thank you . . . very much."

As Charles came up to join them, he wondered why Indira was looking so happy.

The following morning Indira came down to breakfast to find Charles alone in the Breakfast-Room.

"Am I late or early?" she asked, as he rose at her approach.

"Early," he replied. "You went to bed before midnight, which was very sensible of you. The rest of the party stayed up very late gambling and drinking far too much to make an early rise enjoyable."

"I had no idea you were going to gamble," Indira said. "I would like to have seen the tables."

"They were in the next room," Charles replied. "But what do you mean you would like to have seen the tables?"

"I have heard so much about gaming in England, and of course the Chinese play very different games, while the Indians prefer talking, which is usually about politics, and they become very heated on the subject!"

Charles laughed.

"I won a few pounds last night, then slipped off to bed. I wanted a clear head for the Steeple-Chase, which is what the Marquis always has."

Indira looked at him enquiringly, and he explained:

"He always wins his own Steeple-Chase, and I am convinced it is because he drinks very little and is extremely fit."

He lowered his voice as he said:

"Because he is an excellent host, his guests are stupid enough to indulge themselves at his expense. Too much claret does not make for good, hard riding, which we will all need if we are to finish the course."

"I want to ride too," Indira said.

"I heard a lot of talk last night about Lady Sinclair taking part in the race," Charles replied, "but I did not believe it."

"Her Ladyship is quite certain she is going to win."

"Then you must certainly beat her!" Charles said quickly. "You can have one of my horses. I have four with me."

"You must not give me the one you want for yourself," Indira replied. "And Lady Sinclair thinks she is very, very good. So please do not be disappointed if she beats me."

"What is all this?" asked Jimmy, who had come up behind them while they were talking.

"Indira is going to take part in the race, and I only hope she can ride well. We shall feel very guilty if she ends up with a broken neck."

"I can ride anything from a donkey to an elk," Indira said, "but what we are concerned with at the moment is a really good jumper. The Marquis has promised that I can see the course today."

"He did?" Charles exclaimed. "Well, if he offers you one of his horses—jump at the chance! They are superlative."

"I expect he is keeping the best for Lady Sinclair," Jimmy said, "and you realise that if Indira beats her, she will scratch her eyes out!"

Indira looked worried.

"I have no wish to upset her," she said, "and if she wants the Marquis to admire her riding, I will not compete."

"What we want," Charles said in a low voice, "is for him to admire you."

Indira helped herself from a silver dish that was offered her before she answered:

"What you are asking me to do is too difficult, and I think it would be wise to let me leave today."

"If you do that," Charles said sharply, "It will be most ungrateful, besides being very stupid from your own point of view."

Indira gave a little cry.

"I have no wish to be ungrateful. As you must know, I can never thank either of you . . . enough for all you have . . . done for me. It is just that I am . . . very bad at . . . intrigue."

As she spoke she was aware that the Marquis had come into the room.

452

He was looking magnificent in riding-clothes, and his boots were so highly polished that they seemed to reflect like mirrors.

Charles and Jimmy would have risen to their feet, but he said:

"No, please do not move! Good-morning, Lady Mary! I am surprised to see you so early. The rest of my party will doubtless sleep late."

"Lady Mary is very anxious to enter the Steeple-Chase," Charles said, "but to tell you the truth, I am astonished that you are allowing women on the course. I should have thought the jumps were far too high for them."

"I have lowered the first ten," the Marquis replied, "but after that you will find the rest are more difficult than they have ever been."

The Marquis said no more while he refused two dishes which were offered to him and took a small spoonful from a third before he went on:

"Lady Mary is going to see the course this morning, and I know she will be sensible enough to withdraw from the contest if she thinks it is to much for her. If there is a female casualty, no woman will ever be allowed to jump at Ardsley Hall again."

"I promise you I will be very honest about my capabilities," Indira said, "but I find it frustrating to think that men are convinced that no woman can ever equal them in sport if in nothing else."

"How can they?" Jimmy asked before the Marquis could reply. "You can hardly have women jockeys or women gameshots. And how could a woman pugilist stand a chance?"

Charles laughed.

"That is certainly ludicrous! But riding is rather different, and some women ride extremely well."

"In Rotten Row!" Jimmy exclaimed scathingly. "Most of them in the hunting-field look for a gap in the hedge, or the nearest gate."

"You are talking rather scathingly, Overton," the Marquis said, "but I agree with you, women should not compete in men's sports or really in anything else."

"I see Your Lordship has Eastern ideas of women's place in the world," Indira remarked.

The way she challenged the Marquis made Charles look at Jimmy with a twinkle in his eyes.

They both knew Ardsley's views on women.

"Women," the Marquis replied a trifle ponderously, "should be beautiful to look at and entertaining to talk to, but they should certainly not encroach on what are traditionally male prerogatives. That of course includes strenuous games or anything that is dangerous."

He spoke positively and as if there could be no possible argument.

Indira did not reply, but there was a little smile on her lips before she said:

"If Your Lordship will be kind enough to let me see your horses and ride one before everybody else appears who will need your attention, I will go and change into a riding-habit so that I can be ready when you have finished your breakfast."

She did not wait for the Marquis to agree, but went quickly from the Breakfast-Room.

"I must congratulate you, Frodham," the Marquis said when she had gone. "You certainly played the 'Knight Errant' to a very charming and lovely young lady when you saved her from the Highwaymen."

"She is also very intelligent," Charles replied.

"So I discovered last night," the Marquis said, "and I shall be interested to see how she rides, but I expect I shall be disappointed. The type of animal that is available in Eastern countries could not be compared with the horses in our stables."

"No, of course not," Charles agreed. "At the same time, with this innovation of yours, women will at least have a chance to prove themselves as Amazons."

"I hope that will not be the case," the Marquis said sharply. "If there is one thing I really dislike, it is a hard-riding, hard-drinking woman! And that is unfortunately the species which is developing in Leicestershire and in some of the more fashionable Hunting Counties."

"I agree," Jimmy said. "A woman should be beautiful and feminine. At the same time, some of the Cyprians in London look very alluring in Hyde Park on the horses they ride for the Livery Stables."

There was a faint twist to the Marquis's lips as he remarked:

"I also have eyes in my head, Overton!"

"I thought you would not have missed them," Jimmy said quickly. "They cut quite a dash in their colourful habits."

"And in one's pocket!" Charles added ruefully.

As he spoke, he was thinking of one charmer for whom he had bought a very expensive horse, and when their liaison was over he learnt that she had sold it at a profit.

The Marquis finished his breakfast and said:

"I expect you will want to ride too, if we are going to the course. Have you ordered your horses?"

"I will do so at once," Charles replied.

He went from the Breakfast-Room and Jimmy followed him a few seconds later.

Charles was waiting for him in the Hall.

"I have ordered your horse as well as mine," he said. "I am hoping to God that Indira does not make a fool of herself. Things are going very well, and did you realise last night that Lady Sinclair was seething with rage because the Marquis paid her so much attention? She was happy only when Indira had gone to bed and she had him to herself again."

"If you ask me, she is on the way out," Jimmy said. "She is far too possessive with him, and I am sure he is intrigued with Indira, although it is too soon to hope for big results."

"Much too soon," Charles agreed positively.

He walked across the Hall and onto the steps to wait for the horses to be brought to the front door. Then he said:

"I wish now we had told Indira not to ride, but how were we to know that the Marquis had changed his rules and was letting women in on the race?"

Before Jimmy could reply, the Marquis joined them, and at the same time they saw the horses being led down to the side of the house from the direction of the stables.

They were certainly magnificent to look at, their silver bridles glinting in the sunshine, and the horse with a side-saddle was a superlative animal, jet-black except for a white star on his nose.

Charles's horse and Jimmy's were both extremely well-bred, fine-looking horse-flesh which any man would be proud to own, but they could not compare with the magnificent stallion that belonged to the Marquis, and which seemed in its own way to be not only as majestic but also as dashing as he was.

The men were just descending the steps when Indira came running down behind them.

She was looking as alluring as Charles had hoped she would, and even more so, in a very smart summer habit of dark green pique edged with white braid.

The tight-fitting jacket gave her a tiny waist, and her high-crowned hat with its gauze veil trailing behind was extremely becoming.

Charles also noted that her hair was arranged as neatly as any woman might have worn it in the hunting-field, and he thought with a sigh of relief that it was something he had forgotten to tell her.

She might easily have appeared with untidy curls, ringlets, or some other type of coiffure which would have been taboo for any Lady of Quality.

He went towards her, but before he could get there the Marquis was before him, and putting his hands on each side of her waist he lifted her onto the side-saddle.

She placed her leg over the pummel, and with an experienced hand he arranged her skirts over the one stirrup.

She looked down at him and smiled.

"Thank you," she said. "Now will you kindly allow me to get acquainted with my horse, which is something I consider important if we are to show our paces together?"

She bent forward as she spoke, patting the horse's neck and talking to him in a quiet, almost mesmeric voice which made the animal twitch his ears as if he understood.

"I see you are experienced enough to know that is necessary," the Marquis said drily.

"It is especially necessary if one is riding a rampaging elephant or a racing camel!" Indira replied.

He laughed before he mounted his own horse, then they set off, moving slowly away from the house and into the Park.

"There are rabbit-holes here," the Marquis said, "as strangers learn to their cost, so hold in your horse until we are away from the trees."

Charles, however, was concentrating on Indira.

She seemed very much at home in the saddle, and he thought she looked extremely alluring and at the same time so graceful as to appear fragile. He was afraid that if the horse pulled, she might not be able to hold him.

It took them a little time to ride beneath the great oak trees to where on the other side of the Park there was meadowland, and the young grass was filled with cuckoo flowers and cowslips.

The Marquis looked at Indira and enquired:

"Would you like to give *Meteor* his head?"

"I hope he lives up to his name," she replied.

She did not wait for the Marquis to lead the way but touched *Meteor* very slightly with her heel. He sprang forward and Indira knew with a feeling of delight that she was riding a perfectly trained and exceptional animal.

She was well aware that all three men were appraising her and she made no attempt to ride more quickly than they were doing.

She merely let *Meteor* take his pace from the Marquis, and they galloped without trying to race each other for nearly a mile.

Then the Marquis turned his horse and said:

"The Steeple-Chase is a little below us. You can see the beginning of it and the first fences from here."

They all pulled in their horses and the Marquis showed them how he had laid out his Steeple-Chase on some flat fields where he had erected fences which to Charles and Jimmy from that distance did not appear to be very formidable.

"Shall we go down and try them?" the Marquis asked.

They followed him to the beginning of the course. The fences were broad, with plenty of room for all four horses to have jumped them together, but because they knew it was a test, both Charles and Jimmy stood back to let the Marquis and Indira go ahead.

Meteor leapt over the fences almost disdainfully, and at the end of the first five the Marquis drew in his horse to say:

"Now this is where the ladies break away from the male riders. They will turn to the left and jump another five fences which are equivalent to the ones we have just taken. Then they will have a guide to lead them across country so that they can be at the winning-post, where the men will finish, about two miles from here."

"It sounds very gruelling," Charles said.

"When you see the rest of the fences, you will realise that is the right word," the Marquis said with a smile.

"What happens if a lady wins the Steeple-Chase?" Jimmy asked.

"You can surely not accuse me of being parsimonious when it comes to racing," the Marquis answered mockingly. "Instead of a Cup, the winning lady will receive a necklace, which I may tell you is a very attractive one, and I am splitting the two thousand guineas into two portions, male and female, which you must admit is permissible in the circumstances."

"I am sure the winning lady will consider it an achievement, not because of the prizes, but because she has persuaded the noble Marquis to initiate something which puts her on almost equal terms with him."

The way in which Indira spoke made the Marquis look surprised, and Charles gave her a warning glance. Then she said quickly, as if she felt she had said too much:

"At the same time, I think it is a wonderful idea and very encouraging for the women, who are always kept out of anything competitive."

The Marquis moved his horse to her side.

"I have the feeling, Lady Mary, that you are jeering at me!"

"No, no, of course not, My Lord," Indira replied. "And I hope that you will . . . allow me to . . . compete in your . . . Steeple-Chase."

"Having seen the way you took those jumps on *Meteor,* how could I possibly refuse?"

"Thank you."

As Indira spoke she deliberately turned her horse, and he had the strange feeling that while she was excited about the race, she disliked him being close to her.

CHAPTER FOUR

*T*HE MARQUIS, HAVING CHANGED HIS CLOTHES after riding, came down the stairs aware that there was a murmur of voices in the Drawing-Room.

He thought he recognised Lady Sinclair's child-like tone and decided that he did not wish to encounter her at the moment.

He was quite certain she would be reproachful and plaintive because he had been riding without her, and would be exceedingly jealous when she realised that he had been accompanied by Lady Mary.

If there was one thing that bored the Marquis, it was women who became excessively jealous when they had no reason for it. Before he reached the Hall he had come to the conclusion that he had finished with Lady Sinclair.

The suddenness of his decision surprised him, for usually in his many and fiery love-affairs there was a "cooling off" period before he finally made up his mind that he was bored and had no intention of continuing a liaison which no longer interested him.

He was quite ruthless where women were concerned, for the simple reason that he had no respect for married women who betrayed their husbands with him or with anybody else.

It was a sentiment that would certainly have surprised his contemporaries if he had confided in them, but as he had long ago told himself, his principles, if that was what they were, were out-of-date and quite ridiculous.

Nevertheless, every time he went into another man's house to find his wife waiting eagerly for him, her arms outstretched, her lips lifted to him, he despised himself and the woman in question.

Then he told himself that although he had mistresses like every other Gentleman of Quality—it was in its way the same as owning superlative horses or fine paintings—these women were not of any great importance in his life and were very easily dispensable.

Had he had anything to do with young girls, it would have meant, as he was acutely aware, being hurried up the aisle by her parents, ambitious to have the most eligible and certainly the richest bachelor in the country as a son-in-law.

The result was that his leisure hours were inevitably spent with married women who were cuckolding their husbands, and it was part of the scene set by the Prince Regent, whose mistress at the moment was the Marchioness of Hertford.

That her husband was not only complaisant but pleased with the arrangement made the Marquis regard him scornfully and remark to one of his friends:

"Hertford wags his tail round Carlton House like an excited terrier!"

He thought as he crossed the Hall that Lord Sinclair, who had found another "interest," and a very pretty one at that, would doubtless be summoned home to escort his wife until she found another lover.

It did not worry him what either Lord or Lady Sinclair thought. But he knew that he would find it difficult to avoid a scene before his guests returned to London on Monday.

As it was something he invariably encountered when an *affaire de coeur* was at an end, he metaphorically shrugged his shoulders and told himself that Rosie, as she was well bred, would behave like a Lady.

At the same time, he had the uncomfortable feeling that blue blood did not always ensure self-control!

In his experience, women were so distraught at losing his affection that they would not only scream and cry but would threaten suicide in an effort to blackmail him back into their arms.

He thought mockingly that it would have been far more convenient from his point of view if his decision about Rosie Sinclair had not been made so soon after her arrival at Ardsley Hall.

But he knew without argument that the curtain had fallen, and when he saw her again she would not even seem as beautiful as she had when he had invited her to take part in his Steeple-Chase.

It was something he had been very reluctant to do, but because she was a good rider she had pleaded with him at an intimate moment when it would have been very difficult for a man to refuse any request from a very beautiful woman.

'Let us hope she wins,' he thought to himself. 'The necklace will soothe her feelings better than words.'

He knew he was being over-optimistic, for no necklace, however magnificent, however expensive, could compensate a woman for losing him.

In reality he was not as conceited as his enemies thought, and he often found it a handicap rather than an asset that women found him irresistible as a lover, which, when combined with his aura of wealth and prestige, made him outstanding in the society in which he moved.

He had almost reached his Study, where he knew he would find the newspapers which he intended to read before luncheon, when he thought it was likely that Lady Mary would be in the Library.

She had ridden back to the house ahead of him, and he had known, although he had found it difficult to understand, that she had no wish to talk to him intimately, as any other woman would have done.

She had attached herself to Charles Frodham and quite obviously preferred his company.

The Marquis wondered for a moment if because he had rescued her from the Highwaymen, Lady Mary had fallen in love with the young man.

Yet, he was perceptive enough to realise that her attitude towards both Charles Frodham and James Overton was that of a sister for a brother.

He was too experienced with women not to know when there was that little glint in the eyes, that flirtatious curve of the lips, or the vibrations which made a man aware that she was very conscious of his masculinity.

But there was nothing like that about Lady Mary when she talked to the two young men who had brought her to Ardsley Hall, and where the rest of the male guests and himself were concerned, the Marquis was now sure that when they came near her she was actually afraid.

It was something he had never encountered before; in fact, he could not remember in the whole of his life any woman being afraid of him.

'If anything,' he thought cynically, 'the boot is on the other foot!'

Even when he was very young, women had pursued him, and his self-assurance came from having made love to so many, a great number of whom had chased him rather than allow him to do his own hunting.

Just as he had said at White's, he told himself now that women were all the same.

And yet he knew that Lady Mary was different, and he wished to know why.

He opened the door of the Library, and as he did so he heard her voice from the far end of the room say:

"Please . . . leave me alone . . . I want to read this book, which I find very . . . interesting."

There was undoubtedly a quiver of fear in the way she spoke.

The Marquis could not see her because all down the room bookcases jutted out from the wall, and she was behind one which he knew contained the Chinese volume about which he had spoken to her.

"I have no intention of leaving you alone," a man replied, and the Marquis recognised that it belonged to Lord Wrotham, who had sat next to her at dinner the night before.

When he realised that Wrotham was upsetting her, he had thought that it had been a mistake to place him beside her because he was a notorious womaniser who continually boasted of his successes.

However, the Marquis's party had been planned to contain only his personal friends, and those did not include young, unmarried women.

"I have been dreaming about you all night," Lord Wrotham was saying, "and counting the hours until I could see you again."

Indira did not reply, and he asked:

"How can you be so beautiful? You are a temptation to every man who looks at you, and all I am asking, my little temptress, is that you will be a little kind to me."

"Please . . . go away!" Indira replied.

Then she gave a scream.

"Do not . . . dare to . . . touch me . . . you have no right . . ."

She screamed again, and the Marquis realised that this could not be allowed.

He hurried down the room, making his footsteps as loud as possible as a warning to Lord Wrotham.

As he came round the end of the bookcase, it was to see Indira with her back against the books, and Lord Wrotham, having obviously just taken his hands from her, looked round angrily at being interrupted.

"So here you are, Wrotham!" the Marquis said slowly, drawling his words as if he was in no hurry. "One of the servants is looking for you. I think he has a message."

"A message?" Lord Wrotham exclaimed. "I cannot think what it might be."

"You will find the man in the Hall."

Lord Wrotham muttered something beneath his breath and walked past the Marquis and up the Library towards the door.

Only when he had gone did the Marquis look directly at Indira to see an expression of terror in her eyes.

She was clasping a book to her breast with both hands, as if to calm the tumult within her, and he realised that her whole body was trembling.

"I am sorry he upset you," he said quietly.

For a moment she did not reply. Then she said:

"They . . . promised . . . because I am . . . unmarried . . . that this . . . would not happen."

The Marquis looked puzzled and asked:

"Who promised?"

"Charles . . . and James . . . please . . . I cannot stay . . . I want to go away!"

The Marquis did not answer, and she said with a violence which was different from the way she had been speaking before:

"I hate men! I hate . . . them all! I must go . . . into a . . . Convent! There is . . . nowhere else where I can be . . . safe."

The Marquis was completely astounded. Then he said:

"I think you are upset because of what happened yesterday, and I am sorry Wrotham should have behaved in such a stupid manner. But it is one of the penalties you have to pay for being such a very beautiful woman!"

"I hate . . . my hair! I hate my . . . face!" Indira cried desperately. "If I were ugly they would leave me . . . alone . . . and that is all I . . . want."

"I think every ugly woman would give her right arm to look as you do," the Marquis said with a faint smile.

"I am . . . going into a . . . Convent," Indira said decidedly. "Please . . . tell me where I can . . . find one . . . and where they will . . . admit me if I promise to become a . . . Catholic."

The Marquis looked at her to see if she was really sincere.

He prided himself that he always knew if a man or woman was lying, and he was aware that Indira was telling the truth and she really intended to do as she said.

"I would never have imagined," he said slowly after a moment's pause, "that riding as you do, and having a very intelligent brain, you would be a coward!"

Indira started and looked at him almost as if he had slapped her or thrown cold water in her face.

He was aware that he had given her a shock, and she was no longer trembling.

"I am not . . . really a . . . coward," she said after a moment, as if she spoke to herself. "Papa would be . . . ashamed of me if I were."

"I am sure your father would be very ashamed if he thought you would do anything so absurd as to imprison yourself in a Convent just because you have not the courage to face the world as it is."

"But . . . men will not . . . leave me . . . alone."

The Marquis thought it was what most women longed and prayed for, but he said:

"All men are not like Wrotham, and I promise you while he is here in my house he will not trouble you again."

"I . . . think I would rather . . . leave."

"I cannot prevent you from doing so, but I should be very disappointed."

As he spoke, Indira remembered that she not only had nowhere to go, but if she left Charles and Jimmy behind, she would have no protection from Mr. Jacobson.

Lord Wrotham was certainly very frightening, but it was also frightening to think of going alone to London and trying to find somewhere to stay until she found which of her relations were alive and willing to welcome her.

Almost as if the Marquis could read her thoughts he said:

"As I understand it, you have at the moment nobody to travel with, and as you have been through some worrying and shocking experiences, would it not be wiser to give yourself a chance to consider your next move?"

Indira did not speak and he went on:

"I am sure Frodham and Overton will escort you if you wish to go to London when you leave here, but it would be very selfish if you left today and prevented them from taking part in my Steeple-Chase."

Indira gave a deep sigh.

"I am sure . . . My Lord, that I am being . . . selfish and foolish . . . but please . . . please do not let that man come . . . near me again! He touched me . . . and he was trying . . . to kiss me!"

"I have already promised," the Marquis said, "that he will behave himself in the future. I can only apologise that one of my guests should have behaved so outrageously in my house."

464

He knew as he spoke that it was not really an unusual occurrence at Ardsley Hall, and despite Lady Mary's explanations as to why she was travelling alone, Wrotham might easily have misconstrued it and convinced himself that her family was not particularly concerned with her.

Such a beautiful young woman would not usually be allowed anywhere without an elderly and competent Chaperone.

Now for the first time the Marquis found the whole situation rather strange.

He had accepted the story of her not being met at Southampton without query simply because it had not occurred to him to suspect there to be anything unusual about it.

Now he could think of a great number of questions he would like to ask, but he knew it was something he could not do while Indira was still upset.

"What I am going to suggest," he said in a voice that was calm, impersonal, and, he hoped, reassuring, "is that you forget what has happened, and in the short time we have before luncheon let us discuss together the book you are holding in your hand, which I came here to find for you."

"I looked in the . . . catalogue on the . . . table," Indira replied.

There was still a tremor in her voice, but the Marquis knew she was making an effort to do what he wished.

For the first time since they had been talking she took the book away from her breast and looked down at it.

"You are very . . . very . . . fortunate to . . . possess this," she said.

"That is what I have always thought myself," the Marquis replied. "But I assure you that very few of my guests appreciate its age or what it contains."

"But you had it . . . translated?"

"No, that was done by my grandfather," the Marquis replied, "who was clever enough to know how valuable it was, and to employ the greatest scholars of his time to translate it."

"I have heard of 'The Song of Lo Fu,'" Indira said, looking down at the book, "but I like best the little poem by Li Po."

The Marquis was just about to move to her side to look down at the pages of the translation that she held in her hand. Then he thought it might frighten her if he stood too close, and instead he said:

"I have not read it for some years, so suppose you read it to me?"

Indira gave him a little smile.

"I will just read the last three lines," she said.

How many times has the rose flowered?
Do the white clouds as then scatter themselves?
And behind whose dwelling sets the moon?

The Marquis thought her voice was very soft, and that the words seemed to speak to her of the world behind the world.

As if she knew that was what he thought, she said:

"I studied with a Chinese Philosopher, and he taught me that each one of us finds a different meaning in what we read."

"Come with me," the Marquis said. "I will show you something which I am sure you will appreciate."

Indira put the book into its place on the shelf and walked with him to another part of the Library.

There in the centre of the wall was a Chinese cabinet of red lacquer raised above a carved and gilt stand.

It was very beautiful and she had meant to examine it after she had looked at the book, knowing that it was something her father would have enjoyed and that she herself would love to own it.

The Marquis unlocked the doors to the cabinet with a gold key and drew from one of the drawers inside something wrapped in silk.

From it he took out a pottery model of a prancing horse and held it out to Indira.

She gave a little cry of delight.

"A T'ang Dynasty horse!" she exclaimed. "How can you be so lucky as to possess anything so wonderful?"

"It was given to me by my grandfather when I became twenty-one, and he had been given it by his father," the Marquis replied.

Indira touched its glazed surface with the tip of her fingers.

"Only the craftsmen of the T'ang Dynasty," she said as if she spoke to herself, "could catch the vigour and tension of an animal in motion."

"That is what I thought," the Marquis agreed.

"My teacher said," Indira said, her eyes on the horse, "that the sculptured art of the T'ang Dynasty is entirely confident of its mastery of the faith and ability to express vitality and strength of the visual form."

Then as she spoke, thinking of the horse, she thought that might also apply to the Marquis, and a faint flush rose in her cheeks.

Suddenly he was aware that he could read her thoughts, and he told himself that he had never had a more sincere or more unexpected compliment.

And yet in a way he could understand that to somebody as perceptive as Indira, the T'ang Dynasty horse she held in her hands with its expression of pride and vigour was undoubtedly what he aimed for in himself.

Indira stroked the arched neck of the horse, then she gave it back to the Marquis with a little sigh, saying:

"Thank you. I have never seen a more perfect example of T'ang sculpture. I feel that although we know it was originally a tomb figure, it actually lives."

The Marquis took the horse from her, wrapped it again in its silk shroud, and replaced it very carefully in the drawer.

"I think we both know from our studies," he said, "that there is no such thing as death, only life in different spheres."

He was not looking at her as he shut the lacquered doors of the cabinet, but he was aware that she was staring at him wide-eyed before she said in a voice that seemed to vibrate between them:

"How could I have been so stupid as not to realise that before? Of course you are right! I have not lost . . . Papa, he is . . . still with me!"

The Marquis turned to look at her and saw that her eyes were shining almost as if there were a star hidden in their depths.

Then without saying anything more she turned and went from the Library. He knew that she felt for the moment as if she must be alone and could not speak to anybody of what she was feeling.

As he stood there, thinking it was the strangest and most unexpected conversation he had ever had with a woman, what Indira had just said came back into his mind.

"I have not lost Papa, he is still with me!"

Thinking back, he could not remember there having been anything said last night on her arrival about Lord Farncombe being dead, and he was quite sure that it had not been reported in the newspapers.

The Marquis was very precise in his reading, as he was in everything else, and when the newspapers arrived he read the headlines, the Editorials, the Parliamentary Reports, then the Court Columns and the Obituaries of distinguished people, which were printed on the same page.

He was therefore convinced that there had been no mention of the death of the Earl of Farncombe, whom he had never met, but who he was well aware was spoken of highly when people talked of India.

Ever since the victories of Colonel Wellesley—now the Duke of Wellington—at the end of the last century and the rapid expansion of British control of India, it was a frequent topic of conversation in the House of Lords and at the Foreign Office, where the Marquis was often entertained.

He was now quite convinced that there was something strange about Lady Mary and the circumstances which had brought her to Ardsley Hall.

It was something he could not exactly put into words, but it was a tangled skein which he was determined to unravel, and he found himself interested and intrigued in a way he had not been for a very long time.

He joined his guests in the Drawing-Room, and Indira reappeared just before luncheon was announced.

As the Marquis watched her come through the door, he thought for a second that she looked different.

Then he realised it was because for the first time since she had been in his house, she was not looking worried, tense, or apprehensive, but happy.

When Indira went to bed that night, early because she wanted a good night's rest before the Steeple-Chase the next day, she lay thinking how extremely fortunate she had been in coming to Ardsley Hall.

She could not explain to herself now why she had been so foolish in giving way to the despair and misery which had encompassed her like a cloud after her father's death.

She had loved him so deeply and he had meant so much in her life that when he died she felt as if part of herself had gone with him and she was no longer a whole person.

She was sensible enough to know that the shock from which she was suffering was mainly physical, and now she was ashamed and in a way humiliated that her beliefs and her faith, which had glowed like a light, had been tried to the point where she had not applied to her personal sorrow all she had learnt.

She had not realised, as she did now, that her father was not dead but was near her, loving her and being part of her as he had always been.

"How can I have been so idiotic, Papa," she asked in the darkness, "as to have forgotten all we talked about so often? And we both know . . . how much it guided your life . . . and of course . . . mine."

It seemed extraordinary that it should have been left to a perfect stranger, and of all people the cynical, supercilious Marquis of Ardsley, to reveal the truth to her.

Now, as if he had lit a blazing light to show her the way, the clouds had vanished and she could see, hear, and think, and she was no longer unhappy or even afraid.

Looking back, she supposed it was immediately after her father's Funeral, which had taken place within six hours of his death, that she became aware of being menaced by the people who surrounded her.

The burial at sea was very moving and many of the passengers wept in sympathy, although Indira had remained dry-eyed and calm until she was alone.

Then she wept tempestuously, not only at the misery of losing somebody she loved so deeply, but also at the terror of being alone.

After that, everything had seemed a little muddled and indistinct, as if she moved in a fog, and she felt as if everything that happened was a nightmare from which she could not awaken.

'How could I not have tried to reach Papa with my prayers and the vibrations that always existed between us?' Indira thought, and felt as if he was now near her, as he had not been since she believed he had died.

"I am not alone! I am not alone!" she said to herself. "Papa is here, thinking of me, guiding me, protecting me!"

She was quite sure now that it was her father who had helped her to escape from the Hotel and Mr. Jacobson, and who had brought Charles and Jimmy to her rescue.

Also undoubtedly he had brought her to Ardsley Hall so that she should learn how foolish she had been.

She could feel the T'ang horse beneath her fingers, and she knew it was that even more than the Marquis's words which had reminded her that life is eternal and death nothing more than the shedding of an unwanted garment.

"I understand now, Papa, and I am no longer afraid. I am sorry, very sorry that I failed you, and myself, in such a foolish manner."

She felt as if her father was smiling at her, and she could feel the power of the faith in which they both believed seeping back into her and driving out the last remnants of doubt and fear.

"How could I ever have thought of imprisoning myself in a Convent?" she asked herself. "I should have been thinking of ways in which I could spend the money you left me for the benefit of other people."

At the same time, now that her brain was functioning clearly, she knew it was going to be hard to know exactly what she could do in a country which, while she belonged to it, was as strange to her as if she had suddenly found herself living on the moon.

'I must find Papa's relations, and I am sure they will help me,' she thought.

She wondered if perhaps her father's Bankers might be able to help her. Then she remembered that everything in England was in the hands of the firm of Solicitors whom he had trusted.

In any case, Indira was sure that no Solicitors, however honourable, would be the right people to advise her on the spending of her fortune.

Then an idea came to her which made her stare blankly into the darkness.

It was that the one person who could really help her and advise her was the Marquis.

"No, no, of course not!" she said aloud. "He is the last person who must know who I am. To tell him would be to betray Charles and Jimmy, who have been so kind to me."

At the same time, it was difficult not to remember that it was the Marquis and his T'ang Dynasty horse who had not only pointed the way but brought her peace of mind and the courage she should never have lost.

The next morning was bright and sunny, and Indira rose earlier than usual because she was not only excited at the idea of the Steeple-Chase but also, although she would not have admitted it to herself, eager to see the Marquis again.

She had awakened several times during the night to think about him, and found it extraordinary that a man she had come to the house prepared to despise and dislike had instead been the guide, the Guru, which every student of Eastern religion knows appears whenever the pupil is ready.

She thought it would be impossible to explain to Charles or Jimmy what had happened, and she would certainly not attempt it.

But when she had least expected it, the Guru had come, and although she thought that the Marquis would be totally unaware of it and would certainly not be interested, he had during those few minutes in the Library changed her whole attitude towards the future.

Because of what she had learnt in the East she did not for one moment question that this was what had happened or suspect that what had occurred was just chance.

It had all happened in a calm, mysterious way, but the pattern was there. The path that for a time had been twisting and indistinct had still to be followed, and now she was no longer indecisive but determined to go ahead.

'I want to talk to him, and perhaps there are other things he could tell me,' she thought.

At the same time, she was well aware that today of all days the Marquis would not be thinking of her, but of his Steeple-Chase and the many people who would be arriving to take part in it.

When she was dressed, wearing a riding-habit which had come from Paris and which because it was the deep blue of the sea made her skin dazzlingly white and her hair vivid as a flame, Indira went down to breakfast.

She had expected that nobody would be down so early and was therefore surprised to see the Marquis there, and as he rose to his feet at her entrance she exclaimed:

"I did not think anybody would be as early as I am!"

"When I am planning anything as important as a Steeple-Chase," he replied, "I find there are always difficulties at the last moment which have been overlooked, and even fences erected in the wrong way unless I inspect them."

471

Indira sat down at the table beside him and he said:

"I hope *Meteor* carries you to victory."

"I hope so too," Indira replied. "Last night I dreamt I was riding your T'ang Dynasty horse, but instead of galloping over the ground he flew with me towards the moon."

"I suppose that was the influence of the poem, and of course the horse himself," the Marquis said, and after a moment added:

"I too thought about the poem you read to me and tried to sort out the picture it made in my mind."

The Marquis's lips twisted a little before he went on:

"It is something I have not done since I was at Oxford, and I feel as if you have rolled back the years for me. Everything I thought then has become important again, almost as if it was waiting for my return."

"My teacher would have said that when we leave the path, whether by . . . mistake or . . . deliberately," Indira said in a low voice, "the path does not change but waits until we find out the . . . mistake we have made and go . . . back."

The Marquis was about to reply, but at that moment the door opened and Charles came into the room.

"Good-morning, Ardsley!" he said to the Marquis. "Good-morning, Indira! You are very early!"

"What did you call Lady Mary just then?" the Marquis enquired in surprise.

"Jimmy and I call her by her second name because she has been in India," Charles replied, "and anyway, I think it is far more attractive than 'Mary,' which is somewhat ordinary."

"I agree with you," Indira said quickly, realising that he had made a mistake in the way he had addressed her. "It was my mother who chose 'Indira,' and she thought it very appropriate because my father loved everything that was Indian, and they became engaged when they were in Simla."

The Marquis did not say anything. He merely thought this was another link in the puzzle he was trying to solve.

Then other guests appeared for breakfast, all of them men.

The Marquis finished and left the room, and Charles, sitting next to Indira, said:

"I want to talk to you. It was impossible last night after dinner to have a moment alone."

"Yes, I know," Indira replied, "and anyway, I went to bed early."

"You were very sensible," Charles said, "and actually Jimmy and I did not stay up late. I may not win, but I am determined to complete the course."

Jimmy sat down on the other side of Indira.

"We shall be lucky if we do," he remarked. "The jumps are far higher than they were last year."

"I expect there will be some casualties," Charles said, "but I am sure my horse can manage them."

"I would like to have a look at them before we start," Indira said. "Is that possible?"

"Of course it is," Charles replied, "and it is what I want to do myself. We do not want to hang about making desultory conversation with all the other competitors who are already starting to arrive."

"No, of course not," Indira agreed.

She went upstairs and put on her riding-hat and boots and came down again to find Charles and Jimmy waiting for her in the Hall.

As they walked down the steps to where their horses were waiting for them, Charles said:

"I have just thought of something. I do not want to spoil your fun, but I think it is sensible."

"What is it?" Indira asked.

"Seeing the way you ride, and with the horse the Marquis has lent you, you have every chance of beating Lady Sinclair or any other lady. But I think it would be a mistake."

"Why?"

"Because," Charles said, "not only will Lady Sinclair make a scene, but also an event like this is sure to be reported in the Social Columns of the newspapers."

"I never thought of that!" Jimmy exclaimed.

"Well, I have," Charles said, "and if Lady Mary Combe is the acclaimed winner of the Ardsley Hall Steeple-Chase, the Farncombe relations might ask why she is here without their knowledge, and try to get in touch with her."

473

"You are very sensible," Indira said, "so I promise you I will not beat Lady Sinclair. She can have all the honour and glory she wants."

"I am sorry," Charles said. "It seems extremely unfair, and I would not mind betting a considerable sum that you could win."

"It is important for me to ride but not particularly to win," Indira said with a smile.

They reached the horses and she patted *Meteor* and made a fuss of him.

He nuzzled his nose against her and she said in a voice only he could hear:

"You are very beautiful, but not quite as beautiful as the horse I was riding last night."

She was smiling at her own fantasy as Charles lifted her into the saddle, and when he and Jimmy were mounted they rode off to look at the course.

They went slowly, aware that the horses were restless and longing to gallop, but they kept them on a tight rein.

Already there were a number of people gathering in the meadow, and the Marquis's employees were putting the finishing touches to the hedges under his supervision.

They did not ride up to him but went instead onto the higher ground, so that they could see the whole course below them.

"You jump the smaller fences," Jimmy said to Indira, "then come on to the winning-post to watch Charles and me trailing valiantly behind the Marquis!"

"Do you think he will win?" Indira asked.

"Of course he will!" Jimmy said. "There can be no question about that, but I would like to be second."

"That is my place," Charles exclaimed, "and do not dare to do me out of it!"

"I bet you ten pounds I am ahead of you," Jimmy said.

Indira gave a little laugh.

"No, no, you must never bet on yourself. It is unlucky . . . at least, that is what my father always thought."

"Very well," Jimmy said, "but second is where I intend to be."

"You are becoming as self-satisfied and as sure of yourself as Ardsley!" Charles complained mockingly.

They joked with each other for a little while, then Jimmy said he wanted to ride down to look at the last few fences to make sure he took them in style.

He left Charles and Indira alone, and when he had gone Charles asked:

"I may be wrong, but you do not seem quite as worried as you were when we arrived."

"I am all right, thank you," Indira answered, "and I am ashamed of myself for letting two despicable men like Mr. Jacobson and Lord Wrotham upset me."

"Wrotham?" Charles exclaimed. "What has he done? He is a roué, and you are to have nothing to do with him!"

"I thought it would be a mistake to do so," Indira said demurely.

She felt there would be no point in telling Charles what had happened, because she was aware last night that the Marquis had kept his word and prevented Lord Wrotham from coming near her again.

She thought that he glared at her from across the room, but she was no longer afraid because she was quite sure he would not disobey the Marquis's orders to leave her alone.

Now she could see the Marquis below her, riding from one fence to the other and obviously giving orders, which were quickly obeyed.

She was watching him so intently that she started when Charles said:

"I suppose you realise how magnificent you have been and that the Marquis is captivated by you."

"What makes you think that?"

"I know by the way he looks at you, for one thing," Charles answered, "and for another, the way Lady Sinclair was behaving last night made it very obvious which way the wind is blowing."

"I do not . . . understand."

"The Marquis was quite obviously ignoring her, and when she asked him to come and sit next to her at the gaming-table, he deliberately walked in the opposite direction, and she went white with fury."

"I am sorry for her if that is how she . . . feels about . . . him."

Indira hesitated before she added:

"But . . . if she has a husband . . . surely it is . . . wrong?"

"I suppose it is," Charles said, "but you must realise that it is a feather in any woman's cap to be able to say that she has captivated, if only for a few months, the elusive Marquis of Ardsley!"

Indira did not answer, and after a moment he said:

"What is important is that you have played your part to the point where I am quite certain that when you leave on Monday, Ardsley will make it clear that he wants to see you again, and perhaps say even more than that."

"When do you intend to . . . tell him that I am . . . not Lady Mary Combe?" Indira asked in a strange voice.

"I have not yet sorted out the ending of this drama," Charles replied, "but we have tomorrow yet to come."

He smiled, and there was a note of triumph in his voice as he said:

"Make no mistake, Indira, I shall have won my bet. We will have been at Ardsley Hall for three days, and not for one moment, I am quite certain, has the Marquis doubted that you were anything other than what you appear to be."

"I would not be . . . too sure of . . . that," Indira said in a low voice.

Then, to Charles's surprise, without waiting for him she started to ride down the hill towards Jimmy.

CHAPTER FIVE

*L*UNCHEON WAS EARLY and the competitors were all entertained by the Marquis in the big Dining-Room.

There was a buffet, and drinks of every description, including champagne, were provided for his other guests in the Ball-Room.

When Indira, Charles, and Jimmy rode back to the house, coaches were already arriving to line the course, and the spectators had brought elaborate picnic-baskets which were being unpacked by liveried footmen.

"The Marquis certainly does everything in a slap-up manner!" Jimmy remarked.

"I can see it is very exciting for people who live in this part of the country to have a race-meeting all to themselves," Indira said.

As she spoke she was thinking that it was rather like the races in India which she had attended with her father, where huge crowds would gather to cheer on the jockeys and there was wild enthusiasm when a favourite won.

She had also often raced her father when they went riding every morning, and as he had horses imported from Arabia and from Europe, she was used to well-bred animals, although she thought that few of them had been quite as fine as *Meteor* and the stallion which the Marquis was riding.

When they arrived back at the house it was to find Lady Sinclair holding Court and looking exceedingly attractive in a black habit which displayed her pink-and-white-and-gold beauty better than any colour would have done.

She looked at Indira disdainfully and said in an audible voice:

"I always think black is the most suitable habit for anybody who rides seriously. Colours are far too theatrical."

Indira pretended not to hear her and tried not to laugh when Charles whispered: "Meaow-meaow!" at what he had overheard.

When she went in to luncheon she found that the Marquis had thought of her as he had last night, and she was seated not beside strangers but with Charles on her right-hand side and Jimmy on her left.

When she found her place she looked down the table and met his eyes, and she thought he understood that she was thanking him silently for being so considerate.

Because he had so many competitors to entertain, the majority of whom were men, she had assumed he would be too busy even to give her a thought.

But once or twice she realised that he was looking at her, and she hoped that he was not being critical because she was making no effort to entertain anybody except the two men with whom she had arrived at his house.

Lady Sinclair, on the other hand, constituted herself the Marquis's hostess and was showing off in a way that made it obvious that she wished everybody to know that she had a special position in the Marquis's household.

Indira could not help feeling that it was very wrong for her to parade her affection for him and his for her, when she already had a husband, and if Lord Sinclair had been there it would have been a humiliation for him to see his wife in such a role.

Then she told herself that it was not for her to find fault, especially as she was pretending to be somebody she was not and was deliberately deceiving the Marquis.

"Before I leave I will write a letter of apology, but I do not expect I shall ever see him again," she told herself.

The thought was depressing. She told herself it was because she had no friends in England, and she would have liked to feel that the Marquis was a friend and that she could see him again.

Yet she was quite certain that he would have no time for her, for not only was Lady Sinclair fawning on him in a way that seemed almost embarrassing, but other lady riders, two of whom were particularly beautiful, were doing exactly the same thing.

There were, however, only ten women competitors in all, and when luncheon was over and they rode down to the race-course, Charles said:

"Do not be nervous. I am sure you ride better than any of these other females, and you certainly have a finer horse."

"It was very kind of His Lordship to lend me *Meteor*," Indira said. "I feel we understand each other, and you will not be ashamed of me."

"We could never be that," Jimmy said impulsively. "You have been absolutely splendid, and the reason why Lady Sinclair has been behaving like a Prima Donna all through luncheon is because she is jealous of you."

"I cannot think why."

Charles was about to tell her the reason, when he thought that she might be embarrassed and it would spoil her chances in the race.

He had said to Jimmy last night when they went up to bed:

"You know, we really drew a winning card when we encountered Indira in that strange manner. Who would have thought that not only is she beautiful and extremely intelligent, but she rides better than any woman I have ever seen!"

"I was thinking the same thing," Jimmy said, "and if Ardsley is not infatuated with her he damned well ought to be!"

"I think he is," Charles answered, "but he is a strange man, and it is difficult to know what he is thinking."

"I am beginning to think I will lose my money," Jimmy said with a smile, "but it has been worth it. It has certainly given a spice to our visit which I did not expect."

"Nor I," Charles answered, "and, Jimmy, if I am honest, I would like to pursue Indira after we have found her somewhere to live."

"Why not?" Jimmy asked idly.

There was silence. Then Charles said:

"The truth is, I am afraid I am falling in love! So, as I do not wish to have a broken heart, the first thing I am going to do is to find another, 'Clarice' to amuse me, and forget her."

"I suppose, even though she is so rich, your family would not waive their prejudice against a tradesman's daughter?"

Charles gave a laugh which had no humour in it.

"You do not know my family," he said. "They are so stiff-necked, so certain that the earth was made for them to walk on, that they are as bad if not worse than Ardsley."

"Impossible!" Jimmy exclaimed, and they both laughed.

"How are we going to tell him we have made a fool of him?" Jimmy asked after a moment.

"I do not know," Charles said slowly. "I would hate to do anything which would be an embarrassment to Indira, and I think the best thing would be to wait until we have left, then write a letter apologising for deceiving him. We can be quite honest about it and say it was a bet."

Jimmy gave a cry of horror.

"You must be crazy! Ardsley will never forgive us, and we will never be asked here again."

"Well, you think of a better way," Charles said sharply. "After all, we cannot have gone to all this trouble for nothing."

Jimmy thought about it for a moment. Then he said:

"I suppose the only other way would be to say that Indira deceived us, but that seems rather mean."

"And definitely unsporting!" Charles said. "Ardsley has a great deal of power, and he might make himself unpleasant to her, and we can hardly allow that."

"No, of course not!" Jimmy agreed quickly.

They thought for a long time before finally they went to their separate rooms, but both young men were awake for some time, trying to solve what seemed for the moment an unsolvable problem.

As they rode down the course, Charles looked at Indira and felt that his heart was behaving in a very strange manner, and he told himself that he had to be careful.

'She is too damned pretty for any man's peace of mind!' he thought. And he knew, because her eyes were shining and her lips smiling, that she looked very different from the frightened, unhappy girl they had rescued from the hands of her father's crooked Solicitor.

When they reached the starting-point, the horses were already beginning to get into place, and several gentlemen came up to speak to Charles and Jimmy, then looked at Indira in a manner which made it very clear that they wished to be introduced.

Because he was sure it was the last thing she wanted, Charles deliberately ignored every hint they made, while Indira, concerned with making a fuss of *Meteor* and talking to him in her own special manner, did not even notice.

Lady Sinclair arrived looking exceedingly lovely and very obviously aware of it.

She was again playing hostess, and she said to the other women riders:

"It is so delightful of you to come and take part. I know you will help me to show the gentlemen riders that we are worthy of being the first competitors the dear Marquis has ever allowed to race in his Steeple-Chase."

"How did you persuade him to let us in?" somebody asked.

Lady Sinclair lowered her eye-lashes and looked coy.

"You must not ask me such embarrassing questions," she said, "but I can assure you I had to be very, very persuasive."

The innuendo in her words was very obvious, and Indira deliberately moved out of earshot to the other end of the starting-line.

Quite a number of riders were in place before the Marquis came riding up on *Thunderer,* which was the name of his stallion.

He moved in front of them, and the chattering voices died away into silence as it became obvious that he had something to say.

"Now, let me make it quite clear once again," he began. "We all race together over the first five fences, then where the course divides the ladies will take the left-hand fork, where there are five more fences, and will reach what is really the first winning-post."

He paused for a moment, then continued:

"The rest of us go on to where you know the course ends, and I am sure it is unnecessary for me to say that the first person to pass the second winning-post will receive the Ardsley Steeple-Chase Cup and one thousand guineas!"

He saw that one or two of the men look surprised and he added:

"The other thousand guineas will be given to the winning lady, together with an attractive prize which she can place round her neck."

Somebody made a joke about this, and amidst the laughter the Marquis said:

"I suggest you now get into place, and as usual when the flag drops that is the signal for the 'off.' "

As he finished speaking he rode to the left of the starting-line, where Indira was waiting with Charles and Jimmy.

Unlike some of the other horses, *Meteor* was standing quite still, and she had no trouble holding him in, but there was an alertness about him which made her think of the T'ang horse which she had held in her hands yesterday.

Strangely enough, as the Marquis came up to her, she had the feeling that he was thinking the same thing.

"Are you all right?" he asked. "Do not hurry *Meteor* over the first fences, and he will easily carry you ahead for the last five."

"I am sure he will," Indira replied, "and he is looking forward to the race as much as I am."

"I hope . . ." the Marquis began, then hesitated.

Indira knew he was about to say that he hoped she would win, then even as he spoke she was aware that Lady Sinclair had come up behind him.

"I should get into position, Rosie," he said. "Some horses get very obstreperous when kept waiting."

"I am well aware of that, Seldon," Lady Sinclair replied, "but you omitted to wish me luck, and you know I shall not feel lucky without your good wishes . . ."

She paused, then said softly, so that only he could hear what she said: ". . . and your love."

There was a frown between the Marquis's eyes.

He had not missed the way Lady Sinclair had behaved at luncheon, and now he thought that only a very stupid woman would be so indiscreet as to parade her affection for him in public and in such company.

He knew that a number of the County families taking part were very strait-laced and in the past had expressed their disapproval of the Prince Regent and his friends.

While the Marquis was not particular about what was said about him in London, he had always been very careful in the country to protect himself against any hint of scandal.

It was obvious that he was talked about, and he would have been stupid if he had not realised that sooner or later gossip concerning his *affaires de coeur* would be carried almost on the wind from London to Hampshire.

But it usually was a slow process, and by the time Hampshire was discussing some beauty with whom he was said to be infatuated, the whole affair was over and her place had been taken by somebody else.

So when he was at Ardsley Hall the Marquis was careful to see that his parties, rather to the surprise of his friends, did nothing to offend the local hierarchy.

In fact, when he invited any of his more raffish contemporaries to stay, he was very careful not to include any of the local people in his dinner-parties.

As a result, although they undoubtedly talked and were curious as to who was staying with him, it was all hearsay, and they could never actually substantiate what they suspected.

Now he thought angrily that he had made a great mistake in allowing Lady Sinclair to persuade him to let women ride, or even having her as a guest when he was running his Steeple-Chase.

He knew that she was being particularly outrageous for the simple reason that last night he had gone to his own bedroom after saying goodnight to her.

Although undoubtedly she would have expected him to come to her room later to make love to her before saying good-night again, he had merely got into his own bed and gone to sleep.

Ever since she had come downstairs this morning she had been trying to inveigle him into being alone with her, and he was quite certain that she was going to ask him what was wrong.

But adroitly he had avoided a *tête-à-tête,* or even a low-voiced conversation, which was what she was seeking.

He knew now from the expression in her eyes and the hard note in her voice that she was growing increasingly angry.

However, there was nothing more she could say at the moment, and the Marquis calmly moved away.

After looking to see that all the riders were at the starting-point, their horses facing in the right direction, he took his own place in the line, then raised his hand to the starter.

The flag went down and they were off. Indira was careful not to rush the first two fences and to keep *Meteor* firmly under control.

The jumps were easy. Even so, there was one fall and another horse refused, which put those following out of their stride.

Then as they jumped the fourth fence, Lady Sinclair shot ahead and sailed over it in a manner which made it quite obvious that she was now straining every nerve to win the race.

The Marquis thought with satisfaction that once the ten ladies were out of the way, it would make the going very much easier for the men, who would certainly require no distractions if they were to survive the very high fences he had erected over the rest of the course.

He himself always enjoyed a challenge, and although he was aware that he had an advantage in that his horses were superb and he had had the opportunity of practising over this particular course during the past month, he knew too that he had some stiff competition to face.

This was provided by riders who had come not only from Hampshire but from several adjacent Counties merely because they wished to compete against him.

They would do everything in their power to prove their horses superior and their riding as good as his, if not better.

The Marquis thought with satisfaction that if he did win, it would not be an easy victory, and he and *Thunderer* would both have to prove themselves exceptional to keep the Ardsley Cup at the Hall.

He settled down to ride with his usual expertise, which made him seem part of the horse, and he knew as he did so that *Thunderer* was enjoying himself as much as he was, while the other riders were straining and urging their mounts at the first all-male fence.

It was high and certainly formidable, but without exception each horse swept over it, landing without mishap to go on to the next jump.

It was after they had jumped the third fence that the Marquis glanced to his left and thought he must be mistaken.

Then he saw to his astonishment that while the other nine ladies had obeyed his instructions and left the course where he had told them to do so, Indira was still riding with the men and was a little ahead of the field.

"Why the hell could she not have done as she was told?" the Marquis asked himself angrily.

Then as he took the next fence with perfect timing and realised that she had done the same, he thought with a twist of his lips how angry Rosie Sinclair would be and that no other woman he knew would have dared to jump this part of the course as he had laid it out.

Then as he jumped the next fence he heard just behind him a horse fall, and he had a sudden fear that Indira might fall too.

She looked so frail and so graceful mounted on *Meteor* that he could not bear to think of her being thrown to the ground and perhaps injured.

He wondered if he could reach her and order her to pull out of the race, then knew it would be impossible and there was nothing he could do but ride on and hope that by some miracle she would survive.

The next two fences were particularly difficult, and as one rider after another cleared them, the Marquis felt even as *Thunderer* leapt over them that he was willing Indira to clear them too.

Now the field was thinning out considerably. At the same time, riderless horses, which were always a danger, had struggled to their feet and were galloping on regardless of the fact that there was no-one on their backs.

One of them crossed in front of a rider, and he let out a stream of oaths before his horse stumbled on landing and threw him over its head.

When there were only two fences left, the Marquis was aware that there were five riders clear of the rest. Indira was level with *Thunderer,* and only about two lengths behind were Charles, Jimmy, and Lord Neville.

As Lord Neville was on one of the Marquis's finest horses, it was not surprising that he was one of the leaders.

The Marquis knew that although he was a good rider, he was not exceptional, and at the next fence, a very difficult one, he lost nearly a length.

After the last fence the Marquis had arranged that there was a long stretch of flat ground before the winning-post, and it was on this run-in that he knew the best horses would show both their stamina and their speed.

Somehow it was not a surprise when he found himself racing neck-and-neck with Indira.

It was what he might have expected, he thought, and yet at the same time he had never envisaged that his closest competitor for the trophy he had won four years in succession would be a woman.

It was then that he realised what was giving Indira her advantage. *Thunderer* was indeed a slightly better horse than *Meteor,* but he was also carrying a far greater weight.

As they started to race over the flat ground, the Marquis knew unmistakably that this year he had met his match, and he would not win the Cup as he had so confidently expected.

Then as the winning-post came in sight, he was aware, to his surprise, that he was gaining, and *Thunderer* was now a few inches ahead of *Meteor.*

For a moment he thought he must be mistaken, but when he looked again he knew it was the truth.

She was not urging her horse on, as anybody would have expected, but instead was using all her strength to hold him back.

It was so surprising that the Marquis could hardly ask himself why she should do such a thing, before they had passed the winning-post amidst roars of applause, and he was aware that he and *Thunderer* had won the Steeple-Chase by a head.

He rode on a little way until he could draw *Thunderer* in, and Indira did the same.

As the horses slowed down to a walk, he turned to her and said:

"I can hardly believe that any woman could complete such a course, and I should be very angry with you for risking your neck."

"You . . . should be . . . congratulating . . . *Meteor,*" Indira said breathlessly. "He flew over the . . . fences and never put a . . . foot wrong."

"All the same, it was a risk you should not have taken," the Marquis said severely.

She smiled at him and he knew that she was as excited as any other rider would have been.

Then as Charles and Jimmy came galloping towards them, followed by Lord Neville and several other riders, he said quietly:

"I want an explanation as to why you pulled in *Meteor* on the run-in, for I am well aware that you could have beaten me."

He saw the colour come into her face, but before she was forced to reply, Charles had joined them.

"How can—you have done—anything so—crazy?" he asked, his breath coming in gasps between his lips.

"His Lordship was just asking the same question," Indira replied.

"You were wonderful!" Jimmy cried as he joined them. "I would never have believed that any woman could ride like that."

"And no woman shall again," the Marquis said sharply. "I will not allow them to compete another year."

"That is not fair!" Indira cried. "And it would make me miserable to think I had excluded others from this wonderful race."

"We know only too well what you think about women, Ardsley," Charles said with a laugh, "but you must admit that Indira has confounded you and upset all your theories."

The Marquis was saved from answering by Lord Neville, and several other riders who came up, all conveying to Indira their astonishment that she had finished the course.

Then as she blushed and looked a little embarrassed, they reached the crowds of spectators and there were loud cheers and men waving their hands.

At the winning-post itself, Indira saw the other women competitors grouped behind it, and Lady Sinclair was looking at her with an expression of undisguised fury on her face.

Instinctively she tightened her hands on the reins, and as *Meteor* slowed down so that the horsemen riding beside her moved ahead, she looked away from Lady Sinclair, wondering what she should say and if she should apologise to the Marquis for embarrassing him.

Then she saw another face and gave a little gasp of sheer horror.

Standing in the crowd watching her approach was Mr. Jacobson!

For a moment Indira felt as if she could not think and her head was filled with cotton-wool.

Then as if it were the only action open to her, she turned *Meteor,* and before anybody, including Charles, who was beside her, realised what she was about to do, she rode off the course and behind the coaches onto the open meadowland.

There she touched *Meteor* with her whip, and without looking back she galloped straight for the house.

When she arrived, Indira dismounted at the front door and a groom came running to *Meteor*'s head.

" 'Ow did yer get on, Miss?" he asked.

"Meteor came in second," Indira replied.

The groom looked dejected.

"Oi lost me money! Oi was certain ye'd be first."

Because he sounded so disappointed, Indira said:

"I came second in the main race to His Lordship and *Thunderer!*"

The man gaped at her as she walked away and up the steps into the Hall.

She went to her bedroom, and when the maids came to help her she took off her habit and changed into an afternoon-gown. At the same time, she was wondering what she should do.

Mr. Jacobson had found her, and she was thankful that Charles and Jimmy were there to protect her. But she was quite sure he would make trouble, although what form that would take she had no idea.

He could not forcibly drag her to London to marry Lord Bredon if they objected. At the same time, she really had no claim on them, although she was sure they would do everything to protect her.

"You must help me, Papa," she said to her father as she stared in the mirror without seeing her reflection or even being aware that the maid was arranging her hair.

In her mind she spoke to her father, as she had spoken to him last night, without fear.

Instead she felt a calmness that she had not known before, and the terror that Mr. Jacobson had invoked in her when he had first revealed his plan of marrying her to the fortune-hunter had gone.

She knew it was because in some strange, unaccountable way the Marquis had dispelled her terror and unhappiness and had given her a confidence that she had lost from the moment her father had died so suddenly and tragically.

Now Indira was certain he was guiding and protecting her and nothing terrible could happen that she would not be able to cope with once he told her what to do.

Because she was sure that the Marquis's guests would all be coming back to the house to celebrate his victory, she did not go downstairs.

When the maids had left her she sat in her bedroom, thinking of her father and sending out her thoughts towards him so that she could somehow link herself with him.

She had been extremely interested in thought-transference when she was in India, but it was something she had never needed to practise because her father had always been with her.

Now she felt as if the vibrations within herself were seeking his. At the same time, although she found it hard to understand, she felt as if she also vibrated towards the Marquis, and because he was in the same world as she was he would be aware of it.

"I am being ridiculous," she told herself. "He will only be thinking of Lady Sinclair, not of me. But because he . . . understood as no-one else except Papa has ever done . . . I know that I . . . need him."

She must have been in her bedroom for nearly an hour when there was a knock on the door, and when she opened it there was a footman outside.

"Excuse me, Miss, but Lord Frodham wants to speak to you, if it's convenient."

"Yes, of course," Indira replied, "Where is His Lordship?"

"His Lordship told me to tell you, My Lady, he'd be in the Study."

"Thank you," Indira said.

She thought that if Charles wanted to speak to her secretly, it was certainly astute of him to realise that the Marquis would not allow crowds of guests to invade a room which, she was aware, as Charles was, was essentially his own.

She hurried down the stairs, wondering if Charles had seen Mr. Jacobson as she had, and what he and Jimmy would feel about it.

It was impossible to speculate on what they would say or what they would do, but she was not as terror-struck as she knew she would have been yesterday.

A footman opened the door of the Study and she went inside to find both Charles and Jimmy.

She thought they were looking very serious, but as she walked across the room towards them Jimmy said:

"You were magnificent! There is no other word for it! You had everybody who came to watch the race absolutely astounded!"

Indira smiled at him a little shyly before Charles said:

"There is something much more important to talk about at the moment."

"Mr. Jacobson!" Indira said in a low voice.

"Exactly," Charles answered. "I suspected you had seen him and that was why you rode away."

"I thought it was the . . . best thing to . . . do."

"You were right!" Jimmy exclaimed. "And you missed Lady Sinclair throwing a tantrum and screaming at the Marquis."

"What about?"

"About you, of course! She accused him of deliberately sending her and the other ladies on a different course so that you could win the race with him."

"She made a fool of herself," Charles said briefly, "but we have to tell Indira what else has happened."

"What is it?"

Charles drew some papers out of the pocket of his riding-coat.

"Jacobson handed me these," he said, "and quite frankly I do not know what I am going to do about them."

"What are they?" Indira asked.

"One is a writ which orders me to go in front of the Magistrates to explain why I abducted a minor," Charles replied, "and the other accuses Jimmy and me of inflicting grievous bodily harm upon a Solicitor who was merely carrying out his orders."

489

For a moment Indira stared at him as if she could not credit what he had said.

Then she gave a cry of horror before she exclaimed:

"Can he really bring these charges against you? And if he does, what will . . . happen?"

CHAPTER SIX

——— ❧ ———

*T*HERE WAS SILENCE, as both young men considered the question. Then Jimmy said:

"I think, frankly, he is trying to blackmail us. He knows that we will not want a scandal and thinks we will pay to keep him quiet."

"If he brings charges," Charles replied harshly, "he will put a noose round his own neck. After all, there is Indira's evidence that he was trying to force her into marriage so that he could get hold of her money."

Even as he spoke he knew that the publicity such a case would create might destroy Jacobson, but it would also damage Indira's reputation so that no hostess in any strata of Society would accept her as a guest.

Indira clasped her hands together.

"I am sorry . . . so terribly sorry," she said, "that I have . . . involved you in . . . this."

"You could not help it," Charles replied, "and somehow we will give that cheating devil his just dues. I only wish I had hit him harder!"

"It was hard enough for him to bring a charge against you," Jimmy said.

Charles gave a sharp laugh.

"You do not suppose that would stand up in Court?"

Jimmy knew that was true.

Charles was a Nobleman, and it would be acknowledged that he was absolutely justified in dealing as he had with a man like Jacobson, considering that he had been physically menacing a woman.

At the same time, this once again involved Indira, and both Charles and Jimmy knew that somehow they had to keep her out of the mess.

"I refuse to buy him off," Charles said suddenly and violently, "and before we return to London on Monday we have to think of a way making that clear to him."

"It might be a good idea to go and see the Lord Chief Justice," Jimmy said. "He is a friend of my father's, although I have never met him personally."

"Whatever we do, we have to think it out very carefully," Charles replied, "in order to save Indira from being involved."

"But I am involved," Indira said, "and it is very sweet of you to think of me. At the same time, I am only a . . . stranger and have no . . . right to . . . impose upon you."

Charles looked at her and wondered what she would say if he told her she meant very much more to him than a stranger would.

Then he told himself it was too soon to say anything like that, and in any case how could he ask her to marry him, seeing what his family would say about it and how unhappy they would undoubtedly make her?

With an effort he said calmly:

"This is no time for us to make decisions, and we can talk tomorrow when it will be easier than it is now."

He glanced at the door as he spoke, almost as if he expected the Marquis to come in.

"You are right," Jimmy said, "the house is full of people celebrating our host's victory, and there is to be a large dinner-party which the Marquis always gives after the Steeple-Chase."

"If there is to be a dinner-party to celebrate his victory, and if Lady Sinclair is a winner too," Indira said, "I think it would be wise for me to stay upstairs."

As she spoke she thought that Charles was about to protest, and she added quickly:

"As a matter of fact, I do feel rather tired."

"That is not surprising," Jimmy said. "I am tired too, and I never believed any woman could complete that very difficult course as splendidly as you did."

"You really have to thank *Meteor* for that," Indira said with a smile. "At the same time, it would be a mistake for people to . . . praise me when Lady Sinclair is . . . there."

Both men knew that she was nervous as to what Lady Sinclair might say to her or how she would behave.

Seeing the way Her Ladyship had raged at the Marquis and shocked quite a number of his friends, neither Charles nor Jimmy wished for her to be so rude and aggressive to Indira.

"You are quite sure that is what you want to do?" Jimmy asked.

"I am quite sure!" Indira said firmly. "I will send a message to His Lordship to say that I have retired to bed and hope he will excuse me."

Charles nodded as if he thought that was right. Then he added:

"I think you should disappear now, otherwise if the Marquis knows you are downstairs, he might suspect you have reasons other than tiredness for not appearing at dinner."

"Yes, of course," Indira agreed. "And I will go up to my room by a side staircase. Good-night, Charles."

She would have left, but Charles took her hand in his and said:

"I cannot let you go without telling you how wonderful you were! I was terrified when I first realised you were jumping the higher fences with us. Then I just prayed you would complete the course and confound them all."

"Especially Lady Sinclair!" Jimmy added. "I have never seen a more disgraceful exhibition than she made of herself. It was worthy of a Billingsgate fish-wife!"

Charles did not appear to hear him. He was just looking at Indira, until he said in a deep voice:

"We will talk about it all tomorrow. Good-night, Indira, and do not worry. Jimmy and I will look after you."

"Thank you."

He hesitated but did not release her hand.

Then as she looked at him enquiringly he raised it a little awkwardly to his lips.

"The Marquis should give you a special prize for bravery," he said, "and I would like to do the same."

Indira did not blush or seem embarrassed. She merely took her hand from his, smiled at him, then at Jimmy, and slipped out of the room.

Charles glanced at the door after she had left, almost as if he considered following her.

"No-one could be more sensible," Jimmy said. "It would have been disastrous for her to come down to dinner and have Lady Sinclair making snide remarks all the evening, if not being openly rude."

"One thing is quite certain," Charles said, "Lady Sinclair has cooked her goose where the Marquis is concerned. I was watching his face when she was raging at him, and he looked not only more contemptuous than usual but positively disgusted!"

"I was disgusted too," Jimmy said, "and if that is the way in which women with 'blue blood' behave, then all I can say is give me a trades-man's daughter every time."

"I agree with you," Charles answered. "At the same time, I cannot believe most tradesmen's daughters are like Indira."

"I can still hardly believe that she was within an inch of beating the Marquis," Jimmy enthused.

"Well, she was, and what we have to decide now," Charles said, "is what are we going to do about Jacobson."

"If we had had any sense," Jimmy replied, "we should have drowned him when we had the chance!"

Indira reached her bedroom without seeing anybody and crossed the room for a moment to look out at the sun sinking behind the oak trees in the Park. It turned not only the sky but also the lake to crimson and gold.

It was so lovely that she felt as if her whole being reached out to the beauty of it, but she knew that she had to say good-bye.

"Help me, Papa, help me!" she prayed in her heart. "I cannot let these two young men who have been so kind get into trouble because of me. I need all your cleverness and power of organisation to help me at this moment."

Almost as if her prayer had brought her an answer, she walked across

493

the room to tug at the bell-pull which was a strip of exquisitely embroidered satin hanging down from the ceiling.

She went back to the window and waited until there was a knock at the door and the maid who usually attended her came in.

"You rang, M'Lady?"

"Yes, Emily. I wonder if you would be so kind as to ask the Housekeeper to come here as soon as she can."

"I'll fetch Mrs. Baker right away, M'Lady. She's not far away."

The maid left the room, and Indira waited only a few minutes before Mrs. Baker, an elderly woman with white hair, and dressed in rustling black silk with a silver *chatelaine* at her waist, came into the room.

"You wished to see me, M'Lady?" she asked, shutting the door behind her.

"Yes, Mrs. Baker," Indira replied. "I need your help."

"Of course, M'Lady, I'll do anything I can."

"When I returned from the Steeple-Chase," Indira began, "I received a message to say that somebody very close and dear to me had died."

"I'm sorry to hear that, M'Lady."

"You will understand, Mrs. Baker, that I have to leave immediately for London, but I have no wish to upset or cast an atmosphere of gloom over His Lordship's victory-party."

"I can understand that, M'Lady."

"That is why I need your assistance," Indira went on, "and only with your help can I leave immediately without anybody being aware of it."

"Immediately, M'Lady?"

Indira nodded.

"I am needed in London as quickly as I can get there. But it is not going to be easy, because I was brought here by Lord Frodham and Sir James Overton, who had agreed to take me on Monday to some relatives who live about fifteen miles away."

Mrs. Baker was listening attentively as Indira continued:

"Now that my plans have changed, I must somehow get to London, and you can understand I would not wish to spoil their stay here at Ardsley Hall or to disrupt His Lordship's arrangements for dinner."

"I do see it's a problem, M'Lady."

"What I was going to suggest," Indira said, "if you could possibly arrange it, was to have a carriage take me to the nearest Posting-Inn, where after a short night's rest I can hire some horses to take me on to London first thing tomorrow morning."

Mrs. Baker held up her hands in horror.

"Oh, M'Lady, you couldn't do that, and certainly not travel alone!"

"It seems too much to ask," Indira said, "but could one of the maids . . . accompany me?"

"Of course that can be arranged," Mrs. Baker agreed. "It will leave me short-handed when the house's so full, but death, M'Lady, is something none of us can anticipate or arrange to happen at our convenience."

"That is true," Indira murmured.

"What's more," Mrs. Baker went on, her voice warming as she thought out what was required, "I'm sure His Lordship would not wish you to travel in the type of carriage and behind the inferior horses which is all you'll be able to hire at a Posting-Inn."

She paused before she said:

"I'll take it upon myself to see that a carriage takes you to where Your Ladyship'll be staying in London, and of course His Lordship's own horses are stabled along the route so you'll get there very much quicker than you would in a hired carriage."

"Of course you are right," Indira agreed.

"We all have to put our best foot forward, M'Lady, in an emergency."

"I am very, very grateful, and please, will you make quite sure that nobody realises I have left until tomorrow, when I shall be already on my way to London? I will write a note to His Lordship and to Lord Frodham. I know they will understand the circumstances which make me wish to leave at once."

"I think that's very considerate of you, M'Lady," Mrs. Baker said. "There're far too many of those who don't think of other people and are only too ready to inflict their own sufferings upon them."

Without saying any more Mrs. Baker left the room, and a few minutes later Emily and another housemaid came in to start packing Indira's clothes into the three trunks she had brought with her.

She was sitting at the *secretaire* which stood in a corner of her bedroom, and it took her a little time to write two notes, for she had to be very careful what she said.

She was determined to save both Charles and Jimmy from any repercussions arrising from their plot to bring her to Ardsley Hall, for she knew, now that she had seen him, that the Marquis was not a man who would tolerate being made a fool of or deceived.

It struck her that it had been very stupid of Charles and Jimmy to have attempted such a thing in the first place, seeing how much they enjoyed taking part in his Steeple-Chase.

Then with a little smile she thought that if they were really her brothers they were behaving exactly as she would have expected, being young enough to think their plot was fun, without really counting the consequences.

She thought very carefully what she would say, and once again had the idea that her father was guiding her hand as she wrote:

My Lord,

It is difficult for me to tell You how much I have enjoyed Your Hospitality and what a Joy and Delight it has been to ride "Meteor."

I am only ashamed that I deceived Lord Frodham and Sir James, when after they so valiantly rescued me I informed them that my Name was Lady Mary Combe.

This is not true, and my only Excuse is that when they suggested, because there seemed to be no alternative, bringing me to Ardsley Hall, I expected to feel over-awed by Your Lordship and the Company in which I would find myself. I therefore was presumptuous enough not to wish to be seen at a disadvantage. I hope You will understand, and Forgive me.

I learnt after the race was over that Somebody very close and dear to me has died, and I therefore have to leave for London immediately.

I have no wish to disrupt, and perhaps cast a gloom over, the Celebrations Your Lordship has planned with such care, and which I know everybody will enjoy.

It may seem exceedingly impertinent to borrow Your carriage, Your horses, and one of Your housemaids, but there really was no other alternative, and once again, I can only beg Your forgiveness, and thank You from the bottom of my Heart.

I shall never forget the Days I have spent at Ardsley Hall and seeing your T'ang horse, who will, I know, be often in my Dreams.

Thank you, thank you, My Lord, and please forgive me.

I remain, yours gratefully,
* and penitently,*
*   Indira Rowlandson.*

As she finished the letter, Indira read it through and decided that although there were things she might have added or subtracted, there was really no time to write any more.

Quickly she wrote another letter:

Dear Charles and Jimmy,

I enclose a letter for the Marquis, which I think will explain the whole Position without involving either of you.

I can never thank You both enough for being so kind, helpful, and protective towards me. I cannot bear to think of what might have Happened to me if You had not brought me Here. Now you must not be involved any more in my Affairs, and I know that I can manage them myself. Once I get to London I will find people who knew Papa to help me.

Please do not try to find me, and if Mr. Jacobson approaches you, deny all knowledge of where I have gone, but merely say that you do not expect ever to see me again. I think in those Circumstances that his Writs, if that is what they are, will be useless and if what he really wants is Money he will be unable to obtain it if he cannot find me.

Thank You both for being so kind and protective when I needed it most, and I shall think about you with Gratitude for the rest of my Life.

I remain forever in your Debt,
Indira

Indira folded the letter she had written to the Marquis, left it unsealed, and, having written his name on it, placed it with the one for Charles and Jimmy in an envelope large enough to hold them both.

She then addressed it to Charles and left it on the *secretaire,* and hurriedly changed into her travelling-gown and cloak.

By this time the sun had sunk, but she knew there would still be enough light for her to drive some miles from Ardsley Hall before it was dark.

She was just tying the ribbons of her bonnet under her chin when Mrs. Baker came hurrying back into the room.

"Everything's arranged, M'Lady," she said. "I've sent a message to His Lordship to say you're tired after the race and won't be joining his guests at dinner, and the carriage is waiting at a side-door."

"Thank you, Mrs. Baker, you are so very kind," Indira said.

"I've arranged for Johnson to go with you, M'Lady. She's one of our oldest housemaids and is used to travelling. She's waiting downstairs, M'Lady, and there are two footmen outside ready to take down Your Ladyship's luggage."

At Mrs. Baker's command the two men came into the bedroom, picked up the trunks which the housemaids had just finished strapping down, and carried them away.

Indira gave the two maids such a large tip that they were almost incoherent with gratitude, curtseying to her several times, before escorted by Mrs. Baker she went along the corridors of the house and down a staircase which led to the side-door.

Here waiting for her was an elderly maid correctly dressed in a black bonnet and shawl.

"This is Johnson, M'Lady," Mrs. Baker said. "She'll look after you for as long as you want her, then she'll return here with the carriage."

Indira put out her hand to thank Mrs. Baker, who said:

"You are too young and too pretty, M'Lady, to suffer, and I'll be thinking of you and praying that all'll go well for you in the future."

The way she spoke Indira found very moving, and she answered:

"Thank you, Mrs. Baker, and it is not only His Lordship who has made me very welcome since I came to Ardsley Hall, but all of you who have looked after me and been so kind."

She then went through the door and out to where the carriage was waiting.

It was a closed barouche drawn by two horses, and there were a coachman and a footman on the box. As she waved good-bye to Mrs. Baker, she thought how lucky she was to be travelling in such comfort rather than in the inferior type of vehicle she would have to hire at a Posting-Inn.

As they went down the drive and she turned to look back at the house, she felt as if a chapter in her life was closing and she was leaving something which strangely meant a great deal to her, to set off once again into the unknown.

The lights in the windows of the great house glowed golden in the fading light, and involuntarily her thoughts went to the T'ang horse in the Library.

The horse, she thought, had changed her whole attitude towards life, and she felt a sharp pang of regret and an even deeper emotion that she must leave in such a furtive manner.

Then she knew almost as if somebody were telling her so that it was not only the horse she minded leaving but its owner, the Marquis.

He had been her guide, her Guru, and had directed her back to the right path, which she should never have left in the first place.

There was so much more she wanted to learn from him, so much she felt he could tell her, and yet because Charles and James must not be hurt by Mr. Jacobson, she had to leave him without even saying good-bye.

The horses had passed under the oak trees which bordered the drive, and now the house was gradually being obscured by their branches.

Ahead were the massive gold-tipped gates with their attendant lodges and she knew that in a few seconds more the house would be lost to her sight forever.

Then, without her conscious volition, her heart said:

"Good-bye, my guide, my Master, and my love!"

Incredibly, she was aware that she was speaking to the Marquis.

Indira arrived in London on Tuesday morning about noon.

It had been a long journey but a comfortable one, because the Marquis's coachman did not hurry his horses but drove them smoothly and with great care.

Indira stayed three nights at the best Posting-Inns on the way, and as she was travelling with the Marquis's servants she was received with great respect, and was automatically given a bedroom with a room next door for her maid, and a private Parlour.

Because she had no wish to be alone, Johnson had supper with her and proved to be a most interesting source of information about Ardsley Hall and the distinguished guests who were entertained there.

"Forty-five years I've been at the Hall, M'Lady," Johnson said in her prim voice, "and I've seen many changes, and not all of them for the better. But I can honestly say that it's a happy house, and we're very proud of it."

Because Indira was genuinely interested in what the maid had to say, she drew her out and thought when she went up to bed that she had not really missed being at the Marquis's dinner-party.

On Sunday night it was difficult to concentrate on what Johnson was saying, because she kept wondering what Charles and Jimmy had thought when they learnt she had disappeared, and whether the Marquis himself was glad to be rid of her.

She knew it was really her fault that Lady Sinclair had lost her temper and raged at him, and she felt too that he would be annoyed to learn that she had deceived him by giving a false name and pretending to be a titled Lady.

"It is the sort of behaviour he despises utterly!" she told herself.

She hoped that Charles and Jimmy would not be so foolish as to reveal that they were aware of her true identity.

If they did so, it would completely destroy her plan to save them not only from Mr. Jacobson but also from offending the Marquis.

"I am sure, Papa," she said to her father in the darkness, "that I have done the only sporting thing I can do and that you approve. At the same time, I would like to have stayed at Ardsley Hall a little longer and had another talk with the Marquis."

It was not really until Sunday night that she admitted to herself that what she felt for him was very different from anything she had ever felt for any other man.

She had often talked to her father about falling in love, and he had said to her:

"You must not be in a hurry, my darling. As you are very beautiful as well as rich, there will be dozens, if not hundreds, of men who will lay their hearts at your feet, but I am determined to make quite sure that the man you marry is somebody who loves you for yourself—the real you, whom I know and adore."

Thinking back, Indira understood exactly what her father had meant, for until now she had never been alone with a man and there had been no question of flirtations or of anyone making love to her.

Because they were travelling about so much, this was understandable, and also since the parties they had attended were always given for her father, Indira was usually the youngest person present.

She had known that one of his reasons for coming to England was that he wanted her to lead a more social life than they had managed to do in the East, and to meet what he sometimes called "the right type of men."

"What do you mean by that, Papa?" she had asked once.

"You will know what I mean when you meet one," he replied.

She knew now he would have approved of the Marquis, who was a Gentleman in every sense of the word.

He was also a magnificent rider and sportsman, and, unexpectedly—yet of course it must be attributed to fate—he was somebody who had understood what the T'ang horse had meant to her, and the Chinese verses that had been written centuries ago.

"I found him, Papa," she said in her heart, "but I have . . . lost him . . . again. And now I understand what you were talking about."

But to understand did not alleviate the strange pain that she felt in her heart when she thought about the Marquis, and an irrepressible longing to go to him with her troubles and beg for his help.

She knew he would have understood the problems of arriving alone in England without her father, and that he would have dealt very effectively with the traitor Jacobson. At the same time, she was also sure that the Marquis would expect them to find her relatives.

"It cannot be so difficult if I think about it," she told herself.

When she awoke early on Tuesday morning, she had the feeling that once again her father was directing her in doing what was right.

Having breakfasted, she and Johnson went into the yard of the Posting-Inn, where the carriage was waiting for them.

The footman, as he handed Indira into it, asked:

"Where would you wish me to take you, M'Lady, when we reach London?"

As if her father prompted her, Indira gave him the answer.

* * *

501

Early on Monday morning the Marquis had said good-bye to the last of his guests, and as they drove away in Phaetons, travelling Chariots, and Chaises, he walked swiftly across the Hall towards his Study.

He entered it to find Charles and Jimmy waiting for him, both of them looking slightly apprehensive.

"I asked you to wait," the Marquis said without preamble, "until my other guests had departed, so that I could talk to you about Lady Mary, or shall we call her Indira Rowlandson?"

The way he spoke without innuendo in his voice brought a feeling of relief to the young men listening to him.

The Marquis walked to stand with his back to the mantelpiece as he said:

"Suppose you sit down and tell me where she has gone?"

"I am afraid we have no idea," Charles replied.

There was a frown between the Marquis's eyes as he said:

"Are you telling me that she did not give you an address?"

"No."

"But surely you must have some idea which relative has died and caused her to leave in that precipitate manner?"

"I am afraid the answer is again 'No,'" Jimmy said before Charles could speak. "In fact, when we saw her after the race, she did not mention that she was thinking of leaving. She said that we could talk the next day and decide where she should go when we took her to London."

"So that was what you intended to do?" the Marquis asked.

Charles said quickly:

"She had talked of going to some people who live not far away in the country, but I gathered that since she had been here she had changed her mind."

It sounded a little lame, but the Marquis merely said:

"Well, perhaps my Coachman will be able to enlighten us further, but if for the moment you are as ignorant about her arrangements as I am, then there is nothing further to discuss."

"No, nothing," Charles agreed firmly, "but as Jimmy and I are going to London, we will certainly see if we can find her."

The Marquis did not reply, and rising to his feet Charles said a little diffidently:

"I am sorry, My Lord, that you should have been deceived in any way."

"I suppose you have never heard of Miss Rowlandson's father?"

"Rowlandson is quite a common name," Charles replied. "I do not expect he is any relation of the Cartoonist."

As Jimmy thought that any further probing on the part of the Marquis might be dangerous, he interposed to say:

"I think we should be starting for London, My Lord, and if we do hear anything about Indira's whereabouts, we will of course, if you are interested, let you know."

"You can leave a message for me at White's," the Marquis said sharply.

They said good-bye and thanked him for the Steeple-Chase and for entertaining them so well, but they both thought as they spoke that the Marquis was not really attending to what they were saying, but seemed to be preoccupied by his own thoughts.

Only when they were driving off in Charles's Phaeton did Jimmy say:

"Indira certainly got us out of that difficulty very cleverly, but what are we going to do about Jacobson?"

"Nothing," Charles said. "She is right, and I have the feeling he will not make a scene at Ardsley Hall, although he may try to get in touch with us in London."

"How do you think he found us in the first place?"

Before Charles could answer, he exclaimed:

"But of course! You gave your name to the Inn-Keeper. I thought at the time it was unnecessary."

"That is easy for you to say now," Charles replied. "But you know as well as I do that if he had thought us ordinary travellers he would not have produced his best brandy, which you were only too delighted to pour down your throat!"

Jimmy laughed.

"Well, another time you should travel incognito. I can see only too clearly what happened. Jacobson learnt who we were and that we had taken Indira with us. Your groom would have boasted in the stables where we were going. And we were near enough to the Hall to have everybody talking about the Steeple-Chase."

"You are certainly making some good deductions about what occurred in the past," Charles remarked, "but that does not bring us any nearer to finding Indira in the future."

"Do you intend to find her?" Jimmy asked.

"Of course I intend to find her. You know as well as I do that she can no more look after herself than can a babe in arms."

"All the same," Jimmy expostulated, "it was very clever of her to take the Marquis's carriage to London, and one of the maids as a Chaperone to look after her."

"How did you find out all that?" Charles asked curiously.

"I asked the Butler and the Housekeeper. I suspect there had already been enquiries by the Marquis as to how she had left."

"I think she might have told us what she was doing," Charles complained.

"If you think about it logically," Jimmy said, "you will realise that she was thinking of you and me and saving us from being mixed up with Jacobson."

"Yes, that is true," Charles agreed, "and there are very few women who would be so unselfish."

Before Jimmy could speak he added:

"But dammit! I wish she had trusted me! I fear she will get into a lot of trouble if she is on her own, and we will not be there to save her."

The Marquis, as it happened, was thinking very much the same thing.

Now that he knew Indira was not Lady Mary Combe as she had pretended to be, it made him even more apprehensive about her than he would have been otherwise.

Although, as Lord Wrotham had said, she certainly did not look as if she had come from India, he was astute enough to realise that there were many things in England that were strange to her, and that what he accepted as a matter of course, she regarded with curiosity.

'She is so young and so lovely,' he thought, 'It is impossible for her to be on her own.'

He wished now he had questioned Charles and Jimmy far more closely than he had, but he had felt slightly uncomfortable about revealing how very interested he was in Indira.

He also suspected that part of what they had told him had been untrue, although he had no logical reason for thinking so.

What had worried him ever since her arrival seemed now to grow more complicated and more puzzling, so that he went over every conversation he had had with her, and at the end of it was only more bewildered than he had been at the beginning.

It seemed extraordinary that anyone as lovely and as expensively gowned as Indira should be travelling alone, and having appeared from nowhere had vanished into nowhere without his being able to do anything about it.

As he had every intention of finding her, the Marquis concentrated his thoughts on her all the time he was travelling to London.

He had perfected a means of travelling with great speed when it was necessary.

He left the Hall, driving himself in a light Phaeton with six horses. Only a Corinthian with his expertise could have managed such a large team on the main roads and driven until it was dark at a record pace.

He then had an excellent dinner which had been provided by his own Chef at a Posting-Inn, and when he finished, a closed travelling Chariot drawn by a team of four was waiting for him.

Driven by his most experienced Coachman all through the night–fortunately there was a moon–the Marquis slept peacefully until dawn.

After a bath and breakfast he set off again, driving another Phaeton with four perfectly matched horses, which reached London by one o'clock.

At Ardsley House in Park Lane, the Marquis changed his clothes before setting out again, in another Phaeton and with fresh horses, for Whitehall.

He was not feeling tired after the long hours of driving and admitted to himself that the reason for his haste could be expressed in one word– Indira.

The Marquis had always tried to be honest with himself and his feelings.

In fact, he had always known that he despised quite enough of what he found in the world about him and was therefore scrupulously frank when he faced his own emotions about anything or anybody.

Now he admitted, although with reluctance, that his search for Indira was serious to the point where not only his brain was involved but also his heart.

He supposed that he had really fallen in love with her when he had seen her come into the Drawing-Room accompanied by Charles and Jimmy and thought she was the most beautiful girl he had ever seen in his whole life.

Then when he talked to her he had found her so refreshingly different from what he had expected, but he had also been aware that she was in fear of something.

He had been intrigued to the point where he had found it hard to be aware of the existence of any other woman in the room.

He had known when his feelings for Lady Sinclair had altered so suddenly and completely that there must be some reason for it. At the same time, it was something he did not wish to put into words, even though his instinct said it for him.

Now that he had lost Indira and she had vanished in that unexpected and unaccountable manner, he knew he had to find her again.

When after breakfast on Sunday morning he read the letter she had written to him, his impulse had been to rage at everybody in the house for not having informed him that one of his guests had left so suddenly.

But because he had exceptional self-control, when he sent for Mrs. Baker he had appeared to accept with approval the arrangements she had made when Indira had told her she must go to London.

"Her Ladyship was thinking of Your Lordship," Mrs. Baker said, "and I said to her it was very considerate, and many ladies'd want sympathy and condolences, and would be thinking of no-one but themselves."

She thought the Marquis looked approving and went on:

"Although I were worried, M'Lord, that anyone so young and so beautiful should go off alone in such a manner, there was nothing I could do but send Johnson with Her Ladyship, and I asked for one of Your Lordship's most reliable and ablest Coachmen, knowing he would see there was no trouble on the journey."

"That was very sensible of you, Mrs. Baker," the Marquis said. "But Her Ladyship did not tell you exactly where she was staying in London?"

"No, Your Lordship. But the Coachman'll know where when he gets back."

"Yes, of course," the Marquis agreed.

He knew that having deposited Indira he would have taken the horses to the stables behind Ardsley House.

As he was changing his clothes he sent a footman to the Mews, and when he came downstairs it was to find Jackson, a middle-aged man who was an excellent driver, waiting for him in the Hall.

"Good-afternoon, Jackson."

"Art'noon, M'Lord."

"Did you have a good journey up from the country?"

"Aye, M'Lord, very good. We've just arrived, and them new bays be shapin' up well."

"I am glad to hear it," the Marquis answered. "Her Ladyship was not upset by the journey?"

"Nay, M'Lord."

There was a little pause before the Marquis asked:

"Where did you put Her Ladyship down, Jackson?"

"It so 'appens, M'Lord, that Her Ladyship asks me to leave her at some Livery Stables on the outskirts o' London."

The Marquis stared at Jackson in astonishment. Then he asked:

"What was the reason for that?"

"Oi've no idea, M'Lord. 'Cept that's wot 'Er Ladyship asks."

"And when you left her there did you just drive away?"

"Aye, M'Lord."

The Marquis did not speak, and after a moment the Coachman said:

"Oi 'opes I done right, M'Lord, Oi only done wot 'Er Ladyship asks."

"Yes, yes, that was quite right."

The Marquis walked to the front door and outside to where his Phaeton was waiting.

As he climbed into it he thought despairingly that Indira was determined to cover her tracks and that it was going to be more difficult than he had expected to find her again.

However, he drove to the Colonial Office and asked to see Earl Bathurst, who agreed to see him immediately.

The Marquis was aware that the various territories acquired by the British over generations were administered partly by the Secretaries of

State for War and for the Colonies, and partly by great Chartered Companies.

The Earl, who was the Colonial Secretary of State, rose at his entrance and said:

"I am surprised to see you, Ardsley. I thought you were in the country."

"I have just come back to London," the Marquis replied, "and I have one or two questions I would like to ask you."

Earl Bathurst smiled jovially and settled himself comfortably in his arm-chair.

"Ask away," he said.

"First," the Marquis said, "is the Earl of Farncombe dead?"

"Dead? Of course not! He is very much alive, and doing exceedingly good work in India."

"That is what I thought," the Marquis said as if to himself.

"Strange man, all the same. Spent most of his life in the East, and came into the title unexpectedly as the last Earl had no son."

However, the Marquis was not listening, and as Earl Bathurst stopped he asked:

"Have you ever heard in India of a man called Rowlandson?"

The Earl stared at him.

"Do you mean 'Rajah' Rowlandson?"

" 'Rajah'?"

"A nickname," Earl Bathurst explained. "They tell me it is very apt because he is so rich, so important, that even the natives think of him as a Prince."

The Marquis leant forward in his chair.

"Tell me more about him."

The Earl laughed.

"That is going to take a while. He is one of those phenomena that crop up now and again and defy all the laws of average."

"In what way?"

"Well, let me think—what can I tell you about 'Rajah' Rowlandson?" Earl Bathurst asked. "He has made himself the biggest private ship-owner in the East, the biggest conveyor of cargos of all sorts and descriptions. He provides anything and everything anybody wants with a speed which leaves all his rivals gasping, and he is indispensable to the Army, the Navy, and anybody else you like to mention."

He saw the incredulous look on the Marquis's face and added:

"You look surprised, Ardsley, and I do not blame you. But what I am telling you is the gospel truth. Rowlandson is a law unto himself, and there is nobody quite like him—or was. I suppose you know he is dead."

"I had heard that," the Marquis murmured, as the Earl was obviously expecting an answer.

"Died quite recently on the voyage home," Earl Bathurst went on. "I received the information only two days ago. It is a tragedy, a great tragedy, and God knows we have no-one to replace him."

"Do you mean to say that we used him—the British?" the Marquis queried.

"Of course we did!" Earl Bathurst replied. "If our Armies anywhere in the East wanted cannons, guns, tents, or boots, Rowlandson could get them there quicker than anyone else could provide them! The East India Company, with whom he originally worked, found him invaluable."

"Who was he before he started on this strange career?" the Marquis asked.

The Earl laughed.

"You may well ask. The Rowlandsons are a distinguished and respected family in Northumberland. For generations they have gone into the County Regiment, and Rowlandson's father actually became a General! But when 'Rajah' went out to India as the Subaltern, the disorganisation and inefficiency of the ships which brought in the requirements of the troops made him start off on another career."

The Earl paused before he added:

"I believe he borrowed the money from some Indian Nabob and multiplied it a thousand times when he paid it back. Anyway, he is a man who will be greatly missed, not only by a great number of people in the East but also by ourselves."

"Do you know anything about his family," the Marquis asked, "or his relations, and where they can be found in England?"

The Earl shook his head.

"I have not the slightest idea. When I heard 'Rajah' Rowlandson was coming home, I was surprised. He has not been back for years."

There was a long silence. Then the Marquis said in a tone that was surprisingly anxious:

"Do you happen to know the name of Rowlandson's Bank?"

The Earl smiled.

"Now that is an easy question. Of course I do! It is called the Oriental-British Bank. You will find it in Lombard Street. In fact, he owns it!"

CHAPTER SEVEN

———— ❧ ————

INDIRA WAS FRIGHTENED.

Sitting in the Manager's office at the Oriental-British Bank, she found that things were not going as she had expected.

The carriage she had hired from the Livery Stable had moved depressingly slowly, but it had given her time to think out exactly what she should do. In fact, she had been turning it over and over in her mind ever since leaving Ardsley Hall.

She felt sure that the Bank Manager, who had been appointed to the Bank by her father, would be able to help her in every way and first of all to find her somewhere to stay.

She was well aware that she could not stay in an Hotel alone, and she thought perhaps he would be able to recommend some respectable woman, or perhaps even a Lady, who would take her in until such time as she could contact her relations, who again she hoped would be known to him.

However, she felt that she was constricted at every turn by the fact that her father had communicated everything he wished done in England to his Solicitors, and she knew she must have the Bank's support to help her to deal with Jacobson.

When she arrived in Lombard Street she told the carriage she had hired to wait with her luggage, and entering the Bank she asked to be taken immediately to the Manager.

There seemed at first to be some doubt as to whether he would see her. But when she gave her name, a clerk, realising who she was, bowed her obsequiously into a large, important-looking office, where the Manager was seated behind a desk.

When she looked at him, Indira felt her heart sink, for he was an Asian.

She thought it was what she might have expected, remembering that her father had always maintained that when it came to the handling of money, there were none more intelligent and quicker-brained than the Asians.

Yet she had never envisaged that the Bank Manager in England would be one, and she knew that in consequence he would be unable to help her to find suitable accommodations.

Having lived in the East so long, she knew that Asians and Europeans seldom visited one another in their private houses and it would be impossible for her to stay with one as a guest.

The Manager, having commiserated with her over her father's death, expressing most eloquently the consternation and distress it had caused in the Bank, Indira then said:

"Now, Mr. Mendi, I need your help."

"You must be well aware, Miss Rowlandson, that it will be a pleasure to help you in every possible way I can," the Manager replied.

"The first thing I want is a list of the names and addresses of my father's relatives."

The Bank Manager looked surprised before he answered:

"I am afraid I cannot help you there, Miss Rowlandson. I always understood your father directed all his personal affairs through his Solicitors, Lawson, Cruikshank and Jacobson."

"That is true," Indira replied, "but for reasons I will explain later, I do not wish to communicate with them at the moment."

"That makes things very difficult," Mr. Mendi said, "but I will certainly look in your father's files and see if there is anything in them that might be of help."

It took some time to find the files, and when they were brought in there were so many of them that Indira thought despairingly that it might be days or weeks before she had an answer to this question alone.

As she watched Mr. Mendi turn over the closely written pages, which she could see across the desk all concerned money, she began to think frantically that time was passing, and she had no idea where she could stay the night.

Mr. Mendi put down a fat file and took up another.

"I regret, Miss Rowlandson," he said in his precise manner, "that what I have here appears to be concerned only with your father's transfer of monies from one place to another, and there are no personal details of any sort."

This was what Indira was already certain he was about to say, and she was trying to formulate in her mind exactly how she should ask him where she could go when she left the Bank, when the door opened and a rather flustered-looking clerk said:

"There is a gentleman who insists on seeing you, Sir . . ."

Before he had finished the sentence, the gentleman in question, who was behind him, had pushed his way into the room.

Indira looked round indifferently, somewhat annoyed by the interruption.

Then when she saw who was there, she gave a little cry of unrepressed joy, and without thinking she jumped to her feet and ran towards the Marquis, putting out both her hands towards him.

He felt her fingers tremble in his, and he knew she was afraid in the same way she had been the first time he had touched her when she came to Ardsley Hall.

"You are . . . here!" Indira said in a low voice. "I need your . . . help."

"I thought perhaps you would," the Marquis replied.

He looked down at her and for a moment it seemed as if there was no need for words, and they were speaking to each other without them.

Then the Marquis walked towards the desk and held out his hand to the Manager.

"I am the Marquis of Ardsley," he said, "and I feel that as Miss Rowlandson has just arrived in this country, she needs not only your assistance but mine as well."

Mr. Mendi bowed before he replied:

"I am finding it very difficult, My Lord, to locate the late Mr. Rowland-son's relatives, so Your Lordship's help in the matter would be very welcome."

"Surely your father's Solicitors would have their addresses?" the Marquis suggested.

Indira hesitated and to his surprise she looked embarrassed.

"It is . . . impossible for me to . . . communicate with them at the . . . moment," she said when she realised he was waiting for an answer.

"Why?" the Marquis enquired.

At that moment there was another interruption as a clerk came into the office through another door and with a word of apology went to the Manager's side to say something that only he could hear, and hand him a piece of paper.

The Marquis said quietly to Indira:

"How could you go away without telling me where you were going?"

"H-how did you . . . find me?" she parried.

"I have been to see Earl Bathurst at the Colonial Office, who told me a great deal about your father."

Indira blushed and did not look at the Marquis as she said:

"I . . . I am sorry I . . . deceived you."

The Marquis was about to reply, when Mr. Mendi interrupted by saying:

"This is very strange, and forgive me, Miss Rowlandson, but I suppose this cheque for such a large amount is signed by you?"

Indira started and took from the Manager what the clerk had just handed to him and saw that it was a cheque made out for ten thousand pounds and signed "Indira Rowlandson."

The signature was not in the least like her own and there was no need to ask who had presented it.

"It is a forgery!" she said firmly.

"A forgery?" Mr. Mendi exclaimed.

The Marquis bent forward and took the cheque from Indira's hands.

"Is the man who presented this still waiting?" he asked the clerk.

"Yes, Sir."

"Then call the Porters and have him apprehended immediately," the Marquis ordered.

The clerk looked at Mr. Mendi for confirmation and the Bank Manager nodded.

"We must certainly question him as to where he comes from and who has sent him, so do as His Lordship says."

The clerk hurried from the room and Mr. Mendi sat down again in his chair.

"Have you any idea, Miss Rowlandson," he enquired, "who could have forged this cheque?"

Indira drew in her breath and knew there was nothing she could do now but tell the truth.

Driving beside the Marquis in his Phaeton through the crowded streets of the city, she thought with a sense of relief which was almost overwhelming that she no longer had to be afraid.

The Marquis seemed to take over everything that concerned her in a manner which left nobody in any doubt that he was in command, and she knew it was only a question of hours before Mr. Jacobson would be imprisoned awaiting trial.

Before they left the Bank, the Marquis told Mr. Mendi that all communications relating to Mr. Rowlandson's Estate and anything that concerned his daughter were to be sent to Ardsley House in Park Lane.

As they were bowed out into Lombard Street, the Marquis's groom told the carriage Indira had hired to follow them.

The Marquis then drove in a manner which made her feel that he had taken all her burdens from her, and as in her dream she was flying up to the moon.

Since he was concentrating on his horses, they hardly spoke before they arrived in Park Lane, and as she walked across a marble Hall and into a large, comfortable Study lined with books, she felt it had the same atmosphere as the Marquis's house in the country, and it was almost as if she had come home.

He followed her into the Study and said:

"I suggest you take off your bonnet and coat. I am going to give you a glass of champagne. I feel you need it."

As he spoke with what she felt was a kinder voice than he had ever used to her before, she felt her love for him welling up inside her like a shaft of sunlight illuminating everything and sweeping away the shadows.

She had known when he came so unexpectedly into the Manager's office at the Bank that he was like an Arch-angel delivering her from her fears and difficulties, and most of all from the terror of being alone.

She told herself severely that he must never be aware how much she loved him, and that she would never behave in a possessive, over-intimate manner like Lady Sinclair and the other ladies who had fawned over him in the country.

Obediently she put her bonnet and her blue coat down on a chair and, tidying her hair with both hands, walked across the room to stand at the window looking out onto the garden which was at the back of the house.

The fragrance of the flowers in the beds, and the trees with their leaves green against the sky, made her think of the beauty of Ardsley Hall, and she said spontaneously:

"Papa told me how beautiful England was in the summer, but I was so young when I last saw it that I had forgotten."

"I am glad you think it beautiful," the Marquis replied.

He walked to her side and handed her a glass of champagne, and as she took it from him he said:

"I think we should drink a toast because this is a very special day for both of us."

She looked at him in surprise and he added:

"I have been clever enough to find you again, and as you have already said, you needed me."

"I was not . . . expecting the Manager of Papa's Bank to be an Asian. I had assumed he would be an Englishman and hoped he might invite me to . . . stay in his home until I could find . . . one of my relatives."

"You will stay here with me," the Marquis said, "and that is something I want to talk to you about."

"There is . . . something I must tell you . . . first," Indira interrupted.

"What is it?"

"Although I . . . deceived you by . . . pretending to be Lady Mary Combe . . . it was not quite so . . . wrong as it must . . . seem."

She spoke a little hesitatingly, finding it difficult to put into words what she wished to say.

Because she loved the Marquis, she could not bear him to believe that she had called herself a Lady of Title just because she was a snob.

She had not told Charles and Jimmy, but she thought now she must tell the Marquis that she had had a reason for choosing such a title.

"I am sure it is of no importance," the Marquis said, "but of course I will listen to anything you wish to tell me."

"Lady Mary Combe is my . . . cousin, and the Earl of Farncombe is my . . . uncle."

She thought the Marquis still did not understand, and she said quickly:

"Mama was his sister . . . but she died before he became so . . . important, and I knew when I . . . used Mary's name that she would not . . . mind my . . . doing so."

"I am glad you have told me," the Marquis said, "although quite frankly, it is not of the least importance. What I really want is to be told why you minded what I thought."

"Of course I minded!" Indira said quickly. "When you have been so kind, not only when we were in the country . . . but in helping me . . . now at this . . . moment . . ."

There was a pause, then the Marquis said in a deep voice:

"Have you asked yourself why I should be so concerned about you?"

The way he spoke and the fact that he was standing so near to her made Indira feel a little quiver go through her.

Because she was afraid the Marquis might become aware of her feelings, she moved away from him to the centre of the room, where she set down her glass of champagne.

The Marquis did not follow her but merely watched her, thinking that the sunlight on her hair was the most beautiful thing he had ever seen.

Unexpectedly he asked:

"Are you still afraid of me, Indira?"

"A . . . afraid?" she questioned.

"You were afraid when you arrived at Ardsley Hall," he said, "and I knew during dinner you were afraid of Wrotham. When I rescued you from him in the Library, you told me that you hated men, and yet you did not seem to be afraid of me."

He waited, until Indira said in a very low voice, as if she was tracing in her mind a sequence of events:

"You showed me your . . . Chinese poems . . . and the T'ang horse . . . and because of what . . . you said . . . everything changed."

"Everything?"

"What I had been thinking and feeling. You . . . guided and . . . inspired me."

He drew in his breath. Then slowly, as if he was still afraid he might frighten her, he walked from the window to where she was standing by a round table on which there were a number of books.

She looked not at him but at what lay on the table. As he drew near to her he knew that she quivered and he was almost sure it was not with fear.

He stood for a moment in silence before he said:

"When I received your letter on Sunday morning and thought I would never find you again, I went to the Library and took down the book of poems we had been reading. I opened it at random, Indira, and read a poem which seemed to me to be the answer to what I was feeling."

He paused, and as if Indira knew she had to make some response to what he had said, she raised her eyes slowly and, he thought, a little shyly, and then found it impossible to look away.

Softly the Marquis said:

> *Kuan-kuan cry the ospreys*
> *On the islet in the river.*
> *Lovely is the good lady,*
> *Fit bride for our lord.*

Indira did not move as he finished speaking but only waited, and he saw a sudden light come into her strange eyes.

Then as the colour rose in her cheeks like the breaking of the dawn, she made a little incoherent sound and moved towards him.

His arms went round her and she hid her face against his shoulder as he held her very close to him.

"It was a message, my darling," he said, "which I feel neither you nor I can disobey. How soon will you marry me?"

For a moment she was very still. Then almost like the rhythmic movement of the sea or the sound of music, she lifted her face to his and he found her lips.

Because he knew it was the first time she had been kissed and was afraid of reawakening her fear, he kissed her very gently, almost without passion, as one might kiss a child.

Then as he felt her whole body quiver against him, and as he knew her lips, soft and sweet, responded to his, his kiss became more insistent, more possessive.

He knew as he held her close and still closer that the feelings she aroused in him were different from any emotion he had ever known before in his whole life.

Somewhere at the back of his mind he realised that what they were feeling for each other was part of the poems they had read and of the vitality and vigour of the T'ang horses.

It was the beauty of his home and everything that he had once reached out to when he was young, then had lost when he grew older and cynical.

To Indira it was all the wonder, beauty, and glory of the East and the spiritual world she had sensed beneath it. It was inexpressible in words except when she talked with her father, and then with the Marquis.

She knew now that all her studies with her Professors, and what she had felt in the Temples and in the beauty of every country she had visited, could be expressed in one word—Love.

Only when she felt as if the Marquis had swept her up and they were riding amongst the stars did he raise his head and ask in a strangely unsteady voice:

"What do you feel about me now?"

Indira spoke what was in her heart as she said:

"I . . . love you . . . I love you! I know . . . the . . . hidden meaning of your poems . . . is my . . . love for . . . you."

The Marquis did not reply but kissed her with slow, demanding, passionate kisses until her whole body vibrated to his.

Only when the world was forgotten and they were no longer human but like gods did they come back to earth as if the strain was unendurable and for the moment they must again breathe normally.

The Marquis drew Indira to a sofa, then sat down with his arms round her.

"How can I have found you so unexpectedly, when I did not believe you even existed?"

"I never . . . thought there would be a . . . man who would . . . understand what I was . . . thinking and feeling . . . except Papa."

"We have so much to discover about each other," the Marquis said, "and as it will take us a lifetime, we must be married at once so that we need not waste an hour or a day apart when we might be together."

There was a note of passion in his voice which made Indira feel as if what he said was echoed within herself.

Then she gave a sudden little cry that was different and asked:

"Are you sure you should . . . marry me?"

"I have never been so sure of anything in my life as I am that you should be my wife."

"But . . . you do not . . . understand."

"What do I not understand?"

"That perhaps I am not the . . . right person for . . . you."

The way she spoke made the Marquis look at her penetratingly before he said:

"What are you trying to tell me?"

"If I . . . tell you the . . . truth, will you . . . promise not to be . . . angry?"

"I could never be angry with you."

"Or . . . anybody else . . . concerned with . . . me?"

His arms tightened round her and she knew perceptively that he thought she was speaking of a man and was jealous.

"No, no!" she said quickly. "It is not like . . . that. It is just that I have not told you the . . . real reason why I . . . pretended to be my cousin . . . when I came to . . . Ardsley Hall."

"Tell me now."

A little hesitatingly and shyly, she told him of the bet which Charles and Jimmy had made with each other after what they had overheard him saying in White's Club.

The Marquis did not speak, and she finished by saying:

"When they asked me to . . . help them and . . . enquired as to what Papa did, I told them he was a . . . trader."

She looked up at him and now the fear was back in her eyes as she said:

519

"That is in fact what he was . . . and perhaps . . . because I am not . . . grand enough . . . when you think it over . . . you will not wish to . . . marry me."

The Marquis laughed, and it was a very happy sound.

"Can you really be so foolish as not to realise, my lovely one," he asked, "that if your father were a pedlar in Cheapside, or a small shop-keeper, I would still love you and still want to marry you? We have been together, my precious, in one life or another since the beginning of time, and we will be together through all eternity."

"You believe that . . . you really believe . . . that?"

"Of course I do!" the Marquis said. "Charles has won his bet, and I will tell him so when we next see him."

"And . . . you are not . . . angry with them?"

"How can I be anything but overwhelmingly grateful to the two young men who brought you to me?" the Marquis asked. "They shall be our first guests after we are married, and we will never arrange a Steeple-Chase without asking them to compete in it."

He smiled and pressed his lips against her forehead as he said:

"But of course you will beat them to the winning-post, my darling, and me as well."

"I have no wish to beat you at anything," Indira replied. "When I left Ardsley Hall on Saturday evening . . . as I drove down the drive . . . I said in my heart: 'Good-bye, my guide, my Master, my Love,' and that is what you will . . . always be to . . . me."

"Your Master?"

"I want you to . . . teach me about . . . love."

She hid her face against him and whispered:

"I am very ignorant . . . about . . . that, and . . . perhaps I will . . . bore you."

The Marquis was still. In all his many passionate and fiery affairs he had never known a woman who was pure and innocent.

He thought now that nothing could be more exciting or rapturous than to teach Indira, whom he loved with his heart and mind, the inestimable glory of love.

"I will teach you to love me, my adorable one," he said aloud, "to love me as much as I love you!"

"I love you overwhelmingly . . . already," she replied. "My love grows . . . every time I look at . . . you . . . every time you . . . touch me and . . . every time I . . . breathe."

The way she spoke made the Marquis pull her almost roughly against him and kiss her until they were both breathless. Then he said:

"We have to be sensible for the moment, my precious one. I insist that you stay here tonight, but because it would be impossible for me to get a Special Licence for us to be married before tomorrow morning, I must make some arrangements for you to be chaperoned."

"I want to be . . . alone with . . . you," Indira said impulsively.

"That is what I want too," the Marquis agreed, "and after tomorrow you will always be with me, and in my arms, my heart, my mind, and my–soul."

Indira gave a little cry as she said:

"How can you say such wonderful . . . perfect things to me? How can I have been so lucky as to find you when to escape . . . all men I wished to enter a Convent?"

The Marquis laughed, but at the same time, as if he was afraid he might have lost her, he pulled her closer to him.

"I doubt if there is a Convent in existence which could keep you away from me," he said, "and we both know, my darling one, that because we are aware of the Spiritual Force and the power that it gives us, we have a great deal to do in the world for other people. That is our *Karma.*"

"That is what Papa felt," Indira replied, "and he knew it was that same force of which you have just spoken which helped him to be the success he was. He said once that when he was in difficulties or when he was in doubt, he had only to link up with it, and it never failed him."

"That is what we did when I showed you my T'ang horse," the Marquis said quietly. "It spoke to you, and my poems did the same."

Indira smiled.

"I only hope I am a . . . 'fit bride for . . . our lord'!"

"You are perfect," the Marquis declared. "And you can be sure, my beautiful little love, that in this life at any rate we will never lose each other again."

He kissed her passionately, then rose to his feet.

"I have an elderly cousin," he said, "a widow who is not particularly

521

well off, and I know she would be only too delighted to come here for the night. She makes no secret of the fact that she waits hopefully in her small house in Chelsea, until I have need of her."

He smiled as he added:

"I am now sending for her, and will arrange for our wedding to take place in the Grosvenor Chapel, which is only round the corner, first thing in the morning."

Indira drew in her breath.

She loved the way he spoke in his usual authoritative manner. It gave her confidence and a feeling of security she had thought she had lost forever when her father died.

She knew that the two men she loved both had this self-confidence because it came not from themselves but from the inner power in which they believed.

The Marquis walked towards the door, but when he looked back he saw Indira looking at him with such an expression of love in her eyes that he merely stood still and held out his arms.

She ran to him as if she were a homing-pigeon, and he held her close against him to look down into her face, thinking that he had never seen anybody look so radiantly happy.

"Is it true?" she asked. "Or am I . . . dreaming that you . . . love me and your T'ang horse will . . . fly us to the . . . moon?"

"I think we are on our way there already," the Marquis said, "and after we are married and you are mine completely, my darling, we will live in a very special Heaven which every man longs for but few find."

He kissed her as he finished speaking, and Indira thought it would be impossible to know an ecstasy and rapture that was greater than what she felt already.

Then, as if he forced himself to leave her, the Marquis said:

"Go and change, my beautiful bride-to-be, and when I have made all the arrangements for our future happiness, we will have tea together in the room where my mother always sat when she and my father were alone."

"I would love . . . that."

She paused before she added very softly:

"I know without your telling me that your father and mother must have loved each other . . . very much to have . . . produced anybody as

. . . wonderful as you, and perhaps . . . one day . . . that is what we . . . shall be able to . . . say about . . . our children."

The way she spoke brought the fire into the Marquis's eyes. At the same time, it made him feel as if she were something sacred and he should kneel in front of her.

As he kissed her he knew that this was just the beginning of their happiness, and that Indira was right when she said that because their children would be born of love they too would have the power of linking up with the Spiritual Force as they were able to do.

"I love you!" he said with his lips and in his heart, and he knew that the love pulsating through both of them and which made them already one person was also Divine.

This was what he had always sought without really knowing it, and to Indira it was even more simple.

The T'ang horse had carried them to the moon in a dream which had become reality and from which neither of them would ever wake.

Diona and a Dalmatian

AUTHORS NOTE

———— ⟨⟩ ————

ORION WAS FAMOUS for his beauty and he was also a giant. He was endowed with prodigious strength and was passionately fond of hunting. He was always accompanied in his favourite sport by his dog Sirius.

Orion's love-affairs were dramatic and concerned many beautiful goddesses.

When he was killed, he was transported to the sky, where in golden armour, sword in hand, his constellation shines on winter nights. Of course, Sirius is with him.

Dalmatian dogs are aristocrats and have been in England for more than two centuries. Their country of origin has never been decided; some experts say Dalmatia, while others say India or Spain.

They were trained for generations to follow under carriages, and they are also gun-dogs. They are easily trained, are devoted companions and reliable guards, and bark only at persons, not at noises.

CHAPTER ONE

―――― ∽∾ ――――

1819

SIR HEREWARD GRANTLEY LOWERED HIMSELF with difficulty into the large armchair, and wincing with pain he lifted his gouty foot onto a stool.

Then, breathing somewhat heavily, he leant slowly against the back of the chair.

As he did so, a Dalmatian dog trotted across the room towards him, wagging his tail.

He brushed against a glass of brandy which had been placed beside Sir Hereward on a low table and knocked it to the floor where it smashed into several pieces.

Sir Hereward burst into a roar of rage.

"Will you control that damned dog of yours!" he shouted at his niece. "I have told you before, it has no right to be in the house. I will not have it here, it can stay in the kennels!"

Diona ran across the room to pick up the pieces of glass and put them into the wastepaper-basket.

"I am very sorry, Uncle Hereward," she said as she did so. "Sirius did not mean it. He was only coming to greet you because he is fond of you."

"I have enough dogs of my own without yours. Either he goes into the kennels or he will be destroyed!"

Diona gave a cry of sheer horror, and a voice from the other side of the room said:

"I think that is a good idea, Papa! Dogs are a nuisance in the house, as you say, and I have seen Sirius chasing through the woods, which would undoubtedly have upset the birds which are nesting there."

"That is not true!" Diona replied. "Sirius has never been anywhere without me, and because I know it is the breeding season, we have not been near the woods."

"I saw him with my own eyes!"

As he spoke, Diona knew her Cousin Simon was lying and the reason for it.

Ever since she had come to live in the great ugly house that belonged to her uncle, Simon had pursued her with his attentions.

When she had made it clear she would have nothing to do with him, he had become spiteful and made trouble for her.

She was well aware now that he was getting his own back over Sirius because two evenings ago he had attempted to kiss her at the top of the stairs.

She had struggled against him, and when she realised he was stronger than she was, she had stamped violently on his foot, making him yell with pain.

She had run away from him, saying as she did so:

"Leave me alone! I hate you, and if you try to touch me again I will tell Uncle Hereward!"

Because Simon had been waiting for his revenge, he rose now from the table where he had been greedily eating a large breakfast after everybody else was finished and came towards his father.

"Have the dog put down, Papa," he said. "I will tell Heywood to shoot him as he shot Rufus when he grew too old to work."

"You will not shoot my dog!" Diona exclaimed angrily. "He is young, and he does not mean to be clumsy. In fact, this is the first thing he has ever broken in the house!"

"You mean the first thing we have noticed!" Simon retorted.

Diona looked at her uncle.

"Please, Uncle Hereward, you know how much I love Sirius and how much he means to me. He is the only thing I have left that was given to me by Papa."

As she spoke, Diona knew she had made a mistake.

Sir Hereward Grantley had always disliked his younger brother because he was much more popular than he was in the County, and also because he was a better sportsman, a better shot, and far more handsome.

Sometimes Diona thought her uncle had actually been glad when her father had been killed schooling a wild, untrained horse over a high fence.

It was the sort of accident that could only have happened once in a hundred times, and it seemed impossible, since her father had been such an experienced horseman, that it should have happened to him.

The whole County had mourned Harry Grantley, and Diona thought afterwards that her mother had died at the same moment that he had! She had actually pined away and been buried within a year of his death.

This had meant, since her uncle was her Guardian, that Diona had been forced to leave the house where she and her parents had been so happy.

Her home had always seemed to be filled with sunshine, while the huge, draughty, and cold ancestral Manor House where the Grantleys had lived for three hundred years was dark and gloomy.

She had not been there long before she realised that her life was to be made a misery by her Cousin Simon.

The only point in which Sir Hereward thought himself superior to his brother was that while Harry had a daughter, he had a son.

Unfortunately, Simon was not a son of whom any father would be particularly proud.

Although he had now reached the age of twenty-four, he had the mentality of a rather stupid boy of sixteen.

He managed to excel at nothing except in his greed for food and in eating more, Diona thought, than any three men could manage to do.

Simon would be the sixth Baronet when his father died, and as there was no chance of her aunt, who was a semi-invalid, ever having any more children, Sir Hereward did everything he could to make the best of it.

He indulged Simon in every way, spoiling him, hoping that by encouraging him to be more selfish than he was already, in some miraculous manner it might turn him into a man.

It took Diona, who was very perceptive, only a few days to understand her uncle's feelings, and then she felt sorry for him.

But that did not make things any better where she was concerned.

Because in addition to being exceptionally lovely she was also intelligent, she soon realised that she irritated her uncle, and he resented her, just as when his brother Harry was alive he had resented him.

Nothing that she did pleased him, and seldom a day passed when her uncle did not swear at her, usually for some imagined fault, or just because he wished to release his pent-up feelings on somebody.

His wife lay upstairs, whining and complaining and making no real effort to recover from her ill health.

Simon was a continual disappointment, and because Sir Hereward drank too much, he was continually in pain with gout. It had swollen his leg to double its proper size and was now spreading to his hands.

Now, as if the culmination of his anger burst like a boil, he growled to his son:

"You are right. Tell Heywood to dispose of the dog this evening. I have no intention of having my shooting spoilt this autumn!"

Diona knelt down beside her uncle's chair.

"You cannot mean . . . that, Uncle Hereward," she said. "You cannot mean to be so . . . cruel when you know how . . . much Sirius means to me."

Because her voice was very soft and anguished as she pleaded with him, she felt for a moment as if Sir Hereward might relent.

Then Simon said:

"That dog chases everything! I saw him after the chickens yesterday, and if we get no eggs for breakfast it will certainly be his fault!"

"It is a lie! It is a lie!" Diona cried.

But it was Simon's intervention which made up Sir Hereward's mind.

"Give Heywood the order!" he said to his son. "And tell him to make sure the keepers shoot any animal, cat or dog, they see in the woods."

The way he spoke made Diona know that it was no use pleading with him any further.

She wanted to scream at the injustice and cruelty of what her uncle had just ordered.

She was well aware that there was a look of triumph and spiteful satisfaction in her Cousin Simon's eyes as she rose to her feet and walked with what she hoped was dignity from the Breakfast-Room.

Only when she was outside in the Hall and the door was shut behind her did she run frantically up the stairs with Sirius following her.

Not long before his death, her father had bought her Sirius as a present when he was a small wriggling puppy with, because he was more than two weeks old, the black spots already beginning to show on his white fur.

His eyes pleaded for love in a way which made Diona clasp him closely in her arms and know that he was exactly what she had always wanted.

When first her father and then her mother had died, it was Sirius who had comforted her.

He had licked her cheek and cuddled against her as she had cried helplessly and despairingly, knowing that she was completely alone in the world except for him.

There were of course other Grantley relations, but most of them did not live in the same County, and none of them were prepared to offer her a home, especially as she had no money.

Her father had spent every penny of his small capital on the horses he bought with the intention of training them, then selling them for what he hoped would be first-class prices.

The first three or four horses he bought exceeded even his expectations, and he bought more.

"It may seem extravagant," he had said to his wife, "but I have the opportunity of buying some quite unusually well-bred animals from the Estate of an old friend in Ireland who has just gone bankrupt, and I would be a fool to miss it."

"Of course you would, dearest," his wife had replied. "And nobody is cleverer than you are with horses. I am sure they will all show a huge profit."

Thinking of those of which he had already disposed, Harry Grantley was confident that this was true, and when the horses arrived they looked even more promising than he had hoped.

They were of course very wild, and breaking them in entailed patience and very hard work.

It had been great fun to watch him, Diona thought.

He would never let her ride a horse until he considered it safe, and she knew that she was an exceptionally good rider simply because she had ridden ever since she had first begun to toddle.

It was one of the horses from Ireland that had killed her father, and because most of the rest of them were still not broken in, they fetched very little money when her mother sold them.

Nevertheless, they managed to live quite comfortably during the months that followed her father's death.

At the same time, Diona was aware that her mother was growing thinner every day and found it difficult to take an interest in anything except her daughter, and it had become an effort for her to smile, let alone laugh.

Although her composure during the day was heroic, Diona was sure that she spent most of the night in tears, mourning the husband she had loved and lost.

Afterwards Diona could not help wondering if there was anything she could have done to save her mother. However, she knew that her mother had not really been physically ill.

Hers had been a mental and spiritual collapse which made it impossible for her to live without the man she had loved and who had filled her whole life to the exclusion of everything else.

'At least they were happy together!' Diona thought in the cold and misery of her uncle's house.

She had never realised before that it was not bricks and mortar which made a home, but the people who lived in it.

Grantley Hall should have been a beautiful house inside because her uncle was a rich man and the furniture and paintings he had inherited were fine examples of the various periods in which they had been added to the family collection.

But because he was a difficult and disappointed man and there was no happiness in his life, the whole place always seemed to Diona to be dark, gloomy, and as cold as the hearts of those who lived there.

The servants were old and surly, resenting the way they were spoken to and the manner in which they were given orders, but too afraid of losing their jobs to protest.

Outside in the stables there were some excellent horses, and in the kennels there were dogs.

But even they, Diona thought, because nobody cared for them as individuals, seemed to be different from the horses her father had owned and the dogs which had meant so much to her.

At first her uncle had accepted that Sirius should always be with her, sleeping beside her bed and following her wherever she went.

Then she knew that it was Simon who was putting her uncle against the dog, so that he cursed Sirius if he got in his way and would remark disagreeably that "that damned dog is eating us out of house and home."

This of course was a spiteful reference to the fact that Diona had no money of her own, and in fact, as her uncle never ceased to remind her, he had paid her father's debts after her mother's death.

Before that, Mrs. Grantley had struggled to pay off month by month anything her husband had owed, so there had not been a very large accumulation of bills.

Nevertheless, they were enough to make Sir Hereward very unpleasant about them.

He had also, Diona thought, been extremely mean about the servants her father and mother had employed, three of whom had to be pensioned off, while an elderly couple were left as caretakers in the house.

"You can stay here," Sir Hereward had told them, "until I find a purchaser to take this property off my hands. Then I suppose I shall have to try to find you a cottage, or else it will mean the Workhouse."

The way he spoke made Diona cry out in protest, but there was nothing she could do.

Although she thought it was unlikely that Sir Hereward would carry out his threat of sending them to the Workhouse, she knew how much the possibility would upset and worry them.

They would not sleep at nights for wondering what was going to happen to them.

Before she left, she assured them that she would do everything in her power to help them, if and when the house was sold.

"Personally, I think it is unlikely," she said to cheer them up. "Not many people would want to live in such an isolated district as this, and Papa loved it only because it was such a perfect place for riding."

She knew it was also because her father had thought it would be pleasant to be near his brother in the family house where he had been very happy as a boy.

He had told her so often that in his father's time there had always been a welcome for him and his friends before he went into the Army.

He had fought for a number of years before, having married somebody with whom he was overwhelmingly in love, he decided to settle down.

It was then, during the year of peace between England and France in 1802, that her father had moved into the small Manor and been ready, as he had said optimistically, to "start a large family."

Although he must have been disappointed that he was blessed with only one child and that a daughter, he had never let Diona be aware of it.

Actually, it was only after her father's death that she thought perhaps he would have preferred her to be a boy with a chance eventually of succeeding to the Baronetcy.

Of course, there was no reason why Simon would not do that, except that he was obviously not quite normal, and her uncle had no other children.

But she had told herself so often that there was no use in looking back and thinking of what might have been.

She had somehow to face the misery of everyday life at Grantley Hall and wonder frantically if she had any future.

When her uncle was particularly disagreeable to her, she would lie awake at night, wondering if there was anything she could do to earn her own living.

Alternatively, she wondered if she dared write to any of her other relatives and suggest that she might live with them.

But her father's cousins were, of course, also Uncle Hereward's, and she had a feeling that although he did not want her, he would resent her leaving him and would deliberately prevent her from doing so.

"Now that I am your Guardian you will do as I tell you," was a phrase he continually used.

It gave her the feeling that he wanted to dominate her and assert his authority simply because she was her father's daughter.

As she was very sensitive and extremely perceptive about other people, it was not always what they said which hurt her so much as what she knew they were thinking and feeling.

Because her father and mother had loved the country and never regretted missing the excitements of London, although they had both spent part of their lives in the Social World, Diona loved the country too.

Her mother had talked vaguely of presenting her at Court and taking her to Balls and Receptions once she had finished with her lessons and become a débutante.

But her father had died six months before her eighteenth birthday, and she was now getting on for nineteen without ever having been to a Ball or visiting London.

When she was a child, there had of course been parties in the County to which her mother had taken her.

But as she grew older, what she enjoyed far more was hunting in the winter, and being a spectator at the Point-to-Points and the Steeple-Chases in which her father took part.

There she met a number of what were known as the "Country Gentry," but the men who admired her father most were the Yeoman Farmers.

They called her "pretty little Miss Grantley," tipped their hats to her, and invited her into their farms to eat the fresh bread their wives had baked, spread with golden butter from their cows.

But, however kind they were, they were not exactly the sort of friends her mother had envisaged for her.

"I want you to have the same success I had when I was a débutante," Mrs. Grantley would say. "I am not being conceited, dearest, when I tell you I was greatly admired, and quite a number of very charming and wealthy young men asked my father if they could pay their addresses to me."

"Do you mean they wanted to marry you, Mama?"

"Yes, but I did not want to marry them," her mother replied. "I was waiting, although I was not aware of it, until I met your father."

"And when you did?"

"I fell in love with him! He was the most handsome, dashing, exciting man I had ever seen!"

Mrs. Grantley sighed before she said:

"I wish you could have seen him in his uniform! It was enough to make any young girl's heart beat the faster!"

"And he fell in love with you?" Diona asked.

"At first sight!" her mother replied. "And I do not think any two people could be happier than we are."

It was that happiness she missed, Diona thought, happiness that seemed as brilliant as the sunshine.

She thought she could not remember their home when the skies had been grey or the rain had beaten against the window-panes.

Now as she rushed into her bedroom followed by Sirius and shut the door, she felt as if she were fighting her way through a black fog which was suffocating her.

She flung herself down on her knees and put her arms round Sirius, feeling the tears beginning to run down her cheeks.

He was aware that something was wrong and licked her cheek, and as he did so she knew that she could not lose him. If she did she must die too, for there would be nothing left to live for.

Then as she felt Sirius's body warm and close against her, she felt something strong and resolute awaken within her that she had never known before.

She had been so unhappy when she had come to her uncle's house that she had accepted the misery of it like a cross that she must bear because there was no alternative.

When she was abused and cursed for something she had not done, she told herself there was no point in fighting and she would merely apologise humbly and promise to try to do better.

Now she knew she must rebel not only for her own sake but also to save Sirius.

She gave him another hug, and, as if he did not understand but was doing his best to help her, he licked her cheek again, wagging his tail.

Then he sat down to look up at her pleadingly as if he was suggesting that they should go for a walk and get out in the open air.

"That is what we will do, Sirius," Diona said to him. "We will go for a walk and we will not come back. Why did I not think of that before?"

She rose to her feet and locked the door, not that anybody was likely to intrude on her.

At the same time, she realised that she had to be secretive.

Then she spread out on the bed a large silk shawl that had belonged to her mother and began putting into it everything that she thought was an absolute necessity.

There was not very much, for she knew that if she had to walk a long way it would be no use taking something which would weigh her down and be too heavy to carry.

She therefore sensibly placed in the shawl only the lightest things she possessed and two muslin gowns which weighed infinitely less than anything made of a heavier material.

Nevertheless, it seemed quite a large bundle when finally she knotted it together.

She hesitated for a moment.

Then she changed her gown for her best and also put on her newest pair of shoes and her prettiest bonnet, which had belonged to her mother.

She had discarded mourning a month ago because her uncle had said in one of his rages that he disliked having a "black crow" moaning about his house.

Because she still had a little left of the money he had given her to buy mourning-clothes when she had first come to the Hall, she had bought a few pretty gowns from the nearest town.

When she appeared in them he had given his grudging approval until, as if inevitably he had to find fault, he started to complain about how much she was costing him.

However, Diona was glad now that her gowns were new, for the simple reason that they would have to last her a long time.

What was worrying her was that she had very little money left.

She had, however, though it was agony to think of parting with them, a few small pieces of jewellery which had belonged to her mother.

There was her engagement-ring, a brooch which was set with some diamonds which had been her father's present when she was born, and a bracelet, rather ugly but valuable, which her mother had inherited from her own mother and which out of sentiment she had never sold.

"If I sell them they will feed Sirius for a long time," Diona reckoned.

She put the jewellery and the money into a bag which she slipped over her wrist, then collecting her bundle whispered to Sirius to come with her as she unlocked the door.

Sirius thought he was going for a walk and started to jump for joy, but Diona quieted him and he understood.

Because he had been with her ever since he was a puppy, she had only to speak for him to obey her orders.

He never left her side, and the lies Simon had told about his behaviour were even more infuriating because there was not a vestige of truth in them.

Now, knowing it was what she wanted, Sirius walked to heel, and they hurried along the passage to a side-staircase which took them down to a back-door.

Diona avoided the kitchen-quarters because she knew that at this time of the morning the servants would be having their eleven-o'clock tea and beer, and only in the Hall would there be anybody on duty.

Once outside, she started off at a sharp pace down the back drive, which could not be seen from any of the main rooms of the house.

It was also not so wide or impressive as the front drive with its avenue of oak-trees.

She walked quickly on the grass, with Sirius exploring and searching for rabbits but keeping only a little way ahead of her and returning to her side the moment she called him.

It took Diona about ten minutes to reach the back Lodge-gates, which were not so large or well built as those which guarded the main entrance.

She knew that the old couple who lived in this Lodge were both rather infirm and seldom closed the gates unless specially ordered to do so.

There was no sign of them, and as she did not wish to be seen, she hurried past the Lodge and out onto the dusty road.

For a moment she hesitated, wondering whether to turn right or left, but she realised there was really no choice because to go right would take her into the village.

Then just as she was about to walk left, knowing she would have to walk a long way before there was even a sight of a cottage, she saw coming from the direction of the village a horse and cart.

For a moment she wondered if it was somebody she had no wish to see, then with a leap of her heart she realised that it was the Carrier.

She moved on a little way down the road until she was out of sight of the gates.

Then as the Carrier drew even with her, she waved to him.

Everybody in the village knew old Ted, whose sole business was to carry parcels, farm-products, and sometimes people from one village to another.

Now as he drew in his fat, piebald horse he said:

" 'Marnin', Miss Diona! Moight Oi 'elp ye?"

"Please, will you take me with you?" Diona asked.

"Where be ye a-goin'?" Ted enquired.

"I will tell you in a moment."

As she spoke Diona was already climbing up into his cart, and as she sat down beside him she saw that the back of it was full of young cockerels in slatted boxes.

Ted took her bundle from her and put it down at her feet, then as they started off he said:

"Oi ain't seen ye fer a long toim, Miss Diona, an' Oi sees yer dog looks well enough."

Sirius had jumped in after Diona, and now as he disliked sitting on the floor she moved along the hard seat nearer to Ted so that Sirius could be beside her.

The dog was always intensely interested in what was going on, looking from side to side, and she put her arm round him protectively before she asked:

"Where are you going, Ted? A long way, I hope."

"A very long way," he replied. "Oi be takin' these 'ere cockerels to one of th' farms on 'is Lordship's Estate. It'll take Oi all day to get there."

"His Lordship's Estate?" Diona questioned.

Ted nodded.

"Th' Marquis o' Irchester," he said. "They be fer 'is 'ome Farm."

"The Marquis of Irchester!" Diona repeated.

She knew the name, of course, but she had never seen the Marquis, and she was aware that his Estate was in the next County to theirs and nearer to London.

She remembered hearing her father speak of the Marquis's race-horses, and recently she had seen in the newspaper that he had won the big race at Newmarket.

But he had been only a name and she could not remember anything else about him.

They drove for a little way in silence before she asked:

"Do you think there is any chance, Ted, of my getting employment on one of the Marquis's farms?"

"Employment, Miss Diona? Why should ye be wantin' work?" Ted exclaimed in surprise.

"I have run away, Ted!"

"Now what's ye want to go and do a think loik that fer?" Ted replied before she could say any more. "It's not somethin' yer father'd want ye to do."

He paused before he added:

"Fine 'orseman, yer father. Many's the toim Oi watched 'im ridin' to 'ounds, or comin' up to see yer uncle at th' Hall, an' no man could sit a 'orse better'n he."

"That was true," Diona said. "But, Ted, I have to get away. Uncle Hereward has ordered Sirius to be shot!"

Old Ted turned his face to look at her as if he could not believe what she had said. Then he exclaimed:

"That ain't roight! Yer dog's young! There be no reason to shoot 'im!"

"Papa gave him to me just before he was killed," Diona said, "and . . . I cannot . . . lose him . . . I cannot!"

" 'Course not!" Ted agreed. "P'raps some'un'd look after 'im fer ye?"

"That would be worse," Diona said. "He has always been with me, and I would worry in case somebody was cruel to him or did not feed him properly, which would be . . . unbearable!"

There was a note in her voice which told Ted more clearly than her words what she was feeling. Then he said:

"Ye can't look after yerself, Miss Diona. Ain't there some'un ye could go to an' take yer dog with ye?"

"I have thought of that," Diona replied, "but I think Uncle Hereward would insist on my going back to him, and then there would be no chance of my saving Sirius."

There was a silence while Ted digested this. Then he asked:

"Wot you plannin' on doin', Miss Diona?"

"I can work on a farm."

"But ye knows nothin' 'bout cows!" Ted remarked.

"I could learn."

Again there was a long silence as the piebald horse trotted along at the steady pace at which Ted always travelled and which, whatever the weather, always resulted in his reaching his destination and delivering what he carried.

Diona spoke her thoughts aloud:

"What I do know about is horses, and of course dogs."

" 'Is Lordship's got some foin dogs!" Ted remarked. "Sportin' spaniels, most of 'em be."

Diona turned to look at him with an expression of excitement.

"Perhaps he might want somebody to look after his dogs?"

" 'E's already got kennel-men."

"Why not a kennel-woman?" Diona enquired.

"Oi ain't never 'eard o' one!"

"There must be a lot of jobs that a woman could do just as well as a man!" Diona persisted. "I could look after the puppies, and I could take care of the dogs if they were ill, and I could exercise them and of course make them obey me just as well as any man could do!"

There was a long silence until Ted said slowly:

"Oi bin thinkin' of all the 'ouses where they 'as dogs and 'orses, an' Oi ain't never seen no women a-workin' there."

"That is no reason to think they might not employ a woman if they had the chance," Diona said. "Farmers have milk-maids. Why should there not be kennel-maids and women-grooms?"

Ted transferred his reins to one hand and scratched his head with the other.

"Now ye asks me, Oi sees no reason why they shouldn't be," he said slowly. "But Oi knows there ain't no such thing at th' moment, not wot Oi've seen leastways."

"But I could try to get somebody to employ me," Diona said in a small voice. "If they say . . . 'no,' then perhaps, Ted . . . you could think of . . . something . . . else I could do."

She spoke a little hesitatingly because she knew that it had been an unforeseen piece of luck that Ted should be going so far from the Hall.

But, having reached the end of his journey, she must not on any account return with him.

Almost as if he was following her thoughts Ted said:

"Naw, if ye takes me advice, Miss Diona, ye'll go back to yer uncle an' 'ave another word wi' 'im. Ye be too young to go a-wanderin' about th' world on yer own. Ye'll get into trouble, that's what ye'll do."

"If you are thinking of footpads or thieves of any sort," Diona answered, "Sirius will protect me."

"There moight be worse things than that."

"What could be worse?"

Ted could find no answer to this, and they drove on until he said:

"It's noice to 'ave ye wi' me, Miss Diona, but Oi thinks Oi be doin' wrong to takin' ye so far from yer 'ome."

"It will save me from having to walk, Ted. I am running away, and I do not intend to go back!"

Ted lapsed into silence, and they drove on until Diona was just beginning to feel a little hungry, despite the eggs she had eaten for breakfast, when Ted said:

"Oi were a-goin' to stop at The Green Man at Little Ponders End fer a bite, but if ye don't want to be seen, p'raps Oi'd better droive straight on."

"I am very hungry too," Diona replied, "and as I have only been to Little Ponders End once before when I was out hunting, I do not think they are likely to recognise me."

She paused, thought quickly, and added:

"If I take off my bonnet and put a handkerchief over my head, perhaps you could say I was just somebody from the village who asked for a lift."

"That's an idea, Miss Diona," Ted agreed, "an' if ye sit outside Oi'll bring ye some bread an' cheese. The Landlord's not likely to be curious. He's an old man, an' 'alf-blind."

The cottages of Little Ponders End were just in sight and Diona undid the ribbons of her bonnet and put it under the seat.

She then reached into her bundle and found a scarf that she had brought with her in case it grew cold.

She was well aware that it would have been impossible to bring a heavy coat, and the only protection she would have later in the year, if she could not afford to buy anything new, was the shawl in which her things were wrapped.

The scarf was of pale blue silk and did not look very expensive at a distance, although it had belonged to her mother.

She tied it over her head and hoped she looked like one of the village girls who actually would have been wearing a sun-bonnet.

The Village Green when they reached it was empty except for two old donkeys and several ducks on the pond.

There was no need for Ted to tie up his horse, for he immediately began to crop the grass, and he and Diona walked across to The Green Man.

Outside was the usual wooden seat which later on in the afternoon would be occupied by the old men of the village.

Now there was nobody there, and as Diona sat down, Ted went inside.

It was only a little time before he came back with two plates on which were several large slices of cheese and the top of a cottage-loaf.

There was no butter, but Diona cut off a piece of the crust, which she knew had not long left the oven, and when she ate the cheese with it, she thought how delicious it was.

Ted had gone back into the Inn again and returned with two pewter mugs. One was filled with cider for Diona and the other contained ale for himself.

Because they were both aware that it would be a mistake to draw attention to themselves, they ate quickly.

Then Ted went back into the Inn to pay for what they had consumed while Diona walked back to the cart and climbed inside.

Sirius jumped up beside her and they were waiting and ready when Ted returned.

As they drove away Diona said:

"You must let me know how much I owe you."

"Ye be me guest, Miss Diona," Ted replied, "an' if ye be runnin' away, ye'll need every penny for yerself an' yer dog."

"I cannot let you pay for me!" Diona expostulated.

"Ye can pay me when yer ship comes in," Ted smiled, "an' Oi 'opes that won't be very long!"

"So do I," Diona replied wistfully.

As they drove on, she began to think how frightening it was to be going off into the blue with no idea where she would end up.

Then she told herself that however frightening it might be, nothing could be worse than knowing that Heywood, who was her uncle's Farm Manager and a man she had never liked, would shoot Sirius.

She knew that without Sirius she would be more alone in the world than she was already.

"Whatever the difficulties," she told herself, "not only will Sirius and I be together, but I feel quite sure Papa will be looking after us."

If there was one thing her father hated, it was cruelty of any sort, and it had been agonising for him to be forced to have a horse put down because of old age or illness.

Therefore, she knew that he would have been appalled at his brother's cruelty in even thinking of destroying Sirius.

"Papa will help me and look after me," Diona assured herself.

At the same time, she knew that the farther away they drove from the Hall, the more frightened she felt.

For the first time since she had decided to run away she realised how inexperienced and ignorant she was of the world.

She had, thanks to her mother's insistence, been very well educated by not only a retired Governess who lived in the village near their home but also by a Vicar who was a Classical Scholar.

He had instructed her in many subjects, and as he was an elderly man with no family of his own, he had been delighted to teach her.

She had developed such an affection for him that she often thought of him as the grandfather she had never known.

She thought now that if the Vicar were alive she could have turned to him for help.

Then she remembered that even if he had been willing for her to come and live with him, her uncle as her Guardian would have forbidden her to leave the Hall.

'I would only make trouble for people like that,' she thought.

She knew that included her Governess, who was now very old, and a teacher who had been the village School-Master.

He had a wife and several children and he had instructed Diona in arithmetic, algebra, and geometry.

"I cannot think why I have to learn these boring subjects, Mama," she had said once.

"They will make your brain active, darling," her mother had replied, "and what I want you to have is a good education, so that whatever happens to you in life, you will always feel sufficient in yourself."

Diona at the time had not understood exactly what her mother meant.

Because her mother's father had been an extremely clever man who had held an important post in the Foreign Office, her mother had wanted her to be educated as if she had been a boy.

It was only just before she died that Diona had understood the reason for this, when her mother had said:

"I longed and prayed to give your father a son, darling, but you mean so much to him because although you are a woman he can talk to you. You understand each other in the same way as you would have been able to do had you been a boy."

She saw an expression almost of disappointment on Diona's face and added quickly:

"Papa is very proud of you because you are so lovely, but beauty is not enough for a man who has a brain. He wants somebody who can stimulate him with new ideas and amuse him as many wives fail to do."

Mrs. Grantley was almost talking to herself, but Diona kissed her and said:

"I have always wanted Papa to be proud of me, and you know, Mama, how much I love talking to him. But I realise it is all because you were so clever in making me have so many lessons, some of which I found very difficult."

"One day they will all come in useful," Mrs. Grantley said. "That is what my father used to say: everything comes in useful when you least expect it and nothing of any value is ever lost."

Diona realised instinctively that she was not talking of material things, and she said:

"It is rather a lovely idea, like having a treasure-chest inside one's head, which at least nobody can steal from you!"

Her mother laughed.

"That is exactly what I mean, and you have many, many treasures, my darling, which one day you will find are of inestimable value—at least, I hope so."

Thinking now of that conversation, Diona told herself that if she was really to become a milk-maid or, as she hoped, a kennel-maid, it would hardly be a great strain on her intelligence.

"If I were older," she reasoned, "I could perhaps become the Curator in some magnificent Library, but who has ever heard of a Curator with a dog?"

Because it seemed funny she gave a little laugh, and Ted said:

"Oi loiks to 'ear ye laughin', Miss Diona. It be loik yer father. There was never anythin' so wrong that 'e couldn't laugh about it."

"That is true," Diona said, "and as things are very, very wrong with me, Ted, I will just have to laugh and hope they get better."

"Oi hopes so too," Ted replied.

She thought he did not sound very optimistic and felt her spirits drop a little.

Then the horse was climbing a steep incline in the road and when they reached the top she looked to the left and saw silhouetted against the sky a very large, impressive building.

It looked so beautiful in the afternoon sun with a standard flying from the roof-top that she exclaimed involuntarily:

"How lovely! Whose house is that?"

"That be 'is Lordship's," Ted replied, "and the 'ome Farm be just th' other side of th' valley, which's where we be a-goin'."

Diona was silent for a moment. Then she said almost as if somebody spoke to her:

"I am going to the Big House. That is where I know I shall find help!"

CHAPTER TWO

———— ✦ ————

*T*HE MARQUIS OF IRCHESTER had arrived home unexpectedly.

Because his organising ability extended to everything he owned, the servants, although they had no warning, were all on duty at Irchester Park, and with superb expertise his Chef provided him with an excellent dinner only an hour after his arrival.

He had not intended to go to the country so soon after the Season in London had begun to wane, but inadvertently the night before he had heard something of the Prince Regent's plans for his party at Brighton and guessed he would be included.

He had decided the year before that Brighton bored him.

Even if he took a house of his own and did not stay at the Royal Pavilion, it still meant he had to spend long hours there listening to what he considered inferior music and talking to the same people with whom he had already spent most of his time during the last two months.

Although he had a regard for the Prince Regent and they had a great bond in common over their love of paintings and antiques, which a great many of His Royal Highness's entourage did not appreciate, the Marquis decided "enough was enough."

The long-drawn-out dinners at Carlton House would only be echoed at Brighton, where the Prince's Chef attempted to rival every other Chef in the vicinity with the richness of his food and the number of his *entrées*.

Quite suddenly the Marquis felt satiated with it all, but there was another reason too for his precipitate departure.

His love-affairs since the war had given rise to a good deal of gossip, but because he was careful and discreet they never amounted to scandals.

He was punctilious about his *affaires de coeur* as he was about the smooth running of his houses and the perfection of his horses.

But he was so distinguished, so rich, and so extremely good-looking that it was inevitable that he would find himself involved with beautiful women to the point where he knew that one step further and he would find himself in the sort of situation he was determined to avoid.

After serving with great distinction in Wellington's Army, he had also played a large part in the mopping-up operations, which culminated in his being in command of the Army of Occupation.

When finally he returned home, like a great many other soldiers he thought he must make up for the years he had wasted when his chief preoccupation had been to keep alive.

London was waiting to offer every possible amusement and pleasure, and after the privations of war, the food, the wine, and of course the women were very enticing.

The Marquis opened Irchester House in Park Lane and began to give superlative parties which were rivalled only by those the Prince Regent gave at Carlton House.

But as it happened he was most fastidious in the selection of his guests, and it became an honour to receive one of his engraved invitation-cards.

In fact, they were eagerly sought after by even the most spectacular Beauties of the *Beau Monde*.

Ambitious mothers with young daughters realised almost immediately that the Marquis was out of their reach and they would merely waste their time in chasing him.

His predilection, perhaps because of his age, was for sophisticated and alluring married women, or for the extremely gay widows who had lost their husbands in the war.

One of these, and perhaps the most outstanding, was Lady Sybille Malden.

The daughter of a Duke, she had made an extremely bad marriage when, at the age of eighteen, she had become enamoured of Christopher Malden not only as a man but because he looked so alluring in his uniform.

Without it she found him dull, and even before he was killed at the Battle of Waterloo their marriage was described colloquially as "on the rocks."

By this time Lady Sybille was twenty-three years old and very conscious of her attractions.

The moment her year of mourning was over, she arrived in London like a shining star. Her success was immediate and she made the very most of it.

All her lovers were men of importance and also extremely wealthy.

But they were already married, and it was not until six months ago, when she met the Marquis of Irchester, that she began to get other ideas.

Having been unhappy or rather bored in her first marriage, she determined not to marry again until she had extracted the last ounce of pleasure from her present position.

As a Duke's daughter, however daringly she behaved it was unlikely that any of the great hostesses would bar their doors to her, and as an outstanding beauty there was no man who was not ready to lay his heart and most of his possessions at her feet.

That she needed their wealth went without saying, for her father was not a rich man and had a number of sons depending on him, and Malden had, in respect of what Sybille desired, left her very little.

But that did not prevent her from installing herself in a house just off Berkeley Square and patronising the most expensive dressmakers in Bond Street.

When she drove through the Park in her carriage drawn by Thoroughbred horses, she drew every eye.

At the same time, Lady Sybille was aware when she reached her twenty-eighth birthday that she was at the height of her beauty.

She was extolled by every artist of importance, and they pleaded almost on bended knees to be allowed to portray her on canvass, comparing her to Aphrodite, Botticelli's Simonetta, and Fragonard's exquisite women.

But she was acutely conscious that it was only a question of a few more years before she would be watching for wrinkles at the sides of her eyes and the first grey hair to appear on her golden head.

It was then, when she saw the Marquis of Irchester, that she knew what she wanted.

Lady Sybille had been abroad for the last two years, which was why they had not met sooner.

The Prince of an obscure Balkan country had appeared in London and swept her off her feet.

However, she felt that it would be a mistake to flaunt their liaison in front of her English admirers, who were always prepared to disparage foreigners.

She allowed him to take her to Paris, which, recovering from the war, had become one of the gayest cities in Europe.

The success Lady Sybille had experienced there had gone to her head like wine.

But eventually, as her fiery infatuation for the Prince began to fade, she thought it was time to return home.

Her return had been celebrated in a very gratifying manner on her first night in London, when she had attended a Ball at Devonshire House and met the Marquis.

She had, of course, heard of him, but somehow they had never met because she had been preoccupied with other men and he with other women.

Then, having watched him for a short time across the Drawing-Room in which the guests had congregated before they moved into the Ball-Room, she had asked the Duke to introduce her.

Over the next two months the Marquis had become aware—for it was a familiar sensation—that he was being chased, though it would not have been obvious to anybody less astute than he was.

He was not deceived by the remarkable coincidences where at party after party he found Lady Sybille beside him.

Then, when he was riding in the Park or calling to see the Prince Regent, having received an urgent invitation to do so, Lady Sybille would also be there.

At first he had told himself that he was not particularly interested.

She was beautiful, there was no denying that, but he was very fastidious concerning the bestowal of his favours, and at the moment he was actually engaged in pursuing the very alluring wife of an Hungarian Diplomat.

"Pursuing" was the right word, because the Marquis liked to think of himself as the hunter, not the hunted.

Unfortunately, things seldom worked out that way, since the majority of women with whom he came in contact pursued him relentlessly.

Their intentions were so obvious that he often found himself wondering why within serene and lovely foreheads there was not one original thought.

Finally, and it was perhaps the open envy of his friends that decided him, he succumbed to Lady Sybille's blandishments.

At first he was not disappointed.

Although she managed to look like a goddess who had just stepped down from Olympus, there was a very earthy fire on her lips and a tiger passion which could arouse a man's desire to a fever-pitch.

Then slowly, insidiously, the idea occurred to the Marquis that Lady Sybille wanted more from him than a transitory love-affair.

Cynically he had anticipated that, delightful though their association might be, it would not last much longer than any of the others that had amused him since the end of the war.

It was not what Sybille said, she was too clever for that. But the Marquis had an intuition which had served him well when he was commanding troops and gave him what was almost an insight into what a woman was thinking.

Incredibly, because it had never crossed his mind, he was suddenly aware that Lady Sybille intended marriage.

The Marquis knew of course that he would have to marry sometime, and his relatives, when they were brave enough to broach the subject, had made it quite clear that it was his duty to produce an heir.

In fact, several sons were required in order to ensure both the continuance of the title, which was an ancient one, and the preservation of the property.

But he had told himself when he came back from the war that he had no intention of what was called "settling down."

His long years as a soldier had made him feel a great deal older than he was, and he wanted to recapture his lost youth and the feeling of being his own master, which was impossible for any officer who served under Wellington.

"I will marry eventually," he told himself, "but I will not be pushed into it!"

The Marquis had found there was a great deal to do on his Estates, since his father had died three years before he was able to leave the Army.

In his old age his father had neglected a great many things and, what was more important, had chosen the wrong people to be in control.

The Marquis enjoyed every moment of attempting to achieve the perfection he expected.

Only when everything was exactly to his satisfaction did he find that amusement could become a fulltime occupation.

But entertainment was what he was seeking, not the shackles of matrimony, and what he was quite certain would be the inevitable boredom of being tied to one woman who, however beautiful she looked at the end of his table, would probably have a very small brain.

He had actually said to one of his closest friends when they were sitting drinking in White's Club:

"How is it that the majority of women with whom we spend a great deal of our time are so appallingly badly educated that it is impossible to talk to them except on one subject?"

His friend, who had been in the same Regiment, laughed.

"You know as well as I do, Lenox, that an Englishman spends all the money he can afford on the education of his sons, while his daughters are dragged up in a School-Room by a half-witted Governess who is completely incompetent to teach them all that they should know."

"I suppose that is true," the Marquis answered reflectively.

He was remembering that while he had been sent to Eton and Oxford, his sisters had stayed at home in the company of mousey little women whose faces he found impossible to remember.

"I suppose that is why foreign women are, on the whole, far more intelligent," he remarked at length.

"I cannot say that I bother much about a woman's brain," his friend replied. "If she is pretty enough I want to make love to her; if she is not, I ignore her!"

The Marquis laughed, but he found himself thinking of the somewhat banal conversations he had with Lady Sybille on the few occasions when they were not making love.

Then last night at Carlton House he had been aware that she was talking to the Prince Regent in an intimate manner, which for some unknown reason made him suspicious.

He could not hear what they were saying, but there was no doubt that it concerned him.

Inevitably their eyes moved towards him, and although he pretended to be oblivious to the fact, he was very conscious of it.

Then as the Prince rose to greet some new arrivals who had joined them after dinner, he saw Lady Sybille looking as if she were a cat which had licked the cream.

It was then that his instinct told him she was up to mischief as far as he was concerned, and made him move quickly to speak to an Ambassador who had been one of the guests at dinner.

He was determined to find out what was brewing, in case he found himself involved in a manner which he would greatly dislike.

It was the Ambassador who unwittingly gave him the key to the situation.

"I suppose, My Lord," he said, "this is the last party we shall enjoy in this delightful treasure-house before His Royal Highness leaves for Brighton."

"I expect so," the Marquis agreed.

"My wife and I have been invited to the Royal Pavilion," the Ambassador went on with a note of satisfaction in his voice, "and we are delighted that you and Lady Sybille will be there at the same time. His Royal Highness intimated that you would be his guests."

The Marquis looked sharply at the Ambassador, wondering what he was implying.

Then, wagging his finger playfully, the elderly Diplomat went on:

"My wife has told me your little secret, but I promise that I am very, very discreet, and of course I am a fervent admirer of Lady Sybille."

If the floor had opened to reveal a deep chasm at his feet the Marquis could not have been more surprised and disturbed.

Now he realised what Lady Sybille was doing, and he told himself he had been very obtuse.

She was using a weapon that a great number of women had used before her, which was called "Public Opinion."

In her case she had started at the top, with the entourage of the Prince Regent, and now included the Prince himself.

The Marquis had known it to happen before, in the case of a friend who had hesitated on the brink of making a proposal of marriage to a woman who desired him.

It was, however, too late and he had been pressurised into it, not by the woman herself but by her friends and those who admired her.

Choosing a moment when his host was busily engaged with a number of his friends, the Marquis said good-night somewhat briefly and slipped away from Carlton House without speaking to Lady Sybille.

He had driven back to his house in Park Lane, planning what he should do in the same forceful and deliberate way in which he had planned onslaughts against the French.

He knew that the first step was to leave London and go to the country.

On his arrival at Irchester House he had immediately issued instructions to his staff, having his secretary, who had retired to bed, fetched to the Study to listen to what he had to say.

He had then sat down at his desk to write to the Prince Regent to thank him for his hospitality and to say he had been unexpectedly called to the country on family affairs.

He had not written to Lady Sybille, thinking somewhat cruelly that he would leave her to worry as to what had happened and, he hoped, to be uncertain what she could do about it.

Immediately after breakfast he had set off for Irchester Park, driving at a great speed because he felt like a fox going to ground while the hounds were not far behind.

As he reached the country, the beauty of his home and its quiet dignity brought him a feeling of peace that was like a healing hand.

"Is Your Lordship expecting a party?" his Butler asked respectfully after his arrival.

"Not for the moment, Dawson," the Marquis replied. "I have a great deal to do on the Estate and I need a rest."

"Your Lordship will find that here, and it's a great pleasure to have you back, M'Lord."

The man spoke with a sincerity which pleased the Marquis, but once he was alone he began to think about himself, and it made him very cynical.

He admitted frankly that for the last year he had grown more and more bored with the sameness of the hurdy-gurdy of the *Beau Monde,* which never changed its tune.

The same Balls, the same Receptions, the same Assemblies, the same evenings at Carlton House, at Vauxhall, at Ranelagh, and inevitably the same women.

Beautiful, sophisticated, alluring, and desirable, they revealed, as soon as one knew them well, that they were vain, selfish, avaricious, and incredibly brainless, except where it concerned their self-preservation.

"What do I want? What am I looking for?" the Marquis asked himself, and found depressingly that there was no answer.

He told himself that he missed the war, the excitement, the danger, the endless demands upon his attention from his troops.

But at least, and perhaps most important of all, there had been a goal—shining like a guiding star overhead—which was victory.

The war was now won, but the peace, if he was honest, was disappointing.

"What do I want?" the Marquis asked himself again.

It was a question that seemed to be repeating in his mind as he had dinner alone, then walked out onto the terrace to look at the last glimmer of the dying sun behind the ancient oak trees in the Park.

The stars were coming out in the sky and there was a new moon just visible in the translucence of the dying light.

Behind him was the great house that had stood on the same foundations for five hundred years but had been completely rebuilt by his great-grandfather early in the last century.

It was in consequence one of the finest and most outstanding examples of Georgian architecture in the whole country.

The huge State Rooms were each of them perfect in their own way, and the Marquis was the possessor of paintings which were the envy of the Prince Regent and of every connoisseur of art in the country.

Beyond the gardens which he had restored to their original design there were woods which would afford him a great deal of sport in the autumn.

In the valley on the other side there was a stream that wandered through the lower meadows to create a swampland where there were snipe and duck and which later in the year would be Paradise for sportsmen.

Apart from these there were hundreds of broad acres over which he could hunt in the winter and ride the superlative horses with which he had filled his stables since he had returned from France.

"I have everything," the Marquis said firmly. "Why should I want more?"

Then he knew that something was missing—something to which he could not put a name. But again his instinct, from which he could not separate himself, told him that it was essential.

Because he was annoyed at his own restlessness he went to bed early, in the huge State Bedroom with a magnificent four-poster in which many of his ancestors had been born and died, to think about himself.

He had always believed that he was completely self-sufficient, and because he had risen rapidly in the Army he knew he had the gift of leadership.

Some woman—she had not been English—had compared him to Alexander the Great, and he wondered if without really meaning to he had modelled himself on one of the most outstanding men the world had ever known.

Alexander had been not only a great soldier but an intellectual, a visionary, a man who was never satisfied but was always seeking what lay out of reach.

"That is what I am doing," the Marquis told himself, but it did not make for contentment or, for that matter, happiness.

Happiness, he felt, involved the need to strive, the desire to win and to achieve victory.

This, he told himself, was where he came in. The only difficulty was that while in the war he had known exactly what victory entailed, in the peace it was elusive and he could not put it into words.

The Marquis came down the next morning feeling a little more cynical than usual and at the same time ready to mock at himself.

Only when he went out riding on an extremely spirited and obstinate stallion did he forget everything but the age-old fight between man and beast.

He found then the elation of victory which gave them both satisfaction.

He had luncheon alone and spent the time trying to decide whom he should invite to stay.

There were two or three men-friends whose company he knew he would enjoy and who he was sure would be only too willing to obey a summons to Irchester Park.

Then, because he thought they would find an all-male party rather dull, he tried to think of which women he should add to his list.

As was inevitable when he was having a passionate affair with one woman, the others faded into insignificance.

It would, he thought, seem too abrupt if suddenly without any warning he invited those with whom he had flirted before he met Sybille to stay with him in the country.

Besides, he had a suspicion, based on previous experience, that they would still be angry with him for neglecting them and would doubtless have to be placated by a great number of compliments before he was forgiven.

"Dammit all!" he said to himself. "Women are a nuisance and for the moment I can well do without them!"

He had not since he had returned to London installed, as was fashionable amongst his contemporaries, a "Pretty Cyprian" or what was better described as a "bit o' muslin" in a house in Chelsea.

He had at one time considered taking under his protection a particularly alluring little ballet-dancer from Covent Garden.

Then at the last moment, when the words had almost passed his lips, he came to the conclusion that her accent irritated him.

The Marquis had always been fastidious, and, however alluring a woman might be, it was the small things which he found suddenly repulsive and which on many occasions had made him back away at the very last moment.

His close friends found it hard to understand why he should be so particular.

As he never discussed his love-affairs with them, the majority assumed he was more clever at keeping a secret than they were.

They told themselves that doubtless he had a number of women under his protection as well as picking, as they put it, the "ripest plums off the tree" in the shape of the Social Beauties who were as outstanding as Lady Sybille.

"What *do* I want?" the Marquis asked himself for the hundredth time.

Because there was no answer, he sent for a second horse on which to exercise himself during the afternoon.

When he returned at about four o'clock he felt more or less at peace with the world and looked forward to relaxing in the Library, where he usually sat when he was alone, and reading the newspapers.

They had arrived by now, and as he picked them up and glanced at the headlines, he was aware that nothing world-shattering had occurred since he had left London.

He therefore turned to the sporting-pages with much more interest, then suddenly the door of the Library opened and Dawson announced:

"Mr. Roderic Nairn, M'Lord!"

The Marquis looked up in surprise as his nephew, dressed in the very height of fashion, came into the room and hurried towards him with an outstretched hand.

"What are you doing here, Roderic?" the Marquis enquired.

"Are you surprised to see me, Uncle Lenox?"

At twenty-two the Marquis's nephew, who had been given into his care by his eldest sister, a doting mother, was a very prepossessing young man.

He had, however, been spoilt from the moment he was born, and only because he had persisted in saying he must enjoy himself in London had his mother, shedding floods of tears in the process, begged the Marquis to watch over her "lamb."

Lady Beatrice Nairn was a widow, and her husband, a Scotsman, had left her large but unproductive Estates in Scotland. She therefore felt it impossible to leave them to sponsor her son's début into London Society.

Lady Beatrice was convinced that in London Roderic would frequent dens of vice and experience all the temptations of St. Anthony once he became a member of the *Beau Ton*.

The Marquis, however, had taken his responsibilities very lightly.

"The boy has to find his feet, Beatrice," he said to his sister when she beseeched him to prevent Roderic from coming to any harm.

"But he is so very young, Lenox, and so good-looking!"

"So are a great number of other young men," the Marquis replied, "and he cannot remain tied to your apron-strings forever!"

"I am so worried about him, and he has no father to whom to turn in time of trouble."

"There is no reason why he should get into any trouble," the Marquis said a little testily, "and if he does, I will get him out of it."

"That is what I wanted you to say," Lady Beatrice cried. "Roderic has not your strength of character or, if you will forgive me for saying so, your ruthlessness, and I am afraid that any wicked or designing woman would twist him round her little finger."

The Marquis realised exactly what his sister was saying.

At the same time, he thought she was fussing unnecessarily since Roderic, like every other young man of his age, must be allowed to "sow a few wild oats."

Therefore, he had not given his nephew any advice but had merely told him he was there if he needed him.

He had not been surprised when the previous year he had been obliged to pay Roderic's debts, which, although he had not said so, he thought were not really as astronomical as they might have been.

His understanding treatment had resulted in Roderic, who at first had been rather afraid of his distinguished uncle, treating him as if he was a friend and being much more frank than he might otherwise have been.

The Marquis in his long dealings with men knew that this was the best way to ensure that Roderic did not get into any serious trouble without his being aware of it.

In fact, although he thought him a somewhat ingenuous and not over-intelligent young man, he would have been glad to have him serving under him as a Subaltern.

Now as Roderic reached the chair in which his uncle was seated he said:

"I am in trouble, Uncle Lenox, and that is why I had to see you!"

"How did you get here?" the Marquis asked.

There was a little pause before Roderic replied:

"In your Phaeton, with your horses!"

The Marquis's lips tightened for a moment. Then he asked sharply:

"You did not drive them yourself?"

"No, I wanted to, but Sam would not let me."

The Marquis relaxed.

Sam was his Head Groom in London and was exceptionally good with the reins.

"Well?" the Marquis asked.

"I did not know you were leaving London," Roderic said, "and when I went to Irchester House, Mr. Swaythling told me you had come here, and I told him I had to see you at once."

"So he arranged for Sam to bring you?"

"Yes, and I hoped we would break your record."

"How long did you take?"

"Three hours, forty-five minutes."

The Marquis's eyes twinkled.

"Ten minutes too long."

"That was what Sam told me, and I was disappointed."

"I am glad I am still 'top of the form'!" the Marquis said complacently.

"How could you be anything else?" Roderic replied.

"Now tell me why you made this precipitate dash from London," the Marquis suggested. "Are you in debt again?"

"No, no!" Roderic said quickly. "It is not money this time."

The Marquis looked at him a little apprehensively.

"It is a bet I made at White's," Roderic went on after a short pause.

"A bet?"

"I want to win it, and I cannot think of anyone except you who could help me to do so."

The Marquis settled himself more comfortably in the armchair.

"Suppose you start at the beginning."

"It happened yesterday after luncheon," Roderic replied. "We had all had a great deal to drink . . ."

"Who was 'we'?" the Marquis interrupted.

"Oh, my usual friends, you have met them all—Edward, George, Billy, and Stephen."

The Marquis nodded.

They were all young aristocrats who had been at Eton with Roderic, and while the Marquis personally thought they drank too much and did too little, he knew they were the sort of friends his sister wanted Roderic to have, being on the whole what any man would call "decent chaps" without any vice in them.

"We were laughing and talking," Roderic continued, "when Sir Mortimer Watson joined us."

The Marquis frowned.

He knew a great deal about Sir Mortimer Watson and none of it to his credit.

He had deliberately avoided meeting him, although he attended every race-meeting, but by some unfortunate mistake Sir Mortimer had been elected as a member of White's Club.

There had been some unpleasant stories about him to which the Marquis had not deigned to listen, but he was aware that most decent men went out of their way to avoid him.

From a young man's point of view he was bad news.

"There's that swine Watson going up to the Card-Room to pluck another young chicken of its feathers!" he had heard a fellow-member of the Club say the last time he was there.

He had stored it at the back of his mind as another black mark against the man he already disliked.

"He stood us a drink," Roderic was saying, "and then, and I do not know how it happened, we got into an argument as to whether English 'Cyprians' were prettier than foreign ones!"

He paused before he went on:

"Sir Mortimer said the foreign ones were not only prettier but also such brilliant actresses that it was easy to pass them off as being of a much better class than they really were."

The Marquis thought privately that Sr. Mortimer had a point there, and Roderic continued:

"Then Edward, who dislikes Sir Mortimer, started to tell him he was wrong and that not only were foreigners obviously out of the gutter when you looked beneath the paint and powder but that English girls were instinctively better-mannered and better-behaved."

The Marquis remembered that the "Edward" of whom he was speaking was young Lord Somerford, who had recently come into the title and a fortune.

"Of course most of us supported Edward," Roderic was saying. "Then Sir Mortimer bet us one thousand pounds to one in sovereigns that none of us could produce an English girl who could stand up to his choice, who was French and, he said, not only beautiful but could easily pass anywhere as a Lady."

" 'I have never heard such damned nonsense!' Edward replied to him.

'My father's milk-maids are more lady-like than anybody you could import into this country!' "

Roderic smiled before he added:

"We all got very heated, and the result was that we agreed to meet Sir Mortimer in a week's time, each producing an English girl, milk-maid or 'Cyprian,' who will better his exhibit!"

Roderic finished speaking and looked at his uncle a little apprehensively.

"And what do you all have to pay to enter this contest?" the Marquis asked.

"We all stake a hundred guineas on our choice," Roderic replied, "which of course we lose if the judges—Sir Mortimer says they will be independent—choose his 'bit o' muslin' as the winner."

It was what the Marquis expected, knowing that Watson would have made sure of putting five hundred pounds in his pocket before he made the challenge in the first place.

It was the sort of unscrupulous thing he would have expected a man of that calibre to do.

At the same time, he could understand it would be an irresistible challenge to a lot of foolish young men who he had made sure had all had a great deal to drink.

"Well," the Marquis asked aloud, "what are you going to do about it?"

"That is why I have come to you, Uncle Lenox."

"Me?"

"To produce a milk-maid!"

The Marquis laughed.

"My dear boy, you must realise you have been taken for a mug! Watson is certain that none of you will produce anything like this paragon he has up his sleeve, and milk-maids, although traditionally we are told they are very pretty, do not transplant out of their own environment."

Roderic looked sulky.

"That is not being much help," he said after a moment, "and none of us have any wish for Watson to get away with it."

"Nor have I," the Marquis agreed. "He is a man for whom I have a strong dislike, and whom I have no wish to meet."

"There must be something we can do," Roderic said. "Edward has gone off to his own Estate in Hertfordshire and the others are looking round the Dance-Halls. But if there had been anybody new and outstanding in the White House I feel we would have heard about it already."

"I am sure you would have," the Marquis agreed.

"Then what can I do?" Roderic asked desperately.

"Pay up your hundred guineas and admit you are a loser!"

Roderic, who had been sitting near to his uncle, rose to his feet.

"I am damned if I will do that so tamely," he said. "This is not the first time Sir Mortimer has taken me for a ride!"

"No?" the Marquis asked.

"I did not tell you, but I had a very foolish bet with him one night when I was pretty badly 'foxed.' It cost me two hundred guineas, and I was ashamed of it the next morning. Even a 'greenhorn' could not have been so foolish!"

"Then you should have learnt your lesson," the Marquis said. "A man like Watson is always out to make money from those who fall for his tricks, which is exactly what this is."

"I realise that, but I wanted to beat him at his own game," Roderic replied. "Can I have a look round your farms tomorrow, Uncle Lenox? Suppose, just suppose there is a milk-maid or a farmer's daughter who is so pretty that it will take them all by surprise?"

"It will certainly take me by surprise!" the Marquis said. "In fact, I would call it a miracle!"

"That is exactly what I need—a miracle—and I am optimistic enough to believe that they happen."

The Marquis laughed.

"I hope your faith in the Heavenly powers is justified. At the same time, as I have already said, milk-maids, however attractive they may look in the country, are not at their best when they reach Piccadilly."

"You are deliberately trying to depress me," Roderic complained. "Do you know what Billy said to me before I came here?"

"No, tell me," the Marquis said good-humouredly.

"He said: 'The one person who can help you, Roderic, is your uncle.' "

"Why should he have said that?"

"He went on: 'If there is anybody who knows a pretty woman when he sees one and makes certain she does not get away, it is Irchester!' "

"Thank you," the Marquis said. "I appreciate the compliment. But I assure you the women I associate with, Roderic, are not milk-maids, nor, as it happens, are they what you aptly describe as 'bits o' muslin.' "

"Then what can I do?" Roderic asked despairingly.

The Marquis was trying to think of an answer when the door opened.

"Excuse me, M'Lord," Dawson said, "but there's a young lady here insists on seeing you."

"What is her name?" the Marquis asked.

"She wouldn't give it, M'Lord, but she said it was very important she should see you personally."

"You said, 'young lady,' Dawson?"

"I suppose I should say 'young woman,' M'Lord, as she's alone and she's got a big dog with her."

"A young woman with a dog who will not give her name?" the Marquis said. "This sounds like one of your puzzles, Roderic."

His nephew was looking out a window with a sulky expression on his face and did not answer.

"It seems a strange request, Dawson," the Marquis said. "What is the dog doing?"

"I suggested, M'Lord, that the dog remain outside, but she said: 'The dog comes with me, and I wish His Lordship to see him.' "

"I suppose she wishes to sell it to me," the Marquis said drily. "Well, you can tell her I have enough dogs of my own at the moment and do not intend buying any more."

He expected the Butler to leave the room, but Dawson hesitated.

"It's a very fine dog, M'Lord, and an unusual one. It may sound impertinent, but the young woman is very pretty, and it was unusual the way she insisted on seeing Your Lordship."

Roderic turned from the window.

"Pretty? Did you say she was pretty, Dawson?"

"Very pretty, Mr. Roderic, exceptionally so!"

Roderic looked towards the Marquis.

"You heard that, Uncle Lenox? I have a feeling you are wrong and a miracle has called just when we wanted one!"

The Marquis gave a short, dry laugh.

"It is so unlikely, but if it is the miracle you have been praying for, I will pay your hundred guineas for you!"

"Done!" Roderic cried with glee. "Bring her in, Dawson! Bring the young woman and her dog in immediately!"

Dawson looked at the Marquis for confirmation.

He nodded.

"Very good, M'Lord," Dawson said, and went out, shutting the Library door.

CHAPTER THREE

———— ⟨∞⟩ ————

*T*ED TURNED HIS HEAD to stare at Diona in surprise.

Then he said after a moment's hesitation:

"Oi thinks it's a mistake, Miss Diona. Oi sees 'is Lordship's at 'ome, an' Oi suggests ye come wi' me to th' farm."

Diona shook her head.

"No, Ted, I want to go to the Big House first. I somehow know it is the right thing to do."

She could not explain why her instinct told her she would receive help from there and nowhere else; she knew only that that was what she must do if she was to save Sirius.

Then as Ted's horse plodded slowly on she said:

"Promise me, Ted, you will tell nobody where I am. You know if Uncle Hereward gets to hear of it he will fetch me back and destroy Sirius."

"Ye knows ye can trust Oi, Miss Diona," Ted replied.

"Yes, of course, Ted, and I am very grateful to you."

There was a long pause before Ted managed to say what was in his mind.

"If ye're in trouble an' ye wants Oi, tell Farmer Burrows at th' 'ome

Farm to send fer me. 'E know 'ow to do it, an' Oi'll come quick as Oi can."

"Thank you, Ted, you have been very, very kind."

Ted brought his horse to a standstill. He had stopped facing a grass track which Diona guessed would lead to the Home Farm.

She got down from the cart, followed by Sirius, and Ted handed her her bundle.

"Take care o' yerself, Miss Diona," he said, "an' remember, Oi'll come fer ye, if ye sends a message."

"I will not forget," Diona said, "and thank you again, Ted."

She walked away towards the house, knowing that he was watching her go with a worried expression on his old face.

As she reached a grey stone bridge over the lake she stopped.

She realised it would look very strange if she asked to see the Marquis carrying a silk shawl which contained all her belongings.

At the side of the bridge there was clump of bushes.

She put the bundle into the middle of them, thinking it was unlikely that anybody would notice it and steal it before she was able to retrieve it.

She then walked on, with Sirius at her heels, feeling as if a thousand butterflies were fluttering in her breast.

She was frightened, in fact very frightened, but the only alternative was to return to her uncle and plead with him once again.

But she knew that would be hopeless, and even if she had to scrub floors it would be better than losing Sirius.

"I will make it quite clear," she said to herself, "that I am prepared to do anything, but I could be more useful in the kennels than anywhere else."

It did, however, require a lot of courage to walk up the grey stone steps to the front door.

There was no need to knock, for a footman on duty had obviously heard her footsteps, or had been looking through the window, and as she reached the top step the door was opened.

"I wish to see the Marquis of Irchester!" Diona said in what she hoped was the same tone her mother might have used.

The footman did not reply but looked to where a Butler was standing in the background.

He had grey hair, and as he advanced towards her Diona thought that he looked more like a Bishop than a servant.

"You're asking for His Lordship, Miss?" he enquired in a somewhat pontifical voice.

"Yes, I wish to see him urgently."

It was then that an argument started, first because Diona would not give her name, and secondly because the Butler was insistent that His Lordship could not be disturbed unless she would give a reason for seeing him.

However, she was determined that she must, however difficult it might be, meet the one person who she felt could help her.

When finally the Butler, somewhat discomfited by her determination, left her standing in the Hall, she was aware that three footmen were looking both at her and at Sirius with an expression of admiration in their eyes.

"That be a fine dog ye have there, Miss," one of them said tentatively.

Diona was aware that if they had thought her a Lady, as they would have known her to be had she been accompanied by her mother or an elderly Chaperone, they would not have spoken to her.

"His name is Sirius," she replied, "and I have had him ever since he was a small puppy."

"They be very fast, them dogs," the footman remarked, "an' good after game!"

"Yes, I know," Diona said with a smile.

There was the sound of the Butler approaching them from the passage, and the footman lapsed quickly into silence and straightened his back.

Diona waited apprehensively.

"If you'll come this way, Miss," the Butler said, and she knew she had won.

Then she told herself as she walked down the wide passage that this was only the first hurdle.

The big jump lay ahead, and she found herself praying fervently to her father as she walked for what seemed a long way.

"Help me, Papa, please help me!" she said. "You could never allow anybody to do anything so . . . cruel as to . . . destroy Sirius. I must keep him . . . alive . . . I must!"

The Butler opened a door with what she thought was a very condescending air, as if he thought he was making a mistake in allowing her to meet his Master.

Then she heard him announce:

"The young woman, M'Lord!"

With difficulty she forced her feet to carry her into the room.

For a moment she had an impression of books, hundreds and thousands of them, rising from the floor to the ceiling.

Then she was aware there were two men in the room.

One was young and was looking at her in what she thought was a somewhat strange manner.

The other was without question the most handsome man she had ever seen in the whole of her life.

At the same time, she was aware that he was overpoweringly authoritative and exactly what she suspected the Marquis of Irchester would look like.

He was sitting at his ease in a high-backed arm-chair with his legs crossed, and she thought that he looked as if he were a King upon a throne and felt as if she ought to go down on her knees in front of him.

Instead she curtseyed very gracefully, then as neither of the gentlemen spoke she walked slowly towards them.

She was quite unaware that she made a picture such as they had not expected, in her best summer-gown which was a pretty one of sprigged muslin trimmed with blue ribbons.

Her chip-straw bonnet had a wreath of wild-flowers round the crown, and because gloves were too expensive, she wore mittens which did not conceal her long, thin fingers.

She walked forward with the big Dalmatian at her side until she was a few feet away from the Marquis, and because it seemed the right thing to do she curtseyed again.

"You wished to see me?" the Marquis asked.

"Yes . . . My Lord."

"You told my Butler it was very urgent?"

"Very . . . urgent indeed, My Lord."

"I am interested. What is your name?"

There was a little pause before Diona said:

"I am called . . . Diona."

The Marquis raised his eye-brows before he asked:

"Is that all?"

"Y-yes . . . My Lord . . . I have my reasons for not . . . wishing to be . . . known by any . . . other name."

"Tell me why you are here."

For a moment it was very difficult to speak. Then after Diona drew in her breath she managed to say:

"I . . . I wondered if Your Lordship would . . . employ me as a . . . kennel-maid."

As she spoke she saw a look of surprise in the Marquis's eyes, and was aware that the other gentleman, who had not moved since she came into the room, now walked to stand facing her and to stare in a way that she found extremely embarrassing.

"Did you say—a kennel-maid?" the Marquis questioned.

"Yes, My Lord . . . it may seem . . . strange . . . but I am very experienced with dogs . . . and horses for that matter . . . and I need . . . employment."

"I have never heard . . ." the Marquis began.

He was, however, interrupted by Roderic, who exclaimed:

"Why should you not be a milk-maid?"

Diona looked at him and replied:

"I am prepared to be a milk-maid . . . if there is . . . nothing else . . . but I cannot see why, if there are . . . kennel-men, there should not be . . . kennel-maids, and I could . . . do many things which . . . they would find difficult . . . because they . . . are men."

She spoke a little hesitatingly, and the Marquis asked:

"What things in particular had you in mind?"

"A . . . a woman could . . . look after the puppies better than a man . . . especially as often happens . . . when the bitch has too many and some have to be . . . reared by hand. I have always been able to . . . poultice a horse better and less . . . painfully than my father or his . . . grooms could."

She realised as she spoke that in making out a good case for herself she had, without thinking made a mistake.

"So your father has horses?" the Marquis remarked.

"Yes . . . My Lord."

"But he no longer wishes you to help him in his own stables?"

"My father is . . . dead . . . My Lord."

The Marquis noticed the little throb in her voice as she spoke. Diona still missed her father so desperately that it was hard not to be emotional about him.

"And I presume he has left you no money," the Marquis said.

He spoke in a dry, business-like tone, which made it somehow easier for Diona to reply in the same manner.

"That is the truth, My Lord. In fact, I now have to earn my own living, and it is extremely important that I should start doing so . . . immediately."

If she had not been so frightened, she would have appreciated the quickness with which the Marquis said:

"That means, I presume, that you have nowhere to go unless I take you in."

"That . . . is true."

It was then as she spoke that Roderic made a sound that was like a cry of triumph.

"The miracle, Uncle Lenox!" he exclaimed. "I have won my bet! Look at her! You only have to look at her to know that she is exactly what I have been seeking!"

The Marquis made a gesture with his hand as if he thought his nephew was being too impetuous, but Roderic, taking a step towards Diona, asked eagerly:

"Will you take off your bonnet?"

Diona's eyes widened.

"I will explain in a moment," he said, "why it is necessary, but please do as I ask you."

It was certainly a very strange request, but Diona could not think of any reason why she should refuse.

It also flashed through her mind that kennel-maids were not likely to wear the same sort of clothes that she was wearing, and she knew now it had been a mistake to bring nothing serviceable with her.

However, she had brought a riding-skirt that she had put in at the last minute despite the fact that it made extra weight.

572

As she lifted her hands to undo the ribbons of her bonnet, which tied under her chin, the Marquis said:

"I understood you had some reason for bringing your dog in here. Do you wish me to buy him?"

"No . . . no . . . of course not, My Lord! I would not . . . sell him for a . . . million pounds. It is just that he is the reason why I am seeking . . . employment, and why I would like to . . . work in the kennels, because he is . . . always with . . . me."

The Marquis snapped his fingers, and to Diona's surprise Sirius, who was usually somewhat suspicious of strangers, walked to his side.

"He is certainly a very fine specimen of a Dalmatian," the Marquis observed, "and I can quite understand that you would not wish to part with him."

"I have had him ever since he was a small puppy," Diona replied. "He is everything in the world to me . . . and the . . . only thing I . . . love."

She spoke so fervently that she saw the Marquis raise his eye-brows in surprise.

Then she took off her bonnet and pressed up her silver-gold hair, which had been flattened down, and Roderic gave a cry of delight.

"She is beautiful!" he said. "Quite, quite perfect for what I want!"

Diona stared at him, thinking not only that he was a very strange young man but that what he was saying was quite inexplicable.

At the same time, the Marquis, now that he could see Diona's hair, was aware that Roderic had very good grounds for his enthusiasm.

He fancied himself as a connoisseur of women and he had to admit that she was lovely in an unusual way.

She was very young, and yet she was not a pink-and-white or a rosy-cheeked English beauty, which he thought would have been in his nephew's mind when he was seeking for the milk-maid of his imagination and which he was unlikely to find.

Diona's face was pointed and was entirely dominated by her large eyes, and her hair was the silvery gold of the sky at dawn.

She had, he thought, the ageless beauty which one saw in the Greek statues of their goddesses and which he had always thought was a classical beauty now lost in the annals of time.

There was no doubt that with her straight little nose, her perfectly chiselled lips, and her long neck, Diona resembled the statues he had seen many years ago in Greece.

He had also inspected them more recently in the Museums in Paris, where they somehow seemed out-of-place, as if they pined for their native land.

Then he was aware, as he had been since she had first come into the room, that while her strange eyes were the colour of a morning mist, there was an expression of fear in them that he had never expected to see in a pretty woman's face.

He thought as she stood in front of him waiting for his verdict that she might be Phyne before her Judges, whose advocate, when she was accused of impiety, had appealed to the sentiment of the jury by throwing open her dress and revealing the beauty of her breasts.

Then Roderic was crying out:

"I have found her, and I am sure I can make Sir Mortimer look a fool and take the thousand guineas off him!"

"I think you are going too fast, Roderic!" the Marquis said. "The first step must obviously be to persuade Diona, as she wishes to be called, to agree to help you in this momentous task."

The cynical manner in which the Marquis spoke made Diona aware that he had a contempt for what his nephew was talking about, and she said quickly, because she was afraid:

"Please, My Lord . . . all I want to do is to . . . work for you and with your . . . dogs."

"I am considering that possibility, which is certainly an unusual one," the Marquis replied, "but I think you should first listen to what my nephew has to say, and perhaps I should introduce him—Mr. Roderic Nairn—Miss Diona!"

Diona was aware that he was mocking her and it made her feel embarrassed, but she made a small curtsey and was aware as she did so that Roderic's elaborate bow was also a mockery.

Sirius had returned to her side and she put her hand on his head as if it gave her courage, knowing that if she followed her inclinations she would leave and go elsewhere for help.

The difficulty was that she had no idea where to go, and, what was far more important, there was Sirius to consider.

Because she was touching him he looked up at her and licked her hand.

As he did so, Diona glanced at the Marquis and thought in some strange way that he understood what she was feeling and, even more extraordinary, was aware of what she was thinking.

In a completely different tone of voice he said:

"Suppose you sit down and let my nephew explain to you what at the moment must seem not only incomprehensible but rather insulting."

"I am sorry if I appeared rude," Roderic said quickly. "It is just that before you came into the room my uncle informed me that what I was trying to find was so impossible that only a miracle could help me."

He smiled beguilingly as he finished:

"Then you appeared, and there was my miracle!"

Because she felt as if her legs would no longer support her, Diona sat down carefully on a chair that was near the one in which the Marquis was sitting.

It was a high-backed chair with a wicker seat.

She sat down gracefully and Sirius immediately flopped down on the floor beside her.

Holding her bonnet in her lap, she raised her eyes to Roderic Nairn, wondering what he was about to tell her.

Everything since she had come into the room had been bewildering and very different from what she had expected.

She had anticipated that the Marquis might cross-examine her and knew he would think it strange that she would give him only her Christian name.

But she hated lying, and somehow, although she felt it was foolish of her, she had no wish to assume a name to which she was not entitled.

And yet it was essential that nobody should ever learn who she was, for fear of her uncle getting to know where she was hiding.

Roderic seated himself on the arm of a chair and began:

"I expect you know, Miss Diona, that men in London enjoy having wagers amongst themselves, especially if they are members of a Club called White's."

"Yes, I know," Diona replied, "because my . . ."

She was just about to say that her father had been a member of White's.

He had made her and her mother laugh when he told them about the strange bets that were made amongst the members and how they were all recorded in a "Betting Book."

She realised that the Marquis was listening to what was being said and quickly bit back the words that came to her lips, knowing that she had to be very careful not to reveal her identity.

"I and some friends of mine had a bet with another member of the Club," Roderic continued, "that we would find an English girl, preferably a milk-maid, who was more beautiful and more intelligent than a foreigner who he was convinced would be far superior in every possible way."

Diona looked puzzled.

"Surely," she said, "it would be a very unequal contest unless everybody in it came from exactly the same class. After all, most milk-maids are not well educated!"

The Marquis's lips twisted and there was a twinkle in his eyes as he wondered how his nephew would answer that.

He was well aware that Roderic had chosen his words with care so as not to reveal that the contestants were to be ostensibly what he had described to his uncle as "bits o' muslin," who would inevitably be more quick-witted than any country-girl was likely to be.

That Diona should have put her finger unerringly on the weak side of what he had just said amused him, and he realised his nephew was struggling to find a reasonable answer.

Finally Roderic said:

"She does not have to be a milk-maid. That was just a figure of speech. But the girl that Sir Mortimer will produce is, he assures us, not only beautiful and quick-witted but could also pass as a Lady."

Diona considered this for a moment. Then she said:

"I do not think any milk-maid I have ever known would find that possible!"

"But," Roderic argued, "that is just where you are so different, and you said you are willing to be a milk-maid, although I am sure Uncle Lenox will be delighted to have you in his kennels."

He paused to say impressively:

"But first you must win this contest for me, which takes place in a week's time."

"What would I . . . have to . . . do?" Diona asked.

There was a little tremor in her voice because she was frightened.

She had a feeling—and once again her instinct was at work—that she was being pushed into something of which her mother would certainly not have approved and which her father would certainly have forbidden.

He had told her about the Bucks and Beaux who surrounded the Prince Regent and spent a great deal of their time gambling and drinking in the Clubs of St. James's.

She knew that whenever he could afford to go to London he visited White's to see his old friends, and sometimes he would make her laugh about the new members who had joined since he had last been there.

He described the Dandies scornfully, saying they were nothing but "clothes-horses," and he thought even Beau Brummell was excessive in the fuss he made about clothes.

"How any man can want to spend two or three hours a day dressing, God only knows!" he had said once. "It is a waste of precious time and, more important than that, a waste of life."

"I have always heard, Papa," Diona had said years later, after Beau Brummell had left England in disgrace, "that Mr. Brummell was very intelligent."

"He was a wit," her father had conceded, "and he had the brains to make himself an arbiter of fashion and a person of social importance. At the same time, he did not have the self-control to prevent himself from gambling away every penny he possessed. What could be more stupid than that?"

"I agree with you," Diona's mother had said. "At the same time, darling, I think these Clubs often prove a temptation to young men. It makes them want to show off, and inevitably they drink too much to give themselves courage to spend what they cannot afford."

Her father had smiled.

"That is a very good way of putting it, but men must be men, and learn to stand on their own feet."

"I am afraid that often means standing on other people's," her mother had said quietly.

Remembering that now, together with other things her father had said about White's, Diona felt nervous.

"All you have to do," Roderic was saying, "is to come to London and let me take you, not to the Club, for women are not allowed in there, but to somebody's house where you will meet all the other contestants, and of course the foreigner, who will not be half as pretty as you are."

"How will the judges . . . assess the . . . brains of those who are . . . competing against her?" Diona asked.

Again Roderic was having to think hard, and the Marquis's amusement increased.

It was quite a reasonable question after what she had been told, and he thought that perhaps this was something Sir Mortimer himself had not thought out.

"I suppose," Roderic said airily after a pause, "that there will be conversation, perhaps over dinner, and we might even dance afterwards. The judges will be able to see how each girl carries herself and behaves as she eats and dances."

Diona drew in her breath.

It was bad enough to think of being a contestant in a competition of which she was sure her mother would not have approved.

But to dine and dance with a number of strange men at a party which included milk-maids, and to be unchaperoned in a strange house where she did not even know the hostess, was something her mother would never have allowed.

"I . . . I could not . . . do that," she said quickly.

"Why not?" Roderic asked in surprise.

Then, as if he suddenly thought of something he should have said earlier, he added:

"I forgot to say that of course I will pay you a fee for doing this."

He hesitated before he went on:

"I will give you twenty pounds and a gown which will be so fantastically smart that it will knock them all sideways."

Diona stiffened and sat very straight and upright in her chair.

"No!" she exclaimed. "I certainly could not allow a gentleman to give me a gown! I also have no . . . wish to take part in this . . . competition!"

It passed through her mind that if she went to London, and if there were a number of members of White's at this peculiar party of which Mr. Nairn was speaking, there might conceivably be one of her father's friends amongst them.

It was unlikely because most of those who had visited them in the country and occasionally had stayed the night for a Steeple-Chase or a Point-to-Point had been men of her father's age.

Nevertheless, one never knew, and she could imagine nothing that would shock them more than to find her father's daughter pretending to be a milk-maid.

Almost before she had finished speaking, Roderic gave a cry of horror.

"You cannot say that!" he said. "You have to help me!"

As if the straight manner in which she was holding herself and the expression on her face told him better than words what she was feeling, he appealed to the Marquis.

"Help me, Uncle Lenox," he begged, "help me to convince Miss Diona that she is not only the miracle I have prayed for but is more perfect for the part than I ever imagined anybody could be!"

"I think," the Marquis said slowly, "you would find that not only Diona but any other *respectable* milk-maid who has spent all her life in the country would be apprehensive and somewhat shocked by what you have suggested."

"Shocked?" Roderic queried.

Then, as if it had suddenly sunk into him that his uncle had accentuated the word "respectable," he understood what was being said to him.

He moved from the arm of the chair on which he had been sitting and bent forward to say pleadingly:

"Please, Miss Diona, I desperately need your help, and it would be too cruel of you to refuse me without thinking it over very carefully."

Diona did not reply and after a moment he added:

"You say you have to earn money and this is a very easy way to do so. I will make it fifty pounds if you will agree to what I have suggested."

"It is . . . too much!" Diona protested. "And . . . I cannot go to . . . London."

"It is not as frightening as you think it would be," Roderic said, "and I promise to look after you."

He was not aware that when Diona said she could not go to London, the Marquis looked at her sharply and thought that what she was meaning was different from the way his nephew interpreted it.

If there was one thing the Marquis really enjoyed, it was a puzzle he had to solve or a mystery for which he could not find an explanation.

As soon as he had returned to England he had found that what intrigued him most was to discover where the weakest places were on his Estates.

He spent a lot of time in tracking down where money was being wasted or stolen, and where people were deliberately not doing what was required of them for reasons that did not appear obvious on the surface.

Now he found himself suddenly alert and extremely interested in Diona.

It was not so much on account of her beauty, but because she was obviously not of a class to become a milk-maid and must be hiding some secret.

Because he thought Roderic's pleadings might make things more difficult than they were already, he said:

"I have a suggestion to make, and I want you both to listen to me."

Diona turned her face towards him and Roderic did the same somewhat reluctantly.

"I imagine, although I may be mistaken," the Marquis began, "that Diona has come quite a long distance and must be tired. She has already told me that she has nowhere to go if she leaves here, so I suggest that she accept my hospitality for tonight, and she can then after dinner, or perhaps tomorrow, consider your proposition again."

Diona's lips parted, as if she was about to say that what Mr. Nairn had asked her to do was impossible, but the Marquis went on before she could speak:

"I would also like to discuss with my Head Kennel-man whether he thinks it possible for him to find employment for a woman, but I think I am right in saying that I already employ four men to look after my dogs."

He knew as he spoke that he had said exactly the right thing, for Diona gave a little murmur of excitement, and her eyes, which had been dark and frightened, had a sudden light in them.

"Will Your Lordship . . . really do . . . that?" she asked in a breathless little voice.

"I will do so if you will agree to stay the night."

"With Sirius?" Diona asked quickly.

"Naturally he is included in my invitation."

"Then . . . thank you . . . thank you very much . . . I accept . . . most gratefully, My Lord!"

As she spoke she rose to her feet, as if the interview was at an end.

As she did so, the Marquis said:

"I presume you have some luggage with you?"

He spoke cynically, as if he suspected it was unlikely.

Diona flushed as she replied:

"As I was travelling very light, My Lord, I brought the few . . . things I was able to carry in a bundle. I . . . I put them in some bushes . . . on the other side of the bridge."

She thought as she spoke that it sounded a very strange and rather childish thing to do.

The Marquis, however, appeared unperturbed. Then he said:

"Ring the bell, Roderic."

"I hope," he went on to Diona, "as you will be staying here you will give my nephew and me the pleasure of dining with us?"

He had expected her to accept with alacrity, as she had accepted his invitation to stay, but to his surprise she hesitated a moment before she said:

"Would that be the . . . right thing for . . . me to do?"

"The right thing?" the Marquis queried.

"I . . . I am sure kennel-maids do not . . . dine with their employers."

The Marquis smiled.

"You are somewhat of an unusual kennel-maid, Diona, and may I bring to your notice that you are not yet employed by me? So I think that on this occasion at any rate it would be quite in order for you to accept my invitation."

Diona considered what he had said before she replied:

"Thank you, My Lord. I am very honoured to be your guest."

"I keep London hours," the Marquis said, "and dine at eight o'clock. I expect you would like to rest for a little while before we meet in the Blue Drawing-Room a quarter-of-an-hour before dinner. You will be shown the way."

"Thank you, My Lord."

As she spoke the door opened and Dawson appeared.

"You rang, M'Lord?"

"Yes, Dawson. Miss Diona will be staying here for tonight. Put her in the Dolphin Room. She has, I understand, some belongings which she left in the bushes on the other side of the bridge."

Dawson's expression did not alter, nor did he appear in the least surprised, as he replied impassively:

"I'll have it fetched, M'Lord."

"Ask Mrs. Fielding to look after Miss Diona," the Marquis said, "and she will be dining with Mr. Roderic and me."

Dawson bowed his head to show that he understood his instructions, and Diona curtseyed.

"Thank you, My Lord," she said. "Thank you very . . . very . . . much."

The note of gratitude in her voice was inescapable, and the Marquis noticed that some of the fear had gone from her eyes.

As he watched her turn and follow Dawson from the Library, he was wondering why she was in hiding, what she had done to bring her to this situation, and he no longer felt as bored as he had been earlier in the day.

Then as the door shut, Roderic jumped up from the chair to throw a cushion in the air and say with a whoop of joy:

"I have won! I have won! Nobody—and I repeat, nobody—will be able to produce anything half so pretty!"

Then as he caught the cushion and replaced it in the chair he added:

"Thank you, Uncle Lenox! I always knew you were a sportsman, but now I am prepared to drink your health a thousand times and say there is nobody like you."

"I am very gratified," the Marquis said drily.

"I was terrified for one moment she would walk out on me," Roderic said, "but then you cleverly warned me that of course she is respectable. I never would have thought of it myself."

"Of course she is respectable!" the Marquis said sharply. "And what is more, I doubt if she has ever heard of a 'Cyprian' or a 'bit o' muslin,' and even if she had, she would not have the slightest idea what they are."

Roderic stared at him.

"Do you mean that?"

"I think, Roderic, you must learn how to judge people for what they are, and not what they appear."

"But she is on her own. She comes here unchaperoned and asks to see you, and wishes to be engaged as a kennel-maid. What am I supposed to think?"

The Marquis did not reply for a moment. Then he said:

"I think you must reason that out for yourself. I am only warning you, Roderic, that she has obviously run away to hide. If you frighten her as you did when you talked about the party which would be given at this rather debatable contest, she will run away again!"

Roderic gave what was almost a cry of protest.

"I cannot allow her to do that!"

"Then be careful what you say and even more careful how you behave."

Roderic considered this for a moment before he replied:

"If she is as respectable as you are saying she is, she is not going to like meeting Watson's nominee, who will undoubtedly, from the way he described her, be what the French call a 'Courtesan.' "

He did not wait for his uncle to comment but went on almost as if he were talking to himself.

"Although I have never been to Paris I have heard about them. They are a cut above the ordinary *fille de joie'* and expect to be covered in orchids and diamonds by any man who is rich enough to afford them."

Because he suddenly remembered to whom he was speaking, he said:

"Why am I telling you all this? You have been to Paris and know what I am talking about."

The Marquis, who had been listening with his eyes twinkling, said:

"May I suggest that the equivalent of a French 'Courtesan' does not really exist in England, and Watson was well aware of this when he challenged a lot of inexperienced and rather stupid young men who would not have the least idea of what they were up against!"

"Damn him!" Roderic exclaimed. "I call that cheating!"

"Actually, it is a shrewd bit of crookery."

Roderic threw himself petulantly down in a chair. Then he asked:

"Are you saying that we none of us have a chance in hell of beating Watson?"

"I think, on the contrary, that you have every chance," the Marquis answered. "In fact, unless the judges are bribed—and I should make sure they are not under Watson's thumb—Diona would eclipse any French 'Courtesan'!"

Roderic, alert and eager, again sat up.

"Do you mean that, Uncle Lenox?"

"I seldom say what I do not mean," the Marquis replied loftily.

"Then I *must* persuade her," Roderic said, "or rather you must!"

"I have nothing to do with it," the Marquis protested.

"But you must help me, and you know as well as I do that any woman will do anything you want, even jump over a cliff, if you beg her to do so!"

The Marquis laughed.

"Is that my reputation?"

"Of course it is! What was it Edward said the other day about you—'Invincible in war, invincible in bed!' "

As he spoke, Roderic looked at his uncle and saw the frown between his eyes, and added quickly:

"I am only telling you what Edward said, so it is no use being angry with me. Please, Uncle Lenox, you know we have somehow to defeat that ghastly Sir Mortimer, otherwise you will hear him crowing up and down St. James's Street for the rest of the year."

"That is a situation that must be avoided at all costs!" the Marquis remarked. "At the same time, it would be a mistake to be over-confident. Not that Diona would not win, but that she may not agree to take up the part."

He did not hear his nephew's reply but walked from the Library as he spoke.

As he moved along the corridor towards the Hall, his lips, which were often set in a hard line, were twisted in a faint smile which, to those who knew him well, meant that he was definitely amused.

CHAPTER FOUR

―――― ❦ ――――

$\mathcal{A}$s Diona came down the stairs for dinner she felt as if she were taking part in a Play.

Although her mother had often described to her the beautiful houses she had visited as a girl and where sometimes she and her husband had stayed, it was not the same as actually seeing anything as impressive and magnificent as Irchester Park.

Although Diona's bedroom was not one of the State Rooms, it was very comfortable and very attractive.

The bed had a round canopy above the centre of it, and the curtains which came from it were tied with silver ropes at each of the four posts.

She had looked round her with delight, and the elderly Housekeeper had said in what Diona knew was an extremely disapproving voice:

"I understand, Miss, that your luggage consists of only what is contained in this shawl."

As she spoke, Diona saw that a footman had just handed it in through the door to a younger maid who was wearing a lace-trimmed mob-cap with an apron to match.

"I am afraid I am travelling very light," Diona said, "and I was not able to bring a trunk with me."

Mrs. Fielding pressed her lips together, and Diona said apologetically:

"I had to leave home in rather a hurry."

Then, because she felt it was not the Housekeeper's business, she put up her chin and said in a tone which she was sure her mother would have used:

"It is very kind of you to look after me, and this is the loveliest house I have ever seen."

She thought Mrs. Fielding relaxed a little. Then she said with a different note in her voice:

"Are you intending for your dog to sleep here with you, Miss?"

"Yes, of course," Diona replied, "and I promise you he will not be any trouble and is perfectly housetrained."

The Housekeeper sniffed, as if she thought that was unlikely, and Diona added:

"I have had him ever since he was a puppy. He looks after me, and if robbers tried to break into my room I assure you he would be most ferocious!"

She thought the Housekeeper looked at her in a strange manner, but then she smiled.

"I think it's very sensible of you, Miss, to have him with you," she said. "Emily will look after you. Please ask for anything you require."

With that she swept from the room almost as if she were a Queen, and Diona wanted to laugh.

While Emily was helping her to change from what she was wearing into the muslin gown she had brought with her, together with a shawl, Diona kept wishing that her mother were with her so that they could laugh together at everything and also admire the contents of the Marquis's house.

"I hope I shall have a chance of seeing the paintings and everything else," Diona said beneath her breath, and sent up a little prayer that the Marquis would agree to employ her and she would be able to stay here.

When she thought about it, she was very apprehensive about what Mr. Nairn was suggesting to her.

How could she possibly go to London and attend the sort of party he had described?

Although she was very vague as to what it entailed, she knew it was something which her mother would have forbidden her to do.

She thought too that his plan complicated everything.

All she wanted to do was to work in the kennels with the Marquis's dogs and be quite certain that her uncle would never find her there.

In London there might be all sorts of pitfalls, and if somebody should recognise her it would be disastrous.

The whole idea was terrifying.

At the same time, it was a great relief to know that she had somewhere to stay at least for tonight, and to know that not only she but also Sirius would be well fed and it would cost her nothing.

After she had explained to Emily what Sirius had for his supper, she went downstairs while Diona was washing and then came back with a bowl of freshly cut-up meat, which made Sirius jump with joy.

Because Diona was so frightened that he might do anything to annoy Mrs. Fielding, she spread a towel on the carpet before Emily put down the bowl.

However, she was certain that as Sirius was a very tidy eater, there would be no cause for complaint.

It was only after she had rested a little and was putting her muslin gown back on that it struck her that the Marquis and Mr. Nairn would be in evening-dress.

While her muslin gown was very pretty, it was not really what her mother would have thought suitable for the evening.

'I suppose I should have refused to dine with him,' Diona thought apprehensively, 'and asked instead if I could have a tray in my bedroom.'

She knew that would have been very dull, and it was in fact far more exciting to dine with the Marquis. She was certain his company would be very different from that of her uncle.

Sir Hereward always as if by right monopolised the conversation in the Dining-Room at the Hall.

It usually concerned something that had irritated him in the County or on the Estate, and he would talk about it throughout every course, expecting nothing more than an occasional murmur of acquiescence from the other people seated at the table.

Diona could remember the amusing subjects which her father and mother had discussed and how they had argued just for the joy of sharpening their wits against each other.

Her father had always encouraged her to join in.

"If there is one thing I cannot stand," he had said once, "it is young girls with vacant faces thinking only of how much food they can stuff into their mouths."

"You have never known your daughter like that!" Diona's mother had expostulated, laughing.

"I want her to be like you, darling," her father had replied, "pretty and so much more amusing than any other woman I have ever met."

"I love to hear you say that," her mother had replied, "but give Diona a chance. She is very young, and she has not travelled as you have or begun yet to live her life fully."

"She will learn," her father had replied. "In the meantime, talk! I hate bells that do not ring, birds that do not sing, and women who have nothing to say!"

They had all laughed at that. Then when Diona had gone to live at the Hall, because nobody listened to her, she used to think of her father and have imaginary conversations with him.

'Now,' she thought, 'even if I do not have a chance of saying very much, at least I shall have somebody interesting to listen to.'

The Marquis might be frightening, in fact she thought he was very frightening, but at the same time she was sure that anything he had to say would be worth hearing.

She would certainly rather listen to him than to Mr. Nairn.

Dawson was waiting at the bottom of the stairs and she thought, although she was not sure, that he looked a little disparagingly at her simple muslin gown.

Because after she had bought it she thought it looked cheap, she had asked the seamstress who worked at the Hall to add a frill of real lace which came from one of her mother's gowns.

It encircled her shoulders and joined in the front with ribbons she also added which were of blue satin and had come from Paris.

She had enough of the same lace to make a wide frill round the hem, and while the dress as not like an elaborate evening-gown in the manner of those illustrated in *The Ladies' Journal,* it was, Diona thought, definitely very pretty.

The Blue Drawing-Room, into which she was shown, had a crystal chandelier hanging from the centre of the ceiling with what appeared to be hundreds of lighted candles on it.

It made the whole room glow with a soft light. Everything seemed somehow to shine and glitter in a way that lifted Diona's heart and made her feel it was a prelude to something exciting.

Then as she walked over the soft Aubusson carpet towards the end of the Drawing-Room, she saw that standing by the fireplace, which because it was summer was filled with flowers, were the Marquis and Roderic Nairn.

They each held a glass of champagne, and as they turned towards her she realised how magnificent the Marquis looked.

He was even grander than her father had been when he was going to a Hunt Ball or out to dinner with somebody important in the County.

His white cravat was tied in an intricate fashion that Diona was sure was new. It was snowy white against his slightly sun-tanned skin, and the points of his collar were high above it.

His long cut-away coat fitted without a wrinkle, and she knew that he was wearing the new "drain-pipe" pantaloons.

These had been invented by the Prince Regent to save gentlemen on less-formal occasions from having to struggle into silk stockings and satin knee-breeches.

Roderic Nairn looked smart, but the Marquis wore his clothes more casually, as if they were part of himself and he was supremely unconscious of them.

Neither gentleman spoke as she advanced towards them, and only as she reached the Marquis and dropped a small curtsey did he say:

"Good-evening, Diona! I hope you have been properly looked after?"

"Everybody has been very kind, and Sirius would like to thank you for a delicious dinner."

Sirius, upon hearing his name mentioned, wagged his tail, but he kept just behind Diona, as if at their new place he was on guard and determined to protect her.

"Sirius is a strange name for a dog!" the Marquis remarked.

"Strange?" Diona queried. "Your Lordship must be aware that Sirius was the name of Orion's dog, who followed him in his favourite sport of hunting."

The Marquis raised his eye-brows.

He was well aware of the Homeric origin of the name, but he was surprised that Diona should know it.

"I have forgotten all the Greek I was forced to learn at Oxford!" Roderic remarked, as if the omission were something of which to be proud.

"That is rather a pity," the Marquis said, "because in that case you will not realise that Diona's name is obviously a form of 'Dione.'"

Roderic looked blank, and Diona gave a little laugh.

"That is clever of you," she said. "Mama wanted to call me 'Dione' because she said I was the daughter of Heaven and Earth, which of course represented her and Papa."

She laughed again and went on:

"But Papa said 'Dione' was too difficult for the English to pronounce and they would make a mess of it. So he insisted I should be christened 'Diona'!"

The Marquis's eyes twinkled.

"I can see, Roderic," he said to his nephew, "that we are going to have a very intellectual evening! It is a pity that the judges of Sir Mortimer's contest are not listening to us."

"I should like Miss Diona to repeat what she has just said when she is in front of them," he replied.

Because Diona did not wish to spoil the evening by saying she had no wish to enter the contest, she changed the subject by saying to the Marquis:

"I did want Sirius to be called 'Tishtriya,' after the Celestial Dog-Star who is worshipped in Persia, but again Papa said it was too complicated a name."

She paused, then as she thought the Marquis looked cynical she went on:

"I then thought of calling him after another Celestial Dog, the Chinese T'ien-kon, who drives away evil spirits."

As she spoke she thought that T'ien-kon might have driven away Uncle Hereward!

"I think you will find that my dogs have very English names," the Marquis remarked, "for the simple reason that they are named by my Head Kennel-man."

"Have you any Dalmatians?" Diona asked eagerly.

"Two, who are getting rather old," the Marquis replied. "But they are extremely well bred, and I shall be interested to see how they compare with Sirius."

"I shall be very upset," Diona replied, "if Sirius loses on points."

"And I of course shall be piqued if he wins," the Marquis answered.

She laughed with a spontaneous and natural little laugh which the Marquis thought was very different from the affected, contrived laughter of the women with whom he associated in London.

Then, as if she suddenly thought of it, Diona said:

"You must please forgive me if I am not adequately gowned to dine with Your Lordship in such a splendid house, but I came away in rather a hurry, and took from my wardrobe only a few things I could carry easily."

There was a faint twist to the Marquis's lips, as if, she thought, he questioned what she said before he remarked:

"And you thought that very pretty gown in which you arrived would be suitable for a kennel-maid?"

Diona blushed, and he thought perhaps he had been unkind.

There was a little pause before she answered:

"It was only on my way . . . here that I thought of being a . . . kennel-maid as a way of . . . employment. Of course, if Your Lordship does . . . engage me, I will somehow buy the appropriate . . . clothes."

The Marquis did not have to reply because at that moment Dawson announced dinner.

Roderic immediately offered her his arm, saying:

"I think you look very pretty, but I doubt if my uncle's dogs will be able to compliment you as eloquently as I can!"

Diona laughed and replied:

"If you become too eloquent, Sirius may be jealous. You will find he is very ferocious when he is defending me."

"You are making me nervous," Roderic said.

At the same time, he was thinking that when Diona laughed, she looked more entracing than he could imagine any Frenchwoman could look, however eminent she might be as a Courtesan.

However, he was determined to be cautious and not to upset her in any way.

"I am sure Uncle Lenox will be able to persuade her to do what I want," he told himself confidently.

They reached the Dining-Room and Diona gave an exclamation of delight because it was so beautiful.

Painted in pale green, which was the hallmark of Robert Adam, it had alcoves in the walls, in which stood statues of Greek gods and goddesses.

At each end of the room were Ionic pillars supporting the painted ceiling, which depicted Venus with a host of small fat cherubs greeting Neptune emerging from the sea surrounded by mermaids.

The room was illuminated by huge white candles set on carved wooden stands which Diona was sure had come from Italy or Spain.

The candelabra on the table were of silver, and she noticed immediately that there was no white cloth on the table, which was a new fashion which had been introduced by the Prince Regent.

Because she was so excited by everything she saw, as she seated herself on the right of the Marquis she exclaimed:

"Papa told me it was now fashionable to have a polished table without a cloth, but I had never seen one before. I am sure it shows off the silver far better, especially your beautiful George I candelabra."

"I agree!" the Marquis said. "But I am surprised you should recognise the date."

"Why?" Diona asked.

The Marquis knew the obvious retort would be rude. Instead he said:

"When it comes to silver, most people find it difficult to distinguish between the three Georges."

"But George I silver is so much more simple in design," Diona said. "That is why I realise how appropriate it is with your Ionic columns."

The Marquis was quite certain this conversation would leave any Frenchwoman whom Sir Mortimer could produce looking extremely foolish.

However, he was not concerned at the moment with Sir Mortimer or Roderic and their contest, but with unravelling a puzzle and making note of every clue that Diona gave him.

As if Roderic felt out of his depth and was determined to assert himself, he started to talk about horses and the races that had taken place at Royal Ascot.

Diona had not known it until now, but she was not surprised to learn that the Marquis had won the Gold Cup. It had been a spectacular finish, with his horse beating the favourite by a neck.

"I wish I had seen it!" she said. "I have always longed to go to Ascot, and I suppose now I shall never have the chance of doing so."

This told the Marquis without her saying any more that it had been intended she should visit the races, but her hopes had been dashed.

Diona did not continue, but he realised he was becoming more and more intrigued and at the same time puzzled.

There was no doubt that she was a lady, and yet, he asked himself, what lady of that age would be allowed to wander about accompanied only by a dog?

Also, what well-bred young lady would have the courage to go out into the world to earn her own living without any money, or her relatives forbidding her to do so?

It was a mystery and one he was determined to solve.

The easiest way, he knew, was to let Diona give herself away out of her own mouth.

He was too astute and too used to cross-examining soldiers who had got into trouble in Portugal or France, and who invariably lied, to ask too many questions.

Instead, he led Diona on by arguing when she made some particular statement, inviting her to explain herself, and sometimes getting a very revealing answer.

"It would be foolish to ask you if you are fond of riding," he said, "but do you consider yourself a good rider?"

"Papa said I was very good, and as he was outstanding, it is not conceited for me to say 'yes' to that question."

"Did you father do any racing?"

He was aware that Diona hestitated in case the answer she gave should be indiscreet.

Then, as if she knew he had not heard of her father, she replied:

"He often rode in local Point-to-Points and Steeple-Chases, but that was all."

"That makes me think," the Marquis said ruminatively, "that I should have a Steeple-Chase here very soon. I gave orders for the race-course to be repaired, but I have not yet used it, and it would be easy to erect jumps quite as difficult as they have in the Grand National."

"That is a wonderful idea, Uncle Lenox!" Roderic exclaimed. "And if I could ride any of your horses, I would stand a chance of winning!"

The Marquis laughed.

"If you rode them under your own colours, that might be considered unsporting."

"Alternatively," Roderic said, looking at him somewhat slyly, "I could invest in a few good jumpers of my own!"

"Judging from the present state of your Bank-balance," the Marquis retorted drily, "I think that would be a serious mistake."

"Then I should be forced, unless I can borrow from your stables, just to be a spectator," Roderic said complacently.

Because she realised he had got his own way, Diona smiled at him from across the table, and he said:

"If you are going to ride in this contest, I advise you to go down on your knees before Uncle Lenox and beg him to mount you. His horses are far better than anybody else's."

"That is what I have already surmised," Diona said, "and I hope perhaps I shall be allowed to look after them if they need me."

The Marquis sat back in his armchair.

"Are you seriously contemplating being a woman groom as well as a kennel-maid?" he asked.

"I cannot see why not!" she answered a little defiantly. "Horses react in a gentler way to a woman's hand, and sometimes we have the magic which only the gypsies know, which will turn a wild horse into a quiet and obedient one."

The Marquis was interested.

"I have heard how the gypsies can make their horses do anything they ask of them," he said. "Do you really know what their formula or incantation is?"

Diona looked away from him and he knew she was wondering whether she should answer his question truthfully or feign ignorance.

When he wished to do so the Marquis could force people, by means of what he sometimes thought was a magic of his own, to obey him.

He therefore concentrated his thoughts on Diona until she turned her head as if she could not resist the power he was pouring out to her.

"I know a . . . little about their . . . secret ways of making their horses and dogs . . . follow them and do what they . . . wish them to do," she conceded.

"They trusted you with their secrets?" the Marquis enquired.

Diona's eyes, looking into his, flickered. Then she said:

"They trusted Papa, who befriended them . . . and when they had a particularly fine horse to sell they always . . . offered it to him . . . first."

"They did not trick him?"

"No, of course not. The gypsies would never trick a friend, and they looked on us as friends."

"Why?"

The way he spoke the monosyllable was very compelling, and Diona replied:

"They camped on our land and came back year after year. Nobody would ever believe it, but they never touched anything that was ours."

She looked at the Marquis to see if he believed her, and went on:

"We never lost a chicken or an egg, and when they left, everything was tidy, and the only thing to show they had been there were the ashes of their fires."

Diona was looking back into the past, remembering that everybody who had come in contact with her father and mother had loved them.

She thought now that the happiness which radiated from them inevitably made other people feel happy.

It was so very different from the miseries she had suffered with her uncle at the Hall and the darkness and gloom that had enveloped her from the moment she had entered through the door, unwanted and certainly unappreciated.

Her eyes were far more expressive than she knew, and the Marquis watched her, feeling that every moment he was getting nearer to finding out her secret.

Suddenly looking back into the past, her eyes met his and for a moment it seemed as if they were both of them held spellbound by a strange vibration.

It had nothing to do with where they were or who they were, but it seemed part of the eternity from which they had come.

Then Roderic broke the spell, which was somehow as delicate as a cobweb, by saying:

"Let us go on talking about the Steeple-Chase. What will the prizes be, Uncle Lenox, and whom will you invite to take part in it?"

"A number of my friends," the Marquis said, "and of course anybody locally who has good enough horses."

His answer told Diona, almost as if he had broken the dream in which she was living, that one person who most certainly would not take part would be herself.

People with good horses would certainly include some who had known her father and mother and would recognise her as being their daughter.

There would also be those who had come to the Hall since she had been there, friends of her uncle's who had, she knew, looked at her with a flicker of admiration in their eyes.

Although she had had no chance of talking to them alone, and her uncle had invariably snubbed her if she tried to join in the conversation, they would remember her.

One thing she must never do if she was to remain in hiding was to allow any of the Marquis's friends or neighbours to catch sight of her.

She said nothing, but the Marquis was perceptively aware that a shutter had fallen down between them and she had retired into some secret cavern where he could not reach her.

But it only made him more determined than ever to discover what all this was about.

He played with the idea that she had run away from a prospective bridegroom.

Then, with his knowledge of women, he felt he was prepared to swear that she was so innocent and untouched that no man had so much as kissed her and she was completely unawakened.

He was aware that while she had looked at him at first with fear, and then, he thought, with a certain respect and even admiration, she was making absolutely no effort to attract him as a man.

He was quite certain it was because she did not know how to do so.

It was the same with Roderic. He was eager to talk to her and he would, the Marquis thought, with the slightest encouragement have flirted with her.

But the way in which Diona spoke to them both told him that she was completely unselfconscious and unawakened to the idea that there was anything strange in dining alone with two attractive men.

It was obvious that she was so young and ignorant of the world that she was behaving as a child would have done in the circumstances.

Her appreciation of the room and the silver was echoed by her appreciation of the food.

"I have never eaten anything so delicious!" she said as dinner ended. "But there is one thing I cannot understand."

"What is that?" the Marquis enquired.

"If you have Chefs here and in London, which I am sure you do, to produce meals like this every day, how is it possible that you are so slim?"

She had not meant to sound as if she was paying him a compliment but rather simply curious, and the Marquis said:

"I take a great deal of exercise."

"I suppose that is the answer," Diona said. "Papa always complained if we had too many dishes with cream because that made him put on weight and he liked to ride light."

"I, too, have no wish to be too heavy for my horses," the Marquis answered. "And I assure you, Army rations, which I endured for a number of years, are not so enjoyable that I got into the habit of over-eating."

"I admit to having been very greedy this evening," Diona said. "I have eaten far more than I should have done, and have enjoyed every mouthful!"

She laughed, as if she had found the food irresistible, and Roderic laughed with her.

They all went together to the Drawing-Room, as the Marquis said that neither he nor Roderic wished to be left alone with their port. Diona went to the French window that was open onto the garden outside, and stood there.

Her head was silhouetted against the stars and her slim body in her white gown was outlined against the shadows in the garden.

The Marquis watched her and thought she might easily be a celestial being who had come down, as the gods and goddesses of the Greeks and Romans were always prone to do, to entice and bemuse mere mortals.

597

The difficulty from Roderic's point of view, he knew, was that the help he needed was not what Diona would wish to give him.

He had, too, the strange feeling that she might vanish as inexplicably as she had appeared, without giving them any warning of her intention.

Roderic had joined Sirius, who was exploring the garden below them, and the Marquis moved to stand beside Diona at the window.

Her head was thrown back as she looked up at the stars, and he asked a little mockingly:

"Are you beseeching Orion, and I see his constellation is above your head, not to demand his dog back?"

He was speaking lightly and was surprised at the depth of emotion in Diona's voice as she replied:

"No-one . . . no-one shall . . . take Sirius from me! He is mine, and no-one shall . . . hurt him!"

The strength of her feelings seemed to vibrate from her, and after a moment the Marquis said quietly:

"You sound as if somebody has threatened to do so."

Diona looked away to where she could see Sirius, white against the dark shrubs, nosing amongst the bushes.

"I . . . I do not want to . . . talk about it."

There was a little silence. Then she cried:

"May I please ask you a favour?"

"Of course," the Marquis replied.

"Will you promise not to mention to anybody outside this house that I am here, or that I have a Dalmatian with me?"

"You think that if I did so, it might be dangerous for Sirius?"

"Yes . . . very . . . very dangerous! Will you . . . promise?"

"You realise I am curious as to why you should ask me such a thing?"

"I am . . . sorry if I sound secretive . . . but it is of no importance to you . . . and very . . . very important to me that I should . . . remain anonymous."

"I will naturally respect your wishes," the Marquis said, "but if I do what you ask, will you promise me something in return?"

She raised her eyes to his and he saw that she was frightened.

Because he could read her thoughts, he knew she feared he was going to say that she had to do what Roderic wanted.

Instead he said:

"If you are frightened and you think that I can help you in any way, will you come to me for assistance?"

"Do you mean . . . that?"

"I mean it," the Marquis said, "and I will also help you if it is humanly possible to do so."

He heard the little sigh of relief that seemed to come from the depths of her body before she replied:

"Thank you . . . thank you! I knew I was . . . right to come to you the . . . moment I saw your . . . house."

"What do you mean by that?"

For a moment he thought she was not going to answer his question. Then she said, looking up again at the stars:

"What Papa called my 'intuition' told me that I should find help from you, and I was not . . . mistaken."

The Marquis knew, although she had put it so simply, that it was what he felt himself in times of danger, and when he was in a position where his brain alone seemed unable to help him.

It was then that he used his instinct or something more powerful. There were no words to express it, yet it had never failed him.

"So you were sure I would help you!"

Diona turned to look at him again.

"I was still very . . . very frightened!" she admitted.

"And now?"

"I am still frightened . . . but not of you."

"Let me help you to sweep away your other fears," the Marquis said. She shook her head.

"No-one can do that . . . but if I could . . . stay here for a little while . . . Sirius and I would be very . . . very grateful."

"I have already told you that I will consider how I can help you. I do not believe in making hasty decisions, but of course, in the meantime, you are my guest."

He saw the reflection of the stars in her eyes as she said:

"Thank you . . . thank you! Tonight I shall be very . . . grateful for not having to sleep in a . . . hay-stack or under a hedge . . . which I was very afraid would . . . happen."

The Marquis laughed.

"I think you will find the bed in the Dolphin Room is much more comfortable."

She looked away from him, but he had the feeling that she was not seeing Sirius or Roderic moving about at the end of the garden, or the stars reflected in the lake beyond them.

Instead, she said in a low voice, almost as if she was speaking to herself:

"I think Mama would be . . . shocked at my staying here . . . but in a strange way I feel it is the right place to be . . . and that God brought . . . me to you."

When Roderic came back into the room, Diona said, and again the Marquis was surprised:

"I hope, My Lord, you will not think it very rude if Sirius and I go to bed, but I feel very tired. It has been a long day, and because there has been a lot to upset me and make me . . . anxious, it has been more . . . exhausting than a day in the saddle."

The Marquis was used to women making every excuse not to leave him.

They were usually prepared to stay up all night rather than retire, unless of course he went with them. So once again he was surprised, but he merely answered:

"I think you are being wise, Diona, and I suspect that somewhere in your mountain of luggage you have something in which you can ride! So I suggest you join Roderic and me for breakfast and immediately afterwards you can help me exercise my horses."

For a moment Diona stared at him.

Then she made a little sound that expressed how excited she was far more eloquently than words could have done.

"May I really do that?" she asked. "I have a riding-skirt with me, but I am afraid I shall not look very . . . conventional."

"There will be nobody else to see you except for the horses," the Marquis remarked, "and I doubt if they will complain!"

She gave a little chuckle. Then she said:

"At what time do you breakfast? I promise you I will not be late."

"At eight o'clock," the Marquis said. "Of course, if you are asleep, Roderic and I will understand, and we will set off without you!"

He was teasing, but Diona exclaimed:

"I shall be up and dressed by six o'clock just in case I keep you waiting!"

"There is no need for that," the Marquis replied. "You merely have to tell Mrs. Fielding at what time you wish to be called."

"Yes, of course!" she exclaimed. "I had forgotten, because at home I used to call myself."

This was another clue, the Marquis thought, which meant that at home there had not been a large number of servants.

Yet, from the way Diona had behaved at dinner and had helped herself from the many dishes presented by the footman, he realised she was used to being waited on.

She had been quite firm in refusing what wines she did not want, as if it was something which happened every day and she did not even have to consider it.

This and a number of other things she had said and done sent the Marquis to bed thinking about her.

When he was finally alone in the darkness, he told himself that the puzzle with which she presented him was as fascinating as any conundrum he had ever encountered in the past, and far more attractive.

He realised that sooner or later he would have to make up his mind how to employ her, and that would present a number of difficulties he would have to solve.

He could hardly pay her for looking after his dogs and at the same time entertain her in his Dining-Room.

If she was employed at the level of a "kennel-maid," such as Roderic kept talking about, it would be impossible for her to live in what those on the Estate called the "Big House."

He was quite certain that this difficulty had not yet presented itself to Diona, although doubtless it would do so sooner or later, and he wondered what she would make of it.

In the meantime, he was aware, without her even telling him so, that everything that happened was concerned in some way with Sirius, although he was not quite certain how.

Never before had he met a woman whose attention would wander while he was speaking to her because she was wondering if her dog was all

601

right, and who would watch her dog rather than try to draw a little nearer to the man beside her.

It was a very old trick played by beautiful women to show the long, classical line of their necks while tipping back their heads to look up at the stars.

But he was well aware that Diona had done it naturally and had been quite unaware that he was watching her or that the movement might mean something to him.

When she said she must go to bed she had put out her hand towards him, saying as she did so:

"Thank you, My Lord, from the very bottom of my heart for your kindness. Tonight has been a very exciting experience, and I will never forget . . ."

The Marquis expected her to add, as every other woman had done, in a soft, inviting tone: ". . . being with you!"

Instead, Diona finished:

". . . seeing your wonderful house, of which I hope I may see more tomorrow, and having such a delicious dinner."

"I am glad it pleased you," the Marquis said conventionally.

"Sirius must thank you too."

She gave the Dalmatian an order and instantly he sat up on his hind legs.

"Say 'thank you,' Sirius!" she ordered, and he bowed his head.

"Excellent!" the Marquis exclaimed. "I see he is well trained, and of course very sincere in his gratitude."

"We both are."

She smiled, but there was nothing intimate or flirtatious in her eyes, only a sincerity which seemed to have swept away the fear that had been so very obvious when she arrived.

Then she said good-night to Roderic, curtseying to him, and the two men walked with her across the Hall to the bottom of the staircase.

She curtseyed once again, then like a child she raced Sirius to the top of the staircase.

When she reached the top she turned to wave to the Marquis and Roderic, who were watching her from the Hall. It was an impersonal, happy gesture with nothing intimate about it.

Then she was running once again with Sirius along the wide corridor which led to her bedroom.

"She is perfect!" Roderic exclaimed. "Perfect! Oh, Uncle Lenox, I cannot wait to see Sir Mortimer's face when I produce her!"

The Marquis did not reply.

There was a frown between his eyes as he walked back towards the Drawing-Room.

For some unaccountable reason, it annoyed him to think of anything so unspoilt as Diona coming into contact with Sir Mortimer Watson.

CHAPTER FIVE

───── ❧ ─────

SIMON WALKED INTO THE BREAKFAST-ROOM, where his father was already seated at the head of the table.

As he helped himself rather greedily from the silver dishes on the side-table, he asked:

"Any news of Diona?"

For a moment Sir Hereward did not answer. Then he growled:

"She will come back when she is hungry."

Simon sat down at the table and started to eat in the uncouth manner which had always made Diona feel slightly sick.

Then Sir Hereward, who was opening his letters, exclaimed:

"Good God!"

His voice was so loud that Simon looked up.

"What is it, Papa?"

"I can hardly believe it."

"Believe what?" Simon enquired.

Sir Hereward looked at the letter again as if he felt it was deceiving him. Then he said:

"This is a letter from your Uncle Harry's Solicitors to tell me that Diona has been left a fortune by her Godmother!"

"A fortune?" Simon repeated.

"Eighty thousand pounds, to be exact!"

"I thought she had no money!" Simon said plaintively.

"Of course she had no money!" Sir Hereward said sharply. "But her Godmother, a woman I have never even heard of, has left her this large sum, and the Solicitors, quite rightly, have communicated with me as her Guardian."

"But you do not know where she is!" Simon said.

As he invariably stated the obvious, Sir Hereward frowned for a moment, then said as if he was speaking to himself:

"Eighty thousand pounds! And the girl is barely nineteen! I have an idea, Simon, that this will benefit you."

"Me, Papa?"

"Yes, you, my son."

As Sir Hereward spoke he smiled in an unpleasant manner which, if she had seen it, would undoubtedly have made Diona alarmed.

Riding back over the Park, Diona thought that the last three days had been the happiest she had ever known.

Not only had she been able to ride the Marquis's superb horses, but to be with him and Roderic was a joy that made her spring out of bed in the morning, excited because a new day was beginning.

After they had breakfasted they raced one another over the meadowland, riding into the cool of the woods and jumping a dozen hedges.

They were now returning to the Big House for what Diona knew would be a delicious luncheon with conversation that seemed to sparkle as brilliantly as the sunshine outside.

Because she had been starved intellectually ever since her father's death, she found when she went to bed at night that her mind was turning over and savouring not only what had been said but what she wanted to discuss the following day.

She had to admit that most of the arguments which were very spirited were between her and the Marquis.

But Roderic was a good listener, and he also occasionally sided with one or the other of them, which made it more interesting.

Sometimes when she awoke in the night she thought she must have been dreaming.

She would feel that if she lit a candle she would see not the beautiful draped bed of the Dolphin Room, but instead the dark brown velvet curtains of her bedroom at the Hall, which was symbolic, she thought, of the lack of colour in the rest of the house and the people who lived in it.

Because she was so happy she had begun to forget her fear of her uncle and the threat that Sirius would be taken from her.

She had been delighted to find that the Marquis's dogs, though very well bred, as he had said, were no finer than Sirius, and even the kennel-men admitted he was an outstanding Dalmatian.

Now as he ran beside the horses she knew that the exercise he had been having these last few days had been good for his figure, and she thought no dog could be more handsome or more attractive.

At the same moment, the Marquis spoke to her, and as she turned her head she thought the two adjectives might also apply to him.

"I think I have time, Uncle Lenox," Roderic was saying, "to take this horse I am riding over the jumps on the race-course before luncheon. I want to make sure which one I will ride in your Steeple-Chase."

The Marquis smiled, but he did not reply, and Roderic, instead of crossing the bridge which led towards the house, galloped off towards the race-course that was on the other side of the Park.

"He is very enthusiastic!" Diona said as she and the Marquis slowed to a walk to cross the stone bridge. "Do you think he has a chance of winning?"

Before he could answer, she laughed.

"I suppose I can answer my own question by saying: 'Not if you are competing!' "

"Are you suggesting I should be handicapped?" the Marquis enquired.

"Yes, of course you should be," Diona replied, "because you are too good at everything and it does not give us ordinary mortals a chance."

"You are very complimentary," he replied, "and I have a suspicion that you intend to ask me if you can compete in the Steeple-Chase and ride either Champion or Mercury."

Those were the names of the two of his horses she had ridden that had pleased Diona most, but she was surprised that he had noticed.

Then she remembered that it could be very dangerous for her to take part in the Steeple-Chase, and she merely replied:

"I think long before that takes place you must decide whether you wish to . . . employ me, or I must look . . . elsewhere."

As she spoke she knew that every nerve in her body was praying that she would not have to leave Irchester Park or, for that matter, the Marquis.

They had reached the steps leading to the front door before he answered:

"When you have changed, Diona, I want to talk to you. I will be in the Library."

She looked at him quickly and apprehensively, but as he was concerned with dismounting he did not meet her eyes.

She ran upstairs to her bedroom, and as she took off her riding-skirt she wondered frantically what he had to say to her.

Because she had the feeling that it was important, she did not spend any time at the mirror but merely took out some of the pins in her hair which had kept it tidy while she was riding, while Emily buttoned her white muslin gown at the back.

It was very plain but it was new, and the ribbons she had added to it were of the soft green of the first buds of Spring.

Then at the last moment, because she felt that she should perhaps have put on her best sprigged muslin, Diona took two of the little white rose-buds that were in a vase on the dressing-table and pinned them on the front of her gown.

"That's ever so pretty, Miss!" Emily exclaimed.

Diona smiled at her as she ran from the room and down the stairs to find the Marquis.

He was sitting, as she expected, in his favourite high-backed armchair at the side of the fine Adam mantelpiece.

Above it was a shield of the Irchester coat-of-arms painted on wood with his crest at the top.

Walking towards him, Diona thought the Marquis made a picture which should have been painted by some great artist and hung beside his ancestors in the Picture Gallery.

He was not smiling as she reached him, and because there was a serious expression in his grey eyes which she did not understand, she stood in front of him feeling a little nervous.

"W-what is it?" she asked. "I have not . . . done something . . . wrong?"

"No, of course not," he replied, "but I want to talk to you about the future."

Diona felt as if an icy hand clutched at her heart and she asked quickly:

"Has Mr. Nairn been . . . worrying you about his . . . contest?"

"He has certainly mentioned it," the Marquis replied.

"I . . . I am afraid . . . you will be . . . very angry with me," Diona said hesitatingly, "but . . . please . . . I cannot do what he . . . asks."

"Why not?"

"It is something which I know my father and mother would . . . disapprove of my doing . . . and also . . . I cannot go to . . . London."

"Do you intend to tell me why?"

"N-no . . . I cannot . . . do that."

She thought as she spoke that because she was being secretive he might be angry, and she looked down at him pleadingly as she said:

"Please . . . please . . . try to understand . . . you know I am hiding . . . and if I go to London there might be people who would . . . recognise me."

She saw the look of surprise in the Marquis's face before he remarked:

"I thought you told me you had never been to London."

"That is true," Diona said. "At the same time . . . I have met people who have come from London . . . and if I . . . played Mr. Nairn's part . . ."

Her voice broke off, and because she was feeling bewildered and afraid that the Marquis would be insistent with her, she went down on her knees beside his chair.

"Please . . . help me . . ." she begged. "It is all such a muddle . . . and I have been so happy . . . here with . . . you."

The Marquis looked at her and she had the feeling, although he did not speak, that he was somehow reaching towards her and understood.

Then he said very quietly:

"You say you have been happy with me, Diona, and as I also have been very happy with you, I have something to suggest."

Her eyes were on his, and she wondered why he hesitated before he went on as if he was choosing his words:

"I realise that you are in hiding, and I hope one day you will trust me with your secret. In the meantime, as you cannot go on staying here indefinitely, I am going to suggest that I take you to London and keep you safe."

"To . . . London?" Diona asked. "But I have to . . . work."

"Not as a kennel-maid."

"Then . . . what can I do?"

She knew he was feeling for words before he replied:

"I have a small house where you and Sirius would be very comfortable and completely safe. I could not be with you all the time, but we could be together a great deal, and it would be possible for me occasionally to take you with me to one of my other houses, where we could ride."

He realised as he finished speaking that Diona was staring at him in bewilderment, her eyes searching his as if trying to understand.

"I should feel safe with you," she said, "but I do not . . . quite know why you should want me to . . . go to London . . . or how I could earn my . . . living."

The Marquis put out his hand towards her, and after a moment's hesitation she gave him hers. He drew her a little closer and put his arm round her shoulder.

Because he was touching her she could feel his strength and the vibrations passing between them that she had felt before.

"You are very lovely," he said in a deep voice, "and very young, and you must have somebody to take care of you."

The way he spoke gave her a strange feeling in her breast, which she had never known before.

Then, because he was still looking into her eyes, it seemed to her as if his grew larger and larger until they filled the whole world and there was nothing but him.

"We will be very happy together," he said softly.

Then, hearing the door of the Library open, Diona jumped to her feet, and as the Marquis also rose, Dawson came into the room.

"Sir Hereward Grantley and Mr. Simon Grantley, M'Lord!" he announced.

Diona made a muffled cry, and Sirius, who had been lying on the floor beside the Marquis's chair, growled in his throat.

Then, walking lamely because of his gout and leaning on an ivory-handled cane, Sir Hereward came into the room.

He advanced towards them and Diona felt as if she were turned to stone.

There was silence until Sir Hereward was within a few feet of the Marquis. Ignoring him, he merely stared at Diona before he said roughly:

"So here you are! A nice dance you have given me, disappearing in that disgraceful manner!"

It was then that Diona realised she had not drawn a breath from the moment her uncle had been announced, and now she was trembling.

Sirius growled again, and as if the sound brought her back to reality she said:

"I ran away, Uncle Hereward, to . . . save Sirius. You said you were . . . going to have him shot, and I could not . . . lose him . . . I could not!"

"You should have talked to me about it instead of behaving like an idiot," Sir Hereward said.

Then, as if he remembered that was not why he had come to find her, he added:

"You can come home now, and if Sirius behaves himself in the future I will spare him."

His change of tone was so surprising that Diona gave an audible gasp.

Then, as if he could not bear to keep silent any longer, Simon cried:

"What Papa is saying is that now that you are an heiress, you can pay for Sirius yourself and your father's bills!"

"Be quiet, Simon!" Sir Hereward shouted.

He turned his head to reprove his son, and in doing so he seemed to become aware of the Marquis for the first time, for he held out his hand to say:

"Forgive me, My Lord, for intruding upon you unexpectedly, but I only learnt late last night that my extremely undisciplined niece had come here."

The Marquis ignored Sir Hereward's outstretched hand and merely remarked:

"I should be extremely interested to be told what all this is about."

"I will tell you," Simon said in his impulsive manner. "My Cousin Diona has come into a fortune of eighty thousand pounds from her God-mother. Think of it—eighty thousand pounds for a young girl like that!"

"I do not know what you are . . . talking about," Diona cried.

"There is no need for us to discuss our intimate affairs in front of strangers!" Sir Hereward said sharply. "There is a carriage outside, Diona, and you will come home with me now. Then I will explain what you need to know."

"I am sorry . . . Uncle Hereward," Diona answered, "but I am not . . . going to live with you . . . any more. I have been very . . . unhappy, and although I pleaded with you . . . you ordered Sirius to be . . . shot, and I would . . . never . . . risk his being in that . . . position again."

"I have told you that you can keep the dog!" Sir Hereward said angrily.

"You can keep him," Simon chimed in, "because you are going to marry me! And with eighty thousand pounds you can have dozens of dogs if you want!"

"I . . . I do not know what . . . you are . . . saying."

Now because she was so frightened the words seemed to be jerked from Diona's lips.

"Will you be silent, Simon!" Sir Hereward thundered. "Leave this to me."

Quite unabashed because he had been so spoilt that he was not in the least afraid of his father, Simon smiled at Diona in a way that made her flesh creep.

It was the same foolish smile he had had on his face when he had tried to kiss her, and the expression in her eyes now was the same as when she had had to fight him to get free.

Because Sir Hereward felt he had silenced his son, he looked again at the Marquis.

"My apologies, My Lord," he said, "for inflicting my domestic affairs upon you in this unseemly fashion. I will now take my niece away with me, and you will not be bothered with her any further."

Hardly aware of what she was doing, Diona moved a step nearer to the Marquis.

"As I have concerned myself in your niece's affairs," the Marquis said in his most authoritative tone, "I think I am entitled to an explanation, Sir Hereward, of what you plan for her in the future."

"I see no reason . . ." Sir Hereward began.

Then, as if the Marquis forced him to do so, he explained after a pause:

"My niece is an orphan, and I am prepared for her to marry my son, who in due course will inherit my title and Estates."

"And you think your niece will consent to this arrangement?" the Marquis asked.

Quite obviously it was a challenge. Sir Hereward's face grew redder than it was already, and the note of anger in his voice was unmistakable as he replied:

"I am her Guardian and, as Your Lordship well knows, she must legally obey any arrangements I make for her."

As if the full impact of what he was saying penetrated into Diona's mind, she knew that the only thing she could do was to run away and hide.

She tensed her whole body to take the first step towards escaping to run from the room and go on running.

Instinctively the Marquis knew what she was about to do, and he caught hold of her wrist.

As if he had checked her in mid-flight, she turned her head to look at him reproachfully, and he was aware that she was shaking with fear.

At the same time, Sirius, as if he knew what was happening, was now growling menacingly in his throat.

The Marquis's fingers tightened and Diona felt as if he drew her a little closer to him before he said:

"I am afraid, Sir Hereward, your plans are not practical because Diona is engaged to me!"

There was a stupefied silence.

Then as Diona drew in her breath in bewilderment, Simon cried out:

"You cannot have her! She is mine! Mine! Papa said she is to marry me, and she has to do so!"

The Marquis ignored him.

He was watching Sir Hereward, who was well aware of the import of what had been said, but could not think for the moment how to cope with it.

Then as his son's shrill, hysterical voice died away he said heavily:

"She cannot be married without my consent!"

"I am aware of that," the Marquis replied quietly, "but I hardly think you would withhold it."

The two men's eyes met, and while Sir Hereward glared at him, the Marquis's of contempt was unmistakable.

Then, as if Sir Hereward knew he was beaten, he said:

"In the circumstances, I can only hope Your Lordship is fully aware of what you are doing and will not be disappointed."

The Marquis did not reply, and after a moment Sir Hereward went on:

"I imagine the next step is for our Solicitors to discuss the Marriage Settlement."

Again the Marquis did not make any reply, nor did he invite the two men facing him to sit down.

As if he was suddenly acutely conscious that he was unwelcome, Sir Hereward said:

"I shall wait to hear from Your Lordship!"

Without even looking at Diona he started to walk slowly and without much dignity towards the door.

"But, Papa," Simon expostulated, "you promised me! You said I could marry Diona! How can she marry anybody else? It is not fair! And he does not want her money. He has lots of his own!"

Sir Hereward did not answer his son, and as he reached the door he passed through it.

Then as he left it open behind him they could hear Simon's plaintive voice gradually fading into the distance down the corridor outside.

Only when he could no longer be heard did the Marquis release Diona's wrist, and as if she could no longer stand she sank down onto the floor beside Sirius and put her arms round him.

As if he understood that they had passed through a crisis which had left her on the verge of tears, he rubbed his face against her cheek and let her hold him close to her.

The Marquis walked towards the door.

"We will leave for London immediately after luncheon."

It took Diona a moment to realise what he had said.

Then as she murmured: "London?" she found the Library was empty except for her and Sirius.

It was impossible to talk at the pace at which the Marquis was driving, and anyway Diona was thankful that she did not have to ask questions.

She had come down for luncheon feeling more or less composed, having, by a great effort of will, fought against collapsing in tears in her bedroom.

She found when she entered the Library that Roderic was with the Marquis, but she had no idea whether or not he had been told of the uncomfortable drama which had just taken place.

She knew only that she had no wish to speak of it, and as if the Marquis understood what she was feeling, they talked all through luncheon about the Steeple-Chase.

The Marquis gave Roderic a list of the rules of the race and discussed with him who should be invited to take part.

Diona was almost certain by the time the meal was over that Roderic had no idea that in his absence anybody had called to the house.

Also, she thought that strangely enough he did not seem to be curious as to why they should be leaving for London.

She had an uncomfortable feeling that he thought it was on his account and that the Marquis was taking her there so that she would be ready and rested before the contest with Sir Mortimer, which meant so much to him.

'I shall have to explain sooner or later that I am no longer in hiding,' she thought, 'and as my father's daughter I could not possibly be involved in anything like that.'

Yet, she felt she could leave everything to the Marquis. He had saved her once. He could save her again.

At the same time, while she was very uncertain what he was thinking or feeling, at least she felt sure he had no wish to marry her.

The suggestion he had made to her just before Sir Hereward arrived was still puzzling her, and she was trying to understand what he had implied.

She could also, when she thought of it, still feel the strange sensations that he had aroused in her not only by the tone of his voice but when he had put his arms round her.

She thought, although it seemed incredible, that if her uncle had not arrived at that moment, the Marquis might have kissed her.

He had certainly drawn her closer to him, and as he had done so she had felt a sensation almost like a flash of lightning piercing through her, and it had been impossible to breathe, impossible to think.

She wondered what she would have felt if he had kissed her.

Then as they drove on and she stole a glance at him as he concentrated on his horses, he was looking so overwhelmingly attractive that she knew she wanted the touch of his lips.

She wanted him to kiss her and she was sure it would be very wonderful.

Simon's clumsy advances had revolted her, and when she had run away from him she had told herself she hated the whole idea of being touched and would never allow any man to kiss her.

But now, if she was honest, she knew that she wanted the Marquis's kisses, and she wondered desperately if, now that he knew who she was, he would try to kiss her again.

She was aware, and here her instinct was working, that when he had told her uncle that she was "engaged" to him, it had merely been a way of saving her from being married to Simon.

It was not, she was sure, his intention to marry her.

Then as they neared London, suddenly like a blinding light it came to her that she had been very stupid.

What the Marquis had suggested was that he should look after her and keep her safe and hide her as she had wanted to hide, but not as his wife.

Because Diona was so innocent, she had no idea how a man made love to a woman.

She had seen the happiness of her father and mother and knew that if she ever married, that was what she wanted to find with her husband.

However, she was aware that there were other kinds of love, and although everything Simon did and said disgusted her, she knew she attracted him as a woman, which was why he wanted to kiss and touch her.

The Marquis had been very different, but still what he had offered her was not the love she was seeking—the love that was beautiful, sacred, and part of the sunshine.

"He has saved me, but I must not impose upon him," Diona told herself.

She was not quite certain what she should do, but she was afraid that if she was not with the Marquis and being protected by him, her uncle would once again try to marry her off to Simon.

She could not imagine anything more horrifying or more degrading.

The mere idea of being tied to her cousin and in a position where he could touch her made her feel as if she had been thrown into a pool of reptiles.

She must have shuddered, for the Marquis turned his head to ask:

"You are all right? You are not cold?"

"No . . . of course not," Diona replied.

They changed horses a little later, but the Marquis stayed only as long as it took to take one team from between the shafts and replace it with another. Then they were on their way again.

Roderic was travelling with Sam in another Phaeton, and Diona guessed without asking that the Marquis was determined to break his own record, if possible, and certainly to reach London well ahead of them.

When they finally arrived at Irchester House, Diona looked at him apprehensively, wondering what was waiting for her there.

She walked beside him into the large Hall and saw an elderly man come forward to greet him.

She knew from the conversation she had listened to between him and Roderic that this was Mr. Swaythling, his secretary, who ran all his houses.

"You received my message, Swaythling?" the Marquis enquired.

"Yes, My Lord. The groom arrived about an hour and a half ago."

"You have carried out my instructions?"

"Everything has been arranged, My Lord."

"Good!" the Marquis exclaimed.

He turned to Diona and said:

"This is my secretary, Mr. Swaythling, who, with his usual expertise, has managed to provide you with a Chaperone at such short notice."

Diona held out her hand and Mr. Swaythling shook it.

"I hope, Miss Grantley, it will be to your satisfaction," he said, "and I am sure you would like to wash and change after what I am sure was a most precipitate journey. You will find our Housekeeper, Mrs. Norton, waiting for you at the top of the stairs."

"Thank you," Diona said.

The Marquis did not speak, but feeling somehow that she was dismissed, she walked up the stairs feeling alone and shy.

She knew without being told that her status had changed, because Mr. Swaythling had addressed her by her own name.

Mrs. Norton dropped her a curtsey, saying:

"You must feel tired, Miss, coming from the country at the speed His Lordship always drives! I'd be frightened to death if I was in one of those smart new Phaetons that go so fast."

"I found it most exhilarating," Diona replied. "At the same time, I feel I am very untidy."

She had put on her best gown and bonnet to travel with the Marquis, and she was therefore not ashamed of her appearance as she was led into a large and very attractive room which had windows overlooking a garden.

"I understand, Miss," the Housekeeper was saying, "that your luggage has been somehow mislaid, but the dressmakers have been ordered to be here in about an hour's time."

"Dressmakers?" Diona exclaimed.

She was about to say that she could not afford to spend any money on clothes or allow the Marquis to buy them for her, when she remembered that she was now rich.

She had been so concerned with his feelings for her and the way he had saved her that she had almost forgotten that the reason why her uncle had come in search of her was that she had inherited such an enormous sum of money from her Godmother.

It seemed extraordinary, after having been abused and sneered at for being penniless ever since her arrival at the Hall and having repeatedly heard her father criticised because he had died in debt, that she should now be wealthy.

She could remember her Godmother well.

Lady Campbell had been a close friend of her mother's even though she was very much older. In fact, thinking about her now, Diona was certain that she must have been over seventy.

She supposed she might have got in touch with her after her father died, instead of obeying orders and going tamely to live with her uncle.

But she had not actually seen Lady Campbell since two or three years before her mother's death.

She had always been sent a Christmas-card, but she had never thought to write her Godmother, who lived in Northumberland, which had seemed to be at the far end of the world.

'All that time, because Mama loved her and she loved Mama,' Diona thought, 'she was thinking of me and had made me her heir.'

It was easy now to look back and wish that she had behaved in a very different way.

But she had felt so bereft and helpless after losing her father that there had seemed to be nothing she could do but obey her uncle and bow to his unceasing abuse of her.

"I have been weak and spineless," Diona told herself, "and that is something Papa would never have been."

She longed, as so many people had done before her, to "put back the clock."

If only this money, she thought, had come while her father was alive, they could have enjoyed it together.

She could have bought him horses that would have saved him from having to break in the wild ones from Ireland, which had been instrumental in his death.

They would have been able to go to London as her mother had wanted, and she could have been a débutante in the real meaning of the word.

But now it was too late, and she thought that the money, while it would save her from being dependent on anybody, was otherwise not important.

Then she remembered something which really mattered and must be done at once!

Because she was in a hurry to see the Marquis, she did not change her gown, she only washed the dust from her face and hands, with the help of what seemed to be a very experienced housemaid, who arranged her hair.

Then she ran down the stairs to be shown into the Drawing-Room by the Butler waiting in the Hall.

The Marquis was already there, standing with his back to the fireplace, and as she ran eagerly towards him she realised with a sense of acute disappointment that he was not alone.

Instead there was an attractive, smartly dressed, middle-aged woman sitting on the sofa and looking at him admiringly.

"Here you are, Diona," the Marquis said as she reached him. "I want you to feel very grateful to Mrs. Lamborn, a cousin of mine, who at a moment's notice has very kindly come here to act as your Chaperone."

Diona curtseyed and Mrs. Lamborn put out her hand, saying:

"I am delighted to meet you, Miss Grantley. My cousin has been telling me that you have just had the most marvellous news that any young girl could have, and I must offer you my congratulations."

"I always believed heiresses were two a penny," the Marquis said in a disagreeable tone, as if he was determined to quench the enthusiasm in Mrs. Lamborn's voice.

She laughed.

"That is a popular belief. At the same time, a great number of them are excessively plain, and they need money to make them more attractive, which is certainly not the case where Miss Grantley is concerned."

"Thank you," Diona said, feeling that all this was very unimportant.

Then she said to the Marquis in an urgent tone:

"Please . . . can I ask you to do something very . . . urgent for me?"

"What is that?" the Marquis asked.

"If I really have so much money, though at the moment it seems as if it is an illusion, can I send some immediately to the people who were pensioned off when Papa died? Uncle Hereward was so mean with them that I feel they hardly have enough to eat, and the same applies to the caretakers of my old home."

"I am sure Swaythling will do anything you ask him to do," the Marquis replied.

"Then may I go and ask him now?"

"Of course, if that is what you wish."

"Where will I find him?"

As if he were being condescending to a rather demanding child, the Marquis walked across the room and Diona followed him.

As he reached the door he turned to say to Mrs. Lamborn:

"Please excuse us, Noreen."

"Yes, of course," she replied.

The Marquis then led the way across the Hall and down another passage, where he opened the door of what was obviously a secretarial office.

Mr. Swaythling, who was sitting at his desk, rose as they appeared, and the Marquis said:

"Miss Grantley has a number of commissions for you to see to on her behalf. As it will take a little time to obtain the money that she has just inherited, I am of course prepared to be her Banker."

Diona looked at him in consternation.

"I am sorry to be a nuisance," she said, "but I have worried so much about these people who served Papa and Mama so well and who trusted us."

She thought the Marquis's eyes softened as he looked at her before he said:

"In which case it would be a mistake to let them suffer any longer."

"I knew you would understand."

"Then tell Mr. Swaythling exactly what you want."

He would have walked from the office if she had not put her hand on his arm.

"Later I want to talk to you alone," she said.

"Of course," he replied, "but I think first you should get to know Mrs. Lamborn. You will find her very helpful."

Diona thought the way he spoke was different from the way he had spoken to her in the past.

Then as he walked away and she looked after him, feeling somehow lost and lonely in a manner she could not understand, she heard Mr. Swaythling say:

"Come and sit down, Miss Grantley, and tell me exactly what you want me to do."

* * *

It was the following night when she went to bed that Diona told herself despairingly that she had lost the Marquis in a way she could not explain.

Everything had moved so quickly that she felt breathless, and from the moment her uncle had surprised them at the Park, she knew everything had changed.

After they had arrived in London, the four of them had dined together, but Mrs. Lamborn talked of people of whom she had never heard, but who were of course relatives of her and the Marquis.

Roderic was sulking because the Marquis had told him that Diona could not appear in his contest as he had wanted.

He whispered to her, so that Mrs. Lamborn could not hear, that he had been told not to say a word about it in front of her Chaperone, but he felt that he had been let down very badly and that his uncle had been extremely unsporting.

"He might have let me have another look round the country in case there was a milk-maid as pretty as you," he said in a low voice. "At least I could have tried to find one."

"Are you quite sure the Marquis cannot help you?" Diona enquired.

"He said to leave it to him," Roderic said. "But how can I do that, and tamely lose face in front of all my friends if I do not produce anybody?"

Diona smiled.

"If he said to leave it to him, then that is what you should do," she said. "I am sure he will think of something clever and outwit that horrible man."

"I doubt it," Roderic replied.

As this conversation took place at one end of the Drawing-Room while the Marquis was talking to Mrs. Lamborn at the other, Diona thought it was a mistake for them to appear secretive in case she became curious.

Deliberately she rejoined the Marquis and his cousin, but they did not seem particularly eager for her company. In fact, she now felt tired after all that had happened and suggested retiring to bed.

She first took Sirius out into the garden and thought that small though it was, it was like everything to do with the Marquis, beautifully arranged and perfect, with an abundance of flowers in bloom and several tall trees that seemed somehow strange in London.

Then she went to bed to feel unhappy and once again lonely.

* * *

The next day Mrs. Lamborn took Diona shopping from first thing in the morning until late in the evening.

They ate a quick luncheon alone as the Marquis was out, and although he was in for dinner, this time Roderic was not present.

Once again he seemed very much more interested in what his cousin had to say, and Diona found herself sitting silent and feeling that she might just as well be at the Hall listening to her uncle droning on over something that had annoyed him.

But she knew that was not true.

She could at least look at the Marquis, hear him, and be acutely conscious that he was there, and even if he did not respond, she was vibrating towards him and wanting him to notice her.

She felt when they said good-night that he was even more formal than he had been the night before, and when she went up to her bedroom she wanted to run away and hide.

Her common sense told her that what he was going to do was to launch her into Society and, with Mrs. Lamborn's help, find her a husband.

That was what every débutante looked for, and she was intelligent enough to realise that this must be the plan behind the Marquis's campaign to find a Chaperone.

He had arranged to have her beautifully dressed and, as she had gathered from Mrs. Lamborn's remarks, to start the ball rolling to ensure that she was asked to every party that was to take place before the Autumn.

A lot of these would not be in London because the Season was strictly over, but there were still a number of people who remained on at least until the middle of July.

Then, if they were aware of her and of her future, as Mrs. Lamborn had not hesitated to point out, she would be invited to parties in the country which would be given for girls of her own age.

There were, Diona learnt, a great number of hosts and hostesses who had houses near to London.

"Of course," Mrs. Lamborn had said blandly, "Cousin Lenox knows them all."

She named them, starting with Syon House, which belonged to the Duke and Duchess of Northumberland, and Osterley, the Earl and Countess of Jersey's house at Chiswick, but as the list went on and on Diona ceased to listen.

"All I want," she told herself, "is to be able to talk to the Marquis as I was able to do when we were alone at the Park."

Because it hurt her to think of how happy she had been then, when they had ridden together and discussed such entrancing subjects at luncheon and dinner, she tossed and turned in her bed, finding it too hot to sleep.

Then she was aware of a strange sound coming from the garden beneath her window.

Because she was curious, she got out of bed and pulling back the curtains looked through an open casement into the garden.

The moonlight was not yet strong but there were stars overhead, yet the trees cast dark shadows and it was difficult to see anything but the outline of the flower-beds.

Then she heard the sound again and it was like that of an animal in pain.

Because she was looking out the window, Sirius was standing on his hind-legs beside her, peering out and growling as he always did if something upset him.

"I wonder what it is, Sirius," Diona said.

He growled again, and she could still hear the little cry and was sure it was a small animal like a cat which might have been caught in a trap.

Without thinking, she behaved as she would have done in the country. She pulled on her shawl, which was all she had to wear over her nightgown, and opening her door walked down the corridor with Sirius until they came to a side-staircase that she had found earlier in the evening when she had taken him out.

It led to a door between the Drawing-Room and Mr. Swaythling's office, which opened onto the garden.

The key was in the lock and there was a bolt which she pulled back.

Then as Sirius ran ahead of her, searching for the source of the sound they had both heard from her bedroom, she stopped.

As she did so, she gave a scream of terror which was muffled before it left her throat.

Something thick and heavy was thrown over her head, and before she could struggle, she was lifted off her feet.

Then Diona realised in horror that she was being carried by two men across the garden.

CHAPTER SIX

———— ✥ ————

*T*HE MARQUIS CAME IN LATE, and although he was tired he lay for some time, finding it difficult to sleep.

There was a great deal on his mind which he turned over and over before finally he slept.

He awoke with a start and realised that what had awakened him was a very unusual noise.

An animal was scratching at his door, whining as he did so. Then there was a sharp bark, and he was aware that it was a dog.

For a moment he thought he must be in the country and it was one of his own dogs, then as he was fully awake he knew it was Sirius.

He lit a candle, then got out of bed and opened the door. Sirius, who was still scratching on it, seemed almost to fall into the room.

Then he gave a sharp bark, and running away from the Marquis down the passage he stopped and looked back, then returned to do the same thing again.

The Marquis would have been very obtuse if he had not understood that something was wrong and that Sirius was asking him to follow him.

He went back for his robe, which his valet had put on a chair by the side of his bed, and struggled into it. Then he picked up the candle he had just lit and followed Sirius, expecting the dog to take him to Diona's bedroom, which was only a little way down the passage. He wondered what could have happened to her and if she was ill.

And if she was, why had she not rung the bell for the maid?

As he reached Diona's door, Sirius made no attempt to enter, although the Marquis saw that the door was open.

He went in and saw that the bed had been slept in and one curtain was drawn back with the window open.

The Marquis thought it very strange until he returned to the doorway and once again Sirius was running on ahead of him, then stopping and looking back.

The Marquis realised that something was very wrong, and because almost perceptibly he had a vague suspicion of what it could be, he ran back to his own bedroom and began to dress.

As if Sirius understood what he was doing, he came to the doorway, whining to show his impatience, but waiting.

The Marquis pulled on the tight-fitting champagne-coloured pantaloons he wore in the daytime, slipped his feet into the first pair of Hessians he could find in the bottom of his cupboard, and snatched a white shirt from his chest-of-drawers.

He was exceedingly quick because having been a soldier he was used to dressing in an emergency, such as on the news that the enemy was approaching.

As he thought that Sirius's whine grew more insistent, it spurred him on.

As he tied his cravat round his neck in just a knot and shrugged himself into a cut-away coat, he was breaking even his own record for speed.

When he walked towards the door and Sirius immediately began to run down the passage, the Marquis stopped.

He opened a drawer of the cupboard beside his bed and took out a pistol. It was a new model which he always carried when he was driving.

Footpads and Highwaymen were still reported to be holding up passengers on many of the side-roads and it was always wise to be armed.

He slipped the pistol into his pocket, then as if Sirius's continual whine had alerted him to an even greater urgency than he was aware of already, he hurried after the dog.

To his surprise, Sirius did not go down the front staircase but a side one at the end of the corridor, which the Marquis seldom used.

Only when he had reached the bottom of it and saw the garden-door open did he begin to be alarmed as to what had happened to Diona.

For a moment he just stood as she had on the step.

Then Sirius raced across the grass into the shadows of the trees, and the Marquis understood that that was where Diona had either gone or been forced to go.

She would have been taken, he thought, through the gate at the end of the garden which led into the Mews.

There was just enough light for him to see that the door in the wall was not open, because if it had been he was sure that Sirius would have followed her.

But although the door was closed, the lock had been broken, and now he understood what had happened.

As he walked out into the Mews with Sirius, he wondered where on earth she had been taken.

It was obvious that she had been kidnapped and there was no doubt as to who was responsible.

Now the Marquis thought he had been very obtuse in thinking that a man like Sir Hereward would sit back tamely without taking any counter-action when his plans had been upset.

He had been surprised that he had not had any communication from his Solicitors, and now he knew that if he had been more alert and more suspicious, he should have realised it was a danger signal.

Standing in the empty Mews, the only sounds he could hear came from the stables, where the horses were moving about, and he wondered frantically what he could do.

Then almost as if Diona herself were helping him he remembered that Sir Hereward had a London house.

It was just by chance that he should know of it, but he could recall way back in his memory soon after the war ended a very lovely lady saying:

"I shall expect you for dinner tomorrow evening. You will have no difficulty in finding my house in Park Street. It is very small, squeezed in between two large imposing ones, one of which belongs to the Earl of Warnshaw, and the other to Sir Hereward Grantley."

She had laughed and said:

"Although I am squeezed between them, there is no need to be jealous. They are both old and very unattractive!"

Her house, he remembered, was on the other side of the Mews which ran the length of Park Lane, and the Marquis set off in that direction with Sirius beside him.

As he went he remembered something else: the lady in question, because she was careful of her reputation, after his first two visits had given him the key to the door of the garden which lay behind her house.

Unlike his own garden, it was shared by at least ten other houses, but all the times he had used it, which admittedly had been at night, he had never seen anybody else there.

He thought now as he was moving very quickly, almost at a run, that it would be a mistake to ring the bell or knock on the door of Sir Hereward's house.

The servants would have been told to ignore him, and it would be impossible for him alone to break in to find out if Diona was inside.

Instead he passed through Park Street, then he sought another Mews off which he remembered the garden-door opened.

He found it without any difficulty, but it was locked.

He was afraid that if he tried to break the lock, as Sir Hereward had obviously done in his garden, it might make a noise, and he had no wish to attract attention to himself.

He put his hand on Sirius's head, patting him and saying in a voice of authority:

"Sir, Sirius! Sit!"

The dog obeyed him, and the Marquis without much difficulty climbed up the six-foot wall and dropped down on the other side. He then opened the garden-door from the inside and let Sirius in.

The dog seemed to understand what was required of him, as the Marquis, keeping wherever possible in the shade of trees and bushes, crossed the garden towards the houses on the other side.

It was not difficult to pick out Sir Hereward's house, and now as he looked at it he knew his instinct had brought him to the right place.

There was a light in a downstairs room, and, what was more, the curtains were not drawn.

Moving beside the buildings just in case anybody should be looking out the windows, which was unlikely, the Marquis hurried along the side of the garden.

He then turned and walked past two other houses before he reached Sir Hereward's.

He realised that luck was with him, for two of the uncurtained windows were open, and as he drew nearer he could hear what was being said.

First there was a man's voice, rather indistinct, then quite clearly he heard Diona say:

"I will not . . . marry him! I will . . . not!"

Diona had guessed who had kidnapped her as she was carried across the garden.

She was finding it difficult to breathe owing to the heaviness of the cloth that was over her face, and also because the two men carrying her were moving so quickly.

Then she heard a voice, which she recognised as that of her uncle, say: "Mind the door!"

As the men stopped for a moment and she thought they were having to bend their heads, her uncle said, keeping his voice low but with the angry tone she recognised:

"Get out of my way, you damned dog!"

There was a yelp and she knew he must have hit Sirius with his stick.

Then there was the sound of a door closing, and she was aware that while she had been taken out of the garden, Sirius had been left behind.

It was at that moment, although she was trembling with fear and almost suffocated by the cloth over her face, that she knew she must tell Sirius to wake the Marquis because only he could save her.

Ever since Sirius had been quite small she had amused herself not only by training him to the word of command but also by making him obey her thoughts.

It was her father who had told her of the amazing instances of thought-transference that were frequent in India and that Indians could communicate with one another even if they were hundreds of miles apart.

"I do not understand, Papa," she had said. "How can they do such a thing? How is it possible?"

"Scientists have known for a long time that there are waves going round the world," her father had said, "and I think what happens is that we can communicate with one another in the same way."

"In the same way?" Diona had questioned.

"As our thoughts move from us on waves, we can direct them towards somebody we wish to receive them," her father had answered, "and if he is sensitive and perceptive, he understands."

"It is a fascinating idea, Papa," Diona had said, "and I shall try to communicate with you in my thoughts."

"It is something your mother and I have often done," her father had replied. "At times she will answer questions in my mind before I actually ask them."

Because Diona had believed that her father would much rather communicate with her mother than with her, she had practised on Sirius and after a time she had begun to think that she was successful.

She would call him without making a sound, and he would come to her from the other end of the garden.

She was not always so successful when she tried to direct him actively to do something, and as the men carried her for what seemed a long way, she wondered despairingly whether he would understand.

"Go to the Marquis! Fetch the Marquis, Sirius!"

She felt as if she was straining every nerve in her body to reach him, and she was still trying to think how she might save herself when she was carried up a flight of steps and into a house.

She was aware that they had crossed a Hall, then she was set down on her feet and somebody lifted the cloth from her head.

For a moment, because it had been so hot and uncomfortable and also dark, Diona had difficulty focussing her eyes.

Then she saw that she was standing in a large room lit by a number of candles and facing her were her uncle and Simon.

Even though it was what she had expected, she felt herself tremble.

Then she was aware that Simon was looking at her in a way she most disliked, and she nervously pulled her silk shawl, which was all she had to cover her nightgown, closer across her breasts.

"I have brought her here," Sir Hereward said, "and now we had better get on with it!"

He was speaking to somebody behind her, and as Diona turned her head she saw a man who had been sitting at the far end of the room come towards her.

He was wearing black, and she wondered who he was. He was too small to have been one of the men who had carried her and who she thought must have been footmen.

Then as she looked at the man in black she saw the white muslin at his neck and knew he was a Priest.

What was about to happen swept over her with a feeling of horror.

She knew that she was trapped and it was impossible to run away.

Then, almost as if some voice told her to play for time, she gave a little murmur and deliberately collapsed slowly to the floor.

She closed her eyes, hoping that her uncle would believe she was unconscious.

"She has fainted!" Simon cried. "Now see what you have done, Papa! She has fainted, or is she dead?"

"Of course she is not dead!" Sir Hereward said angrily. "Fetch a glass of water!"

"Where from? I do not know where there is any!" Simon replied.

"Ask one of the servants, you fool!" Sir Hereward thundered.

Diona heard Simon stumble across the floor and hoped he would not find the water too quickly.

Now, although she was vividly conscious of her uncle's heavy breathing as he stood beside her, she was still trying to send out a cry for help, but now it was to the Marquis.

If Sirius had obeyed her, he would have awakened him by this time, but she wondered frantically if the Marquis would have any idea where to go.

She knew her uncle had a house in London, but he seldom used it, except occasionally when he had a meeting or a dinner to attend and he stayed the night.

Never since she had gone to live at the Hall had she been to the London house, and she thought that because the Marquis did not know her uncle and he was of no particular importance, he was unlikely to know where he lived.

Then some flicker of hope that he would somehow save her made her try again to reach him.

As her father had told her the Indians did, she thought of her cry for help flying out on a wave towards him, and she visualised his face as he received it.

"Help me! Help me! Save me! Please . . . save me! I . . . love . . . you!"

Even as she tried to transmit those last three words, she knew he did not love her, and in consequence she was afraid that he would never know how greatly she needed him.

She heard Simon coming back and her uncle say:

"Is that the water? Now lift her head and force it down her throat!"

"Supposing she does not drink it?" Simon asked.

The Priest spoke for the first time.

"I will do it," he said.

Diona was aware that he knelt down beside her and Simon must have handed him the glass.

As he put his arm under her head and raised her up, she was aware that he was almost as repulsive as her cousin.

There was something nasty, if not evil, about him, and she wanted to shrink away from his touch.

He was obviously more experienced than Simon.

He pressed the rim of the glass against her lips, and although she tried not to drink, as she felt the water trickling down her chin and onto her nightgown she felt forced to take a sip or two.

"Come on, come on!" Sir Hereward was saying impatiently.

"I think she is coming round, Sir," the Priest said.

"If not, throw the water in her face!" Sir Hereward ordered.

Because she had no wish for that to happen, Diona made a feeble movement with her hands, then pushed the glass away from her mouth.

"That is better!" Sir Hereward said. "Now get up on your feet, and let us have no more delays!"

"I . . . I feel . . . ill . . . Uncle Hereward!" Diona murmured.

"You will feel a damned sight more ill if you do not do as you are told!" Sir Hereward replied. "Help her up, Simon, and once she is standing we can start the Service."

Clumsily Simon pulled her to her feet by one arm, with the Parson doing the same by the other.

Because Diona felt she had no alternative, she stood up and put up her hand to push her hair away from her forehead.

"Please . . . Uncle Hereward," she said, "let me . . . have something . . . decent to wear."

"When you are married you can go back and fetch your clothes," Sir Hereward said. "At the moment there is no point in keeping your bridegroom waiting."

He was sneering at her as he had sneered so often before at the Hall, and Diona retorted:

"If you are intending to marry me to Simon, I will . . . not make the responses! I will not . . . marry him!"

Because she felt she had nothing to lose, she went on:

"How dare you . . . kidnap me in this . . . disgraceful manner! It is an . . . outrage, as you are well . . . aware."

"Do not speak to me like that!" Sir Hereward shouted. "You were a penniless orphan when I took you into my house, fed you, clothed you, and paid your improvident father's bills, and this is all the thanks I get!"

"It is not a question of thanks," Diona replied. "I am quite prepared to thank you for what you did for me, even though I was very unhappy in your house! But I will not . . . marry your son, who . . . as you well know, is not . . . fit to be the . . . husband of . . . anybody!"

She knew as she spoke that it was a most provocative thing to say, but because she was fighting a lone battle and there was no hope of being saved, she was no longer afraid of her uncle.

She knew she must die rather than allow Simon to kiss her and touch her, and that if she was married to him she would kill herself rather than live with him as his wife.

Crimson in the face with rage at her insolence, Sir Hereward glared at her and said sharply to the Parson:

"Start the Service—get on with it!"

"I will not . . . marry him! I will not!" Diona cried.

Sir Hereward raised his stick.

"Then I will beat you until you do as you are told!"

He moved towards her and Diona gave a cry of fear.

Then there was a sudden bark and Sirius jumped through the window and landed on the floor.

On hearing Diona cry out, without waiting for the Marquis he had leapt through the window and rushed towards her.

He jumped at her, barking now with excitement because he had found her, and as Diona gave a little sob of happiness because he was there, the Marquis climbed onto the window-sill.

It took him a moment to swing both his legs into the room, and as he did so Sir Hereward, moving with surprising quickness, put his arm round Diona's neck.

He dragged her back from the centre of the room and stood with his back to the wall, holding her as if she were a shield in front of him.

The Marquis, on his feet now, stood for a moment looking contemptuously at what was happening.

The Priest and Simon were staring at him in sheer astonishment, and Sir Hereward, almost throttling Diona with the tightness with which he held her, was glaring at him as he slowly drew a pistol from the pocket of his coat.

"You are trespassing in my house, My Lord!" he said. "You will kindly remove yourself immediately or you will have what will be reported as a regrettable accident!"

"Are you seriously threatening to shoot me?" the Marquis asked.

"I shall not hesitate to do so if you interfere," Sir Hereward replied.

His pistol was pointing at the Marquis's heart.

Diona, gasping for breath because her uncle's arm was squeezing her throat, thought frantically that he meant what he said and if the Marquis tried to save her he might be killed.

It flashed through her mind that rather than let that happen, she must acquiesce to her uncle's wishes and marry Simon, and she thought she must tell him so.

She tried to speak and she must have moved, because her uncle's arm tightened, and instead of words there was once again a stiffled scream of pain.

Sirius, who had been watching her, unable to understand what was happening, at least knew she was being hurt.

Springing at Sir Hereward, he jumped up as if to bite his arm.

Sir Hereward raised his pistol in order to get it out of reach of the dog, and as he did so, with the unerring aim of a first-class shot the Marquis, whose hand was holding his pistol in his pocket, shot him through the arm.

The explosion seemed unnaturally loud in the room and it echoed and re-echoed.

Sir Hereward staggered and with a bellow of pain dropped his pistol on the floor. He also released Diona to put his left hand to the wound on his right arm, and she ran across the room to fling herself against the Marquis.

She could not speak, she could only hold on to him as if he were a lifeline in a tempestuous sea.

The Marquis put his left arm round her and walked slowly backwards towards the door.

"If any of you are thinking of stopping me," he said, "it would be a mistake!"

"You have no right to shoot my father!" Simon cried as if he had suddenly found his voice.

The Marquis did not bother to reply.

He only looked contemptuously at the Parson, who had cringed away, his Prayer-Book in his hand, and as if he had been accused of doing something illegal the Cleric said:

"It is not my fault! I only did what he told me to do!"

The Marquis did not deign to reply.

He knew exactly the type of Parson Sir Hereward would hire.

There were many of them in London who would perform a Marriage Service anywhere that was convenient if they were paid enough, and then in registering it would swear that it had taken place in a consecrated building so as to make it legal.

The Marquis had reached the door and he opened it still facing the three people in the room.

By this time Sir Hereward had sunk down in a chair and the blood was spreading from the lower part of his arm over his hand.

The Marquis pulled Diona through the door to the Hall and closed it behind him.

There was a footman staring at them by the front door, and when they walked towards it the Marquis was aware that Diona's feet were bare.

He bent and picked her up in his arms, and as the man opened the door for them he said:

"You had better send for a Doctor for your Master. He has injured himself!"

He did not wait for the footman to reply but carried Diona down the steps and along the street.

She hid her face against his shoulder, and at first he thought she was crying, but then he was aware that her hand was holding tightly to the lapel of his coat as if she was afraid she might lose him.

She was very light and it did not take the Marquis long to walk back the way he had come.

Sirius followed them, his tail wagging as if he knew that he had been particularly clever in bringing them together again.

The Marquis walked through the door he had left open into his garden, and, as if she was aware of it because his feet no longer rang on the cobblestones, Diona raised her head.

"You came!" she murmured. "I was sure that Sirius would somehow . . . tell you . . . what had . . . happened to me."

"He told me!" the Marquis said quietly.

"I tried to . . . tell you . . . where I was."

"I found you," the Marquis said, "and I was in time."

As if the fear of what might have happened was still there, Diona turned her face again against his shoulder, still holding tightly to the lapel of his coat.

The Marquis carried her into the house through the garden-door, but instead of going upstairs he walked along the passage which led to the front Hall.

The night-footman was drowsing comfortably in the big padded arm-chair by the door.

When from the few lighted candles that were still burning in the silver sconces he saw his Master appear, he got quickly to his feet.

"Light some candles in the Drawing-Room!" the Marquis ordered.

The footman ran to obey and the Marquis carried Diona into the room. When two candelabra were burning brightly he said: "That is enough," and the footman left them.

It was then that she turned to look up at him.

Her fair hair was streaming over her shoulders and her eyes seemed to hold in them the light from the candles as she said almost as if she could hardly believe it:

"You . . . saved . . . me! You . . . saved me!"

"I saved you," the Marquis repeated.

He put her feet to the floor but he did not take his arm from round her shoulders, and when she was standing he pulled her against him roughly and his mouth came down on hers.

She wanted to cry out at the wonder of it.

But he was kissing her possessively, demandingly, and insistently, as if he had been afraid to lose her and was proving to himself that she was safe and with him.

He kissed her and it was as wonderful as Diona had thought it would be, only so much more so, and although his lips were hard, demanding, and at first almost painful, she was not afraid.

She knew that it was what she had wanted, what she had longed for, and she had not lost the Marquis as she had thought she had.

Because she was so soft and small and her lips were very sweet, innocent, and inexperienced, the Marquis's kisses grew more gentle, then they were infinitely tender.

Now as he kissed her Diona felt not only lightning flashing through her body as it had done before, but also as if it gave her everything she had sensed was part of love, and which she had thought she would never know.

It was the beauty of the flowers and the stars, the moonlight and the shimmering silver of it on the water.

It was music, the music she had heard in her dreams, the sunshine, and the love that she had missed when she had left home to live at the Hall.

It was everything which was perfect and yet it was all in one man.

She knew as he kissed her and went on kissing her that she belonged to the Marquis, and her heart, her soul, and her body, if he wanted it, were all his.

Only when he raised his head did she manage to say:

"I . . . love you . . . and I knew that the love I was . . . sending to you would . . . bring you to . . . me."

Her words were almost incoherent, and the Marquis did not answer.

He only kissed her again until she felt as if the lightning flashing within her turned into fire, and flames seemed to flicker through her to touch her lips and meet the fire that was on his.

Unexpectedly he picked her up again in his arms and lifted her onto the sofa.

"You have been through so much," he said, "that I am going to give you something to drink. God knows, we have both earned one!"

Diona wanted to cry out that she wanted nothing but him, but he had moved away from her.

He went to the grog-tray which stood in a corner of the Drawing-Room, on which she knew by now there was always a bottle of champagne in a silver ice-cooler.

He poured out two glasses and brought her one. Then he sat down on the edge of the sofa to look at her.

The expression in his grey eyes made her feel rather shy and she was suddenly conscious that she was wearing nothing but a thin nightgown and that while the Marquis had been kissing her the silk shawl had slipped from over her shoulders.

She tried to pull it a little farther over her and the Marquis smiled.

"Who would believe that so many fantastic things could happen to so small a person?" he asked.

"But . . . you came . . . just in time."

"You have to thank Sirius for that."

Sirius, who had been lying contentedly on the hearth-rug since they had come into the Drawing-Room, heard his name and pricked up his ears.

"Did he tell you what had happened to me?" Diona asked.

"He told me very eloquently," the Marquis answered. "First he woke me by scratching and whining at my door. Then he led me into the garden and I saw that the lock was broken."

"I have tried to teach him to do what I want by thought," Diona said, "but I was afraid that because I was so desperate he would not understand."

The Marquis looked at her questioningly.

Then, stumbling a little over her words because she was still excited by the Marquis's kisses, Diona told him what her father had taught her about the transference of thought.

She explained how all the time the men were carrying her away with a heavy blanket over her face she had tried to send orders to Sirius to wake him and tell him to save her.

The Marquis listened. Then he said quietly:

"After that, I think you sent out thought-waves to me."

"Did you feel them?"

"I am sure I did!" he replied. "They made me remember where your uncle's house was, and Sirius and I came through the garden to hear him threatening to beat you."

Diona gave a little cry.

"I was playing for time," she said. "but I am a . . . coward . . . and if you had not come at exactly that moment . . . I am afraid I could not have . . . delayed the marriage any . . . longer."

The Marquis took her hand and raised it to his lips.

"I have never known anybody quite so brave," he said, "or so wonderful!"

She looked at him wide-eyed because of the way he spoke.

Then he rose and took the glass from her hand.

"Now I am going to insist that you go to bed," he said. "You have been through a great deal, far too much in fact, and we will talk about it again tomorrow."

"I . . . I do not want to . . . leave you."

"I know, my darling," the Marquis answered, "and I have no wish to leave you, but I have to be sensible for us both."

He put down her glass, then holding out his hands to help her to her feet he said:

"Besides, you have to think of Sirius. He too needs his beauty sleep!"

Diona laughed as he meant her to do.

Then as she stood, seeming very small without shoes and looking up at him with her fair hair waving over her shoulders, her eyes very large in her small, pointed face, the Marquis said:

"We have so much to say to each other, but I know, even though you will not admit it, my lovely one, that you are exhausted."

Diona knew this was true, but she was surprised that he was aware of it.

He picked her up in his arms again.

"I can walk," she protested.

"I like carrying you," the Marquis answered, "and you are so light that you might be one of the nymphs who I am quite certain still live in the lake at the Park."

"I was sure they were there," Diona replied, "but I did not say so to you in case you thought I was too . . . fanciful."

"I knew they were there when I was a child," the Marquis said, "and I am certain of it now that I am grown up."

He gave a little laugh as he carried her out of the Drawing-Room and up the stairs.

The night-footman stared at them in surprise.

The Marquis carried Diona to her bedroom and set her down in the centre of the bed. Then, taking off her shawl, he pushed her gently backwards against her pillows and pulled the sheet over her.

"Go to sleep, my precious one," he said, "and dream of nothing except that you are safe, and Sirius and I will never let this happen again."

Because there were no words in which to tell him how much she loved him, Diona merely held out her arms.

He kissed her until she felt as if the room were spinning dizzily round her, and she thought they were moving up through the ceiling and into the starlit sky.

She wanted him to kiss her and go on kissing her, but he said in a strangely hoarse voice:

"Good-night, my darling."

He took her hands from round his neck and placed them on her breast.

As he stood looking down at her, the expression in his eyes made her feel as if a light lit them both and they were not on earth but flying among the stars.

Then the Marquis blew out the candles and going from the room shut the door quietly behind him.

For a moment Diona could hardly believe he had gone.

She had become so close to him and was so much a part of him that it was as if he were still with her and she with him.

Then as she shut her eyes she found herself saying over and over again:

"Thank You . . . God . . . thank You! This is love, and what I always . . . wanted! Thank . . . You! Thank . . . You!"

CHAPTER SEVEN

———— ✇ ————

$\mathcal{D}$IONA AWOKE WITH AN IRREPRESSIBLE FEELING of happiness.

She lay for a moment thinking how wonderful everything was and how never again would she be so frightened or so lonely as she had been before the Marquis came into her life.

Then she realised that Sirius was looking at her over the edge of the bed, and it was he who had awakened her.

"I expect you want to go out," she said.

She pulled the bell and almost immediately the housemaid who looked after her opened the door.

"Will you ask somebody to take Sirius out into the garden?" Diona said. "And please ask them to stay with him."

"Very good, Miss."

As Sirius bounded towards the door, knowing he was to be taken out, Diona added:

"What time is it?"

"Nearly eleven o'clock, Miss."

Diona gave a little cry of horror.

"I had no idea it was so late!"

"His Lordship gave orders, Miss, that you was not to be woken!"

Diona sat up in bed.

"Is His Lordship downstairs?"

"No, Miss. He's gone out, and said he'd be back for luncheon, and Mrs. Lamborn told me to tell you when you woke that she's gone out shopping."

As by this time Sirius was at the end of the passage, the maid hurried away.

Diona got out of bed and pulled back her own curtains.

As she did so, she looked down into the garden, remembering how last night she had been kidnapped by her uncle, and if it had not been for Sirius and the Marquis she would by now be married to Simon.

The mere idea made her shudder.

Then she told herself that all was finished.

She was quite certain that after the Marquis had shot her uncle in the arm he would now leave her alone, and anyway there was no reason to think any more of him or of Simon, or of the miserable time she had spent at the Hall.

She felt as she had when she lived at home, that the sun was shining, the birds were singing, and everything was so wonderful that it was like being in a special little Heaven which was all her own.

She put on one of her prettiest gowns, hoping that when the Marquis saw her he would admire her in it.

Then, because she did not wish to miss a moment of his company when he returned, she ran down the stairs with Sirius, who had come back while she was dressing, behind her and went to the Library.

It was a very different room from the large and impressive Library at Irchester Park. There were far fewer books, and yet it was a Library, and she knew it was the Marquis's favourite room.

She thought one of the reasons was that there were some magnificent paintings of horses on the walls.

She stood looking at them, thinking how well the Marquis rode and what a joy it was for her to ride with him.

The door of the Library opened and she turned round expectantly, but it was not the Marquis who came in, but one of the most beautiful women she had ever seen.

She was very elegantly dressed in an elaborate gown which must have been extremely expensive, and her high-crowned bonnet was trimmed with small curled ostrich-feathers in peacock-blue.

There were diamonds glittering in her ears and round her neck, and she was so spectacular that Diona found herself staring at her almost rudely until as the lady came farther into the room she remembered her manners and curtseyed.

Then she realised that the newcomer was looking at her with an unmistakable expression of dislike.

"So it is true!" she said sharply. "I was told that the Marquis had a young woman staying here with him, but I did not believe it!"

Her tone of voice was aggressive, and Diona answered:

"Yes, I am staying here, but I am chaperoned by His Lordship's cousin, Mrs. Lamborn."

She felt it was rather strange to have to explain herself to this lady, whoever she might be.

But if she had thought to appease her by such an explanation and sweep away the expression of anger in her beautiful eyes, her words seemed to have the opposite effect.

"Who are you and where have you come from?" the lady asked in an even ruder tone of voice.

Because Diona felt almost bemused and her behaviour was so unexpected, she answered as if she felt compelled to do so:

"My name is Diona Grantley, and I came to London with His Lordship two days ago."

"Imposing yourself upon him, I suppose," the lady said. "Well, let me tell you that your presence here has caused a lot of gossip which is extremely bad for his reputation. Chaperone or no Chaperone, he is too young and too important to have young women staying in his house, and the sooner you leave the better!"

"L-leave?" Diona faltered.

"Yes, leave."

"I . . . I do not . . . understand."

"Then let me make it clearer! I am Lady Sybille Malden, and the Marquis, upon whom you have thrust yourself, and I are to be married!"

"M-married?"

As she spoke Diona felt as if the ceiling were falling in on her head and the room suddenly seemed very dark.

"Yes, married," Lady Sybille repeated, "and I have no wish to have my future husband made a laughingstock. I suppose it will not have occurred to you that such behaviour would be interpreted in a manner which must damage him in the eyes of the Social World."

"I . . . I did not . . . realise that."

"Well, now you do," Lady Sybille said abruptly, "and the sooner you get out of here and go back to where you came from, the better it will be for him and for me!"

She stared at Diona, seeing the sunlight on her pale gold hair and the worry in her large, strangely coloured eyes.

Then, as if the sight of such things made her lose her temper completely, Lady Sybille stamped her foot.

"You heard what I said!" she cried. "Get out, and stay out! His Lordship belongs to me!"

The way she spoke was so vehement that Diona gave a little cry, and without attempting to say any more she ran from the Library, down the passage, and up the stairs to her bedroom.

She knew now why the Marquis had not asked her to marry him.

How could she have been so foolish as to think when he kissed her last night that she belonged to him and could be with him forever?

Standing in the centre of her bedroom, she wondered frantically where she could go, and without him to protect her she knew she must hide again.

Then, like a child who had been hurt, she knew she must go home.

It flashed through her mind that her uncle might find her at the Manor, then she was sure that as he had been searching for her, he would have been there already and would not trouble to go back again.

"Anyway, that is where I must go," she told herself. "There is nowhere else."

She went to the wardrobe, and as she did so she saw on a chair a large round hat-box which must just have arrived from Bond Street with some bonnets which Mrs. Lamborn had bought for her the previous day.

She took them out, and pulled from the hangers in the wardrobe several gowns, not choosing them but taking whichever came to hand, and flung them into the hat-box.

She then added her nightgown and her hairbrush.

As the box was now full, she put the lid back on it and tied it with the ribbons that were affixed at the sides.

It was heavier now than when it had contained only a few bonnets, but fortunately the gowns which Diona had packed were very light.

She found the shawl, which had belonged to her mother, in which she had carried her things when she had first run away from the Hall.

She put a bonnet on her head, and only as she took from a drawer a pair of gloves and a satin bag in which she carried her handkerchief did she realise that she must have some money.

For a moment she wondered frantically if she could manage without it. Then, as if her mind took over from her emotions, she knew how she could get some.

Carrying the hat-box, with Sirius behind her she walked slowly down the stairs, and as the footman on duty hurried to take the box from her she said:

"I have to join Mrs. Lamborn at the shops. Will you please call me a Hackney-Carriage?"

"I could send to the stables, Miss," the footman said.

"I think that is unnecessary," Diona answered. "Mrs. Lamborn will have a carriage with her, and it will not take me more than a few minutes to join her."

"That's true, Miss," the footman agreed.

He opened the front door to go out into Park Lane in search of a Hackney-Carriage, and the moment he had gone Diona walked quickly to Mr. Swaythling's office.

She opened the door to find, as she had expected, that he was sitting at his desk, and when he saw her he rose to his feet with a smile.

"Good-morning, Miss Grantley. Is there anything I can do for you?"

"May I have some money?" Diona asked.

"Of course!" he replied. "How much do you want?"

"I have some rather expensive things to buy this morning," she answered. "Would it be possible for me to have twenty pounds?"

She was aware that Mr. Swaythling raised his eyebrows as if he was surprised at the large amount, but he answered courteously:

"Yes, of course, but I think you will find it more convenient to have fifteen pounds of it in notes."

"That is a good idea," Diona agreed, opening the satin bag which hung from her wrist.

Mr. Swaythling put the notes and five golden sovereigns into the bag.

"Beware of pick-pockets," he said jokingly.

"I will," Diona answered, "and thank you very much."

"I hope you will find everything you want in the shops."

As Diona left him he sat down again at his desk.

By the time she reached the Hall, the footman had fetched the Hackney-Carriage and had lifted her hat-box into it.

"I want to go to *Madame* Bertin's shop in Bond Street," Diona said, and the footman gave the order to the Cabman, who drove off.

Because it was a hot and sunny day the carriage was open, and as soon as they had travelled a little way down Park Lane, Diona raised her voice to say:

"I have changed my mind."

The Cabman, high above her, turned his head slightly so that she knew he had heard, and she went on:

"Will you please take me to The White Bear in Piccadilly?"

The Cabman nodded and drove on, as they did so, Diona thought it was lucky that she knew where she could hire a Post-Chaise.

It was only by chance that she was aware of it, but she remembered that when Roderic had arrived with Sam twenty minutes after she and the Marquis had returned from the country, he had said:

"Of course you beat us! You had the best horses. Those that Sam was driving were so slow I would have done better in a Post-Chaise from The White Bear at Piccadilly!"

"You insult my stable!" the Marquis had retorted.

Roderic had then laughed.

"I am only piqued because you drive so much better than anybody else, as you well know."

"Now you are flattering me," the Marquis had replied, "which makes me suspicious of what you are going to ask for in return."

They had all laughed, and Diona had thought, as she had so often before, what fun it was to hear the two men joking with each other.

Because it was such a strange name, "The White Bear" had lingered in her mind.

When the Hackney-Carriage turned in to the courtyard, she knew she was cleverly covering her tracks so that not only her uncle but also the Marquis would be unable to find her.

"He might not want to, or, alternatively, he might think it was his duty to discover what has happened to me," she told herself.

But she knew that the one thing she could not bear was his kindness now that she knew the truth.

"He is to be married," she went on, "married to that very beautiful lady, and I am a fool to have thought for one moment that I might mean anything to him."

She paid for the Hackney-Carriage and engaged a Post-Chaise with two horses, which was expensive, but it did not seem to matter.

Ten minutes later, with Sirius beside her, she was being driven through the crowded streets, which as soon as they got outside the City gave way to the open country.

She was going home because it was the only place where she belonged.

But she knew that she had left her heart behind with the Marquis, who was to marry Lady Sybille.

The Marquis walked into White's Club, and the moment he appeared Roderic rushed up to him.

He was obviously very excited as he drew the Marquis aside to ask in a conspiratorial whisper, although he could not repress his elation:

"How did you manage it? How could you have been so clever?"

The Marquis smiled faintly.

"I imagine from what you are saying that Sir Mortimer's contest will not now take place."

"He has just informed us that, owing to unfortunate circumstances which he could not explain, he has to withdraw his wager."

"Good!" the Marquis exclaimed.

"What did you do? How did you contrive that it should be cancelled?" Roderic asked.

"I think the whole thing is best forgotten," the Marquis replied.

"You cannot leave me curious for the rest of my life," Roderic persisted.

As if the Marquis realised that would be a cruel fate, he said:

"You really have to thank one of my friends who found out with whom Sir Mortimer was intending to confront you."

"A French Courtesan!"

"Exactly!"

"But you somehow persuaded her not to come to England," Roderic said, as if he was beginning to grasp what had happened.

"One of my friends has persuaded her," the Marquis replied, "that Paris is far more amusing, especially as he is there!"

Roderic gave a whoop of joy.

"Uncle Lenox, you are a genius, and I am eternally grateful to you for saving my face, and incidentally, so are the rest of my friends. It was impossible for them to find anybody in the country—or for that matter in London—who is both beautiful and intelligent!"

"Next time beware of Sir Mortimer," the Marquis said, "and avoid taking his bets."

"We will," Roderic agreed. "You may be quite sure of that! 'Once bitten, twice shy'!"

He saw the expression in the Marquis's eyes and added a little ruefully:

"Twice bitten, as far as I am concerned!"

"Well, I am glad I have been able to help you," the Marquis said with a smile, and walked away to speak to a friend who was beckoning him.

He did not stay long in White's, but drove back to Irchester House, thinking of Diona and feeling it was urgent that he should see her.

He had wanted to do so as soon as he awoke, but he knew that after such a disturbed night it was important for her to sleep.

Now his need of her seemed to intensify almost as if she were communicating with him as she had done when her uncle had kidnapped her.

Without meaning to, the Marquis urged his horses to go faster.

Only as he drove up to his house and saw Mr. Swaythling waiting for him on the doorstep did he have a sudden fear that something was wrong.

As he stepped down from his Phaeton to join Mr. Swaythling, his secretary moved with him into the Hall and said in a low voice:

"Will you come to my office, My Lord? I have something to tell you."

"Yes, of course," the Marquis agreed.

He walked in silence into the office, and when the door was closed he asked sharply:

"What is wrong?"

"I thought you would want to know, My Lord, that Lady Sybille Malden is here and has been for over an hour."

He saw the Marquis's eyes darken and went on:

"When she arrived she walked into the Library, although a footman tried to show her into the Drawing-Room, and Miss Grantley was there."

The Marquis was suddenly tense, but he did not speak, and Mr. Swaythling continued:

"I may be worrying unnecessarily, My Lord, but Miss Grantley came to see me twenty minutes after Lady Sybille arrived and said she was going shopping."

Mr. Swaythling paused as if he thought he was making much ado about nothing.

Then he went on quickly:

"She asked me for twenty pounds because she said she had some things to buy, and I did not think there was anything strange about it until Mrs. Lamborn returned just now, saying that Miss Grantley had not joined her as I had expected she was going to do."

"How did she leave here?" the Marquis asked.

"In a Hackney-Carriage, My Lord."

"A Hackney-Carriage? There are plenty of horses in the stables!"

"The footman informed me that he did suggest he should fetch a carriage, but she said she was joining Mrs. Lamborn, and that is what worried me, My Lord."

There was a deep scowl between the Marquis's eyes as he asked:

"Did Miss Diona take anything with her?"

"She carried a large hat-box," Mr. Swaythling replied. "The footman said it was rather heavy, and of course she had her hand-bag."

The Marquis was still as he was obviously thinking.

At that moment there was a knock on the door.

Mr. Swaythling crossed the room to open it.

Outside was the housemaid who had looked after Diona.

"Excuse me, Mr. Swaythling," she said, "but I understand His Lordship's with you, and I thought I should bring this downstairs right away."

"What is it?" Mr. Swaythling asked.

"A note I found in Miss Grantley's bedroom on the dressing-table. I didn't know she'd gone upstairs again, and I've only just discovered it."

"Thank you," Mr. Swaythling said, taking it from her.

He shut the door of the office and handed the note to the Marquis.

He felt as he did so that he was undoubtedly right in thinking that Miss Grantley had not been going shopping as she had said she intended to do.

The Marquis opened the note. It was very short, and he read:

Thank you for saving Me from Uncle Hereward, and thank You too for all your Kindness. I hope You will be very, very Happy, but because it is harming You to have me staying here, Sirius and I are hiding where No-one can find Us.

Do not worry about Me. I am sure I shall be safe.

Thank You again so much,

Diona

The Marquis read the letter through twice, then he said in a voice which Mr. Swaythling, who had known him for a long time, found hard to recognise:

"If you were alone in the world and hiding, Swaythling, with only twenty pounds between you and starvation, where would you go?"

Mr. Swaythling stood thinking, then he said:

"I cannot imagine where Miss Grantley would go in the circumstances. She has no home and . . ."

He got no further. The Marquis gave an exclamation.

"What was the address she gave you the other day when she asked you to send some money to her father's pensioners?"

Mr. Swaythling searched amongst the pile of papers on his desk, found what he was seeking, and held it out to the Marquis, who took it and walked towards the door.

"Where are you going, My Lord?" he asked.

"To the stables," the Marquis replied.

"You have not forgotten that Lady Sybille is waiting in the Library?"

"Let her wait!" the Marquis replied and was gone.

Late in the afternoon Diona arrived back at the Manor House where she had lived with her father and mother.

It had been a long journey, but she had let Sirius stretch his legs every time they changed horses, and the Landlords at the Posting-Inns had persuaded her to have something to eat and drink.

She had not been hungry because she felt as if there were a great stone in her breast which grew heavier every mile which took her farther away from London and the Marquis.

She could think only of his handsome face and the wonder of his lips when he had kissed her last night.

She had felt then as if he carried her up to the stars and they were no longer human beings but part of the celestial world.

'I shall never be happy again,' she thought to herself.

She felt desperately afraid of the future, when she must hide and go on hiding for fear that her uncle would find her and make her marry Simon.

Yet somehow when she walked into the house which had been her home all her life, it was as if she were enfolded in her father's and mother's arms, and they were there to look after her and protect her.

Old Mr. and Mrs. Briggs were overjoyed to see her.

They had not yet received the letter from Mr. Swaythling telling them that their pensions would be increased, but Diona sat down in the kitchen and told them a great deal of what had happened since she had last seen them.

Because she had known them ever since she was a child, she felt they were part of her family.

When she related how her uncle had tried to marry her to her Cousin Simon, they were as shocked and horrified as she thought her mother would have been.

"I knowed, soon as I set eyes on that young man, there was somethin' wrong with him," Mrs. Briggs said. "He were just like poor Jake in the village, who's always been laughed at for bein' a 'Looney,' and no-one'd ever think o' marryin' him!"

"You understand now why I have to hide," Diona said.

She had been right in thinking that her uncle had gone to the Manor to search for her.

He had not come himself, but had sent one of his grooms, a surly man who, despite their protests that they had not seen her, insisted on searching the house.

"It were a insult, Miss Diona, that's what it were, not to have our word took," Briggs said.

"I do not think Uncle Hereward will look for me here again," Diona answered. "If he does, I shall have to hide in the woods or in the cellar until he leaves."

"We wouldn't let him have you, don't you worry yer head about that," Mrs. Briggs said. "Now you go upstairs, dearie, and change into somethin' cool while I start cooking you a nice dinner."

Diona did as she was told, but when she reached the First Floor she did not go into what had always been her own bedroom, but into her mother's.

It was a very attractive room because although they had very little money, Mrs. Grantley had exquisite taste.

When Diona opened the shutters she found that the Briggses had kept the room spotlessly clean.

The white muslin curtains which draped the big bed in which her mother and father had slept had been washed, and so had the muslin skirt to the dressing-table.

Diona opened the windows and let in the fragrance of the roses which her father had trained to climb up the wall outside.

She felt even more vividly than she had before that her father and mother were somehow with her and looking after her.

What was more, the atmosphere of love, which she had missed so despairingly when she had gone to the Hall, enveloped her again.

It took away a little of the unhappiness she felt at leaving the Marquis.

At the same time, now that she was no longer driving in the Post-Chaise, she felt as if her whole being cried out because she had lost him and his love.

"He is to be married!" she tried to tell herself, but somehow she could only long for his arms round her as they had been last night.

She could feel his lips on hers and hear him saying in that deep voice which made her heart turn over in her breast:

"God, how I love you!"

"And I love him!" she said aloud, as if her mother were there listening to her. "I love him until he fills my whole world . . . the sky and the sea, and I shall never . . . never love . . . anybody else!"

She gave a little sob as she added:

"It was the way you loved Papa, so I know you understand. But what am I to do now that I am all alone?"

As she spoke she felt Sirius's cold nose on her hand and she knew he understood that she was unhappy.

She put her arms round him and said brokenly:

"There is only us, Sirius, you and me alone again, and you will have to look after me because there is nobody else."

She sat for a long time in her mother's room, then as the sun was sinking in the sky she knew it would soon be dusk.

She changed her gown, hanging up in her mother's wardrobe those she had brought from London almost as if she were showing them to her.

The dress in which she had travelled was dusty, and she put it on one side to ask Mrs. Briggs to give it a shaking.

Then she put on one of the gowns which Mrs. Lamborn had bought for her in Bond Street.

It was elegant, yet very suitable for a young girl, made of white crêpe and trimmed with small white roses.

It was so much more attractive than anything she had owned before, and Diona knew as she glanced at herself in the mirror that she had bought it to please the Marquis.

Now he would never see her in it and she might just as well throw it away for all the interest it had to her.

Because once again he filled her thoughts and her mind to the exclusion of all else, she went from the bedroom, thinking that she would go downstairs and talk to the Briggses.

At least it would take her mind for a few minutes from all she had lost and would never find again.

She started down the stairs and Sirius had already reached the Hall when she heard the sound of wheels outside the front door.

The door was ajar because Briggs had not closed it after he had let her in.

Diona was suddenly afraid that after all her precautions her uncle had found out that she had left London, and had come again in search of her.

Even if it was not her uncle, it was important that nobody local should know she was here in case they might talk.

There was nothing she could do but run for safety, and she opened the first door she came to in the Hall.

It was the Study which had been her father's special room, and like the Marquis his paintings were of horses and the books which filled the shelves were mostly about them too.

The shutters were still closed over the windows and the room was dark. Diona ran to a corner where she knew there was a large armchair behind which she could hide.

She crouched down, thinking that if anybody looked in they would not see her, and she drew Sirius close against her, putting her hand over his mouth to tell him he must not make a noise.

As the house was so small, it was easy to hear somebody push open the front door and walk across the polished floorboards.

It was a man, and Diona felt herself tremble.

She had guessed how it had been possible for her uncle to find her at Irchester Park.

She knew that Ted, the Carrier, would never have broken his word of honour, but she felt certain that what had happened had been that her uncle and Simon—especially Simon—had talked about the fortune she had inherited.

The people in the village, eager that she should learn of it, had been determined to do all they could to help find her.

Somebody had undoubtedly seen her travelling in the Carrier's cart.

While ordinarily they would not have thought of informing her uncle of the fact, because they imagined they were doing her a good turn they had hurried to the Hall.

Once her uncle knew she had been with Ted, it was easy to discover where he had been going that day.

That was what must have happened, and now Diona was praying that whoever had called unexpectedly would not realise she was here.

Then, with a sudden constriction of fear that seemed almost to choke her, she remembered that when she had arrived she had taken off her bonnet, a new one trimmed with a wreath of white flowers, and left it on a chair in the Hall.

Because she was so upset, her fingers must have tightened on Sirius, for he moved restlessly and gave a little whine.

As Diona quieted him, the door of the room opened.

Crouching down behind the chair, she held her breath.

Then, wrenching himself from her arms and barking with joy, Sirius ran to whoever was standing in the doorway, jumping up excitedly.

"Diona?"

It was the Marquis's voice that said her name, and as she got unsteadily to her feet she could see him silhouetted against the light.

Because she could not help herself, because he was there and she had thought she would never see him again, she ran across the room.

He held out his arms and pulled her against him. Then he was kissing her as he had the night before.

He kissed her demandingly, possessively, in a way which made her feel as if nothing mattered, nothing was of the least importance except that she belonged to him.

A long time later, when they were still standing in the doorway, the Marquis asked in a strange, unsteady voice:

"How could you run away in that extraordinary fashion? How could you leave me after what I said to you last night?"

It was difficult for Diona to reply, because he had carried her up into the sky and it was almost impossible to come down to earth again.

Then in a small voice which he could barely hear she answered:

"I . . . I was . . . hurting you . . . I was . . . harming you by being at your . . . house in London."

"Who told you that nonsense?" the Marquis asked.

"L-Lady Sybille . . . and she said you were going to . . . m-marry her!"

The Marquis drew Diona out into the Hall.

In the last light of the sun coming through the windows on each side of the door he looked down at her.

He saw the radiance that was still in her face because of his kisses, and the worry that was just coming into her eyes because of what she was remembering.

Her lips were red and soft from his, and the pale gold of her hair was like a halo round her small pointed face.

The Marquis stood looking at her as if he had never seen her before. Then he said very quietly:

"Put on your bonnet. I see it is on the chair."

Because she was so bemused by what was happening, Diona did not seem to understand, and the Marquis moved a few steps and picked up the bonnet.

He put it gently on her head and tied the ribbons under her chin.

Then as she still stared at him with an expression of love that she could not disguise, the Marquis took her by the hand and drew her out through the front door.

His Phaeton was covered with dust, although the horses looked comparatively fresh, and at their heads was a groom who habitually drove with him and whom Diona had seen before.

He grinned at her and touched his hat.

As he did so, the Marquis picked her up and lifted her into the Phaeton.

Then as he took up the reins the groom jumped up into the small seat behind and the Marquis drove off.

Only as they turned out of the gate and onto the dusty road which led to the village did Diona find her voice and say:

"Where . . . are you . . . taking me?"

"To the Church!" the Marquis replied.

She looked at him as if she could not have heard him aright.

"The . . . Church?"

"We are being married! The Parson is already there waiting for us."

Diona was stunned into silence.

Then as just ahead of her she saw the little grey stone Church where she had worshipped every Sunday and where her father and mother lay in the Churchyard, she managed to ask:

"B-but . . . how can you . . . marry me?"

"Very easily," the Marquis replied with a faint hint of laughter in his voice, "and it is something I should have done much sooner! I am taking no more risks of losing you again!"

He drew up his horses outside the Church, jumped down from the Phaeton, and went round to lift her down to the ground. She said as he did so:

"Is it right for you to . . . marry me?"

"It is something I am going to do," the Marquis answered, "and I think, my darling, it is what we both want."

He looked down at her as he spoke, and as she looked into his eyes she knew it was not what they said to each other that mattered. It was that they were indivisibly linked together and were already one person.

The Marquis put her arm through his and drew her to the porch.

As she reached it she heard the soft strains of the organ, and as they entered the Church she saw the Vicar waiting for them on the Chancel steps.

He had taken the place of the old man who used to teach her, and both her father and mother had liked him and thought of him as a friend.

Then the Marquis was drawing her up the aisle, and a few seconds later the Service began.

Driving back the short distance to the Manor, Diona could hardly believe that she was married.

At the same time, she knew that when the Marquis had made his responses in his firm voice, and she had heard her own soft and a little frightened reply, her dreams had come true.

The music that had filled the Church had come not only from the organ but from their hearts.

She had felt that God was blessing them and so were her father and mother, and they were telling her that this was what they had wanted for her.

"I am married!" Diona whispered to herself, and added: "And I love him more than I can ever say!"

It seemed to her that nobody could have had a more perfect wedding, surrounded by the love which she could feel vibrating not only from the Marquis but from her father and mother.

And of course, although he had been very unobtrusive, from Sirius.

He had followed the Phaeton without her being aware of it, and only as she reached the Chancel steps had Diona seen that Sirius was standing beside her almost as if he were taking the place of her father, who would have given her away.

He stood there all through the Service, not moving or making any noise, and she knew that his love was very important and something she could not do without.

As they returned to the Manor and the Marquis once again lifted her down from the Phaeton, Sirius ran ahead of them into the house as if he was leading them in.

The Marquis and Diona walked across the Hall, and as the door of the Sitting-Room was open he drew her inside.

While they had been at the Church, Mrs. Briggs had opened all the windows and the room was filled with the fragrance of the flowers in the garden.

The Marquis shut the door, and now as if there was no hurry he very slowly undid the ribbons of Diona's bonnet.

As she looked up at him, feeling that everything had happened so quickly and unexpectedly that she could not think, but only feel, he put his arms round her and drew her against him.

For a moment he did not kiss her, and she had the feeling that the solemnity of the Service was still with him as it was with her.

Then very gently and tenderly he kissed her forehead, both her eyes, and lastly her lips.

At first it was a kiss without passion, a kiss of dedication, and it made her feel like crying.

Then as she pressed herself close against him, his lips became more insistent but beguiling, as if he wooed her with kisses, and she felt her whole being quiver with the wonder of them.

The Marquis raised his head.

"You are mine, Diona, mine, and I will never lose you again."

"I love you . . . I love you."

The words had been pulsating in her all day and had intensified when she had seen him again. There was nothing she could do now but try to express her love.

"I love you!" she said. "But . . . I feel you should not have . . . married me."

"But I have married you," the Marquis said, "because I love you more than I can ever love anybody else in my life, and because, as you well know, my precious, there is something inescapable between us."

He kissed her again before he added:

"We can neither of us ever be complete without the other."

"How can you say such . . . wonderful things to me?" Diona asked. "It is what I feel . . . but I never thought you would . . . feel it too."

The Marquis smiled as he replied:

"I felt it literally from the first moment I saw you, but I fought against it, telling myself I had no wish to marry anybody."

"But . . . Lady Sybille said . . ."

"Forget her!" he interrupted. "She is of no importance in our lives. I suppose I was foolish to have taken you to London, but I did so for your sake."

"For my . . . sake?"

"Because you are so young, and because you have seen so little of the world, my darling, I thought I ought to give you what I called a 'sporting chance' to meet other men, just in case you found one you loved more than me."

Diona gave a little cry.

"How could you . . . think such a . . . thing? Of course I could never . . . love anybody more than you! It would be . . . impossible!"

"I made a mistake, and I was certainly punished for it," the Marquis said. "I have never been through such agony as last night when I realised you had been kidnapped, and again today when I learnt that you had left the house because of some nonsense Lady Sybille had said to you."

"You did not . . . promise to . . . marry her?"

"I have never asked any woman to marry me except you!"

Diona laughed.

"You never asked me! That is why I thought, when she told me you had promised to marry her, that you were still thinking of . . . hiding me away in some . . . little house where we could be together . . . but I would not be your wife."

The Marquis pulled her roughly against him.

"You are to forget all that! I was still most foolishly trying to preserve my freedom and my independence. I might have known it was a losing battle."

He thought she did not understand and went on:

"I love you, and my whole heart went out to you, and yet I suppose like most men I was afraid of being tied to one woman who might bore me."

Diona stiffened.

"Suppose . . . I do bore . . . you?"

"I know that is impossible," he said. "I have certainly not had any time since I have known you to be bored! It has been a case of one drama after another! I think I am now entitled to a rest, or rather a honeymoon."

"Is that what we are . . . going to . . . have?"

"Tomorrow we are driving to Dover to board my yacht."

Diona's eyes widened.

"Where are we going?"

"Anywhere you wish," he replied. "The world is very large, and there are many places I want to show you, and I want to make love to you there before we come back to take up our responsibilities together."

"It sounds so wonderful, so very . . . very . . . wonderful!" Diona said breathlessly. "You are quite . . . certain you will not be . . . bored?"

"Is that what you expect to be?"

"I am . . . afraid."

"Have you forgotten," he asked, "that we think the same, we feel the same, and we are joined by our waves of thought?"

"You heard . . . me last . . . night."

"And again today," the Marquis replied, "and I think, whether you were aware of it or not, you were calling to me and drawing me to you all the time you were travelling from London to here."

Diona put her head against his shoulder.

"I thought you were to be married to Lady Sybille," she whispered. "It was . . . a misery I can never express . . . I wanted to . . . die."

"You will never leave me again."

His lips found hers, and he kissed her until the room disappeared and there was only the scent of roses and the music which came from their hearts.

"I love you . . . I love you!" Diona was saying.

But she was not certain whether she spoke aloud or if it merely vibrated through her body from her mind.

Much later, when the only light came from the stars outside the uncurtained window and the moon that was just creeping up the sky, Diona moved in the Marquis's arms.

"Are you awake?" she whispered.

"I am too happy to sleep," he replied.

"Are you . . . really happy? Not . . . bored . . . or cynical . . . or blasé?"

He laughed.

"I doubt if I ever will be any of those things again. And what about you, my darling? I have not hurt you or frightened you?"

Diona drew in her breath.

"I had . . . no idea that . . . love was so wonderful!"

She kissed his shoulder before she said:

"Being with you is . . . like being in Heaven! At the same time . . .
it has made me so very . . . very happy that we should be here together
. . . in the house that I know is . . . filled with love and in the same bed
in which Papa and Mama slept and were the two happiest people in the
whole world."

"With the exception of us," the Marquis corrected. "I am convinced,
my beautiful one, that no man has ever been so fortunate as I am, and I
shall fight as I have never fought as a soldier to protect you, to guard you,
and to keep you from harm either physically or mentally."

Diona gave a little murmur of happiness and moved even closer to him
than she was already.

"I love you . . . I love you!" she said. "There are no . . . words to
. . . express what I feel, except . . . those three."

"They are all I want to hear," the Marquis said. "But you can love me,
my darling, without words. Every time I touch your body I feel it respond
to me, and every time I look into your eyes I know they are telling me
things which are so ecstatic that they are inexpressible except to me."

"You say all the things I want to say," Diona said. "How can you be so
. . . wonderful?"

"That is what I want to be," the Marquis replied, "and I think, my
precious, just as I know how much happiness your father and mother gave
to everybody, that we must try to create the same love wherever we go."

Diona gave a sigh that came from the very depths of her being.

"How could I ever have doubted that Papa and Mama were looking
after me?" she asked. "They told me to come and find you at the Big
House, and although at first I was frightened of you . . . I think I must
have known almost from the very beginning that you were the man I
wanted to be with for the rest of my life."

She paused to ask:

"You are . . . quite sure it will not . . . hurt you socially to have
married me . . . and not somebody far more . . . suitable?"

The Marquis knew she was thinking of Lady Sybille, and he answered:

"You are not the only one, my adorable wife, who runs away. The reason why I was at Irchester Park when you came there was because I too had run away–from London and a certain woman who was trying to inveigle me into a trap."

For a moment his voice was hard. Then he said in a different tone:

"But of course, like you, I believe it was fate that put me in exactly the right place at the right moment, when you came to ask for my help."

"Of course it was fate!" Diona agreed. "Or, actually, it was Sirius, for if he had not knocked over Uncle Hereward's glass of brandy, and if he had not awakened you in time to prevent me from being married to Simon, I would not be here now."

The Marquis's arm instinctively tightened round her as she finished:

"It is all such a glorious . . . exciting story, and I feel I have read it in a book rather than . . . lived it myself."

"Perhaps you should put it in a book," the Marquis said, "and we must certainly one day tell it to our children."

He could not see the blush that rose in Diona's cheeks, but he sensed it was there.

Then as she hid her face close against him he heard her whisper:

"Do you think . . . perhaps you have . . . given me a . . . baby?"

The Marquis smiled before he answered:

"It is something we can make sure of, if that is what you want!"

"I have never known . . . until now, how one . . . starts a baby," Diona said softly, "but it is so very . . . very wonderful . . . and I want not . . . one baby . . . but several . . . so please, will you go on . . . making love to me?"

"I can answer that question very easily," the Marquis replied. "I shall love you, and make love to you, my beautiful one, until the stars fall from the skies and the moon no longer shines."

As he spoke his lips were moving over the softness of her skin, and his hand was touching her body.

Once again little shafts of lightning were moving through her, and at the same time she felt as if the sunshine she had always associated with happiness was burning in her breasts and on her lips.

It seemed to intensify until as she felt the fire in the Marquis's kiss she surrendered herself to the ecstasy and joy he aroused in her.

It was something so perfect, so Divine, that she knew God blessed them.

Then as the flames within them leapt higher and higher and the Marquis made her body his, she knew they were also one in their minds, and their souls, for all Eternity.

ABOUT THE AUTHOR

———— ❦ ————

$\mathcal{B}$ARBARA CARTLAND, the world's best known and best-selling author of romantic fiction, is also an historian, playwright, lecturer, political speaker and television personality. She has now written over 636 books and has the distinction of holding *The Guiness Book of Records* title of the world's bestselling author, having sold over 650 million copies of her books all over the world.

Miss Cartland is a Dame of Grace of St. John of Jerusalem; Chairman of the St. John Council in Hertfordshire; one of the first women in one thousand years ever to be admitted to the Chapter General; President of the Hertfordshire Branch of the Royal College of Midwives; President and Founder in 1964 of the National Association for Health; and invested by her Majesty the Queen as a Dame of the Order of the British Empire in 1991.

Miss Cartland lives in England at Camfield Place, Hatfield, Hertfordshire.